THE NYCTALOPE vs. LUCIFER

also by Brian Stableford
The Wayward Muse
The Stones of Camelot
The New Faust at the Tragicomique

also translated and annotated by Brian Stableford

News from the Moon and Other French Scientific Romances (*anthology*)

by Paul Féval
Anne of the Isles and Other Legends of Brittany
The Black Coats: 'Salem Street
The Black Coats: The Invisible Weapon
The Black Coats: The Parisian Jungle (*forthcoming*)
John Devil
Knightshade
Revenants
Vampire City
The Vampire Countess
The Wandering Jew's Daughter

by Paul Féval **fils**
Felifax the Tiger Man

by Pierre-Alexis Ponson du Terrail
The Vampire and the Devil's Son

by Villiers de l'Isle-Adam
The Scaffold and Other Cruel Tales
The Vampire Soul and Other Sardonic Tales

also forthcoming
The Vampire Captain
(*by Marie Nizet*)

THE
NYCTALOPE
VS.
LUCIFER

by
Jean de La Hire

translated, annotated and introduced by
Brian Stableford

A Black Coat Press Book

Acknowledgements: We are indebted to Marc Madouraud, Philippe Ethuin and Jean-Luc Buard for research assistance.

English adaptation, introduction and afterword Copyright © 2007 by Brian Stableford.
Cover illustration Copyright © 2007 by Denis Rodier.

Visit our website at www.blackcoatpress.com

Introduction

The Nyctalope vs. Lucifer, which was first serialized in the Parisian newspaper *Le Matin* from November 25, 1921 to March 30, 1922 is of some historical importance as the first superhero novel, at least in one definition of the term "superhero."

There had, of course, been many previous literary heroes whose physical prowess had been highly exceptional–Edgar Rice Burroughs' *Tarzan of the Apes* (1912) is perhaps the most obvious example–but whose abilities were straightforward exaggerations of the capacities of ordinary men rather than specific and explicitly paranormal "superpowers." There had also been characters who were enabled to play heroic roles by virtue of their possession of some such paranormal gift, including several gifted–like C. H. Hinton's *Stella* (1895)–with invisibility. None of the latter had, however, yet become established as a serial crusader for justice who made a career out of using his (or her) superpower to combat evil on a regular basis. La Hire's Leo Saint-Clair, a.k.a. The Nyctalope, on the other hand, went on to do exactly that, thus laying down a template that was to be adopted by such US pulp magazines as *Doc Savage* (launched in 1933) before providing the core mythology of US comic books from the late 1930s onwards.

As might be expected from a first step into such exotic territory, *Lucifer* is tentative and awkward–so tentative and awkward, in fact, that it probably seemed rather weak-kneed and inept even to some of its contemporary readers, let alone modern readers familiar with the flamboyant and highly-developed spectrum of contemporary superheroism. It did, however, strike enough of a chord with its contemporary readers to warrant the extrapolation of a series; in its day, it was a popular success. It is hard to imagine a similar popularity being achievable today, but the novel certainly serves to illustrate the manner in which a remarkable trend first got started, in terms of its generative pressures and narrative temptations. No one nowadays is likely to think territory, *Lucifer* a good book, but it is by no means an uninteresting one; its naivete is revealing, not only in terms of the primal evolution of its particular subgenre but in terms of the broader evolution of daily serial fiction and the techniques developed to deal with its challenges. Although newspaper serials of that kind are long dead–never having made much impact anywhere but in France–the same narrative challenges and techniques are manifest throughout the world in television soap operas.

Lucifer is, therefore, offered to 21st century English and American readers as a literary curiosity, which casts some light into the murky background of some of the most popular–if least respectable–forms of contemporary fiction. Like many aged ancestors, it is a trifle embarrassing, as much because of its crude attitudes as the clumsiness of its literary technique, but it is, nevertheless, a significant link in the history of modern entertainment. It is a link that has been missing for some considerable time; this translation will hopefully situate it where interested readers will be able to find it.

The creator of the Nyctalope was born in Banyuls on January 28, 1878, into an obscure aristocratic family which had long been impoverished by various social upheavals. His birth-name was Adolphe-Ferdinand Célestin d'Espie de La Hire. His family claimed descent from one of the knights who fought with Jeanne d'Arc, although its most famous member by far was the mathematician and astronomer Philippe de La Hire (1640-1718), who has a theorem and a lunar mountain named after him.

Biographical sketches claim that La Hire's parents cherished the fond hope that he might embark upon a military career before he yielded temptations of the *fin de siècle* and set out for Paris, with the intention of devoting himself to *livres et l'amour*, but that is the sort of *cliché* that is standard in literary biographies of the period. He arrived in Paris too late to jump on to the Decadent bandwagon while it still had some momentum, but he did manage to associate himself briefly with its dwindling twilight, becoming a close friend of Pierre Louÿs–a chapter in La Hire's otherwise unpublished *Mémoires* was extracted and printed by Louÿs enthusiasts as a significant insight into the author's life.

La Hire began his literary career with high ambitions, selling much of his early work to Fernand Xau, the editor of *Le Journal* and the humorous periodical *Gil Blas*. He worked for a while as secretary to Colette's husband, "Willy," and wrote a brief memoir of that time in *Ménage d'artiste: Willy and Colette, étude biographique et critique [An Artistic Household: A Biographical and Critical Study of Willy and Colette]* (1906). The latter was issued by his own publishing imprint, Adolphe Espie, which published numerous novels and volumes of poetry as well as issuing a short-lived periodical, *La Revue des Lettres*, whose contributors included Paul Adam and J.-H. Rosny Aîné.

La Hire's two novels in the salacious tradition of Willy's works, *Vengeance d'amoureuses [Lovers' Revenge]* (1905) and *Trois Parisiennes [Three Parisian Women]* (1906), were both issued under the Adolphe Espie imprint. He also founded the similarly-inclined *Bibliothèque Indépendante* in 1904, although he handed over editorial control in 1905 to Marguerite Weyrich, who was presumably his sister-in-law; he had married Marie Weyrich–also born in 1878–a short while before. The *Bibliothèque Indépendante* published La Hire's non-fiction book *L'homme et la societé [Man and Society]* (1907) and Marie's novel *Modèle nu [Nude Model]* (1908).

Marie de La Hire was also an impressionist painter of some note, and her later works tended to the avant-garde; they included a *"Croquis Dada" [Dada Sketch]* (1920) presumably inspired by her friendship with the Dadaist poet and painter Francis Picabia. She had earlier tried her hand at popular fiction, though, contributing *La fiancée fantôme* [*The Phantom Bride*] to a Tallandier imprint whose chief stock-in-trade was sensational fiction by the likes of Fortuné du Boisgobey, Jules Mary and Arthur Bernède. It was her husband who "sold out" more conspicuously, though, presumably in order to provide a secure financial foundation for his family; he accepted a contract in 1907 to supply one of the most downmarket Parisian periodicals, Maurice Bunau-Varilla's *Le Matin*, with serial fiction, thus ruining his literary reputation irreparably.

Serial fiction of this sort was by then in its third generation. The *roman feuilleton* had become established as the leading vehicle of French popular fiction in the 1840s, when serials by Alexandre Dumas and Eugène Sue had become key assets in circulation wars waged by daily newspapers catering to the ever-widening audience provided by the march of literacy. After a distinct hiatus caused by the Revolution of 1848 and Louis-Napoléon's *coup d'état* of 1851, *feuilleton* fiction was firmly re-established, enjoying a new heyday in the 1860s when such writers as Paul Féval and Ponson du Terrail began the formularization of crime and adventure fiction, but that too was interrupted by the Franco-Prussian War of 1870. Restored to health again, the native tradition was exposed to significant competition in the 1890s when popular fiction translated from English, German and Italian began to appear in much greater profusion. Although it remained robust in the face of that competition, French popular fiction became markedly defensive, consciously playing to its established strengths and carefully cultivating its own idiosyncrasies even as it absorbed the influence of trends begun in other nations–and, in parallel, saw its own innovations borrowed, copied and extrapolated elsewhere.

In the first decade of the 20th century, this complex pattern of mutual influence was well-set, as was an exaggerated stratification of the marketplace that worked on the not-entirely-justified premise that popular fiction–especially crime and adventure fiction–was mostly consumed by relatively uneducated male readers unable or unwilling to cope with much literary sophistication. Although Dumas and Sue had certainly not escaped the oppression of having their work regarded by the worthies of the *Académie Française* as essentially worthless, Féval and Ponson had suffered considerably more. By 1900, the disdain with which writers of *feuilleton* fiction were regarded in opinionated literary circles had reached an effective maximum.

New recruits to the field had various strategies available by which to armor themselves against that disdain, including the kind of capitulation that allowed writers to disdain their own work while pocketing the money it brought in. It was to this company that Jean de La Hire belonged; not only did he refrain from putting much literary effort into his work, but he deliberately employed methods and devices of which he was scornful. After 1907, he was a bad writer by design, and was glad to be bad by design, because it protected him from the awful possibility that he might still be bad if he tried to be better.

Like several other fellow-travelers of the dead-but-not-quite-buried Decadent Movement–the most conspicuous examples being Théo Varlet, Gustave Le Rouge and "Claude Farrère" (Charles Bargone)–La Hire decided that the kind of popular fiction that offered most scope to his prostituted imagination was what is nowadays termed "science fiction." Although Jules Verne's literary career had been started and shaped by a contract to produce works that might be serialized in publisher P.-J. Hetzel's family magazine, Verne had avoided much of the stigma that *feuilleton* fiction had attracted during the last three decades of the 19th century, and had gone on to become a beloved national institution.

Vernian fiction had become popular enough to warrant the founding of specialist magazines such as the *Journal des Voyages*, and although such fiction moved steadily downmarket, it benefited almost as much from crime fiction in the 1890s by the importation of English influences–in this case the enlivening influence of H. G. Wells. By 1907, Wells had given up scientific romance, and that whole genre was in steep decline in England, but its less pretentious equivalent was still relatively healthy in France. La Hire's first serial for *Le Matin* was *La roue fulgurante* [*The Fiery Wheel*] (1907), the extravagant account of an alien abduction by a spacecraft which appears to anticipate the notion of "flying saucers." (It was later reprinted under the title *Soucoupe volante* [*Flying Saucer*] and helped to popularize that term.)

La roue fulgurante was presumably a little too extravagant for some of *Le Matin*'s readers, because La Hire reverted to more modestly Earthbound adventure fiction thereafter. (One of the key features of daily serial fiction is its urgent responsiveness to reader reaction, which operates within serials as well as between them.) Most of his subsequent works in this vein retained an element of scientific romance, however–and more than one ventured into space–although they invariably embedded their inventions within the conventional story-arc of crime fiction, thus anticipating the contemporary genre of "technothrillers." The hybridization of the two genres had become virtually inevitable, by virtue of the pressure of "melodramatic inflation."

Once crime fiction became formularized, routinely focusing on heroes who operated in the context of long series, the threats faced by those heroes were highly likely be subject to an escalating scale of menace. Unlike real crimefighters, who have to take whatever cases are presented to them by the whims of chance, in no particular order, fictional heroes are pressurized to outdo their previous efforts in meeting each new challenge, lest their readers become jaded. Sherlock Holmes graduated from trivial puzzles to a climatic confrontation with a "Napoleon of Crime" allegedly responsible for most of the evil deeds committed in London. His rivals often set out from the benchmark he had created, swiftly working their way up from mere Napoleons to veritable Lucifers. By the same token, the heroes themselves had to become larger than life in order to match these escalating threats on more-or-less equal terms. Once Sherlock Holmes had established an unsurpassable paradigm of human deductive ingenuity and Tarzan a similar ideal of natural human virility, the temptation to stray into the realms of the supernatural and the superscientific became considerable. La Hire was part of a group of *feuilletonistes*–including Gaston Leroux, Arthur Bernède, Gustave le Rouge and Maurice Renard–who began to explore the possibilities of such hybrid fiction with some determination and vigor.

La Hire's first venture into the proto-technothriller genre was *L'homme qui peut vivre dans l'eau* [*The Man Who Could Live Underwater*], serialized *in Le Matin* in 1908. The eponymous Icthaner is not the hero of the novel, though, being merely the hapless subject of a biotechnological experiment carried out by the villains. The hero is an engineer named Severac, the inventor of a new kind of submarine. One of the minor characters who assists Severac's cause is, however, a man named Jean Sainte-Claire.

When the arch-villain of *L'homme qui peut vivre dans l'eau* joined forces with a whole company of evil masterminds for a more ambitious Martian adventure in eccentric megalomania in *Le mystère des XV* [*The Mystery of the XV*], serialized in *Le Matin* in 1911, he was again opposed by a Sainte-Claire, this time forenamed Leo, Jean's son, a fearless explorer whom we are told is known as the Nyctalope because of his ability to see in total darkness.

Nothing more was heard of the Sainte-Claires in the next decade. La Hire reverted to more orthodox Vernian fiction in the long *Le corsaire sous-marin* [*The Submarine Pirate*] (1912-13), which features one of many clones of Verne's Captain Nemo, but soon thereafter *feuilleton* fiction suffered one of its frequent *bouleversements*, its consumption and development being inhibited by the Great War of 1914-18. La Hire was not reduced to inactivity in those years, however; *Le Matin* continued to appear and La Hire continued to supply it with serial fiction, including the long futuristic fantasy *Au-delà des ténèbres* [*Beyond Darkness*] (1915-16), whose protagonists employ suspended animation to escape the woes of the 20th century, awakening in the 30th.

When the war was over, La Hire continued his sciencefictional experiments with a explicitly Wellsian account of *Joe Rollon, l'autre homme invisible* [*Joe Rollon, the Other Invisible Man*] (1919)–one of several works he issued under the pseudonym Edmond Cazal–and it was at this point that he apparently became convinced of the viability of superheroism as a device of literary crimefighting. When La Hire returned to his Sainte-Claire character, he now became "Jean de Sainclair the Nyctalope." Not only was his alias given much greater prominence, but his surname was shortened, so that it became less a celebration of a key disciple of St Francis of Assisi and more a symbolic combination of sanity (or soundness) and clarity. This did not last, however. In the next volume in the series, the Nyctalope's name reverted to being "Leo Saint-Clair" without any explanations.[1]

---

[1] In order to maintain the continuity of the series, we have chosen to use the name "Leo Saint-Clair" throughout the book (*note from the publisher*).

Nevertheless, it was a significant move, for the new Sainclair / Saint-Clair was opposed by an equally symbolic archvillain, whose alias and character represented a deliberate attempt to reach a new extreme.

La Hire's "Lucifer" was by no means the first archvillain to be credited with a satanic aspect–Paul Féval had teased his readers with the notion that Colonel Bozzo-Corona of the *Habits Noirs* might be a literal incarnation of evil in the 1860s–but La Hire was determined to make the most of the parallel in attempting to design a new archetype of evil for a new historical and scientific era. It was not possible, of course, for La Hire to compose proto-technothrillers in and after 1919 in exactly the same way that he had done before and in 1913, because the world had altered very considerably in the meantime.

The Great War had not solved any of the political problems that had motivated it; its net result was to render all the ambitions entertained by the European powers that had started it hopelessly redundant. Europe, which had been the economic and political heart of the world order, smashed itself up so badly that economic hegemony was handed to the United States of America on a chipped plate. The war had been widely advertised as a war to end all wars, which would centralize and consolidate imperial civilization; yet, it had not only contrived to shatter all imperial dreams but had made future wars more likely–and had established beyond the shadow of a doubt that modern armaments of war had evolved to the point at which the next war was far more likely to obliterate civilization than to save it.

In this ideological context, the ambitions, methods and apparatus of archvillainy were bound to take on a new satanic significance; the real world had demonstrated that it was just as prone to melodramatic inflation as popular fiction, and the melodramatic inflation of popular fiction could no longer be regarded as a merely literary device. The first confrontation between a superhero and villain was bound to be supercharged in more ways than one.

To modern comic book readers and cinemagoers, the Nyctalope is bound to seem rather feeble as a proto-superhero. His superpower consists of being able to see in the dark–absurdly trivial by comparison with the sorts of abilities possessed by the likes of Superman and Spider-Man. Even in the context of a vast ensemble, like the multitudinous mutants whose star players are the X-Men, he would have difficulty nowadays qualifying for a minor role. As a mere practical ability, in fact, Saint-Clair's nyctalopia plays relatively little part in the plot, and no role at all in the novel's eventual climax. A contemporary writer's first priority would have been to engineer a situation in which the Nyctalope's supreme victory would be predicated on his plunging the final battle into darkness at the crucial moment–which he would have been very easily able to do, given the novel's obsession with electric lighting–but La Hire could not be bothered.

La Hire forgetfulness in giving due emphasis to his protagonist's superpower illustrates the primitive nature of his understanding of the literary logic of superheroism, but it also serve to highlight the fact that the heavy and repeated emphasis of Saint-Clair's alias within the story owes more to its metaphorical than its literary significance. The relatively trivial fact that Saint-Clair can actually see in the dark is less important than his symbolic status as a paragon of moral and scientific Enlightenment. His nickname is primarily an amplification of his surname; his preternaturally *sain* and *clair* sight is the antagonist of moral rather than actual darkness.

In this respect, too, the Nyctalope is bound to be found wanting by modern readers. The particular brand of sanity and clarity he aspires to represent and embody is obsolete now, irreparably tarnished by its nasty racism, its silly sexism and its confusedly hypocritical attitude to violence. While the racism and sexism might conceivably be excused as typical products of their era, largely taken for granted by all popular novelists of the day, Saint-Clair's prevarications in regard to the legitimacy of murder and torture are more difficult to forgive, because of the blatant inconsistency of his conduct–whose inadequacy even he and his creator occasionally notice and shamefacedly admit. This moral confusion becomes increasingly obvious as the novel's plot unfolds, exemplified by the uncomfortable manner in which the hero gets through his first confrontation with Lucifer's extended family, when he only escapes being crushed with casual and contemptuous ease by virtue of the implausible and morally dubious intervention of another character–whose subsequent treatment by author and hero alike might easily be reckoned abominable, and whose belated recognition in the novel's final lines might be seen as adding unctuous insult to casual injury.

Although it certainly qualifies as a narrative flaw, the moral confusion of the novel is one of its most interesting aspects from a purely historical viewpoint. Mature exercises in superhero fiction, precisely because of their relative sophistication, handle such issues much more dexterously–which is to say that they dodge them with far greater skill and grace. La Hire, pioneering the territory, did not know enough in advance to be able to dodge them, and ran right into them. Had he been able to plan his work more elaborately, he would probably have done much better, but the very essence of daily serial writing is that it cannot be planned in advance. The writer of such fiction is obliged to make up his story as he goes, not only because he does not know at the beginning how long it might be required to last, but because he does not know what running modifications he might be forced to make to its plot in response to reader response. He must start, and remain, infinitely adaptable–despite the fact that, once he has published an episode, he is bound by its limitations forever, unable to cancel out errors or steps that turn out to have been taken in the wrong direction, let alone readjust his groundwork to support new ideas and reactive editorial instructions.

All serial fiction tends to be messy, but the more successful such fiction is in the course of serialization, the messier it is bound to become–and *Lucifer*, whose serial version eventually extended to some 200,000 words, became very messy indeed. One of the effects of that messiness, however, was to strip bare the inherent problems of the nascent genre to which the serial belonged, and *Lucifer* exposes the problematics of superhero fiction in no uncertain terms. Anyone who aspires to create a paragon of moral clarity, a writer of newspaper serials or comic books no less than an academic philosopher or the founder of religion–has either to tackle essentially contentious issues head on, matching seemingly-immovable obstacles with hopefully-irresistible forces, or fudge those issues as best he can. La Hire would undoubtedly have fudged them if he could, but he was unable to lay the groundwork properly, and had to do things the hard way. In consequence, his scheme fell apart–but that is not at all surprising. How much better do the writers of modern television soaps do, with a century of accumulated experience to draw on?

La Hire went on to pen many more accounts of the Nyctalope's crime-fighting exploits, but I shall leave the description of those later works to Jean-Marc Lofficier's account of the character's career in the Afterword. La Hire interspersed the Nyctalope's adventures with other items of popular fiction, including scouting adventures and other science fiction thrillers. He attempted to continue working through World War II just as he had worked through World War I, but the cost proved much higher. In January 1941, he was given joint editorial control of J. Ferenczi *et fils*, the publishing company that had issued paperback editions of many of his serial novels, and in April of that year. the company was renamed *Editions du Livre Moderne*, in which guise it was "Aryanized" by the occupying Germans. La Hire was fired in December, but the association returned to haunt him in September 1944, when Paris was back in French hands.

La Hire and his co-editor, André Bertrand, were among a number of publishers blacklisted by the Syndicat des Editeurs for collaboration with the Nazis. He was arrested in May 1945 and tried in December; the judgment confirmed his permanent exclusion from the world of French publishing. He escaped from custody in February 1946 while being transferred to a hospital, but was condemned in absentia in 1948 to ten years' imprisonment and the loss of his citizenship rights. He never returned to serve the sentence but was still in disgrace when he died on September 6, 1956. He was, however, survived by the Nyctalope, the penning of whose adventures were taken over by his son-in-law, according to a pattern that was to become normal in respect of successful superheroes.

The central presence within it of a proto-superhero is not the only feature of *Lucifer* that recommends it for attention as a historical artifact. It is very much a product of its time in several ways, of which two might be singled out for special attention: its occultism and its futurism.

La Hire's use of occultism may seem a trifle belated, given that the "occult revival" of the 19th century, assisted and guided by such movements as Spiritualism and Theosophy, had been as much a product of the *fin-de-siècle* as literary Decadence, and had suffered a similar fade from fashionability after 1900, although one element that proved more robust than most was hypnotism. The literary mythology of hypnotism had been given a considerable boost by George du Maurier's account of Svengali in *Trilby* (1894) and the notion had been readily observed into such popular thrillers as George Griffith's *A Mayfair Magician: A Romance of Criminal Science* (1905). The paperback edition of the latter novel (issued under the title *The Man with Magnetic Eyes*) carried an advertisement inside its front cover offering to sell readers a "simple method that anyone can use to develop the powers of personal magnetism, memory, concentration [and] will-power... through the wonder-science of suggestion".

Although many of the references La Hire drops into his plot are to such 19th-century figures as Allan Kardec and Eusapia Palladino, it is significant that that they are juxtaposed and interwoven with another set of references, to Pierre and Marie Curie and other discoverers of the scientific mysteries of radioactivity. The combination is not as incongruous as it may seem nowadays, and was certainly not untimely. One of the less obvious of the Great War's many effects was to bring about a temporary renaissance of certain aspects of the occult revival. An entire generation of young men had been slaughtered on the battlefields of northern France and Belgium, leaving behind a generation of grieving mothers and fathers, very many of whom clutched at the straws of solace offered by Spiritualism.

The most prominent British victim of the renewed craze was Arthur Conan Doyle, creator of the archetypal master of criminal detection, Sherlock Holmes, and the bombastic scientist Professor Challenger. Holmes was spared explicit degradation, but Challenger was not, being forced to capitulate with the forces of unreason in *The Land of Mist* (1926); Doyle went on to prove that relentless logic applied to dodgy premises can produce spectacularly ludicrous results when he became a vociferous champion of the Cottingley fairies. In this intellectual climate, La Hire's revivification of "occult science" and his attempts to support that revival by simultaneous reference to hypnotism and radioactivity was likely to strike a sympathetic chord with many of his readers.

Although scientists had been much more successful in debunking Spiritualist delusions once the early gullibility of William Crookes and Oliver Lodge had been replaced by a sterner skepticism, the general intellectual thrust of occult science had always been to absorb rather than repel. The cardinal philosophical difference between occultism and natural science is that the former is expansively holistic, while the latter is painstakingly reductionist in its method. Occultists seek mysterious echoes and murky equivalences of meaning everywhere, and are obliged by their most fundamental assumptions to interpret all new scientific discoveries as resurrections or extrapolations of ancient esoteric wisdom. Such discoveries as electromagnetic waves–especially radio waves and X-rays–inevitably seemed glorious to occultists, not because of their technological potential but because they seemed so utterly and intrinsically magical, echoing powers of telepathy and clairvoyance attributed to ancient magicians. Of all such discoveries, none seemed more significant or so beautifully symbolic as the discovery of radium, which was immensely difficult to purify but, once isolated within a test-tube, glowed in the dark!

It is entirely apposite–and, indeed, was probably inevitable–that the satanic archvillain opposed by a superheroic nyctalope in 1921 should be an hypnotically-talented occultist, and that his apparatus of putative world domination should be fuelled by radium; the combination is an entirely natural process of syncresis. A few years later, of course, no such association would have been possible, and the precautions taken by Professor Lourmel and the Nyctalope to insulate themselves from the magical power and mystical significance of radium would have been unthinkable. *Lucifer* was published within a narrow window of opportunity, which was gradually curtained as post-War enthusiasm for Spiritualistic solace foundered on the rock of practicality, and shuttered with a brutal slam when it was realized that the workers charged with exploiting the luminosity of radium in painting the hands of watches were dying in droves of oral cancers because they licked their paintbrushes to give them finer points. In 1921, no one knew how slyly lethal radiation would prove to be, or how profoundly the symbolism of the radium glow would have to be altered.

La Hire's futurism was equally timely. Although modern terminology would categorize *Lucifer* as science fiction, and the terminology of its own day would probably have identified it as Vernian romance, it might perhaps be most aptly described as a futurist fantasy. It is certainly not a futuristic fantasy, because it is very insistently set in the present day, but it is very obviously preoccupied with themes that were central to the futurist manifesto issued by Filippo Marinetti, which had been published in the Parisian newspaper *Le Figaro* in February 1909, where La Hire presumably read it. The three central themes of Marinetti's futurist–speed, technology and violence, with the primary emphasis on speed–are all conspicuously fetishized in *Lucifer*

The story told in *Lucifer* is particularly intoxicated with calculations of speed, the narrative being constantly preoccupied with the velocities attainable by new cars, aircraft and express trains. It is similarly obsessed with technological applications of electricity to lighting, means of communication and the provision of motive force; all of La Hire's interior descriptions are careful to include information regarding the positioning of the electric lights, and most of his interior settings are equipped with neat arrays of electric switches. Although such inclusions became a favorite means by which La Hire routinely padded his prose, there is no doubt that he was trading on a genuine fascination that he expected his contemporary readers to appreciate and share, because it reflected and magnified the ongoing transformation of their own domestic and industrial environments. Once the inhibiting effects of the Great War had been removed, there was a dramatic increase in the perceived pace of social life as a cataract of technological innovations previously reserved for military use burst into the commercial and domestic arenas; 1921 was the year in which this process generated its greatest excitement, putting the roar into the "roaring twenties."

The use of violence in *Lucifer* seems far less striking to the modern eye than its idiosyncratic uses of speed of technology, but that is because standards have shifted so dramatically in the interim. In this respect, more than any other, melodramatic inflation has raised the stakes across the board within the whole spectrum of action/adventure/thriller fiction, and anything written in 1921 now seem pathetically tame in the scope and detail of its violence. What Lucifer and Saint-Clair actually do to their various victims, on stage and off, was to be far outshone when American pulp fiction and Hollywood movies initiated an accelerating process of positive feedback in the 1930s, whose products were exported to the rest of the world in the wake of World War II. Within its own tentative context, though, the story told in *Lucifer* does aim to fetishize both the threats and the actual assaults trailed in the first few chapters and periodically reiterated thereafter.

Differences between the use of parallel terms in the French and English languages caused some difficulty in the translation of *Lucifer*, the most obvious being the fact that "nyctalope" has almost opposite meanings in the two languages. The Latin term *nyctalopia* is quite unambiguous in meaning "night-blindness"—i.e., an inability to see in the dark—but English dictionaries conscientiously note that the term is sometimes mistakenly used in English to signify the complementary phenomenon of "day-blindness," for which the correct term is *hemeralopia*. In French, this confusion had proceeded to such an extreme by 1921 that *nyctalopia* was not only mistakenly used to refer to day-blindness but to the ability, rather than the inability, to see in the dark—the 1924 edition of the *Petit Larousse* makes no reference to the etymological confusion, simply defining *nyctalopie* as "*Maladie des yeux, dans laquelle la vision, très faible pendant la jour, augmente notablement avec le déclin de la lumière.*" [A disorder of the eyes, in which vision that is very weak in daylight is considerably increased with the decline of light intensity.]

Even in French, therefore, the Nyctalope's ability is not exactly in accordance with the dictionary, but it does tend in the same direction. In English, calling someone a Nyctalope would imply the opposite—someone whose night-vision is reduced rather than enhanced. I have, however, retained the name on the grounds that it is sufficiently esoteric in its implications not to cause readers any significant difficulty.

Difficulties of a not-dissimilar sort also arise in association with the powers attributed to Lucifer. These are subject to subtle modification in the course of the story, but they are introduced in the early chapters by the description of their effects on three victims. In each case, the term La Hire initially uses to the condition of the afflicted is *envoûtée*–a word that has no direct English equivalent.

15

It is unclear exactly how the significance of *envoûtée* in French differs from that of *ensorcellée*, which is transposable into "ensorcelled," "spellbound" or "bewitched." *Enchantée*, whose English transposition, "enchanted,", is very similar in its English implication to "bewitched," is used rather differently in French, but bilingual dictionaries usually feel free to offer "enchanted" as a makeshift English equivalent of *envoûtée*–a substitution that has to be reckoned problematic in the particular context of *Lucifer*, where La Hire seems to be using *envoûtée* because it is more easily investable with pseudoscientific implications than *ensorcellée*–although he soon broadens out his own terminology to take in such terms as *maléfice*, which refers to malevolent spells cast by witches.

Had La Hire so wished, he could have employed the ready-made pseudo-scientific jargon of Mesmerism or hypnotism, but he evidently made a deliberate decision not to do so in the opening of his story, where he attempts, via Louis Mattol, to draw a sharp contrast between Lucifer's *envoûtement* and conventional hypnotic phenomena. That distinction is significantly eroded in the course of the plot, but it would be wrong nevertheless for a translation to employ that kind of terminology from the outset. I, therefore, decided to translate envoûtée as "under a spell" to begin with, broadening my terminology as La Hire broadens his to take in such alternative terms as "bewitchment," and sometimes referring to Lucifer as an "sorcerer" as well as a "spell-caster." This seems to me to be as close as the English language can get to the intended implications of La Hire's terminology, although it is, admittedly, slightly unsatisfactory.

The text posed few other problems in translation, but I have made several slight modifications to it. Although the repetition of information–including the verbatim reproduction of entire paragraphs–is a deliberate device employed by La Hire to pad out episodes whenever his inspiration runs thin, it occasionally becomes unbearably tedious, and I have cut about a number of substantial passages in which the unnecessary repetition of information seemed inordinately excessive and numerous individual sentences or subclauses. Although it seemed inappropriate to conceal the author's flagrant racism by relentless censorship, I have modified its expression in several instances by cutting terms that had no function other than gratuitous insult. I have also corrected a few of the author's trivial "continuity errors," although I have let some of them stand (usually calling attention to them in footnotes) in order to retain the flavor of the original.

The version of the text that I translated is that of the first paperback book edition, published by Ferenczi in 1922, which was divided into two volumes titled *Lucifer* and *Nyctalope contre Lucifer*. The sections of the text are numbered separately in the two paperback volumes, but I have amended the numbering to restore a single sequence.

Brian Stableford

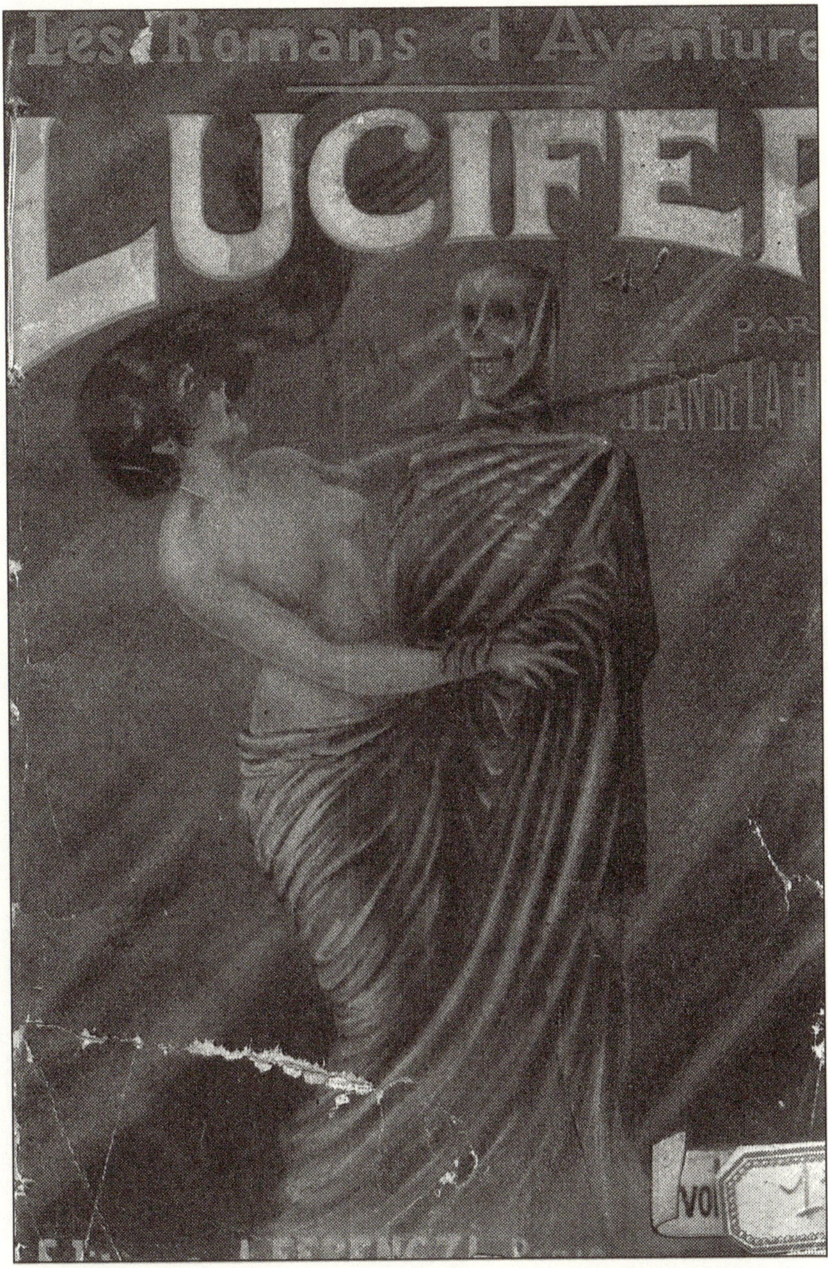
Les Romans d'Aventure
LUCIFER
PAR

Part One: Occult Power

I. Irène's Torture

Always logical and often ferocious, Destiny has its frightful ironies. Who would have thought that the life of the celebrated Professor Onésime Lourmel, of all people, would be turned upside-down by a tragic and mysterious catastrophe?

At 50 years of age, Professor Lourmel, holder of the chair of neuropsychology in the Faculty of Medicine, clinical director of Sainte-Anne Asylum and member of the Academy of Sciences, was one of the busiest men in Paris. Without neglecting his professorial, therapeutic and academic duties in the slightest, he found the time to contribute assiduously to the *Revue des sciences psychiques*, to write a monthly column for the *Annales de la psycho-névrose* and to make a brief study tour every six months, in the course of which he visited two or three provincial or foreign psychiatric hospitals.

Despite working so hard, Professor Lourmel–a robust, cheerful and sociable–did not turn his back on the world. In the exceedingly comfortable house he owned in Auteuil, he had created an environment eminently representative of Science and Frenchness. That environment was also redolent with grace, elegance and beauty, for the Professor liked pretty women, frequented the theaters and reserved one of the best boxes at the Opera by subscription.

A bachelor, Professor Lourmel left the practical management of his existence to his sister Luce, who was five years his junior, but Mademoiselle Luce could not be anything more than the finest of stewards, and the Professor would have suffered what he would have described as "emotional solitude" had he not devoted all his tenderness to his orphan niece, Irène. He had seen to her careful upbringing and had married her off to a young man whom she had met during her vacations in the house in Auteuil. On the threshold of her 20th year, Irène had realized every young girl's dream by marrying Raymond de Ciserat, a naval lieutenant, the son of the illustrious gynaecologist C.-G. de Ciserat, a colleague and friend of Professor Lourmel. "Old Ciserat," as he was known in the Faculty of Medicine, had died on the day that his son graduated from the naval college, and Professor Lourmel had served as Raymond's father thereafter. On the eve of the marriage, he said, not without emotion: "I had two children. I shall have them always, since I have married them to one another. They know that my house is theirs whenever they desire, as they desire, and to the extent that they desire."

Raymond and Irène knew this so well that they spent the two weeks following their marriage at the house in Auteuil, and it was only after devoting a

19

fortnight to "Uncle Onésime" that they left to spend a long honeymoon touring Italy and Sicily. After that journey—which was to last four months, from April to July inclusive—Raymond de Ciserat, with he full permission of the Admiralty, was due to organize and direct a submarine expedition financed by the recently created Subtranslatlantic Company. It was understood that Irène, who was as intrepid as she was beautiful, would accompany her husband in this routine mission.

Throughout the month of April, Uncle Onésime received a letter every day bearing the joint signatures of Irène and Raymond. They came to him from Nice, San Remo, Genoa, Florence, Milan and Venice. On May 1, however, he received no letter. There was none on May 2 either. Anxious, and already quite angry—for the famous Professor was extremely irascible by nature—Lourmel sent a telegram to Venice, to the last address given by the young couple.

May 3 went by without his receiving a letter or a reply to his telegram. Mademoiselle Luce, who was helpless, had a terrible time. The Professor's dolorous anxiety and irrepressible wrath were, in combination, a frightful thing to behold. All the same, it would have been a mere comedy, in the end, if Raymond and Irène's silence had had some banal cause—an abrupt departure from one place to another, postal delays or a few days' excursion into a region devoid of modern communications. Mademoiselle Luce patiently enumerated all these possible explanations; Lourmel acknowledged their plausibility, but his anxiety and anger were not at all diminished.

On May 4, that anxiety and that anger were suddenly transformed into an inexpressible anguish and a powerful fury, repressed by a cold determination—because Lourmel had received a letter, which was expressed in these terms:

Uncle, I could not use the telegraph for I would be thought insane—and if I expressed myself in a telegram, in discreet terms, you would not understand me. Today, I see that I must speak clearly, to say this: Irène is under a spell. *I am in torment. It will surely be the death of me. Come—come to our aid! I am in despair. Come!*

Raymond
Hotel Danieli, Venice.

When this letter was brought to him and he read it, Professor Lourmel was in his office at Sainte-Anne Asylum, in the company of his laboratory assistant, Louis Mattol. Mattol, his most distinguished student, was impassioned by the difficult task of turning the so-called "occult sciences" into exact sciences. As white as a corpse, with sparkling eyes and a hoarse voice, Lourmel said to his astonished assistant: "Listen, Mattol!" And he read Raymond de Ciserat's amazing letter aloud, emphasizing the words. Mattol went pale, just as the Professor had. He loved Raymond and Irène like an older brother. Although he addressed the young woman politely as "*vous*," he always addressed the young officer as "*tu*."

When the letter ended, the Professor looked at his assistant without adding a word, with the searching and surgical expression he used to hypnotize the occupants of the asylum. Mattol understood the question implicit in that insupportable gaze, and simply said in a firm voice: "Master, I believe in the reality of what are called spells."

"Do you know of actual cases?" the Professor asked, dryly.

"I know of three."

"Irrefutable?"

"Inexplicable–other than in term of psychic compulsion."

Professor Lourmel read Raymond's letter again and put it on his desk. Then, his voice still dry and hard, although his body was seized by a sudden tremor, he asked: "Did you ever meet Colonel de Rochas, Mattol?" [1]

"I never met him," the assistant replied, "but I've read his books and made notes on them."

"I met him. Listen! One day, this happened: on one side of a large room, a woman was sitting, facing the wall. In the most distant corner was a table, and on that table was a photograph of the woman. Standing at the table, Colonel de Rochas touched the photograph with his fingertip. Immediately, the woman felt the touch. The Colonel scratched the image twice with his fingernail, on the right hand and the left arm. At the same instant, two red stigmata–the bloody scratches of a fingernail–appeared on the woman's left arm and right hand. This was witnessed by the mathematician Poincaré, the gynaecologist Ciserat and I, the neuropscholologist Onésime Lourmel. The Colonel called it the first stage of *bewitchment*."

The Professor fell silent.

"The incident is known to me," Mattol murmured, impassively. "The story was published in *La Justice* on August 2, 1892. Colonel de Rochas did more thereafter, Professor."

"I know."

No longer able to contain himself, Lourmel got up abruptly and thumped his desk hard with his fist, causing several books, pencils, a penholder and bottles of ink to jump into the air. He let out a terrible growl, his entire body agitated by wrath, while tears of anguish sprang from his eyes.

"Mattol," he said, "we'll leave this evening for Venice. I'll inquire, investigate... It's necessary to identify the spell-caster, to find him, to capture him. By all the gods that men have invented, and by the God they suspect but do not know how to define, I swear that I shall strangle this villain with these very hands!" He raised his clenched and quivering fists above his head, then let them fall heavily back upon the desk. "Go to my house, Mattol," he said, dully. "Tell Luce to make the necessary preparations for the journey, then go pack your own suitcase. Meet me at the Gare de Lyon at 8 p.m. We'll take the Paris-Milan train. I'll send a telegram to Raymond. Do you have a revolver?"

"Yes, a Browning."

"Bring it–and buy one for me; I don't own one myself. Perhaps before strangling the man, I'll be obliged to put bullets into his legs so that he can't escape. Strong though I am, I'm also slow; I'm not 20 years old any longer, and I can't run very fast. Go, my friend, go!"

Mattol went out.

After a pause, Lourmel groaned. "But if I arrive too late to save her, then... Oh, then I shall have to devise tortures for that monster... Slow tortures!"

In Venice, nor far from San Marco, stands the Hotel Danieli, a palatial old building with exceedingly comfortable rooms. At 6 p.m. on May 5, two people were alone in one of its sitting-rooms: Irène and Raymond de Ciserat. They were seated beside a round table charged with refreshments. Irène was stretched out in a rocking-chair, with her head slumped on her left shoulder and her eyes shut. Raymond, seated in an armchair, had turned towards his wife and was looking at her with passionate tenderness. They were each as pale as the other. Irène's face, with lowered eyelids, wore an expression of suffering, while Raymond's, with eyes wide open, bore the marks of fatigue, insomnia and an extraordinary nervous tension. His hands were on his knees, clutching a newspaper, convulsively tearing it up without his being aware of it.

From time to time, the young officer's eyes went to the clock to measure the passing of time. He had received the Professor's telegram the previous night; Irène and he were both awaiting the arrival of their learned, powerful, ingenious and energetic uncle, in whom their only hope of salvation rested. Raymond had decided to blow his brains out if his wife succumbed to the frightful and capricious sickness that had mysteriously descended upon her.

Suddenly, Irène opened her eyes–her beautiful blue eyes, formerly so bright with happiness, now horrified and flooded with tears. She looked at her husband and found the loving strength to smile at him. Then, in a feeble but fearful voice, she asked: "What time is it?"

"6:15," Raymond replied. Letting go of the rumpled, twisted and torn newspaper, he reached out tenderly to take his wife's hands in his, adding: "The train arrived 20 minutes ago. Uncle and Louis will waste no time..."

At that moment, a resounding voice was heard on the quayside outside, crying: "Wait, Mattol!"

"They're here!" Raymond said, getting to his feet. "I'll go welcome them. Will you go to your room?"

"Yes–call Lili."

Lili was Irène's foster-sister. Having become Madame de Ciserat, Irène had taken on little Emilie Dupal–usually known as Lili–as her chambermaid. Intelligent, devoted and alert, the young woman was the perfect servant for the new bride. Raymond had only to make a gesture to bring Lili running–she had been doing a little sewing in an adjacent waiting-room. Immediately, with a firmer tread than might have been expected, in view of her seemingly-infinite lassitude, Irène de Ciserat went into the little three-room apartment that the newlyweds occupied on the first floor of the hotel. Lili followed her.

Two minutes later, Professor Lourmel erupted into the sitting-room, with Raymond de Ciserat and Louis Mattol to either side of him. "I want to see her right away!" the Professor said, with contained violence. "She isn't in bed, you say? You went out this morning? Good–that reassures me a little, but I must see her. Take me to her! Take care of the suitcases, Mattol, I beg you."

While Mattol occupied himself with the luggage and the rooms that the naval officer had reserved for them that morning, Raymond led Lourmel up to the first-floor apartment. Lili had gone. In the little room where she was waiting, Irène leapt up to put her arms around the Professor's neck and hug him, then immediately let herself fall into an armchair. Covering her face with her hands, she burst into tears.

"There, there!" said Lourmel. "Calm down, little one. I must know everything, in detail. We must talk calmly, if we are to act effectively thereafter." He took off his hat and gloves and threw them on a table. Taking the young woman's hands in his, he drew them aside and studied her tearful face. "You can hardly sleep," he said, "and you can scarcely eat anything. A few more days of that and you'd be a complete mess. We must take countermeasures. We shall fight, and fighting is always healthy sport. There–you're better already! Don't cry any more. Raymond, sit down in that armchair. That's good. You must both answer my questions clearly, concisely and without digression. We shall conduct a sort of medico-legal inquest. A certain coolness and serenity is required."

The Professor's voice, words and expression seemed to enliven Irène. She raised herself up; her cheeks became less pale, her eyes less fearful.

"Mattol has come with me, little one," Lourmel went on, addressing himself to Irène. "He'll be useful to us, as much by virtue of his specialist knowledge as his character. I swear to you that we shall save you. Enough preliminaries–I shall begin the interrogation. How did this affair begin?"

Irène and Raymond looked at one another. The young woman drew the necessary courage from her husband's ardent eyes. She turned to her uncle, who was sitting facing her and slightly to the right, and she spoke in an emotional voice, her forehead pink with embarrassment.

"It was during the night of April 28. I woke up suddenly, convinced that someone had kissed me on the left cheek. I thought that it was Raymond and I put out my hand–but as I opened my eyes, I saw, by the light of the electric night-light, that Raymond was asleep. I thought I had been dreaming and closed my eyes again, smiling–but the sensation of being kissed was immediately renewed, on the right cheek this time, and as if the lips were moving over the skin. I sat up, astonished, and passed my hands over my face. Then, the kisses were on my hands, along my arms, so strong and so strange that I was afraid. I cried out: 'Raymond! Raymond!' Immediately, the kisses ceased, but I felt such a violent blow on my left shoulder that it thrust me back upon the pillow."

She fell silent, shivering.

Immediately, Raymond took up the story: "Her cry woke me up. I leaned towards her–and the terrified expression on her face made me leap out of bed. I turned up the electric light. Assuming that Irène had had a nightmare, I took her in my arms to comfort her, for she was trembling in every limb. She was reassured, little by little. Laughing and crying at the same time, she told me what she had just felt. Naturally, I thought it was a nightmare, and I uncovered her left shoulder to kiss it, as one does with a child who has suffered a minor injury–but I was stunned by amazement. The shoulder was reddened, already slightly swollen, exactly as if she had received a blow from a little hammer! Instinctively, I put my finger on it, and Irène let out a cry; the bruise was extremely painful.

"The idea of a hammer-blow only came to me later, uncle, when I reflected on the dimensions and form of the little contusion. At first, though, once the initial shock had passed, what I thought and told Irène was that her nightmare had caused her to make a violent movement and that she had bumped into the bedhead or the corner of the night-stand. I held Irène in my arms and it wasn't long before she went peacefully to sleep."

"Good!" said the Professor. "What happened next?"

Irène, now very pale and making an effort to suppress her nervousness, continued: "I was quite tranquil during the next day. Raymond and I spent almost all of it visiting various churches. The bruise on my shoulder troubled me slightly, but in the belief that I had had a nightmare, I laughed about it. That evening, at 6 p.m., while Raymond stayed in the hall to smoke a cigarette, I came into the bedroom to change my dress. I was undressed, facing the full-length mirror, while Lili was rummaging in my trunk, when... Oh, uncle!"

"Go on, child, go on!" said Lourmel, taking hold of the tremulous hands that Irène had held out towards him, as if imploring his aid.

"Well, I felt myself seized around the waist, from behind, while burning lips showered rapid kisses on my shoulders and the nape of my neck, brutally. I was petrified. All at once, I felt a bite on my left shoulder, very close to the wound inflicted the previous night–and in the mirror, I saw tooth-marks appear on my flesh! *But there was no one there, no one behind me!* Lili was on the other side of the room, half-buried in the trunk. No, *there was no one!* I suddenly felt ill... Oh...!"

Wrenching her hands way from her uncle's fingers, Irène covered her face and threw herself violently backwards, in the grip of a terrible nervous tremor.

Professor Lourmel, impassive but pale and tight-lipped, stopped Raymond with a gesture as the young man was leaning towards his wife. Then he took a little box from his waistcoat pocket, from which he extracted a Pravaz syringe and a needle.[2] The syringe was full of liquid, slightly tinted with yellow. "Give me your right arm, Irène," he said, in a voice of irresistible authority.

She obeyed, and shielded her eyes with her left hand. The Professor turned back the sleeve of her silk dress; with a sure hand, he plunged the needle into the white flesh of the plump arm. The piston forced the liquid in. The needle was withdrawn, carefully wiped and returned with the syringe to the box. Replacing it in his pocket, the Professor said to Raymond: "We'll let her rest. Continue."

The anxious officer pulled himself together, and spoke in a clear and rapid voice. "I was called into the room by Lili, who came on to the staircase and said: 'Madame has cried out and fainted!' I found Irène stretched out like a corpse on the bedroom carpet. I carried her to the bed. Straight away, I noticed the new wound, which was exactly like a nasty bite. The skin was not broken, but the marks of teeth stood out whitely in the middle of a violet bruise.

"I questioned Lili. She didn't know anything. Our attentions revived Irène and I was able to obtain an account of the frightful event from her. This time, there was no question of any unconscious gestures, nightmarish sensations or involuntary contusions. Irène was wide awake, calm, smiling and happy when she had felt the hands pressing her waist, the lips kissing her shoulders and neck and the teeth biting into her flesh–and the bite was there!

"We were unable to eat dinner or sleep. Not until morning did we become drowsy, after having said a thousand stupid things–anxiously on my part, in terror on Irène's. Finally, though, we got up again. On the following day, as the weather was beautiful, we resolved to carry through the plan we had formulated the previous afternoon: an excursion to the monastery of Saint-Lazare.

"A hired gondola was waiting for us. It was a round trip of several hours. We took a nice cold lunch. Lili came with us. Everything went well, except that Irène and I were haunted by an obsession from which nothing could distract us– endless questions with no plausible answers. Finally, with the help of the brisk air of the lagoon, Irène recovered some of her appetite. After that, the monastery proved interesting. We were heading back towards Venice, slightly less tormented, when the gondolier, coming alongside the public gardens, pointed at an old woman sitting on the damp steps. He said to us: 'There's a witch–the most famous on these shores. For a lira, she'll tell you about the past, present and future–but she's from Toledo, and although she's been in Venice for 20 years, she can only speak Spanish. People understand anyway–they always understand!'

"The old woman was already leaning over. She stared at Irène and took her hand in an authoritative manner–but she barely glanced at it before drawing back. Interlacing her fingers in a pitying manner, she looked at Irène with eyes full of sadness. '*Ay, probrecita,*' she murmured. '*Hechizaa! Hechizaa!*' And she fled, whimpering. Silently, the gondolier plunged his oar back into the water– and I noticed, as we left the gondola in front of the hotel, that he looked at Irène with a sort of fearful pity. For her own part, Irène was calm, indifferent, seemingly unconscious, having not even thought of asking me what the witch's words had meant.

"As for me, despite my familiarity with the Spanish language, I did not know the meaning of the word *hechizaa*–but I hastened to find out. Having left Irène in the care of Lili, who was helping her to undress, I went to the hotel library. There I found a Spanish/French/Italian dictionary. I searched for the word *hechizaa*. It means *spellbound* or *bewitched*. Spellbound! That was a ray of light for my mind, but for my heart, it was an atrocious shock!"

With a sigh, Raymond de Ciserat fell silent. He lowered his head and placed a hand over his forehead. Then, with a sudden shiver, he went on; his eyes were sparkling and his voice was harsh. "The phrase was not unfamiliar to me. Louis had often spoken to me of strange phenomena. At his suggestion, I had read recorded accounts of a number of genuinely troubling experiences–but I had always remained skeptical before. At that moment, however, I was convinced. The bite–the visible bite! And a conviction imposed itself on my mind and my heart: the conviction that, somewhere in the world, there was a man–a coward and a monster–who loved my wife and who had embraced and tormented her at a distance! And my wife had actually experienced the embraces and the tortures of that man!

"I didn't want to believe it. I said to myself: *I shall watch and observe*. That is what I did–and that night, the night of April 30, was a terrible one. Irène was seized and beaten, struck–even scratched! You will see the wounds on her left side. I held her in my arms, but I could not protect her. It was horrible! In the morning, I wrote to you. We no longer had any other hope but you. Irène, look at me!"

Hurling himself to his knees in front of his wife, Raymond seized her hands. In a transport of love and anguish, as she leaned over him, he threw himself upon her and they hugged one another, sobbing. Professor Lourmel got to his feet. Drawing himself up to his full and imposing height, he towered over the entwined spouses curled up in the vast armchair and looked down at them with an indefinable expression of tenderness and sorrow. Then, his eyes became bright and piercing again, almost icy. "Irène, Raymond," he said, gravely, "have faith. Mattol and I will be the stronger. Answer me, Raymond–what has happened since the night of April 30?"

"Nothing!" said the naval officer, dully. "But as every minute passes, we tremble in anticipation of the minute to come."

"I want to see these stigmata. Get into bed, Irène."

The spouses got up and, still entwined, went into the next room. When they had disappeared, Lourmel went into the anteroom, where he found Lili. "My girl," he said, "go and tell Monsieur Mattol that I want to see him. Wait with him in the sitting-room. I'll be in the bedroom. You must both come and join me when I call for you. Close and lock every door behind you."

"Yes, Professor," the servant said. She went out.

When Lourmel had subjected Irène to a physical examination, the young woman, a little calmer, put on a dressing-gown. Lourmel then called Mattol.

Followed by Lili, the intern came into the bedroom; he kissed Madame de Ciserat's hand. In response to the Professor's invitation, everyone sat down.

Succinctly, but without omitting anything, with the clarity of a mathematical demonstration, Lourmel acquainted Mattol with the facts as reported by Irène and Raymond and the observations that he had made. "The bruises are irrefutable," he concluded, "as are the superficial scratches that I have examined. The former have the appearance of having been produced by quite violent blows with a little hammer; the latter are exactly what one would expect if the skin had been broken by a fork with three sharp prongs. We therefore find ourselves confronted with material phenomena that cannot be doubted. What has caused them? Struck by the manner in which the phenomena were produced, and also by the word spoken by an alleged witch, Raymond believes that a *spell* has been cast, and this despite the profound skepticism that he formerly professed with regard to mysteries of that order. Irène does not know what to think; she lives in continual terror. But we must know the cause to suppress the effects, and there are two conceivable hypotheses–can you see what they are?"

"Yes, Professor," the assistant replied, gravely. "The two hypotheses are, on the one hand, a complex case of somnambulism, hypnotism and suggestion, and, on the other, an explicit case of spell-casting."

"Perfect!"

"Professor," Mattol went on, ardently, "I do not believe that the former is the case. It would imply defects and disorders in Irène and Raymond that are not evident in either of them. You know both of them too well, and I know Raymond too well, to have the least doubt on that subject. I see no sign in them of any somnambulism or hallucination sufficient for Raymond to have subjected Irène, unconsciously, to the physical phenomena that she has felt and you have established, especially without Irène having actually seen Raymond acting in that extravagant and brutal manner. Lili was in the room during the second phase of the phenomena, while Raymond was downstairs in one of the hotel's reception-rooms. The problem is complicated by the fact that Lili herself would have to be involved in the somnambulistic and hallucinatory vertigo. Everything indicates that that is not the case.

"As for the possibility of suggestion, autosuggestion–in which Irène would be her own victim–it might have enabled her to go so far as to experience sensations of any kind, but not to the extent of causing cuts and bruises. In thaumaturgy, such cases are possible and do occur–but scientific experience tells us that they only occur in certain subjects predisposed to ancient, profound and dominant cerebral defects; this is not the case with Irène, whose mind, in addition to having been educated by you, is calm, logical, reasonable and immune to all excessive imagination. As for Raymond, you know as well as I do how sound his brain is. Thus..."

"There is nothing more probable than bewitchment?" said Lourmel.

"That is my opinion, Professor."

There was a pause. Irène had abandoned her hands to Raymond's, and her large blue eyes, full of fear and sorrow, were imploring help that her one true love was, alas, incapable of providing. Raymond, incessantly squeezing and caressing his wife's hands, was looking back and forth at his uncle and his friend, pleadingly.

"Mattol," said the Professor, "you have studied these questions more than I have. I will admit that a spell has been cast, with the reservation that this admission will not be definitive until I have personally witnessed the production of the phenomenon. That's understood, then. But what is the remedy?"

"There is but one," Mattol replied, unhesitatingly.

Irène and Raymond, breathless, were hanging on their friend's every word. Lourmel fixed his eyes on his pupil. "Which is?" he asked.

"Firstly, to identify the spell-caster."

"Good! And then?"

"Then, to have a material image of him, a photograph, painting or figurine, charged with the subject's sensibility—which is to say that it must have been in contact with his flesh for several minutes. By means of such an image, we might in turn cast a spell on the spell-caster. Or, better still, we could find the spell-caster himself and kill him."

"There's no other cure?" Lourmel said, simply.

"No, there's no other," Mattol said, curtly.

"In that case," the Professor said, turning to Irène, "it's you, my child, who must guide our first step. You've heard Louis. He is knowledgeable, to the extent that anyone can be knowledgeable in matters that exact science has not yet penetrated. What he says is true, to the extent that a statement can be true based on experiences that are still insufficiently numerous for a theory to be safely established. Various speculations, of a more or less practical kind, have been set before you. We have talked; we shall now act—and it is the first step of the action that we must all take together, by trying to identify the spell-caster: the unknown entity whose victim you are. Let's see Irène—summon all your usual reason, all your calm, all your fine intelligence. Do you feel that you are capable of reflecting, remembering and considering this question with us coolly?"

His warm, sonorous voice carried a sort of suggestive force; it radiated energy and will-power; Irène received its beneficial influence. She had already withdrawn her hands from Raymond's grip, as if to collect herself. She closed her eyes. Her beautiful pale face recovered some color. When she opened her eyes again, they were a deeper blue and shone more brightly; they were almost hard beneath the dampness of restrained tears. In a very calm voice, in which all her will-power was perceptible, the young woman said: "I'm ready, uncle."

Professor Lourmel stroked his short, bushy white beard with his right hand and tapped his thigh with his left. "Good!" he said, with evident satisfaction. "Don't hold anything back. Do you suspect someone? Someone who might have pursued you—pardon me, little one; excuse me, Raymond, but we have so few

28

words at the service of our thoughts!–with his desires, his love, his spite, his jealousy, his hatred?"

Irène closed her eyes. Her facial expression was untroubled, merely displaying the concentration of an avidly-searching mind. Several minutes ran by without anyone pronouncing a single word or making a gesture. Not a breath was audible. Lourmel, Raymond, Mattol and Lili all wore the same anxious expression as they studied Irène's face. That face suddenly reddened violently. The young woman's entire body shivered. "Ah!" she cried, putting her right hand to her forehead.

She opened her eyes, which turned passionately towards Raymond. "Yes, that's it!" she said to him. "That must be it! You shall be the judge. I remember... Oh, things that I had completely forgotten! I remember them now, quite clearly, in every detail, as if it were yesterday. And the man's features...! Yes, yes, it can't be anyone but him!"

She fell silent, after emitting a great sigh; her eyes never left Raymond's face. The latter took his wife's hands very gently, and caressed them. "Speak, Irène." he said, tenderly. "Speak!"

"And be calm, little one–very calm," the Professor added, slowly.

Overcoming her emotion, Irène began to speak. "It was last winter, during the big party you gave, uncle, in honor of the American Professor Jameson, when he visited Paris. You were at sea, Raymond. I had just danced with you, Louis. I had gone into the library in order to rest for a while. I had been alone there for a few minutes when a man I did not know, and had never even seen before, came in. I thought that he, too, was seeking solitude, and that he would leave when he saw me–but no! He came straight towards me. I can remember him exactly: tall, very thin, smoking a cigarette, with red hair and a moustache, and a sort of fixed smile–a *rictus sardonicus*–upon his lips. His eyes were some indefinable color between yellow and green, but were dark and sparkling nevertheless, profoundly sunk into their orbits, with long red eyelashes. He was elegantly-dressed, apparently relaxed, feline and powerful. I had that entire impression then, although it was certainly unconscious–and it all came back into my mind a few minutes ago, appearing before my eyes with an intensity that frightens me!"

Irène shuddered and her eyes closed–but she opened them immediately, and they expressed a wild willfulness.

"The man came forward," she continued, "bowed to me, and said, without any preamble; 'Mademoiselle, I have an income of 3000 francs a year, I belong to a great Polish family and I am 35 years old. I saw you this evening for the first time. I looked at you for an hour–and I love you. Will you give me permission to ask Professor Lourmel for your hand?' "

Irène laughed nervously, and went on: "I was stupefied–but not for long. Suddenly, emerging from the profoundest depths of my soul, the horror of that individual overwhelmed me. 'You are mad, Monsieur!' I cried. 'And you repel me! Go away, this instant!' Then, as I now remember, the man smiled strangely, accentuating his rictus. Without saying a word, he raised his right hand above me. I slumped back in the armchair, overtaken by a strange somnolence. I must have kept my eyes open, however, for I could still see, as if in a dream–or, unable to help myself, a nightmare. I saw the man go straight to a shelf, on which there was a large family photograph album. He opened it, riffled through it, and withdrew three items. Then, returning to me, he untied the ribbon that was wound twice around my hair, and used it to attach the three photographs together..."

"Ah! I understand!" Professor Lourmel exclaimed.

"I deduced as much!" murmured Mattol.

"What? What do you understand? What have you deduced?" said the astonished Irène, as if waking up from a dream.

But Raymond, who was listening with anxious avidity, leaned over her ardently. "Go on, Irène," he begged. You were saying: '...used it to attach the three photographs together...' "

"Ah! Yes!" After blinking for a moment, she went on hurriedly: "He attached the three photographs together, and slid them over the skin along the nape of my neck, between my shoulders and into the cleavage of my silk dress. Then, he took me by the hands, forcefully, looked me straight in the face and made me shut my eyes, although–I remember it perfectly–I wanted to keep them open. A short time afterwards, I sensed that he had withdrawn the photographs and perceived that he had gone. I must have fallen asleep right away, for, if I'm not mistaken, I was woken up–I don't know how much later–by you, uncle."

"That's right!" said Lourmel, gravely. "I, too, remember it well. Everyone had gone and I had not seen you for an hour. I thought you were in your room, but Lili corrected me. I searched for you and found you profoundly asleep in the big armchair in the library. I woke you up. You burst out laughing, and embraced me joyfully–and you went to bed without mentioning the red-haired man."

"I didn't remember anything," Irène affirmed, with evident sincerity. "But just now, doubtless under the influence of your words and Raymond's ardent presence, a veil suddenly seemed to be lifted from my mind and I saw that whole scene again..."

"That's normal," said Mattol.

"And the photographs?" the Professor asked.

"Have they really disappeared?" cried Irène.

"You haven't opened the album since then?"

"No, I don't think so. I would certainly I have noticed the absence of three photographs and would have mentioned it to you."

"All the more so," said Mattol, "since the photographs are certainly of you, Irène. It's thanks to them that the red-haired man was able to put you under a spell."

"My God!" groaned the young woman, shivering again and hiding her face with her hands.

Raymond sat down on one of the arms of her chair, put his arms around her and kissed her on the forehead.

"I discovered the absence of the photographs a few days later," Professor Lourmel said. "I thought that Irène had taken them. I remember remarking that the missing photographs were of her, for the album was quite familiar to me: one in a tennis costume, one in an evening dress, taken from the front, and one in the same evening dress, in a rear view with the face in profile. It was when I was correcting the proofs of my report to the Academy on a new study of the nervous system. I was excessively preoccupied with the corrections, and immediately forgot about the photographs, which I suppose I never mentioned to you."

"Never," whispered the young woman.

"And you never saw the man again?"

"I have not seen him since."

"Did you notice him that evening, Mattol, in the crowd swarming in the drawing-rooms, the dining-room and the library?"

"No, Professor," Mattol replied. "I didn't notice him."

"But he's the one we have to find!" cried Raymond.

There was a brief pause for reflection.

Irène raised her head and squeezed her husband's hands. She looked alternatively at her uncle and Mattol with an anxious expression. Raymond's eyes were fiery and his face expressed the rage and hatred that were seething in his heart; he saw the abhorrent image of the red-haired man, the enigmatic sorcerer who—no doubt seemed possible—was Irène's impudent and cowardly torturer.

"But to what end?" Raymond suddenly spat out. "Is it merely for revenge, or does he have some plan? Ah—we must find out who he is, find him, seize him and kill him!"

"Yes, we must find out who he is," the Professor repeated, determined and somber in his calm. "Anticipating an enormous influx of visitors, I had placed Richard in the hallway, charging him to obtain the name and address of each guest. I wanted the list to later pay homage to Professor Jameson. A long table was placed across the hallway, leaving only a narrow passage. Richard was sitting at the table with the guestbook, the pen and the ink. To the left were three hired valets in charge of the cloakroom. That should have worked very well."

"Good!" said Mattol. "I can confirm that, having passed through myself."

"Then the wretch's name can be found in the register!" cried Raymond.

"I hope so—but the book has been sent to Professor Jameson in New York."

"We'll go to New York!" said Irène and Raymond, in unison.

"Yes, of course," the Professor agreed. "But it will take two days to get to Le Havre, plus six days or thereabouts from Le Havre to New York. That makes eight. Then there's the time of the return journey. From now until then..."

He fell silent. Everyone understood. Every face went pale. Lili, almost hysterical, could not suppress a sob.

"Besides," Mattol put in, "the man could have given a false name."

There was a long anguished silence. Then, turning to Mattol, the Professor continued, his voice, his expression and his body language displaying his impatience. "Let's see, my dear friend. You know how to get to the bottom of these matters. Isn't there any means of impeding the spell and attenuating its effects? Isn't there any force, obstacle or barrier that can be interposed between the spell-caster and his victim?"

Mattol replied slowly and carefully, under Irène's and Raymond's pleading gaze. "Experiments in this area are still at the stage of groping timidly in the dark. However, it seems to me that a change of physical environment, if the change is unknown to the spell-caster, might disorientate him and render him almost powerless."

"What do you mean by *physical environment*?" Raymond asked.

"I mean the dominant element, in terms of volume and density, between the spell-caster and his victim. All this is barely at the theoretical stage, based on scant empirical evidence, but in the present case, that dominant element is *air*. We can do nothing about the spell-caster, but we can change the physical environment of the victim. Isn't the Subtransatlantic Company's submarine stationed at Le Havre?"

"Ah, Louis!" cried Raymond, throwing himself towards his friend. "I understand! We'll go to New York by submarine!"

"Is that possible, at the present stage of the company's organization?" asked the Professor.

"Yes, yes!" said the naval officer. "Two exploratory submarines are ready to go to sea–the *Lampas* and the *Synancée*. It's the *Lampas* that was assigned to me for my mission."

"We'll obtain its use for the voyage," the Professor said.

"And by traveling at the greatest possible depth," Mattol went on, "we'll put a cushion of water between the red-haired man and Irène, of such volume and density that his spell will be unable to penetrate it, the natural elements being incompatible for the transmission of the will-power's effluvia..."

"And the phenomenon of spell-casting is nothing but the transmission of an extraordinarily powerful will," murmured the Professor.

"When shall we leave?" Irène asked.

"Tomorrow. We must be ready to take the 2 p.m. train to Milan and Paris."

"When shall we be in Le Havre?" Irène asked, shuddering.

"About 30 hours later–on May 7, in the evening."

"And at sea?"

"Two hours after our arrival in Le Havre," said Raymond de Ciserat.

Dusk had invaded the room during this conversation, but no one had thought of switching on the electric light. As Raymond pronounced the words Le Havre, the sonorous and repetitive sound of the dinner-gong became audible.

"Will you go down, my dear?" Raymond asked his wife.

Irène smiled valiantly. "Yes, I'll go down! All of you, it now seems, form a rampart around me. You've suffered even more than me, my dear, and we have both been disabled."

The young woman pressed herself fondly against her husband, who smiled and said to her: "We hadn't thought of the submarine, of physical environments and incompatible elements, effluvia and will-power..."

But their smiles did not last long.

When the lights had been switched on, the three men went into the sitting-room, leaving Irène in her bedroom to dress for dinner, with Lili's help. Scarcely two minutes had gone by when a scream resounded, followed by panic-stricken cries for help. Without a second's hesitation, the three men hurled themselves forward.

In her petticoat and camisole, Irène had collapsed in an armchair, in front of the petrified Lili. The unfortunate young woman, her face contorted in horror, was frantically trying to defend her throat, lips and cheeks from the hands and lips of someone who could not be seen, but whose brutal contacts left red marks and light scratches on the recently-powdered delicate skin.

For several minutes, in Raymond's powerless arms, in front of the terrified Lili and under the observant eyes of Lourmel and Mattol, Irène was prey to the cruelties and the even-more-odious caresses of he mysterious spell-caster. Then, abruptly, she felt nothing more. She looked at Raymond and breathed out, exhaustedly. "It's finished!" she said–but her throat and shoulders retained stigmata which, superficial as they were on this occasion, forbade the wearing of a low-cut dress. Madame de Ciserat, therefore, put on a high-necked dress–because, having regained her courage, she was determined to go down to the hotel dining-room for dinner.

A well-stocked table was set in the quietest corner, half-hidden by a folding screen. When Irène appeared with Raymond, her uncle and Mattol were already there. They sat down together.

"I've just checked the timetable," Lourmel said, immediately. "There's a train for Milan and Paris at 11:15 p.m. tonight. We must not delay any longer. I've telephoned the station and reserved three sleeping compartments. We'll be in Paris tomorrow, and on the morning of the following day, we'll board Raymond's submarine in Le Havre. We'll see Professor Jameson in New York. I've searched my memory, and I'm sure that I saw him in a one-to-one conversation, for several minutes, with a tall, lean red-haired gentleman..."

"Oh, uncle!" said Irène. "Do you really remember that?"

"Yes."

33

No more was said. What was there to say? The young woman and the three men were so profoundly and intensely united that they were thinking the same things at the same moment, and knew it. Words were unnecessary.

At 11:15 p.m., Professor Lourmel, Louis Mattol, Raymond and Irène de Ciserat, with Lili, climbed up into the compartments reserved in a carriage which would be attached to the Paris express in Milan. The journey passed without the slightest incident. In Paris, Lourmel's limousine was waiting at the Gare de Lyon.

As they went along the Grands Boulevards, they embraced Aunt Luce–who was mortified by anguish–and reassured her as best they could. Two extra trunks full of clothes were loaded into the automobile and they caught the train for Le Havre, where the arrived in the early morning.

Two cars from the Subtransatlantic Company, whose local director had been alerted by telegram, were waiting for the travelers. They went directly to the main quay, where the offices of the company and the apartments of its senior managers were located. Facing this edifice, in the old harbor, floating docks had been established to shelter the submarines *Lampas* and *Synancée*.

Following Raymond and the director, Irène got down from the cars that had brought her from the station. As she crossed the pavement to go into the sumptuous building, she was passed by a man who slipped a piece of paper adroitly into her hand and whispered, very quietly and rapidly but quite distinctly: "For you alone, on your life!"

The man disappeared around the corner of the building, presumably into a street at right-angles to the quay.

A little apartment, consisting of a bedroom, a sitting-room and a bathroom, was put at the disposal of Irène and Lili for the three or four hours that would pass before the embarkation. Professor Lourmel, Raymond de Ciserat and Louis Mattol had important matters to discuss with the company's director.

As soon as she was left alone in her room, while Lili was running a bath, the distraught Irène ripped the envelope open.

During the journey, she had not suffered any undue sensation. As she had an optimistic temperament, a cheerful character and a heart exultant with love, and as Raymond wanted nothing more than to see her happy and to be happy for and with her, both of them had allowed themselves to be overtaken by hope, by the illusion that the nightmare might be over and done with... But here was this letter: a letter written in red ink on sulfur-yellow paper, in bold and angular handwriting; a letter that Irène had to read twice before she understood it properly.

Irène, you now know a little of my power. And now, I want you to accept into yourself, into the innermost privacy of your being, the loyal, determined and absolute decision to be mine, entirely mine, undividedly and forever, far from Paris, beyond France.

I could, solely by the exercise of my will-power, bring you to me, without any possible struggle on your part–but no! I want you vanquished, consenting and submissive. I want your yes *to flourish on your lips in consequence of the decision of your own mind. I want your slavery to commence by virtue of your own choice.*

There are two alternatives between which you must choose.

Either you will make the decision that I ask–and I shall know that it has been made simply by the fact of your mental acceptance–or I shall kill, at a distance and with frightful tortures, first your Aunt Luce, then your uncle Professor Lourmel, then your friend Louis Mattol, and finally, your husband Raymond de Ciserat. Then I shall take control of you, despite anything you might do, and you will live with the remorse and shame of having sacrificed, uselessly, the four people that you love.

To make the desired decision, I will give you until June 10. Should you fail to do so, your Aunt Luce will die at midday on June 11, after 12 hours of torture.

I add that, once you have made the decision, I will give you the appropriate instructions to render it effective.

A woman who will soon be by my side, who hates me–whom you will love, mourn and replace–cursed me one day by throwing in my face a formidable name. That name pleased me. I desire no other, and I sign myself :

Lucifer.

II. Monsieur Narbonne's Strongbox

In Paris, at the very moment when Irène de Ciserat was reading the letter from the terrifying sorcerer who proudly signed himself "Lucifer," Monsieur Mathias Narbonne was the dolorous victim and terrified witness of an extraordinary event.

The whole world knew Mathias Narbonne as a billionaire philanthropist. French, Parisian and Montmartrian, by a marvelous caprice of destiny, he had made a fortune in Argentine and Brazil. Fortunate speculations–which were, moreover, entirely honest–based on the latent state of war between permanently-revolutionized Mexico and the avidly expectant United States had multiplied that fortune tenfold in three years.

A billionaire to the point that the slightest operation, whether industrial, commercial or merely financial, added further millions to his billions, Narbonne returned to France, Paris and Montmartre at the age of 50, and had an exceedingly tasteful house built in the Rue d'Orchampt, overlooking the city, from which flowed a hundred rivers of gold.

Hospitals and universities; numerous families and unwed mothers, miners' cottages consigned to mourning by firedamp; maritime villages starving for lack of fish; agricultural regions devastated by some forgotten savagery or caprice of nature–in brief, everyone who toiled and suffered in France, Italy or Belgium–received aid and remedy, abundantly and intelligently administered, from "Monsieur Mathias." Whether in person or through the mediation of three or four women of mature years, noble spirit and clear mind, his generosity was usefully and justly shared, at least in France, Italy and Belgium. "I had to make a choice," Narbonne said, with his natural good humor. "Considerable as it may be, my fortune is not sufficient to soothe all poverty in any of the world's five continents. I am French, and I have always considered Belgium and Italy to be the sisters of France–during the Great War, they acted nobly–so I am a Franco-Italo-Belgian philanthropist..."

Narbonne was a philanthropist to the tune of 500 millions a year, on average–and 500 millions, judiciously employed, without "compensating commissions" or "aid committees," can dress and cure a great many wounds on an annual basis.

On May 7, the philanthropist, who had been awakened at 5 a.m., as was his habit, spent two hours getting dressed and at breakfast. Then, accompanied by the godson who served as his secretary–who appeared at 7 a.m. precisely–he went into his study, a large room illuminated by two huge bay windows looking out over the immensity of Paris.

"First, let's make the weekly assessment of the state of the coffers, André," Narbonne said.

36

A large office desk occupied the middle of the room. Its two sides, each furnished with 20 drawers filled with files and accounts, served both the master and the secretary, who habitually sat facing one another. While the broad and cheerful light of the Sun, already high above Paris, and the pure morning air entered through the two open windows, André d'Arbol sat down on one side of the desk. On the other side, with his back turned, Narbonne marched towards the enormous bronzed steel safe which took up an entire wall-panel between the southern corner of the wall and the door to the library. It was then that the extraordinary event occurred.

As he was opening the safe and extending his right hand into its interior, Narbonne released a sharp exclamation, withdrew his hand and took a step backwards.

"Oh! What is it?" said André.

"Christ! A bandage, quickly... A piece of string, a handkerchief–it doesn't matter!"

André leapt to his feet, dumbfounded.

Very pale, with his face contracted in pain, Narbonne put his left hand around his right wrist and squeezed hard. He displayed his right hand; blood was running from the palm, which had been pierced right through as if by a stiletto-thrust.

André brought a ball of string out of a drawer and made a skilful ligature above Narbonne's right wrist. The blood ceased flowing almost immediately. In the meantime, the philanthropist had recovered his characteristic impassiveness. "André," he said, "telephone Dormoy. He's bound to be at home at this hour. Tell him to come immediately, with what's needed to make a dressing. Tell him it's a penetrating wound–a knife-thrust right through the hand." Monsieur Dormoy was Narbonne's close friend and physician.

Five minutes later, a succinct explanation had been made over the telephone. "Now, let's think!" said Narbonne.

André immediately hung up the telephone, went to the open safe and looked into the compartmentalized interior of the vast steel box. "How the Devil did it happen?" he muttered.

"Yes–how, by thunder? There's nothing in the strongbox that could pierce a hand this fashion."

There was, indeed, no trace of a blade, nail, stiletto or dagger in the safe. "Then again, even if there were some instrument capable of cutting or piercing," André went on, still bewildered, "what force could have seized it, brandished it, and brought it down with sufficient violence to..."

Narbonne had now folded his right arm over his breast. The index finger of the injured hand was curled up between two waistcoat buttons. It was as if the arm were held in a sling pinned to the shoulder or knotted about his neck. The two men stood together, looking into the safe. "I don't understand," the philanthropist murmured.

37

"Me neither," muttered his secretary.

"Let's sit down and wait for Dormoy."

Each of them went to his habitual place, facing one another across the huge desk. Narbonne, who was very pale and still suffering considerable pain, shut his eyes; André d'Arbol's confused gaze went from his employer's face to his wounded hand and back again. Both understood that speech would be in vain, so neither of them expressed his nebulous and tumultuous thoughts.

Their silence and immobility lasted scarcely ten minutes before the arrival of Monsieur Dormoy, who lived near the corner of the Rue d'Orchampt at No. 104, Rue Lepic. He was shown in by Michel, the philanthropist's manservant.

Doctor Olivier Dormoy was a 45-year-old Burgundian, with neatly-brushed dark hair and a goatee beard. He was an excellent practitioner, cheerful and good-hearted. He displayed his astonishment frankly. "What?" he cried, from the doorway. "A dagger-blow? How? Where from?"

"Dress it first, my friend," Narbonne said. "We'll talk afterwards."

"Fine! D'Arbol, my dear chap, please fetch a bowl of some sort, two hand-towels and boiling water."

The petrified Michel remained on the threshold, watching and listening, unable to believe his eyes or his ears. André revived him with a shove, pushed him into the corridor and went out. A minute later, he returned with the items he had been instructed to fetch. Water was always on the boil in the kitchen.

Meanwhile, Dormoy had opened a small case that he had brought with him, displaying his surgical instruments. He untied the wrist, releasing the blood flow, then secured it again with a tourniquet. Then, after having carefully examined the strange wound, he applied a gauze dressing to each face of the hand and suspended a sling from the shoulder of his patient's jacket. It was all completed in a quarter of an hour, without a word being spoken.

When it was over, Narbonne drank a small glass of rum which André had brought him. "Very good!" the philanthropist concluded. "You can assure me, Dormoy, that it's not serious?"

"I can assure you of that, my dear friend. You'll experience a certain difficulty opening and closing your right hand for some while, but nothing essential was cut. I'll renew the dressing every morning. In a fortnight, you won't need the sling any more."

"Thank you."

With his left hand, Narbonne pointed to two armchairs, one of which was André's and the other reserved for visitors, placed to one side of the office desk. The secretary and the physician sat down. Michel took away the bowl, the water-jug, the blood-stained hand-towels and the rum glass. The whole study was tidy and sunlit.

Narbonne sat down in his usual place. After a moment's meditative silence, he said, very gravely: "Dormoy, my friend, what has happened is extraordinary. Listen." With minute care, he related the facts, omitting no detail of his movements and gestures.

Dormoy, utterly astonished, went to examine the interior of the safe, whose door was still open. As he came back to resume his seat, the physician murmured: "You amaze me, Mathias! If I hadn't known you for 30 years, and hadn't known André since he was born, I'd think both of you were mad. I'd think that André had stabbed you in the hand with a dagger he'd since thrown out of the window... but I know you both. You tell the truth. In which case..."

"In which case?" Narbonne said, impassively.

Dormoy shrugged his shoulders. "I don't know," he mumbled. "I have no idea..."

There as a dull ringing noise. André reached out over the desk and pressed one of a dozen ivory buttons fitted into a crystal plaque.

One of the study doors opened and Michel came in, bearing a tray on which letters and newspapers were piled up. "One registered letter," he said. "The postman's waiting."

The receipt-book was on top of the pile of envelopes and newspapers. André took it, opened it, and signed the name *Mathias Narbonne* in the necessary place. He picked up the registered letter, emptied the tray and returned the postman's receipt-book. Michel went out.

When the door had closed, André slit the envelope of the registered letter, brought out a piece of paper, unfolded it and–without looking at it–placed it on the blotter in front of his employer.

Narbonne looked at the unfolded letter and immediately exclaimed: "By thunder! What's this? André, Dormoy, come and see!"

The young man and the physician came to stand to either side of their master and friend and leaned over. They looked at one another in stupefaction over Narbonne's bowed head. Then they turned back to the piece of paper.

This is what they had seen, and read:

To M. Mathias Narbonne,
Rue d'Orchampt, Paris.
May 6,
If the postal service is efficient in Paris, this letter will reach you a short time after an invisible dagger will have pierced your right hand. It would have been just as easy for me to deliver this blow straight through your heart. That is what I shall do at midnight on June 10 if you have not, in the meantime:

1. Made a formal decision, definitive and irrevocable, without any loopholes, to cease all your benevolent works and to put an end to your philanthropic career.

2. Deposited at the Swiss-Russian Bank in Geneva, in the name of M. Eiger Nott, the sum of 100 million Swiss francs, which M. Nott may then withdraw without impediments, on demand, with only sufficient proof of his identity (birth certificate and passport).

Understand that any attempt at trickery, or the arrest of M. Nott, my representative, will be severely punished. There is no lack of places on the human body where a trenchant instrument can be buried to a greater or lesser depth.

Midnight, June 10–do not forget!

Lucifer.

III. The Vestal of the Rue Favart

Elsewhere, in the course of the morning of May 6, an unexpected occurrence upset the management and staff of the Opéra-Comique and filled the hearts of the most intimate admirers of the marvelous La Païli–a singer of genius and one of the prettiest women in the world–with anguish.

At 9 a.m. precisely, Monsieur Lerond, the director of the Rue Favart's Temple of Music, went into his office and said to the office-boy: "Bring Monsieur Lysor in as soon as he arrives. I'm also expecting Mademoiselle Païli; don't keep her waiting for a second–it's unnecessary even to announce her."

Octave Lysor had been the composer in fashion for six months. The idol of the great concert-halls, having had two simultaneous prodigious successes at the Monnaie in Brussels and La Scala in Milan, he had written a score for the Opéra-Comique based on a posthumous libretto by Edmond Rostand, which the *cognoscenti* had praised to the skies. Scarcely 30 years old, he augmented his glory with the triple prestige of youth, virile beauty and vast intelligence. The harshest critics did not contest his genius. He was called the "French Wagner," to signify the immensity of his talent rather than to indicate its quality, for his music had nothing in common with that of the god of Bayreuth.

A year before, a star of the first magnitude had dazzled the theatrical and musical sky with an incomparable brilliance. In the course of an audition granted to a few candidates by Monsieur Lerond, a divinity of the stage and song had been revealed, whom no one had previously seen or heard: a beautiful young French girl, born to a Parisian father and a Florentine mother, who had been signed under the name Laurence Païli. Three months later, she was universally famous as "La Païli."

With a voice of crystal and gold, an innate sense of stagecraft, a curious and cultured mind, a dark beauty of disturbing magnificence and the supple slenderness of a figure worthy of Diana, La Païli had only needed to appear three times at the Opéra-Comique to be worshipped as a divinity. Immediately, a legend had grown up around her–a legend which, extraordinarily, was exactly true. Rich, by virtue of a fortune left to her by her father–who had been killed in a car accident–and proud, with a heart as noble as it was delicate, she did not, and never had had, a "friend." She lived in virginal purity with her mother, an excellent woman and the mistress of a well-ordered household comprised of a cook, two chambermaids, a chauffeur and an old Italian manservant who played the role of factotum.

The existence of this actress was as pure, as simple and as transparent as that of any earnest young girl of an upper-middle class household. The newspapers, whose business is to make jokes, thus designated Laurence Païli as "the vestal of the Rue Favart," "the Diana with the soft smile," "the white star" and

41

other virginal paraphrases. A great respect surrounded La Païli everywhere–a respect as sincere and profound as the authentic admiration which no one could help feeling when they had once seen and heard her.

Sitting down at his desk, Monsieur Lerond set about opening the daily correspondence, which he annotated rapidly with a pencil, divided into four piles, and threw into a basket. He had devoted five minutes to this work when the office-boy announced Monsieur Lysor, stood aside to let him enter, then went out and shut the door.

"*Bonjour*, my dear director," the composer said, throwing his light overcoat on to a chair. How goes it? I was afraid I might be the last to arrive."

"Faith," replied Monsieur Lerond, laughing and shaking Lysor's hand, "I thought the same three seconds before you were announced. Our diva is usually so punctual! We said 9 a.m.–it's six minutes past. I'm astonished that she isn't here. We'll all have lunch together, maestro!"

"Ah!"

"Yes–are you free?"

"If I wasn't, I shall be."

"Naturally. One isn't often lucky enough to have lunch in town with La Païli. We can get a table at midday, and we'll have all the time until 5 p.m. to get everything organized. I haven't had any news of Laurence for two days, but she's a woman of her word. She must have studied your score. The matter will be settled this afternoon. Tomorrow, we'll be able to get *La Carmélite* under way. What a pity that Rostand is dead! He would have eaten with us–and what a glorious trio I would have had at my table: La Païli, Edmond Rostand and Octave Lysor!"

"A quartet, you mean," said the smiling composer, "for Madame Lerond..."

"That would, indeed, be true," said Monsieur Lerond, simply. "By virtue of her talent, her beauty and her intellect, my wife is, as you opine, worthy of such artistic peers. She is visiting her family for a few days... business matters... oh, nothing serious, but her presence was indispensable. There will only be Laurence and you at my table. God! There's the telephone! Why, it's 9:15 a.m. Can our diva possibly...?"

Monsieur Lerond had unhooked the receiver, and he modified the tone of his voice. "Hello! Hello... Yes, it's me... on behalf of whom...?"

After a pause, he resumed: "Madame Païli? Yes, I'm waiting for her." He turned his eyes towards Lysor, and murmured anxiously: "There isn't a hitch, I hope." Immediately recalled to the telephone conversation, he smiled, saying: "Yes, of course, my dear Madame, it's me... Good day... Yes, I'm can hear you very well..." There was a pause, then: "Hello! No! You don't say... It's not possible... No, no, I haven't seen her... and Monsieur Octave Lysor is here, waiting with me... Oh...! No...! You're imagining things... Should we come?... Both of us...? Very well! Immediately!... Yes!... Yes!"

As he progressed through this sequence of replies, Monsieur Lerond had changed his tone, his expression and his attitude. To the attentive and astonished eyes of the composer, he represented first surprise, then bewilderment, then anxiety, then anguish. After the second "yes," Monsieur Lerond, still standing up, replaced the receiver mechanically. Pale and agitated, he said in a dull voice: "Quickly, quickly, my dear friend. Let's go! Is your car downstairs?"

"Yes."

"Let's make haste."

"Give me an explanation!" pleaded the young maestro, as he took up his overcoat.

"I don't have one myself! I'll tell you what little I know in the car. Where are my gloves? Oh, there they are. Let's go!"

In the car, which sped as rapidly as possible towards the Rue La Fontaine in Auteuil, where La Païli lived, Monsieur Lerond could offer no more response than this to Lysor's questions: "Laurence disappeared yesterday evening. Her mother, a decent woman, doesn't know what to think."

"But how can such a thing have happened?" the young composer persisted.

"I don't know any more than you! Nothing more was said on the telephone."

It seemed to the two men that the Rue La Fontaine was very far away, so long was the route and so great their impatience. Finally, though, the car came to a halt. "Follow me," said Monsieur Lerond.

Lysor had never been to La Païli's home, having only had one conversation with her, a week previously, in the director's office at the Opéra-Comique. He followed Lerond. They went up three floors, and pressed electric bell. A distressed lady's maid with tear-stained eyes appeared; they passed through a hallway to a large drawing-room, where they waited for three minutes. Then a handsome brunette woman of 45 appeared, plainly dressed, her face distraught, although her manner was determinedly calm.

"Octave Lysor, Madame Païli," murmured Monsieur Lerond, politely, before immediately adding: "Well, my dear Madame, was it really you that I spoke to on the telephone? I haven't gone mad? Mademoiselle Laurence..."

The mother, who had already sat down soberly, began to speak in a contained voice while the two men took their seats: "I'm determined not to lose hope, and yet... You'll give me advice as to what to do? This is the situation: for four days, Laurence has seemed to me to be depressed and agitated at the same time, with a kind of terror in her eyes, all of whose expressions I know. To my questions, she replied: 'Leave me alone, Mother. A touch of spleen... It's nothing!' She was studying your work, Monsieur Lysor, *La Carmélite*–about which she was, at first, passionately enthusiastic. The day before yesterday, though, and especially yesterday, she interrupted herself continually to fall into somber reveries. Does she dislike it, after all? I asked myself.

43

"Yesterday, at 4 p.m., a messenger brought a telegram for her. I was here, next to the piano, at which Laurence was sitting. She read the message–then, screwing it up into a ball, she threw it in the fire and burst into tears. She wept..."

Tears sparkled in Madame Païli's eyes. She paused and wiped her eyelids with a handkerchief that she was holding in her left hand. Passing the fingers of her right hand across her forehead, she made an effort and continued; "I was upset, as you can imagine. 'What on Earth is it, Laurence?' I asked. 'Nothing, Mother,' she replied, 'nothing... It's not worth the trouble... It will be over soon... Leave me alone, I beg you.'

"I left the room, to hide my own tears from my daughter. I went to my room to pray to God. I stayed there for an hour with the door closed, alone, racking my brains between my prayers, trying to understand...

"It was 5:45 p.m.–I glanced at the clock as I went in–when I returned to the drawing-room. Laurence was no longer there. The score wasn't on the piano. I went to my daughter's room; there was no one there. In the bathroom, in the whole apartment–no Laurence. I summoned the cook, the two chambermaids, the chauffeur–no one knew anything. No one had seen my daughter go out.

"Then, I had a moment of panic. I searched everywhere. There was no note addressed to me, but the beaver-fur hat and wrap that Laurence sometimes wore over her interior furs for professional journeys–which is to say, to go from here to the theater where she keeps all her stage costumes and evening gowns–had disappeared.

"I made an effort to calm myself. I got dressed and came down, as if to go out. As I passed the lodge, I engaged the concierge in casual conversation. He had seen Laurence go out. There you are, I said to myself, she's at the theater.

"I took a taxi and hastened there. There was no one in her dressing-room, to which I have a key. The concierge at the stage entrance had not seen her. I was on the point of asking to see you, Monsieur Lerond, but it occurred to me that I might be acting too precipitately, and that my questions might compromise my daughter. Was she not free to do as she pleases? Myself, I have nothing; I live on her fortune and her earnings. She is the sweetest of daughters. I had never had the least complaint against her. What right had I to meddle in her se-cret life–since it was now obvious that she did have secrets? I conquered my apprehensions, my dread, my terror, and resolved to wait. I went back home.

"Our servants–all four of them–are like a family. I did not hide my anxie-ties from them. We spent the night waiting, they at their posts and me in my room. Nothing. Finally, this morning, a short while ago, this is what I received... And it was then, in desperation, that I telephoned you..."

So saying, the mother extended her right hand towards a little table and took up a folded piece of blue-tinted paper, which she held out to Monsieur Le-rond. She was unable any longer to retain her tears, which ran down her cheeks and were lost at the corners of her lips or fell on to her bosom. The composer leaned forward and both men read what was written there in a sorrowful stupor. They recognized the highly original handwriting of a great artist. It said:

My beloved mother,

I am obliged to undertake a journey which will last some considerable time. I cannot tell you any more on pain of profound misery for both of us. In my writing-desk, to which you have a key, you will find my checkbook. The checks inside are all signed; you have only to write in the sums to obtain the money you need. Pay compensation to Monsieur Lerond, if he demands it.

Give my apologies to Monsieur Lysor; I have taken his score with me. He has a copy, so he will lose nothing. He must search for another interpreter, alas!

Mother, do not doubt your daughter. I love you, and you alone. I do not love any man; this is not an adventure motivated by my own will. Oh, I cannot explain—that is forbidden. Keep my departure secret, and when it is necessary to speak to them, demand that Messieurs Lerond and Lysor keep it too.

La Païli is still your little Laurence. I will come back, mother, I promise you. Wait for me, without ceasing to love me and respect me.

Mother! Mother! Oh, what distress...

Laurence.

IV. The Nyctalope

On that same morning, Leo Saint-Clair was suddenly taken by the idea of going to lunch in a restaurant in the Parc de Saint-Cloud. The weather was delightful, with a clear sky studded with light clouds, gentle sunlight and a breeze perfumed with all the aromas and languid with all the sensuality of spring.

Leo Saint-Clair alias the Nyctalope! Who in the world does not know that name and its reputation? Officially sanctioned, but free to act on his own initiative, he had organized, at his own expense, an expedition that had forced the surrender of the last dissident warlords in Southern Morocco. He had discovered and rescued the King of Spain, who had been abducted and imprisoned by a gang of terrorists. In China, accompanied by 30 volunteers, he had captured and killed a triumvirate of brilliant but insane masterminds who had been planning to turn their vast Asiatic empire into an hellish anarchist's haven, subject only to their bloody and barbaric whims. For these deeds, and others no less peremptory, he was famous throughout the world—but he was more famous still because he merited the strange title of Nyctalope.

He was of medium height, slim and muscular, wiry and athletic—a complete and consummate athlete. His face and profile were Gallic, but without a moustache, like a clean-shaven Vercingetorix.[3] His features were handsome and clean-cut and his expression virile. He had incomparable eyes, which were most often brown, but sometimes green and sometimes yellow. In poor light, the irises of these eyes dilated, for Leo Saint-Clair could see in complete darkness, not as well as in sunlight, but as well as any man might in the evening twilight on the Algerian coast in summer, when a clear sky surrounds the Moon and the swarming stars—well enough to read, without difficulty, the printed text of a newspaper. In semi-darkness, Saint-Clair could see much better, with a more precise perception of details, than in the light of noon. For this man, therefore, darkness did not exist, so long as he had is eyes open. It was largely to this nyctalopic faculty that Saint-Clair owed his success in his mad enterprises—in which it had amused him, more than once, to risk his life.

May 7 was Leo Saint-Clair the Nyctalope's 35th birthday.[4] He had a habit of saying, and thinking, that the most intense sensual experiences are to be found in solitude—entirely alone, if one's heart is free; in the company of one other, if one is prey to amorous passion. Saint-Clair had returned from the Sudan only ten days previously and had not yet made an appearance in his various circles of acquaintance, having departed 14 months and a half before that to flee the place where his beloved mother had died of pneumonia; he still had grief in his heart, and had no appetite for any other company than his own. This is why, on that particular morning, when he had woken up with a powerful sense of renewal and serenity—as if the dear dead woman herself had wished that life would

46

return to the forehead she had kissed while rendering her last sigh–Saint-Clair thought of taking a walk in the Parc de Saint-Cloud.

It's Monday, he said to himself. *There won't be many people on the further pathways, and no one in the new luxurious restaurant in front of the Terrace. Let's go! I'll build up a healthy appetite with a brisk walk in the park.*

The Nyctalope lived in the Rue Nansouty, on the edge of the Parc Montsouris in the 14th *arrondissement*. He had bought a little townhouse with an artist's studio, which he had converted into a very comfortable library and trophy-room. His household included a manservant and a chauffeur, sturdy fellows who were intelligent and resolute, companions in his adventures, loyal to the last drop of their blood and the last thought in their skulls. There was also a concierge-groundskeeper and his wife, a fine cook whose talents were well-suited to Saint-Clair's delicate tastes. The Nyctalope was both gourmet and gourmand, all the more so because he was well aware that, when he was on his expeditions, he had to content himself with dried meat, smoked fish, processed cheese, pressed figs, coarse dates, biscuits that had to be broken with a hammer–in sum, anything that could serve the purpose of human nutrition.

"Corsat," said Saint-Clair to the manservant, who had arrived in his dressing-room to administer his daily massage, "tell Pilou that we'll be lunching in Saint-Cloud today. We'll leave at 9 a.m. You'll come too. Warn Sidonie and tell her that for dinner, I'll only want boiled eggs with tomatoes and baked endives. Fetch two bottles of the '96 Chateau Margaux–I distrust vintages that I haven't chosen for myself."

Having taken these precautions, Saint-Clair–feeling healthy and youthful, illuminated by a serenity he had not known for 15 months–climbed into the car that was waiting for him in the enclosed courtyard of his little house. Pilou, who was sitting at the steering-wheel, looked like a young English general in his eccentric uniform. In a similarly correct manner, Corsat closed the door and took the seat next to the chauffeur. The concierge-groundskeeper, Choiffour, opened the gate and gave a military salute as the low-slung roadster went past.[5]

Just as the rear wheels were passing through the gateway, however, Saint-Clair sat up straight and said: "Stop!" The car came to an abrupt halt. Then, in the silence of the deserted quarter, the four men were able to hear quite clearly the repetition of the sound that Saint-Clair's super-refined hearing had already caught, which had prompted him to give the order to halt: it was the ringing of a telephone.

If such a simple thing caused the Nyctalope's return to his home, it was because the ring had an exceptional quality. The telephone installed in the studio was a special line, private and secret, which only served one of Saint-Clair's correspondents: Monsieur Alexandre Prillant, an illustrious politician and intimate friend of his, who was presently President of the Council and Minister of the Interior. Furthermore, Monsieur Prillant did not always use that special line to communicate telephonically with Saint-Clair. Normally, he asked the operator to connect him, just like anyone else, and the call would cause an ordinary instrument in the smoking-room or the ground floor of the house to ring–which would not have been audible outside. For the President of the Council to use the secret telephone, it must be a matter to extreme importance.

Saint-Clair snatched up the receiver.

"Is that you, Leo?" said a voice that he recognized–Monsieur Prillant's–gravely.

"Yes, Alex," Saint-Clair replied.

"Are you free?"

"Yes."

"Can you come straight away?"

"To your house or the ministry?"

"My house. Immediately?"

"Yes–my car's in the courtyard. I was going to spend the day in the country."

"Forget the country. I need you. It's serious."

"I'll hurry."

"Thank you."

On hearing that word, Saint-Clair buttoned his coat, went downstairs, leapt back into the car and said to Pilou: "Monsieur Prillant's house–quickly!"

Choiffour opened the gate again and the roadster shot out. The Nyctalope's car only took a quarter of an hour to go from the Rue Nansouty to the Avenue Kléber, where Alexandre Prillant lived.

Monsieur Prillant was waiting for his young friend–the explorer was 15 years younger than the statesman–in his study. Outside his public duties, the Minister, who had been widowed three years before, devoted himself entirely to his belatedly-born son named Henri–a handsome, robust and intelligent boy of ten, for whom he entertained greater ambitions of happiness than he had ever entertained on his own behalf. Prillant had adored his wife, and his son was his only consolation; he said sometimes that if misfortune were to overtake his son, the Sun would turn black for him, and life would no longer be anything but gloom.

"Dear God, what's the matter?" cried Saint-Clair, at the sight of his great and powerful friend.

Alexandre Prillant's face was livid and drawn; his eyes were hollow and burning with fever–but the two vertical wrinkles between his furrowed eyebrows testified that the decisive will of a man of mature years remained intact within this man of 50, tormented by some atrocious pain.

After shaking Saint-Clair's hand, Prillant asked him to sit down, then sat down himself. "Something horrible is happening," he said, in a slow, dull voice with a grave and sonorous tone. "Henri is dying, by slow degrees, of intermittent strangulation."

"What?" said Saint-Clair, startled.

48

"Yes! Listen, and don't interrupt–the minutes are worth as much as hours. I shall be brief, in any case. With you, the essentials are sufficient...

"You know that, for ten days now, France has been threatened by a general strike, fomented clandestinely by Communist organizations and planned by the Confédération Générale du Travail, to express solidarity with the agricultural workers, who have been on strike for two weeks."

"I know."

"Today, at noon, a meeting was to have taken place between the delegates of the CGT, the Association Patronale des Mines and the government. I convened the conference and I was to chair it. I'm sure that it would have concluded with an agreement; tomorrow, there would have been a universal return to work on entirely new terms, the general strike would have been called off, and social peace would have been ensured in our nation for at least a decade..."

"I know that–I believe you."

"Well, my friend," Prillant went on, in a voice that was now slightly tremulous, "since that conference was announced, exactly six days ago, I have received a telegram like this every morning. This is today's–take it and read it. The other five were identical."

Prillant pushed a sheet of blue-tinted paper, folded in two, towards the corner of the desk where Saint-Clair was sitting. Saint-Clair took it up impassively, and read:

To Monsieur Alexandre Prillant,
President of the Council, Minister of the Interior
Call off the conference. Discourage the APM by a curt refusal to negotiate. Oppose the proposals of the CGT by refusing point-blank to see them. Otherwise, your son Henri, to whom I am applying strangulation every six hours, will be completely asphyxiated and killed at noon on May 7.
Lucifer.

Saint-Clair remained motionless and mute for 30 seconds. He was very pale. Then he raised his head and gazed at his friend; his large eyes were fiery. "This isn't a sinister, joke, is it?" he said, dryly.

Prillant shook his head. Making an effort to remain calm, although his voice was plaintive with suppressed emotion, he replied: "Four times a day, at regular intervals–at 6 a.m., noon, 6 p.m. and midnight–my beloved Henri's throat is violently seized by invisible hands. He is choked and strangled. He suffocates; he croaks; he almost expires. Then the strangulation abruptly ceases. The marks of the strangler's fingers remain visible..." There was a silence charged with anguish; then Prillant began speaking again. "For the first three days, I observed and reflected, swearing everyone here to silence regarding the unimaginable phenomenon. On the evening of the third day, I telephoned Professor Lourmel, but he had just left for Italy. Immediately, I summoned the Prefect of Police and the head of the Sûreté. They instituted a general surveillance in post offices of people sending telegrams. On the evening of May 4, 5 and 6,

49

three women were arrested–three Alsatian women. They were immediately interrogated, examined and studied. They had acted under the influence of hypnotic suggestion; their will was not their own and they could not remember anything. Then, in desperation, I called you."

Prillant fell silent.

After a terrible pause, Saint-Clair simply said: "Why do you not obey this Lucifer?"

Prillant replied with the same simplicity. "Never! The circumstances, the facts, my reputation, my ideas relating to the present social conflict–everything indicates that I am the one man in France, at this moment, who can prevent France from falling victim to a Communist Revolution in years to come! My duty as a Frenchman, a Minister and a civilized human being is to act..." He stiffened, seeming to draw himself up in his armchair. His face was implacable. "My son Henri," he said, in a voice that was hoarse but firm, "will probably die at noon when I, the President of the Council of Ministers of the Republic, the supreme holder of authority in France, will open the meeting from which an agreement will emerge between labor and capital."

"And afterwards?" said Saint-Clair, still impassive.

"Ah! Afterwards..." The father let his face fall into his hands and a sob shook his entire body–but he got up immediately, abruptly straightening his nimble and vigorous body. "Afterwards," he said, determinedly, "I shall devote everything I have–my power, my fortune, my grief and my hatred–to avenging my son."

Saint-Clair also got up, though, and clasped his friend's hands almost brutally. "Alex," he said, his tone curt, his voice authoritative and his gaze fixed, "do you trust me?"

"Yes, completely," Prillant affirmed, forcefully.

"If I say that your son will not die, will you believe me?"

"Yes, I'll believe you!"

"And you will do your duty with serenity–with total serenity?"

"Yes, absolutely."

Saint-Clair laughed–a peculiar laugh of bravado and triumph, terrible in the circumstances. "Well," he said, "I tell you this, my friend–your son will not die."

"Oh, Leo..."

"Shut up. It's time to act. Where's Henri?"

"In his room, with his English governess and his tutor."

"The same ones he had 15 months ago?"

"Yes, Miss Ellen and Monsieur Verfeuil."

"Is he dressed?"

"Yes. I saw him before I telephoned."

"Good. I'll take him away."

"You..."

"Will you hesitate now?" Saint-Clair said, interrupting.

"No, no! Go–take him! Provided that you save him, do whatever you wish."

"I'll take him away. I don't know when I'll be able to return him to you–a week, a fortnight, a month... but he'll live! Have no doubt about that, by God!"

"I don't doubt it, Leo. Do you know, then...?"

"I suspect... I deduce... Oh, the hell with it–Yes, I know!"

"Explain then, as briefly as possible."

"No! We must act now, and talk later."

"You're right, as always. Come on, then."

Henri Prillant had not forgotten his "Uncle Saint-Clair" who, like an uncle who was both genuine and marvelous, brought or sent him the most miraculous toys. The children that Henri played with in the Trocadéro gardens and his friends' houses never had such things.

Containing his emotion with difficulty, Saint-Clair said to Henri: "My boy, I shall cure the illness that has afflicted you from time to time for several days. Furthermore, your father is allowing me to give you a great treat. Can you guess what?"

"What? What is it?" said the child, his eyes avid with curiosity.

"A journey–a lovely journey in a motor car. We're leaving straight away. Papa says we may–isn't that so?"

"Yes, yes!" said Prillant, smiling but almost weeping with emotion.

"Oh, in a motor car!" cried the child, clapping his hands and then throwing his arms around Saint-Clair's neck.

Three minutes later, the explorer climbed back into his roadster with Henri and Miss Ellen. Monsieur Prillant and the tutor Verfeuil brought blankets and coats.

"Pilou," Saint-Clair said, in the curt, incisive tone that the Nyctalope's voice took on in matters of life and death, "it's 9:30 a.m. It's necessary to be in Le Havre by 11:30 a.m. It's 228 kilometers..."

"We'll be there, boss! The tires are brand new, and I have three spare wheels. Even if one bursts, we'll get there. There are stretches where I can do 150 kph..."

"Good–I'm counting on you and your machine." Turning to Prillant, Saint-Clair went on: "Can you reach the director of the Subtransatlantic Company in Le Havre by radio within an hour?"

"Yes, if I take care of it myself," the Minister replied.

"Good. Have their top man in Paris send the director in Le Havre the following message: *Prepare the submarine* Lampas *for an immediate departure and submersion at 11:30 a.m. and place it at the disposal of Leo Saint-Clair.*"

Then, in response to a "Get going!" the car moved off, carrying the enraptured Henri Prillant wedged between Saint-Clair and Miss Ellen.

The 228 kilometers were covered in an hour and 52 minutes. Having left the Avenue Kléber in Paris at 9:30 a.m., Saint-Clair and little Henri arrived at the main quay in Le Havre at 11:22 a.m. The car stopped in front of the pontoon hangar in which the *Lampas* and the *Synancée* were moored. The Lampas, already outside, was maneuvering slowly in the harbor, scarcely a cable's length away. Saint-Clair, leaping out of the roadster, saw a silhouette and a face he recognized on the submarine's gangway.

"Ciserat!" he cried.

"Saint-Clair!" the naval officer replied.

A dinghy was moored nearby; Saint-Clair leapt nimbly into it. "Miss," he said, "pass me the child and get aboard."

The Englishwoman obeyed, rapidly and dexterously.

The explorer took the oars and soon came abreast of the submarine.

"You, here!" said Ciserat, assisting his friend, the young woman and Henri to climb on to the gangway. "Who's the child? Is he yours? I don't know–the radio message that was passed to me as we were about to depart didn't explain anything."

"You talk too much, old chap," Saint-Clair said. "Get the young lady aboard, and the boy–who is the only son of Alexandre Prillant, President of the Council and Minister... do you hear? Get aboard, get going, submerge! Before noon, the *Lampas* has to be under 100 meters of water."

At that moment, a head appeared at one of the open hatchways between the conning-tower and the gangway, which led down into the submarine's interior. On seeing that head, Saint-Clair cried out in amazement. "Oh! Professor Lourmel! So you're not in Italy?"

"I have been," the Professor said, climbing on to the bridge. "I heard you– what's happening?" He looked at the child and frowned–then experienced the sudden illumination of which brains of genius are capable, went to Saint-Clair and whispered in his ear: "Another case of spell-casting, eh?"

Saint-Clair started. "What do you mean, another?"

"Yes, my niece, Ciserat's wife. In Venice... Phenomena of torture by supernatural means. Mattol, my pupil, had the idea of the opposition of milieux– but for you, in similar circumstances, to have thought of the *Lampas*... of sheltering underwater... you must believe that..."

"I don't believe, I know! God's blood! Too much talking. At midday..."

"One more minute, Nyctalope!" the Professor commanded, in a masterful voice. "Since you're certain, you surely aren't leaving with the infant?"

"Oh, I'm not leaving. I have a investigation to conduct."

"I thought so, Saint-Clair. I, too, need to investigate, to punish..." And he called out: "Mattol! I'm getting off! The suitcases, quickly!" Then, to Ciserat, he said: "Not another word. You heard and understood. Be calm. Once we're in the dinghy, depart and submerge. Poste restante, New York, a fortnight hence."

Mattol emerged, looking slightly haggard. A sailor passed him the suit-cases, which he threw into the moored dinghy. Lourmel had already quit the gangway. Saint-Clair followed him. As they passed an open hatchway, Irène de Ciserat suddenly appeared in front of the explorer. An exclamation sprang to his lips, but she put the index finer of her left hand to her lips, instructing him to be silent, while her right hand thrust a folded piece of white paper into his. She knew Saint-Clair, having met him at least 20 times at her father's dinner-parties. He took the paper and went on.

At another hatchway, Ciserat helped Miss Ellen and Henri into the submarine. Mattol followed them. Lourmel and Saint-Clair got into the dinghy and cast off the mooring-rope.

Ciserat gave his orders. The waters behind the *Lampas* became agitated. Sailors appeared and set about dismantling the guard-rails and walkway of the gangway. Then they dived into the hatchways, which were sealed. There was a metallic clicking sound, distinct at first, dull thereafter. Ciserat remained alone on the conning-tower–and the *Lampas* drew away, towards the harbor entrance.

Saint-Clair and Lourmel watched it mutely from the quay, on to which they had just climbed, a few paces away from the roadster. When they had seen Ciserat wave his cap in the air and the *Lampas* disappear behind the curve of the quay where the semaphore tower was, they looked at one another, smiling.

"He's saved!" said Saint-Clair.

"She too," said Lourmel.

"But it's a provisional measure," Saint-Clair said, gravely. "It's necessary to make it definitive. We must return to Paris. We'll eat in the car–after that, you must tell me about your adventure, and I'll tell you mine. Have you identified the spell-caster?"

"No, have you?"

"No–I only found out about it three hours ago."

"Amazing!"

"Bah!" Saint-Clair shrugged his shoulders. "If he learns of our intervention, he'll try to kill us before I can be on his trail–but can he? Let's get going! To Paris, Pilou–but first, go to the Place Gambetta and stop at the restaurant there for five minutes. That'll give you and Corsat time to buy a roasted chicken, three bottles of Moët, bread and fruit. We'll lunch on the road. Don't worry, Professor, I've a complete picnic basket in the car! It will be comfortable and proper–but I warn you, we'll be doing 80 kilometers an hour. I have motoring goggles for both of us, though."

By the time the roadster drew into the courtyard of the little house in the Rue Nansouty, three hours later, Saint-Clair knew every detail of Irène de Ciserat's painful adventure and Professor Onésime Lourmel had learned the whole story of the tragic blackmail to which Alexandre Prillant was subjected.

Once they were in the house, the explorer entrusted his guest to Corsat, who led him to the little guest-apartment on the first floor, where he was able to shave while his clothes were brushed. Before going to his own dressing-room, Saint-Clair went into the studio and finally brought out of his pocket the piece of paper that Irène had given him aboard the *Lampas*. He read it.

It was the letter containing Lucifer's ultimatum–the letter that had been given to Irène on the quayside in Le Havre.

Saint-Clair re-read the letter, then put it into his wallet with the telegram that Prillant had left with him. He put the wallet on the table, along with several other objects–a chronometer, a matchbox, a bunch of keys and a Browning. Then, he undressed, washed, rinsed and dried himself rapidly and put on fresh underclothes and flannel pajamas.

Rested and refreshed, with his feet bare inside his oriental slippers, Saint-Clair went down to the smoking-room on the ground floor where Professor Lourmel was waiting for him. As he passed through the studio, he picked up his wallet, which he threw on a table. After that, he went straight to the little desk in the corner of the room which bore a telephone, notepads and various directories.

On one of the pads, he saw a note in Choiffour's handwriting–the concierge answered all telephone calls in his master's absence. It said: *Monsieur Mathias Narbonne asks to be informed as soon as Monsieur de Saint-Clair returns. The matter extremely serious and urgent.*

The Nyctalope had met the celebrated philanthropist in America. He had a presentiment, which immediately expressed itself aloud: "Ah! Is this another matter concerning the mysterious Lucifer?" Turning to Lourmel, he said: "We must start a sort of council of war. I think there will be at least four of us–perhaps more. My intuitions are rarely mistaken. Monsieur Narbonne, whom you know, wishes to talk to me about an extremely serious and urgent matter. Is he involved too?"

"I wouldn't be surprised," the Professor said. "Our national philanthropist is an ideal target for the hatred of a malefactor of this Lucifer's sort."

"We'll find out."

Unhooking the telephone receiver, Saint-Clair dialed Narbonne's number. He got through immediately.

"Hello? Monsieur Narbonne? Oh, it's you, d'Arbol. Yes–what is it?... Oh! Oh! The case is not an isolated one... Ah, Monsieur Narbonne! Good day!... Yes! You are not alone... No, not on the telephone... What?... Very well, we'll be waiting for you... Who, us? You'll see... Understood."

He hung up, then remained silent and still for a minute, while the interested Lourmel waited patiently. Then he unhooked the receiver again.

"Hello!... Hello Mademoiselle, my name is Leo Saint-Clair. Yes... Perfectly. Get me the President of the Council... Yes, at the Place Beauvau. Thank you."

There was another pause, during which he remained still. Then: "Hello, is that you, Alex?... Yes, it's me, Leo... All is well. The child is safe. I'll tell you how and where... Right away, if you can spare two hours... Yes? Perfect. Come, then... You'll find two important people here... Who? Professor Lourmel and Monsieur Narbonne... Perfectly... Hurry... Understood!"

Saint-Clair replaced the receiver, this time definitively. Then, addressing the Professor, not without a certain solemnity, he said: "My dear Professor, I have the pleasure of informing you that, under the chairmanship of Monsieur Prillant, the meeting of the mineworkers's employers and the delegates of the CGT has just concluded with a solid agreement that guarantees France, save for some unforeseeable catastrophe, at least ten years of social harmony. And I can also tell you that the same Monsieur Prillant will be here in 20 minutes, shortly preceded by Monsieur Mathias Narbonne." He changed his tone to add, in a more familiar manner: "It's useless to say anything more until they're here— we'd only have to repeat ourselves. Cigars and cigarettes are here—I'll have some water brought in, sugar, fruits, rum... Is that all right by you? Good!"

Mathias Narbonne and André d'Arbol arrived first. Their car, a saloon devoid of luxury but solid and comfortable, had scarcely parked on one side of the courtyard when a horn sounded and the concierge had to open the gate again. It was Monsieur Prillant's limousine. Saint-Clair appeared at the door of the house.

The statesman and the philanthropist knew one another, naturally. They shook hands, then Narbonne and André exchanged brief cordial greetings with Saint-Clair. Afterwards, in the smoking-room, there was a short conversation between Prillant and Lourmel, while the philanthropist gave a concise explanation to Saint-Clair in a low voice.

When the hats and gloves had been taken away by Corsat, everyone sat down around a table, on which bottles, carafes, glasses, and fruits—both fresh and dried—had been set out, along with spoons and knives, boxes of cigars and cigarettes, a few blotting-pads and paper and pens.

There was a moment of silence while everyone concentrated his thoughts.

"My friends," Saint-Clair said, eventually, "let us first summarize the facts in chronological order.

"First, Mademoiselle Irène de Ciserat is subjected to some kind of strange abuse in Venice, the observation of which led Professor Lourmel and Louis Mattol to conclude that she was under a spell—a phenomenon that falls into the category of what are nowadays called the occult sciences.

"Second, young Henri Prillant, age ten, is subjected to partial strangulation four times in every 24 hours, at regular intervals—strangulation that can only be explained supernaturally.

"Third, Monsieur Narbonne receives in his right hand–which is presently bandaged and supported by a sling–a dagger-blow that transpierces it, under conditions that again require the admission of a supernatural factor.

"Further:

"First, in Le Havre, while crossing the pavement of the main quay, between the car that had brought her and the building that she was entering, Mademoiselle Irène de Ciserat is intercepted by an unknown man, who slips a piece of paper into her hand, then disappears round the next street-corner. This is the piece of paper. It is a letter. I shall read it."

When the letter had been read, Saint-Clair–without taking any notice of the violent emotion that his listeners did not even think of hiding–calmly put the piece of paper down to his left. Drawing another sheet of paper out of his wallet, he continued.

"Second, every morning for six days, including today, Monsieur Prillant has received a telegram. The six telegrams are identical. A police operation allowed them to arrest three women–the intermediaries who sent the last three telegrams; their examination at Saint-Anne revealed that they had acted under the influence of hypnotic suggestion, that they came from various villages in the Haute-Alsace, that they did not know one another and that they had no memory of the messages they had sent from Parisian post offices. I will read you one of these telegrams."

Saint-Clair read, while his audience–even Prillant, who was already perfectly familiar with the terrible message–listened intently. The uttering of the infernal signature resounded, lugubriously and menacingly, in the silence they maintained, while the impassive Saint-Clair put the paper down to his left and withdrew a third sheet from his wallet.

"Third," he said, without pausing, "in the post brought to him by his manservant shortly after the piercing of his hand, Monsieur Narbonne received this registered letter. I will read it after calling your attention to this skull engraved at its head..."

He showed the sinister image all around, and began reading again. Having read it, Saint-Clair put the letter down to his left and set both his forearms on the table, with the palms of his hands flat.

"Finally," he said, still calm, his delivery slow, precise and emphatic, "I make particular note of one fact: Mademoiselle Irène's statement reveals to us that, before her marriage, she was obliged to reject an impromptu proposal of marriage made by a mysterious red-haired man on the occasion of a party given by Monsieur Lourmel in honor of the American Professor Jameson. The disappearance thereafter of three photographs of Irène has been established.

"These, then, are the facts.

"One: after investigating Irène's case, Professor Lourmel and Louis Mattol have concluded that a spell had been cast. Two: as soon as I was apprised of Henri's situation, I, too, concluded that a spell had been cast. Three: knowing now what happened to Monsieur Narbonne, I conclude that it, too, was the result of a spell. This conclusion is corroborated by the fact that the spell-caster revealed himself and confessed his responsibility in the letters that he signed Lucifer.

"The objectives of the three spells are also revealed by the spell-caster himself. He desires to possess Irène; he intends to annex Monsieur Narbonne's billions; and he wishes to foster Communist anarchy in France.

"It is up to us, on the one hand, to ensure that these three objectives are unattained, and, on the other hand, to prevent Lucifer from taking revenge on his victims–or anyone else he may choose.

"Without any communication between us, thanks to our relative familiarity with the so-called occult sciences, Mattol and I immediately thought of the same protective device: the antagonism of milieux–the *Lampas* and its submersion under the sea. The cushion of water will form a shield between the designated victim and the projection of the spell. I was familiar with Ciserat's preparations for submarine explorations and knew about the *Lampas*, too. I hastened to shelter Henri Prillant therein before the fatal hour, just as Irène's relatives did the same to protect the young woman from the threat of further abuse.

"As to the rest, Irène will not submit to the demand made of her. Monsieur Prillant has not submitted either, since the conference has taken place and reached its fortunate conclusion. This, my friends, is where we are now. The exposure of these facts was necessary, but now, all that is in the past; we shall speak of it no more. The future lies before us. What are we to do? First, Monsieur Narbonne, do you intend to capitulate?"

"Never!" said Narbonne, firmly. "I summoned my solicitor this morning and added a peremptory codicil to my will, which gives my entire fortune to certain benevolent causes, by means of a simple and inexpensive foundation. When the lawyer left, I said to André: 'Now let's wait for June 10. If I should die...' He did not dare say to no–I would not have taken it well! But while talking about the supernatural–for that seemed to me to be the only explanation–and trying to counter his objections–for André has remained a skeptic despite it all–I thought of you, Saint-Clair. Your knowledge is encyclopedic, and you have done such astonishing things! Besides, I, too, now have the resource of a submarine!" And the brave Monsieur Narbonne burst into laughter.

"Let's deliberate, then," said Saint-Clair, "and decide what to do next."

Part Two: The Nyctalope in Pursuit

I. An A to Z of Paris, via X and Y

At 6 a.m. on May 8–the day after the council of war held against the mysterious Lucifer at the Rue Nansouty, Leo Saint-Clair, the Nyctalope, went to Saint-Anne Asylum. He left Corsat, his Burgundian manservant, and Pilou, his Provençal chauffeur-mechanic, at the main door.

The three men were dressed in almost exactly the same light and comfortable costume: grey jackets and trousers, traveling caps and worn kid gloves, with aviator's boots for their master and cycling shoes for Corsat and Pilou. The Burgundian was carrying three monastic robes rolled up and secured with string, while the Provençal was furnished with a gusseted suitcase of medium dimensions, containing necessary articles of toiletry, a medicine kit, some changes of underwear and various scientifically-perfected burglar's tools.

The Nyctalope and his two adjutants were armed with special pistols–invented and constructed by Saint-Clair himself–containing capsules of liquefied air, which propelled 8mm bullets over a range of 500 meters, with neither sound nor smoke, and which could be fired ten times without reloading.

At the asylum, Saint-Clair was met by Professor Lourmel. Two minutes later, he witnessed the release of the three Alsatian women arrested after dispatching telegrams addressed to Monsieur Prillant from three different post offices at the same hour on three consecutive days. They had been questioned while awake, and then again while in a hypnotic trance, and had given no other response, in strongly-accented French, than: "I don't know!" Whatever the question was, the response never varied: "I don't know!"

On seeing them walk away, clad in banal costumes like chambermaids of the modest sort, having given no evidence that they knew or recognized one another, the Nyctalope decided to follow the most lively of the three. For private convenience, he named her Dorothée–for these unconscious emissaries of Lucifer had no papers and had not uttered any name that might permit their identification.

Saint-Clair shook Lourmel's hand in the large doorway and began following the enigmatic Dorothée; Corsat and Pilou walked behind him. Ten meters away from the asylum's exit, they overtook the other two women, who were being trailed by two of the cleverest of the Sûreté inspectors especially assigned to Monsieur Prillant.

The three women immediately set off in different directions. Dorothée, without a moment's hesitation, took the Boulevard Saint-Jacques and headed straight for the Métro station, changing her traveling bag from one hand to the other several times over. The two others, hypnotically entranced, slowly went along the Rue de la Santé, gradually drawing apart with the utmost carelessness, one encumbered by a suitcase, the other by a bundle. Saint-Clair soon lost sight of them, concentrating his attention henceforth on Dorothée. She was a slim, rather frail girl, more nervous than the women of the Rhineland usually were–assuming that her origin could be accurately judged from her accent.

The Nyctalope never wasted mental effort on the construction of useless hypotheses. He had no idea what Dorothée would do. He did not speculate as to where she might lead him; he simply followed her, determined to do so until she arrived at her lodgings, or until her attitude or some intervening event demonstrated that she was quite disorientated and lost.

All the same, the Nyctalope could not help being surprised when, after Dorothée had led him to the Gare de Lyon, he heard her ask for a second-class ticket to Marseille at the window serving the Burgundy lines. Although he had formed no conjectures, he had not expected the German woman to set off for the Mediterranean.

Everything about the young woman–the abrupt accent, unsoftenable even by a long sojourn in another country, the cut of her dress, her footwear, the shape of her hat and her general appearance–testified that scarcely a week had gone by since she had quit the banks of the Rhine. But she was not returning to her own country; she was going to Marseille!

"We'll follow her!" said Saint-Clair. He bought three second-class tickets to Marseille.

Resisting the temptation to engage in vain conjectures, Saint-Clair restricted himself to observing Dorothée. She seemed every inch the traveler: a trifle distraught, sulky and fatigued, but decisive and at ease, quite accustomed to the course of events. She bought a fashion magazine and one of those magazines that are to literature what a *pot-pourri* is to music. She read, drowsed, stared at the countryside, ate in the restaurant car, relaxed in the corridor of the carriage and slept upright, wedged in the corner of her compartment, with two cushions hired on the platform at Paris. After getting off at Marseille at 9:40 p.m., she left the station, hesitated momentarily in between the five or six hotel omnibuses standing there, then boarded the one whose conductor, more enterprising than his counterparts, had grabbed her luggage.

Saint-Clair found a fiacre, climbed into it with his two companions, and gave the name of the hotel that had been on the front of the omnibus Dorothée had taken. He arrived there before her, overheard the number of the room that was given to her, and arranged to have the room next door, which was free. By chance, Pilou and Corsat were already accommodated on the same floor.

At 9:35 a.m. on the following day, they set off again in the direction of Ventimiglia, with tickets for Antibes. There they all wound up–taking sufficient precautions to ensure that Dorothée did not know that she was being trailed–at a third-rate hotel situated not far from the station.

At the hotel desk, Saint-Clair heard Dorothée say: "I'll be staying three full days, and I'll take my meals in my room, at the full-board rate."

Saint-Clair, Corsat and Pilou sat down around a table in a little garden overlooking the hotel entrance, on which a servant deposited a bottle of lemonade and three glasses. No one else was there.

"You, Corsat," the Nyctalope said, "won't budge from the hotel. Stay in the garden or the lobby, from which you can keep an eye on the whole ground floor. You, Pilou, will follow Dorothée whenever she goes out. She intends to spend three whole days in Antibes."

"Three whole days!" proffered Pilou, in the familiar but respectful tone that he and Corsat both adopted when talking to the Nyctalope. "Let me have some time off, boss. This is practically my native land."

"Yes, I know–you were born in Vallauris. Neither of you will sleep or eat, of course, except when Dorothée's meals and repose afford you the opportunity. As for me, I'll be wherever circumstances dictate that I should be–and you'll make a complete report whenever we meet up. Whichever of you doesn't see me during the day must deposit a succinct, complete and clear report in the usual place, under the old folded newspaper in the drawer of the night-stand in my bedroom. Is all that understood?"

"Understood, boss," the two men said, in unison.

"Good."

Saint-Clair got up and left the garden. He only had to take a few steps to find himself beside the calm waters of the cove of Saint-Roch, which were pale blue that day. He followed the shoreline in the direction of old Antibes. Then, having passed a little jetty, he climbed the steps that led to the terrace overlooking the harbor. There, he stopped for a few minutes, studying the quays, the lighthouse and the several boats and small ships that were anchored in the tiny port. Then, he began walking again, at a leisurely pace, along the seafront promenade.

The afternoon sky was a deep blue. The sunlight was joyously bright and the serene air was possessed by a sort of voluptuous languor that was profoundly invigorating. To the left was the bay of Nice, green and silvery, overlooked by the snowy peaks of the violet Alps; to the right was the bay of Antibes, with the indentations of the Plage de la Salis and the Cap d'Antibes, with its pines, palm-trees and countless multicolored roses, which perfumed the breeze as it passed over them.

The view was incomparable, the sensations delightful. Saint-Clair forgot all about the enigmatic Dorothée and the mysterious Lucifer, because this sight and its associated memories–one of the white villas on the Cap d'Antibes, shrouded by pines, eucalyptus trees, palms and roses; the memory of Juan-les-Pins and its beach; Vallauris and its gardens, its flowing waters and its orchard– caused the Nyctalope to recall the most poignant weeks of his entire existence.

"How I loved her!" murmured Saint-Clair, leaning on the parapet and fixing his gaze on the terraced rooftops of a sunlit villa on the flank of the Cap d'Antibes. "We were there. No one knew her name or mine. In Paris, her mother and her friends thought she was staying with a relative, our accomplice. Three weeks, during which we both delighted in one another...

"A virgin, and such an innocent mind! It seemed that it truly was her awakening to life, and that she had not lived until then! How marvelous her beauty was! Oh, the sensuousness of the days and nights! Laurence, my Laure, my only love! Were we right to part, voluntarily, at the height of our joy, so that our happiness could not become banal as we accustomed ourselves to it, under threat of satiety? We wanted our love to be like a flower in our lives, snatched from our fingers by a gust of wind before it could fade. We wanted our embraces to be a memory to which no other could compare, in all the days and nights to come...

"And it's true that I cannot think of you, my splendid Laure, without loving you still, and desiring you, and calling out to you...

"Since we separated–after which you abruptly became the illustrious La Païli and I acquired fame under the name of the Nyctalope–we have not seen one another, nor heard one another's voices, nor read one another's letters... nothing!

"Where is she now, my lover of the Cap d'Antibes, Juan-les-Pins and Vallauris... Of the sea and the roses, of clear springs and odorous fruits, of the beds of carnation-petals, where her mermaid body and spreading hair... Where is she now? Against what stage-setting is she preparing, at this very moment, this evening's triumph? Laurence, Laurence, how I wish I could forget you! Why has destiny brought me back here, by the strangest of routes, beneath this sky, before this sea, within view of that shuttered villa and its enchanted garden?"

Supporting himself on his elbows, Saint-Clair put his forehead in his hands and closed his eyes. Minutes fell into the past. Then, he drew himself abruptly upright.

"Let's go," he said, aloud. "That's enough dreaming. Let's get back to work."

He turned his back on the Cap d'Antibes, went along the seafront boulevard and through the network of old streets to the Place Nationale, where the post office was. He addressed an encrypted telegram to Monsieur Alexandre Prillant, whose deciphered text read: *Am in Antibes, probably for three days.*

Afterwards, he went back to the cove of Saint-Roch via the market-place and the marine port. Corsat was alone in the garden, sitting at a table with a bottle of lemonade and three glasses. Saint-Clair leaned over him, his gaze questioning.

"She went out five minutes ago," the Burgundian said. "Pilou's on her heels, of course."

"That's good."

61

He went up to his room, turned the key and shot the bolt. He released the secret catch of the suitcase which Pilou had deposited on a table. With the aid of a few small instruments, he had no difficulty in opening the communicating door between his room and Dorothée's.

In the course of the journey, during a long halt at Toulon, Dorothée had scribbled in pencil on a few pages of a little notebook that she had bought from a newsvendor on the outskirts of Marseilles. Saint-Clair surveyed the room with an investigative gaze. The enigmatic woman's traveling-bag was not on any of the tables, nor on the floor, but the Nyctalope immediately noticed that the key of the mirror-fronted wardrobe was not in the lock. He opened the wardrobe with a turn of his lock-pick; the bag was there.

Two minutes later, seated beside the open wardrobe, he was rifling through the notebook. If some noise outside were to announce the arrival of the young woman, everything would be back in its proper place in less than 20 seconds, and Saint-Clair would be back in his own room.

Thirty-two of the notebook' pages were covered with lines written skillfully and concisely in Gothic script, without any corrections.

The woman must be educated, the Nyctalope thought. *At any rate, she's well-accustomed to writing. Let's see!*

Saint-Clair read, wrote and spoke half a dozen languages almost as well as French; German held no secrets from him. He read very quickly. As he knew that he was alone, he did not bother to keep his face impassive, and his expression soon testified to his considerable satisfaction.

Having read everything, he replaced the notebook carefully in the bag and locked the wardrobe again. He went back into his room–without closing the communicating door–and opened the window overlooking the garden. He whistled the eight notes of the scale, clearly and carefully-spaced. Then, he closed the window again, lit a cigarette and paced pensively back and forth across the room while he smoked.

Three minutes went by; then the door opened soundlessly. Corsat came in, closed the door behind him and waited. Saint-Clair continued pacing back and forth while the cigarette was still sweet, but when the tobacco took on the bitter taste of moist nicotine, he threw the butt into the empty fireplace and stopped in front of the Burgundian.

"When Dorothée comes back in," the Nyctalope said, "you must follow her immediately, without bothering with Pilou. Climb the staircase directly behind her. In the corridor, you must slow down as you follow her, as if giving her time to open her door, which is locked. When she's on the threshold, about to go in, you must be immediately behind her. Push her inside violently with one hand; put the other one over her mouth, to prevent her crying out, and go in with her. That's all. Go!"

"OK, boss."

Corsat returned to his seat beside the table in the garden. He ordered another bottle of lemonade, carefully filled a stout short-stemmed pipe and began to smoke.

Up above, Saint-Clair reopened the window, sat down in a position from which he could see the garden and filled a pipe that was narrower and longer-stemmed than Corsat's, just as carefully as the Burgundian. He too began to smoke.

Time passed.

A distant clock had just sounded the last chime of 7 p.m. when Saint-Clair abruptly put down his pipe and drew himself away from the splendors of the setting Sun. He had just seen Dorothée walking towards the hotel, some 20 paces from the garden. He waited, standing by the window. Three meters behind the young woman, Pilou appeared. One behind the other, the followed and the follower came into the garden.

Saint-Clair whistled the eight notes of the scale as before, but very rapidly, save for the first one, which he prolonged. Then he closed the window.

Pilou, pressing his pace, overtook Dorothée and climbed the steps to the main door in front of her. He went up the staircase precipitately, ran along the corridor, and came into his employer's room without knocking, rapidly closing the door behind him.

"No time to talk," said Saint-Clair. "Stay close to me–and when I say go, help Corsat tie up the girl without a sound." They both took up positions behind the communicating door between the two rooms. It stood slightly ajar, so that Saint-Clair could see what he needed to see.

Footsteps sounded on the landing, then in the corridor, followed by the noise of a key inserted into a lock and being turned. Hinges creaked.

The door opened. Dorothée appeared, tall and slender, with Corsat behind her, taller and broader. The young woman took a single step–and a strong hand came up, grabbed her head, and plastered itself over the lower part of her face.

"Go!" said Saint-Clair, throwing the communicating door wide open.

Pilou slipped through. In less than a minute, the doors to the corridor were firmly closed, locked and bolted. Dorothée, bound and gagged by Corsat and Pilou, was seated in the only armchair. Terrorized, her eyes already moist with tears, she looked up at Saint-Clair who stood in front of her. He immediately began speaking very softly in German.

"Please don't be afraid, Fräulein," he said. "No one will do you any harm–but it is necessary that you do not make a noise. Will you promise me, by blinking your eyes three times, not to cry out or to attempt to resist? These men will release you then, and leave you alone with me. I need to tell you some very important things–and also to save you from the abominable power that has made your life a martyrdom for two months. Yes, yes, I know everything you have suffered–but I shall save you! Come on–promise me now, Fräulein."

Dorothée's long blonde eyelashes were lowered and raised again convulsively, three times.

"Go into my room!" Saint-Clair ordered Corsat and Pilou.

They disappeared immediately–but in order to keep track of everything that was said and done, they left the door slightly ajar and watched and listened.

The young woman's dolorous face and mystified eyes soon became calm again. Her features took on a surprisingly trusting and relaxed expression. Dorothée was already submissive to the magnetism of the Nyctalope's gaze and will-power. Her body seemed to collapse slightly into the armchair and she babbled in German: "Who are you? What do you want?"

"Whoever I am," Saint-Clair replied, in the same tongue, "I wish you nothing but good. Yes, look at me–and don't resist. That which has been done so many times to your detriment, I shall do for your benefit. Go to sleep, Edwige, go to sleep–that is what I want!"

"You know my name too?" she whispered, already in the grip of the magnetic influence.

"I know what I know," the Nyctalope supplied, gravely. His beautiful long hands–which, when necessary, had a grip of steel–had been making ritual passes in the air a moment earlier; now they brushed the young woman's forehead and temples caressingly. The woman whom he had called Dorothée before the little notebook had revealed that her name was Edwige–the enigmatic instrument of Lucifer, one of his slaves–fell into a hypnotic trance.

There followed a long dialogue in German: affirmations and energetically-formulated questions; answers extracted, with difficulty at first, then more easily, then extended by details spontaneously furnished by the works of a memory that had finally been unlocked and freed.

"Edwige!" intoned the Nyctalope, "Edwige! Hear my words and obey! I am more powerful than the demon who has, until now, dominated you and imposed his will upon you. It was by virtue of my influence that, when you came out of the hospital in Paris, you were progressively freed from his infernal grasp. Thanks to me, you had the strength to flee, and instead of turning towards the Rhine, you came to the Mediterranean. You are now trying to sail for Brazil, where you have been offered employment. Is that what you want to do?"

"Oh, yes! Yes! But I am suffering! I was never able..."

"You will be able to do it, thanks to me. Answer my questions. I want you to. I order you to. Where did you meet the evil man?"

"In Colmar."

"On what date?"

"December 25... Last year..."

"In what circumstances? Where were you? What were you doing?"

"Beside the Nortmund family's Christmas tree... In a house called *The Willows*... In a corner of the big drawing-room. I was the children's governess..."

"Governess to the Nortmund family's children? You?"

"Yes. I had succeeded in passing myself off as a native of the Alsace..."

"What did the evil man look like?"

"Tall, red-haired, thin, with fiery eyes–terrible!"

"Tell me his name?"

"I don't know it."

"Had you seen him before?"

"Never."

"How did he come to be there?"

"I don't know... Everyone in the world was there... There were a great many faces unknown to me..."

"What did he say to you? What did he do to you?"

"He did not speak to me. He looked at me, while putting his hands on me... And I felt my soul passing through them. That was all, that evening."

"Afterwards? Speak! Tell me everything. I want you to, Edwige. I command it!"

"The next day, as I came out of evening Mass, alone, I encountered him again. He looked at me. I had to follow him, without his saying a word to me. Outside the town, he took me by the hands and said: 'You are mine!' Oh, the horror, the horror! He took me to an isolated house. I could not put up any resistance. I went back to *The Willows*, broken. I was questioned, for I had the face of a dead woman. I could not say anything, except that I was tired, very tired..."

"Afterwards? Keep talking, Edwige. Talk."

"Afterwards, months passed. I was able to believe that it was a horrible nightmare. Then, one day, I received an envelope in the post which contained nothing but a card bearing this message: *Next Sunday, at 4 p.m., I shall be waiting for you outside the Basle Gate. Burn this card, be silent, and come.* I obeyed in every detail. He took me to a little house on the bank of the Lauch, on the right bank–a little red house. He... Oh, the horror, the horror! Then he put me into a trance, dictated a series of orders, gave me a wallet containing money and a blue envelope... That same evening, I took the train to Paris and I..."

"Enough! I know the rest. But the man, the man–where did he come from?"

"I don't know."

"He never called himself by any name whatsoever?"

"Never."

"What language did he speak?"

"German."

"With what accent?"

"Without any particular accent... Correct speech... No specific provincialism... Classical German–yes, classical..."

"You know nothing about him, then? Nothing but his features, his thinness, his voice..."

"His voice was harsh and imperious, metallic, his elocution often too rapid and jerky."

"Good! What about the house–the little red house on the right bank of the Lauch. Is that all?"

"That's all... And I'm glad that's all, for now you won't make me say any more. I'm tired, so tired..."

"You'll sleep peacefully, Edwige. And you'll rest... And you'll forget this whole nightmare."

The Nyctalope took the young woman by the waist, raised her up gently and carried her as far as the bed, where he set her down. By means of the appropriate rhythmic movements, he made her pass from the hypnotic trance into a natural sleep. He drew the curtains, went to make sure that the door to the corridor was securely locked, then went back into his own room and bolted the communicating door.

To Corsat and Pilou, who were standing there waiting for him, he simply said: "There's a train to Paris at 8:48 p.m. You'll be there tomorrow morning. Get the car and go immediately to Dijon. Wait for me there at the Hotel Terminus. Get your personal belongings out of the suitcase. Keep the portmanteau."

"Yes, boss," the two men said, in unison. But Corsat, stiffening into a military pose, immediately added: "Boss, would you permit me, on behalf of both of us, to ask one question?"

"Spit it out."

"How did you already know what you needed to know in order to interrogate the young woman in such a fashion?"

"I'll satisfy your curiosity," the Nyctalope said, smiling. "It's as well, in any case, that you know everything about this business, which will take us a long way, I think, along difficult roads, at the end of which we might have to fight something worse than death. When we stopped at Toulon, I saw the woman scribbling extensively in a notebook. I went through her bag and read it. Edwige is obsessed with keeping an intimate diary. Freed from the hypnotic bonds in which Lucifer had wrapped her, she felt her own personality reemerge and wrote an account of that liberation. Conscious of the subjection to which she had been forced, horrified by what she remembered of the past, she wanted to put as much distance as possible between the past and the present. You heard what I said to her? So now you know as much as I do."

"So are we going to Colmar, boss?" asked Pilou.

"Not to Colmar, but to Mulhouse. I shall go to Colmar alone, by rail, carefully disguised. You've only just time to lighten the suitcase and buckle the portmanteau–get on with it! We'll meet again in Dijon. I'll be there on the early hours of May 11, arriving on the Calais-Mediterranean express at 3:57 a.m."

"We'll be there before you, boss," Pilou assured him.

"I'm counting on it."

He shook their hands, took up his hat, left the room and the hotel, and went to dine at Cap d'Antibes, at a certain table in a particular room in a certain hotel. He ordered the waiter to set a bouquet of three white roses, which had scarcely begun to fade, in the place opposite, where Laurence Païli had once sat.

II. La Païli's Lover

On the following day, May 10, at 9:30 a.m., Leo Saint-Clair collected an encrypted telegram at the Antibes post office. Its second part upset him profoundly for several minutes, during which he had to retreat to the darkest corner of the drab post office, leaning against the wall to prevent himself from falling over. The telegram was from Monsieur Prillant, and was thus comprised:

1. Two women separately en route towards Strasbourg and Mulhouse. 2. Laurence Païli disappeared, leaving mother desperate note ordering her to remain silent. Mother confided in me despite supernatural threats. Have Laure's note for your review. Alex.

Laure, disappeared! Madame Païli, subjected to supernatural torments! It was only natural that the unfortunate woman, despite that abuse, had trusted Monsieur Prillant, for she and he were the only people in the world who knew about the love between the Nyctalope and Laurence Païli–whom he called Laure and whom the crowds in Paris, Vienna, Rome and New York had ostentatiously nicknamed "the vestal of the Rue Favart."

Laure, vanished!

So she's in Lucifer's power! howled the Nyctalope, within himself. And he had to learn this in Antibes, in the corner of the world that had been their lovers' Paradise!

The minutes of Saint-Clair's terrible emotion were long-lasting and extremely painful. Finally, though, the Nyctalope recovered himself, morally and physically. He seized a telegram form and cabled to Prillant: *Am coming. Leo.*

Then he ran to the hotel. In a matter of moments, his powerful love for La Païli had generated a new plan of action. He ate a hasty meal, wrote a few letters and was at the railway station at 1:24 p.m. to catch an earlier train.

That train stopped at Dijon for seven minutes. That was enough for Saint-Clair to leap on to the platform and talk to the assistant station-master about Corsat and Pilou, who would be awaiting him in vain at the Hotel Terminus that night. At 9:10 p.m., he was in Paris. A taxi, whose driver was stimulated by a huge tip given in advance, took him to the Avenue Kléber, where Alexandre Prillant was waiting for him. Within five minutes, he knew everything about Laurence's disappearance that Monsieur Prillant knew, by virtue of the very complete account given to him by Laurence's mother. He read and re-read the poignant note left by the singer.

At 10 p.m., Saint-Clair and Prillant left the Avenue Kléber in the statesman's limousine; Saint-Clair told his companion everything that had happened regarding Edwige. At the central telephone office, he was put in direct communication with the Hotel Terminus in Dijon and spoke to Corsat and Pilou in person. He directed them to go to Vesoul and wait for him the next day in front of the Prefecture.

While Saint-Clair was calling Dijon, Prillant telephoned the head of the Sûreté, who arrived ten minutes later aboard a powerful racing-car driven by an élite mechanic. Saint-Clair and his suitcase replaced the head of the Sûreté in the deep and narrow quilted bucket-seat, while the latter climbed into the President of the Council's limousine.

At 10:28 p.m. exactly, the Nyctalope left Paris by the Porte de Vincennes. The Sûreté car covered approximately 350 kilometers, going from Paris to Vesoul via Troyes, Chaumont and Langres, at hurricane speed. At 1:12 p.m. on May 11, Saint-Clair transferred from the police car to his own roadster, which was waiting there for him in front of the Vesoul Prefecture.

The jubilation that Corsat and Pilou had initially felt quickly vanished when they saw the intense emotion that was displayed on their master's face. The Nyctalope's features were as white and still as marble. The eyes alone were alive–but what unholy fire burned within those eyes!

Saint-Clair was now fighting to save from torture–and perhaps death as well–not only Irène de Ciserat, Mathias Narbonne, Henri Prillant and other unknown victims, but La Païli, Laurence Païli, his beloved Laure...

With the same hurricane speed that the Sûreté car had manifested in transporting the Nyctalope from Paris to Vesoul, the roadster, piloted by Pilou, carried La Païli's lover towards the Trouée de Belfort.[6]

III. The Little Red House

The villa named *The Willows* was located north-east of Colmar, ten minutes walk from the town center. It was a large 18th-century dwelling surrounded by beautiful gardens, through which a stream meandered, bordered by magnificent willows.

The Nortmunds, while remaining French at heart, had settled in 1871 in their estate in Alsace, where they owned important mills and a large agricultural domain.[7] Despite the difficulties the family had experienced as a result of the severe, reserved and hostile attitude it had adopted after the annexation by Germany–maintaining it without weakening from generation to generation–when Colmar became French again in 1918, they were the first to celebrate the end of their 45 years of punishment.

The Nortmund family now consisted of six persons: the grandfather, Charles, who bore his 74 years heartily; his son Louis and his wife Blanche, respectively aged 40 and 37; and the couple's three children, Paul, Pierrette and Jacqueline. The boy had just started at Saint-Cyr;[8] the two girls, much younger than their brother, since they were only 12 and 10 years old, were taught at home by their mother and a qualified governess.

Having left Corsat and Pilou at Mulhouse with the car, Saint-Clair was able to take a train almost immediately to arrive in Colmar at 7 p.m. on May 11. At Mulhouse, to avoid detection by the enemy, he had taken the trouble to pass through several hotels, changing his appearance every time and making his exit through another door than the one by which he had entered–or via a window, when that was feasible. In such cases, he paid in advance for a room for 24 hours, and carried no luggage except for a light overnight bag containing the wigs, clothing and accessories necessary to his transformations. By the time he caught the train to Colmar, even his Burgundian and his Provençal would no longer have been able to recognize him. He had the physiognomy, the appearance, the gait and the stiff elegance of a lean Pomeranian junker-turned-commercial-traveler.[9]

Saint-Clair would scarcely be noticed in this guise in Alsace, where men of that sort passed too frequently through the towns to attract any attention, unless they were possessed of some particular eccentricity. He would be able to go anywhere in Germany, if it became necessary, and encounter nothing en route but sympathy. On the other hand, he would cause a certain sensation at *The Willows*, where the Nortmunds were not accustomed to receive pure-bred Prussians.

To the porter who opened the little gate within the main gate giving access to the villa's gardens, Saint-Clair gave a business card engraved with the words *Heinz von Kraft, Commercial Representative, Berlin, London, Paris, Rome*. In a secret compartment of his overnight bag, the Nyctalope kept an assortment of business cards bearing various names, professions and nationalities, as well as half a dozen blank passports, duly stamped and authorized.

"Please will you give my card to Monsieur Nortmund and tell him that I need to talk to him about serious and urgent matters–serious and urgent, I emphasize–of personal concern." This was proffered in German, in an appropriately arrogant manner.

The porter pouted, read the name on the card for a second time, looked his visitor up and down disapprovingly, and finally pointed to a central pathway furnished with rustic benches, which led directly across the lawn at a slight upward slope, to the steps of the villa. "Wait there," he muttered, "on one of those benches. I'll give the card to the footman. I don't know whether Monsieur Louis is receiving visitors today, especially at this hour, when the dinner-bell will soon be rung."

While the pretended Heinz von Kraft went to sit down on a bench, the porter went into his lodge, pressed the button of an electric bell and came out again. A black silhouette appeared on the white steps at the far end of the path, came down and crossed the lawn, advancing rapidly. This was a footman, to whom the porter gave the card and repeated, in French, what the visitor had said. The valet darted an astonished glance at the impassive Heinz von Kraft and went back along the path at the same rapid pace.

A few minutes went by; then an alarm bell trilled in the porter's lodge. "Would you care to follow the path, Monsieur," said the latter, bowing slightly in the visitor's direction. "The footman will admit you."

"There we go!" Saint-Clair murmured, in satisfaction. "There's organization here, order, discipline and alacrity. If Monsieur Nortmund's physiognomy pleases me as much as the approach to his house, I'll tell him everything; he'll be an indispensable auxiliary, and his villa will be the comfortable headquarters necessary to my operations–which, I believe, will not be on a small scale."

The footman took his overnight bag and introduced him into a simply and economically furnished study. Saint-Clair was then confronted by a tall, broad-shouldered man of powerful appearance, with austere clean-shaven features. His calm eyes were a profound blue; his chestnut-colored hair was cut and brushed.

"I am Louis Nortmund," the man said, in French, in a voice that was clear and cold. "You had yourself announced in a singular fashion. What are these serious and urgent matters of which you speak, which concern me personally? Be brief and clear, please. I can only give you a few minutes." He remained standing, and did not invite his visitor to sit down.

"Perfect!" cried the fake Heinz von Kraft. "You are as good as I had hoped, Monsieur Nortmund, and we can talk constructively. But one question before anything else, to which I ask an immediate response: do you know the name Leo Saint-Clair, alias the Nyctalope?"

71

Although he was extremely surprised to hear these words—in French, pronounced with the purest and most distinguished Parisian accent—emerging from the mouth of a junker with a military gait reborn as a commercial traveler, Monsieur Nortmund replied with a certain emphatic patriotic pride: "Who does not know, not merely the name, but also the features, reproduced a thousand times over in the newspapers, and the universally-admired exploits of the great Leo Saint-Clair, the Nyctalope?"

Saint-Clair laughed lightly, assumed the expansive gaze that gave him an irresistible power of seduction, and said: "I am not Heinz von Kraft, Monsieur, and the manner in which you have just answered me obliges me to blush with elementary modesty in revealing to you that I am Leo Saint-Clair, the Nyctalope."

"You!" cried Nortmund.

"Me. Would you care to show me to a bathroom and return my overnight bag, which the footman who admitted me very obligingly took away? I shall erase the von Kraft disguise and reveal my true face, with whose features the newspapers have familiarized you. Then I shall explain myself."

Without a word, Monsieur Nortmund led his strange visitor to his own bathroom. An instant later, he brought the overnight bag himself and withdrew again.

It required a quarter of an hour for the Nyctalope to transform himself into his own self again. When that was done, he went out by the door through which he had entered, and found Monsieur Nortmund waiting for him in the corridor.

"Let's go downstairs, Monsieur," said the businessman.

They returned to the study, whose windows were now closed. It was brightly lit, not merely by the 12 electric bulbs of a chandelier but by six lamps set in three wall-brackets. Nortmund studied the Nyctalope in this intense light.

"Ah, Monsieur!" cried the Alsatian, with his arms outstretched, his eyes laughing and his whole face transformed by joy, "what great pleasure and happiness you give me! Leo Saint-Clair, the Nyctalope, under my own roof! Oh, I shall not question you; you shall speak when you wish. My father and I, our servants and our workmen, our friends and our fortune, are all at your service—for I assume that, to come into my home in the guise of a Prussian squire, you must be on some sort of expedition or exploration, a hunt or a war... Something difficult, delicate and perilous. But it's dinner time—have you the time to join us?"

"Certainly!" said Saint-Clair, shaking both the Alsatian's hands, glad to find him so devoted and enthusiastic beneath his frosty and slightly egotistical exterior. "You delight me, my dear Monsieur! Yes, I have the time to dine. But first, a precaution, if you please. Are you absolutely sure of the discretion and fidelity of your servants—all your servants, or at least those who have seen Heinz von Kraft and will see Leo Saint-Clair?"

"Yes, absolutely sure. What do you want me to do?"

"Gather them here, show me to them, and tell them that—for reasons of the utmost gravity—Saint-Clair has been von Kraft and will become him again, and have them swear on oath not to tell a living soul, or talk among themselves, about von Kraft or Saint-Clair, for any reason whatsoever."

"That's fine!" said Monsieur Nortmund. "Would you care to wait for me here. It will take five minutes—there's no need to bring them here. I'll assemble them and talk to them."

Five minutes later, he returned, not alone but with his father and his wife. Monsieur Charles and Madame Blanche Nortmund greeted the famous explorer with the utmost cordiality and the most delicate discretion. Saint-Clair was treated as a very dear friend welcomed after a long separation. Immediately afterwards, the butler announced that dinner was served, and everyone went into the dining-room.

The conversation was entirely worldly, but a trifle earnest, for Saint-Clair could not set aside his troubles and preoccupations completely. After the meal, Madame Blanche retired and the three men went back to the study.

The reliability and fidelity of the servants was so well established that there was no need to subject it to further proof, but Saint-Clair asked that the doors and windows should be firmly closed and the curtains drawn. He began talking in such a well-tuned voice that his companions immediately adopted a very quiet tone by way of imitation.

"Messieurs," he said, "First hear me out without interruption. Afterwards, you can reply and ask me questions as you please." Briefly, clearly, and with the intense liveliness that he could give to the slightest anecdote, he recounted the fourfold story of Irène, La Païli, Mathias Narbonne and Henri Prillant. Then, he related the details of Edwige's adventure, and afterwards fell silent.

There was a long silence. While the Nortmunds reflected, the Nyctalope waited, studying the father and son with his sharp eye. They were similar in their build and their features, save that Louis' chestnut-colored hair had become silvery white in his father, Charles.

Finally, after exchanging a brief glance with his son, Charles Nortmund fixed his calm eyes on Saint-Clair's and said, simply: "There's little to add. Edwige, whose abrupt and seemingly-motiveless departure we could not explain, has been replaced—and that's all we can say about her. As for ourselves, relative to this Lucifer, I repeat what Louis has said to you. My son and I, our servants and workmen, our friends and our fortune, are all at your disposal. You are the master here: give your orders!" Getting to his feet, Charles Nortmund offered both his hands to the Nyctalope. The latter shook them, smiling. .

They sat down in their armchairs again. "Thank you," Saint-Clair said. "I accept, but I hope that I shall have little to ask of you. For tonight, this: my car and my usual assistants, my manservant Corsat and my chauffeur Pilou, are at Mulhouse; if they did not receive fresh instructions from me by telephone by 9 p.m., they were to come straight here."

"It's 9:40 p.m.," Louis said. "I'll give orders for the main gate to be opened for them and a room with two beds to be prepared–and a place in the garage for the car."

He got up to leave, but Saint-Clair stopped him, saying: "Then, a room for me. Corsat and I will only sleep until 3 a.m.; Pilou will stay in bed because he needs more rest than Corsat. With the latter, I shall go to a little red house on the bank of the Lauch."

"May I come with you to act as guide?" Louis said, with avid enthusiasm.

"Certainly!" the Nyctalope agreed, and added: "What we learn at the little red house will determine our next step." He made a gesture, and Louis went out. Then, addressing Charles Nortmund, he continued: "Meanwhile, my dear Monsieur, I would like you, if I leave Colmar tomorrow, to coordinate matters here– to transmit to me, whenever and wherever it may be convenient, any information that arrives at the Central Commissariat of Colmar regarding the two women who are being followed by the Sûreté's inspectors, and who left Paris heading for Strasbourg and Mulhouse. You must introduce yourself to the Commissaire with this card. It will accredit you, in accordance with instructions received from Monsieur Prillant." From his wallet, he took a small red card marked with what looked like shorthand symbols.

"When should I go to the Commissariat?" Monsieur Charles asked, as he took the card.

"As soon as you hear from me, your son, Corsat or Pilou, that I am no longer in Colmar. Naturally, I shall let you know at an opportune moment when, where and how you should send me the information communicated to you by the Commissaire. You must always have a plausible public excuse for your twice daily visits to the Commissariat, of course."

"That's easy enough," said Monsieur Charles, with a smile.

"And now, I must sleep."

"I'll take you to your room. Will you need to be woken up?"

"No–my eyes will open at the stated hour."

"Very well. On awakening, you have only to ring and Louis will wake Corsat–and everything will be ready. Will you eat before leaving?"

"Yes."

"Good."

Monsieur Charles did not leave the Nyctalope alone until he had been rapidly assured that the room and the bathroom reserved for him had everything that a guest might need.

Hours passed, while some of the inhabitants of *The Willows* devoted themselves to peaceful sleep and others maintained an excited vigil. At 3:05 a.m., on a damp, dark and starless night, the Moon being almost continuously veiled by enormous black clouds moving slowly across the sky, three men left the villa's grounds by the little iron gate at the rear of the gardens. It let them out on to a broad path following the right bank of the Lauch.

These three men were the Nyctalope, Louis Nortmund and Corsat. They all wore little Basque berets of the kind that cling to the skull, which the wind cannot blow off and which never fall off in a struggle or during strenuous exercise. Corsat was wearing a belt furnished with leather pockets filled with various objects.

The distance from the iron gate to the wall encircling the red house was three kilometers. The hands of Louis' watch stood at 3:45 a.m. when they arrived.

Louis only knew the little red house by virtue of having seen it a hundred times while passing along the riverside path when out walking or hunting. The path curved around an ancient but well-constructed wall, surrounding a garden in the middle of which stood the house. All of it—ground floor, first floor and a mansard roof enclosing the attics—was visible the path. The garden seemed to be abandoned, its fruit-trees having reverted to their wild state, while tall grass and brambles had invaded every part of it. The house seemed dead, the doors and windows permanently closed. Along the Lauch, the encircling wall plunged into water that was almost stagnant at that point, replete with viscous vegetation and reeds. On the western side, the wall was pierced by a gateway from which extended a path some 20 meters long, at right angles to the road.

The house reportedly belonged to a bachelor from Strasbourg, whom no one knew and had ever seen. The place was very isolated, far from any frequent traffic. The riverside path had nothing but wild hedges for two kilometers downstream and three kilometers upstream. These hedges protected a strip of fallow land five kilometers long and half a kilometer wide, belonging to the same mysterious proprietor of the red house. The riverside path did not, in fact, lead anywhere; at the extremity of the strip of abandoned fields, it ended in a cul-de-sac in a little fir-wood.

All these details had been given to Saint-Clair by Louis during their walk to the house.

When Louis said "Stop!" in a low voice, they were at the place on the path which overlooked the wall. Corsat and Louis knew that the Nyctalope could see everything in the now-total darkness as clearly as in daylight: the wall, the unkempt garden, and the house, which appeared to them only as variously-nuanced shadows.

After two minutes of observation, Saint-Clair whispered to Louis: "Thank you, my dear Monsieur. I have no further need of you now, but you may wait for me here if you wish. It is impossible for you to follow me into the house without a light; you would bump into everything and make too much noise. Corsat, on the other hand, is used to following me through the darkness..."

"I'll stay here and wait for you. One word, though..."

"What?"

"If I were to make too much noise, as you say, who would hear me? Do you suppose that the little house might be inhabited?"

"The red-haired man brought Edwige here twice. If there is anyone in there, we have no reason to believe that it will be anyone but him."

"That's true. I'll wait here, then. But I'm strong enough to climb the wall. If I hear a gunshot, I'll come running."

"Yes, a gunshot or a whistle-blast," said Saint-Clair. Without another word, he moved off, not towards the wall but along the road, in the direction of a little path leading to a gateway in one of the other "terrestrial" walls, the "aquatic" side only being bordered by a narrow strip of vegetation.

Corsat followed him, his footsteps muffled. He was guided by his hearing, instinct and habit more than by sight, for the night was pitch dark. A cold wind blew in gusts, not high in the atmosphere but almost at ground level. The crowns of the poplars were scarcely rippled, but the bushes were trembling.

The two men soon reached the door in the wall. "It's tarred wood, solid and firmly shut," said Saint-Clair, in a voice that only Corsat could hear. "The keyhole is shiny. Someone has been here in the recent past, more often than the Nortmunds and others suppose. Pass me skeleton key No. 8."

There was a slight click of steel and Corsat, having verified with his fingertips the number engraved on the shaft of one of the instruments contained in one of his leather pockets, passed the requested skeleton key to his boss.

In 20 seconds, the door opened silently. They crossed the threshold and the Nyctalope pushed the door to without engaging the lock, so that they would be able to get out again without resorting to the skeleton key.

A winding path extended from the wall to the house through a minuscule virgin forest comprised by inextricably interwoven branches, shrubs, bushes, brambles and grass. The Nyctalope observed that the path was frayed to a greater extent than the abandoned appearance of the house might lead one to expect.

Someone comes here often, Saint-Clair thought. *Might I find a bird in the nest?* While he walked on soundlessly, silently followed by Corsat, all his senses were acute; his nyctalopic eyes distinguished the least detail in the gloom, including shades of color and subtle contours. His nostrils flared, discerning the various odors of the Earth, the plants and the nearby water. His ears perceived a multiplicity of nocturnal sounds. All his nerves were raised to an attentive pitch of sensitivity. On the trail of a mystery, the Nyctalope became a force as scrupulous in his perceptions as he was formidable in his effects.

The minuscule forest extended all the way to the wall of the house. The sinuous pathway led to a low-set door in a recess in that wall. The Nyctalope stopped; behind him, Corsat immediately became still.

"There's no window in this façade," Saint-Clair whispered. "There's only one entrance–this one, closed off by a wooden door with two tiny holes for special keys. Pass me the two."

With his customary skill, Corsat touched, chose and seized the requisite key. Saint-Clair tried it in one of the locks, but in vain. It had no more success in the other lock. "The three!" he demanded.

The second attempt was similarly checked by both locks. "We'd have to cut through the door around the hinges," he said. "Too long. Follow me."

He moved along the wall, followed by Corsat. The branches and bushes that their hands pushed aside gave rise to sounds that blended in with those of the wind in the trees. The two men rounded a corner of the house and moved along the façade parallel to the wall bordering the water, a dozen meters distant. There were neither bushes nor grass there; the ground was clear, stony and flattened.

"There's a flight of three steps," Saint-Clair whispered to Corsat. "A door flanked by two windows; two more on the first floor; wooden shutters, closed." He climbed the three steps and examined the door. "The same double lock as down below. No point in trying. We'll go up to the roof. The rope! Don't move."

Corsat opened one of his leather pockets and took out a skein of rope, which the Nyctalope took from his fingers. It was a sort of silken lasso the thickness of his index finger, about 20 meters long, admirably light, flexible and sturdy, with knots placed at intervals. A ball, made of lead shot and rubber inside a felt capsule, was fixed at one end.

With the lasso in hand, Saint-Clair stepped back to the riverside wall. He looked at the roof of the house and saw two chimneys. He chose the closer one. He rolled one end of the rope around his left wrist, while his right hand gripped the cord some 50 centimeters from the ball. He swung it, whirled it rapidly around, then threw it–and the ball, lifting the rope behind it, looped itself around the chimney, along with four meters of the lasso. Saint-Clair pulled it tight. The rope dangled down the wall as far as the steps, where the Nyctalope rejoined Corsat.

"I'll go up first," Saint-Clair said. "Here's the rope–get hold of it! When I pull on it, climb up."

The two men were wearing rubber-soled shoes. Their hands went from knot to knot; their feet made no sound on the old roughcast façade. Under the pressure of the taut rope the cast-iron guttering creaked–a slight noise lost in the sounds of the windswept night.

On the roof, on the far side of the chimney, the skylight of an attic interrupted the uniform alignment of the slates. This skylight, whose glass was rippled and murky, stood 20 centimeters ajar.

Saint-Clair smiled and shrugged his shoulders. "One can pose as Lucifer," he said, "but one can't think of everything."

The Nyctalope reached through the opening and seized the notched iron rod that served to open and close the window, which was soon wide open. The two men passed through, one at a time, the first giving the second the necessary instructions. As the darkness was still opaque, Saint-Clair said to his companion: "Attic lumber-room with floorboards. One trapdoor, three meters to the left. Come on."

They moved as lightly as cats. On one side, the trapdoor was furnished with a ring, to which a cord was attached. The cord passed over a little pulley suspended from a roof-beam, and descended again to pass through a hole in the floorboards. Saint-Clair wedged the cord between the casing and the wheel of the pulley so that it would not budge, and calmly lifted the trapdoor, setting it back completely. He looked through and saw a landing, a section of wall with red hangings, a banister and a flight of stairs, apparently descending all the way to the ground floor. There was a ladder mounted on the wall, hanging from an iron hook. The pull-cord hung down from the trapdoor to the landing.

"The ladder's too far away for me to grab it, even if I lean out as far as possible," Saint-Clair said, "but the drop's only three meters. We'll suspend ourselves at arm's length and let ourselves fall on to our toes, together. OK? Are you there? Now!"

The floorboards creaked loudly under the weight of the two men. They stayed still, knees bent, in silence. For Corsat, the darkness was total. The Nyctalope saw a narrow corridor leading to the staircase, in whose rear wall there was an uncurtained window. There were two doors to the right and one to the left. There were numerous damp stains on the red cloth of the old wall hangings.

Suddenly, the silence was broken by an exclamation: a brief, harsh and brutal "oh!"

Instinctively, Saint-Clair and Corsat stood up and stiffened, avidly attentive. They both turned in the direction from which the sound had come—the partition wall with the two doors.

A few seconds after the exclamation, there was a whole series of successive and simultaneous sounds: the metallic creaking of mattress-springs, the groans of a thick and coarse human voice, muffled footsteps on an uncarpeted floor, the scrape of a match...

A beam of light showed under the nearer door,

Almost immediately afterwards, Saint-Clair and Corsat heard the man behind the door getting dressed, muttering bad-temperedly and talking to himself in a low and slurred voice. It was impossible to make out a single word clearly, but the occasional syllable and the rough consonants testified that the monologue was in German. The man's footfalls on the bare floor suggested that he was slow and heavy, presumably fat.

Saint-Clair and Corsat had already taken action. They were flat against the wall to the right and left of the door, their heads slightly turned and their hands free, ready to leap, to grab, to hold. "When he opens the door," the Nyctalope ordered, "grab him, cover his mouth, put him on his bed and roll him up in the blankets, stifling him."

"Yes, boss!"

They waited, calm and joyful in their anticipation.

The heavy tread approached; a clumsy hand drew back a bolt, turned a key; the door opened wide... and it was as if two lithe jaguars had leapt upon a gorilla!

The enormous man scarcely had time to release a raucous groan and to raise his hands defensively. A large handkerchief was crammed into his mouth; he was gripped by four bruising hands of steel, while two human bodies frog-marched him backwards to his bed. He was rolled up in his bedclothes like a piece of meat in a pastry. Then, with the light curtains abruptly ripped from their rail, he was trussed up from his ankles to his shoulders. His head was uncovered, and he saw two men leaning over him, one to his right and one to his left.

At the head of the bed, on a white wood night-stand, stood a candle in a wrought-iron candlestick, which illuminated the prisoner's face. His brutal skull was covered in thick short-cropped red hair. He had blue-grey eyes and his coarse skin was clean-shaven, with neither beard not moustache. It was the head of a brute, to be sure, but an intelligent brute; the forehead was high and broad, the eyes expressive, the lips eloquent.

If this man is a humble nonentity, the Nyctalope thought, scrutinizing the immobile features, *he's not a vulgar nonentity. If this man is truly devoted to Lucifer, he won't talk unless he's subjected to physical pressure. Before interrogating him, it'll be as well to search the whole house.*

There was a bunch of keys on the night-stand, next to the candlestick. Saint-Clair saw them and took them. "Corsat," he said, in German, "this fellow must have Herculean strength. Don't trust entirely in the blankets and curtains. Dagger in hand, my friend! If the prisoner shows any sign of trying to escape, stick the blade in his thigh, then in one or other of his arms, until he calms down. There's no need to kill him, but if he gives any trouble, a few little cuts will thin his blood nicely. Watch him! I'll be back in a few minutes."

Saint-Clair went out, perfectly calm, leaving behind the light of which he had no need. First, he wanted to make sure that there were no other men in the house. He drew his pistol by way of precaution as he went down to the ground floor. Thanks to the bunch of keys, he did not foresee any difficulty in the domestic expedition.

The ground floor consisted of a corridor leading from the bottom of the staircase to the main entrance, one empty room, a cellar containing wood, coal and two cases of champagne—one of them opened—and a kitchen furnished with instruments indispensable for the exercise of the unrefined culinary arts. There was no living being there, but there was scarcely any dust to be seen; the furnished rooms gave the impression of having been used frequently, if not continually inhabited.

Saint-Clair went back upstairs. He already knew that there were three doors there. One, which stood open, was the room where Corsat was guarding their prisoner. The second, on the same side of the corridor, gave access to a little bedroom furnished with a made-up bed, a dressing-table, a plush carpet and a full-length cheval-glass of superior quality. There were two sets of curtains on the window, a blue velvet door-curtain and blue cloth hangings surmounted by tasteful paintings. The wardrobe contained male clothing, hats, shoes and underwear, all devoid of marks of origin, bearing no owner's monogram or initials.

Saint-Clair went out, closed the door again and crossed the corridor diagonally to open the final door—but he quickly ascertained that none of the keys in the bunch would fit the lock, and saw that it was of such quality that a simple skeleton key would not suffice to open it.

We'll have to use the cutter, he thought.

Saint-Clair only wanted to question his captive on matters he could not resolve for himself. To open the firmly-locked door and find out what was inside was something for which the Nyctalope did not need anyone else. He went back to Corsat. "The cutter," he said, laconically.

The Burgundian's right hand was playing with a large-bladed knife, sharp-edged and pointed. His left hand opened a bag suspended from his leather belt and drew out an instrument somewhat reminiscent of a small, flat camera.

Saint-Clair had put his Browning back in his pocket. He took the instrument, returned to the closed door, made two adjustments to one face of the apparatus—which was furnished with little buttons and winged screws—and set one of its narrow sides it against the wooden door, level with the lock and ten centimeters from the frame. A scarcely-perceptible scraping sound then became audible as something moved back and forth with an accelerating rhythm. Little by little, the Nyctalope moved the instrument downwards, and a groove two millimeters wide appeared above it. The apparatus was an automatic saw, operated by a compact electric battery of unprecedented power and capacity.

Saint-Clair made three grooves, one parallel to the fame and the two others at right-angles to the first, The rectangle of wood thus detached contained the lock, which remained fixed—but the door yielded to a shove by the Nyctalope's knee, after which he immediately dropped to a kneeling position.

There was a loud bang, then another.

"Don't move, Corsat!" cried Saint-Clair. "It's only an automatic pistol, fired by the opening of the door. There'll be one more shot, I think."

"OK, boss."

The faint radiance that emerged obliquely from the prisoner's room scarcely illuminated the threshold of the third room, but there was no darkness for the Nyctalope. Experienced, skillful and prudent—the kind of prudence that goes with courage and temerity, as will-power goes with love and passion—he waited for the third shot, kneeling down by the wall next to the door-frame. It was not long in sounding. As Saint-Clair had anticipated, the automatic pistol had a built-in delay for the third shot, but the bullet buried itself harmlessly in the wall, as its two predecessors had.

Access to the dark room was now straightforward, and probably free of danger, but the Nyctalope waited, inspecting it carefully before entering. He had placed the electric cutter on the floor. His Browning, fitted with a silencer, was in his right hand. He moved forward darting glances into the corners he had not been able to see from the doorway.

"No one, and no visible hiding-place," he murmured.

All the same, he remained ostentatiously armed, for he mistrusted the bookshelves that were set to the right and the large mirror to the left, set above a low-slung divan, along its entire length. They gave a suspect appearance to the room, further emphasized by the licentious paintings hanging on the walls and the hardbound books arrayed on the shelves, whose titles were worthy of that which a bibliophile might call "my Inferno." Facing the immense divan, to the right of the fireplace that was flanked on the left by the bookshelves, was a beautiful wardrobe whose three panels were mounted with mirrors. The keys were set in three ornamental locks delicately sculpted in copper.

Saint-Clair opened the middle compartment. Feminine apparel appeared, exhaling a perfume that was less suggestive of an elegant socialite as of a rich courtesan unafraid of migraine–a very strong, insistent, subtly inebriating perfume.

"There we go!" said Saint-Clair, shrugging his shoulders as he closed the wardrobe door. "It's the *débauché*'s boudoir..." Mechanically, he opened one of the side compartments, and started. "Oh! This is much more serious! Our *débauché* is a torturer by methods more direct than spell-casting. He'll have to pay the account of a Spanish inquisitor when I get my hands on him!"

Trembling with furious indignation, Saint-Clair slammed the narrow door of the second compartment into its frame. What he had just seen inside was nothing less than a complete collection of handcuffs, whips, restraints, canes, switches, metal gags and chokers. He did not even deign to look in the third compartment.

Resisting with all his might the supposition that Laurence Païli might have been brought here and lodged in this place of cruelty and debauchery, Saint-Clair left the room. He put his Browning back in his pocket and went to plant himself in front of the captive, over whom Corsat was watching attentively.

"You–what's your name?" he asked, in German.

The brute grunted, looked down in a surly fashion and said nothing.

"Talk, idiot," Saint-Clair said, rudely. "If you don't, you'll make the acquaintance, on your own account–do you understand me?–with the pretty toys I've just seen set out and suspended in the left-hand compartment of the wardrobe over there."

The man shuddered, grunted again and said nothing.

The Nyctalope waited for about a minute, his lips peevish, his brows knitted and his eyes hard and terrible. Then he turned round and went back to the "infamous room," as he had privately named it. He returned almost immediately,

81

carrying a pair of handcuffs, a metal gag and a sort of short-handled knout whose six cords were tipped with steel balls armed with tiny spikes.

The man looked at it in a kind of fearful daze.

Letting the gag and the knout fall on to the bed, Saint-Clair skillfully handcuffed the captive, whose wrists Corsat swiftly brought together in response to a glance from his boss. Immediately afterwards, Saint-Clair struck the prisoner brutally on the chin with the index finger and middle finger of his left hand, stuck rigidly together. The man howled and, with his right hand, Saint-Clair crammed the metal gag into his mouth. The man remained motionless, seated on the edge of the bed.

Then, Saint-Clair seized the knout, raised it and struck it against the wall, where the spiked steel balls ripped holes in the colored paper. "I'll count to ten," he said, in a dry, cold and implacable voice, stressing the German syllables. "If you want to talk, to answer my questions in full, raise both your index fingers, while the other fingers remain folded. That will be the signal to put an end to the blows that you will receive, and which, until now, you have had the hideous pleasure of inflicting–for I've guessed that you play the role of torturer here, under the orders of the infamous monster who calls himself Lucifer. Do you understand me? Yes? Take the knout, Corsat! I'll count to ten. When I've finished, strike this filth on the body and the limbs. Don't spare the head–and strike powerfully. Be pitiless. If he runs around the room, pursue him. The jackal won't suffer the hundredth part of the tortures that he's surely inflicted on his master's innocent victims!"

Corsat did not say a word. He seized the knout and raised himself up to his full height beside the seated man. Saint-Clair began counting slowly, leaving about five seconds between each number: "One... two... three... four..."

The man had not even enough moral fiber to wait for the first blow. As Saint-Clair said "five," he raised his index fingers and his porcine eyes became basely pleading.

"I expected as much," said Saint-Clair, disgustedly. "This torturer's valet is a coward. Bring him along, Corsat. We'll be better off in the dining-room downstairs. It doesn't stink like a trough, as this room does. Don't worry about the lasso or the cutter. We'll go out via the roof, because I want to leave all the doors locked. Light the electric lamp and snuff out the candle. Good. Follow me–and if the fellow stumbles, a rap on the head with the knout will bring him to his feet."

Five minutes later, Saint-Clair and Corsat learned that their captive was Heinz Kroon. For an hour, they listened to him talk, the Nyctalope restricting himself to asking curt and precise questions when necessary.

IV. After Kroon's Revelations

The *Schwarzwald*, or Black Forest, is a German mountain range which terminates to the east in the Rhine valley in the Grand Duchy of Baden and Wurtemburg. This steep chain is 260 kilometers in length. Its highest peak, the Feldberg, is exactly 1,425 meters high. Despite the relative modesty of its altitude, the *Schwarzwald* is one of the coldest parts of central Europe; snow is found there in summer. Its most densely-forested part has no large towns, only isolated habitations in the midst of the wildest scenery.

The most forbidding part of these hirsute mountains–which the black firs drape in perpetual mourning and where the mists move from morning until evening over damp uneven rocks–lies in the south-west, within a radius of about 30 kilometers from the intersection of the 48th degree of northern latitude and the 6th degree of eastern longitude. The sources of the Danube are there: nameless springs bursting from huge unexplored grottoes descend in heavy waterfalls into unknown abysses, and centuries-old firs on mossy crags overhang frightful precipices, at the bottom of which rivers sometimes cascade along serpentine paths at breakneck speed.

There, overlooked by a circle of steep mountain slopes, and itself overlooking a circular valley where a few human beings eke out a living as primitive farmers, is to be found a strange, romantic edifice with vertiginous walls, set on a rocky peak around which an improbable staircase spirals. The clouds in the sky and the mists of the Earth mingle around its flanks, continually gathered and dissipated by the mountain winds. This is the castle of Schwarzrock.

From Freiburg-in-Brisgau, which is a town in Baden, to the wild valley of Schwarzrock, by the paths that are the most direct, if not the most difficult, is about 50 kilometers.

On May 12, at noon, Leo Saint-Clair, Corsat and Pilou left Colmar in a small hired car, which did not look like much but had a good engine. Saint-Clair had become once again a thoroughly convincing Heinz von Kraft, commercial traveler, suitably transformed by false whiskers and clothes cut in the local style. Corsat could easily have passed for a colleague of a less well-bred sort, and Pilou–who had a genius for make-up and disguise–was playing the role of a Swiss chauffeur who had followed a thousand other trades in his time, in an admirably natural fashion. It goes without saying that Corsat and Pilou, who had been prisoners of war in Thuringia in 1917-18, spoke German as easily, if not quite as purely, as Saint-Clair.

The three adventurers spent the night of May 12 getting their fill of sleep in a patriarchal hotel in Freiburg-in-Brisgau. At 8 a.m. on May 13, comfortably equipped as tourists, they left Freiburg on foot after Heinz von Kraft had told their host that he would spend a week walking in the Black Forest with his friend and chauffeur, who would play he role of domestic servants during the pleasure-trip.

In the mountains, the time lost in going upslope is regained going down. That day, Saint-Clair and his auxiliaries covered 32 kilometers between Freiburg and the place where they slept, which was a forest hamlet furnished with a humble inn.

At 10 a.m. on the next day, they arrived on the crest of the mountainous circle enclosing the valley of Schwarzrock. This circle was linked, via a deep and narrow gorge, with one of the valleys extending towards the Danube, but that almost-impassable gorge served only to export the valley's melted snows in torrents and streams. The only routes into it were steep zigzagging paths leading from the distant roads to Baden and Wurtemburg, which were few and scarcely practical–for the valley's inhabitants, who numbered about 30, almost never left it, and rarely saw four strangers emerging from the gap in the course of a year.

"We're here, finally!" cried Saint-Clair, when he saw the castle of Schwarzrock planted atop it black rock in the middle of the enormous depression. He sat down amid a chaos of loose stones beside the breach in the crest that hollowed out the pass giving access to the valley. His companions imitated him. Their clothes were uniformly somber, and there were no shiny objects among their equipment. Blending in with the slope, they were completely invisible from the castle or the hovels in the valley.

The three men looked at the edifice, inaccessible to anyone who was not invited–into which, however, all three of them expected to enter the following night. The fortified building had ironclad doors and loopholes garnished with electric cables. On its highest tower, active by day and by night, there was a sort of microphone receiver, which captured the least noise produced within a radius of 500 meters of the natural and artificial rocky mass and transmitted them to resound, separately, with varying intensity and quality, in various items of apparatus fixed to the walls of a "listening room."

This was, in fact, the place where the formidable and monstrous Lucifer lived, and from which the fluid emanated that had attacked Irène de Ciserat, wounded Mathias Narbonne, half-strangled little Henri Prillant, irresistibly attracted Laurence de Païli and directed Edwige and her unconscious fellow cat's-paws. It was also, perhaps, the place where that same Laurence Païli was being held captive, subjected to unknown tortures for the demoniacal pleasure of some devil with a human face.

The Nyctalope was shivering with impatience, tremulous with an enormous and profound anger, all the more terrible because he had to contain it. The hour had not yet come for him to unleash himself. If only it would arrive...

Saint-Clair summoned up all his reserves of strength–but would not the mysterious enemy be wilier, stronger, better-prepared to defend himself and better armed for attack and riposte alike? With his elbows on his knees and his

84

chin and cheeks in his hands, the Nyctalope stared at Schwarzrock for a long time.

That May day had an exquisite gentleness. Pierced, shredded and dissipated by the Sun's rays, the mists climbing from the dank depths of the valley reached half-way up the enormous column of rock and vanished without attaining the castle walls. An east wind was chasing the last clouds away, sweeping clean the hallucinatory blue sky. In that enchantment of spring, where even the dark firs seemed to take on a hint of the plain's greenness, Schwarzrock appeared ever blacker and more sinister.

Two hours passed. No more mist, no more cloud; the Sun was almost at its zenith in the azure sky.

"Let's eat!" said Saint-Clair, in a low tone. "But let's go behind that curtain of bushes and rocks. That little patch of grass will be ideal for an afternoon nap. We have to wait here until night falls—eight hours in which we must take turns to sleep, if we can, and play lookout. Our limbs will need to be well-rested, at any rate. Do we know what we need to do? We'll eat several times, in small doses; that way digestion won't slow us down, and we can go without eating for 24 hours, if need be. Then, my friends, get used to the idea that Death lies in that castle, waiting for us, ready to seize us in a myriad different ways. Above all, my friends, above all... but I'll tell you that later, when we go to face our moment of peril. Let's eat now, smoke a little and rest."

That was what they did. When the afternoon had run its course, though, as the Sun disappeared and dusk slowly extended it darkness, there were still two eyes on the crest of that mountainous circle watching the castle, the spiral staircase and the green valley where a few grazing cows appeared as slowly-moving stains.

Nothing happened. No one came out of the castle and no one went in. No silhouette appeared on the walls, on the towers, or at the narrow windows. Schwarzrock would have seemed uninhabited, had not occasional slight puffs of white smoke emerged from an invisible chimney and climbed vertically into the sky above the edifice, which was dark brown where it reflected the light, and black in the shadows.

"Let's get ready!" Saint-Clair said, once the Sun had vanished.

It was not without emotion that Corsat and Pilou devoted themselves to the preparations that their boss had instructed them to make, verbally and by example. All the tourist equipment was gathered into a bundle and buried under stones between two bushes. The cord-soled sandals on their feet were replaced by socks and hobnailed boots. Over his usual flannel and linen underwear, each of the three men put on a sort of leotard, which covered everything from the ankle to the neck. A balaclava helmet and gloves of the same texture were suspended from each belt. Each supple leather belt supported a silent Browning, a dagger in a scabbard and a pair of secateurs whose crystal shafts were covered in felt. In addition, Corsat's belt was furnished with a satchel containing the electric cutter and various other instruments, motors and tools.

For some time, electricity had played a role in almost every adventure that Saint-Clair and his auxiliaries had undertaken, and the most elementary prudence advised them to arm themselves in advance with the means to counter electricity used as an item of attack or defense. The Nyctalope never set off on an expedition without all his accessories being set out in the boot of his car, in a suitcase, a tourist bag or a vagabond's sack.

"We're ready," he said, after inspecting Corsat and Pilou with a swift glance. His face was calm and grave, and his eyes softened as he added: "Above all, my friends, remain masters of your own will!" He paused, thought for a second, as if choosing his words very carefully, then continued: "If our presence is detected, the weapon that we have most to fear is the enemy's will. Remember my explanations. You must, therefore, attend to your own will, stiffen it and render it inflexible. If you feel your moral force growing weak, stiffen all your muscles and all your sensibility, say to yourself: 'I do not want to give way; I shall not give way!' and continue to act physically according to the requirements of the moment. We might be obliged to separate. If so, the peril will be tripled, for while we are together, our combined wills will be unbreakable. Finally, my good comrades, companions in joy and in pain, remember that we are fighting to safeguard innocence–and, I am sure, to save humanity from an unimaginable slavery. Now, my friends, for the happiness of all the days that I still have to live, let's clasp hands and go forth!"

Corsat and Pilou had listened calmly. They gave their hands to Saint-Clair. Their embrace was fraternal. "Don't worry about us, boss," Corsat said. "We'll hold on, or die."

"Yes, boss," said Pilou the Provençal, simply.

"Thanks!"

Night had fallen, its blackness scarcely relieved by the stars, which were being blotted out by a light mist. Thanks to their habit of making nocturnal excursions, Corsat and Pilou could see well enough in the open to follow the Nyctalope without making any sound. Silence was the most important thing, to begin with; they had to move forward without knocking over and stones or falling over themselves. It was necessary not to rattle a pebble against a rock to disturb the silence of the night. In the valley of Schwarzrock, the silence was absolute: no crickets sang; no frogs croaked; the sheep and cattle on the land made no sound; and there was no wind in the fir-trees. Every five minutes or so, a bird would trill in the distance, but its lugubrious, regular call only made the silence more apparent.

Black on its enormous crag, its battlements and towers silhouetted against the slightly less black sky, the sinister castle seemed higher than the mountains. The three adventurers, as intrepid as madmen, as resolute as desperadoes and as calm as sages, went as silently and lightly as shadows to meet their Destiny.

Part Three: Schwarzrock

I. Baron Glô von Warteck

In the enormous and profound cul-de-sac formed to the north by the abyssal valley of Schwarzrock, there was a house lurking under a rocky cliff between two clumps of fir-trees. The valley was relatively warm, by virtue of its orientation, which sheltered it from the north wind but allowed the sunlight to penetrate via the gorge. The flanks of the circle were more funnel-shaped in the east-south-east section of the compass. In addition—a rarity in the Black Forest—the valley of Schwarzrock divested itself completely of its winter snows in the first days of May, particularly in the sheltered vicinity of the house in the north. This large, stout house was made of stone and wood, with an overhanging roof sustained by thick, squared-off tree-trunks, which established a sort of courtyard around the habitation.

At 8 p.m. on May 14, a man and a woman were sitting in front of a little fir-wood fire in the hearth, in the big communal room which, in Black Forest cottages, serves as a kitchen, a dining-room, a dining-room and a master bedroom. The children, relatives and servants, if any, sleep in outbuildings at the back of the house or in closets flanking the attic.

The man and the woman, dressed like all mountain peasants, were both tall, with grey hair, coarse features and blue eyes. They were peeling apples, throwing the flesh into a cauldron half-full of water and the peel into and old wine-case. They were working slowly and silently.

Suddenly, while the cuckoo was emerging from the clock to signal that it was 8:30 p.m., a dull sound was heard, like the noise of a hammer striking a full wine-cask in a cellar. The man and the woman lifted their heads. Their eyes became fixed and their hands became motionless. The sound was immediately followed by an equally loud rattle; then, after ten seconds of silence, three equally-spaced blows.

The man and the woman stood up, letting their apples and paring-knives fall to the ground. Turning to the back of the room, they waited respectfully. In a loud voice, and very distinctly, in a Wurtemburg accent, the man said: "Thy servants are ready, Our Lord!"

Exactly a minute went by. Then, without the slightest noise, the enormous and heavy dresser rotated from left to right, its right-hand side forming a pivot and disclosing a cavity smaller in its dimensions than the item of furniture. At the back of this cavity, an invisible door silently opened, abruptly displaying a rectangular patch of light brighter than that which was spread by the electric bulb suspended from the ceiling. In that lighted rectangle, a human form was silhouetted in black. Then, the door must have closed again, for the brightness vanished, and a man came forward into the room, while the enormous dresser slid back into place.

The two peasants bowed deeply, and said: "Welcome, Our Lord Baron."

"Good evening, Zucht; good evening, Adelheid. Where are the boys?"

"Out hunting, Our Lord," Zucht replied. "But they'll soon be back."

"I hear them, Our Lord," said Adelheid.

The sound of footsteps was, indeed, audible outside.

The exterior door opened and two hearty fellows appeared, one immediately after the other, their rifles in their hands and their game-bags slung over their shoulders. The second closed the door behind him while the first, on seeing who was present, bowed and said: "Welcome, Our Lord Baron."

"Welcome, Our Lord Baron," his brother repeated, bowing in his turn.

They raised their heads again and waited in the same respectful attitude as their parents.

Baron Glô von Warteck, Lord of Schwarzrock, was dressed in an elegantly-tailored formal jacket made of fine black velvet, trousers whose creases described a straight line all the way to his black suede shoes and a white silk shirt with an abundant collar and flounced sleeves. His skin was only a little less pale than his shirt. He was perhaps a little too tall and a little too thin, but his appearance would have been more attractive if he had not had the harsh and wretched face of a sly and savage Mephistopheles.

He had a large bony head, thickly sewn with thick, matted red hair that no comb could ever have straightened for more than a few minutes. His face was transected mid-way by a long and bushy red moustache. It was the face of a pirate or a Kalmuk, with jutting cheekbones and distorted features.[10] It was a terrible and diabolical face by virtue of the eyes, which were green and yellow, cruel and viperish, dark and sparkling at the same time, set deeply in their orbits beneath long red eyebrows. It was a unsettling face, which must have easily turned repugnant on occasion, first because of the *rictus sardonicus* formed by the lips, and then because of the strange stillness of those same lips–which were as thin as if the mouth had been cut by the slash of a razor, but sometimes swelled to the point of making the jaw seem fleshy. They were set above a chin that was too long, too pointed and curved like the chin of one of the three witches in Macbeth.

All that made Baron Glô von Warteck a fearsome presence as he confronted Zucht, his wife and his sons. His green and yellow eyes, cold and commanding, expressed a will so powerful that he had had no actual need to formulate the question he had asked, perhaps automatically, a few minutes earlier, as to the whereabouts of the sons. As his eyes fixed themselves, by rapid turns, on Zucht and Adelheid, then on Franz and Berthold, the peasants trembled.

"Yes, yes, Our Lord Baron!" said Adelheid, in a terrified voice, clasping her hands together in supplication, answering the Baron's next, unformulated question. "Yes, Minna will be docile. All of us—her father, mother and two brothers—have begged and prayed for the sake of our peace. She consents! Your sacred desire will not need to be imposed. Minna will come to Your Lordship's castle of her own free will. I have only to alert her to your presence..."

Baron von Warteck stood stiff and motionless in front of the pleading woman and the three petrified men. Despite his singular thinness, he would have given a spectator to this scene the impression of comfortable, easy and unlimited physical power.

Adelheid fell silent, bowed and ran to a door set in the wall to the left of the bed. She opened it and called: "Minna! Minna!"

A soft voice replied: "I'm coming down, mother."

The sound of footsteps, muffled by thick indoor slippers, was heard in the attic, then on a staircase whose wooden steps creaked. A young woman appeared on the threshold of the door, which her mother had left open when she returned to her husband.

The Baron ceased projecting his will-power then, for Zucht, Adelheid, Franz and Berthold stood at ease, though still respectfully. All four smiled in an amicable and contented manner at the graceful Minna. She was a pretty German girl of 18, blonde, rosy-cheeked and innocent, with candid blue eyes. She was of medium height, plump and much more refined and well-groomed than the peasants of the Black Forest usually are. Her hair had been very thoroughly combed and she had been carefully dressed in the multicolored costume which is considered in the theater to be traditionally Tyrolean.

With a slight smile and a troubled expression, Minna came timidly towards the Baron, curtsied, and said in a child-like voice: "I am entirely at the service of Our Lord Baron."

Glô von Warteck's eyes glinted. For a second, his face expressed an indefinable cruel satisfaction. He raised his right arm and held the hand above the blonde head, as if he were taking possession of the young woman.

"Embrace your mother, father and brothers, Minna," he said, in a strangely sonorous fashion, dry and metallic at the same time, "and get a cloak."

Four times over, the child was seized, hugged and kissed, in a very restrained and bizarre fashion, sad and joyful at the same time, full of regret but nevertheless proud: an emotion as indefinable as the satisfaction expressed by the face of the formidable Baron.

Then, Minna went to a corner of the room and unhooked a hooded cape. She threw it over her shoulders and put up the hood. She bowed down again before her master and waited.

"Farewell, my faithful servants," the Baron said to the family. He put his hand on Minna's shoulder and added: "Come, child."

With her, he marched towards the cavity that had been uncovered again by the half-rotation of the dresser. The door opened in front of him and the couple advanced into the rectangle of light. Noiselessly, the door closed and the dresser slid back into place.

The Baron and Minna walked, more rapidly now, through a large subterranean tunnel devoid of woodwork or masonry. The rock was bare, oozing damp. If human hands had played any part in making the tunnel, it must have been several hundreds of years ago–but it could only have been a few years ago that galvanized iron brackets supporting electric lights had been fixed to its walls, to the right and to the left, and parallel grooves etched in the rocky floor to channel the trickling water.

At first, the tunnel was level, then it began to climb perceptibly; then there was a succession of staircases, inclined planes, curved to a greater or lesser degree, and large flat areas whose walls bore black doors, reinforced with iron and enormous locks. Masonry, some ancient and some recent, some intact and some repaired, now alternated with bare rock, dry or slick, with no more irregularities or oozing trickles of water. Then there were walls, some made of rock and some contrived, covered with neatly-carved and polished oak panels, evidently maintained with daily care. There were no more brackets, but wrought iron chandeliers with numerous electric lamps, which lit up automatically as the Baron approached and were extinguished in his wake.

Minna, visibly impressed with admiration, but bewildered, slightly afraid and disorientated, was still moving at a rapid pace, as if drawn along by the hand that still rested on her shoulder, occasionally clenching momentarily.

Finally, the Baron stopped.

They were in a large vestibule where the wall-panels were partly dressed with loose tapestries. The huge central table, sturdy and polished, was surrounded by ceremonial chairs of the sort used by burgraves.[11] Only four of the 50 or 60 lamps held by an immense chandelier were lit.

The Baron and Minna had halted in front of a tapestry with two sections, one falling in wide straight pleats while a double-stranded cord lifted the other. In the gap, between two fringes of gold, was a white-painted door.

After standing still for a moment, Warteck put out his right hand and opened the door. He went through it, with Minna close beside him. The man and the young woman matched strides, passing through a small room decorated in white and gold, in which two electric lights sustained by gilded bronze Cupids lit up to either side of the fireplace as they entered. Another door stood open, and Warteck paused on that threshold.

If little Minna had been capable of making an observation, she would have noticed that the Baron's left hand, which was still resting on her shoulder, was trembling continuously–but the girl was in no condition to notice such a small detail. In her mental confusion, she did not even take full account of what she saw: a room decorated in blue and silver, fully-charged with luxury in its carpets, tapestries, furniture, statues, cushions and its canopied bed. Electric wall-lamps gave out a soft, filtered light.

90

At the back of the room, on a low divan, between two pairs of immense curtains, which must have masked windows, a young brunette woman in a long white dress had just stood up abruptly, assuming a defiant and combative attitude. Her head was thrown back proudly; her eyes were cold.

Shoving Minna abruptly into the room, Baron von Warteck said, in a tremulous voice: "Madame, here is what I promised you."

He stepped back, closed the door, turned round, crossed the other room at a rapid pace, went along one side of the vestibule, and suddenly disappeared; one of the tapestries had lifted up in front of him, and had then fallen back, leadenly.

II. The Overhanging Turret

Outside on the mountain-slope, at the same moment, the Nyctalope came to a halt.

"Careful, Pilou! A crevice... Two meters wide. If we jump it, we risk making a noise."

"A bridge, then?"

"Yes."

Pilou was a former gymnast of the first rank. The life that he led with the Nyctalope had not allowed him to get rusty. The night was not so dark that one could not see the ground three meters ahead. Twenty centimeters from the edge of the crevice, Pilou stood up straight, lifted his arms in parallel, made his entire body stiff and fell forward. The tips of his toes did not moved forward an inch; on the other side of the crevice, his forearms struck the rock, his flat palms pressing down with all the force of his taut muscles. Thus Pilou made a gang-plank, by which means Saint-Clair and Corsat crossed over the precipice in two rapid steps.

The Burgundian seized the Provençal's wrists; ten seconds later, they were standing side by side–and the three adventurers continued their descent of the pathless mountain slope, with Saint-Clair in the lead.

There were so many rocks, bushes and clumps of firs that their progress was slow, but when they finally reached the grassy plain on the concave valley floor, they advanced with strides that were large, rapid and regular. They made no noise, heading straight for the foot of the monstrous crag supporting the castle. They arrived in less time than it had taken them to descend the mountainside flanking the vast natural basin in at whose center Schwarzrock loomed up like the jet of a fountain.

Saint-Clair sat down; his two companions did likewise. For their benefit, the Nyctalope spoke in an even voice, without stressing any syllables, so quietly that it was imperceptible to any ears but those very close by and accustomed to hearing it.

"While we were walking," he said, "I studied the castle from a decreasing distance. I noticed an overhanging turret, so vertiginously attached to the main tower that any thought of reaching it from outside would seem like madness. When he installed his electrical defenses, Lucifer cannot have given the slightest thought to including that turret within his system. That's point one.

"Point two is that the turret is occupied; its three mullioned windows,[12] which are disposed in such a way that their base-line forms half of a hexagon, were all lit up for a few seconds. I'll wager that it's a woman's bedroom or sit-ting-room, because I could make out ribboned curtain-loops through the trans-parent lace curtains. Then other, opaque, curtains were drawn, for the windows to the right and left were totally obscured; only the window in the middle retained a thin vertical line of light–the interval of two curtains that do not quite meet." He paused, then continued in the same tone: "My friends, we must climb straight from here to that overhanging turret, which is directly above our heads."

After another pause, Pilou said: "How high?"

"I'll calculate," Saint-Clair said, in an assured tone. "There's between 65 and 80 meters of rock, with a flat section formed by the spiral stairway at about the 38th meter. Parenthetically, the question of using the spiral stairway is not even worth raising; Kroon specified that certain steps, whose numbers he did not know, are tricked out with electrical circuit-breakers; when a foot touches them, a signal immediately sounds in the listening room. To resume, 80 meters of rock with a flat section, which must be avoided, at about the 38th meter; 20 to 25 meters of wall to the sculpted supports of the corbel–which is to say, to any one of the three windows. That gives a maximum total of 105 meters to scale..."

"Vertically," said Corsat.

"Perfectly," said Pilou.

"And silently," the Nyctalope reminded them.

After another pause, Pilou said: "That worries me, naturally. Our three lassos each measure about 60 meters from end to end. That's fine for you and Corsat–but I have to attach the cord.

"Yes," the Nyctalope said, simply.

Of the three, while Saint-Clair was capable of almost anything and Corsat excelled in operations of strength, Pilou took the principal role whenever the abilities of a first-rate gymnast were indispensable.

"To begin with," Saint-Clair went on, "you have a cleft in the rock over there to your left."

"Height?"

"About five meters."

"And after that?"

"A meter or so to the right of the top of the crack, there's a ledge. That's all; above that, I can't see anything but smooth rock, which even overhangs slightly. But I'll be damned if you can't find anything more–at that distance, rock like this always looks as smooth as a hand."

"Right."

"On your way, then!"

"And if something should happen–what's the signal?"

"None," said Saint-Clair, curtly. "Any signal, whatever it might be, would be overheard by others. The order of the day is conquer in silence–or die."

"OK, boss. Pass me the rope, Corsat."

Corsat had been busy. He gave Pilou the three silken lassos with the leaden weights, tied end to end in such a manner as to make a single long rope rolled up into the least possible volume.

Pilou attached it to the back of his belt. "The night's pitch dark," he grumbled.

"So much the better," said Saint-Clair.

"I won't be able to see any better on that rock than in a tunnel."

"You can smell, you can touch, you can guess..."

"It'll be OK, damn it! I won't fall."

Pilou always grumbled and complained, in seeming reluctance, before undertaking anything genuinely difficult or perilous–but then, having given that Platonic satisfaction to his spirit of independence and natural indolence, and having estimated the real difficulties that he had to surmount, he got to work with all the more coolness and resolution, jubilant in advance with the triumph he would enjoy when he had done his part. The brave lad was gloriously naïve, his vanity so puerile that it became touching. He took off his boots and suspended them around his neck, saying, "I'll do it, then, damn it."

"I don't see any alternative," Saint-Clair said, impassively.

"That's true. Goodbye, boss! Goodbye, old boy!"

Pilou's hands were seized by Saint-Clair and Corsat, who were certainly more emotional than they would have seemed, had their faces been visible.

Pilou moved to the left, to the fissure that the Nyctalope had mentioned; henceforth, as one might imagine, all his movements were acrobatic, executed with passionate attention. Corsat saw nothing but a shadow that was gradually lost in the darkness, fading and disappearing into the opaque black mass of the rock supporting the sinister castle.

Negotiating the fissure was child's play to Pilou. The two sides of the cleft could have been as smooth as the edges of a gash in a slab of butter and Pilou would have climbed it, buttressing his limbs and entire body between the walls of the crevice. In fact, the cleft, like all those produced by weathering in the mass of a rock, was irregular, its edges riddled with cracks. Child's play!

Having reached the upper extremity of the cleft in 20 seconds, Pilou supported himself, with his right hand on a projection and his left knee in a hollow, while he searched to the right for the ledge the Nyctalope had mentioned. He found it, hooked himself upon it by the right hand and tested its solidity. Ten seconds later, he was standing upright on it, his belly and breast pressed to the rock.

There the difficulties began.

Pilou could see absolutely nothing. Although the sky was clear, the night was very dark; besides which, a mist had formed. The rock was a black wall, which lost itself in the bizarrely blurred darkness of the vapor.

Pilou put the fact that he had eyes out of his mind.

"Damn!" he muttered, between his teeth. "I'd never dare look the boss in they eye again. I know full well that this woman he loves–but whom I've never seen–is in the castle. So I have to get up there and attach the rope, or I might as well let myself fall and be crushed. No matter! It'd be the first time, all the same, in the course of an adventure, that there's nothing we could do." While he indulged in this monologue, his arms were above his head and his groping fingers were searching blindly. "Ah! A hole. Ugh! Not very big. I can hardly get two fingers into it–but that's enough for a foothold, to search higher up. Let's go!"

The calm, slow, sublime struggle proceeded: one man against the law of gravity, the inhospitability of perpendicularity and the natural non-adherence of a human body to the side of a rocky crag, in the dark. Except that it was not entirely in the dark, for Pilou knew that the Nyctalope's lynx-like eyes were watching him, following him and judging him.

With his fingers, fingernails, armpits, elbows, knees, breast, belly, thighs and every other part of his body, simultaneously reptilian and angular, supple and hard, Pilou searched, groped before gripping, set himself flat, suspended himself, swayed, hauled himself up, stretched himself out and repeated the process, slowly and prudently, breathing evenly and in a calculated fashion.

And he climbed.

He climbed.

An hour went by, then two.

Pilou resumed his tranquil monologue. "Good! There's the flat section he mentioned, about 38 meters up: the spiral stairway. Mustn't lean, with any part of the body, on any of those steps hollowed from the rock. If that step were one of those that had been transformed into a circuit-breaker! One encounters such hazards. What am I saying? These nasty hazards are all around. I could do with five minutes rest, though. Ah, there's a ledge. A bit of a slope, it's true, extending diagonally beneath four, five, six steps. Large enough for me to lie down on my back, for a start, then... Let's see. It's a matter of combination. Then I'll stand up and grope overhead. If I can't find anything to hook myself on and get over the flat section without touching any of the steps, I'll have to... Oof! It's good to breathe lying one one's back. If I could only find somewhere to attach the lasso, this ledge would serve as an excellent first base; the boss and Corsat would be perfectly able to sit down on it and rest. But where should I attach the lasso? It's only 60 meters long, and I have 105 to climb. It ought to be at least halfway. I'm not yet high enough, since I've got about 67 meters still above me– and once it's attached, the lasso won't give me more than 58 or 59 at the most. Well, I won't be supping bouillabaisse in a hour... There's isn't any, anyway, since we're in the holy land of... That's enough! Jump to it!"

He stood up. He groped about. Above his head, the rock overhung, forming a vault over the stairway. Standing on the narrow ledge at the edge of the stairway–which had neither parapet nor guard-rail–he moved his arms, searching with his fingers to the right and the left for a crevice or a projection from which to suspend himself. Then he froze, petrified.

A luminous square had abruptly appeared in the rock beneath the vault, directly in front of him. His face was only separated from that unexpected peep-hole by the width of the stairway.

Pilou remained petrified for no more than ten seconds. The sight of the head of a living man within the peep-hole brought him to his senses. He thought of the silent Browning. He reached for his belt, seized it, took aim...

In the meantime, the man in the lighted window had made a movement of his head and gestured with his arms; a noose shot out from the square hole, which passed over Pilou's head, slid down over of his shoulders and was pulled taut at the very moment when he pressed the trigger.

The man in the peephole opened his eyes and his mouth wide, vomited up a gush of blood and disappeared, collapsing like a marionette whose strings had been cut.

For his part, though, Pilou lost his balance and toppled backwards. He tried in vain to grab hold of something... and fell. He dragged with him the cord whose tightened slipknot pinned his arms to his torso–the cord that slid over the sill of the peep-hole and the lip of narrow ledge on which he had rested.

I'm dead! Pilou thought. *Adieu!*

Doubtless, in one of those seconds that seems to take years to elapse, he knew the infinite despair of one who is young and strong, and yet is about to die.

The Nyctalope, from where he was sitting with Corsat, could not see the peep-hole, but he could see the luminosity projected therefrom. He saw the noose fall over Pilou's shoulders and torso, and he saw Pilou fall.

"Stand up, Corsat! Give me your hands! Pilou's falling!"

The Burgundian obeyed instantly, although he only understood the last two words.

Pilou, at the end of a fall of some 37 meters, was received by an elastic trampoline formed by four arms, linked in two pairs. The arms flexed, and the bodies to which they belonged leaned towards one another, buckling into a kneeling position. Pilou lay between them like a cadaver.

"Put him on the ground!" whispered the Nyctalope. "Look up. If you see a light, warn me. I'll take care of Pilou, if he's not dead–but listen, to reassure you a little, Pilou is attached to a rope. The rope, doubtless extended by something from which it unwound, opposed by some resistance, extended relatively slowly–but for that, the shock would have broken our arms and would have killed Pilou instantly. I think, therefore, that he's only fainted. Ah! Good man! He held on to his Browning so tightly that he didn't let go even when he fainted. And it was all done, in the end, without any noise... He's alive. Corsat! He's alive! Get the rum!"

Corsat took an object from one of the pockets suspended from his belt. It was a small screw-topped aluminum flask covered in felt. Pilou absorbed half of its contents in a single gulp, opened his eyes, shivered, and propped himself up on his elbows before springing abruptly to his knees.

"Careful, Pilou!" Saint-Clair said. "No noise! Yes, I've put your pistol to one side, and the rope that seized you was able to support you during your fall, fortunately, slowing it down and deadening it."

"Then I'm alive, boss!"

"So it seems."

"Good God, three times over, and God's blood!"

It only needed five minutes for Pilou to recover himself entirely, to tell his story, and to conclude: "Since the whole of the knotted rope did not fall with me, because the impulsion provided was not sufficient to draw all of it through the peep-hole, it must be fixed up there!"

"Perhaps firmly enough," Corsat said, "to bear the weight of a man climbing up."

"Right!"

"We'll have to pull on it first to make sure."

"Naturally!"

Saint-Clair did not say a word, so his approval was taken for granted. Consequently, the Burgundian and the Provençal groped for the slipknot, found it and drew out a few meters of rope between their hands. Having drawn it taut again, they hauled on it; it resisted. They made more effort; it still held firm.

"I'll climb up," Corsat said.

"No, that's my job," Pilou replied. "I've partly failed in my mission. My honor's at stake."

"It's not a matter of honor," the Burgundian retorted, ardently but still in the customary whisper. "There's danger up there. It's a matter of strength, which is my province."

"No, damn it, it's mine! Climbing 38 meters up a slippery rope is a matter of skill."

"Let's go, then!"

"Right!"

"Stand aside!"

"No, you stand aside!"

"Come on, boys!" the Nyctalope said. "It's matter of strength, skill and initiative, all at the same time. Up there, it will be necessary to choose, decide, command and act in new circumstances—so I'll go up first. You'll both hold the rope down here. Then Corsat will come up, because I might need his strength right away, while Pilou holds the rope taut. Then, when Corsat has arrived, Pilou will climb up last, because he'll need all his skill to climb a loose rope that no one is holding still. That way, each of us will make the most of his abilities."

When the Nyctalope spoke, one did not debate; one obeyed. Holding the rope in both hands, Pilou and Corsat pulled it taut. In order to resist their traction, it must indeed be very firmly attached within the redoubt, cellar or room behind the peep-hole.

With one bound, Saint-Clair leapt upon the shoulders of his two men. He grabbed the rope and began to climb, moving his arms and legs rhythmically in a slow and measured fashion. His ascent would have been easier if he had braced his feet against the rock, but he thought that he might risk dislodging fragments of stone, so he climbed like a gymnast.

When he found himself immediately below the platform provided by the stairway, he remained immobile for a moment to catch his breath and recover all of his usual calmness; then, pulling himself up by his elbows, he performed a somersault, facilitated by the rope, and found himself standing on the narrow ledge on which Pilou had lost his balance.

The little window was still illuminated. It was wide and deep enough for a man of ordinary corpulence to pass through it. No noise was coming from it. The Nyctalope cold not see anyone or anything between the angle of the opening and the masonry wall at the back of what seemed to be some sort of bunker—a grotto hollowed out by human hands.

He assured himself that his pistol was not wedged in its holster, and that the traction of his thumb and forefinger would suffice to draw it out. Then, holstering it again, he suspended himself from the rope and moved along it, folding his legs to make sure that they did not touch the steps. He shoved his head and shoulders into the hole with a single thrust of his back. He saw that the interior of the redoubt resembled a sentry-box, and that there was no one in it but a man lying on the floor beside a camp-bed. His chin, neck and shoulders were stained with dark red blood.

He crept forward, disengaged his arms and hands and let himself fall head-first upon his palms, then disengaged his feet and stood up straight.

"Here I am," he murmured.

His photographic eyes rapidly surveyed the room's four walls, floor and ceiling. It was square, with one door. There was a table and a chair to the left. Under the peep-hole, there was a windlass, to which the completely-unwound rope was secured. A camp-bed and a cupboard were located to the right, a bare wall at the back. The bloody corpse lay on the smooth stone floor; Pilou's bullet had gone right through the neck, from one ear to the other, severing both carotid arteries. The dead man was dressed in the grey-blue uniform of a German infantry soldier, with boots and a round peak-less cap. An electric light was set in the middle of the ceiling. In the left-hand corner, between the wall with the door and the wall with the peep-hole, on a table fitted to the angle, was a simple telephone apparatus. On the table, there was a stout Browning, fully loaded, a pot of tobacco, a pipe, a lighter and an old hardbound book: Goethe's *Hermann und Dorothea*. Under the table, there was an empty bucket and a tin-plate jug half full of water. The peephole was equipped with a little glazed casement, pulled back inwardly to the left, and a thick wooden shutter, pulled back to the right. At the foot of the bed were two washcloths, both dirty.

"A sentry post," Saint-Clair murmured. "Why the windlass, the rope and the slipknot, when other, more scientific, means of attack and surprise are possible? We'll find out, if it becomes necessary to know.[13] Let's wait for Corsat."

While waiting, he inspected the door. "No lock and no bolt–just a simple catch. The sentry has neither the right nor the means to shut himself in. But does he stay here all night or is he relieved?"

Saint-Clair went to the cupboard fixed above the camp bed, opened it and made a swift inventory of its contents. "Four metal plates, two sets of cutlery, with knives, two goblets, two napkins and a dozen books! Ah, what's this?"

It was a card on which numbers, names and figures were set in four triply-divided columns. The names were arranged in bracketed pairs. The figures were the days of the month. The first 13 numbers were crossed out in red pencil. The total number of pairs of names was 20, the list being replicated identically three times over, numbered one to ten, 11 to 20 and 21 to 30. Only the 31st had two bracketed names that had not previously been repeated in triplicate.

"Good!" said Saint-Clair. "Sentries are stationed here in pairs, three nights per month at ten-day intervals, and there's an extra pair for months with 31 days. The first 13 nights of May have passed, crossed out in red pencil. This is a calendar; the numbers are the sentries' identification numbers. From noon on May 14 to noon on May 15, the two sentries are Wolf and Ragh, Nos. 43 and 44."

He leaned to one side. The left breast of the dead man's tunic was marked with two fours, stamped on white cloth sewn on to the breast pocket.

"Here's Ragh, No. 44," said Saint-Clair. "Where's Wolf?"

At that moment, he hard a slight sound outside. He turned towards the peep-hole, in which Corsat's head was soon framed. Saint-Clair beckoned with his finger. The Burgundian entered in the same manner as his boss. He had scarcely had time to stand up when the noise of someone in heavy boots clattering down a flight of stone steps became audible on the far side of the door.

"Quickly!" said Saint-Clair. "Put the corpse on the bed, as if the man were sleeping with his back to the door. Pull up the covers to hide the bloodstains. Good! Come here! When I jump, you jump! The same as Kroon in the red house."

When the door opened, Ragh seemed to be asleep. Saint-Clair and Corsat were standing in the corner, masked by the opened door.

A man came in. He pushed the door shut with his heel and the latch clicked home. He had a loaf of bread under his left arm, and his right hand was raised to deposit a mess-tin on the table. Two of the tin's four compartments were full.

Good! thought Saint-Clair. *I was right. Wolf had gone to fetch dinner. The bed is for the two guards to sleep on, in turn, during their 24-hour shift.*

Having set down the bread and the mess-tin, Wolf turned to the bed. "That pig, Ragh!" he growled, in the purest German of Berlin. "He'd sleep his life away. If I were a bad comrade, I'd report him for shutting his eyes during my absence. Fortunately... *Ach*!"

99

While advancing towards the bed, still talking, to wake his companion, Wolf had turned his head slightly and seen the peep-hole, the rope and the naked windlass–but he had no time to reflect further on these unusual things. A large hand crushed his lips upon his teeth, while other hands immobilized his arms. Two bodies weighed upon his, and legs entwined with his, forcing him to his knees. He tried to fight, but he was lifted up, tipped backwards, stunned by a punch to the head. His jaws were forced open and something like a napkin was forced into his mouth, to serve as a gag, before he could utter a sound. His arms were secured to his body by his own belt and his legs were rolled up in a blanket.

Utterly bewildered, Wolf retained sufficient consciousness to see two men bending over him, one of them armed with a knife. He heard words pronounced in a low voice in French–a language he knew quite well, having spent five years working in a hotel in Nice before the war.

"If he struggles, I'll stick the blade in his throat. Undress the other one, Corsat, and put on his uniform, including the cap and boots. Watch out for the blood on the breast and shoulder–wipe it off as best you can. We must be quick. Ah, here's Pilou. Pass me the satchel that's preventing you from buttoning the tunic. Good!"

Wolf almost fainted with terror, partly by virtue of the realization that his comrade was dead and partly on seeing a third person come through the peep-hole–but the man with the knife prevented him from falling unconscious by saying to him, in French: "Wolf! I can see in your eyes that you understand what I'm saying. You'll understand this even better: I'm going to undress you, because I need your clothes. One suspect gesture and my second comrade–who has just come in–will put a bullet in your head like he one that killed Ragh: a bullet fired from a silent pistol. Silent, you understand? Watch him, Pilou. If he flinches, kill him!"

When such words are pronounced, with supportive gestures, by an individual with the Nyctalope's features and eyes, one obeys them if one does not wish to die. Wolf did not wish to die. Not only did he remain meek when he was untied, but he hurried to undress himself to demonstrate his good intentions. In response to an order from Saint-Clair, he bundled up his clothes, including his cap and boots, and secured it with his belt.

"Pilou, put that on your back. If necessary, you can disguise yourself within a minute, as Corsat is. I'll hang on to the satchel. You, Wolf–answer me!"

"Yes, Mein Herr."

"The steps behind that door–do they go further down?"

"No. This guard-post is in the deepest hollow in the rock."

"Are there other hollows?"

"Yes."

"What purpose do they serve?"

100

"As barracks and store-rooms."

"Where does the staircase lead, exactly?"

"Firstly, to the central rotunda of the store-rooms. Secondly, to the landing of a circular corridor, which is the lowest floor of the castle. Thirdly, to the armory where all the other staircases and corridors leading to the castle terminate."

"Are there guards stationed in the armory?"

"No, but all the doors are electrified."

"What is the purpose of this sentry-post?"

"To capture anyone who passes by alive."

"What if there are two, thee or four?"

"The first is to be taken alive and the others reported; if the Baron wishes, they can be struck down before reaching the top of the stairway."

Saint-Clair laughed. "The most ingenious provisions are sometimes defeated, as you see. So there's no way to get into the castle from here except by way of the armory?"

"Yes."

"Are there patrols by night?"

"No, electricity protects everything."

"Where had you come from with this food?"

"The troops' kitchen, which is installed in a cellar like this one, in a corridor off the rotunda with the barracks and store-rooms."

"How do the troopers communicate with the Baron?"

"By telephone–there are no human intermediaries."

"How many men are there in the castle, in total?"

"I only know 30, including Ragh and me, but there are others–I don't know how many."

"What time is the curfew?"

"It sounded about half an hour ago. You won't find anyone in the rotunda or the circular corridor. All the doors are closed and electrified, except the one to the kitchen, which stays open for the benefit of the two men on watch here–everything is made available to us in extreme abundance but wine and spirits, which we never touch. At 8 a.m. the doors are de-electrified and normal life resumes: intense circulation, armed patrols..."

"What do you know about the castle and what goes on there?"

"Nothing–absolutely nothing! I've never been into it. I've never been further or higher than the guard-room. Those within the troop who know something say nothing, because there are spies among us, and the least indiscretion–no matter how trivial or inconsequential–is punishable by death. I ought to tell you that you must take me with you when you leave, if you wish me to live. Otherwise, I'll be electrocuted."

"We'll take you," Saint-Clair said. "Corsat, gag him and tie him up again. Get rid of the corpse–push it under the bed. Quickly. Follow me Pilou!"

He went to the telephone and manipulated it delicately, using forceps taken from the satchel.

"There's a risk that the Baron will telephone," he said. "In that case, Corsat, you'll reply that all's well. If anyone comes, kill them silently. It's a pity, but we have the alternative, at every moment, of killing or being killed. No hesitation, Corsat–strike! It's 10:30 p.m. If neither Pilou nor I has returned by 4:30 a.m., leave by the peep-hole, slide down the rope and return to Colmar. Wait three days, then tell the whole story to Monsieur Prillant in Paris."

"Yes, boss."

"Good! Come on, Pilou. More talk will lose time. Let's see–if we can't do anything tonight, we'll get going after the 8 a.m. awakening. If that's the case, we'll have plenty of time before then to find out what else Wolf knows and to form a plan of action. Stay alert, Corsat!"

Followed by Pilou, Saint-Clair left the sentry-post and went up the lighted staircase. The rotunda was also lit. The numerous doors there were all closed except one, leading to the kitchen. There was no one in the kitchen. A concert of snores was audible behind one of the doors.

"Let's try the circular corridor," said the Nyctalope.

They went up the next flight of steps, which came to an end on a landing in the form of a vaulted cellar. To the right and left of the lighted landing were the openings of two dark tunnels: the orifices of the corridor that made a tour of the castle's base, along whose length various loopholes and peep-holes had been cut in the masonry, permitting the valley and surrounding mountains to be observed.

While moving from the sentry-post to the landing, Saint-Clair had observed the orientation of various points relative to the overhanging turret that was probably inhabited by a woman, where heavy curtains had been drawn across lighted windows.

"It's to the right," he said.

Still followed by Pilou, he took the tunnel to the right. They were soon in total darkness, the light from the landing no longer reaching them. Pilou's only guide was the flow of slight sounds that his finely-turned ears picked up, but he followed the Nyctalope step for step around the corridor's various bends.

When the Nyctalope stopped abruptly, Pilou stopped behind him.

They were beside a peep-hole, with neither a casement nor a shutter, where the night without was slightly less darkly-inscribed than the night within. Beyond this rectangle of attenuated darkness, a kind of perpendicular white beam was distantly discernible.

Saint-Clair leaned out, looked up and then drew back. "We're almost facing the overhanging turret," he said to Pilou. "The guard-room, close by, separates us from the apartments on this floor that are within the turret. The castle's structure, at this point, forms an angle that puts us, relative to the turret... Look, Pilou! The wall is old and our daggers are sturdy. Can you make your way from the peep-hole to the turret, then attach the lasso? Then I can rejoin you."

"I'll go see, boss. Hold on, here's the lasso. I'll keep the other end attached to my belt. You let it out as I go. Your dagger?"

"Here it is. Wait a moment."

The peep-hole was wide enough and deep enough for both men to be able to pass through it, but two thick iron bars forming a cross divided it into four rectangles that were too small. The Nyctalope used the electric cutter to saw through the bars at the four ends.

Pilou lay flat on his belly within the peep-hole. Leaning out, he made out the overhanging turret, vaguely outlined in the darkness but marked by the per-pendicular line of light. He groped along the wall to the right and planted a dag-ger; the mortar displaced by the blade made a slight sound. He tested its solidity by leaning on the hilt. Then, using it as a point of support, he slid forward in a serpentine fashion, put out a leg and searched the ancient and corroded stone with his bare foot for a usable foothold. Then, he moved on.

Drawing the rope with him as the Nyctalope unwound it, Pilou planted the second dagger, suspended himself from it, and searched with his toenails for another foothold in the cracks where the mortar had crumbled away from the masonry. Drawing out the first dagger, he planted it again, higher up. Then, he repeated the operation.

Once he had arrived at the overhanging turret, whose mullioned windows were lavishly embellished by sculptures, Pilou had no difficulty finding a deeply-excavated item of scrollwork, in whose protrusions he looped, wedged and knotted the lasso. He pulled on it and it held firm. He buttressed himself between the two mullions and remained immobile.

The Nyctalope, not without anxiety, had watched the brave Pilou accom-plish this vertiginous and perilous acrobatic feat, approximately 105 meters above the ground. When he saw Pilou become still, he took a deep breath. Per-sonally, he never gave any fearful thought to what might happen. He made his exit from the peep-hole feet first. When the greater part of his body was outside, he braced himself with his shoulders and attached the taut rope to the cross formed by the iron bars. The cross, when placed in the peep-hole in a certain manner, was immobilized by the tension of the rope, which it served to attach and maintain.

Creeping along the rope, Saint-Clair suspended himself limply over the void. He could not support his feet against the wall, because the rope was ex-tended too tautly between the peep-hole and the turret–but it was child's play to him to move hand-over-hand while suspended, towards the tower. He arrived there, quickly braced himself between two colonnades that stood out in sharp relief, found a sill with his foot and was soon standing upright, with his breast pressed against a casement-window with 20 small lights. Pilou was next to him.

"Come on!" whispered the Nyctalope. He was at the right-hand window; he wanted to move to the central one, so that he could see into the turret's inte-rior through the gap between the two opaque curtains. They slid easily from colonnade to colonnade, thanks to the sharp relief of the sculptures, ledges, borders, uprights and mullions.

When he reached he middle section of the central window, Saint-Clair looked in.

Pilou heard him exhale and saw him clench his fists, with his forehead, his lips and his chin stuck to one of the little panes of glass. Pilou leaned back slightly, with his arms extended, and leaned sideways so that he too could look in through the gap in the curtains–and he was able to make out a very beautiful woman in a white dress.

Her hands were clasped between her breasts and she was weeping. She was weeping desperately, her face tragic and immobile, and the tears were running down her pale cheeks, which were very pale indeed.

III. The Invisible, Immutable, Insurmountable Wall

Leo Saint-Clair, the Nyctalope, was endowed with that prompt, clairvoyant, resolute intelligence which discerns the detail of a set of facts with lightning speed, which instantly forms hypotheses within the framework of those facts, and which acts immediately in the most propitious manner, with regard to the desired outcome.

Saint-Clair saw before him, tearful and desperate, a woman he had recognized instantly: the only woman whom he truly loved. And that woman was in the formidable castle of Schwarzrock, where a man reigned who was undoubtedly not far removed from considering himself to be an incarnation of Satan–a human Satan, cruel, lustful, ambitious, avid and pitiless, armed with an unfathomable occult power...

"Laurence!" he murmured. "Laure, my love... My life!"

The time that elapsed while Saint-Clair remained immobile and inactive, pressed against the array of small lights that garnished the central window of the overhanging turret, was no longer than three minutes: three minutes during which he observed, hypothesized, decided. Then, immediately, he acted.

It was the simplest and easiest action in the world–but one after which no retreat was possible. The only alternatives were to triumph, to die, or to become Lucifer's slave... Except that there was a fourth possible dénouement, which Laurence Païli's lover could not, and did not, envisage.

He acted, then–which is to say that he held himself in place by gripping a sculpture with his left hand, his two feet resting securely on a solid ledge, and he used his right hand to rap on a glass pane with the pommel of his dagger, which Pilou had returned to him.

He rapped–and immediately saw Laurence shiver. Her eyes changed expression and fixed themselves upon the narrow gap between the two huge curtains suspended in front of the trifenestral balcony forming the overhanging section of the turret.

Saint-Clair rapped again, and Laurence Païli–no longer weeping, her visage expressing nothing but immense amazement–took several steps forward. Hesitant and decisive at the same time, thinking impossible things and daring to imagine, nevertheless, that they might be realized, Laurence came right up to the curtains, lifted her lovely bare arms, seized the heavy cloth in both hands and drew the two sheets apart.

Oh, Leo! Is it possible? Him! Here! These cries of happiness, exclamations and questions were all confined to Laurence's thoughts. She had opened her mouth, but no sound came forth. She remained immobile and rigid, her arms outstretched, her hands clenched in the two parted curtains. Her head was thrust forward, her avid eyes fixed on the face she saw behind the tiny transparent pane, illuminated by the bright pure light of the electric chandelier. That face! How could she have failed to recognize it? It was that of the only man...

He saw that he had been recognized, and he smiled.

Suspended above an abyss into which the least accident might precipitate him–at the bottom of which his body would be crushed–having decided to get into that room, where he might be ambushed and killed, and resolved to do anything to snatch this woman away from the monster who had certainly tortured her, Saint-Clair smiled. It was the smile of a gentle and happy lover, a smile so marvelous in its youthful, calm and confident serenity, that Laurence, seeing nothing but that smile, forgot everything that surrounded, threatened and loomed over her–and her lover, unexpectedly brought by some miracle of which she had not dared dream–and she, too, began to smile.

That was the commencement of an unforeseeable scene: a scene at first astonishing, then terrifying, then maddening, which would convince the Nyctalope of the power of the man he had set out to fight.

Having smiled, and thus filled one another with happiness, Leo and Laurence understood one another. She knew that she could open the window, and he knew that she knew it. And, indeed, the young woman unclenched her hands, let go of the parted curtains, and with her arms already reaching out, tried to take a step towards the central window, from which she was only separated by a distance of approximately one and a half meters–a distance represented by the extent of the projection forming the overhanging part of the turret.

Laurence wanted to go forwards. She managed half a stride, her bosom extended and her right arm slightly outstretched–but the stride was suspended; she could not complete it.

After she had stood with her left foot upraised for a few seconds, she lowered it slowly to the carpet, lowering her arm at the same time. Her face immediately–for the beautiful captive had a quick mind and knew what Lucifer could do–expressed a violent and nameless terror: a terror that made her entire body tremble, and so suddenly enfeebled her muscles that she subsided, her legs buckling, her arms loose, her hands slack.

Saint-Clair watched all that. He did not understand the cause, but he measured all the consequences of the effect with a single flash of thought. He did not hesitate.

"Pilou," he said, brace your back against my chest, if you can; wedge your legs against mine, if necessary. My left hand has a secure hold. You must have both hands free. Diamond and mastic. If someone comes, we're dead, so be quick! Get that window out in such a way that it stays intact, and can be replaced if necessary."

On receiving an order exposing him to danger, Pilou grumbled before obeying, when he had the time–but on this occasion, there was no time to spare. In consequence, Pilou obeyed immediately.

While Pilou got into position and worked with the diamond and the mastic to cut out and pull away a window, noiselessly, Saint-Clair replaced the dagger in his right hand by the silent Browning. *If anyone comes,* he said to himself, *I'll kill him. Laure's there. First, we must free her, whatever it costs. Since we can't get to the rooms on the circular corridor without passing through the electrified guard-room, we'll have to go that way. Laure will have to suspend herself from my shoulders, with her arms around her neck. Pilou will help me. The first thing is to free Laure! But why has she collapsed like hat, in despair, evidently incapable of the slightest movement?*

In front of him, the two leaves of the window came apart and opened, Pilou having lifted the interior catch with his left hand, reaching through the hole he had cut through the pane.

A lithe catlike leap carried the Nyctalope on to the balcony formed by the overhanging turret. Laurence was still watching him with terrified eyes. She tried to lift her arms and reach out to him, but the gesture was interrupted midway. "Ohhhh!" she moaned, dolorously. "I can't." The terror expressed by her eyes was mingled with desperate supplication.

Saint-Clair was only separated from Laurence by two paces. He took one—and then...

He experienced the frightful horror of suddenly feeling a mysterious and invisible obstacle in front of his fists, his forehead, his breast and his knees, against which even his indomitable will was powerless!

The Nyctalope had the impression that he was pushing, with all the force of his taut, forward-thrusting body, against crystal glass of perfect clarity and transparency, which was quite invisible. But when he realized that there was no glass there, and that his hands, face and entire body had been interrupted by an object devoid of material existence, he immediately understood why Laurence had collapsed on the far side of the same immaterial object. An acute sensation of the crushing disproportion of the forces deployed by the man against whom he was at war flashed through him, and he was chilled by fear.

Pilou had come in behind him. Discreetly, he had taken up a position in a corner of the balcony, saying to himself: *The curtain will hide me. Whatever the boss does, he won't think about me until he needs my help. If I'm hidden, I won't be remembered inopportunely, but I'll see everything, and if I see that it's necessary to intervene to save him, I'll be ready.* He had two free hands, ready to seize a dagger or a Browning.

When Pilou saw Saint-Clair's face take on the same terrified horror and the same despairing and desperate supplication as the woman's, however, and saw them as motionless as two statues, five centimeters apart from one another, one standing up as if stretched out and the other sitting on her haunches as if folded up, he felt the chill of the cold breath of mystery. Still lucid, he fought against his fear–and as there was no other action he could perform but marching forward, he marched. He moved straight ahead, thus approaching Saint-Clair diagonally from the flank.

It was then that the Provençal's right elbow brushed against the invisible obstacle. By virtue of a natural reaction of the muscles, Pilou lifted the elbow and leaned to his right–and felt himself stopped short. "What?" he said. Immediately, he turned his head, then his entire body. He lifted both hands and plunged forward–but was stopped dead. His eyes, the curvature of his mouth and all his other facial features took on that same terrified horror, and he was frozen by fear in his turn.

Sufficient time had now elapsed for the Nyctalope to overcome his distress and regain control of his momentarily-paralyzed senses. While keeping his eyes closed, he used his hands to wipe beads of sweat from his forehead, cheeks and bare neck. He shook his head violently and breathed in through flared nostrils. Calm again, he opened his eyes.

"No more panic!" he said, in a low voice. "Let's observe and reason." For him, reason followed observation as thunder follows lightning.

His hands groped, testing the obstacle. His gaze was no longer directed at Laurence Païli but at the objects in the room to the right and the left.

No glass, however perfect, he said to himself, *could have this transparency. Then again, glass would produce a noise when my hand struck it. I already had a intuition; now I have an incontestable certainty. The obstacle doesn't produce any sort of noise when struck; my hand is stopped dead, as if the air itself had acquired solidity without becoming visible–an impossibility, in the familiar order of things.*

The same obstacle is raised before Laure, who is five centimeters from me. If I rap it hard, my hand feels the reaction. If I touch it gently, my hand does not experience any sensation of cold or warmth; the obstacle is the same temperature as my fingers, my hand, my lips, my cheeks or my forehead, according to which part of my body comes into contact with it. Finally, the most powerful effort of my tensed muscles bracing my shoulder has not the slightest effect on the hardness, stability, solidity or immobility of the obstacle. What conclusion can be drawn, except that this invisible, immutable, insurmountable wall is an immaterial wall? It is the effective result of the command You shall go no further! *pronounced by someone whose will imposes itself absolutely, without any relativity.*

Very well! For the present, nothing can prevail against it. But if the material body cannot pass through, the immaterial gaze can, so light passes through. Air also passes through, since I can smell perfume–her unforgettable favorite perfume, a mixture of fern and iris. Will sound pass through it, then?

Saint-Clair did not wait any longer to try the experiment. He mustered the most serene calmness, and whispered, in an interrogative fashion: "Laurence?" Immediately, he thought: *She heard me. Sound passes through. We can talk to one another. Wait! Someone might come at any minute. We must pronounce none but useful and effective words.*

In response to the appeal of her adored lover, arrived by virtue of some prodigy and stopped, like herself, by some other prodigy, the young woman had stood up, all her terror abruptly banished by the victorious invasion of hope.

"Leo!" she replied. "Leo!"

He heard her, and understood that she loved him every bit as much as before. He was glad of that, but he restrained his happiness so as not to distress her. Clearly, unhurriedly, and in a voice that was low but whose least inflexions were audible, he said: "Laure, I shall free you, perhaps tomorrow, during the day, and perhaps the following night. Be happy, but do not let your happiness show. Make sure that nothing is modified in you or your surroundings. Do you understand? Answer me."

"Yes, yes–everything! Oh, Leo..."

"I must hurry. Danger might surge forth at any second, and I suspect that it would be mortal. No wasted words–reply to my questions quickly and briefly. In Paris, you were subject to suggestion, irresistibly drawn away from your home, isn't that so?"

"Yes."

"A red-haired man, thin?"

"Yes."

"He's here?"

"Yes."

"Do you see him often?"

"Twice every day, at midday and 6 p.m., he makes me sit down at his table."

"What does he want from you?"

"Everything!" The young woman blushed violently.

"He doesn't force you?"

"No, he wants me to make the decision myself."

"He has told you that you'll never leave the castle?"

"Yes, and he has proved that, even if all the doors before me were to open, I still would not be able to leave. The same invisible thing that stops me, and has stopped you, here..."

"Good. I understand. He horrifies you?"

"Oh, Leo, do I need to..."

"But no physical violence?"

"None–not yet."

"Why not yet?" Saint-Clair demanded, shivering.

"He has forced me to witness incomprehensible tortures... Several young women... Oh, the poor things!" Laurence, her face martyrized, closed her eyes– but she opened them again, attentively, in response to Saint-Clair's voice.

"He has threatened you, if you do not yield?"

"Yes."

"What deadline?"

"May 31."

"Today is May 14. We have more than enough time. Do you know the red-haired man's name?"

"He has told me that his name is Glô von Warteck, a German Baron, although he was born to a cosmopolitan Hindu and a Russian of Mongol extraction. Sometimes, mockingly, he calls himself Lucifer, sometimes he claims to be the Antichrist." [14]

"What do you know about the castle? Enumerate, in order, what lies outside this room."

"This room, a corridor, a large staircase, a dining-room, a library, then a little corridor, perfectly straight, and a narrow spiral staircase, and, finally, a vast round room with five windows, from which one can see the whole of a circle of mountains. In the middle of that room there is a bizarre machine, concerning which he said to me: With that, and before long, I shall set the entire universe beneath my feet. He added, while looking at me: But you, I only wish to hold of your own free will–and then you shall see me, with the entire universe, at your feet."

Saint-Clair suppressed a surge of anger. Calmly, he went on: "What else do you know about Lucifer and the castle?"

"Only this: the servants never speak and he never speaks to them. He commands them by the power of his thought and his will, and he reads their thoughts. This is a Castle of Silence–an abominable silence! I have heard no other voice but his and that of a young woman who, shortly before you arrived, he consented to give me as a servant–and whom he will torture for hours in order that she can describe her suffering to me. Oh, the monster! But that's all I know, alas. Nothing more."

"One more question. Has he spoken to you about people he has tortured at a distance?"

"No, never. He only talks to me about personal matters–nothing, save for the sentence regarding the universe at his feet, but gallantries and atrocious threats..."

"That's good!" Saint-Clair concluded. He added: "Is the invisible wall still there?" He struck it. "Yes." Then he went on, smiling: "Laure, my beloved, my life... wait and hope. Some time during the day, or the following night, I'll come back–and I'll take you away! I'll go back now–it's imperative."

He put his ten fingers to his lips, in a bunch, and blew a kiss to Laure, who smiled at him divinely and replicated his gesture. Immediately, he turned round. "Follow me, Pilou!" he said. "Replace the window."

During this dialogue, the Provençal had had plenty of time to recover his composure. He did not understand the miracle of the barrier preventing any forward movement into the room, but, since the boss accepted the "miracle," what could he do? He had accepted it, calmed himself, listened and devoted himself to reflection, ready to do anything as soon as it became possible–and when Saint-Clair gave his order, he obeyed immediately.

When the Nyctalope was outside, his feet on the sill and his hands gripping the sculptures, Pilou went out, braced himself against the Saint-Clair's legs, closed the window again, took up the pane that he had left on the ledge, and worked rapidly to replace it. He was ingenious and skillful. He had cut out the pane by cutting through a line of old mastic. New mastic, carefully applied, covered the old mastic, overlapping it slightly to hide the rectangular cut and to hold the glass in place, so well that one would have had to inspect the pane at very close range to suspect that a section had been removed and replaced. The light coming from the interior provided sufficient illumination for the work.

In the meantime, Leo and Laurence continued looking at one another, smiling at one another, penetrating one another with their love, which they had recovered in an intoxicating fashion, even more profoundly than when they had separated voluntarily.

"It's done, boss," Pilou murmured.

"Good," he replied. "I'll go back first. Then detach the rope and make your way back in the same manner that you came."

A quarter of an hour later, the Nyctalope and Pilou went back into the sentry post, where Corsat was waiting for them quietly, guarding Wolf.

IV. The Nyctalope's Plan

As was his habit when he did not think secrecy necessary, Saint-Clair immediately brought Corsat up to date with the relevant facts–but he talked in Castilian, because the Burgundian and the Provençal knew the language of Alphonse XIII, while Wolf undoubtedly did not understand a word of it.

"Pilou, too," he concluded, "was stopped by the invisible wall erected by the incomprehensible power of Baron Glô von Warteck, alias Lucifer. Explanations, I can't provide–I don't know anything, although everything will doubtless be explained eventually–but actions, we can take, and must. I have a plan. This is it."

While Corsat and Pilou listened gravely, and Wolf, seated on the bed, watched them avidly, Saint-Clair outlined his plan. Again, he concluded: "It's risky. To anyone who told me what I've just told you, I'd say *it's mad!* and it is; but to leave without trying to impede Lucifer, or saving Mademoiselle Païli and the others–after having killed Ragh, cut and extracted the bars of the peep-hole in the round corridor–taking Wolf with us, as I promised him explicitly to do, would put Warteck on his guard and render it impossible for us to get into the castle again. It would condemn Mademoiselle Païli and many others to..."

He paused, put his hands to his head and groaned–but he continued almost immediately: "I thought of getting Monsieur Prillant to pressure the government of Baden into ordering an invasion of Schwarzrock, Warteck's arrest and the liberation of his victims... but there are two alternatives, either of which would be worthless. The government of Baden might be sincerely resolute in prosecuting the monstrous crimes that are being committed here, or it might only be resolute in appearance. In the former case, there is the uncertainty and risk of a operation of war, inevitably publicized before the decisive attack, against an enemy whose weapons and resources are unknown. In the second case, the enemy would be warned by the very people who were preparing to attack him. In either case, Warteck would have time to disappear; he only needs an aircraft to take off from some terrace of the castle or some subterranean opening out in the mountain. At the very least, he would take his revenge on the victims who are in his power. No! No official intervention! We must act alone–and quickly. This time, though, it really will be a matter of success or death. Strictly speaking, I could, by modifying my plan slightly, execute it alone. Corsat, Pilou, you could..."

"Not a chance, boss!" the Burgundian cut in curtly, while Pilou, more peremptory still, contented himself with a shrug of the shoulders and a smile.

"Good!" said the Nyctalope. "I understand–and I expected no less of you. Thank you, my good, brave fellows. Since everything's been said, let's not lose another minute. To work!"

The rope that had earlier been drawn forth by Pilou's weight was fixed to a hand-cranked windlass riveted to the stone floor, and passed over a pulley suspended from the plastered ceiling. The windlass and pulley were so well-oiled that their functioning only produced the slightest sound. While Corsat turned the windlass and rolled up the rope, Pilou extracted Ragh's body from under the bed. When the rope was fully wound, the body was set within the slipknot. It was almost nude, because Corsat had put Ragh's uniform on over his black leotard.

"Wolf," Saint-Clair said to the captive, "you must choose. Would you rather be attached with the corpse, lowered into the valley, accompanied by Corsat halfway up the mountain, and then left to your own resources, assured of death if you return to the castle in order to betray me—or would you rather enter my service, to work with me and these two men against the infamous criminal who reigns over this castle, to obey me as these men do, and to leave here with the guarantee of an official position with a suitable salary, and more than one property producing an annual income. Choose!"

"*Ach!* At your service, Monsieur!" said Wolf, enthusiastically, when his gag was removed.

"Take note of the fact that the slightest indication of treason on your part will immediately be rewarded by a dagger in your heart or a bullet in your brain."

"I'll serve you faithfully," Wolf promised. Solemnly, with his right arm raised—for Saint-Clair had untied him as he was speaking—he added: "I swear it on my blood and on my life, in the name of God. I don't know the master of Schwarzrock; I never promised him fidelity; I haven't touched this month's pay yet; I don't..."

"Enough, Wolf," said the Nyctalope, dryly cutting him off. "You've chosen; you've sworn; your life will answer for your fidelity. Excuses are futile and I don't judge you. You're an instrument that God has put into my hands, that's all. If the instrument is sound, I'll use it; if it's false, I'll break it. The rest is between God and your conscience; it's none of my business." Turning to the Burgundian, he added: "Go on, Corsat!"

Then, while Corsat attached himself to the rope, running it under his armpits and placing his feet on the cadaver's shoulders, Saint-Clair said: "Wolf, help Pilou to pass the corpse through the window. Corsat will follow. I'll take the windlass."

The corpse and Corsat disappeared. Saint-Clair slowly let out the rope. When the rope was fully extended, he sat down on the bed, sat Wolf and Pilou down on stools and said: "Silence and rest, until Corsat gets back."

Corsat was gone for an hour. His return to the foot of the rock on which Schwarzrock stood was signaled by a slight vibration of the rope extended from the pulley to the window.

"Pilou, Wolf, pull him up!" Saint-Clair commanded.

113

A few minutes later, when the rope was almost completely coiled around the windlass, Corsat leapt from the window into the guard-post. "It's done, boss," he said. "The corpse is in a fissure in the rock, hidden beneath brush and stones."

"Good." Addressing the ex-sentry, Saint-Clair said: "Wolf, tell us every last detail of what you did in the 24 hours preceding your present tour of duty, minute by minute, and every aspect of the orders in force here. Listen hard, Corsat, for this is of particular concern to you and me."

Wolf talked. Saint-Clair interrupted frequently, to obtain precise details of places, facts, persons, times and words. When Wolf had finished, Saint-Clair looked at his watch.

"Twenty-five past midnight," he said. "Still nearly nine hours before we take action. Pilou, you and I will sleep, if possible. Corsat and Wolf will stay on watch until 6 a.m., then we'll take over until 9 a.m. Then, the execution of my plan will begin in earnest."

The hours passed without incident. Everyone within the mysterious castle seemed to be asleep. Saint-Clair and Pilou dozed, lying side by side on the bed, while Corsat, speaking in a whisper, tirelessly extracted from Wolf everything that he knew or suspected about life in the castle. He obtained no more than a fragmentary repetition of the account already given.

At 6 a.m., the four men divided up the food that Wolf had brought the previous evening. As Saint-Clair, who was completely absorbed, remained silent, the others did not say a word. When the frugal meal was finished, Saint-Clair said: "Corsat and Wolf, three hours of sleep for you now."

"Honestly, I'd rather not, boss," Corsat replied. "It's impossible for me to rest lying down, immobile. Let me sit here, and get up from time to time to walk from one side of the room to the other."

"Monsieur," said Wolf in his turn, "Let me stay on watch. If anything happens—a telephone call or visit, it's better that..."

The Nyctalope cut him off. "So be it," he said. "I wasn't giving you an order. If anything does happen, it's unlikely that you'll have to do anything but keep quiet, at least until I judge it opportune to tell you what to do."

"Whatever it is, I'll do my best to obey."

"I'm counting on it, Monsieur Wolf."

Silence fell again.

Sitting at the foot of the bed, his elbows on his knees and his head in his hands, Saint-Clair was lost in thought, with his eyes closed. Pilou, squatting on the windlass with his back to the wall, was smoking blissfully—for he always found a means, even when dressed in a leotard, to carry his pipe, tobacco and lighter. Corsat walked back and forth at the back of the room. Wolf, seated on a stool with his back against the table, watched Saint-Clair relentlessly.

Two hours passed. The electricity cut off automatically as soon as the light of day rendered artificial lighting unnecessary. No sound was heard, inside or outside the castle.

At 8 a.m., Saint-Clair–who had consulted his watch periodically–raised his head, his eyes attentively open. Fifteen minutes passed, then 15 more, then another 15. Then the Nyctalope got up and, with a slow movement that made his powerful muscles stand out beneath his leotard, he stretched himself. Pilou quickly emptied his pipe, which disappeared, and stood up next to Corsat, who was already immobile.

Understanding that the moment for serious action was imminent, Wolf got up and stood where he was with similar rigidity. Saint-Clair looked at him then, with eyes stranger than any he had ever seen before: deep grey eyes, unsustainably penetrating, calm and terrible. "If I'm not mistaken, Wolf," Saint-Clair said, in a faint voice as calm and terrible as his eyes, "you told me that you possess a certain password which is only used once every 24 hours in the castle, and is not used again for a month, which the captain of the castle guard communicates secretly to the two sentries when they are relieved?"

"Yes, Monsieur," said Wolf, emotionally.

"You also told me that after a particular ring, this password, given on the telephone, has the effect of causing the master of Schwarzrock to come here immediately, alone."

"Yes, Monsieur."

"Finally, you told me that if the master of Schwarzrock considers the use of the password to be justified, the two sentries who have sent the summons receive a reward of 10,000 marks each–but that, on the contrary, if the summons does not seem to the master to be justified, the two sentries are punished by spending six months in the dungeon with their feet in irons. That is to ensure that the master is not disturbed, except by reason of an occurrence of the utmost seriousness–which must be one of those specified by a numbered list on the notice-board on which the guards' orders are posted."

"Yes, Monsieur."

"You stated, too, that the unique password must be immediately followed by the order number of the occurrence promoting the extraordinary summons."

"Yes, Monsieur."

"Now, Wolf, recite the list of occurrences, in numerical order. Go on–I'm listening."

Very pale, in a slightly tremulous voice, with his eyes lowered before the Nyctalope's unsustainable gaze, Wolf recited: "One: the death or insanity of one of the sentries. Two: a danger of insanity or death to both of them. Three: the capture of some individual. Four: the sounding of the horn. Five..."

Saint-Clair raised his hand and Wolf fell silent. "What is this horn? Do you know what it sounds like?"

"Yes, Monsieur."

"Go on,"

"It's a horn whose sound, once heard, is unforgettable. In order to justify a summons, the horn must be blown, somewhere in the valley or in the mountains to sound one long blast followed, after an interval of about 30 seconds, three short blasts."

"And do you know what that signifies–in what circumstances the horn is blown?"

"No, Monsieur."

"That's all right. Continue."

Wolf resumed: "Five: the entry into the sentry post of a man other than the sentries or the captain of the guard. In such a case, the first thing is to render it impossible for the man to move or cry out. If several men enter, one sentry must raise the alarm immediately, while the other must shoot as many of the intruders as possible, without any word of warning. Inaction is forbidden. Six: the death or insanity, or the danger of death or insanity, of the captain of the guard." After a pause, Wolf concluded: "That's all, Monsieur."

Saint-Clair closed his eyes for a minute or two. Then a smile wandered over his lips, and he opened his eyes again. "If I'm not mistaken," he said, "you also told me that to summon the captain of the guard here, it's sufficient that something should happen which is not among the five incidents on the list, but in respect of which neither of the sentries dares take the initiative?"

"Yes, Monsieur."

"Very well, Wolf, I'm satisfied." Addressing Corsat and Pilou, Saint-Clair said in his usual voice, as if he were continuing an ordinary conversation: "Wouldn't it be interesting to announce number four? What might be the reason for sounding the horn, and what would happen if I ordered Wolf to act as if it had sounded? I find it intriguing, and I'm tempted... as you are, too, no doubt? But no–we must restrain our curiosity, my friends, at least for the moment. All the more so because number six fits in with my plan and modifies it most conveniently, exactly as if it had been created for my benefit. Number six, moreover, like numbers one and two, implies that one can go insane here as easily as one might die!"

Corsat and Pilou nodded their heads and stood up straight again, impassively. They knew that what the boss said in this fashion, in perilous circumstances, was the prelude to some forceful and decisive action.

The Nyctalope's eyes, face and voice immediately resumed the quality that had petrified Wolf without depriving him of his intelligence. He turned back to the man and said: "First, summon the captain of the guard."

Wolf obeyed without hesitation. He turned on his heels, went to the telephone, pressed the bell with one hand while the other lifted the receiver, and spoke into it, spacing his words and emphasizing each syllable.

"*Woechter! Ja! Bisher Hauptmann! Woechter!*"

116

"Corsat, Pilou," Saint-Clair said, "the execution of the plan will commence now. Wolf, you'll greet the captain and tell him that Ragh, lying there on the bed, appears to have fallen ill a few moments ago. Understood?"

"Yes, Monsieur."

"Good."

Corsat, still wearing Ragh's uniform, lay down on the bed with his face to the wall, while Wolf extracted a spare smock and denim trousers from the cupboard. Saint-Clair and Pilou, once the latter had disencumbered himself of his equipment and Corsat's satchel, which he hid under the bed, stood flat against the wall, where the opening door would hide them from the view of whoever came in. Wolf, in order to play his role as best he could, went to stand next to the bed.

Three to five minutes might have elapsed, or only one or two—for the march of time accelerates and slows down by turns in such circumstances, in step with the thoughts progressing through the waiting minds. Then footsteps were heard of a man shod in heavy boots descending a staircase. The door opened and a man came in—an enormous human colossus, bare-headed, with the neck, shoulders, arms and hands of a brute beast!

Saint-Clair did not see the face of this formidable fellow—who, having entered and violently kicked the door shut with his heel, went straight to the bed, grumbling inarticulately. He saw, though, that the figure was at least two meters tall, with shoulders, hands and a stride to match. He had not thought to ask Wolf what sort of physique the guard captain had.

Good God! he said to himself. *If I'd known... Will we be able to bring such a man down without his being able to cry out? If his voice is proportionate to his...*

But the *hauptmann* was leaning over the fake Ragh; the moment had come. Saint-Clair nudged Pilou and they both leapt forward. At the same time, Corsat turned round, with a cushion in his hands.

While Corsat, setting the cushion on his chest, flung his powerful arms around the neck of the colossus, violently burying his face therein, Saint-Clair leapt on to the *hauptmann*'s huge back as if mounting a horse, and delivered two crashing ju-jitsu blows to the sides of the man's head, behind the ears. Meanwhile, Pilou rapidly secured the man's legs by means of his lasso, wound it around the torso, encircled one wrist, pulled it taut and knotted it, then encircled the other wrist, tightened it and knotted it again. Then he breathed out, having completed his task within four seconds.

After these four seconds, during which time the *hauptmann* was experiencing to the paralyzing effects of surprise, he stood up with a furious thrust of his back, lifting up Corsat and his cushions, Saint-Clair's ju-jitsu blows having only caused him a sharp pain that served to increase his strength tenfold. However powerful that strength was, though, he could not shake Saint-Clair loose, nor cause Corsat to fall, nor disorientate Pilou.

117

The Burgundian clung stubbornly to the man's skull, stifling him by crushing his face into the cushion. When the *hauptmann* got up, Corsat profited from his new position to clamp his knees about his victim's flanks. Saint-Clair repeated the blows of his fists more powerfully, generating an agony so extreme that nine men out of ten could not have borne it longer than the time necessary to cry out and fall unconscious. Pilou, bracing himself against the man's heels and knees, forced him to fall forwards on to the bed.

The *hauptmann* snarled and shook his body, like a bull trying to shake off banderillas,[15] resisting the pain that threatened to render him unconscious and the pressure that had provoked his fall–but his snarl, muffled by the cushion, was barely perceptible. His movements only maintained their violence for a dozen seconds or so. His resistance might have been effective if the pain had not been ceaselessly renewed and pressure of the spiral slipknots had not continually increased upon his calves, knees and thighs, crushing them together–but the human package fell upon the bed, which collapsed with a groan, its legs breaking and its metal frame and mattress ending up flat on the stone floor.

That will force me to modify my plan, Saint-Clair thought, while still in action. *The bed won't be presentable for when Lucifer comes in–and the enormity of such a brute couldn't be hidden under it even if it were intact. Ah, if I'd known...but it's too late. How can the plan be adjusted?*

Saint-Clair jumped to the ground. Pilou and Corsat had forced two napkins into the stunned *hauptmann*'s mouth, and they rapidly tied him to the bed-frame itself, skillfully enough that, if he should recover consciousness, he would not be able to get to his feet or make more noise than it is prudent to make within a sentry-post. They had already made too much.

There was a moment's silence and rest then, during which their respiration became normal and their minds recovered the requisite calmness, which the rapid and violent struggle had disrupted slightly.

"Let's go," said Saint-Clair. "It's decided." He looked at Wolf–who had not moved during the fight, having no orders to follow–and his voice took on an extraordinary gravity and solemnity, although it maintained its muted tone. "To the telephone!" he said. "Send the summons, pronounce the password, and follow it with the number six, which signifies the death or insanity, or the danger of death or insanity, of the captain of the guard. Wait, Wolf! Pilou! Behind the door as before! Corsat–grab the *hauptmann* by the legs, as if you were restraining him. And you, Wolf–after the telephone call, grab his arms. Both of you will be leaning over him, with your backs to the door. You, Wolf, when the door opens, will stand up slightly, look to the side of the door, and say, very rapidly: 'Sir, the captain had gone violently mad. After his fit he fainted, and we were able to tie him up; it was only afterwards that I was able to send the summons to your lordship.' And you will do nothing further, Wolf–is that understood?"

"Yes, Monsieur."

"When Lucifer is in front of the *hauptmann* at your side, Corsat, you'll seize him by the throat. Pilou and I... that's good! Wait a moment longer, Wolf..."

All of this seemed quite simple, sure, and easy to execute. They had succeeded with the *hauptmann*, who was a colossus. Why should they not succeed with Baron Glô von Warteck, who was no greater than the human average in physical terms?

In physical terms!

What about mental terms, though? In terms of thought, will-power and psychic powers whose extent was still unknown? What might he be capable of doing, in a struggle against enemy wills? What would he do?

At the first hint of action against him, as soon as he could take account of it, whether by intuition or by evident fact, might he not be capable of thinking and willing in such a manner that contrary thoughts and intentions would be nullified? Might not Wolf, Corsat and Pilou then find themselves petrified, incapable of movement or gesture?

And what about me? the Nyctalope asked himself. A violent anguish gripped his heart. For the first time in his life, he hesitated over an action that he wanted, and had planned, to carry out—but he rebelled against the anguish and the hesitation. "The action is desired, planned, necessary, obligatory!" he whispered. "The principal condition of success, in all things, is action."

He pulled himself up to his full height and said, coldly: "The telephone, Wolf! And may God go with you!"

Wolf obeyed. He did not know what he was risking. He was ignorant of the true power of the individual he had formerly considered no more than his master. He had seen these three enigmatic beings accomplish unexpectedly difficult things with ease. Even if the overlord of Schwarzrock was as strong as they were—for it was surely impossible for him to be stronger!—these three men, with his aid, would overcome the Baron. Interesting things would be seen in the castle then!

Thinking along these lines, Wolf went to the telephone.

Corsat and Pilou were already in place. Saint-Clair joined Pilou, and they listened.

Wolf rang. Then, emphasizing each syllable of every clearly-enunciated word, in the emotionless voice of a corporal commanding an exercise, he said: "*Herrlichkeit! Ja! Herrlichkeit, Woechter. Woechter, ja! Rosen Laura. Nummer sechser. Sechser, ja!*" [16]

Oh, what a chill penetrated the profoundest depths of Leo Saint-Clair's soul when he heard the password. The unique password, which would never be used again as a password, was composed of the two forenames of the woman he loved, and for whom he would shortly be risking his life. His hatred of Lucifer was further exacerbated. *Oh, let him come, let him come!* he thought. *My iron will against his occult power!*

119

To calm himself. he began counting off the seconds: one, two, three, four, five, six, seven...

At 82, he stopped.

The door opened. It opened without any noise of footsteps being audible. It opened, and was slowly closed again.

A man was standing there, motionless in he middle of the room—a man who was looking at the demolished bed to which the stunned *hauptmann* was tied, and over which two men were leaning, one of them Wolf and the other bearing only the uniform of Ragh.

Saint-Clair and Pilou could only see the man's back. He was bareheaded. He had untidy red hair, worn long at the top of the skull but cut short at the nape of the neck and about the ears. That hair glittered in the sunlight coming through the window, whose broad beams cut diagonally through the room, and in which impalpable dust-particles danced. He was tall and thin, dressed in a well-tailored smoking-jacket and a shirt with a white silk collar and cuffs, the latter turned back and the former turned down.

Saint-Clair made these observations during the time in which Wolf, half-turning towards the door, said very quickly, in a voice that was slightly strangled by the twist in his neck: "Sir, the captain had gone violently mad. After his fit he fainted, and we were able to tie him up; it was only afterwards that I was able to send the summons to your lordship."

Without replying, the red-haired man walked towards the bed, thrust Wolf aside with a gesture, and leaned over to examine the *hauptmann*'s face.

At that moment, Corsat, Saint-Clair, Pilou and Wolf himself, moving silently rapidly and precisely, grabbed him, gagged him and tied him up. They sat him down like a mannequin, facing the door with his back to the wall, on the *hauptmann*'s legs.

Then, Saint-Clair experienced a bizarre sensation: an abrupt warmth and a sort of itch in his neck and shoulders. Without being able to account for it, his attention was irresistibly directed away from the red-haired man and drawn to something that was happening behind him. Saint-Clair stood up, turned round... and a sharp cry escaped his lips. He was rooted to the spot, while Corsat, Pilou and Wolf, alerted by his cry, stood up and turned around simultaneously. Like him, they were frozen.

Standing before them, immobile in the middle of the room, a man was looking at them. He was bare-headed; he had untidy red hair, worn long above the forehead but cut short above the temples and the ears, and that hair was glittering in the sunlight. He was tall and thin, dressed in a smoking jacket and a white silk shirt, with its collar turned down and its cuffs turned up. It was exactly the same man, seen from the front, that Saint-Clair had seen from behind 30 seconds earlier, and on to whom, with Pilou, Corsat and Wolf, he had hurled himself.

Wolf, Corsat, Pilou and Saint-Clair saw, standing before them in the middle of the room, at liberty, the man that they had just that instant gagged, tied up and seated on the *hauptmann*'s legs, on the bed, against the wall. He had the same red eyes, the same vulture's beak of a nose, the same razor-slash of a mouth, the same square and bony chin...

Impassively, the red-haired man made a gesture.

Saint-Clair, Corsat, Pilou and Wolf had to turn their heads slightly–and without entirely losing sight of the man standing at liberty before them, they saw behind them, unquestionably, the same man, bound, gagged and sitting down...

V. The Ultimatum

About 12 hours earlier, when the Nyctalope, having been trapped on the balcony of the overhanging turret, had then disappeared through the window, Laurence Païli had remained stunned for several minutes. Then, gradually recovering her composure and her awareness of her surroundings, she got up, took a step back and drew the curtains closed again.

She felt so tired and feeble that she could not stay on her feet and let herself fall into a large, profound and high-backed armchair. She set about thinking. She could not believe that the prodigious appearance of her lover, the words spoken on either side, the promise of salvation and his disappearance out of the window above the vertiginous abyss, had been no more than the illusory plot and unreal vicissitudes of a nightmare.

Since she had been drawn away from her mother, her apartment, her art and her theater by an unknown force like that which draws iron filings irresistibly toward a magnet, the young woman had certainly known troubled hours, when hallucination and reality became confused to the point at which she believed that she had suffered fits of dementia. Since she had found herself captive in this fantastic castle, over which incomprehensible mystery reigned, she had certainly been subjected to fantastic dreams in the course of her disturbed sleep, in regard to which she had asked herself, when she awoke, whether they might not have been a inexplicably incoherent succession of material facts. Above all, the phantasmagorias to which the enigmatic and terrifying Baron Glô von Warteck had subjected her, sometimes with advance warning and sometimes without, had been well-designed to make it difficult for Laurence Païli to know, more often than not, what was real and what was not. This time, however, she had an infallible interpreter: her love! Then again, she knew, with certainty and with faith, what Leo Saint-Clair the Nyctalope was capable of accomplishing.

How had he known? How had he got here? She would find out in due course. But he had come to save her, because he loved her still, as she had never ceased to love him, never doubting it for a moment. What was more, he had given orders. She could not, in consequence, do anything but obey. And obedience, in this instance, was simply to be strong and to hope, to prepare herself and to wait.

She became strong as soon as these reflections were complete. Shivering with joyous hope, she prepared herself—which is to say that she went into the dressing-room adjoining her bedroom, set about twisting and arranging her hair into a solid bun, and dressed herself from top to toe in all the clothes she had been wearing on he day when, subjugated by that irresistible occult summons, she had left Paris. Baron Glô von Warteck, while filling wardrobes and two chests of drawers with enough clothes to comprise ten *trousseaus* for La Païli's usage, had not taken away from her anything that she had brought to Schwarzrock.

That night, Laurence did not sleep at all. Sitting in the armchair, she revisited the divine months of her love-affair with Leo Saint-Clair at Cap d'Antibes. Sometimes laughing, sometimes crying, sometimes a little girl intoxicated by love, sometimes a woman proud of her happiness and avid for its recommencement, glorified by all the various beauties with which passion can sublimate the features and the expressions of an amorous young woman who is already physically beautiful, Laurence Païli awaited the return of her liberator.

Daylight came and, some while thereafter, the hour when two servants brought the usual breakfast into the singer's room. Nothing was lacking in Schwarzrock. Coffee, milk, chocolate, butter, fresh cream, honey, wild strawberries gathered at dawn, fresh hens' eggs, raw or boiled, cold meats and smoked ham, sliced bread and brioches with butter, all in pretty vessels of rustic porcelain, were loaded on two platters, which the bearers deposited on the table. The third servant–of a rank superior to the two others–had unfolded a double cloth in linen and lace, and laid out the silverware and the crystal glassware.

This morning, absorbed as she was in her amorous expectation, Laurence noticed that the chief servant was no longer the superb Italian woman of the preceding days but the little German blonde with blue eyes whom the Baron von Warteck had shoved into her room the evening before, after an awful warning. Knowing then, and only for less than an hour, to what frightful tortures the child–so young, so pretty and so evidently naïve–was destined, Laurence had not had the strength to talk to her. Dreading that she might burst into tears in front of the nonplussed girl, she had sent her away, confiding her–according to the Baron's will–to the Italian woman who performed the functions of senior chambermaid.

Unfortunate girl! Laurence said to herself as she saw her laying out, not unskillfully, the tablecloth, silverware and glassware. *But my departure will save her from the tortures to which she would have been subjected because of me. How sad she is! I shall talk kindly to her.*

Laurence called, softly: "Minna!"

Zucht's daughter turned her peach-tinted round face and blue eyes towards "the Lady," and smiled.

In German–for the singer spoke all six of the major European languages– Laurence said: "Is it you, Minna, who will henceforth supervise my table service?"

"Yes, Madame," Minna replied, "and also in the drawing-room." She blushed and added: "Madame might care to be indulgent in the early days, for I have never served before, and..." She hesitated.

Laurence sought to encourage her with a gesture and a smile.

"And I must keep Madame company," Minna continued, without overmuch assurance, "after dinner this evening. Madame might care to pardon me if

123

I do not know how to talk, or play music, or read aloud in an elegant fashion... I'm only a peasant, but I shall be happy to please Madame, and I shall make every effort to serve her, in every way, as best I possibly can... and to love Madame, if Madame will permit it, and..."

But Minna could say no more. She snatched up her apron and hid her face—which had reddened deeply—and burst out sobbing.

Impassively, with rigid features and mechanical gestures, as if they were unable to see or hear anything, the two serving women finished their work. They were handsome girls of 18 or 20 from the canton of Lucerne, strong and sturdy but bovine in expression. When everything was arranged as it should be, they stood side by side on the other side of the table, with their arms by their sides, splendidly indifferent. Next to these powerful females, the German girl seemed to be a porcelain figurine.

Suddenly, Minna's hands released her apron, her arms fell and her body stiffened as if standing to attention. Her tears dried up and she became immobile, mute, impassive, under the command of an occult will that had abruptly possessed her, from afar or nearby.

It was not without a certain astonishment that Laurence had listened to what Minna had said. When she saw her break off her sobbing to become an automaton like the two Swiss girls, as the Italian woman had also been, she understood. She was beginning to unravel a few of the innumerable enigmas that composed the strange existence of Schwarzrock, all day and all night long. With raised eyebrows, she said to herself: *Hold on! Why did the monster allow the child the liberty to see, think and speak for a few minutes? That's strange! Neither the Italian girl nor the Swiss girls, who are destined to play the same role of martyr as Minna, ever had that liberty in my presence.* She then shrugged her shoulders. *What does it matter? I shall leave with Leo. These girls will not suffer "in my honor," as the monster said, mockingly. As to whether they continue to be automata or not, what can I do about it? I must think of Leo and myself, and of no one and nothing else, in order to be strong and ready. I must eat. I'm hungry, anyway. I'm hungry for the first time since I left Paris. All this looks delightful. I ought to eat, and I want to.*

Leaving her mantle, her hat and her gloves on a little side-table placed by the armchair, Laurence got up, walked to the lavishly-garnished dining-table, sat down on the chair that Minna automatically pushed forward and set about eating heartily, silently served by the two Swiss girls, whom Minna directed, equally silently, impassive in gesture and expression.

Neither of the Swiss girls seemed to notice that "the Lady" was wearing a dress this morning that was very different from the indoor clothing in which they had previously seen her—a simply-tailored dress of a neutral grey-brown color. Minna, similarly, appeared to pay no heed to the mantle, the otter-skin hat, the traveling-gloves and the tanned leather handbag on the side-table.

Laurence Païli made these observations, and a few others, while she was eating, and said to herself: *They must be totally hypnotized, mere puppets whose strings the monster pulls without even thinking about it specifically. It's an astonishing thing!* She stopped eating, her hand suspended, and went pale. *I cannot get used to the idea that, if he wished, I would be like these three girls, devoid of thought and will...*

Repressing that emotion, which often seized her, she shrugged her shoulders, smiled, and resumed: *Once I'm with Leo, I'm sure these spells will no longer be able to have any effect on me...*

Thereafter, she thought exclusively of the future and her face expressed a serenity that was youthful, confident and absolute. As she finished the meal, however–the only agreeable one she had had since leaving Paris, and the most copious–and got up to wait for the table to be cleared and for the servants to leave her apartment, she suddenly stood stock still, stupefied. The three young women presented an extraordinary aspect, which recalled to Laurence's mind the appearance of freedom that the sensitive Minna had momentarily taken on.

What! she thought. *Are all three of them free now? What's happening, then?*

Indeed, the two Swiss girls and the German girl were no longer automata. Their stances were no longer stiff. Minna smiled. The others had an air of naïve confusion, as if they were astonished to feel alive. They were not clearing the table mechanically, as usual; they were looking around in bewilderment and admiration, as if they had never seen the room before, even though they had been coming into it three times a day for a week.

Minna was visibly surprised to see that, at 9 a.m., the bedclothes had not been disturbed. She dared to say, with an ingenuous and charming familiarity: "What! Didn't Madame go to bed last night?"

A keen curiosity sprang up in Laurence's mind, along with the thought of incalculable consequences. Without replying to Minna's question, she went hurriedly to the balcony formed by the overhanging turret, whose large curtains she had already opened. With a resolute step, but very anxiously, she marched past the curtains through the space that had always been impenetrable to her, although the servants had always passed through it without encumbrance when going to open or close the windows. She moved through the space that had formerly been occupied by the invisible, incomprehensible wall–the immovable, invincible object that had separated her from Leo on the previous evening, standing between imprisonment and liberty.

"Let's see!" Laurence said, aloud–and immediately released a cry of joy. The invisible wall was no longer there. The enigmatic obstacle had been removed. The passage was clear!

Quivering with instinctive joy, Laurence went as far as the window, turned around, and passed again over the patch of carpet on which her feet had never been able to tread. She went back and forth three times, as if to fortify her certainty.

The two Swiss girls and the German watched her from a distance in amazement, their naïve eyes expressing a hint of dread. Laurence saw that and she laughed lightly.

"What I'm doing astonishes you, doesn't it?" she said. "If you only knew how much more you three have astonished me! Let's see, you two are named Marie and Gertrude, aren't you?"

"Yes, Madame," the two Swiss girls replied, in unison,

"Good. Now, come here and stand directly in front of me... Good. Kneel down. You don't understand? That doesn't matter. Obey me meekly–and with a smile... A spontaneous smile, Mesdemoiselles. Ah, you're laughing? Very good. You're ravishing when you laugh. Now join your hands, as if you were praying to the good Lord. Perfect! Don't move! You too, Minna–come here! Stand to my left, very close to me, Put your arm around my waist. Yes, you dare! Lean your head on my shoulder. Oh, what a pet you are! Now you'll repeat, all three of you together, what I say to you, yes?"

"Yes, Madame," said the three young women, amused by this unexpected game, whose motives and profound purpose they could not guess.

Still smiling lightly, but very pale, in a voice a trifle dulled by emotions, as if she were conducting an experiment of the utmost gravity, Laurence went on: "To please me, very greatly, you will repeat exactly..." After a brief pause, she pronounced: "Baron Glô von Warteck, Lord of Schwarzrock, is an abominable criminal."

Minna, Marie and Gertrude shuddered, their faces expressing astonishment tinged with dread. A communal hesitation made them look at one another.

"Very good!" cried Laurence, who was entirely serious now. "You hesitate, so you understand the enormity of your pronouncing such a sentence. Your minds remember, reason and judge–you are, therefore, free! Well, to prove to me that this freedom is truly without restriction, at least for the moment, pronounce in your turn–which will give me great pleasure, I assure you–the sentence that I repeat: *Baron Glô von Warteck, Lord of Schwarzrock, is an abominable criminal.*"

Then, hesitating no longer, smiling faintly, like little children who are afraid but who brave the danger, Minna, Gertrude and Marie pronounced, almost in unison: "Baron Glô von Warteck, Lord of Schwarzrock, is an abominable criminal!"

"Bravo! And thank you! You're charming girls, and I want to hug you. You first Minna, then you, Gertrude, then you, Marie. Get up, and attend to your duties."

But the three servants, having stood up, remained immobile and perplexed. Their duties? Evidently, their minds having been freed, they did not know what their duties ere. No longer hypnotized, they did not remember what they had been doing every day at about this hour.

Laurence Païli, satisfied, was about to tell them what their duties comprised, when an abrupt transformation overtook the three young women. They stiffened, holding themselves straighter, with impassive faces and expressionless eyes. They moved, jerkily. Within two minutes, the table was cleared and put away in the corner and the leftovers were taken out. Then, supervised by Minna, the two Swiss girls went into the dressing-room, did their work there quickly, as they did every day, came back into the bedroom and stripped the bed, in which no one had slept, in order to remake it, as they did every day.

While this was going on, Laurence usually retired to a little room in a large alcove where there was a Pleyel grand.[17] She usually played, reading from a score or improvising according to the whim of her fingers. This morning, though, she watched the three servants at work. By the time the three young women left, after bowing in her direction like puppets, Laurence had established that their normal automatism had been entirely restored.

As soon as she was alone, she ran to the balcony of the overhanging turret. The invisible, immutable, insurmountable wall stopped her dead in her tracks.

"For a few minutes, then," Laurence concluded, "voluntarily or otherwise, the monster was occupied–absorbed to such an extent that his thoughts were entirely monopolized. The portion of his thought that is ordinarily devoted, by day and by night, to the maintenance of the invisible wall and the control of the three servants, was no longer evident here. Why? What caused that phenomenon?"

For a few minutes, Laurence Païli searched for an answer to this question, but she understood that the answer could only be determined by knowledge of events of which she was ignorant and could not at present discover. She did not, therefore, persist in trying to resolve a problem that was currently insoluble.

All the while that she was pondering these extraordinary incidents, she was still waiting for Leo Saint-Clair. He had promised that he would return, during the day or the following night. The morning went by without Laurence Païli growing impatient. She had absolute confidence. She waited.

At 12:30 p.m., Glô von Warteck did not arrive–as he had done several times–to invite her to have lunch with him and escort her to the dining-room. The three servant girls brought her lunch, to which Laurence did justice. They served it automatically, without a word or an intelligence glance.

During the afternoon, incapable of reading or playing music, the young woman continued to wait, fidgeting fretfully. She rang for Minna several times, to ask her questions and give her orders. The German girl did not reply to a single question and only obeyed certain orders, mechanically. Silence was imposed upon her and her mind had no power of choice. Several times, also, Laurence went to the balcony; the invisible wall was always there.

At 4 p.m., she had afternoon tea.

Dusk fell. The lamps in the chandelier and the wall-lamps were lit. Laurence extinguished some of the lamps by turning off their switches. Then she dined, but without appetite and very lightly. The servants turned back the bedcovers, set out her nightgown, brought water, sugar and fruit, and went out after bowing stiffly. The curt ringing of a shrill bell, followed by a grating sound, warned Laurence that the doors of the room and the dressing-room were electrified, inviolable under pain of death.

The night began—and Laurence waited.

Little by little, the anxiety characteristic of long waiting, during which hope and despair alternate, gripped her heart, hammered in her brain, made here limbs grow heavy, and exasperated her nerves.

She waited, and her suffering gradually increased.

She began to feel tired. She had not slept for 36 hours; she had not been able to sit still all day. At 10 p.m., she felt harassed. She was so badly in need of sleep that even the anguish of waiting, with its terrible alternatives of hope and despair, could not keep her awake.

Slumped in the armchair, she did not fall sleep immediately. She tried to fight, and prolonged a painful drowsiness for more than an hour. Finally, though, fatigue proved the stronger. With a heavy head, an exhausted body and weakened nerves, Laurence Païli slipped into a dreamless sleep, which resembled—save for the gentle movements of light respiration—the sleep of death.

When Laurence opened her eyes it was broad daylight. The curtains were drawn; the breakfast-table was set; the three servants were standing beside it, immobile and stiff, their faces expressionless—and Baron Glô von Warteck was standing in front of her, smoking.

He waited while she rubbed her eyes, came fully awake and stood up, quivering and ready for a fight—a desperate fight, since Leo Saint-Clair had not come. He bowed deeply.

"Mademoiselle," he said, with ceremonious sarcasm, "I beg you to do me the favor of allowing me to be present during your breakfast this morning, for I have some very important and very urgent things to tell you. We shall talk, if you will deign to answer me, as soon as you have dismissed the servants." He smiled, his red eyes aflame with desire, hatred, cruel irony and triumphant joy. "Very important," he repeated, "and very urgent things, Mademoiselle!"

Under Lucifer's gaze, Laurence felt a sensation she had experienced several times before in the last few days, as if her thoughts were whirling in her head. Following the encouraging appearance of Saint-Clair, and in consequence of the observations she had made the previous day regarding the three servants, Laurence Païli was extremely lucid this morning, ready for combat. She knew that the turbulence of her thoughts was usually followed by a sort of gentle prostration, when she was conscious of not being entirely the mistress of her own will, and of not possessing her ordinary freedom of decision. Until now, she had given in to that turbulence and that prostration, to the partial installation of another soul within hers–but today, following the long and profound reflections of the previous day, she believed that she had divined the truth regarding the incomprehensible phenomena in whose midst she had lived and had to live. Holding to that truth, Laurence Païli found herself abruptly determined to fight.

When she felt the turbulence, therefore, she experienced a sort of renaissance of her entire being, and she brought all her will-power to bear in resisting the vertigo. She decided that she ought not to close her own eyes in order not to see the monster's–for he would see that and take action in consequence!–but to concentrate her own gaze and to turn it inside herself. Her goal was to produce the effect of being possessed by an obsessive idea so powerful and all-penetrating that although one's eyes are wide open and fixed, they actually see nothing of what they appear to be looking at.

On doing that, Laurence knew instantly that she had resisted effectively, because the scarcely-commenced turbulence broke up, the prostration was not produced, and she had the very clear sensation of being entirely the mistress of her own will. But Laurence was a professional actress. *I must not only resist him without his knowing it,* she told herself, *but also let him believe that he is dominating and annihilating me to the same extent as on other occasions.*

She recalled the successive attitudes that she had adopted, involuntarily, on those other occasions; this time, she simulated them voluntarily.

He will believe that he is reading my thoughts, she said to herself, *and subsequently substituting his thought for mine, in part. My God! Can I be stronger and more cunning than he? I must, else I shall be lost. For Leo must certainly have run into difficulties, if only temporary ones, in the execution of his plan.*

The very facility with which she was able to extend this inner monologue convinced Laurence of her victory. She played her role. Her clear and staring eyes became indecisive, as if misting over–which permitted her to escape, by a means less fatiguing than the first, the fascination of von Warteck's eyes. Then, she became weak at the knees, let herself slump into an armchair and remained still for a moment, with her eyelids half-closed and a puerile smile on her lips. Then she got up, went to the table with a hesitant tread, sat down and began to eat.

Always keeping in mind that she might have need of a great deal of strength and endurance, as circumstances required, she ate her fill. When she had finished, the servants cleared the table mechanically and disappeared.

Laurence got up again. The proof was now conclusive. Throughout the meal, she had felt the effluvia of a mind and a will that were not hers whirling around her own, like a noisy swarm of hungry mosquitoes. This time, she had extended a mosquito-net around her by means of her own will, coldly resolved to fight until there was a definitive victory–or a defeat worse than death.

Good! she said to herself. *It's a good game–let's carry on playing it!*

She took a few steps, went to sit on the divan beside Baron Glô von Warteck and lowered her head into her cupped hands, while leaning her elbows on her knees. Her eyes stared ahead, expressionlessly.

"Very important and very urgent things?" she said, slowly, in the voice of a little girl. "Well, Monsieur, I'm listening!"

During the time that had elapsed since he had repeated the sentence *Very important and very urgent things, Mademoiselle!* Glô von Warteck had not paid any particular attention to his victim. His reflexes functioned habitually in respect of the special, very attenuated hypnotism that he was accustomed to use on Laurence while waiting. He was preoccupied by the events of the previous day and by what he intended to accomplish today. That certainly made the self-recovery that Laurence was attempting to achieve much easier. It also permitted the young woman's artfulness to be exercised without any risk of opposition.

Thus deceived, due in part to his own fault, and not knowing that he was deceived, Baron Glô von Warteck continued, so to speak, to spin the wheels of the formidable mechanism of his will-power without gaining any power over Laurence. He had made a plan the day before. He had come here to execute the part of it that concerned Laurence, and he did so mechanically, without suspecting that Laurence, instead of listening submissively in such a way that she would react in the desired fashion and obey, was observing, reflecting and calculating, and was responding to the exact necessary to maintain her role.

The conversation was curt, and the play of his features hardly varied–for Lucifer retained an absolute impassivity throughout, his expressionless eyes fixed on Laurence's left temple. From the very first words, Laurence was petrified, while a tumult of despairing anguish and tenacious hope whirled in her brain, this time without opposition. When it replied to the hard and emphatic voice of Glô von Warteck–who was speaking in French–Laurence's voice was always the whisper of a perplexed and terrified little girl.

"Mademoiselle," he said, "your lover, Leo Saint-Clair, the Nyctalope–yes, your lover, for I have read many things in your thoughts, especially while you slept, and there is nothing I do not know about your past–is in the castle. He is my prisoner. He would obviously have attempted to free you. How did he know that you were here? I would know that soon, if I wished to know it, but it is unnecessary for several reasons. His life is in your hands. Do you want him to remain alive?"

"Yes, yes... alive! Don't kill him!" Laurence moaned.

"I repeat that his life is in your hands. You know that I would only have to will it for you to stretch yourself out at this very moment, smiling and abandoned, on this divan... but no! You know already that I do not want to have you in that fashion. I want you to come to me of your own free will, exercised after a choice on which all your sentiments have had their influence.

"Never, I tell you!" Laurence said. "I will never be yours by choice."

"You will be mine after making a choice, or by the force of my will–but in the second case, it will be a Hell for you and for those you love. Today I speak to you for the last time, with one more element to make you yield. Listen!"

"I'm listening," Laurence said, shrugging her shoulders. "You know very well that I can't help listening."

"Firstly, the final deadline expires at midnight on June 10. Today is the May 15. You have a calendar here. You shall not see me again until midnight on June 10–unless, by a violent mental effort, you summon me before then to say: 'I am yours, my beloved!'

"Secondly, from today until June 10, or until the moment when you summon me, Leo Saint-Clair and his two companions will be, at any moment and according to my whim, subjected to physical and moral torture, which they will come every morning, at 9 a.m., to describe to you in person. You will see the stigmata of the physical torture in their flesh, and what they tell you will enable you to judge the extent of their moral torture.

"Thirdly, from today until midnight on June 10, or until the moment when you summon me, Minna, Gertrude and Marie will be violated and tortured according to my whim–and every evening, at 8:30 p.m., after you have dined; they will also tell you in detail to what they have been subjected, and how they have suffered.

"Finally, if, at midnight on June 10 at the latest, you do not come to me in the manner that you know I desire, Saint-Clair and his two companions will be put to death–after having witnessed for 24 hours the spectacle of your giving yourself to me, and meeting an exactly similar fate to Minna, Gertrude and Marie in my hands.

"This ultimatum is the last, because since 9:10 yesterday morning, I now have in my power the person you love most in all the world: Leo Saint-Clair, the Nyctalope!"

VI. This Holofernes' Judith [18]

"Since 9:10 yesterday morning..."

When Baron Glô von Warteck had pronounced these six words, Laurence could hardly help crying out, getting up and manifesting the joy produced by the certainty added to a discovery she had made, whose consequences she could not have foreseen, but of whose supreme importance, as a matter of life and death, she now had an intuition.

"Since 9:10 yesterday morning..."

Here we go! Laurence said to herself. *Lucifer is not omniscient, since he doesn't know what happened here, between 9:10 and approximately 9:30 a.m. His mind has its weaknesses, since he can't take account of what he doesn't know. His psychiatric gift is limited, since he hasn't read in my mind the one fact that I was determined he should not read. His power is not absolute, since he has not been able to force me, by the ordinary mechanism of his will, to have no secrets from him. Finally, his faculties of intelligence, observation, deduction and his mastery of himself are not perfect, since he has, without any necessity, pronounced the worlds that have enlightened me:* since 9:10 yesterday morning...

Long after Baron Glô von Warteck had left the room. Laurence Païli continued sitting on he edge of the divan, with her elbows on her knees and her chin in her cupped hands. The expression on her face gradually changed, at first merely pensive and grave, then contracted, as if by wild and tragic resolution and then been fixed in horror and infinite despair. Finally it became calm, as white as alabaster, as she sat with her eyes closed and a delicately serene smile on her lips, like that of a young woman who had died while enraptured by a happy thought.

An hour went by, a second, a third. Then, a door suddenly opened and the three servants came in. While they laid the table for lunch, like automata, Laurence went into the dressing-room, get undressed, and put on slippers and an elegant dressing-gown. Then she ate, with a good appetite, but silently and pensively. She did not spare a single glance for Minna, Gertrude and Marie, who cleared the table when she had finished and disappeared.

Until 2 p.m. Laurence smoked Egyptian cigarettes, paced back and forth, established that the invisible wall was there, and then went to let down her hair, allowing the beautiful black tresses to undulate gently over her shoulders, down her back and along her bare arms.

Suddenly, blushing abruptly then immediately becoming quite pale again, she stood still in the middle of the room, her sparkling eyes taking on an implacable resolution.

"Oh, if I had a weapon!" she murmured. "If I had a revolver, or a dagger... but no! Everything here that might serve as a club or a hammer is solidly fixed. The bronze chandeliers and the clock are bolted to the marble. The central heating means that there's no fireplace equipped with fire-irons and a basket of logs, with one of which I might strike to kill, or at least to stun. No weapon at all! The silver forks and knives that are brought to my table are so slender... oh, he's taken every precaution! The bread is sliced, the meat cut up into little morsels. No, no–the search is futile. There's nothing at all. To fight and conquer, I have nothing but my will, my body, my hands... and if I'm mistaken... if I can't reproduce the phenomenon of 9:10 to 9:30 yesterday morning with greater intensity... if it's impossible for Leo to profit from the phenomenon while it lasts... if, in the end, my sacrifice is futile... well, I'll allow myself to die!"

She breathed in deeply, like a diver about to hurl himself into the abyss– and, after concentrating her thoughts, she slowly pronounced, in a whisper: "Baron Glô von Warteck, I summon you. Come!"

The previous day, at 9:10 a.m., when Leo Saint-Clair had seen two identical red-haired men at the same time–one free and standing in front of him, the other tied up and sitting behind him—he had thought at first that he was prey to a hallucination. Immediately, though, he, Corsat and Pilou saw Wolf, acting as if he had received a very precise verbal order, set about ungagging and untying not merely the seated man but the *hauptmann* too.

The three captives established then that there were indeed two red-haired men, for they saw both of them in front of them, with the spluttering and sweating *hauptmann* to their left and the livid and tremulous Wolf to their right. Then they experienced an abrupt vertigo, and they perceived vaguely that one of the two red-haired men made some strange gestures in their direction. They felt themselves grow weak at the knees and faint–and everything ceased to exist.

When they recovered consciousness, they were in a high-ceilinged room with bare stone walls, into which daylight entered through four narrow glazed loopholes. The room was round and the loopholes marked the extremities of two perpendicular diameters, along whose imaginary lines were set four camp-beds. Each bed was occupied by a man: Saint-Clair, Corsat, Pilou and Wolf, each dressed as he had been in the sentry post. The three Frenchmen even had their weapons–Brownings and knives.

To his great amazement, Saint-Clair saw their equipment, including Corsat's satchel and Pilou's lassos, set on a round table in the middle of the cell. The four men, opening their eyes at the same time, pushed themselves up with their elbows into sitting positions. They looked at one another, and saw that they had all seen everything. The Frenchmen made certain that their Brownings had not been unloaded.

Almost immediately, Saint-Clair began to speak, quickly and briefly. "Are you entirely lucid, Corsat, Pilou?"

"I think so," Pilou replied.

"Me too," said Corsat.

"Let's put it to the proof. Reply to some questions. How many individuals comprise the Nortmund family, You, Pilou..."

"Six," the Provençal replied, without hesitation. "The grandfather, the father, the mother, one son, two daughters,"

"What are their names? You Corsat..."

Straight away, the Burgundian said: "Messieurs Charles and Louis, Madame Blanche, Monsieur Paul, Mesdemoiselles Pierrette and Jacqueline."

"Good. And you, Wolf–do you know why you're here, with us?"

"I only know," Wolf replied, dejectedly, "that we have not long to live."

"What makes you so certain?"

"This round room with four beds is legendary among the castle personnel. They call it the vestibule of death. To my knowledge, eight men have already been shut up here for offences that were more or less serious but were all punished by the same penalty: death. I saw them–two on the first occasion, three on the second and third occasions–for whenever men are condemned to death, all the castle staff, men and women like, file through this room, coming in by that door and going out by the one on the right. Then they're never seen again–never again! We're in the vestibule of death. Nothing can save us now."

"Well, that's another question," said the Nyctalope. "We say nothing can save us now when we see death before us, a millimeter and a second away, in distance and time–and then...! Isn't that right, Corsat and Pilou?"

"Dead right!"

"To a T!"

At these words and the two exclamations that followed, Wolf's blue eyes opened wide. "*Ach*," he said, "you're mad!"

"Perhaps," said Saint-Clair, smiling. "Since you consider us to be utterly lost, you must think that nothing can make the situation worse?"

"I do think that," said Wolf, with fatalistic resignation.

"Then you won't have any difficulty answering the questions I put to you."

"None, Monsieur–but I warn you that I told you everything I know in the sentry post. Everything!"

"So you didn't know that there were two physically identical Barons von Warteck?"

"I had no idea."

"You didn't mention this vestibule of death."

"Indeed–but it's the only thing, I swear to you, that I omitted."

"Prepare your soul for death, then, Wolf, since you're convinced that you're going to die. If I can save you at the same time as the rest of us, though, will you consent to live?"

"Certainly–but you can no more save yourselves than you can save me."

"We'll see! Prepare your soul for death, Wolf–but also for life. In the meantime, my companions and I will examine the situation.

Throughout this dialogue each of the four men had stayed exactly as he was immediately after their awakening, Saint-Clair sitting up, Corsat leaning to his left on a hard bolster, Pilou leaning to his right on the edge of the bed, Wolf sitting crossways, his legs dangling. Turning away from Wolf, who was facing him, Saint-Clair turned to his right, towards Corsat, then to his left, towards Pilou, and said: "Come together!"

Each one moved to sit at the foot of his bed, facing the central table. In that position, Saint-Clair only had to extend his arms to seize Corsat's left hand and Pilou's right, provided that they extended their arms too. Given that their bedheads touched the wall beneath each of the loopholes and that the beds were about two meters long; given also that in order to touch the table in front of them the three men had to lean forwards and reach out their arms; and given, finally, that the table was about a hundred and fifty centimeters in diameter, the exact dimensions of the vast circular room cold be calculated.

"Let's see," said Saint-Clair, after having made the calculation, by virtue of his habit of leaving no observation neglected. "What do you think about what happened to us? Corsat?"

"I only know this," Corsat relied. "To have left us our weapons, and to have had my equipment, my satchel and those two lassos set down at our disposal, the red-haired twins must be very sure of their power."

"Fair enough," Saint-Clair agreed. "You don't have any thoughts about the scene in the sentry post, then?"

"None. It's too complicated. I'll leave that to you, boss."

"What about you, Pilou?"

"Me, I only have one question."

"What?"

"Why did we faint before the red-haired twins, without being struck, touched, or even slightly brushed by anything whatsoever?"

"Because the sight of a second red-haired man identical to the first disorientated us," Saint-Clair replied, "and the newcomer simply put us into a hypnotic trance." After a moment's pause, he continued: "Personally, knowing what I know, I wouldn't give a farthing for our lives. There's no use bluffing any more. We've found ourselves facing death 20 times before, Corsat and Pilou, and I've always said to you: 'Bah–we'll escape yet!'–for I was sure that we would escape. And I was right, for we're here. This time, though, while repeating what I said to Wolf, that it's only necessary to despair of life when one is actually dead, I say to you: 'it will be very difficult, and perhaps impossible, to escape again!' To succeed, we shall have to bring to bear all of our will-power. Will-power, will-power, will-power! Three times I say it to you–for that's the issue: to exert our will, and to do it powerfully enough to prevail, despite the terrible will that opposes us.

135

"Doors that are bolted or electrified, walls that are thick and steep, armed men–all that is nothing. Imagination, coolness, courage and decisiveness are all that's needed to defeat them. Here, though, it's a mind that we must overcome– and with our own minds, essentially! Corsat, Pilou, my good men, we let ourselves be taken by surprise once, and Lucifer hypnotized us. That's stupid–and so dangerous that we are now prisoners, in graver danger of death than we have ever been before. I'm not at all sure that we can save ourselves; I scarcely dare to nurture the hope–but I desire it with all the might of my being... all the might of the love that is the intimate foundation of my being.

"Why are there two red-haired men? It might be explained by the birth of identical twins, or skillful make-up. Therefore, the question is unimportant. What is important is this thought: only one of the two red-haired men is endowed with the psychic power; only one of them is the true Baron. That was the second of the two–I mean the one who was the second to enter the sentry post yesterday. We may have to distinguish between them, for safety's sake. How can we make that distinction? I have no idea.

"So Corsat, Pilou, my orders are: Keep your will-power taut, so that it cannot be subjugated for a second time. Is that understood?"

"Understood," the Burgundian and the Provençal said, quite simply, in unison.

"Well, now we have only to wait," Saint-Clair concluded. "Since it is evidently impossible for us to control the circumstances, we must fight the kind of war dictated to us by the circumstances created by Lucifer."

Ah, if only the Nyctalope had been able to foresee that it would be Laurence Païli who would have to prepare herself to create the "circumstances" in the midst of which the supreme battle would unfold! But he could not foresee that–and it was better, moreover, that he could not foresee it. It would have caused him more suffering than the threat of death.

"Nevertheless," he continued, in a cheerful tone that was terrible in its faintness, as he rose to his feet, "there is no known case of prisoners who are condemned to death, but who are determined not to die, who do not first dedicate themselves to a minute examination of their prison. Let's subject it to intense scrutiny; it might perhaps be helpful."

"The examination won't take long," said Pilou.

"Wolf!" called Corsat.

"What?" During Saint-Clair's discourse, the man had remained immobile on the edge of his bed, prostrated by a sort of resigned stupor.

"What time did the processions past the condemned in which you took part take place?"

"It was shortly before the midday meal on each occasion."

"We won't have a long time to wait, then," the Burgundian stated. He added: "I'm eager to see the faces in the procession. It ought to be funny, for they'll surely be open-mouthed, and then we'll be certain that..."

"Do you need that to be certain, idiot?" asked Pilou, mockingly.

"It'll be a sort of sentence for us, that procession... regarding the condemnation, inasmuch as the sentence isn't communicated to the condemned man..."

Corsat and Pilou continued their idle chatter in a whisper, while watching their employer make a slow tour of the room.

Saint-Clair tipped over the four beds, measured the four glazed loopholes with his hand–each of them was a handspan-and-a-half wide and five deep–and examine the two facing doors. The latter were black-painted iron, exactly fitted to their granite frames without any visible locking mechanism; struck with the hilt of a dagger they resounded vibrantly, the noise echoing in the depths of corridors, staircases and immense rooms.

"Wolf!" said the Nyctalope.

"Yes, Monsieur?"

"By which door did you enter?"

"That one." Wolf pointed to the one on the left of his own bed, which was facing Saint-Clair's.

"Good–so you went out of that one?"

"*Ja.*"

"How did you approach the first? Enumerate."

Docilely, Wolf enumerated: "Guardroom; straight staircase; corridor at right-angles; spiral staircase hollowed out of the thickness of the tower wall; the door."

"Good." Saint-Clair paused, pensively. He remembered what Laurence had said–word for word, for he had a powerful memory: "a narrow spiral staircase, and, finally, a vast round room with five windows, from which one can see the whole of a circle of mountains." *And in that room,* Saint-Clair said to himself, *is the mysterious machine: the machine that will give Lucifer so much power that he claims that, with its aid, he will have the entire universe at his feet. Now, there's only one round tower with windows and loopholes which overlooks the other parts of the castle. I observed that from outside. The height of its windows is greater than the height of the mountains. Here are the loopholes, from which I too have seen the entire circle of mountains. I must, therefore, be immediately underneath the room in which the mysterious machine is hidden. That's important–very important.*

"Corsat! Pilou!" In a low voice–for there might be a listening device, and what the Nyctalope had just realized had to be kept secret from everyone except his two associates–he communicated his discovery to Pilou and Corsat. Then he said to Wolf: "And the other door?"

"Descending spiral staircase within the wall; circular corridor; then the right-angled corridor, the straight staircase and the guardroom."

"Good. Listen, Wolf. You're broad-shouldered and square-backed, with solid thighs and calves. Could you bear the weight of two men for ten minutes, one atop the other?"

"Yes, certainly."

"Very well...when you're fatigued, say so, and Corsat will replace you. Place yourself here, between the table and your bed. Pilou, climb on to Wolf's shoulders, standing upright. Perfect! Now me. Provided that no one's spying on us through some hole...!"

Saint-Clair climbed up Pilou's body, which was standing on Wolf's shoulders, and stood up on the Provençal's shoulders. In this manner, with his two arms half-extended above his head, he could touch the round ceiling of the room—the vault above which was the floor of the room containing the machine. Taking a dagger from its sheath, he had no difficulty introducing the blade into a narrow and short crack that he had noticed from below, and which he believed to be an interstice produced by the slight displacement of two badly-set stones.

Immediately, he let out a soft laugh.

"Down!" he said, in a low voice.

He climbed down, then helped Pilou down, and said: "Even Lucifer doesn't think of everything. Does he know that vault is only an optical illusion? To begin with, the tower must only have had one floor: a tube, with a large staircase with landings extending all the way from the ground to the high platform serving the loopholes and the battlements. Then the stairway was taken down and stairwells hollowed out in the rock, and the tower was divided into several floors, each with one room, with ordinary floorboards and ceilings. To give the stone-walled rooms a medieval appearance, though, vaults were fashioned out of flexible laths of chestnut and skimmed with cement, as if to paint an optical illusion. We'll wait until after the midday meal. In less than a quarter of an hour, thanks to our mechanical cutter, that vault, ceiling and the floorboards above will be pierced by three parallel holes large enough to let us pass through. And then, as for the machine... everything will be easy, if Lucifer has not thought to establish a fluid wall around us, or one of his other scientific sorceries..."

Saint-Clair fell silent and cocked his ear, as did his three companions. A bell was ringing, its sound muffled by distance.

Wolf shivered, and murmured: "The procession!"

"That's it, then," said Pilou. "We're condemned to death?"

"*Ja.*"

Wolf, letting himself fall to the edge of his bed, sat there as if petrified.

"This will be curious," said Corsat, simply.

"Sung in the key of D," said Pilou, mockingly.

"Will-power! Will-power, my friends!" said the Nyctalope, gravely. He sat down at the foot of his bed, his hands on his knees. Corsat and Pilou sat down too, one of them upright, the other with his legs folded, his heels tucked up against his thighs, his arms crossed and his chin on his wrist. They waited with great interest, determined to preserve their composure and to remain masters of their own will. They soon perceived the muffled tread of rapidly-approaching feet.

Suddenly, without the slightest noise, one of the iron doors opened wide and a man appeared. It was the *hauptmann*. As he came in, he searched the three French prisoners with his eyes, studying them with such a hostile expression that Saint-Clair murmured to Corsat and Pilou: "What pleasure that man will take in making us suffer, if ever he has us in his power!"

The *hauptmann* immediately took up a position at the foot of Wolf's bed. With Saint-Clair, Corsat and Pilou before his eyes, he watched the procession. He had an automatic pistol in his right hand.

Is that a precaution against us? Saint-Clair wondered *Or against someone who... but no, it cant be against anyone but us. Hasn't Lucifer enveloped the* hauptmann *in a wall of protective fluid, then? Why have we been left to think and act so freely? It's true that it's within this prison, firmly closed and doubtless carefully watched... Since I got into Schwarzrock I've established the existence of enigmas that seem to me to be entirely contradictory. If these contradictions are not deliberate on Lucifer's part, might it be that Lucifer is only possessed of a limited and intermittent power? Hmm–all that's very interesting. To all the peremptory motives I already have for wanting to live and emerge victorious, I can add another: to know; to understand and elucidate these enigmas, explain the mysteries, draw down the veil of the Occult...*

While maintaining this internal monologue, the Nyctalope, even more attentively than Corsat and Pilou, watched the procession–but he did not count the men passing before him, because he knew that Corsat and Pilou were counting. Instead, he studied their faces.

Although none of them attained the gigantic proportions of the *hauptmann*, the bodies passing before him were almost all athletic–but their indifferent or resigned physiognomies displayed mediocre intelligence. Many had the faces of brutes, with the cruel and avid eyes of pigs at a full trough. They marched heavily and rhythmically, falling into step in response to an order given outside the entry door–a cadence that continued through the exit door, but was forcibly disturbed as they reached the staircase. They were all dressed in the same uniform. Every tenth man had one, two or three canary-yellow chevrons on his sleeve.

Then, without any gap, there were the women: plump women from northern Germany or tall, broad women from the Teutonic cantons of Switzerland. Their expressions were mostly bewildered. Saint-Clair noticed that they were all beautiful or very pretty, young, hale and sturdy. They were uniformly dressed in the picturesque Tyrolean costume popularized by *laïtou* singers in the music-halls of the world.[19] Their skirts were very short, their arms bare, their blouses and bodices low-cut.

As they passed by, the men and women looked to their left and right at the condemned men. There was stupidity and cruel joy in the eyes of the men, perfect indifference in the eyes of the women, who did not even show curiosity. Several passed without turning their heads to the left or the right.

Suddenly, there were no more tramping feet at the entrance. The *hauptmann* left his place, fell in behind the last woman and left, after turning his head momentarily to dart a second glance of hatred and ferocious joy at the Frenchmen.

One after the other, the doors closed again, soundlessly. The procession was over. Saint-Clair had not thought to measure the time it had taken. "How many men?" he asked.

"Fifty-eight," replied Corsat.

Saint-Clair turned to the German. "Wolf!" he said. "Twenty-eight more than those you know, including you and Ragh. How many women, Pilou?"

"Thirty," the Provençal replied. "Even if that's all, it's a large staff."

"Which knowledge teaches us nothing," Saint-Clair concluded. "Wolf!"

"*Mein herr*?"

"When will they bring us a meal?"

"Never," Wolf replied. "We're condemned to death. We'll have nothing more to eat and drink, and no one else will come to see us. If we're executed after the usual interval, it will be tomorrow. This afternoon and tonight, we can rest easy."

"Very well, this afternoon and tonight, we'll be working to get out of here. Corsat! Pilou!"

"Boss!"

"Do you feel that your heads are quite free, your brains clear? Have you a clear consciousness of your hope of escaping death, and your determination to realize that hope?"

"Yes, boss, yes!" replied the two men.

"Perfect. If you feel your thinking becoming foggy, your hope faltering and your determination becoming hesitant, tell me immediately! By uniting our mental strength, we'll be better able to resist when Lucifer judges it useful to nullify our free will. Now, silence for an hour!"

The Nyctalope lay down on his bed, closed his eyes and started thinking about everything that had happened to him since Monsieur Prillant had summoned him. Only nine days had passed since then, but what events, enigmas and mysteries those nine days had brought! The Nyctalope applied himself to the task of examining those facts one by one, connecting them logically and deducing hypotheses. In brief, according to his own expression, he *studied the map*.

It was a disconcerting map, in which the blanks of unknown countries were more numerous than the colors and annotations of explored regions–but the latter were no longer isolated from one another, as they had been at first. *I'm beginning to get my bearings here,* Saint-Clair said to himself. Work prevented him from thinking about the probability of imminent torture and death.

As for Corsat and Pilou, they lay down like Saint-Clair, to Wolf's bewilderment, and soon went to sleep.

When the hour was up, Saint-Clair woke them up. They stood up, rubbed their eyes and were instantly ready for action. By their frank expressions and smiles, their employer saw that they were as free as he was.

"Let's go to work," he said. "Stand there, Wolf. Pilou, get on top of him. Corsat, pass me the cutter–then watch the doors. If anyone comes in, kill him! Make certain–use the mute Browning. It's no longer a matter of being careful of what might happen; every obstacle must be struck down pitilessly. Our lives and other lives that are dear to us–and useful to he world–are dependent on our victory. We must conquer or we shall surely die."

This was said in a tone that engraved the words even within Wolf's soul and exalted him to the point of regaining his courage and confidence. In the position of an athlete carrying a "human pyramid," he made the solid pedestal on which Pilou and Saint-Clair stood, one atop the other.

Plied by the experienced hands of the Nyctalope, the cutter began eating into the ceiling.

Two, three, four minutes ran by.

Suddenly, the cutter was no longer purring. "Curse it!" Saint-Clair groaned. "The invisible wall!"

His hands and his head had just been violently pushed back. His knees had buckled and it seemed to him that his skull was touching the ceiling–although the deeply curved ceiling was now a meter above him. His hands, holding the cutter, could no longer be lifted above his head. He understood immediately.

"The invisible wall! Down!"

He leapt on to the table, and from there to the floor. Pilou got down from Wolf's shoulders.

"*Ach!*" the German said. Saint-Clair, Corsat and Pilou looked at him, and saw him become petrified, his face impassive and his eyes blank.

The Nyctalope understood again; his companions guessed.

"Beware, friends!" Saint-Clair said, in a forceful voice, as he seized both of them by the shoulders with fraternal pressure. "Beware! The invisible wall is surrounding us–it's a perfidious assault against our freedom of thought, our will! We don't want to give in, and we shall not give in!"

He drew them backwards and sat them down beside him on a bed–and they looked at one another in turn, mingling their soul with his, mustering their strength. Then, when he saw that they were resisting hard, he spoke to them. They replied. If Wolf had been able to hear them, he would have heard them passionately recalling, sometimes earnestly and sometimes laughing, adventures they had previously undertaken in Africa and Oceania. To escape the present power of Lucifer, Saint-Clair, Corsat and Pilou were taking refuge in the past.

That lasted for hours–hours of daylight and of darkness, and then of daylight again. During those hours, Saint-Clair, Corsat and Pilou were talking and fighting, uniting their strength–but they grew thirsty, then hungry and starved of sleep. They felt fatigue overcoming them. They became afraid that they might soon be too weak, and began to think that they could not hold out for another day...

Wolf lying on his bed nearby, was like a dead man, his eyes closed and his breathing imperceptible.

At noon on May 16, Saint-Clair, Corsat and Pilou could do no more. The felt their minds misting over and heard their speech becoming thick and slurred.

At 1 p.m., their sight became troubled.

"No, no!" howled Saint-Clair, exasperated.

With a last outburst of will-power, he repelled the infernal power and tore his companions away from it. Half an hour passed, during which they were able to retain the illusion that they could get the upper hand–but at 1:45 p.m., they were plunged into the fog again. At 2 p.m., they were desperately conscious that they were going under, and they clasped one another by the hand, sobbing...

Now, it was on May 16, at the first stroke of 2 p.m. that Laurence Païli pronounced the words: "Baron Glô von Warteck, I summon you. Come!"

What the young woman had learned, observed and deduced permitted her to pose the problem in these terms: *Leo is in Lucifer's power. If there were nothing but bolts, locks and walls between Leo and liberty, I would be unworried–but there are occult forces, the fluid barriers that the monster can dispose.*

Now, I know that at a certain moment yesterday, when Lucifer concentrated all his efforts go capture Leo, he "forgot" his other victims–or, rather, the psychic power that he had to employ against Saint-Clair alone diminished the intensity of his other fluidic actions. For one reason or another, or perhaps both, at the time when Lucifer overwhelmed Leo yesterday, the invisible wall ceased to exist and the three servants recovered their free will.

At present, Leo is much more the prisoner of the monster's psychic forces than of the doors and walls of Schwarzrock. I must, myself, put Lucifer into such a state of general forgetfulness that the effects of his fluidic action will cease everywhere. Leo, who is invariably attentive to all phenomena. will perceive the change and profit from his moral liberty to free himself physically. Perhaps he will even be able to procure weapons and return here–and then he will kill Lucifer!

The only question is whether I can, by myself, throw Baron Glô von Warteck into such an state of ecstasy that he will be thoughtless for at leas an hour, devoid of will-power by virtue of being utterly consumed by sensations of pleasure...

Laurence was so preoccupied with this question that she had no consciousness of the heroism and sublimity of the sacrifice she had just resolved to make.

She stood upright, shivering and pale-faced, with sparks in her eyes. Her hair flooded over her shoulders, hanging down as far as the hollow of her back in admirable waves and curls. Her voluptuous figure was tightly molded in the silk of her robe. She waited, facing the door from which the man would emerge

142

whom she wished she could strangle with her own hands: the man whom she would gladly and remorselessly throw to a herd of starving hogs; the man to whom she was about to give her splendid and chaste body, in its entirety, to save Leo Saint-Clair, the man she loved...

She waited for Baron Glô von Warteck.

And Baron Glô von Warteck appeared.

The entire world admired Laurence Païli; she was an incomparable artiste, as prodigious an actress as she was a stirring singer.

Whatever it pleased Lucifer to think himself—magus, sar,[20] cabalist and occultist as he really was, theoretical genius and diabolical inventor as he had shown himself to be by virtue of his mysterious machine—Baron Glô von Warteck was also a man: an ardent, passionate man burning with all the fires of Hell; an admirer of physical beauty, like the true Satan, the fallen archangel. How could he resist the eyes and all the bodily attributes of Laurence Païli? How could he divine the comedy in this superb offering?

Confronted by the prospect of possessing a woman, every man is vainglorious. Warteck attributed his own victory to the prestige of his exorbitant personality, because he knew that a woman like La Païli dreaded neither torture nor death—and because he did not know that Laurence had seen Leo Saint-Clair, and expected to be avenged and purified by him...

Deceived, seduced and overcome by the gaze the smile and the entire attitude of this captive Venus, he fell to his knees, with a rictus that attempted to be a gallant smile, saying—in a voice raucous with desire—"Here is Hercules as the feet of Omphale!"[21]

But the singer thought: *Here is Holofernes before Judith. When Leo arrives, perhaps I shall already have been able...*

And she leaned forward, offering her lips to those of the Lord of Schwarzrock.

VII. The Nyctalope in Action

It was at that same instant that Saint-Clair, Corsat and Pilou experienced an abrupt sensation, as if a strong current of cold air were passing over them, sweeping their foreheads and purifying their brains.

They stood up as one, let go of one another and looked at each other drunkenly, conscious that they had been freed from a mental slavery that was even more terrible and degrading than physical slavery. They felt completely free.

"Sing the song–free!" cried Pilou.

"Free!" repeated Corsat, bursting into laughter.

"Damnation! What happened?"

"It's not important," Saint-Clair put in, curtly. "We're free, so back to work! We mustn't lose a minute. We don't know how long our liberty will last, since we don't know its cause. To work! Wolf! Wolf!"

"Hey, Wolf!"

"Get up, Wolf!"

Corsat and Pilou shook the sleeping German. Thanks to their shoving, he came out of his leaden sleep quickly enough. He was hauled to his feet and pushed into position directly beneath the section of ceiling in which Saint-Clair had earlier begun to cut an opening large enough to pass through. Pilou climbed on to his shoulders, and Saint-Clair onto Pilou's. With his Browning in his fist, Corsat kept watch on both doors.

Five minutes went by before Saint-Clair threw the section of the vault that he had cut away on to one of the beds. "Corsat–electric torch to Pilou!"

The Burgundian took a little fishing-torch from his satchel and threw it adroitly to Pilou, while their employer disappeared into the hole in the ceiling. Almost immediately, Saint-Clair's voice commanded, "Corsat, blunt chisel to Pilou!" Then, "Pilou, come!" and, when Pilou had rejoined his boss, "Corsat–send Wolf up!"

The Provençal's lasso was uncoiled and suspended from the orifice in the ceiling to the foot of a bed. Prodded, supported and pushed by Corsat, Wolf climbed up and disappeared. Saint-Clair's voiced sounded again: "Corsat, gather everything together! Grab the section of ceiling that I threw down just now, and climb up!"

Two minutes later, there was no one in the prison. The hole in the ceiling had been blocked; given its height, the suspect spot would have had to be examined with particular attention to make out the thin oval line of the section, all the more so because the loopholes let in the daylight so parsimoniously that the vault was perpetually in shadow.

Despite its arching frame, which advertised great solidity, the artificial vault would not have been strong enough to support the weight of four men had Saint-Clair not taken the precaution of arranging Corsat, Pilou and Wolf at the periphery, where the frail carpentry of the vault was braced against the circular wall. "Don't move," he said. "If I need you, I'll call you by name. And no noise!"

They were in a sort of round cupboard. Its center was occupied solely by the vault of the prison, whose culminating point touched the floorboards of the room above–boards sustained by enormous cross-beams with intervals approximately a meter wide. At the periphery, though, there was a good two meters of height between the base of the underlying vault and the floorboards above. It was dark within, Pilou only having switched on the electric torch in order to get himself and his two companions into position–but the darkness was no hindrance to the Nyctalope. He had wasted no time in choosing the most convenient interstice. By poking the blunt chisel between two badly-fitted planks, he assured himself that there was nothing above the boards but a thick carpet. He immediately brought the electric cutter into play.

If there's anyone in the room with the machine, he told himself, *we're lost– but there's no way round that. I have to risk it.*

And he risked it. After two minutes' work, he was reassured.

At this point, if anyone is following the vibration of the blade from above, he won't have the patience to– Saint-Clair cut the thought short in order to express a contrary notion. *Sorry! If he's not stupid, he'll have the patience to wait, to see it through–and he'll reap the benefit of waiting, for he'll still be the stronger, even if he has a rudimentary weapon. When I poke my head through the hole I've made, that person, holding himself back slightly, has only to drop a noose over my head and strangle me, or hit me over the had with something hard, stunning me... Bah! I have to risk it.*

And he risked it, knowing full well that in any adventure, the best chance of success is to confront risks–even unknown risks–resolutely.

As the blade cut through one, then the second, then the third and finally the fourth side of the cavity the four cross-beams, a slender ray of light marked its passage–a narrow crack through which passed the bright daylight that undoubtedly illuminated the room above: the room of the machine.

Because thoughts identical to the Nyctalope's were running through the sagacious minds of Corsat and Pilou, the Provençal and the Burgundian put out their hands in unison when the blade had only 20 centimeters to go, each touching one of Saint-Clair's shoulders. He turned to face them, his face illuminated by the daylight coming through the rectangular crack excavated by the blade.

"Now, what?" Saint-Clair whispered, stopping the cutter.

"I want to go first, boss!" replied Pilou, in the scarcely perceptible voice that all three of them adopted in such circumstances.

"No, me!" said Corsat.

"Enough, my friends!" the Nyctalope commanded. "I was expecting that. But I don't want to risk your lives. There's one man here who's expendable, and he will take the chance. Besides, if there's someone waiting for us up there, Wolf's appearance will be so astonishing to him that we might gain a few seconds while surprise suspends his action. Bring Wolf here and stand well to his right and left, so the three of you won't weigh too heavily on the same part of the vault. Good—wait!"

He set the cutter in motion again. A moment later, he drew the instrument back and passed it to Corsat one-handed, while the other hand kept the square piece of floorboard in place. It was only sustained by two centimeters of wood and carpet, which remained intact.

"Here, Wolf!" whispered Saint-Clair. "As soon as the opening is made, you'll put both your arms out, put your weight on them, brace yourself on your elbows, stick your head and shoulders through, then the rest, very quickly. Do you understand?"

"*Ja!*"

"Will you do it?"

"*Ja!*"

"Good. Pilou, get ready to follow him immediately."

"Understood, boss!"

"I'll go next, then Corsat last. Hands on Brownings or daggers, in case there are men up there—we must get through!"

"We will, boss."

"I'm counting on it. Are you ready, Wolf?"

"*Ja*, Monsieur."

"Go!"

Saint-Clair lowered his left hand. The square of board sagged and was immediately seized and pulled by his right hand. There was a dry, muffled crack as it broke away—and through the square gap went Wolf's hands, arms, head, shoulders and torso. Buttressed so as not to weigh upon the vault, Corsat pushed him upwards, while Pilou, getting a handhold on the edge of the opening in his turn—but with only one hand—went up with Wolf, his head level with the German's shins.

Wolf and Pilou passed through within 15 seconds; Saint-Clair followed immediately in seven, then Corsat in eight. Within half a minute—as measured by Pilou, who had checked at his watch twice—all four stood up on a thick carpet, in a large round room flooded with sunlight.

There was no one in the room but themselves. At least, the four men could not see anyone from where they stood—but when a dry click sounded behind them, all four turned on the spot.

They stood up as straight as pickets, their eyes widening and their mouths falling open to emit exclamations that only came out as hoarse rattling sounds.

With empty orbits, a worm-eaten nose and teeth displayed in a rictus, the very image of Death was marching towards them, in the form of a huge walking skeleton. In the phalanges of its ten bony fingers, it gripped two glinting metal cylinders.

A quarter of a hour before, in another part of the castle, two men had been chatting a little and smoking a lot.

In addition to the large central tower, which stood at least ten meters higher than any of the castle's other structures, Schwarzrock had four square corner towers, none of them raised up much higher than the central battlements. These four towers marked the cardinal points of the compass rose. The part of the castle in which the apartment reserved for Laurence Païli was accommodated was in the south-western façade.

Each corner tower was not only linked to the central tower by corridors and internal staircases but by a kind of stone gangway which, passing over the roof of the intermediate building, formed a straight pathway open to the sky. Four gangways extended from terraces on the four square towers to four open bays set in the wall of the round tower, opening into the room where the machine was. As the wall of the central tower was two meters thick, each of the four arched bays was defended by two iron doors and an enormous intermediary grille.

The two men who had been chatting a little and smoking a lot were in the southern tower. They were wallowing in large leather-upholstered armchairs on each side of a vast fireplace where logs were burning. They were surrounded by glass-fronted bookcases filled with books, a massive table charged with pieces of paper, a writing-desk and various office utensils, a few oak stools, a side-table–positioned between them–carrying smoking paraphernalia, two large earthenware tankards and an enormous jug of beer.

One of these two men was the red-haired man whom Saint-Clair and his companions had tied up and sat down in the sentry-post beside the recumbent *hauptmann*. The other was the *hauptmann* himself. Before their desultory conversation had started, they had both been moving automatically, their faces bleak and their eyes expressionless, standing next to the empty fireplace on the two sides of he sided-table, each one stuffing his long porcelain pipe. Suddenly, they had shivered and looked at one another with joyous surprise. In a hoarse voice and a low tone, the red-haired man had said–in German, of course–"We're free, Fritz."

And the colossal *hauptmann* had grunted, in his thick voice: "We are indeed free, Hunter!"

There was a pause, then Fritz the *hauptmann* asked: "What's happening, then?"

"*Ach*!" said he red-haired Hunter, shrugging his shoulders. "I saw *him* going into her room."

147

Fritz made a strange gargling sound in his throat, which was laughter, and said: "I understand why *he* isn't thinking about us, then. Between her and the prisoners, *his* mind must be somewhat preoccupied–there's nothing left for us. Let's take advantage of it, Hunter!"

"Let's, Fritz!"

The called a manservant, ordered a fire and beer, cheerfully finished stuffing their pipes, sprawled in the large armchairs, which they placed at a comfortable distance from the fire, and they smoked, drank and chatted a little–very little, and only about the excellence of the freshly-brewed beer, the usual draw of their pipes, large armchairs whose upholstery molded itself to their occupants, and a blazing fire on a brisk May afternoon, when the snow had not yet cleared the mountains...

In that temporary liberty to which the redoubtable tyrant had abandoned them, Fritz the *hauptmann* and the red-haired Hunter indulged an animal enjoyment of the pleasure of being alive.

They had enjoyed a quarter of an hour of the pleasure of animal existence when something, abruptly and unexpectedly, snapped them out of that pleasure and imposed upon them, more unexpectedly still, the unprecedented and immediate necessity of acting without orders. They had to act with initiative, by themselves, unaided by any but their own minds, because they were free; Lucifer no longer governed their will in the manner of a radiotelemetrist guiding the flight of an aircraft or a pilot-less ship at a distance by means of the spectrum of Hertzian waves.

This thing, this unexpected thing, was the simple ringing of a bell: a bizarre, crystalline ringing whose pitch was continually raised and lowered, very rapidly. This ringing sounded from inside a plain wooden box fixed to the wall between two bookcases.

At the first ring sounded. its pitch rising, the red-haired Hunter and Fritz the *hauptmann* both went pale, extracted the amber mouthpieces of their pipes from their teeth, looked at one another, and then turned to look at the noisy box.

At the second ring, whose pitch descended this time, Hunter and Fritz got up, set their pipes on the side-table, and looked at one another again, livid and indecisive, as if terrified.

At the third ring, they leapt towards the box as one. Hunter, arriving first, pushed a little lever fixed under the noisy box from right to left. It fell silent immediately.

"It's the skeleton, Fritz!" said Hunter, his voice blank.

"*Ach*!" Fritz groaned. "The walking skeleton!"

"Out there."

"Are our men in revolt?"

"Or urged by curiosity?"

"Impossible!"

"Impossible, indeed!"

"The prisoners then...?"

"Also impossible. The doors are closed."

"And we alone know how to open them."

"Fritz!"

"Hunter!"

"What shall we do?"

"Yes, what shall we do?"

"Go there."

"See and kill."

"Or be killed, if the electricity hasn't..."

"No other way."

"None indeed! But the master will torture us for years if, for whatever reason, we infringe the defenses and invade the zone where she is..."

"He didn't anticipate the case of the skeleton..."

"Perhaps he did and perhaps he didn't."

"In that case, Hunter?"

"In that case, Fritz, we've already stood here talking for too long. Let's go! And may God or the Devil..."

They each had a stout Browning, Hunter in the pistol-pocket in his trousers and Fritz in a leather holster suspended from his belt. They took them in hand and, without further hesitation, set off at a run. The red-haired Hunter went ahead, with Fritz the *hauptmann* behind him.

The door to the gangway opened with a click, as if impelled by a sudden gust of wind. The red-haired man and the *hauptmann* ran along the narrow stone pathway following the crest of the roof that formed a "parting of the waters" between the south-western and south-eastern buildings of Schwarzrock. The former was light on his feet and lithe, the latter heavy and lumbering, but they were as fast as one another.

When they arrived at the wall of the tall central tower, Hunter touched a stone, then another, and yet another. The tapered iron door opened. They passed through and the door closed again. Within the arch, an electric light immediately lit up and the two men found themselves confronted with an enormous grille barring the narrow gallery from left to right and top to bottom.

Hunter knelt down and touched two floor-level stones in succession. The grille opened. They passed through and the grille closed again behind them. Only one door now separated the two men from the room where the machine was, the room where the skeleton had walked...

Hunter touched three stones, this time above his head–but the final door did not open.

Hunter and Fritz looked at one another, astonished.

"You try it," said the red-haired man.

"The *hauptmann* raised his right arm and touched the three correct stones–but the door remained shut.

149

In front of the door which they had tried to open, but which had not opened–the only door separating them from the room where the skeleton had walked, from which no sound emerged–Hunter and Fritz suddenly shivered and their teeth began to chatter.

They were afraid!

At that same instant, on the other side of the door, Saint-Clair suppressed the emotion that had petrified him momentarily–and which still petrified Corsat, Pilou and Wolf, who stood behind him.

When the human skeleton appeared, marching towards them, holding its two metal cylinders, they had been rooted to the spot for several seconds. Already, with a gesture as mechanical as its gait, the skeleton had slowly raised its arms, at the end of which the cylinders gleamed–but this gesture revealed something to Saint-Clair, which the skeleton's left arm had previously hidden. That thing was a long spiral of insulated electrical wire, attached to the wall at a socket and trailing behind the skeleton's left foot, disappearing into the heel.

"Get down!" ordered Saint-Clair, in a voice that was contained, dry and imperious.

He fell to the ground on his side, immediately imitated by his three companions.

"Corsat–the scissors, quickly!"

Two seconds later, he had a pair of scissors in his hand. Reaching forwards with lightning speed, he cut the spiral wire close to the heel. The skeleton, no longer maintained in equilibrium by the automatism of its march, abruptly fell forwards, as if hit by a bludgeon, and collapsed entirely, with a rattle of bones.

"Get up!" Saint-Clair ordered.

A door had just opened in front of them–the door behind which the red-haired Hunter and Fritz the *hauptmann* were waiting, which had finally opened when Hunter had touched the three stones for a third time. Every mechanism, however perfect it might be, has its malfunctions, which are often inexplicable, and it was some such malfunction that had kept the door shut twice when it ought to have opened.

At the sight of the two men and their bewildered attitude, Saint-Clair understood that the red-haired man was not the real Baron Glô von Warteck but merely his double–a servant devoid of any occult power. He laughed briefly and said, in French: "Corsat! Pilou! We, who knew how to cut off the electricity and make the skeleton collapse, know how make it impossible for these men to..." He broke off and said, in German, changing his tone to one of command: "Hands up, you two, or I'll shoot!"

He pointed his silent Browning at the *hauptmann*–but it was the red-haired man who cried "Living men! We need living men!" He leapt to his left, towards a copper lever that was glinting in the sunlight, and pulled it down.

150

The *hauptmann* had not put up his hands and Saint-Clair had pulled the trigger–but the big man had dropped to his knees. The bullet ripped through his right ear. Coming to his feet, the *hauptmann* threw himself head first at Saint-Clair. The latter, struck in the side, lost his balance. He staggered, trying to stay on his feet, but he was grabbed by the legs and brought down.

Corsat immediately leapt on to the *hauptmann*'s shoulders.

"No!" Saint-Clair cried. "My hands are free–stand aside!"

Corsat understood, and leapt back, at the same instant that Saint-Clair shoved the barrel of his weapon against the *hauptmann*'s forehead and pressed the trigger again. There was no smoke and no noise, save for a brief groan and the collapse of a heavy body. Fritz the *hauptmann* was dead, his extended body and wide-flung arms sprawling on the floor.

Saint-Clair got to his feet with a single motion. He saw immediately that Pilou had disappeared. "Where has he gone?"

"In pursuit of the red-haired man," Corsat replied.

"Where?"

"There!" Corsat pointed to the doorway, now closed again, through which the *hauptmann* and that red-haired man had appeared.

"He'll get back to us, or we'll get back to him. There's not a moment to lose. I know which way to go. Come here, Corsat, Wolf!"

Saint-Clair recalled the young woman's words very well: "*This room, a corridor, a large staircase, a dining-room, a library, then a little corridor, perfectly straight, and a narrow spiral staircase...*" With the incalculable rapidity of overstimulated thought, he said to himself: *If we follow that itinerary in a contrary sense, we'll arrive at the door of her room. Whatever the cause may be, we are not subject to Lucifer's control; the invisible wall is no longer around me, so there is a chance that it's no longer around her either. As for the electrified doors, it's merely a matter of finding and cutting the electrical conductor...*

It did not take him more than a minute to discover the secret mechanism that opened the little door beyond which he saw, as he had expected, a spiral staircase. It was pitch dark, but the Nyctalope did not even notice that. As he went down the stairs four at a time, turning vertiginously around the central column, Corsat switched on the pocket-lamp and followed him.[22]

Wolf followed Corsat; he had not understood the words spoken in French but he had guessed, having heard his name pronounced, that he was to go with Corsat. He knew, besides, that there was no salvation for him, save by the hand of this extraordinary man–extraordinary in his presence and his actions, if not his goals, of which the poor chap knew nothing–so he followed Corsat, who ran after the Nyctalope.

After the spiral staircase, there was an iron door, a narrow corridor, short and straight, an iron grille, a wooden door, a large room furnished as a library, a second wooden door, a padded enclosure, a little dining-room decked out in a luxurious Medieval style, two padded wooden doors, a curtain, a large landing and a monumentally large descending staircase with only twenty steps, another landing similar to the one above, a corridor sumptuously hung with ancient tapestries, a door...

"There it is!" said Saint-Clair–and stopped in front of the door.

Corsat and Wolf stopped behind him.

VIII. From Minute to Minute

The things that one expects to be the most extraordinarily difficult and complicated are sometimes the simplest and easiest, as human anticipations are often thwarted by destiny.

The door in front of which the Nyctalope, Corsat and Wolf came to a halt was that of the apartment in which the celebrated Laurence Païli–Laure, the woman that Leo Saint-Clair loved–was held captive. Between himself and that door–or, at least, the opening of that door–the explorer had expected to find a thousand obstacles.

Now, the door was unmasked by any curtain. Tall, broad, with only one panel in sculpted and polished oak, it had a gleaming brass handle to the left, a third of the way up. In the case of an ordinary door, if it is unlocked, one turns a handle more or less similar to that one, and the door opens. But this door would undoubtedly be better defended than the garden of the Hesperides, and the invisible dragon that guarded it would not be as easy to slay as the one that Hercules had to dispense with before collecting the golden apples from the three daughters of Atlas! [23]

With his heart beating rapidly, Saint-Clair said to himself: *If it were sufficient, in order for me to avoid electrocution, to insulate myself before leaning on the handle long enough to open the door...*

In the meantime, he slid his fingers and hands into a pair of gloves taken from one of the pockets in his leotard–and he depressed the handle very, very gently. His eyes and ears were alert, attentive to the least indication of danger.

Little by little, the handle turned, just like an ordinary handle–but without any noise, because the mechanism was carefully maintained. When the handle was fully depressed, Saint-Clair instinctively made the gesture that one makes when one has just turned a door-handle–which is to say that he pushed. He pushed–and the door opened! It simply opened–and nothing else happened!

To Saint-Clair's great amazement, he was able to cross the threshold. Corsat and Wolf followed him. Behind the three of them, the door remained open.

They found themselves in a large antechamber hung with old tapestries, with waiting-chairs to the right and the left but no other furniture. There was no window; a fretted brass lamp, converted into an electric light hanging from the ceiling, shed a soft light. There was only one other door, facing the first. Saint-Clair went straight to it, and–this time without taking any precaution–tried it. It did not resist. With an expansive gesture, he pushed it abruptly open to reveal a large rectangle of sunlit brightness, and the vision of a large and high-ceilinged room flooded with light, fully carpeted, filled with furniture, luxurious ornaments–and, at the back, the balcony of the overhanging turret...

"Don't come in! Oh, don't come in!" exclaimed Saint-Clair, in a voice that was as fearful as it was unexpected–choked, imperious and pleading at the same time, and furious too.

He slammed the door violently behind him and ran forwards.

What a spectacle confronted him!

Stretched out on the huge low divan, with her bare legs hanging down and her feet lost in the fur of a polar bear skin, Laurence Païli lay as if dead. A tunic of white silk and lace, crumpled and ripped to shreds, scarcely covered her body. Her spreading hair covered her right shoulder and side, while a trickle of blood ran over her bare left shoulder. Her arms, one of which was dangling down as far as the white bearskin, were wide apart, forming a cross. Her lips were slightly apart and her eyes were closed; her face, turned towards the sunlit turret, had the pallor and calmness of death.

Next to the divan, on the Persian carpet beyond the edge of the white bear-skin, a red-haired man, similar in every respect to the red-haired man who had fled up above with the Provençal on his heels, was lying on his side. His legs were folded and his arms were outstretched in front of him; his clenched fingers were plunged into the pile of the carpet. He too had the livid face of a corpse, but with a fixed expression of frightful rage, for his eyes were still open, terrible in their fixity!

Saint-Clair felt utterly overwhelmed and helpless. "Come on, then!" he groaned. He pulled himself together and stood there, with the two bodies in front of him.

"She... dead? That blood... and him, dead too? How... why?" He was stammering. He understood. "Oh, no, no!" he moaned. "I must be calm... and act when necessary. Come on! I must regain my strength..."

As he looked at the red-haired man, saying to himself, *That one's obviously Lucifer*, he saw the recumbent body move, uncurling slightly. The fingers opened, extended... and the eyes...

Then, there was a shout–many shouts, a tumult, Pilou's voice, Corsat's voice, calling: "Boss! Boss! To us! Here!"

He turned round, ran to the door, opened it and saw Corsat and Pilou in the antechamber, holding the red-haired man and lifting him up like a mannequin, while he lashed out at their arms and legs, howling in German. Further away, in the corridor, a crowd of men was hesitantly pressing forward–but they were already being pushed aside by newcomers with resolute faces, armed with stout Brownings. They stopped in response to an abrupt command: "Halt!"

Immediately, in response to a second command, the first four in the vanguard rushed upon Corsat, Pilou and Saint-Clair–but they bumped into one another; the Nyctalope had struck them down, with no other sound than the click of his Browning's automatic loading device.

There was a momentary stupor among the attackers. Pilou abandoned the weight of the red-haired man–who was no longer struggling–to Corsat and said to Saint-Clair: "There are 50 of them. Eventually, one or other of them will kill you, boss! I know how we can get out. Corsat can cover the retreat and shield himself with that living puppet..."

"Wait!"

Everything that had happened since Saint-Clair had emerged from the room in response to his comrades' appeal had taken less than a minute. He turned round, ran back into the room, searched for a dressing-gown, found a cloak and wrapped it around Laurence Païli's body–asking himself all the while, with atrocious anxiety, whether she was dead or had merely fainted. Carrying his lover's body in his arms, he returned to the antechamber, where Pilou seized him by the elbow, drew him on and pushed him forward, preceded at a run by Wolf.

Only then did detonations resound behind them.

"You'll kill him!" Corsat howled. "You'll kill him!" He had set the red-haired man on his back, in such a manner as to shield himself completely. He ran after Saint-Clair and Pilou.

Several seconds of running brought them into a wide corridor. Then Wolf stopped short, letting the emburdened Saint-Clair overtake him, along with Pilou, his Browning in his hand, and Corsat, with the red-haired man suspended behind him as a shield. When they had all passed by, Wolf slammed a door shut, the noise echoing from vault to vault like a cannon-shot.

Immediately, shouts were raised behind the door, and blows rained upon the iron mass–but Wolf had taken the lead again and they all ran. They went down staircases at top speed, at the risk of stumbling and fracturing their skulls or limbs. They stopped abruptly in front of a main door.

"Your cutter," said Wolf.

Pilou took it from Corsat's satchel. Within a minute, the door was opened, the section of wood holding the lock having been excised. They were in a stable; there were horses and harnesses. A man stood up behind a shallow partition, but Wolf knocked him down with a blow of his fist.

"The cutter–over there!" Wolf said to Pilou, pointing to another large door.

While Pilou went to work, Wolf saddled a horse–an example so rapidly followed that two minutes later, four horses were galloping across the plain encircling Schwarzrock. On leaving the stables they had found themselves at the base of the enormous rock, in an ancient grotto communicating with the castle by means of a sloping gallery, in which a staircase had been built.[24]

Gunshots sounded from above, fired from the ramparts and the towers, but they were out of range.

The horses reached the bottom of a zigzag pathway, which climbed up to the principal pass serving as a communication link between the circular plain and the outer regions of the Black Forest.

"Up there!" said Saint-Clair. "That's salvation, for they won't dare follow us up there in large numbers."

155

The horses set off along the steep path. Wolf's was at the head; the second carried Saint-Clair and the still-inanimate Laurence; the third bore Corsat and the terrorized red-haired man; the fourth was mounted by Pilou.

At that moment, Zucht and his two sons, Franz and Berthold, came running out of the house at the extremity of the valley; they were armed with rifles. Simultaneously, six saddled horses emerged from the stables of Schwarzrock, carrying six men armed with lassos.

Three minutes later, the Zuchts and the horsemen met at a crossroads, and one of the men from Schwarzrock said to Zucht: "They must not be killed. They must be taken alive–those are the Baron's orders. Shoot down the horses if our lassos are ineffectual or if we're killed, and bring back the fugitives alive."

"How many are there?" asked father Zucht.

"Four men, with one woman and Lord Hunter, whom they've kidnapped."

"We'll take the short cut," said father Zucht. "We'll get to the pass before them."

"Good! We'll follow the path. Two of their horses are doubly loaded, so they'll make slower progress than we will. Above all, don't kill them! Rather die than kill–that's the order. There's torture, remember!"

"That's understood!"

The three Zuchts plunged into the trees, while the six horsemen urged their mounts on to the bare path that zigzagged up the mountain.

Imagine that strange scene. In the 20th century, in the heart of a civilized country–in a steep and thickly-forested region, admittedly, but an inhabited and policed region, where tourism companies have planted signposts and installed benches at "viewpoints"–four men were fleeing on horseback, carrying a woman who was unconscious or dead and a subdued captive. These four men had Brownings in their fists and were determined to kill or be killed rather than being captured. Nine men were pursuing these fugitives resolutely, firmly determined to capture them or be killed! Did no policeman or forest ranger intervene? No–for the plain surrounding Schwarzrock was private property, the domain of Baron Glô von Warteck. His gamekeepers were the three Zuchts, and no policeman had the right to go into that immense domain without a legal warrant properly issued by the judiciary authorities.

No one dreamed of asking the legal authorities to take action against whatever lay within that girdle of mountain and forest known as the domain and barony of Schwarzrock–for a barony and its domain are regarded, in Germany, as an element of a nominally-defunct empire. The fugitives, therefore, could expect no help from anywhere or anyone against their pursuers; their entry into the castle had made them *disappear*. The pursuers knew that no one except the Baron would care if the fugitives were killed–but the Baron would send them to their deaths, if they did not succeed in capturing them.

156

Once the pass was traversed and the fugitives were on the other side of the mountain, however, it would be a different matter. The domain of Schwarzrock finished at the horizon made by the mountain chain forming the circle. There was a low dry-stone wall up there, built years before and maintained on a daily basis by the Zuchts, which marked the boundary. On the other side of that wall, at intervals of 500 meters, stood trees with stripped trunks bearing placards on which it was written that any trespass within the bounds of the domain would be at the risk of death, by reason of numerous wolf-traps, and, furthermore, was formally prohibited, under penalty of imprisonment. In four places, facing one another in pairs, the wall allowed the passage of pathways by which one could enter or leave–paths framed by high rocks forming mountain passes–and although there was no gate closing them off, notices saying *No Entry* were continually renewed, painted in black on a white background.

Once the pass had been traversed, therefore, and the wall left behind, one was no longer on Baron Glô von Warteck's land, but in the territory of the Grand Duchy of Baden, which had been transformed since 1919 or 1920, at least in appearance, into something more-or-less democratic and republican. Then, any discharge of firearms would certainly attract policemen, forest rangers and other official guardians of Baden. On the other hand, it was necessary not to put overmuch trust in that, since it was incontestable that Baron Glô von Warteck, mysterious as his castle was, was not a man to whom the Baden authorities paid particularly close attention. And strangers wandering in the Black Forest often suffered accidents–the sort of accident that might involve a gunshot or a fall into a deep precipice. As for a fight, or a capture with a view to sequestration–and abduction–well, the policemen and forest rangers of Baden, if by chance they found themselves in proximity to such an occurrence, might well have the elementary prudence to see nothing. What good does it do, after all, to get mixed up in other people's business, when one does not have specific orders in one's pocket, with a duly signed arrest warrant?

Such were the reflections made by Leo Saint-Clair as he urged his horse on–for he had seen the wall and the notices two days earlier. Instead of repeating what he had said earlier about their being saved because they would not be pursued in large numbers, therefore, he concluded: *If anyone catches us, we must kill them! We can only save ourselves by stopping the pursuit–by bringing down the pursuers.*

Although he and his companions had seen the six horsemen who had come out of the stables galloping across the valley, they had not seen the three Zuchts.

All the reflections that Saint-Clair was able to make regarding these contingencies did not, of course, prevent him from simultaneously devoting the greater part of his mind, and all of his heart, to his primary preoccupation: Laure's condition. That condition remained unmodified. Saint-Clair held the young woman in front of him, seated sideways, with her side leaning against his breast. Her head was tilted back in his folded left arm, slightly tilted to one side

157

so that he could see her dear face–the face of a dead woman, unarguably! No breath passed between the teeth and the slightly-parted lips. No respiration, however imperceptible, stirred her throat or her bosom. All her limbs were quite inert. Even so...

Yes, the lover, attentive to all these indicators, said to himself, *Even so! That suppleness in her joints, that warmth in her flesh... this is no dead woman! If she no longer lives, what killed her? The blood trickling over her shoulder and left side was nothing: a rip in the ear-lobe, a platinum earring having been torn away in the course of the struggle in which the dressing-gown was reduced to tatters. The cut in her ear has already closed, the blood having clotted. Strangled? No–her neck is unblemished, without he slightest bruise. What then? Is she dead or alive? She certainly isn't breathing–but cases of catalepsy have been observed in which respiration seemed to have stopped...*

"Halt!" cried a muffled voice. It was Wolf, who was following the example set by Corsat in exercising the initiative he had received an hour before. As Saint-Clair, Corsat and Pilou came abreast of him, he pointed to a white rock that loomed up to the left 300 meters away. "There's a short cut that leads straight to the pass. It turns off on this side of that white rock, I've just seen three men go up it, with rifles slung over their shoulders. They'll get there before us and set an ambush."

"And behind us," Pilou said, "the six horsemen are gaining on us. Listen."

They listened. Twenty-four iron horseshoes were striking the rocky path, displacing stones whose consequent rolling could easily be distinguished.

The Nyctalope did not hesitate. "We're in enemy territory," he said, coldly, "fully engaged in hostilities in a war without mercy. I presume they'll only shoot at our horses, and will make any sacrifice to take us alive, for they want us to suffer more than death. We must defend ourselves and save ourselves. The life and liberty of millions of people depends on our liberty. It's necessary that you keep that constantly in mind. We must be merciless. Corsat, Pilou, dismount. Hide here, to the right and to the left, and shoot down the six men who are pursuing us. Because the guns make no sound, you should each be able to kill two before being spotted, and you'll have to strike the last two down quickly, in case they're able to immobilize you in some unforeseen manner. We must expect them to use gas, or something else. I'm astonished that they haven't fired shells containing asphyxiating gas at us. All that will doubtless be explained, and other things besides..." [25]

He paused, listened, and murmured, after having satisfied himself; "We have the time." He went on: "I'll lead both your horses. As the path leads through the woods now, they won't see that two of our horses are riderless. As soon as the job's done, catch me up quickly–we'll slow down to a walk in the wood."

While listening, Corsat and Pilou had dismounted and tied the silent and passive red-haired man securely to one of the horses. He seemed utterly dazed, with the eyes of an idiot and slack features.

"Let's go!" said Saint-Clair.

While Corsat and Pilou, Brownings in hand, hid themselves behind rocks and bushes to the right and left of the path, Wolf urged his mount forward. Saint-Clair followed, still holding Laurence tightly, leading the other two horses by the bridle.

Ten minutes later, during which he had heard three cries and the sound of something heavy rolling downslope with the pebbles, Saint-Clair was rejoined by the Provençal and the Burgundian. "It's done," said Pilou, mounting his animal. "The six men were unarmed, although each had a lasso."

"Good," said Saint-Clair.

Corsat, who said nothing, and did not want to untie or displace the red-haired man, simply took the bridle from his employer's hand and walked beside the horse,

Shortly afterwards, they arrived at the extremity of the wood. The road zigzagged over the bare mountain, which was crowned by an irregular wall, between two crags separated by a large breach: the pass through which it was necessary to go, close to which the three riflemen must be lying in ambush.

They stopped. They could not see anything moving. in the light of the sun–which was still high in the sky–pebbles shone here and there. The scene was calm, serene and bright, and the silence as now absolute.

"I see their strategy," Saint-Clair said, in a low voice, as if talking to himself. "The six horsemen would have captured us with their lassos when the three awaiting us up there shot our horses, or at least obliged us to rein them in. A stupid strategy–it's not Lucifer who's in command of Schwarzrock at present. He can't have made a full recovery if, as I dread, he still lives. I ought to have put a bullet in his head and another in his heart–but I was only thinking of Laure! Then again, to kill an unconscious man, even when he's an enemy of that magnitude... no!"

He fell silent, looked at Laurence, stifled a sob and turned towards the Burgundian. "Corsat, I'm entrusting this woman to you. You must return her to me or be dead. Wolf, stand guard over the red-haired man and our horses. Pilou, dismount and come with me. Corsat, if you hear a shot without it being immediately followed by a whistle-blast, I'll be dead. In that case, wait for Pilou for a quarter of an hour, then flee. And–listen to this, Corsat... If you see that this woman is about to be recaptured by the men of Schwarzrock, my friend, plant your dagger in her heart. Perhaps she's dead already, but if she's alive, I don't want her to wake up in front of that monster. If she knew what was going on and were able to speak, she'd beg you to kill her. So kill her!"

Corsat was very pale. He received the beautiful inanimate body in his arms, wrapped in its white mantle. "I'll kill her, boss!" he said, hoarsely.

"Good. Thank you, on her behalf and mine. Come on, Pilou!"

Saint-Clair had considered the possibility that the three men Wolf had mentioned might also be equipped with lassos. To risk approaching the pass without first rendering the three men harmless would, therefore, be foolish. They might also be first-rate marksmen, capable of bringing down Saint-Clair's, Corsat's and Pilou's mounts with three simultaneous shots. While a fourth shot was fired at Wolf's head or heart, two lassos might immobilize Saint-Clair and Corsat. Thanks to the disposition of the rocks to either side of the path, the three assailants would be able to act virtually without being seen by their victims.

Even given all that, they might still have been able to triumph, but to risk a fight in such circumstances would be deplorable. It was much better to take the enemy by surprise, if possible, and to risk being wounded or killed in doing so—for it might well be the case that if they could not take them captive, the men of Schwarzrock would be licensed to kill them, so long as no stray bullet could strike the woman...

This was why Saint-Clair and Pilou, creeping through the bracken at the edge of the wood, made rapid progress in the direction of the narrow path on which Wolf had seen the three men. It could not be very far away, since it led to the pass.

"Without any doubt," Saint-Clair said, "it must wind through the chaos of that landslide of black rocks over there. Anyone could climb up there without being seen. While the path zigzags through the rocks, it will serve us as well as it served them."

"We'll fall upon them before they see us, boss!" Pilou murmured.

"I hope so. Faster!"

The Nyctalope was not mistaken. A visible path meandered through the chaos of black rocks.

"Excuse me, boss!" Slithering like a snake, Pilou went on ahead before Saint-Clair could object—and in the absence of a formal order, the positions of the two men could not be reversed, for the path was too narrow for Saint-Clair to overtake Pilou unless Pilou stopped and moved aside into some cranny. Saint-Clair did not give any order. He sometimes rewarded the devotion of his men by permitting them to look out for him, and that was the reward they most desired. One can imagine the prudence with which they advanced, albeit with all possible haste.

The tall rocks looming over the path projected a continuous shadow through which they slid, sometimes hugging the left-hand side of the natural wall and sometimes the right. Their dark leotards rendered them nearly invisible. They paused for a few seconds at each bend in the path—for just enough time for Pilou to stick out his head and see what lay ahead. Then, they set off again, lithe and alert, their Brownings in their hands.

Suddenly, at one such bend, Pilou whispered: "Wait, boss!"

"Are they there?"

"Yes."

"Have they stopped?"

"Yes."

"Why?"

Footsteps sounded, though, and Pilou raised his hand in warning. After a minute, the footsteps faded away. "Two have gone," Pilou whispered. "One's still there."

"In ambush?"

"Yes."

"The place must overlook the other path. Pilou!"

"Boss?"

"Is he positioned in such a way that we can attack him and gag him without his having the time to...?"

"Yes. He's kneeling down, with his back to us. He's concentrating on the path."

"His rifle?"

"Propped up against the rock beside him."

"How far away is he?"

"Twenty meters. Along the path to the right-hand side, though, there's a ribbon of rock, bare and smooth, on which our footsteps won't make any noise."

"I want to avoid killing him, since it's possible," Saint-Clair said. "We won't shoot him if he doesn't hear or see us. The gag?"

"I have it in my hand–a headscarf."

"Good! I've got the cord. Let's go–but keep your hand on the butt of your Browning, half-holstered. If we have to shoot, the weapons can be drawn and cocked in less than a second. If we can get close enough to him to jump him, the weapons will fall into their holsters. Ready?"

"I am."

"Go!"

"Right!"

Pilou rounded the rocky outcrop from whose shelter he had made his observations, without the risk of been seen, thanks to indentations that masked everything while permitting the passage of rays of light. Saint-Clair followed him immediately. Their thick rubber soles made no noise. There were no stones on the rocky ribbon that formed a sort of irregular sidewalk which would have rolled away if accidentally kicked, because the ribbon was steeply inclined towards the middle of the path. The two men sometimes had to put their shoulders to the rock and brace themselves in order not to slip; fortunately, the rock was dry.

Saint-Clair and Pilou gazed steadfastly at the broad back, thick neck and Tyrolean hat of the kneeling man, who was intently watching a patch of ground that Pilou and Saint-Clair could not see.

161

Suddenly, the man sat back on his heels, while maintaining his kneeling position, and his right hand reached out to his rifle–but he never completed the gesture. Pouncing like a cat, Pilou landed on his back and wrapped his large scarf twice around the man's head, covering his mouth. The man fell backwards, his arms raised–but two hands seized his wrists and rapidly bound them together.

The man found himself laid flat on his back, his feet tied together as quickly as his hands. His furious eyes were wide open.

Saint-Clair leaned over him. "No harm will come to you, friend," he whispered, in German, "if you stay still. My companion is tightening your bonds so that you can't get free. I'm going to use the muzzle of my Browning to stuff the scarf further into your mouth, and my comrade will attach a second gag made out of your own scarf. That way, it will take a long time for you to free yourself from the gag, even if you rub your neck against the rock."

"He'll get there in the end, though," Pilou said.

"Of course–but we'll be far away by then. He won't be able to give chase, because it will take him even longer to work through the cords tying his arms and legs. I'll disarm him completely: his ammunition belt–empty the cartridges from his rifle, Pilou–his hunting-knife... perfect! I saw a pool of water in the middle of the path, ten paces..."

"I know where it is, boss–I understand!".

Pilou went to the pool, which was quite deep, and gently lowered into it the ammunition-belt, the unloaded rifle and the eight cartridges removed from its magazine. He slid the hunting-knife into a nearby fissure, in which it disappeared entirely.

"That's one!" said Saint-Clair, quite satisfied by not being obliged to kill the man, and hoping to do the same with the others.

"Shall we go?" asked Pilou.

"Yes."

They went on, leaving the recumbent man where he was. Pilou was now in the lead. After five or six minutes, they were able to ascertain that they were only 100 meters from the pass, as a bird flies. They redoubled their concentration, because the other two ambushers could not be far away.

Almost immediately, they stopped, holding their breath. A man was standing three paces in front of them, rifle in hand, with the butt under his arm. His back was turned to them, but he undoubtedly had the sensation of being watched, for he made a movement of his head which displayed three-quarters of his face.

"Don't move! Silence!" growled Saint-Clair, in a restrained voice. His Browning was aimed in a threatening manner. Immediately, still speaking in German, he added: "Pilou–fire at the rock to demonstrate that our weapons make no noise."

The Provençal fired. There was a dull impact as the bullet flattened, but no other sound.

The man was not stupid. He understood that if he opened his mouth, a bullet in the head would kill him instantly and cut off his cry before it could even emerge from his larynx. His sacrifice would be futile, for the deadly bullet would do its work without any detonation to testify that it had been done. As for firing his rifle, that was impossible–for the good reason that he no longer had it. As prompt as his master, Pilou had seized the butt of the rifle and snatched it away, during an instant of hesitation immediately after he had received the order to fire at the rock. He had kept the rifle in his left hand while the right drew the Browning from its holster and fired; it was all done with Pilou's incomparable rapidity and sureness of movement.

"Surrender or die–choose!" Saint-Clair went on. "Reply quietly."

"I surrender," the man said, sheepishly.

"Bind and gag him, Pilou. He has a scarf. He must also have a handkerchief–use his bootlaces." Then, addressing his captive, he continued, as calmly as if he had been engaged in the most ordinary conversation: "It must have been your brother that we met back there. He resembles you strongly."

"Yes, he's my brother," the man replied, as Pilou tied him up before gagging him.

"I would have been able to kill him even more easily, for we seized him before he saw us–but I'm content to render him incapable of crying out or getting to his feet for some time. If you don't want the third man to lose his life, tell me where he is and how I can best take him by surprise. The first two coups have succeeded, by virtue of good luck–I'm afraid that the third..."

The man responded straightforwardly, his gaze calm and direct. "The other man is my father, Adalbert Zucht. I'm Franz, the younger son; the one over there is the elder, Berthold. In the absence of any direct order from our father against you–whom I shall recognize if ever I see you again–you may count on the fact that Berthold and Franz Zucht will not forget that you spared our lives. We are not Prussian brutes, but honest and loyal mountain men of Baden. Don't kill my father! He's up there–look! That white stone hides him from us as it hides us from him. He's covering the pass. You can surprise him by continuing along this path, which turns sharply around the rock. He has no reason to expect an enemy from that side, so he won't be on his guard–but he has fine ears, and he's very quick. Don't kill him! He speaks French, as I and my brother do."

"We shan't kill him," Saint-Clair said, gravely, in French, "provided that he doesn't shoot at us. If he does, we'll be obliged to break his arm, at least, for if his first shot misses–as I'm almost sure it will–I can't permit him to fire a second. But we'll hurt him as little as we possibly can. You've spoken well, and I believe that your thoughts match your speech. I trust your word. Will you swear to me that, from this moment on, you'll be neutral? if so, you'll be untied and not gagged.

"I swear!" said Franz, raising his hand.

"Can you answer for your brother?"

"I'll answer for him."

"Good. Go set him free. Untie him, Pilou. Take back your rifle, Franz—but don't make any noise going down to your brother."

The Nyctalope could read the eyes of men. He knew that Franz Zucht would not play false, so he let him return to Berthold. With Pilou, he immediately began the ascent towards the white rock behind which Adalbert Zucht lay in ambush.

Like his sons, the father was watching the zigzag road, his mind concentrated on the pedestrians and riders who might arrive at the pass by that means, if Berthold and Franz or the six horsemen with lassos had not stopped the little troop already. If any one of the fugitives—man, woman or horse—escaped the lassos, Adalbert was ready to kill a quadruped or break the leg of a biped, for his sight was keen and his rifle-bullets always hit their intended mark.

Saint-Clair and Pilou no longer had to be wary of anyone but Adalbert, and it was not important for them to make no noise during and after the mountain man's capture.

"Slowly!" said Saint-Clair to Pilou. "We must get behind him. The white rock is set in such a way that we can go round it on either side. I'll go left, and arrive in Zucht's sights without appearing to see him. He'll shout "Hands up!", certain that I won't try to put up a fight, since he'll be pointing his rifle at me. Indeed, I shan't fight—but as I put up my hands and all his attention is fixed on me, you grab him from behind and immobilize his arms. It doesn't matter if he cries out."

"What if he has time to pull the trigger?" Pilou objected.

"Bah! I'll watch his fingers. Anyway, the jolt you give him will deflect his rifle and the bullet will go over my head. I'll be all right. Understood?"

"Understood, boss."

"Let's separate, then. You follow the path; I'll go that way, through the maze of rocks. I'll be upset, though, if on of us has to break the man's arm."

The ensuing scene was brief, and such that Zucht kept the secret of his humiliating stupor until his dying day.

After making a noise intentionally, Saint-Clair stood up, emerging from behind a large flat stone with his back turned to the old mountain man—who, ready to fire, immediately cried: "Hands up! Turn around!"

Manifesting fearful surprise, Saint-Clair obeyed. Contentedly, without any suspicion, Zucht lifted up his rifle. At the same instant, Pilou leapt on him from behind and immobilized his arms, using is thighs to press them against his sides. With a gesture as skillful as it was unexpected, Pilou snatched the rifle away with his right hand, while putting his left over Zucht's eyes, completely blocking his sight.

"Franz! Berthold!" Zucht cried. "Help! Help!"

Saint-Clair spoke briefly, with goodwill. Father Zucht calmed down. The sons arrived. Everything was swiftly explained, after Berthold had prudently ascertained that the white rock screened them completely from any watchers in the castle–where it was probable that powerful binoculars were trained on the pass, with attentive eyes behind them.

The result of the brief conference was that the three Zuchts were left at the places along the path where they had been surprised and vanquished, duly bound and gagged, disarmed and slightly roughed-up.

"Don't worry about us," Franz said. "Within an hour, someone will come from the castle to find out what became the six riders, their horses and us. We'll be untied before we get hungry or thirsty. The six dead men will say nothing. Berthold and I will tell that part of the truth which would have been the whole truth if we hadn't talked. As for father, his humiliation and surprise are too sincere for his to have any need to talk or dissemble. He'll keep quiet. We'll play our parts–our lives are worth a few petty lies, although Our Lord the Baron isn't to be trifled with..."

"Why are you submissive to that man?" Saint-Clair asked. "Couldn't you live somewhere else–and even here, aren't there laws of the land that..."

"Let's not speak of that, Monsieur!" said Berthold, frowning. "Bind and gag my father here, then my brother, over there, then me, further away–and go! If I might be permitted to offer you some advice, never come back. Those who escape Our Lord the Baron once never escape him a second time."

Nothing more was said.

Saint-Clair stayed behind the white rock, where he tied up and gagged poor Adalbert Zucht–who had aged a great deal in those few minutes. Meanwhile, Pilou went with Berthold and Franz, whom he accommodated according to their desire. Then the Provençal ran to the place where Corsat and Wolf were waiting, with Laure–still unconscious–and the prostrate red-haired man.

A quarter of an hour later, Saint-Clair having picked up Laurence again, the little cavalcade went through the pass without any difficulty. They went down the mountain as quickly as possible. At a carefully-chosen spot in the forest, as they had arranged several days earlier, Louis Nortmund met them with a large limousine.

"Finally!" the Alsatian cried. "I was beginning to fear that you had suffered some misfortune..." He stopped immediately when he saw the young woman held in Saint-Clair's arms. He thought she was dead. Very pale, he set about unwrapping her.

IX. Dead or Alive?

The horses were abandoned. Pilou took the wheel, with Wolf and Corsat squeezed into the front seat beside him. Saint-Clair and Louis Nortmund installed Laurence Païli as comfortably as possible in the back of the vehicle, then sat down facing her, on the tip-up seats attached to the partition. They placed the red-haired man, still silent and stupefied, between them.

For the benefit of the impatient Nortmund, Saint-Clair gave a quick summary of events. Then, leaving the industrialist to his utter amazement, he devoted himself to planning ahead while the car headed at top speed for Vieux-Brisach, where they could pass into Alsace without hindrance because Monsieur Nortmund knew the customs officers and forest rangers. In any case, Saint-Clair's suitcase–which was in the car–contained official papers adequate to overcome any difficulty that might present itself.

"First, Laure!" Saint-Clair concluded. "It's necessary to bring her out of this cataleptic state–for she's alive! I cannot and will not accept that she's not alive!" He looked at the young woman's inanimate face for a long time with an expression of infinite love and infinite pity. "After that, I'll go to see Professor Lourmel and tell him everything I've observed. He'll have news of Irène and little Henri, whom Mathias Narbonne will have to join on the *Lampas* in New York. Then I'll return to my war against Lucifer. It won't be long! It's him or me; one or other of us must die, before the survivor's eyes, by June 10–the date when Lucifer has sworn to unleash his wrath. Twenty-four days at the latest, since it's now May 17."

While the limousine sped on through the night, the Nyctalope continued thinking hard, watching Laurence Païli all the while, continually asking himself, in the depth of his being: "Is she dead? Is she alive?"

Thanks to Louis Nortmund, who had only to show himself at the frontier to be waved through without difficulty, they crossed the Rhine at the new bridge at Vieux-Brisach. They turned into Neuf-Brisach and went through Wolfgantzen, Andelsheim and Horburg to Colmar, where they went into *The Willows* at daybreak.

The Nortmunds got busy. A new guest-room was opened, aired and warmed up. Blanche Nortmund and her maidservants laid Laurence Païli on a low bed, after undressing her, massaging her, and dressing her again in a delicate nightgown. The vaporous whiteness of the nightgown was not as white as her face, which was that of a living corpse, although her body was scarcely chilled and her flesh was youthful, supple and solid.

In Colmar, there was an old physician from Strasbourg named Jacob Goulden, retired but highly reputed, very knowledgeable and wise: the medical oracle of Alsace. Summoned by Louis Nortmund, Doctor Goulden was welcomed by Saint-Clair, who showed him Laurence Païli, saying: "Can she be revived, doctor?"

Goulden remained alone with Madame Blanche by the motionless body. An hour later–60 minutes that Leo Saint-Clair spent wandering in the garden, experiencing 60 years of anguish–Goulden summoned the Nyctalope and the Nortmunds. "She's alive," he said. "Yes, she's alive. I don't know any more. Her exact state is neither catalepsy, nor a hypnotic trance, nor a faint, nor ordinary sleep. I've tried every known means of exciting her sensibility. Useless! Nothing! It's an unprecedented case, at least for me. I've never seen, nor read, nor heard of anything like it. Her body's alive, unquestionably–it's scarcely breathing, but it is breathing. Nourishment is impossible–I've tried, but nothing passes... so I don't know..."

"That's enough about the present," Saint-Clair said, calmly. "Tomorrow, and the day after...?"

"In my opinion," the doctor said, modestly, "she'll die slowly for lack of food. She'll fade away. But as her vital functions are reduced to an infinitesimal minimum, her present state might last for weeks without any other modification than a progressive loss of weight. The body will devour everything within that can nourish it–then, when there's nothing left by bones, shriveled muscles, drained nerves and atrophied organs, the body will die."

"And you don't see any possibility of an awakening?" asked Saint-Clair, as calmly as before.

Doctor Goulden made a gesture expressing helpless ignorance. "Anything is possible in nature," he said, softly. "We only know what we have so far been permitted to discover–which is very little–and science itself is clouded by a thousand uncertainties.

"So what do you advise, doctor?"

"That two intelligent experienced and conscientious nurses should take turns of duty by day and night in the young woman's room, observing intently. At the slightest sign of change in her present state, call a physician–always the same physician, preferably a neurologist. While waiting, make every attempt to stimulate life..."

"Very well," said Saint-Clair. "You undoubtedly know Professor Onésime Lourmel, doctor?"

"Certainly! I've met him twice at his surgery in Paris, and have had the honor of receiving him in my home while he was passing through Strasbourg five years ago."

"He's the one who will care for the patient."

"In that case," the physician concluded, nodding his head, "if a strangely sleeping body of this sort has one chance in a thousand of returning to life, this young woman's eyes will reopen! Professor Lourmel can work miracles."

Eight hours later, Leo Saint-Clair was in Paris, having driven the Nortmunds' large limousine from *The Willows* to the little house in the Rue Nansouty with the Nortmunds' chauffeur beside him.

In the rear section of the vehicle–to whose wheels new tires had been fitted before departure–were Louis Nortmund and his wife Blanche, watching over Laurence Païli, who was laid out on the soft cushions of the back seat. Following behind, in the Nyctalope's roadster, were Corsat, Pilou and Wolf with the red-haired Hunter, who was still befuddled. They drove like the wind.

Meanwhile, Charles Nortmund and Doctor Goulden telephoned from Colmar to put Professor Lourmel in the picture–so effectively that when Saint-Clair carried Laurence's inert body into the guestroom of the house in Rue Nansouty, he found Professor Lourmel, flanked by two nurses, waiting by a made-up bed.

"Doctor Goulden has given me the details of the case," the professor said, immediately. "Lay the child down there; these ladies will look after her. I'll examine her, in case I can offer a fuller diagnosis than my colleague. Go take a warm bath to calm your nerves, my dear friend–you need it. Then eat, drink and sleep. I don't want to see you again until you've recovered your usual balance. I won't leave your Laurence in the meantime, I promise you. Then I'll talk to you about her–and other people too. You can't do any more now. Go! That's an order! Bath, table, bed. Get out!"

Held upright by the prodigious empire of his will-power over his muscles, although his nerves and entire body were exhausted. Leo Saint-Clair replied: "You'll understand Laure's case better after I've told you..."

"No! No, by thunder! No!" cried the professor. "I don't want to hear you or see you until you've eaten, drunk and slept. Do you want to collapse on the spot, like a puppet with its string cut off? Tell me afterwards–and I will, indeed, understand Laurence's case better. I'm talking too much! Get out!"

He shoved Saint-Clair out of he room, slammed the door and turned the key in the lock, rudely.

Aided by Choiffour, Sidonie had prepared everything: the bath, the table, the bed. As he got undressed in the bathroom, Saint-Clair asked after Corsat, Pilou, Wolf, their captive, Madame Blanche and Louis Nortmund.

"Corsat, Pilou and Wolf are splashing about in tubs in the laundry," Choiffour replied. "Monsieur and Madame Nortmund have gone to the hotel with their chauffeur; they told me to tell Monsieur that they will stay there for a week, after which they'll return to Alsace. As for the red-haired man, Corsat and Pilou have kept him with them, and he's doing everything they say. Monsieur will permit me to say that the man is very obedient, and that it's very funny to see him imitating Corsat and Pilou..."

Rinsed, fervently massaged, rubbed with alcohol and enveloped in a thick dressing-gown, Saint-Clair ate and drank. Then he listened at the guestroom door, remaining there for five minutes. He heard absolutely nothing, and assumed that Lourmel and the two nurses were observing Laure. As he was tottering with drowsiness and fatigue, he resisted no longer and went to bed, aided by Choiffour.

"Can he wake her up?" he mumbled, already semi-conscious. "Can he prevent her from dying? How shall I find her? Dead? Oh, no! Living?" Almost as soon as he lay down, though, he fell asleep, no longer capable of movement or thought.

It was May 17. There was a chronometer on the mantelpiece of the large study-bedroom where Leo Saint-Clair was lying, minutely regulated according to the conventions established by all the astronomers in the world: the personal chronometer of the director of the Paris Observatory, who had made a gift of it one day to the explorer Leo Saint-Clair. The chronometer's movement persisted for 365 days without rewinding; on February 29 in leap years, the key was given a quarter turn to rest it just enough to accommodate the extra 24 hours. It was, in brief, the most precise chronometer in the world. As the Nyctalope fell asleep, at the very moment when his will-power and conscious life were temporarily annihilated, while time itself moved on incessantly, it indicated 16 hours 12 minutes and 18 seconds.

Part Four: Drama in the Bermudas

I. Irène Appears and Disappears

Nine hundred kilometers east of South Carolina in the Unites States of America, between 31 degrees 53 minutes and 32 degrees 20 minutes north latitude and 64 degrees 20 minutes and 64 degrees 45 minutes west longitude, isolated but not lost in the Atlantic Ocean, is an archipelago that few Europeans know, save for a few hundred Englishmen. It is the archipelago of the Bermudas. It is composed of 300 islands and islets, populated by 12,000 inhabitants, of whom 4,000 are white. Surrounded by reefs, which extend far out to sea, many of which are only exposed at low tide, the Bermudas are separated from one another by narrow channels.

Any manual of geography will inform you that the principal island is only 30 kilometers long and one or two kilometers wide, that it is named Bermuda, and that its town, Hamilton, is the capital of the archipelago. If your curiosity is sufficiently engaged to make you read further, you will also know that the climate of the Bermudas is warm and salubrious; that the soil is very fertile wherever the rock is covered by earth; that coffee, cotton, sugar-cane and other excellent and useful things are cultivated there; that whales were once hunted in the vicinity; and, finally, that although the islands were discovered in 1522 by the Spaniard Bermudez, they remained unoccupied until the Englishman Somers was shipwrecked there in 1609–and what would you expect that Englishman to do but found a colony? Which he did.[26]

Other Englishmen came, who were not shipwrecked, but who continued the colonization ardently. First of all, naturally, they made the Bermudas into a strong military position, then a penitentiary and place of forced labor, and finally an active center of commerce with the Antilles and North America. Since then, the Bermudas have been one of the most prosperous of England's colonies. His Britannic Majesty's Governor resides in his capital, Hamilton. There, he can find out everything, without delay, about whatever happens under his government, thanks to wireless telegraphy, recently established in the more populous islands, with a central post office under the roof of the government in Hamilton.

There was, however, one rather remarkable thing that Sir Ernest Bernd, Governor of the Bermudas, did not know, and which the wireless telegraph could not tell him, but which might one day cost him dear. This was that his forebear Somers had not been the only man, nor he first, to "colonize" the Bermudas. A strange family cast away there had established itself, lived as best it could, struggled, prospered and labored in secret. And now...

It is a truly extraordinary story, an adventure rare in the chronicles of humankind, which is worth telling, succinctly, in some detail.

On February 16, 1608, in good weather and at low tide, two hours before sunset, a Dutch ship dropped anchor a few cables south of the tip of the southernmost of the Bermudan reefs. It lowered a launch propelled by six oarsmen.

Mooring on the first visible reef, the launch disembarked a man, a woman, two boys aged six and eight, a five-year-old girl, a bundle of clothes and underwear, a box of biscuits, one keg of wine and three of water, one bundle of fishing-rods and one of various utensils, a barrel of gunpowder, two muskets, a bullet-mould, lead ingots and various trunks of personal effects. Having done that, the officer took the rudder of his launch, which was already heading away from the reef towards the ship, doffed his hat to the group abandoned on the reef and pronounced gravely, in German: "May God protect you, Baron Glô von Warteck, your wife, your sons and your ward—and may Satan, who has lost you, flee before the radiance of that divine protection!"

It was a beautiful speech—but the echoes it might have awakened in the soul of Baron Glô von Warteck did not prevent him from perceiving almost immediately that, as the tide rose, the reef would be almost entirely covered by the waves within the hour. Only a central platform about a dozen meters square—which bore a meager vegetation, half-terrestrial and half-marine, presumably being inundated only by the most powerful waves of major storms—would remain uncovered at high tide.

"Diana!" the Baron said, rudely. "We have scarcely an hour to get ourselves and our possessions to shelter. Night's falling and the sea's climbing. Hurry!"

The Baron and his wife were young and sturdy; the two sons, Rupert and Norbert, already had muscles and character; except for little Grisyl,[27] who was taken to the platform first, they all toiled on the reef for three quarters of an hour. When the tide arrived at its normal height for the season, the waves were breaking two meters below the narrow space where, sheltered by the skillfully piled-up bales, boxes, barrels and trunks, the marooned man, woman and three children huddled together all night.

Why had they been abandoned? Because, in Germany, Baron Glô von Warteck and his wife, having acquired an evil reputation as sorcerers, necromancers, instruments of the Devil and regular attendees of the Sabbath, had been sentenced to deportation to the Americas—and the secret sentence confided to the captain of the ship on which they were embarked was to disembark them "with the means to work and to defend their lives for at least a month on the first desert island that God and his winds might discover."

At low tide, after a night when he had scarcely slept, Baron Glô von Warteck—the first of that name—set about examining his domain: a frightful rock between 100 and a 150 meters long and wide, of which a mere dozen square

171

meters was above water at high tide. It was impossible to live there. Other reefs and islets were visible to the north, and islands with vegetation–life!

"With the boxes, the trunks and the barrels–which we'll empty right away–and everything that floats," the Baron said, "we'll make a raft. We'll load it with our possessions and ourselves. Via the reefs and the islets, we'll reach one of those islands by nightfall. I'll make oars with two long spars from one of the boxes. To work!"

Everyone was about to obey him when he suddenly cried: "Hey! What's that I hear?"

It seemed to him that the rock beneath his feet sounded hollow. He rapped forcefully with his foot: there was a dull resonance, which everyone could hear. What terrible thought then surged into the mind of Baron Glô von Warteck?

The German folded his arms. Towards the distant archipelago of the Bermudas–inhabited, no doubt, by tranquil indigenes–he turned a face that was formidable, by virtue of the implacably ferocious expression of his eyes and mouth. Then he turned his face eastwards, seemingly menacing the people of Europe–the persecutors of the Warteck family–from afar, across the ocean. A curse sprang to his lips. "Ah, if Satan is here," growled the Baron, "may Satan come to my aid! For I have an idea!"

Then he tapped his foot again, imperiously.

"Wife," he said, "there's a hollow here–a hole, an excavation or perhaps a cave. Perhaps this reef, this rock, is nothing other than the peak of a submarine mountain, and is concealing our future kingdom below sea-level. If my intelligence does not deceive me, it's there"–he tapped his foot again–"that my dynasty will reign, waging war against all men, from century to century, until our great-great-grandchildren will avenge us by reducing all humankind to slavery. The pick! The pick!"

He rapidly fitted a handle to the heavy and pointed cast-iron pick-axe that was among the tools abandoned along with him by courtesy of the ironic mercy of his judges. Striking here and there, sounding with small and prudent blows, he searched for the point at which the cavity reached, so to speak, the angle of its vault. He soon found it.

"Good!" he said. "I can break into the vault here, without going too deep."

The pick-axe scratched the rock, and then bit into it.

Silently watched by his wife, Diana, who was carrying Grisyl in her arms, and by the interested Rupert and Norbert, Glô von Warteck labored for a hour without pause or rest, apparently unhurriedly and without getting tired. Then, abruptly, the pick slid into a hole–the vault had been breached.

It was the work of a few minutes to enlarge the hole, round it off, and give it sufficient diameter for Rupert to pass through it. One of the trunks was wrapped around several times by a strong braided leather cord. The Baron quickly untied it, and looped one end around Rupert's torso, under the armpits. He knotted it carefully between the shoulders.

"My son," he said, "enough daylight should enter the hole by this orifice for you to estimate its approximate dimensions and its principal dispositions. Observe everything at your leisure, and shout for me to pull you up again. Then tell me exactly what you've seen."

Rupert was only eight, but he was strong, intelligent and earnest. He was also taciturn, speaking rarely and saying only what was necessary. He did not reply to his father. Gravely, after an adoring glance at his mother–who was smiling, but pale–he disappeared into the cavity.

Glô gradually let out the cord that slowed down the child's slide. Then he held it taut, as the child weighed upon it. About seven meters of cord was extended. Suddenly, it slackened.

"Rupert's found a foothold," he said.

A voice came up from below, clearly: "Hey! I'm untying the cord. I can walk."

They waited for a full half-hour, not without a certain anxiety. Finally, the cord moved slightly, and Rupert's voice was heard again: "Hoist me up again, father, please!"

He reappeared. His expression was still grave but his eyes were shining contentedly. "Father," he said, "first there's a small oval space, from which I passed into a hole, just large enough for me to fit into it but longer than my body, through a thick vault. I was then in a larger space that was almost round, 40 paces across, with a flat floor and inwardly curving walls–all quite dry, without a trace of damp. It was there that I untied the cord. Then, on this side"– Rupert pointed eastwards–"a narrow and high crack leads, after ten or 15 sloping paces, to another cavity. I was able to go into it because my eyes had adjusted to the darkness–the daylight scarcely reached it.

"I remembered that I had some of those tiny yellow-headed candles in my pocket, which light up when you strike them against a stone. I lit them, one after another. I saw that the third cave was a little less spacious than the second. It was square in shape, and one of its faces had six alcove-like openings of various depths. One of them had a hole that went almost straight down–I didn't risk trying to go down that one! Finally, I noticed that the side-walls of the alcoves were crumbling slightly, and that the dust, when I put a little on my tongue, tasted like iron. That's all I know, father."

Glô von Warteck shivered and his hard grey eyes sparkled with joy. "Diana," he said, "in there is where we'll live. I'll make panels to block the tunnels leading to the oval space and the large round one, and I'll blow up the first vault, on which we're standing, so that the entire reef will be flooded even at low tide. I have a plan!"

He seemed to grow taller as he stood there. He brandished his fist towards the east–towards Europe, the civilized world that had cursed his wife and his children and rejected him from its bosom. "Damn you, mankind!" he howled.

All that day the Wartecks toiled, taking everything they possessed down into the round cave and arranging it there.

"The ocean will be relatively calm until the new moon," Glô said. "We have time before the equinoctial high tides."

They did not lose a minute, only interrupting their labor to eat and to sleep, and only to the extent that was indispensable. Shrewd and skillful, swimming like a dolphin and gliding between the rocks like an eel, little Norbert spent all day fishing and gathering crabs and mollusks. His father accompanied him sometimes to collect certain marine plants: edible seaweeds that made excellent vegetables. Sometimes, at low tide, Rupert hunted among the rocks, armed with a long cord with a lead ball on the end, and killed birds of various sorts which came to feed on the tiny creatures swarming in the weed.

The natives of the islands, in their dug-out canoes, occasionally strayed into the vicinity of the Hollow Rock, as the Germans called their refuge. Then Norbert, Rupert and Glô hid in the clefts, watching the unsuspecting men with a sort of hateful avidity.

On the 17th day of their new life, the Wartecks–who were all fishing, hunting or gathering on the reef at low tide–saw a canoe arrive that was only occupied by two naked men, light-brown in color with oily hair, armed with harpoons. Glô quickly gave instructions to little Norbert; then the Baron, Diana and Rupert hid while the younger son and Grisyl–both naked–took up a position close to the orifice of the Hollow Rock and began whining and weeping loudly: poor little castaways deposited there alive by the caprice of the waves!

The two natives, at first astonished, then curious and finally moved to pity, came closer. They beached their canoe on the rock, disembarked and ran towards the desperate children–but they were attacked, knocked down, tied up and carried off. Loaded with fragments of stone and swathed in seaweed, the canoe was sunk in one of the little coves surrounding the reef, in such a fashion that it could easily be re-floated. "It will be useful later, before it rots away," Glô said.

The two captives were transformed into slaves, manual workers indispensable to their current enterprise and future plans.

The interior of the Hollow Rock was eventually fitted out to the Baron's satisfaction. The second orifice–the one that led from the oval cavity to the second, known as the Round Room–was furnished with three trapdoors, providing three hermetic seals. The uppermost one was made entirely of stone, with invisible hinges, incrusted in such a way that it appearance did not differ in any respect from the surrounding rock, and was not separated from it by any evident discontinuity.

Judiciously-placed holes were bored and stuffed with gunpowder; when the Baron lit the fuse that was connected to all these mines, there was a series of detonations and little volcanoes. Rocky fragments of various sizes rained down profusely. After that, large waves broke over the reef even at low tide, sweeping it from one end to the other, because the superior section forming a platform above the highest waves had been razed. Between waves, the part of the rock where the stone trapdoor was located was exposed to the air; one could open it and close it hurriedly without a single drop of water entering the gap. When the sea was calm, the place remained dry for hours, and one could leave the three panels open in order to go out and to ventilate the grottoes. At high tide, though, the ocean covered the reef completely, leaving no evidence of its existence save for a foaming whirlpool.[28]

Months, then years, passed.

In the Hollow Rock, the Accursed Ones and their slaves–the latter population soon being augmented and subjected to merciless selection–worked doggedly. Glô von Warteck invented, experimented, fabricated and constructed relentlessly.

The Englishman Somers was shipwrecked on one of the Bermudas. He founded a colony. Other Englishmen came, building up the colony.

In the Hollow Rock, Baron Glô von Warteck died at the end of his 69th year and Rupert succeeded him. Well in advance of the deaths of Diana and Glô, Norbert was married to Grisyl, who was a distant cousin and they had three sons, of which the eldest was named Glô–Glô von Warteck II.

The Hollow Rock had an amphibious grotto which could be filled with water and emptied at will, connected to the sea by a submarine canal that could be opened and closed. It was the ingenious Norbert who constructed the first diving-suit; his son, Glô II, subsequently devised the first submarine. English engineers were captured, for the Accursed Ones had need of skilled workmen. They bored deep into the submarine mountain, hollowing it out and exploiting its resources. The Wartecks found inexhaustible quantities of iron oxides there, whose combination made the rock magnetic and which produced iron of superior quality.

Much later, after Glô IV read a book stolen from a ship that the Accursed Ones had attacked and sank, they were able to obtain electricity by immersing metallic electrodes at various depths in the sea and connecting them in a certain way. By this means, Glô IV drew electric fluid, force and light from the ocean.

The passing years accumulated into a century, then two centuries. The year eventually came when a certain Sir Ernest Bernd was named Governor of the Bermudas by one of His Britannic Majesty's Ministers.

Bernd had no more idea than his predecessors how to account for the occasional disappearances of young men and women from among the people under his authority. Nor was he any more able to discover the cause of occasional perturbations affecting his telegraphic apparatus, and, in consequence, radiotelegraphic communication within the Bermudas. Nor had he any more idea how to explain the fiery radiance that lit up the sky from south to north on certain nights, whirling from one horizon to the other. The first phenomenon was explained by accidents at sea and sharks, the second by unknown magnetic phenomena, the third by meteors undetected by astronomers.[29]

Thus it was, the Bermudas having been unaware of the existence of the formidable and populous Hollow Rock for 313 years, that there came a day which the calendars of the Christian world called May 17, 1921. And on that day, there came a fugitive instant of time, which the astronomical chronometers indicated as being, in Paris, the eighth second of the 12th minute of the 16th hour–which corresponds, in the Bermudas, to the instant designated as 11:12:08 a.m. For Sir Ernest Bernd and his Bermudan administration, it was a little before a quarter past eleven in the morning.[30]

That day, as on every other day, a von Warteck descended from the original Baron–Grisyl VII, a relative of Glô XIII of Schwarzrock–was on watch in the "listening room" of the Hollow Rock. This listening room was a sort of round cell established in the dome of a submerged peak forming a sort of camel's hump with the Hollow Rock, which was about a hundred meters away. The apparatus within it infallibly registered everything that made a sound on or under the sea within a radius of several thousand miles. Error-free messages arrived there transmitted by a combination of aerial and underwater wireless telegraphy, and the reports, instructions and orders of the master of the Wartecks of the Hollow Rock, Rupert VI, were transmitted therefrom.[31]

That day, it was a Grisyl who was on watch, for in the secret realm of the Hollow Rock, the Warteck women had the same rank and duties as the Warteck men–duties appropriate to each one's physical and mental qualities. This Grisyl was a young woman, perhaps 20 years of age, with short-cropped white hair, white eyebrows and eyelashes, pink eyes and a candle-wax complexion, having the same discoloration as all the present Warteck race. Twelve generations of the same family does not live in artificial light–first of candles, then phosphorescent reflections, then electric lamps–without paying a price. By means of rational hygiene, however, these submarine troglodytes had retained solid bones, strong muscles and efficient nerves. Grisyl was a sturdily-built young woman with a good figure. She was dressed in a sort of grey linen pajama-suit, with its collar turned down over a grey flannel chemise, and leather sandals on her feet.

Seated on a straight-backed stool in front of a narrow table bearing two open ledgers and a fountain-pen, Grisyl was reading a monthly scientific journal published in Boston, Massachusetts, by the light of a single electric lamp set in the ceiling, when there was a clicking sound behind her, like that of castanets. The young woman raised her head, pushed the journal to a corner of the table, and looked at the chronometer fixed on the wall in front of her. At the same time, she reached out her right hand and pressed one of the 18 mother-of-pearl buttons arranged in three rows of six to one side of the table. Ten lamps lit up, vividly illuminating the listening room and all of its apparatus. The same hand then seized the fountain-pen, while the left drew the ledgers towards her, and Grisyl wrote on the first line of page 594:

17 - 05 – 21 – 11h 12' 8"

Then she looked at a black screen set above the chronometer, where white dots and dashes appeared, spaced according to the conventions of the Morse alphabet. While she watched, Grisyl translated them and wrote down the translation in German in the ledger:

Submarine Lampas, *left Le Havre May 7, destination New York. Not hurrying. Will probably go astray at sea, often submerged. Capture it. Irène and Henri aboard. Separate them from others, to be treated as prisoners, put to work. Glô XIII. Schwarzrock.*

The screen became black again. The castanets fell silent. The transmission had ended.

"Strange!" said Grisyl, in a low voice. Why has Our Lord informed us only today of a departure that took place on May 7–ten days later! The *Lampas* may already have reached New York. No matter! The message is no less urgent. Better wake up the *Grottenmeister*, who must still be asleep." Rupert VI, the master of the Hollow Rock, bore the title of *Grottenmeister*–Master of the Grottoes.

Grisyl was about to press one of the mother-of-pearl buttons when a small bell tinkled behind her. Leaving her finger suspended, she turned her head to the left and looked at a map of part of the Atlantic Ocean, on which the Bermudas were placed at the exact center. A luminous point appeared on the pale blue map.

"Ah!" said Grisyl. "Is that the *Lampas*?"

She looked attentively. The luminous point had appeared north of the Bermudas, at the intersection of the 41st parallel and the 55th meridian, close to the latitude of New York. The point was moving from east to west, and slightly to the south, as slowly as the minute-hand of an ordinary watch. Impassively, Grisyl lowered her suspended index finger and pressed the nacreous button. The funnel-shaped loudspeaker of a phonograph opened out in the partition wall to her left. She turned to the funnel and spoke into it, emphasizing the syllables: "*Grottenmeister?*"

A metallic voice immediately emerged from the loudspeaker, equally emphatic: "Yes, I'm listening."

"Message from the Lord of Schwarzrock," Grisyl said. She repeated it.

"Is that all?" said the metallic voice.

"No. The map indicates the submarine moving west-south-west at 41/55."

She pressed the same button again and the loudspeaker closed up again, becoming a sort of black lump on the partition wall.

Curiously following the progress of the minuscule point of light on the map, Grisyl waited. A quarter of an hour went by, then she suddenly murmured: "*Ach*! The *Uberalles* is setting out!"

Another luminous point lit up on the map, seemingly emerging from the cluster of raised black dots in the center which marked the Bermuda archipelago. This point, moving almost as rapidly as the second-hand of a watch, was heading north-north-west.

Grisyl picked up the fountain-pen and rapidly scribbled some figures on a corner of the journal. In solitude, one acquires the habit of expressing thoughts aloud, and she murmured: "If the suspect submarine doesn't change its direction or its speed, the *Uberalles* will catch up with it between 16:00 and 17:00 p.m. on the 61st meridian. If it is the *Lampas*, I'd certainly like to see this Irène!"

She leaned her elbows on the table, put her plump chin in her cupped hands, and sat quite still, her eyes fixed on the map–but her eyes soon misted over in reverie. Grisyl's face softened into a sort of femininity, which soon became so intense that the young Valkyrie of the Dark might have seemed almost charming.

It was, indeed, the *Lampas* that was making its way in the direction of New York, completely submerged, in the vicinity of the 41st north parallel.

There was as much difference between the *Lampas* and the submarines built before and during the Great War as between an exploratory sailing vessel of 50 years ago and the Prince of Monaco's yacht. The *Lampas*, a luxury vessel built with all the most up-to-date technology, judiciously installed with comfort in mind, was a sort of submarine yacht, on which 20 passengers could live very agreeably, while her crew did not have to suffer any of the many and various discomforts typical of naval submarines at sea. As for the danger, that had been reduced to a minimum by ingenious provisions to ensure individual and collective salvation even in the least favorable circumstances.

Having left Le Havre on May 7, the *Lampas* could have entered the port and harbor of New York six days later, had that been the wish of its commander, Lieutenant Raymond de Ciserat–but what need was there for haste? They had gone to sea with the aim of protecting Irène de Ciserat and little Henri Prillant from the spells cast by the enigmatic monster Lucifer, and they believed that that goal would be attained by reason of the antagonism of the contrasting environments surrounding the victims and the sorcerer.

Irène was installed in a cabin communicating on one side with her husband's cabin and on the other side with the cabin occupied by her chambermaid, Lili. Little Henri Prillant and his governess, Miss Ellen, occupied a double cabin. Louis Mattol, who was performing the duties of physician, had naturally taken the cabin reserved for the ship's doctor, next to the first mate's.

Restricted in size, but quite sufficient and very comfortably furnished, these habitations were located in the stern of the *Lampas*. In the submarine's mid-section were the commander's and first mate's stations, the latter also known as the "chart room," and various controls, with their associated machinery. In the bow were the crew's and other officers' stations, and a storage-hold, divided into compartments. Along the sides were the ballast-tanks, each one flanked by a diving chamber.

The crew was 26 strong, including the commander, the first mate, the doctor, the purser and four other officers: the second mate, the engineer, the stoker and the chief diver. Under normal circumstances, the *Lampas* would have carried a staff of scientists of various kinds, bent on discovery–but it was not a scientific expedition that the submarine was making on this occasion.

From the beginning, it seemed that Louis Mattol's theory of the antagonism of elements had been correct and justified. Ten days went by without Irène de Ciserat and little Henri suffering any mysterious and terrifying maltreatments. When the commander handed the watch over to his first mate–a young long-haul captain named Jacques Saincer–he, Mattol, Irène and Miss Ellen engaged in animated conversation, with increasing cheerfulness and hopefulness. They conjectured interminably about the significance and gravity of the news that they were bound to receive in New York, transmitted by uncle Lourmel, of Saint-Clair and the struggle to which the Nyctalope had committed himself. Since they had been able to check the sorcerer's occult power at the first attempt, thanks to Mattol's science and the existence of the *Lampas*, they did not doubt that the monster would be definitively vanquished soon enough.

On May 17, when the on-board chronometers indicated 16:28 p.m. in local time, Jacques Saincer was at the commander's post, with two submariners manning the apparatus. He suddenly released an exclamation of astonishment, while the two men were bewildered by the phenomenon that had provoked it.

This strange phenomenon was that all the needles of the instruments in the conning-tower, magnetic or not, flickered madly for about half a minute, and then turned in the same direction, fixed but quivering.

"What's this? What does it mean?" murmured Jacques Saincer, as bewildered as his men. Immediately thereafter, he leapt down from his seat, his eyes wide and his ears cocked, stammering: "What's happening? Cloadec! Kermor! Do you see? Do you understand?"

The men, pale and shivering, did not reply.

What was happening would, indeed, have confused any navigator. All the needles were in motion again, describing a quarter-circle within their frames. Those which served to indicate the direction of the submarine signified that its heading was now south-south-west, not west-south-west as it had previously been. At the same time, Saincer, Cloadec and Kermor experienced the very clear sensation that the *Lampas*, without reducing its speed, had made a sharp turn to port, changing direction by at least 86 degrees!

The first mate had not given any order to change direction, and Cloadec–whose hand was on the tiller–had done nothing to effect such a change. Even so, the incomprehensible change had taken place.

It did not take Saincer long to collect himself. "Stop!" he ordered.

Kermor transmitted the order to the engine-room. The propellers were disengaged, then re-engaged almost immediately, turning in a contrary direction. The *Lampas* should first have slowed down, then stopped–but the apparatus indicating her speed marked an increase in the rapidity of her submarine glide. The vessel was shaken with violent tremors, to the point at which the three men had to hold on tight in order not to fall over.

"What's happening? What can be happening?"

In a little room between the cabins and the chart room, Irène and Raymond were chatting, while Mattol read an article in a scientific periodical and Miss Ellen was playing dominoes with little Henri. They were all aware of the abrupt change of direction; as they stood up, the sudden lurch sent Henri tumbling to the floor, threw Irène on to a divan and Miss Ellen against the table.

"Hey!" said Mattol, clinging to his armchair. "What's going on?"

The movements stopped almost immediately; in the conning-tower, Saincer had shouted an order to disengage the propellers. The most amazing phenomenon of all, however, was that the *Lampas* was moving southwards with frightful speed–a speed that she had never attained before, and which the engines were incapable of imparting to her. This speed, registered by the instruments, was also perceptible, if not estimable, by virtue of the creaking and grating sounds that every part of the submarine was emitting.

Ciserat went into the command-post.

"What's happening, Jacques?" he demanded of Saincer, who had graduated with him from the Naval Academy, and with whom he had maintained a close friendship.

"I've been asking myself that question for five minutes," the mate replied, his wide eyes going from one item of the apparatus surrounding him to the next. "We were heading west-south-west, as we should, at the normal speed of 30 knots. Then we turned sharply to port. The vessel didn't respond to the reversal of the engines. Now, with the propellers disengaged, providing no motive force, we're heading south-west at 60 knots! I swear that it's as if some marine monster has taken us in tow and is dragging us along–it's insane!"

Raymond de Ciserat, who had listened attentively to his friend and subordinate, felt a chill. Excited as he was, Jacques Saincer was no more insane than Cloadec and Kermor, who were standing at their posts.

"A marine monster? A giant squid?" Ciserat said. "No, it's impossible. The *Lampas* isn't as easily manipulable as a nutshell. It's something else. Let's go to the shaft–come to think of it, have you listened to the microphone?"

"Oh! No!" cried Saincer.

Ciserat raised his hand, opened a sort of little port-hole which uncovered an acoustic microphone, and listened for a moment. His face was not long delayed in expressing great surprise. "Strange!" he said. "Nothing! Absolutely nothing! Let's go–if there's any further bizarre occurrence, telephone me, Kermor!"

Followed by Jacques Saincer, the commander left the conning-tower and went along a narrow corridor, illuminated–as was the entire vessel–by small electric bulbs.

The "shaft" was a novelty of submarine navigation, constituted by the stem of the vessel. It was not constructed as a solid piece of metal but as a hollow tube of proven strength and rigidity. A telephone with four outlets connected the shaft to the conning-tower. The shaft could hold four men clutching hand-grips, with their feet on metal rungs, each one with a telephone-receiver to his left at head height. When an index finger pushed a polished ivory button above the left hand-grip, communication was established with the command-post.

In addition, the tube was pierced four times, always at head height, by port-holes furnished with thick lenses enclosed between copper shutters, about eleven centimeters in diameter–which is the distance, in the majority of human faces, between the extremities of the two brow-arches. In response to telephonic orders given by duly authorized observers in the shaft, the shutters opened and two electrical projectors located on the port and starboard sides of the *Lampas*, at about a third of her length, directed unprecedently powerful and penetrative searchlight-beams ahead of the vessel. It was then possible to look into the sea ahead of the *Lampas* through any one of the port-holes, or all four, to a distance of some 500 meters, by means of a beam about 50 meters wide at the extremity of the visual field. Objects, animate or otherwise, inevitably seemed blurred, as if by a light shimmering fog; naturally, the closer they were approached, the clearer they became and the more details became observable. Even at the most extreme distance, though, they were sufficiently distinguishable.

The entrance to the shaft was a narrow, low-set hole that one stooped to go through, and which terminated the central corridor running from the poop to the prow of the *Lampas*–a corridor situated directly above the keel, which communicated via ladders and hatchways with every other part of the submarine.

Once in the shaft, Ciserat on the higher rungs and Saincer beneath him, the former gave the signal. The portholes opened; the sea was illuminated... and the two men uttered a dull exclamation.

Their entire bodies trembled and their fingers clenched on the aluminum handholds. Their mouths fell open, misting the lenses to such an extent that they were soon unable to see anything at all–but they had already seen what here was to be seen.

It was unimaginable. It was insane.

Ciserat was the first to recover his composure. Briskly, he wiped the lens with his sleeve, and it became clear again. Saincer imitated him almost immediately.

"Do you see it?" Ciserat said. "It's no more than 100 meters away! No doubt about it–it's the stern of another submarine. That's what's towing us. How? By what means? There aren't any tow-ropes! None! How, then?"

"It's difficult to make it out because of the turbulence of its wake, with such speed!" stammered Saincer. "All the same, there's no doubt. We're in tow. But how? What's tying the *Lampas* to that machine?"

"What is it?"

"I don't know."

They spoke at the same time, hardly listening to each other, their minds in turmoil, all their scientific and maritime suppositions having been overturned. Suddenly, a loud voice sounded overhead. "Well, what is it? Raymond? Saincer? Can you hear me? Are you listening?"

They got hold of themselves. "Is that you, Mattol?" Ciserat said, in a relatively controlled voice. "Good. It's enough to stupefy anyone, you know. Do you see it?"

"Do I see it? I've been here for a quarter of an hour. I wondered what you were doing. Have you discovered it?"

"Discovered what?" said Saincer.

"Discovered the tether by which that damned submarine is towing us."

"No, we haven't discovered it!" Ciserat growled, becoming frustrated.

"Don't get upset, Raymond! I'm not a mariner; that's why I'm not distracted by any preconceived ideas or familiar technology. The tether that attaches us to that fantastic craft is clearly an invisible chain, which cannot be cast off or severed, except at the will of its user. A chain against which we are as powerless as a corpse inside a lead coffin welded shut; a chain which, without a doubt, is the result of the satanic will of Lucifer. That chain is called *electromagnetism*."

A dazed silence reigned in the shaft. The three men stared through the unshuttered portholes at the submarine that was drawing the *Lampas*, her crew and her passengers along.

To what prison? To what tortures?

"Irène! Irène!" moaned Ciserat. Then, pulling himself out of his pitiful state, the naval officer proclaimed: "I shall defend her! I shall save her!"

Ciserat then closed the portholes and passed through the manhole, followed by Saincer.

They went through the narrow corridor to the chart room, to which they immediately summoned the four junior officers. They held a council, discussing all the ideas that the abnormal situation of the *Lampas* suggested, and the formidable danger that threatened her passengers.

Meanwhile, in the common room, Irène de Ciserat and Miss Ellen could not hide their anguish from little Henri, who, seeing their distraught faces, began crying and calling out "Papa! Papa!" with infinite distress.

In the control-room of the *Uberalles*–which, propelled forward by its electric motors, drew the metallic mass of the *Lampas* towards it and maintained her in its wake by means of a powerful electromagnet fitted to its poop–two men were standing, one in front of a compass with his hands on a steering-wheel, the other in front of a rectangular table carrying instruments whose dials were equipped with luminous numbers and flickering needles.

The first, who was tall and thin, seemed to be bald, because his short-cropped hair was almost colorless. His square, bony, hairless face was the color of candle-wax; his red eyes had lashless lids. His rigid impassiveness was sinister. He was dressed in a grey cloth pajama suit, a flannel shirt with its collar turned down and leather sandals. This was Rupert VI, known as the Ageless Man, the father of Glô XIII of Schwarzrock and the ruler of the secret domain of the Hollow Rock: the *Grottenmeister* himself.

The second, who was small and broad-shouldered, had woolly hair and an olive complexion. His pointed nose, thin lips and slightly slanting eyes indicated a mixed Indian and Chinese heritage. Captured at sea by the pirates of the Hollow Rock when he was only 15 years old, serving as a cook on an Antilles brig, he had immediately shown such intelligence that Rupert VI had made him successively his pupil, his secretary, his lieutenant, and finally the second-in-command of their submarine, the *Uberalles*.

This man was perfidy incarnate, a glacier covering a volcano of passion. He had but one moral quality: a boundless admiration for and an infallible fidelity to Rupert VI–but woe betide the man or woman to whom he took exception, for whatever reason, if Rupert did not intervene in time! This disquieting individual, who was as cold and ingeniously cruel as any human could be, was named Malta. He was not wearing the grey Warteck uniform, but that of their rare subordinate officers: a blue cotton jacket and trousers, an unstarched grey linen shirt with the collar turned down, and espadrilles.

There was rarely any conversation in the control-room of the *Uberalles*, whether Rupert was here with Malta or Malta was in command with his usual pilot. While they made their way towards the Bermudas, with the *Lampas* in tow, hours passed without a word being spoken by the Ageless Man or his companion. Suddenly, however, the latter said, in German: "We'll be in port in five minutes, *Grottenmeister*." His voice was fluid and rather unctuous.

"Relax the magnetism gradually, in proportion to our speed," Rupert replied, his elocution harsher and more emphatic. "Once we've docked, according to the orders I gave in advance, the *Lampas* will be taken over and held by the dockyard electromagnet. You'll direct the operation thereafter. Grisyl will assist you and take special care of Irène and Henri. Take the others to the weaving-mill, then report to me."

"Yes, *Grottenmeister*."

That was all.

The port of the submarine domain of the Hollow Rock was a large basin constituted by a grotto connected to the sea by three electric locks. Powerful pumps could empty the basin in less than a quarter of an hour. A dockyard was disposed here, furnished with several electromagnets, which maintained the *Uberalles* in whatever position was required for the various operations of making repairs, painting and cleaning required by its frequent usage. There was another, simpler berth to one side, which served as a resting-place.

The port was, of course, connected by watertight doors to the cave-complex that constituted the domain of the Hollow Rock–which, in reality, comprised several rocks and a system of excavations extending for kilometers within the granite mass of the submarine plateau whose peaks formed the reefs and islets of the Bermudas.

The *Uberalles* went into the basin, whose huge lock-gate opened in front of it. As for the *Lampas*, its bow was now stuck to a plate-like electromagnet fixed vertically in the stern of the *Uberalles*. It too came into the basin–but there, once it was above the dock, Malta cut the current to the electromagnet and the liberated *Lampas* began to sink, its ballast-tanks being full. In addition to its own weight, it was drawn down by the magnetic fittings of the dock, to which it was affixed as if welded to it.

Maneuvering so as only to be attracted by the magnetism of the other berth, the *Uberalles* settled gently and remained immobile. Then, Malta having given the requisite signals, the pumps started up, and the basin rapidly became completely dry. It was roughly oval in shape. At one of its extremities were the entry and exit locks and the valves for filling and emptying them; at the other extremity two galvanized iron stairways led to the arched doors.

One of these doors opened and Grisyl appeared. At the same time, a kind of cargo-door opened in the starboard side of the *Uberalles*, throwing out a gangway to the galvanized iron mats on the floor of the basin. Rupert, Malta and five other men descended this gangway.

Rupert went up the stairway at whose top Grisyl stood waiting and disappeared, after receiving a smile of respectful welcome from the young woman. Meanwhile, Malta led the five men towards the *Lampas*. Grisyl ran to join them. "Malta!" she said. "What are the *Grottenmeister*'s orders?"

After a ostentatious bow and an obsequious smile, the other replied: "To seize the passengers and crew of the *Lampas*, without striking a blow or risking anyone's life. I'll wait for them to come out, which they'll soon be able to do..."

"Indeed," said Grisyl, laughing. "They must be impatient to know what has happened to them, and I imagine they'll only be able to find that out by poking their noses outside."

"Yes, miss. And when they poke their noses out, as you put it, they'll breathe in the soporific gas with which the whole basin will be filled. Five minutes–and we'll only have to gather them up. The *Grottenmeister* ordered that you are to attend specifically to Irène and Henri. While we wait, I must make sure that the *Lampas* is undamaged and that no water has penetrated its hull."

Turning to his five men, Malta gave a few brief orders. They ran into excavations whose low doors opened and closed, then reappeared carrying rolled-up rope-ladders. In the next five minutes, all of these were thrown down and fully extended, and Grisyl, Malta and the five men clambered over the hull of the Lampas, examining it from top to bottom and from one end to the other. One thing that astonished the investigators, to which Grisyl called attention, was that two hatchways were open, one to port and one to starboard, above cavities that were unquestionably ballast-tanks.

"That's peculiar!" Grisyl said. "Did you know, Malta, that in this new class of submarines, the ballast-tanks are connected to the sea by portholes or hatchways?"

"No, but it hardly matters."

"Doubtless–but we'll have to seek an explanation."

"Naturally, miss. And of other things too, I suppose. Our *Uberalles* must be greatly superior to this *Lampas*, but all the same, according to the reports of our agent in Le Havre, its has some unfamiliar newly-perfected mechanisms, knowledge of which will be useful to us..."

"There's no sound from within."

"Oh, the *Lampas* has a double hull reinforced within by thick mufflers and layers of cork; no sound escapes. We mustn't delay, miss. The *Grottenmeister* is impatient–any possibility of conflict is to be avoided."

"Let's go, Malta. We'll stop on the last step of the stairway. When we see their conning-tower opening, we'll disappear. You'll leave the ceiling-lights on?"

"Yes, miss."

"Perfect. They'll be able to see through the periscopes. As the soporific gas is colorless, and as transparent as oxygen... *Mein Gott*! It will be amusing to watch them fall asleep."

Ten minutes later, in the listening room–where a young and athletic Norbert was on duty–Grisyl and Malta leaned over the polished center of the table, from which the ledgers and the fountain-pen had been removed. Suspended above the table was the lower section of a special periscope, which projected an image of the interior of the basin on to the table, in two ovoid hemispheres. The *Lampas* was divided longitudinally into two parts, one showing the underside and the other the view from above its hull.

"*Ach*!" said Grisyl, after waiting for a quarter of an hour, "They're taking their time. Nothing's opening up. They aren't very curious. They're afraid of something–not very brave."

"Hum!" Malta grunted, dubiously.

Five minutes passed, then five more, and then another five...

"The *Lampas* has been immobile for half an hour, and nothing has moved!" Grisyl cried. "Not the propeller, nor the rudder, not the hatches. Something's amiss!"

"We ought to report and get further orders, miss."

"Yes, we've waited long enough." She took a step to her right and pressed one of the mother-of-pearl buttons. The telephonic loudspeaker emerged from the partition.

"Hello!" said Grisyl. "*Grottenmeister*?"

There was a brief silence, then a metallic voice emerged from the conical funnel. "Yes, I'm listening."

"There's no movement aboard the *Lampas*. Immobility and absolute silence. The microtelephone isn't registering any sound, and the periscope isn't moving."

"I understand." There was a pause, during which Grisyl and Malta waited gravely, without moving. Suddenly, the metallic voice resumed: "Ten men with gas-masks and four gas-jets. Force an entry into the *Lampas*, turn on the gas-jets. That's all."

"Understood, *Grottenmeister*." Grisyl pressed the button; the funnel closed up. "I'm on it!" the young woman added.

Throughout this scene, the Norbert on duty had been standing next to the table, saying nothing. As Grisyl smiled before going out with Malta, he piped up: "It is very curious! I'll leave the periscope and the microtelephone on. I'll keep watching you until you get into the *Lampas*."

"Yes, you should," Grisyl said—and left, with Malta.

The enigma was puzzling, and would have caused terrible anguish to any friend of the *Lampas*'s passengers. It was inconceivable that, after all that had happened to the submarine, its crew and passengers would show no signs of life. Everyone would have expected that, once the *Lampas* was immobilized, Raymond de Ciserat would make an effort to take account of the phenomena whose plaything he had been, and of the place where he was now beached. The hatches should, therefore, have opened, the searchlights should have come on, and men should have appeared on the conning-tower...

But nothing had moved; no one had appeared. The *Lampas* was like a lead coffin enclosing none but the dead.

What, then, had happened to Irène de Ciserat, little Henri Prillant, Miss Ellen, Mattol, Lili, the commander, the first mate, the purser, the four junior officers and the 18 sailors and engineers? Why was none of them switching on a searchlight, opening a porthole or a unlocking a hatch? Were they dead? If so, what had killed them? Were they merely asleep? Under the influence of what agent, gaseous, liquid or emotional? It was a mystery.

As these thoughts crossed their minds, the curious and anxious Grisyl and the avid and impassioned Malta hastened to issue orders and take action, in order to find out without further delay.

Wearing air-tanks on their backs and helmets that were hermetically sealed at the shoulders, Grisyl, Malta and the ten men climbed down to the *Lampas* by means of the rope-ladders, which had been left in place after the first brief inspection. Four of them were carrying gas-cylinders and jet-nozzles like those used to spray acid. Another, who marched at the head, was carrying an oxy-acetylene torch.

The entire party went to the conning-tower and surrounded it, nozzles in advance. In response to a signal from Malta, the man with the torch projected a long continuous jet of blue flame on the steel hatchway sealing the conning-tower. The metal softened and melted...

Malta made a gesture. The torch was extinguished. Another man, armed with a steel crowbar with a wooden shaft, set to work quickly and efficiently; the hatch was opened. The procedure was repeated on a second hatch. Then the gas was projected into the conning-tower, in profusion.

Five minutes elapsed.

One after another, the four gas-spreaders descended into the *Lampas*, preceded by the man with the torch and followed by Grisyl and Malta. The other men, furnished with various tools, brought up the rear. The last two had large leather straps slung over their shoulders, which could easily be improvised into a stretcher for a wounded, sleeping, unconscious or dead body.

As the troop slowly advanced further into the French submarine, however, Grisyl's curiosity and Malta's expectation changed into surprise, amazement, and then into the kind of atrocious anguish that the presence of an illimitably impenetrable mystery generates–for Grisyl, Malta and their ten men became more and more convinced that the submarine *Lampas* was devoid of human life. There was not a single man, woman or child to be found, nor even one of those small animals–cats, white mice, guinea-pigs–that submariners like to keep as pets, and which often prove useful as indicators of poor air quality.

There was no living person aboard. The passengers and crew? Absent–vanished! No one! From the poop to the prow, from the keel to the top of the conning-tower, the *Lampas* was deserted.

When Grisyl and Malta were absolutely certain of this incredible and incomprehensible fact, they both felt a cold chill of fear.

II. The Murder of Sir Ernest Bernd

That day, in his gubernatorial mansion in Hamilton–a beautiful and pleas-antly comfortable house devoid of any undue ostentation–His Britannic Maj-esty's Governor of the Bermudas, Sir Ernest Bernd, awoke with that serenity which puts one in a thoroughly good mood. For a week, Sir Ernest had had the immense pleasure and joy of entertaining his father's best friend, the great American savant Professor Lionel Jameson, who, accompanied by his charming daughter Jessie, had come to study the flora and fauna of the Bermudan islets and reefs.

To tell the truth, it was the mischievous Jessie who had convinced her fa-ther of the urgency of this research. "Sir Ernest has written to tell me, father," she had told him, "that you're sure to find rare and previously undiscovered specimens..." This was because Jessie was in love with Sir Ernest, whom she had met in England shortly before the young Englishman was appointed Gover-nor of the Bermudas–while Sir Ernest, desirous of a career in the colonial serv-ice, had only applied for and obtained the Governorship of the Bermudas in or-der to be as close as possible to New York, where Professor Jameson and his daughter were usually resident. The two young people had devoted all their lei-sure-time to writing letters, which, obstinately presented to her father by Jessie, with her comments, had persuaded the savant to go there to study a fauna and flora that are actually quite well-known.

Science is often the plaything of love.

So Professor Jameson and his daughter had come to the Bermudas, where they became, as was appropriate, the guests of their friend the Governor. Sir Ernest exercised his ingenuity in arranging excursions, which provided opportu-nities for pleasure and sentiment to Jessie and himself while maintaining the appearance of petty scientific expeditions.

To the north-east of the archipelago, a few miles beyond the northernmost reefs, there is a remote islet, which Sir Ernest declared to be more interesting than all the rest. So it was, primarily because it was beyond the range of the simple motor-launch that sufficed for ordinary excursions, making it necessary to embark on the Governor's private yacht–which could not approach the island too closely because of the surrounding reefs. A skiff would have to be lowered to take the Professor and two sailors there, leaving Jessie and Sir Ernest aboard the yacht, all alone–the crew being irrelevant in the circumstances. Jameson was certainly not a meddlesome father; even so, a serious and pleasant flirtation be-tween a couple who are not yet officially engaged can only be genuinely serious and pleasant when the young man and the young woman can put some distance between themselves and their mentors.

On the morning of May 17, therefore, they embarked on the *Blue Rose*.

The day was everything for which Ernest and Jessie had hoped. The young Governor forgot his government for eight hours. Eventually, though, the skiff and Jameson came back from the islet–"Flora non-existent; fauna banal," the slightly irritated savant declared–and climbed back board the *Blue Rose*, so they had to think about returning to Hamilton. Sir Ernest gave the expected order to Captain Wallis, the yacht's commander, and the ship raised its anchor and set off for Bermuda.

Jameson, Captain Wallis and his wife, Sir Ernest, Jessie, Doctor Simpson and the mate O'Mersey [32] were all on deck, variously standing or sitting, leaning back or bracing both hands on the guard-rail and chatting, when a booming sound was heard on the port side. Turning abruptly towards the ocean, they all saw something describe an aerial trajectory like a leaping dolphin and fall back into the water with a splash.

"Oh! What's that?"

"Strange!"

"A flying fish?"

"Enormous, if so!"

"And a round head–you saw it."

"A dolphin? No!"

"I think..."

But Professor Jameson did not say what he thought, for the sea parted under pressure and a second projectile shot out, described a similar trajectory and fell back–then another, yet another, then two at the same time, then a whole series of jets, one after the other or simultaneously. Astounding! Captain Wallis, who was a marvelous mathematician by nature, automatically counted 31, with perfect accuracy.

Jameson, who was an observer by nature and by virtue of his scientific training, took note of their shape and characteristic details. Before the 30th phenomenon had even been produced, he concluded: "Diving-suits!"

"Look! They're coming up again! They float!"

"But where have they come from?"

"There are only three deep-sea divers in the Bermudas."

"Has a ship sunk?"

"No–we've only seen two sails, which disappeared over the eastern horizon."

"A submarine, then?"

"And its entire crew might have be saved by means of its diving-suits..."

"I don't see any other explanation."

Captain Wallis had given the orders demanded by the circumstances. The *Blue Rose* came about, lifebuoys were thrown overboard and the yacht's three boats put to sea. Rescuing shipwrecked sailors is a matter of duty. Besides, they appeared to be expecting to be rescued, with the most absolute confidence and tranquility. Half-submerged in the water, assembled into tightly-knit groups of three or four, the suited divers floated gracefully, bobbing in the waves. There were definitely 31, of which one–in a group of four–was attached to another by a sturdy line. It took two hours to get them all aboard the yacht.

As they gradually arrived on deck, they were carried by crewmen–the divers seeming to be stunned, entirely incapable of walking, although their boots were not lined with the usual lead-laden soles–into the vessel's capacious hold. When the first helmet was unscrewed, the sailors exclaimed: "A woman!"

"Yes, I'm Miss Ellen Rake. Where's little Henri? Where?"

"Don't worry, miss, he's here, and in good condition, I think." This was the voice of Raymond de Ciserat, whose helmet had been removed at the same time as that of the English governess, and who hastened to unscrew the helmet of the diving-suit to which the young woman was attached by a line. Meanwhile, the bewildered sailors unscrewed a fourth helmet, revealing the head of another woman.

"Irène!"

"Raymond!"

"All safe and sound."

"Yes–and Lili!"

"I'm here, Madame."

Other divers were arriving.

Mrs. Wallis and Miss Jessie offered their cabins to the two young women, who were fussing over a boy of about 12, who was being extracted asleep or unconscious, from a rolled-up eiderdown that was in the diving-suit with him.

Lili hastened to join Irène. Doctor Simpson arrived at a run. Sir Ernest gave orders to the purser. The sailors unscrewed more helmets. There were shouts and exclamations in French and English, and bursts of laughter.

"Mattol!"

"Yes, intact. How are Irène and Henri?"

"They've been taken to a cabin with Miss Ellen. There are women aboard, and a doctor."

"Good! I've got time to breathe, then! What extraordinary luck to find an English yacht here!

Jacques Saincer's head appeared above the copper collar of his diving-suit. Mattol burst out laughing and cried: "Don Quixote in his armor!"

The French sailors smiled in amusement. What a noise! What a fuss! Lieutenant O'Mersey handed out glasses of whisky, which an English sailor had brought on a silver tray.

"Roll call!" cried the mate in charge of the *Lampas*'s crew.

"Present! Present! Present!" came the responses, from all sides. When that was over, the mate turned to Ciserat–who was adjusting his dress–clicked is heels together with a military salute, and reported that no one was missing.

While the four junior officers from the *Lampas* attended to their men–assisted by Lieutenant O'Mersey, who spoke French–Captain Wallis briefly introduced himself and Sir Ernest Bernd to Ciserat, Saincer and Mattol. Ciserat reciprocated, and immediately asked to know how Irène, Henri, Lili and Miss Ellen were. The Governor and the captain showed them the way to the cabins, preceding them.

Little Henri was lying on a divan in the lounge. "He's sleeping the most peaceful sleep in the world," said Doctor Simpson, whom Captain Wallis immediately introduced.

"An injection of chloral, at Lourmel's dosage, works every time," said Mattol.

Irène took Raymond's hand and smiled. Wearing a tennis-dress, her hair still in slight disarray from the helmet, she looked ravishing.

Mattol spoke English fluently. He conferred with Simpson for a minute. Entrusted to Miss Ellen and Lili, with precise instructions, Henri Prillant was carried away. Mrs. Wallis and Miss Jessie, enraptured by the marvelous adventure, had prepared a bed for him in a triple cabin.

Jessie came straight back to the lounge. She had not been present during the various introductions and had not heard any of the names. That was when Jameson arrived. Until then, he had stayed on the bridge of the *Blue Rose*, attentive to the possible appearance of some other projectile. He had not been in any hurry to see the people who had emerged in such a singular manner from the bosom of the Atlantic. He would have liked two or three more to emerge, to verify the exactitude of his observations and his calculation of the elevation of their trajectory above the surface. After a full quarter of an hour, convinced that no diving-suit had been delayed, and, consequently, that the ocean was not hiding any more, he went down to the lounge, where a sailor had told him that the principal newcomers were to be found. Scarcely had he entered the room when he stopped, opened his eyes wide, opened his mouth, raised his arms and suddenly found it difficult to speak. Eventually, he exclaimed, in a voice hoarse with surprise: "Ciserat! Mattol! Miss Lourmel... or, rather, no, Irène... Madame de Ciserat! And Lieutenant Saincer!" He drew breath, then continued in French: "Where the Devil have you come from?"

He embraced Irène and Raymond, whom he had known as children, and introduced his daughter Jessie to them. She laughed heartily at making the acquaintance, in such an extraordinary manner, of people about whom her father had spoken to her thousands of times. Jameson then shook Mattol's hands–he had seen him often in Professor Lourmel's laboratory in Paris–and exchanged an equally vigorous handshake with Jacques Saincer, with whom he had chatted for a long time in the course of the party that Lourmel had held "in his honor" a few months before, at his house in Auteuil.

"Where are the Professor and Mademoiselle Luce?" he asked. "Why aren't they in diving-suit too?"

While Mattol replied, more seriously than seemed appropriate to Jameson, in the apparent circumstances, the savant also noticed the unexpected expressions worn by Irène and her husband Raymond: a mixture of heartfelt sadness, deep sorrow and animal dread...

He resumed his austere expression. "Something serious, Ciserat?" he said, laconically, in English.

Raymond spoke English even better than Mattol. "Yes sir, very serious. We were on our way to New York to see you."

"Lourmel isn't...?"

"No, no! Our uncle is very much alive, and Aunt Luce too. It's not that."

"Can you talk–tell me everything?"

"Yes."

"May these gentlemen be present?" He indicated Bernd, Wallis and Simpson.

Ciserat looked at his wife, who blushed slightly. "Yes," she said, courageously. "It's best that these gentlemen know. Might they not find themselves in the position of having to defend Henri and us..."

"And Jessie?"

"Certainly," said Irène, with a spontaneous surge of affection.

Jessie, serious now, shook Irène's hand, which she had taken hen her father named the young woman.

Jameson looked at Ciserat. "Then..." he began.

"Will you permit me?" Sir Ernest said, cutting in. "We'll arrive at Hamilton in less than two hours. It's almost dinner time. Our friends are welcome to join us–and Monsieur Ciserat can tell his story this evening, in my drawing-room, beyond the reach of any indiscretion. The walls here..."

Sir Ernest Bernd was right; everyone accepted this advice.

A mere three hours later, Raymond de Ciserat told the story of all the extraordinary events that had occurred since the party given in Professor Jameson's honor and offered his explanations, while the scientist and his daughter, Sir Ernest, Captain Wallis and his wife, Lieutenant O'Mersey and Doctor Simpson listened with avid interest. Louis Mattol and Jacques Saincer were also present.

Meanwhile, the crew of the *Lampas* were entertained by the crew of the *Blue Rose*. Miss Ellen and little Henri Prillant–who was still asleep, and probably would not wake up until the following day–were given a bedroom, sitting-room and bathroom in one of the guest-apartments of the gubernatorial mansion. Another of these apartments as given in its entirety to Monsieur and Madame de Ciserat and Lili–who was with Mrs. Wallis's chambermaid at that moment, choosing day and night apparel for Irène from the rich Englishwoman's wardrobes.

Ciserat also spoke about Leo Saint-Clair, who had brought Henri Prillant to the *Lampas*. "The Nyctalope must certainly be on the trail of this monstrous sorcerer who calls himself Lucifer. We don't have any news, of course. We were hoping to obtain some in New York, at the *poste restante* or at your home, Professor."

"Something may have arrived at my home," the savant said, "but I gave instructions for my correspondence to be kept during the two weeks I had decided to spend here."

"Whatever may be taking place in Europe," Ciserat said, "between the Nyctalope and Lucifer, we have been able to verify the foundation of Mattol's theory of the antagonism of milieux relative to the phenomenon of spell-casting. Since the departure from Le Havre, Irène and Henri have enjoyed absolute peace. Everything was going as well as possible aboard the *Lampas* when suddenly, at 4:28 p.m., when we were about 500 miles from the Bermudas..."

And Raymond de Ciserat recounted the *Lampas*'s astounding adventure. His audience listened as if petrified. He concluded: "It was the diving master, in the course of the council we held after leaving the shaft, who came up with the idea of putting on the diving suits without the lead soles and inflating them sufficiently to give us enough buoyancy once we were outside. Then, one after another, we went into the ballast tanks, opened the exit hatches and slipped into the sea. The effect of the speed we had acquired helped to counter our own tendency to rise rapidly to the surface, or else we would probably have suffered the consequences of too rapid an ascent.

"Our emergency diving-suits are designed in such a way that one can get into them fully-dressed from top to toe. We were thus able to appear before you, once removed from out suits, in a state of relative decency. The only difficulty was posed by little Henri. There was no diving-suit in his size. He might panic. There was a risk of asphyxiation or of bumping his head against the metallic edge of the helmet. Irène thought of the eiderdown at the same time as Mattol thought of the soporific injection, and I attached Henri Prillant's diving-suit to Miss Ellen's, as requested.

"We all took with us the few valuables and precious objects that we possessed, and the 31 passengers of the *Lampas* slipped out of the hatches in the ballast-tanks..."

Raymond de Ciserat paused there, and he turned to Captain Wallis, his expression further emphasizing his seriousness. "Captain," he went on, "you are a seaman first and foremost, as I am myself, and you are doubtless asking yourself how it is that I, a naval officer given command of the *Lampas* by a company that trusted me, could have abandoned the submarine, in apparent defiance of all traditions of honor, thus causing my employer a heavy loss..."

"Yes, I was indeed asking myself that!" said Captain Wallis, with brutal austerity.

"This is my answer, Captain," Ciserat said. "Firstly, the case had been foreseen in which, to save my wife Irène and little Henri Prillant, the son of a universally-admired French statesman, the entire crew of the *Lampas* and her commander might be obliged to separate themselves from the vessel. After putting to sea from Le Havre, I received by wireless telegraph, from the chairman of the board of the Subtransatlantic Company, a formal order to abandon the *Lampas* in any circumstances in which I deemed that remaining aboard would put the spell-caster's victims in grave danger. Secondly, in the case in which that abandonment would be made in such circumstances that I lost control of the *Lampas* and all influence over its destiny, I was authorized to take whatever measures those circumstances seemed to me to dictate for her conservation or her destruction.

"I took those measures, Captain! I think—and I do not believe that I can be mistaken—that the first man who touches the wheel of the *Lampas*, and causes it to turn at least a quarter of a circle, is bound to belong to the band of affiliates and accomplices of Lucifer." Ciserat paused, and looked around the little assembly. Save for Mattol and Saincer, the entire audience as holding its breath; even Irène did not know what the lieutenant was about to say.

There was an anguished silence; then Ciserat said, simply: "The man who turns the wheel a quarter of a circle—whether he has already done so or will do so in the future—will cause the detonation of a charge of melinite. In three seconds, the submarine and its hijackers will be annihilated."

There was another silence. Then Ciserat concluded, in a changed tone: "So we left the *Lampas* in diving-suits, and were lucky enough that the *Blue Rose* and Sir Ernest Bernd..." Smiling with gratitude, Raymond de Ciserat offered his hand to the Governor, who shook it cheerfully and cordially, without any trace of arrogance.

Once the facts were all spelled out, an unlimited field opened up for hypothesis. Questions were put to the eight men and three women assembled in the little room. What, exactly, was the mysterious submarine? Where was its home port? What extraordinary means were at its disposal? How had Lucifer known that Irène and little Henri were aboard the *Lampas*? How had the submarine contrived to intercept the *Lampas*? There were many others—a potentially-infinite number.

The conversation lasted until 2 a.m. in the morning. In the end, two decisions were made: one, that a wireless message would be sent to Professor Lourmel; two, that the passengers and crew of the *Lampas* would await his instructions in Hamilton, along with Professor Jameson and his daughter.

The Bermudas communicated with Paris via New York. On that May 18 at 3 a.m., Sir Ernest Bernd sent an encrypted radiotelegram to Professor Lourmel in Paris, whose decoded text read:

Lampas *captured, drawn with electromagnet towards unknown destination by ultrafast submarine. Have all emerged secretly in diving-suits. Are guests of Governor of Bermudas. Irène and Henri well. Have found Jameson here. Awaiting instructions. Ciserat.*

As they had talked enough, and had no more work to do, everyone went to bed.

The Governor, his friends and his guests met up again for lunch at 1 p.m. It hardly needs to be said that the crew of the *Lampas*, accommodated aboard the *Blue Rose*, anchored in the harbor, had been ordered not to come ashore, while all the Governor's staff had sworn not to say a word about the existence of the French guests in the town. The latter were resolved not to leave the grounds of the mansion unless it was strictly necessary.

The afternoon of May 18 was spent by those awaiting Professor Lourmel's response chatting, constructing elaborate hypotheses, playing chess, reading and smoking. Henri Prillant, who awoke hale and hearty, no longer astonished by anything, amused himself as best he could with Miss Ellen and the two young daughters of Captain and Mrs. Wallis. He suffered no supernatural ill-treatment and Irène was as undisturbed as the child. Would the nightmares of past days never return? Oh, how happy they would be once they were certain of that!

They dined cheerfully, all of the diners having more reasons to rejoice than to be sad. After an evening of music and singing–Irène and Mrs. Wallis both had beautiful voices and an abundance of musical talent–everyone went their separate ways for the night.

That night, alas, the ignorance in which the Governors and inhabitants of the Bermudan archipelago had lived, with respect to the Hollow Rock and the Wartecks, was to cost Sir Ernest Bernd dear–and not only him, but his fiancée and several of his guests.

The gubernatorial mansion of the Bermudas had been built above cellars partly hollowed out from the rock. After a fire, the mansion had been reconstructed on its existing foundations in 1843. Although they were not filled in, most of the cellars remained totally unused. No sommelier had ever risked his shoes or slippers down there. The nearest two or three, where casks and bottles were stored, which were lit by electricity, also served as a lumber-room for the officials and the servants. As for the more distant cellars, they were empty, sealed by ancient wooden doors reinforced by iron, which no one had dreamed of inspecting for many years–either to close them, if by chance they stood ajar, or to open them to see what might lie behind them.

At 1:54 a.m. on May 19, one of those dismal and abandoned distant cellars was suddenly illuminated by a radiant light, moving in a circle, which seemed to spring from the ground. By way of a prelude, a square meter of the floor had been silently lifted up in the darkness, as if it were hinged and a hand were shifting it to one side. The light then sprang forth, turned through a circle, and moved upwards. A hand appeared, holding the instrument from which the light came. The upraised hand was followed by an arm and the entire body of a man dressed in blue cotton, with espadrilles on his feet.

Standing up in the cellar, this human being ceded his place in the square cavity to second, with pale short-cropped hair, a face that was grave and childlike at the same time, dressed in grey flannel and shod in leather sandals.

"Careful, miss–the ground's damp here," said the first, in German, in a voice scarcely perceptible even to the person for whom the words were intended.

"Don't worry, Malta." Grisyl drew herself up to her full height beside her short and stocky companion.

Four more men appeared in succession, dressed in black outfits that combined the functions of jackets, trousers and shoes. Beneath their feet, the cloth was reinforced by flexible rubber soles. Their bare heads all displayed pale, freshly-shaven skulls.

Grisyl, Malta and the four men all wore narrow leather belts, from each of which hung a shielded electric lamp, a coil of braided leather rope, and a sheath furnished with a knife that was both sharp-edged and pointed. There was nothing else, except that one of the four men had some sort of box on his back. from which a flexible tube extended, whose exceedingly fine extremity he held in his left hand.

"The information the *Grottenmeister* received was very precise," Malta whispered to Grisyl. "I know the house and I could find the two rooms with my eyes closed. The locks are oiled and I have a duplicate of Sir Ernest's own master-key."

"Let's go!"

"As you order, miss. I'll go first."

"Naturally."

The sinister sextet moved on silently: a line of shadows, the first being preceded by the beam of his own little lighthouse, often prudently eclipsed. Malta, the guide, went forward as confidently as if he were walking through his own house

Three empty cellars were traversed, the doors simply pushed open. Undoubtedly having been oiled in advance, they creaked no more than the door of a strongbox. Then there was a lumber-room and a cellar full of French red wine. So many bottles! Sir Ernest Bernd was a man of taste.

There was a rotunda and a flight of steps, then an arched door with a modern lock, almost new, which Malta's master-key opened without the slightest difficulty. They arrived in an office with a glass door.

"This corridor leads to the main hallway, miss. The stairs go up to the first floor. There's a large landing, with a straight corridor all the way to the back. The Ciserats' apartment and Henri's room are on the left, the second and third doors."

"Very good, Malta. Go on–I'll follow you."

They went up the stairs, across the landing and along the corridor, to the second door. It was no longer Malta's lamp but Grisyl's that illuminated the door obliquely. Malta had both hands free now. The key was inserted in the lock and given a prudent half-turn, but a further half-turn as immediately interrupted.

Malta shrugged his shoulders.

Grisyl had guessed the reason. *My God, these French people are careless!* she thought. *The door isn't even locked.*

Raymond de Ciserat was, in fact, not careless, but confident of the security that is always offered by the house of a powerful man who has received you as a friend. With a mechanical gesture, he had pushed the little bolt on the inside of his bedroom door, but he had not even thought of turning the key of the access door to the apartment.

There was a vestibule and a sitting-room; then Grisyl, Malta and their four black-clad followers came to the room in which Raymond and Irène were sleeping, side-by-side and face-to-face, in a large bed. The husband's right hand rested on his wife's bare shoulder.

Malta introduced an instrument into the lock, which seized the key lodged on the other side and turned it slightly, thus disengaging it from the vertical slit beneath the round hole of the lock. That done, Malta stepped aside and made a sign.

The man who was carrying a receptacle on his back came right up to the door and slipped the pointed end of the tube he held in his left hand into the vertical slit. He passed through about 20 centimeters of tubing, and then he turned a little tap mounted on the tube. All this was done without the slightest sound, but when the tap had been turned there was a slight continuous hiss, like gushing gas–a sound so slight that it was almost imperceptible.

Then they brought out tightly-folded hoods of fine silk from the pockets of their various suits, unfolded them, and pulled them over their heads. Rubber bands held the hoods tightly under the chin, the ears and around the nape of the neck. The hoods were slightly inflated over the mouth and nostrils, for they were reinforced at those places by several wads of thick cloth steeped in some liquid. The holes that permitted the wearers to see were furnished with a material that was very thin, very flexible and as transparent as crystal.

Six minutes passed, counted off by Grisyl on a watch fixed to her left wrist. She made a sign. The man closed the tap, retracted the end of the tube and took three steps back. Then, with the master key–which, in the very modern locks of the mansion, functioned even if a key was engaged on the other side–Malta opened the door. The bolt shot by Ciserat put up no resistance, because the usual screws holding the bolt-socket had been replaced by thinner and shorter screws, which easily slid out of the original holes. The door was pushed gently open, leaving the socket and its four screws suspended with the bolt. Malta collected them delicately as soon as the door was opened, and put them back in place when it was closed again, having slid back the bolt.

Meanwhile, Grisyl had gone in rapidly, her little torch in her left hand. She stopped beside the bed, illuminating the bedhead. Irène and Raymond were sleeping on their sides, facing one another. Irène was facing the door from which Grisyl had come. "Yes, she's beautiful!" the Warteck girl murmured, beneath her hood, after a moment of contemplation. "Our Lord is right to love this woman... She has all the beauty of the fine and elegant Latin people." She leaned over to look at Ciserat's face, his back being towards her. "And the man! I've never seen one so handsome! How delightful it will be when all these people are reduced to slavery, and we shall have thousands and thousands of such beings to serve and please us..."

Grisyl reached out her right hand and ran her fingers through the black masculine hair–but someone touched her arm. She turned round hurriedly. "All right, Malta! You go–I'll stay on watch here."

With two men, one of whom was carrying the gas cylinder, Malta went out through the open door.

Grisyl seized the hand that Raymond had rested on Irène's shoulder and slid it gently over the pillow. Then she went around the bed, turned back the bedclothes to uncover the sleepers, passed her hands and forearms under Irène's body and lifted her up effortlessly. In the meantime, the two remaining men had removed a sheet and spread it on the carpet. Grisyl deposited the sleeping Irène thereon and carefully wrapped her up, leaving her mouth and nostrils free. She lifted her up again and entrusted the precious burden to one of the two men. She made sure that he was holding the delicate body in his arms and against his chest in such a way as not to do her the slightest harm. Then she looked back at Raymond.

If the *Grottenmeister* had not expressly forbidden it, she thought, she would gladly have abducted that man! Almost immediately, though, Malta reappeared. He beckoned from the threshold. Grisyl stood aside to let Irène's carrier pass.

In the corridor, Grisyl saw that the other kidnapping had been equally successful; a man was carrying a package composed of a blanket wrapped around a little body, the head protruding. *A pretty child!* she thought. *Are all of them like that in France?*

There was no further delay–but as they arrived in a group on the landing, a door opened. A man appeared in the large rectangle of light produced by the open door, clad in white pajamas with red stripes. It was Sir Ernest Bernd, who, being unable to sleep and perhaps perceiving the faint noise of the company's muffled footsteps, had come to see what it was, without the slightest apprehension. At the unexpected sight of the group, he froze. He opened his mouth–but it was already too late! Malta had leapt forwards immediately, his right arm raised, his left clutching his dagger–and thrust the long, pointed blade into Sir Ernest's throat, all the way to the hilt.

The Englishman was scarcely able to emit a choked death-rattle. His knees buckled, and he collapsed. Malta seized him in both hands and supported his weight, staggering under it and taking two forward steps, but contrived to prevent the body's fall on to the waxed floor making more than a very soft thud. Then he stood up, withdrew the dagger and fell into step behind his companions, who had passed by without any emotion.

Sir Ernst Bernd's corpse remained in the middle of the floor, lying on its back with the arms outstretched, in the muted light coming through the open door. The blood running from his cut throat gradually spread across the floor, slowly coagulating.

III. The Nyctalope Intervenes

At 8 a.m. on May 20, Leo Saint-Clair went from his dressing-room into Laurence Païli's bedroom. He was dressed to go out. The nurse on duty had just opened the windows; the pure air of the Parc Montsouris was perfumed with the odors of spring and the joyous light of the Sun was flooding the room.

"How is she?" Saint-Clair asked.

"No change," the nurse replied.

Laurence was lying on the bed. Her head rested on a pillow that was barely creased; her outstretched hands emerged from the broad sleeves of a full-length white flannel nightgown; a light but warm linen sheet covered her to as far as her breasts. She did not seem to be breathing at all. Her face and hands had the appearance of someone who had only just died, serenely and without suffering. Thus her lover had carried her into the little house in the Rue Nansouty on the afternoon of May 17; thus he had seen her throughout May 18 and 19; thus he found her on the morning of May 20.

On the previous day, and the day before that, Professor Lourmel had spent long hours in the room, observing her in her dead-alive state. On May 18, he had left without saying a word. On May 19, he had said: "I don't know, I don't know... sometimes, I seem to see a light at the end of the tunnel. I'll think about it, consult my files, compare the case with others that I've studied previously... until tomorrow, my friend." And he had left the Nyctalope to the first darkness that his eyes had ever despaired of penetrating.

On the evening of May 19, Saint-Clair had watched over Laurence for a long time, assisted by a senior nurse, who was eventually replaced by another. Then he had gone to bed, for he had projects planned for the next day and he needed to rest, to sleep, to be free from thought for a few hours.

On the morning of May 20, he did not wait for any further response than the one the nurse had given. He gazed at his beloved Laure for a long time, kissed her forehead—which was cold, but did not have the frigidity of a cadaver—and said to the nurse: "When Professor Lourmel arrives, please ask him to telephone Monsieur Prillant immediately."

"At the ministry?"

"No, Avenue Kléber."

"Yes, Monsieur."

Corsat was waiting in the antechamber, holding his master's hat and gloves. "Pilou's ready," he said.

"Good. Have you seen the red-haired man?"

"Just now, boss. Still stupid."

"And Wolf?"

"Oh, he'll do anything you want. You're his God!"

Saint-Clair did not smile. He put on his gloves and continued: "When the Professor arrives..." but he interrupted himself abruptly. The special electric bell that Choiffour used to announce an important visitor rang in the vestibule. A car could be heard drawing up in the courtyard.

"The Professor already?" Saint-Clair said. He left the antechamber, crossed the hallway, opened the window and leaned out. "It's Lourmel, running–there's news!"

The Professor was indeed running from the door of his car to the steps at the entrance to the house. Saint-Clair went down, with his hat and gloves on. He met Lourmel at the foot of the stairs, in the ground-floor hallway.

"Grave news, my friend!" said the scientist, breathlessly.

"Let's go in here, my dear chap!"

The grave news was imparted and important decisions were taken in the Nyctalope's study, without either man giving a thought to taking off his hat and gloves–all in less than ten minutes.

"Yesterday evening, from Prillant's secretary, I got a copy of this translation of a coded radiotelegram transmitted by the British Ambassador, sent from the Bermudas via New York and London."

Saint-Clair took the piece of paper the Professor was holding out to him and read the message.

"Wait!" said Lourmel, with a terrible calm. "That's not all. That's nothing! This is more serious–20 minutes ago, Prillant gave me a second radiotelegram from the same source, transmitted by the same route. It seemed to me that yesterday's could wait until the morning to be passed on to you–we both need our rest–but this morning's made me leap into the car. Fortunately, I was dressed, about to go to Sainte-Anne. Here!"

On the second piece of paper, which he grabbed, Saint-Clair read:

During night, Irène abducted from Raymond's side. Henri abducted from Miss Ellen's. Disappeared without trace. Complete mystery. Ernest Bernd dead, throat cut. Raymond half-insane. Jameson and I confounded. Mattol.

Saint-Clair remained silent for a moment, a piece of paper in each hand. Then, in an unemotional tone, as if he were talking about something else entirely, he said: "Ernest Bernd, if I'm not mistaken, is the Governor of the Bermudas?"

"Yes. I looked it up yesterday, after the first radio message."

There was another brief silence. Then, still in the same neutral tone, Saint-Clair said: "This happened in the Bermudas–thousands of leagues from Schwarzrock..."

Another silence followed, longer than the first two. Lourmel waited, gravely. The Nyctalope was deep in thought. Finally, with his eyes flashing, his entire body taut, Saint-Clair said: "Take these telegrams back, my friend; I know them by heart now. I presume that Prillant telephoned you..."

"Just now!"

"To tell you to pass them on to me, and that he and his resources are entirely at my disposal?"

"Precisely. He's waiting at the ministry."

"I was on my way there when you came in. Nothing has changed, save that instead of leaving this afternoon for Schwarzrock, I shall now be leaving this morning for Hamilton in the Bermudas. But what about Laure?... Oh, keep her alive for me! I confide her to you, Professor. I'll take Pilou, but Corsat, Choiffour and Wolf will stand guard here like ferocious dogs. Keep me informed of her condition by daily radiograms. For Prillant's sake, and yours, too, my dear Professor, I must save Henri and Irène. I'm on my way–promise me that you'll keep Laure alive!"

"We aren't death's masters, Saint-Clair," Lourmel said, shaking his head.

"This time, you must be!"

"I promise you that I won't leave this house until you return."

"Or until I ask you to bring Laure to me, alive!"

"In that case, I'll come! But save Irène!"

"I swear to you that I'll do everything I can."

"Go, my friend."

"*Au revoir!*"

Lourmel opened his arms; the two men embraced. Then, without another word, the Professor left the study and went to the staircase that led up to the floor where Laurence Païli's room was.

Left alone, the Nyctalope pressed one of the summoning buttons inlaid into the corner of the table. Corsat appeared almost immediately. "Listen, my faithful friend," Saint-Clair said. "I'm leaving on a long journey. I don't know when I'll be back. I'm leaving you here with Choiffour and Wolf. Stand guard over Laure like merciless misers over a fabulous treasure! No one is to enter or leave the house but Professor Lourmel and people specially designated by him–and keep watch even on them."

"Yes, boss."

"And if you learn–with certainty, of course–that I am dead, there are two alternatives. If Laure has opened her eyes and returned to normal life, show her the documents that have informed you of my death. If she is still in her present state, you will kill her by stabbing her in the heart, for she must not fall into Lucifer's hands again. Swear!"

"I swear, boss!"

"Good. Fetch me the red-haired man–I'm taking him away."

Five minutes later, a car moved out into the Rue Nansouty and headed for the city center. Driven by Pilou, it carried the impassive Saint-Clair and the red-haired man, docile and seemingly unconscious.

Monsieur Prillant was waiting in his office for the Nyctalope. The moral strength of the great politician was well-known; because it was hidden behind a smile, his adversaries sometimes accused Monsieur Prillant of skepticism, but if the Minister's most fervent detractors had witnessed that morning's conversation between the two friends, they would have seen admirable character where, until then, they had only wanted to see political opportunism.

The blow that had struck Monsieur Prillant had been extremely cruel. A late arrival in the conjugal life of the statesman, the adored Henri was his pride and joy. Already in his declining years, all his hopes were concentrated on the child. He had that illimitable tenderness for his son which makes paternal love the most noble, the most beautiful and the most altruistic of the sentiments. Alexandre Prillant's appearance, when he welcomed Leo Saint-Clair into his office, was one of sorrowful gravity. The two men shook hands for a long time, communicating so profoundly by non-verbal means that they only said aloud what was absolutely essential.

"What are you going to do, Leo?" the Minister asked, without preamble.

"I was going to Schwarzrock to kill Lucifer," the Nyctalope replied, "but all that's changed. Since your son is evidently in other hands than Lucifer's, the monster's death might not be enough to save him. Henri must be found and recovered urgently. I'm going to the Bermudas."

"Good."

"I'll need one of the four aircraft commissioned by the Minister of War that were delivered a fortnight ago."

"With a pilot?"

"Yes."

"Do you have a preference?"

"Yes, Girard. Right away–I'm ready to depart."

"Fine. In this regard, the pen and the telephone are as worthless as one another. Let's go to the Rue Saint-Dominique. We'll get General Benoît and take him with us to Le Bourget. He'll give the order. You'll be airborne while we watch."

"I've got my car!"

"I should think so!"

A light overcoat, bowler hat and black gloves were on a nearby chair; Prillant put them on, saying: "Let's go! Is your car at the side-door in the Rue Cambacérès?"

"Yes."

"We'll go that way, then."

General Benoît, the Minister of War, was an aviation specialist; he had accepted the portfolio on condition that all the relevant services should be put into his hands. A particular friend of Monsieur Prillant's, he knew all about the frightful and enigmatic affair. Naturally, he knew the Nyctalope, whom he had been able to see and admire in action a few years earlier in Equatorial Africa.[33]

In a few words, the President of the Council informed the Minister of War what was required of him. The general did not hesitate. "Captain Girard is the pilot and commander of the RC3–it's the best of the four. Here's the duty roster–yes, Girard's at Le Bourget. Let's go!"

In the car, Saint-Clair introduced the mentally-impaired red-haired man to General Benoît, as he had previously introduced him to Prillant, and he gave a succinct account of what had taken place at Schwarzrock.

"Are you taking him to the Bermudas?" the general asked.

"Yes," Saint-Clair replied.

"Why?"

"Because he's a valuable hostage, and perhaps a means of action, whom I intend to keep close at hand."

"I understand."

They said no more, for their minds were overflowing with tumultuous thoughts, and Prillant was suffering too much to pronounce or listen to unnecessary speech.

In the quarters occupied by the colonel in command of Le Bourget airfield–a new building erected just outside the perimeter of the field–the Ministers and Saint-Clair were received by an orderly, who led them to the colonel's office. The orderly was immediately instructed to fetch Captain Girard, and not to say a word about the presence of the two VIPs.

While they waited for the famous military aviator, the colonel prepared the administrative documents necessary to send Captain Girard on a secret mission aboard the RC3, then signed them. Just above the Minister's signature, one of these papers bore the flowing inscription in red ink:

As an exceptional measure, effective for the duration of this mission, the co-pilot and military mechanic will be replaced aboard the RC3 by, respectively, Monsieur Leo Saint-Clair, commander-in-chief of the reserve battalion, and Monsieur Pierre Pilou, first master-engineer in the naval reserve.

There was no mention of the man who would occupy the fourth place, normally reserved for an officer who played the role of observer. In fact, that place would be taken by the red-haired man, whose name and rank were unknown. All the documentation had been drawn up, signed, countersigned, franked, registered and filed by the time Captain Girard arrived.

Captain Girard was 28, of medium height, lean and muscular, dark-haired and clean-shaven. His eyes were bright and energetic, but also soft. He had been awarded the Legion of Honor, the Military Medal, the Croix de Guerre with eight palm-leaves and 20 foreign decorations. He had been wounded three times, but no longer felt any after-effects. He had a cheerful disposition, with something of the street urchin about him. He was the bravest of young men and the most adolescent of heroes, a man of a hundred contrasts, all fusing into a single forceful entity when necessary. In brief, he was a fine fellow, worthy to serve alongside the Nyctalope.

The illustrious explorer and the celebrated aviator did not know one another personally. General Benoît introduced them to one another, adding:

204

"You're under Monsieur Saint-Clair's orders, my dear Girard, from now until he hands you back to your colonel."

"It's a great honor for me," Girard said, simply.

The Nyctalope, poring over a large map that the colonel had spread out, set about explaining calmly what they were going to do. "Two flights of approximately the same length: from here to the Azores, from the Azores to the Bermudas. Each leg is about 3,000 kilometers–ten hours, at 300 kilometers an hour. We'll leave at noon. Is that possible, captain?"

"It's possible," Girard replied.

"We'll arrive in the Azores at 8 p.m. local time," calculated Saint-Clair. "We'll refuel on the island of Terceira, on a suitable field I know near the town of Angra do Heroismo. The Governor of the Azores resides there. He has a motor yacht; he'll see to our supplies. We'll leave again at 10 p.m. and we'll be in the Bermudas by 6 a.m. local time. You and I will take turns piloting the plane. I'm bringing my mechanic, Pilou, and a passenger whose hands and feet will be tied securely to his seat."

Girard nodded.

"Do you have aviation suits for Pilou and me?" Saint-Clair added.

"Certainly."

"The passenger only needs to be wrapped up in a great coat."

"Oh, the wind-deflector's an efficient screen, and we'll have foot-warmers," the captain said, laughing.

"Make the preparations. When will you be ready?"

"In ten minutes, Monsieur Saint-Clair, in front of my hangar."

"We'll follow you, then. I assume that the cloakroom...?"

"Is over there, yes."

Ten minutes later, Saint-Clair and Monsieur Prillant embraced and exchanged a few words. Their voices were not tremulous, but their eyes were misty. "I'll bring him back to you or die out there!" Saint-Clair promised.

The red-haired man was tied up in the RC3. Pilou started the engines–a very easy and rapid process for such a machine, with an operator like Captain Girard.

After another embrace and handshake, Monsieur de Prillant and General Benoît left to return the Paris in the Nyctalope's car, driven by a military chauffeur stationed at the airfield. Saint-Clair climbed into the RC3 and installed himself next to Girard, who gripped the steering-column and lifted up his right hand. The engine roared; the aircraft moved forward, drew away and took off smoothly. It climbed into the air, described a quarter of a circle, and headed directly south-west.

The four aircraft of the RC series were capable of covering 4,000 kilometers without pause. The RC3 had a margin of 1,000 kilometers per stage, since each leg of its planned journey was approximately 3,000 kilometers. With pilots as skillful as Saint-Clair and Girard, and a mechanic like Pilou, the double trip would be perfectly straightforward. The RC3's hull was equipped with floats as well as wheels, so it could land on water and travel over a calm sea, or even a moderate swell.

They crossed the coast to the south of Saint-Nazaire. Apart from sighting a few ships and noting changes in wind direction–always benign–the journey to the Azores took place without incident. The Sun was setting over the sea when the RC3, then piloted by the Nyctalope, landed smoothly on a patch of relatively flat bare ground 500 meters from the agglomeration of dwellings forming the town of Angra do Heroismo on Terceira.

Leaving his traveling companions with the aircraft, Saint-Clair went on foot to the Governor's residence. The Nyctalope had friends in Portugal; he had solicited the help of one of them, a Minister of State, and was seen immediately. Half an hour later, the Governor accompanied him back to the RC3; they were followed by men and pack-animals carrying drums of fuel.

And the RC3 resumed her flight.

The night was magnificently clear; moonlight played on the crests of the calm ocean waves. Saint-Clair slept until 3 a.m., well wrapped-up in his seat. Then it was Girard's turn; he snored like Saint Peter all night. Pilou dozed, waking up from time to time to listen to the engine and accomplish one or other of a mechanic's small but very important duties. As for the red-haired man, whether his eyes were open or closed he was as motionless as a mummy–although the disposition of his limbs did not permit much movement.

The Sun rose behind the aviators. When Captain Girard awoke, having snored with as much regularity as the engine if not the same force, he saw that the ocean below them was sprinkled with islands. "The Bermudas?" he said.

"Yes," said Saint-Clair.

They consulted a large-scale map, quickly locating the island of Bermuda and Hamilton.

"That grey field there, to the right of the patch of houses and trees, seems very suitable to me," Girard said.

"Indeed!" Saint-Clair approved–and he took the aircraft down, describing a prudent spiral.

"I was sure, my dear friend, that you would come by plane," said Louis Mattol. "I expected you today, but not so soon! For the moment, Raymond is no use to us. He's in a state of prostration that renders him incapable of action. If his Irène isn't returned to him within a fortnight, he'll go completely mad, I think. He's already getting there, I fear. His existence has become mechanical and I can only keep him calm with potassium bromide. Fortunately, there's a good pharmacy in the town. Captain Wallis has taken on the duties of interim Governor. We haven't broadcast the news of Sir Ernest's murder; he's thought to be confined to bed with angina. Miss Ellen is confined to her room, distressed and weeping almost incessantly. Professor Jameson's daughter, Jessie, is looking after her and Raymond, assisted by Mrs. Wallis and the good Doctor Simpson. We–you and I, and you too, Captain, I presume–can therefore devote ourselves entirely to the mission."

"Certainly," said Girard.

Talking all the while, Mattol led Saint-Clair and the aviator to Professor Jameson's apartment in the Governor's mansion. The latter was waiting expectantly in a room fitted out as a library-cum-smoking room, which he had adopted as his workroom during his stay in the Bermudas. He greeted Saint-Clair–whom he had met through Professor Lourmel–warmly, and was equally effusive with Captain Girard, with whose fame and accomplishments he was familiar.

The door was firmly closed and they sat down. "What do you know, Mattol?" Saint-Clair said, immediately.

"I'll skip over the observations and deductions," the young scientist replied. "These are the results. Firstly, the doors were opened without any breakage, but after some preliminary trickery with the interior locks."

"So the enemy must have at least one accomplice within the mansion," Saint-Clair said.

"Yes, at least one–the enemy probably learned from that accomplice that Irène and Henri were here in the mansion, and in which rooms."

"Probably."

"Secondly, Raymond and Miss Ellen were kept asleep by the emission of a soporific gas, which permitted the abductors to remove Irène, Henri and their clothing without Raymond or Miss Ellen hearing or seeing anything at all. Thirdly, the slitting of Sir Ernest's throat was not premeditated. The Governor would still be alive if fate had not dictated, for some unknown reason, that he would step out of his apartment as the abductors were doing, or had just completed, their work. That's all!"

The Nyctalope started. "That's all?" he said. "You don't know..."

"Oh, there's a whole heap of things we don't know. Where did the abductors come from? How did they get into the house? How many of them were there? And the electromagnetic submarine..." Between the aircraft and the mansion, Mattol had given Saint-Clair and Girard a brief account of the extravagant adventure of the *Lampas* and her occupants.

"We've constructed hypotheses, naturally," the young doctor went on, "on the assumption that the abduction of Irène and Henri is merely the second act of a drama, whose first act was the capture of the *Lampas* by the electromagnetic submarine..."

"One moment!" Saint-Clair said. He turned to Professor Jameson. "Isn't it possible, sir," he said, "to equip the poop, the prow and the flanks of a submarine with devices analogous to electromagnets, which would function as contrary poles and would therefore nullify the attractive force of the electromagnets of a submarine enemy?"

"Yes," Jameson replied. "According to the easily-applied principle that two bodies with the same electrical charge repel one another. To feed the electromagnets, though, our submarine would have to deploy more electric power than the machinery of the submarines we know could furnish."

"What about the *Synancée*, the *Lampas*'s sister-ship?"

"It can't be done. I've already thought of that and calculated..."

"So it's impossible for us," Saint-Clair said, coldly, "to fight the enemy submarine at sea with similar weapons?"

"Yes, quite impossible," Jameson replied, bluntly. "I have no knowledge of the source of the enemy's electrical power, or the means by which it's deployed. We only know one application of that power–the electromagnet that afflicted the *Lampas*–and that application is indeed presently impossible for us."

"Very well," Saint-Clair said, calmly. He turned to Mattol. "Have you taken precautions to ensure that the accomplice has not run off, if he is on the staff of the mansion?"

"I've instituted a roll-call; an unauthorized absence will reveal the guilty party. Wallis has not authorized any absence."

"Perfect!" Saint-Clair wore a smile and an expression which would have seemed terrible if their significance had been understood. He meditated for a few seconds, then continued, his voice calm and incisive. "Mattol, my friend, find me a room in the mansion, very large and secluded, in which absolute darkness can be created by closing the curtains and masking every opening with blankets, hangings, carpets or whatever. Have Monsieur Wallis give the order that all the people in the mansion are to assemble in that room. All of them, you understand–including Captain and Mrs. Wallis themselves–and as quickly as possible! We mustn't lose a minute. When I've done what I have to do, and only then, you can introduce Captain Girard and myself to Captain Wallis and his wife. Get going, Mattol! Professor Jameson, will you please accompany Mattol while he takes the necessary steps? Thank you! Girard and I will wait until everything is ready. When the room is secure, save for one door, and everyone is assembled there, including you, Mattol will come to fetch us. Oh–don't forget this! Turn on all the electric lights in the room. And take care, my dear chap, that no one leaves the room while Mattol comes to fetch me. Is that understood? Good. See you soon."

When the Nyctalope gave orders in a certain voice, while his eyes flamed in a particular way, even a Lionel Jameson was not in the least inclined to raise an objection or a question. One obeyed without saying a word, whether one understood or not, immediately.

"Have you a cigarette?" the Nyctalope asked.

"Yes," said Girard, a slightly dazed and overcome with admiration.

"Give me one. I could gladly smoke for at least a quarter of an hour."

It was not a quarter of an hour but almost double. Saint-Clair was finishing a second cigarette when Mattol reappeared.

"It's done."

"Good." Saint-Clair got up; the captain immediately followed his example. "Wallis didn't raise any objection?"

"None," said Mattol. "He's one of the most ardent of your countless admirers, my dear chap. He'd obey you in everything, except against England and his King."

"So much the better–it simplifies things. Let's go, Girard. Follow us, my dear Mattol. Wait! When we arrive, arrange everyone in such a way that by setting myself two or three paces in front of them, standing on a chair or a table, I can see the entire assembly and observe every one of them, at least from the waist up."

"Understood," Mattol said, simply.

As one might imagine, the people who knew that the gathering in the ballroom of the mansion had been called by order of the Nyctalope were on tenterhooks. What did that prestigious person intend to do? Why had he called this strange assembly? Why the opaque defenses against the daylight? The staff who did not even know that the celebrated Leo Saint-Clair was present, however, and who knew little or nothing about the recent dramas that had prompted that presence, simply obeyed Captain Wallis, wondering what it all meant.

They were not long delayed in finding out.

On the point of entering the room by the only practicable door, Saint-Clair stood aside and let Girard and Mattol precede him. Hidden behind one of the sections of the open door, he heard the slight noise of the rearrangement. Then there was a relative silence–an expectant silence.

Not seeing Saint-Clair, Mattol came out again, and was immediately restrained by a hand on his shoulder. "Is there a single switch controlling all the lights?" Saint-Clair asked, in a low voice.

"Yes."

"Where is it?"

"In the room."

"Good. Go back in. Position yourself close to the switch. Turn the lights off. And don't move."

Mattol obeyed.

The huge room was abruptly plunged into darkness. The darkness was total, because Saint-Clair came in at that moment and shut the door. He had taken the key from outside; he put it back into the lock from inside, turning it twice to make sure that it was properly engaged. Then he removed the key and slipped it into his pocket.

Some 50 people were assembled in that immense pitch-dark room, who could not see one another, no matter how close they were standing, and could not even see the palms of their own hands; for the moment, they might as well have been blind. Leo Saint-Clair, however, could see quite clearly, almost as well as in broad daylight.

He walked into the profound darkness, light on his feet. He brought a chair, set it down on the carpet, and climbed up on it. Thus placed, he was overlooking three rows of men and women, standing a few paces in front of him. One after the other, he looked carefully at every man and every woman, all of whom had their eyes wide open in the darkness, seeing nothing.

Suddenly, in a vibrant voice, Saint-Clair spoke in German, emphasizing the syllables and separating the words. "Attention! I shall have the lights turned on again, and will then unmask the accomplice, servant, spy and slave of Baron Glô von Warteck!"

The majority of the assembled men and women were English, Bermudan or American, and did not understand German. These words meant nothing to them, and each one maintained the same stance, their faces expressing no more than the expectation they already had.

A few—Wallis, Jameson, Jessie and two NCOs in the mansion guard—understood, and unconsciously registered their impression by a slight change of attitude and a rapid modification of their features. The two NCOs, in particular, widened their eyes and raised their eyebrows; having understood the sentence, they wondered why it had been pronounced.

But the Nyctalope could see!

Avidly attentive, his eyes surveyed the crowd, ready to pick out what Saint-Clair expected to discover—and his nyctalopic eyes perceived a man, the fourth from the right in the second row, who shuddered violently at the pronunciation of the name "Glô von Warteck," then stood on tiptoe, stretching his neck and turning his head to the right and the left. His worried eyes were desperate to distinguish some indication of danger in the darkness!

The man could see nothing, though. He knew that other men were stationed to either side of him, in front and behind him, into whom he would certainly bump if he made any attempt to flee. Besides which, weren't all the doors closed? Immediately, the man's face expressed terror, distress and the interior struggle between his contrasted feelings, impulses, hopes and anxieties.

The man slid his right hand into his back pocket, brought it out again clutching the butt of a Browning, and placed it in his jacket pocket. Then he stood still.

The Nyctalope had not missed any of these facial expressions or arm-movements. He smiled, and waited a little while. There were many people in the room who were holding their breath, oppressed by the mystery concealed by the darkness in which the strange words had sounded.

The Nyctalope, having waited long enough, got down from the chair silently. He did not take his eyes off the ill-fated man and walked towards him on tiptoe, as light and quick as a cat. Those to whom he passed close could not see or hear him, for he did not disturb the silence of the enveloping darkness. He turned at the right-hand end of the second row and arrived behind his man.

Spreading his arms, he reached forward with both hands–and those hands suddenly seized the man's arms brutally and precisely, squeezing them bruisingly.

"Mattol! The light!" shouted Saint-Clair.

All the lights were instantly switched on. There was a swelling murmur and movement, and a circle formed around two men: the Nyctalope and the struggling spy.

It was a brief struggle. The spy's arms were pressed against his sides by the hands that were crushing his muscles, while the base of his vertebral column was struck by a knee as hard as a hammer. He swayed backwards, and was immediately lifted up, thrown forward on to his face, held down by a body lodged on top of him.

Mattol and Girard ran forward.

There was an explosion; the hand of the vanquished man had pulled the trigger in his pocket. The bullet skimmed the floor and grazed the heel of a woman, who screamed and was immediately surrounded–but the Nyctalope, aided by Mattol and Girard, were quick to disarm the spy. He was lifted up in response a curt order and dragged away by Girard and Mattol, followed by Jameson, while Saint-Clair introduced himself to Captain Wallis and said a few words to him.

Wallis climbed up on a chair and ordered that the most absolute secrecy must be maintained regarding everything that had just taken place. He had a Bible brought in, repeated the formula of the oath, and everyone there repeated it with their right hand on the Holy Book. Enigmatic in his icy impassiveness, Saint-Clair watched the ceremony from beginning to end. Then, when everyone else had left the room, he took Wallis's arm and said peremptorily: "Let's go interrogate the spy now, Governor."

The spy had been taken to Professor Jameson's workroom. When Saint-Clair and Wallis came in, they saw the man standing up with his back to a bookcase, facing a window in the full glare of daylight, with his hands bound. He wore the livery of the Governor's footmen, save that the surcoat had been replaced by a small waistcoat; the man had been summoned to the assembly while he was off duty, chatting in the inner courtyard with a comrade. He was about 30, well-built, with a florid complexion, clear blue eyes and a forceful face. He seemed quite calm; his stance was relaxed, without any affectation of distress. He stared calmly at Wallis, then tried to meet the Nyctalope's gaze with similar placidity–but he went pale, turned his eyes away and lowered his head.

Damn! thought Saint-Clair. *This one isn't someone like Wolf. I'll have difficulty getting anything out of him...* Aloud, he said "Mattol!" Drawing the young scientist into a corner, he whispered: "Would you be able, within a few minutes, to put the red-haired man into a hypnotic trance and bring him here in such a way that he seems to be walking freely at your side, and make him say a few words at a designated moment?"

"Yes. There's a scarcely perceptible somnambulistic state into which I can put him and he can be made to pronounce words that I have dictated to him in advance when, for example, I tap the back of his neck with my finger—provided that there are only a few words."

"Good. Here are the words." After a brief pause, Saint-Clair said—in German, which Mattol understood and spoke perfectly—"*You may speak. I release you from your oath. The important thing is to preserve your life, for later.*" He added: "Is that too long?"

"No," said Mattol. "I'll repeat it—correct me if I make a mistake." He did so.

"Perfect," said Saint-Clair. "It's necessary that the red-haired man arrives here with his wrists bound within a quarter of an hour. Is that enough time?"

"Yes."

"Good. Pilou will accompany you, revolver in hand. It's necessary that the red-haired man must walk naturally, of course, as if he were awake, that he appear somewhat resigned to his misfortune, champing at the bit and contemplating his revenge. Can you instill that attitude in him?"

"Yes, very precisely."

"Go on then, my dear Mattol. If all goes well, we'll be on the track of Irène and Henri within 30 minutes at the most. While you're getting the red-haired man ready, I'll tell this fellow what's necessary for your work to have its effect. Since we're inferior to the enemy in weapons of war and preparatory organization, we must combine trickery with force. I don't like making use of a lie, but on this occasion, lies alone can compensate for our scientific inferiority and our lack of military readiness. Then again, against a Lucifer, any weapon is legitimate. Go, my dear Louis!"

Mattol left. Saint-Clair closed the door and went to stand almost facing the captive, leaning on a cupboard close to the window. To his right, on one side of a large table loaded with books and papers, Captain Wallis, Professor Jameson, Captain Girard, Lieutenant Saincer and Lieutenant O'Mersey were seated on chairs or armchairs. Two seats were still free.

"Captain Wallis," said Saint-Clair, gesturing towards the spy, "would you care to tell us under what name this man succeeded in attaching himself to Sir Ernest Bernd's domestic staff?"

"James Conquett," Wallis replied.

"Thank you. Whatever his nationality may be—probably Prussian—his English must be perfect, or he would not have been able to play the role of spy so successfully. We'll employ the English language, then, which is more familiar to us than German. If he pretends not to understand, I'll translate into German. Anyway, what I have to say is quite simple."

He turned his head slightly, to face the captive more directly, and used his clear and incisive voice of "sympathetic authority"—as Professor Lourmel put it—to say: "James Conquett, you belong, over and above all intermediaries, to

Baron Glô von Warteck of Schwarzrock, the master of the formidable organization of which you are an insignificant cog. I, Leo Saint-Clair, the Nyctalope, have fought the Lucifer of Schwarzrock personally. I took him by surprise in his castle, captured him, took him prisoner and extracted him from his fortress."

James Conquett smiled in haughty incredulity and shrugged his shoulders.

"You don't believe me?" Saint-Clair said, also smiling. "I understand that. The manner in which I unmasked you, however, without making the least inquiry, must have taught you that I have the power to... but words are unnecessary. In a few minutes, Baron Glô von Warteck will be brought here, in person, with his hands tied–a captive like yourself."

The spy went pale and his gaze lost its impudence.

"The Baron," Saint-Clair went on, "has agreed to talk in exchange for my promise to set him free once I have liberated all the persons his men have carried off, with whom I am primarily concerned. Since the Baron is my prisoner, though, things have happened of which he is ignorant. To be specific, he has been unable to tell me, because he does not know anything, about the latest exploits of his affiliates–which is to say, the abduction of Irène and Henri and the Governor's murder. You, on the other hand, know everything, since you were the guide and instrument of the kidnappers and the assassin."

Saint-Clair fell silent. He checked that the captive's Browning, which he still held, was loaded. Then he raised his head again, brought up his right hand, placed the weapon against the captive's ribs, and said: "You must talk, as your master has talked, or I'll kill you."

Conquett replied briefly, in German: "You may kill me. I won't talk."

Saint-Clair smiled. "Yes, I know," he said, in English. "I only had to look closely at your face, when I came in, to see than you're a man of resolution–honor, even... That special honor which does not hesitate in its service, even against a young woman or a child. I know that the fear of death won't make you talk. Even so, I tell you that I'll kill you–and I will indeed kill you, because you're no use to us mute, and I have no time to waste on useless encumbrances. That's settled, then–if you don't talk, I'll kill you."

There was a brief pause, a frank stare, then the voice became harder: "But it's Baron Glô von Warteck himself who will decide whether that sentence is to be carried out or annulled. Yes–in person. He's coming here. He'll either tell you to talk, or not to talk. In the first case, you can only obey, and you'll save your life and liberty. In the second case, your death will immediately follow the order of silence given by your master. It's all quite simple and clear. You've been informed, so we have only to wait for the master of your life or death, Baron Glô von Warteck of Schwarzrock."

Jameson, Wallis, Girard and the others–who all knew about the existence of Lucifer's double, and who guessed what instructions Saint-Clair had given Mattol–admired the profound artistry, skill and rigorous logic that the Nyctalope had shown throughout this affair.

After the Nyctalope's last words, everyone waited in silence. Conquett, his head bowed, occasionally darted an upward glance at his adversary. The others remained immobile and grave, prey to a dull anxiety. The Nyctalope, having asked Girard for a cigarette, calmly began smoking, leaning back against the cupboard beside the window, looking at the spy.

Finally, there was a noise of footsteps on the antechamber's floor. A door opened and Mattol appeared, standing aside to let the red-haired man precede him. The latter, whose hands were bound, was followed by Pilou, Browning in hand. Saint-Clair stubbed his cigarette out in an ashtray, bowed to the red-haired man moving towards him, and gestured to the vacant armchair, which was the nearest to the window. Mattol marched in step with his subject; the hypnotist's powerful mind was intimately linked to that of his subject. Mattol gave the red-haired man a mental instruction to sit down and the red-haired man sat down, facing Conquett.

After that, the red-haired man acted exactly as was required for Conquett not to have the most minimal and fugitive suspicion of the formidable comedy that was being played. Mattol specified every detail of his action, one by one, as if he were accomplishing them himself, and his hypnotized subject carried them out.

The red-haired man's attitude seemed perfectly natural: dignified, depressed and a trifle sullen, his fixed stare, furrowed brows and firmly-set jaw expressing a determination to be revenged: an attitude minutely imagined and suggested by Mattol, who was using all his intelligence to support the Nyctalope in this business.

As for Conquett, he held himself rigid when the red-haired man came in, with his chest pushed out and his features fixed, looking straight ahead: the stance of a Prussian soldier on parade before a field-marshal. He certainly had no doubt that this was his master, the terrible Lord Glô von Warteck of Schwarzrock!

"Sir," Saint-Clair said to the red-haired man, gesturing towards Conquett, "I have unmasked and captured the spy working on your behalf in the mansion of the Governor of the Bermudas. You are too well-informed not to know every one of your subordinates individually, whether you have seen them in the flesh, carefully studied their photographs or merely taken telepathic account of the essentials of their physiognomy. So, although you have come straight from Schwarzrock and James Conquett has been living in Hamilton for years, you can answer me. Do you recognize this man, your spy?"

The red-haired man fixed his heavy gaze on Conquett. Nodding his head, he replied in English–doubtless because Saint-Clair had spoken in that language–"Yes, I recognize him."

"Good. Thank you, sir. Now, just as you have decided your own fate by accepting your defeat and its immediate consequences, you must decide the fate of this captive."

"How so?" said the red-haired man, with a peevish movement of his head.

Saint-Clair smiled slightly in observing Mattol's consummate refinement–but no one saw that smile. He replied: "I need this man to talk–to reply without restraint or hesitation to all my questions. If he talks, his life will be saved and he'll be set free at the same time as you. If he remains silent, I'll blow his brains out on the spot with this Browning. The man has guts and isn't afraid of death. Order him, then, to talk or to keep quiet. His life and death are in your hands."

Without any ostentation, Saint-Clair calmly raised the Browning.

Conquett betrayed no emotion, save for a slight flutter of his facial muscles.

The red-haired man raised his head and appeared to reflect. Gently, without Conquett being able to see it, Mattol–who was standing behind the armchair–touched the nape of his subject's neck with his index finger.

Fixing Conquett with a slightly softer gaze, the red-haired man spoke clearly in German, reminding the captive of his fatherland. "You may speak," he said. "I release you from your oath. The important thing is to preserve your life, for later." And–as if he wanted to indicate to his conquerors that his role was finished, and that his humiliation was sufficiently complete–the red-haired man got up and walked towards the door, followed by Pilou.

Conquett shivered as he left. His voice choked by emotion, he said: "I'll talk, Our Lord Baron!"

Intuiting that the terrible comedy required appropriate closure and imitating Saint-Clair–who bowed respectfully–the entire audience rose to its feet, unsmilingly, and bowed as the red-haired man went past. They were unsmiling because their hearts were overcome by emotion; thanks to the Nyctalope's ruse, they would discover the retreat to which Irène de Ciserat and little Henri had been taken–and might, perhaps, be able to strike a mortal blow against the horrible and tenebrous power of Lucifer.

IV. To the Hollow Rock

"No, my dear Professor, no!" said Saint-Clair to Jameson. "It is my intention to interrogate the red-haired man hypnotically about the mysteries of Schwarzrock–for one thing, it's necessary, and for another, it will be exciting, and I crave that more than you can imagine–but not now. The interrogation would bring out a great many facts and would take hours, supposing that that you could succeed where Professor Lourmel failed. Were we to do it now, it would be as many hours lost in the quest to save Irène and Henri, who might at this very moment be groaning in pain and subject to unimaginable tortures. First, Irène and Henri–then we'll think about the red-haired man and Schwarzrock!"

"You're right, my friend," Jameson replied. "Excuse me–and give me your orders. I'll obey like the most humble of your soldiers."

"Thank you, Professor." The Nyctalope shook the hand that the old man held out.

This brief dialogue took place a few minutes after the conclusion of the interrogation of James Conquett. Warned by Saint-Clair that the promise of his life and liberty would, of course, only be kept if the facts demonstrated the veracity of his revelations, the spy had talked as abundantly, as precisely and as clearly as the Nyctalope had demanded. They were still in the study, from which Conquett had just been taken to be imprisoned in a secure and well-guarded place.

After shaking hands with Jameson, Saint-Clair paused for thought. Then, addressing the entire company, he said: "My friends, as the revelations of the spy have demonstrated, every step in the expedition that we are about to undertake will carry the risk of death, or an even worse fate. You're all ready, regardless?"

"Give your orders; we'll obey!"

"Right!"

"We're your soldiers!"

"Onward, Saint-Clair!"

"Yes! Yes!"

All these enthusiastic replies were simultaneous. Saint-Clair smiled. "Here are my orders," he said, immediately. "You, Captain Wallis, are Governor of the Bermudas. Remain here and make sure that the enemy does not appear in daylight to attack us from the rear."

Wallis gave a military salute and bowed.

"You, Professor Jameson, will establish radio contact with Professor Lourmel and tell him everything that has happened–in code, of course. Keep him up to date with everything that happens here in my absence and whatever I might be able to let you now about my actions."

"All right!" said Jameson, simply.

"As for Mattol, Girard, Saincer, O'Mersey, you'll come with me. I'll bring Pilou, and also Miss Ellen, for there are instances in which having a woman with us might prove useful, especially if she is resolute and devoted. We must all be dressed in a suitable manner for the struggle in which we're about to engage. Arm yourselves with knives and Brownings and equip yourselves with electric torches, coils of light and strong rope. Pilou and I will have our silent revolvers and our special instruments. Go–I want you back here in a quarter of an hour. Send Pilou to me, my dear Wallis, and entrust the red-haired man to trustworthy guardians. As for you, my dear Doctor Simpson, remain here; a physician will be useful and might be indispensable. When you come back, Mattol, my friend, bring Miss Ellen."

"Armed?"

"No–she'll only need a pocket torch."

Everyone went out, leaving Saint-Clair alone. He sat down, leaned his elbows on the table and put his head in his hands. Staring into the void, he meditated.

Twenty minutes later, six men and a woman were making their way through the mansion's cellars. The Nyctalope led the way, followed by Miss Ellen, Pilou, Mattol, Girard, Saincer and O'Mersey. The first and last held electric torches in their left hands. Saint-Clair passed without the least hesitation from the cellars in use to the abandoned ones, stopping in one that appeared to have no other issue than the one by which they had entered.

"As I thought," he whispered, "they've taken care to erase their tracks. They walked backwards, raking the ground with a flat piece of wood." He paused, then went on: "Stand over here, to this side. Put the light out."

They obeyed and the Nyctalope set about examining the cellar floor in the darkness. Looking around, he had observed that the walls and ceiling of the cellar were all bare rock, without any masonry–smooth black rock without any holes or cracks, save for the small entrance. There was no passage; the solid mass, gleaming with damp and stained here and there with moss, saltpeter and that earthy foam which often garnishes the walls of tunnels, was not conducive to the subterfuge of a hidden door.

"The passage is in the last cellar," the spy had said, "but I don't know whether it's in the wall or the floor." The walls being immediately discounted, the Nyctalope studied the floor. It was covered with a sort of damp black sand. The irregularly-undulating sand seemed to have been disturbed in several places–here it was hollowed out a little more profoundly, there it was pitted with a little hole–but Saint-Clair soon noticed that a square meter of ground near the back of the cellar was more uniformly flat. He leaned over and touched various points in that area.

Ah! he thought. *This square is hard, while the rest is very soft.*

He knelt down and dug in the sand with his hands, rapidly ascertained the dimensions of the hard surface, and saw that it was indeed a distinct slab a meter square. "Help me, Pilou. Turn on the light–stand there–dig there, following that line and that one. I'll take care of the other two."

Hands and knives worked quickly. When they reached solid rock, the square slab was revealed to be 25 centimeters thick.

"It's a trapdoor whose edges are supported by the rock," Pilou said.

"Yes," Saint-Clair said. "It will certainly be retained underneath by a transverse bar or a carefully-fitted bolt, but it's necessary to lift it. Our cutter won't go through metal and the rock is volcanic–and we mustn't make any noise."

There was a silence, while Pilou's fingers tested the neatly-fitted panel and the Nyctalope reflected. The others waited, their eyes fixed upon the panel, illuminated by the torch that Pilou hand set on the ground.

"Am I to be stopped by the first obstacle?" Saint-Clair groaned.

If there had been no danger in making a noise, two steel pick-axes, vigorously plied, would have smashed the slab to pieces, thick and hard as it was; according to the detailed revelations made by Conquett, though, it was necessary to avoid making a noise. The Wartecks' submarine refuge was certainly very distant, but the subterranean tunnels formed veritable echo chambers and the listening room was at the far end.

The Nyctalope could not help thinking–for he knew how vain and superfluous regret was–if only Conquett had known the location of the Hollow Rock relative to the Bermudas! *I could have gone there in a diving-suit. Is it to the north, the south or some other point of the compass? There's only the subterranean passage. But what's to be done about this stone square so neatly fitted into its rocky bed? What's to be done?*

He looked at it minutely, his gaze passing slowly along the four sides of the thick trapdoor. *Ah! There! What's that?* Already kneeling, he leaned over. A spark of light sprang into his mind and his eyes sparkled with joy. "Look at that, Pilou!" He pointed to a thin circular line on one of the vertical sides of the trap, about a centimeter in diameter. "I'll wager that if I press my finger on that roundel, it'll sink in. It's an electric button, Pilou! Conquett was telling the truth when he said that he didn't know everything, and that what he could tell me was very little by comparison with what he didn't know. The Wartecks foresaw the possibility that one of them might be obliged to spend a considerable time in the mansion, or merely in the cellars, having closed the trap behind him."

"Yes, boss," Pilou said. "But if you press it, and the button activates a warning bell as well as opening the trapdoor..."

"I've thought of that–but I think it's a risk worth running. There are always risks."

"I know that!"

"We must take the chance! If we were always sure in advance of winning, life would be too easy. Have you any means of forcing the trap open without trying the button?"

"No, boss."

"Me neither. We've been here for a quarter of an hour. I've examined every possibility. If I don't press the button, the only alternatives are pick-axes or retreat. Picks make a din, retreat is cowardice. So I'll run the risk and take my chances. There!"

Saint-Clair put his index finger on the button and pressed. As he had anticipated, the minuscule disk sank in. Soft clicking and smooth sliding sounds were heard–and slowly, as if moved by clockwork, one edge of the square trap-door rose up, while the other was maintained by hinges, whose gleam the kneeling Nyctalope saw right away...

At that moment, Grisyl was on duty in the Hollow Rock's listening room. This time, she was not reading. The scientific journal was on the table, closed. Sitting down, leaning on her elbow with her fingers on her temple, Grisyl was daydreaming...

Since she had seen the dark-haired man, Grisyl had read no more. A new emotion was making her heart beat faster and a strange melancholy had softened her rude soul–which, until now, had augmented its native barbarity with all the terrible dryness of the exact sciences. For three days, for the first time in her life, Grisyl had been singularly aware of being a woman rather than an insensible lever in the distant but ever-present hands of Lord Glô von Warteck of Schwarzrock.

She was daydreaming... and her reverie was animated by imprecise visions comprised of what little she knew about the life of human beings on land. So little! She had only ever read scientific textbooks and technical journals–but sometimes, the echo of a story in one of the journals, or the narration of an anecdote serving as a term of comparison, had informed Grisyl that there were, among the men and women of the land, beings who enjoyed a bizarre sentiment called *love*: beings who formed couples... couples like that of the captive Irène and the dark-haired Frenchman who slept beside her when she was in her bed... How handsome he was, that man! Beside him, Malta was coarse and crude, the black workers were monsters,[34] and as for the red-haired men of the Warteck race... no! Grisyl had never thought that there was anything in common between them and these sentiments of "love" which, on the land, sensuously united certain men and certain women...

A clicking sound cut into Grisyl's nebulous dream and dissipated it abruptly. The clicking came from her right and was followed by an intermittent ringing sound, prolonged for about 15 seconds. She turned her head and looked at the bell emitting that sound with frank astonishment.

"Someone is opening trapdoor No. 1!" she murmured. "Who can it be? None of us stayed behind and Schurmer doesn't know the secret. Can it be Raymond de Ciserat, who wants to retrieve his wife and, after searching hard, has managed to...? Poor man!"

Minutes passed. While talking, the girl had gotten to her feet. She remained immobile, leaning over slightly with her hands flat on the table, her eyes staring at the bell, which was still vibrating. Her pale face reddened; a shudder shook her shoulders and a kind of groan escaped her lips.

"Poor man!" Grisyl repeated, letting herself fall back into her chair and clutching her head.

More minutes passed, but the young woman did not move. Scarcely perceptible words emerged slowly from her mouth, punctuated by pauses and sighs. "What am I doing? What's happening to me? I should have called the *Grottenmeister* a quarter of an hour ago to tell him that, for the first time ever, trapdoor No. 1 is open! I must! But I can't... For whoever's coming will die! He'll die! Am I mad?" She pulled herself together violently. She was livid and her eyes were wide. "Yes! I'm mad! By not giving the signal, I'm condemning myself to death, without saving him! But why should I save him, anyway? What is he to me? An enemy! Yes, an enemy! But then–no! Oh, I don't know! But if I can save him..."

She became stiff. Emitting something like a sob as she exhaled, she closed her eyes. Slumped in her chair, she extended her right arm. Her hand was over the quadrilateral panel where the electric switches were aligned. She pressed one–and the telephonographic funnel expanded in response to the customary signal. Her voice became hard and emphatic and she said: "Hello? *Grottenmeister*? Hello? Trapdoor No. 1 has been opened!"

The news must have seemed so extraordinary that the other believed that he had misheard or had misunderstood. The metallic voice challenged her, demanding: "What did you say? Repeat it!"

Grisyl repeated: "Trapdoor No. 1 has been opened."

The metallic voice questioned her again: "And there was no telephone message from out there?"

"No, nothing," Grisyl replied.

If, for some extraordinary reason, an affiliate–which is to say, a Warteck, Malta or a visiting officer from distant Schwarzrock–had opened trapdoor No. 1, he would immediately have explained his action over a telephone line that extended from the Hollow Rock to the entrance of the cellars beneath the Governor's mansion. In the absence of a telephone call, the trapdoor could only have been opened by an enemy.

"Very well!" said the metallic voice–and the funnel closed up again.

Although she was subject to the strict discipline by which the mysterious society of the Hollow Rock was ruled, Grisyl enjoyed certain privileges. She could have herself relieved at her post by her brother or one of her cousins. At that moment, she did not want to stay there. An irresistible power, an enigmatic force suddenly throbbed within her heart and was urging her to run towards the enemy–not to fight him, but to try to save him. She did not even think of fighting that impulse. She pressed one of the buttons and waited, shivering.

A door opened, giving way to an athletic, pale-skinned, blond young man.

"Take my place, Norbert," Grisyl said.

"As you instruct, my dear sister."

The door was still open; Grisyl left the listening room.

At the same moment, a bell sounded three times in the guard-post where Malta was playing a game with a dozen black men, which involved hurling daggers at target 15 paces away. A telephone funnel opened in the wall and a metallic voice shouted: "Malta! Malta!"

Malta was balancing on his supple legs, leaning slightly forwards, with a short-hilted dagger braced against the thumb of his outstretched right hand. He released the sharp weapon abruptly, and it embedded itself in the center of the target. He stood up again and replied: "Hello! Yes, I'm here!"

"Malta!" the voice continued. "Trapdoor No. 1 has been opened. Take six unarmed men and the soporific gas. No dead or wounded–just captives. When it's done, come back and report immediately."

"Yes! It will be done!" Malta bellowed. He was amazed and delighted: amazed that trapdoor No. 1 had been opened, delighted that he had to take captives, because that offered the pleasant and tasty prospect of a spectacle in which various tortures would be inflicted on human beings until they died...

Quickly, he selected six men.

The guard-post was flanked by a room serving as an arsenal and cloakroom. Within two minutes, the six black men were masked and one of them was equipped with the gas apparatus. They were clad in coarse linen jackets and trousers, with bare feet. They suspended lassos from their belts and each of them attached an electric lamp to his chest, unlit for the moment. Malta removed his own jacket and put on a sort of armored vest, made of a material that was as supple as flannel but was impenetrable to a bullet from a Browning or an ordinary rifle, as well as the point of the sharpest stiletto. He put on a mask and armed himself with a rubber truncheon. He too hung an electric lamp from a hook attached to his armored vest, this one illuminated.

"Forward!" he ordered, hoarsely.

After the trapdoor had been opened and Pilou had picked up and extinguished his torch, the Nyctalope ordered his companions not to move. He went down into the square hole alone. There was a galvanized iron staircase there, a meter wide and not too steep for comfort. The Nyctalope counted the steps as he went down: "Twenty!"

He found himself in an irregular space, quite empty. There was a rectangular excavation in its rock wall, whose sides were partially plastered. The excavation was extensive. Because there was no darkness for Saint-Clair, he could see that the tunnel turned sharply to the left about 30 paces from the cave.

They can come down, he thought, *but no noise*! He went back up into the cellar. He walked over to his companions, who were immobile in the darkness, and spoke to them in a whisper that was distinct enough for all of them to hear. "Pilou will walk directly behind me, and Miss Ellen directly behind him. No lights until I give the order to light up. I'll tie a cord to my left wrist and you can all hold the cord, two paces apart. I'll warn you about the state of the ground if there's a risk of stumbling. Tread lightly and silently. Your rope, Pilou! Good! Here it is, miss! Good! Now take hold of it, one after another, Mattol, Girard, Saincer, O'Mersey. Wait while I knot the rest of the coil. Here, O'Mersey. Good! I'm going to set off now. Nine paces to the trap–you'll each perceive the movement as your predecessor goes down. There's a stairway of 20 steps, then level ground. Be wary! When I have an order or a warning to give, I'll whisper it to Pilou and he'll pass it on. That's it–I'm on my way."

As the six men and the women went down the stairway, it creaked slightly, but it was almost nothing.

They left the trapdoor opened and marched on.

Saint-Clair was certainly apprehensive of the possibility that opening the trapdoor had triggered an electrical mechanism notifying the people of the Hollow Rock of the unexpected invasion of their subterranean dwellings, but–as he had said to Pilou–risks had to be run. Conquett's revelations had not indicated any other way or means of attempting to get into the Hollow Rock, within whose labyrinth Irène and Henri were undoubtedly detained.

Saint-Clair had one trump card to play in the terribly dangerous game that he and his companions were playing, and that was his nyctalopia. He expected that the enemy would come to meet him and would set some kind of trap, in order to avoid unnecessary combat and to capture those who had dared to penetrate the as-yet-inviolate secret domain of the Wartecks without firing a shot. It would be so easy–there were a thousand sure means: a door that let them pass but closed automatically behind them, sealing them in a cage, or a projection of soporific gas...

Yes–but the Nyctalope, a headstrong player, balanced these reasonable pessimistic reflections against others of an optimistic stripe, perhaps less reasonable but no less forceful: *I can see clearly where the enemy might not suspect my presence, since the darkness remains total. I shall avoid traps by that means. Then, I have the nose of a Sioux Indian; I'll sniff gas at a distance and we'll retreat–temporarily. Then again, I swore to Prillant that I'd succeed or not return, and I'll succeed! I must and I will. Lourmel is watching over and caring or my Laurence, and I must bring back his Irène. That too I promised... Conquer or die, no hesitation. To conquer, one must act, and I have no other course of action but marching against the Wartecks along this very road. Onward, then!*

While he talked to himself, the Nyctalope made progress at a sure and rapid pace, followed with admirable confidence and truly heroic courage by a woman and five men, each as determined as he was to conquer or die.

Conquett did not know, and had thus been unable to inform Saint-Clair, that the Hollow Rock was situated in a part of the Bermudan archipelago that geographers call "the south-west barrier reef," exactly 11 kilometers, as the crow flies, from Hamilton. Conquett also did not know that the partly-natural and partly-artificial tunnel secretly linking the town of Hamilton to the Hollow Rock followed a rather capricious zigzag course, initially through the mass of the island of Bermuda itself, then through a prolongation of that island that was below sea-level. These zigzags increased the distance considerably, with the result that the distance from the cellars of the Governor's mansion to the first of the innumerable grottoes comprising the strange domain of the Hollow Rock was 17 kilometers and 650 meters.

The Nyctalope and his companions marched on, moving at five kilometers an hour because the ground, sometimes sandy and sometimes rocky, sometimes damp and sometimes dry, was relatively even, devoid of significant rough spots and only moderately sloped. The tunnel made numerous turns, but it was almost invariably high and wide, with no natural or artificial obstacles.

From time to time, the Nyctalope glanced at the watch buckled to his left wrist. For the first half-hour, he walked without astonishment; it did not seem extraordinary that the tunnel was two or three kilometers in length. After five kilometers, though, he began to be surprised. This Hollow Rock was a long way away! He had originally imagined it to be situated in Hamilton Bay, west-south-west of the town, but the compass he occasionally took from his jacket pocket indicated that they were going south-south-west. There was no possibility of error, though. Until now, the tunnel had been unique, without any transverse gallery, cul-de-sac or appendage. Besides, when the ground was damp or sandy, easily visible footprints demonstrated that people had passed back and forth this way.

After an hour of silent marching, therefore, the Nyctalope paused; the line became motionless behind him. They were in between two abrupt turns, which made this part of the tunnel into a kind of rectangular room.

"Wait for me here!" Saint-Clair whispered in Pilou's ear.

He untied the cord from is wrist and went to the far end of the "room." Beyond the corner, the corridor curved away along a semicircular path. There was no one there. There was no noise, save for the slight splashing of water-drops falling from the ceiling into a puddle at 20-second intervals.

Saint-Clair went back to his companions. He had sensed that they were a little tired by that long march through the darkness; he wanted to give them a rest and the comforts of light and speech. It was to find out whether this was practicable that he had gone forward a little way to reconnoiter.

"Light up, Pilou—and you too, Mattol!"

One luminous jet was followed by another.

Saint-Clair signaled to the others, only using gestures, that they too could switch on their electric torches and gathered his companions into a circle. All the faces were illuminated; they were a trifle strained to begin with, but soon relaxed. Miss Ellen's eyes were so cold and resolute that they were frightful to behold. Saint-Clair smiled at the young woman, and his own gaze softened immediately.

"It's much further than I imagined," the Nyctalope whispered. "Be patient. Remember that the darkness through which you're advancing isn't dark to me. I'll guide you with the certainty of avoiding any trap set for us, unless..."

"It's not danger we fear," said Mattol. "It's the instinctive dread, born of the dark, of falling into a trap without being able to do anything useful."

"That's what I thought," said Saint-Clair, nodding his head. "But here you are, full of aplomb. Let's go forward again."

"Forward!" they said, in chorus.

Saint-Clair reattached the rope to his left wrist. The lights were extinguished and they returned to their march.

Another hour passed.

Would this interminable tunnel lead them all the way to the Devil? There was another corner a few paces ahead of them.

"Halt!"–and the Nyctalope left his companions again, to reconnoiter, but as he turned the corner, he stooped short and stood to one side, only poking his head around it.

Still very distant, two tremulous and blinking lights were coming towards him. *Is that a patrol doing its rounds*, Saint-Clair asked himself, *or an expedition that is ignorant of my presence? Or are they coming in response to a signal announcing the opening of the trapdoor? Oh, yes! That stem, that nozzle the man at the head has, clutched in his fist–it's a gas-cannon. They're no more than 500 meters away at the most. I've got an idea! And I've got time. It may be necessary to kill–bah! They're the enemy, and they killed Sir Ernest!*

The Nyctalope turned round and ran to rejoin his companions. He talked, all the while steering them into the darkness with a brief touch or a slight shove.

"No Brownings!" he said. "Daggers only. You alone, Pilou, can fire the silent Browning if I order it. The rest of you, go over there, to the left; there's a protruding rock that will hide you. I'll be opposite you on the right, lying down in the angle of the wall and the floor. I'll take care of the gas-carrier. When I say 'Go!', pounce! There are six or seven, no more, with torches–don't light yours. If they all go out, stay where you are. I'll be able to see and act regardless–I'm stronger in the dark than 20 men. No one stick out a head–we don't want to be seen. Wait–and when you see torchlight dancing on the opposite wall, be ready–my 'Go!' will not be long delayed. Come on, Pilou! You'll lie directly behind me. If I miss the gas-carrier, fire at him..."

"But we two can knock them all over before they know we're here, boss."

"No! I want prisoners! One of them might talk. We know so little! And I have an idea..."

He drew Pilou towards him and made him lie on the ground belly-down in the angle of wall and floor; then he lay down himself.

What strength it took to suppress the sounds of respiration and the beating of the heart, to remain calm...

The soft tread of rapid footsteps was heard. The feet were bare, or shod in sandals with soles of rope or robber.

Abruptly, a beam of light became visible, sliding from left to right and then upwards. Then another...

Twenty paces from the place where Saint-Clair had stuck out his head, eight masked individuals were coming forward, two in front, the others forming two ranks of three. One of the two in front, although dressed like a man, had to be a female. Although the mask concealed the features, there was nothing hidden about the pale-blonde hair—which was, to be sure, cut short, but in a very feminine fashion and slightly wavy. Her neighbor was holding something two-handed, in the manner of a rifle raised to fire: the jet-nozzle of a tube that led over the shoulder to a grey cylinder, broader than the back from which it was suspended.

With his elbow on the ground, the Nyctalope aimed his Browning.

Five seconds went by; then he pulled the trigger. There was only a slight click, with no flicker of flame, smoke or detonation.

The man he had targeted fell head-first, as if pole-axed, spreading his arms. Sprawling on the ground, he moved his legs reflexively, let out a death-rattle, and did not move again.

One of the six men uttered a muffled curse and leapt backwards, but the woman, preceding the men—who had stopped short—said "What's this?" in German, leaning over the stricken man.

It's definitely a woman, a young woman, thought Saint-Clair. Immediately collecting himself, he said: "Go!"

Pilou leapt up, Browning in hand. Miss Ellen appeared, dagger at the ready. Then, in a group, Mattol, Girard, Saincer and O'Mersey.

The black men were unarmed. They moved aside. Thanks to the enemy's instinctive recoil, Saint-Clair and Pilou were already past the gas-nozzle whose tap was closed and whose carrier was already dead. Grisyl, dazed by Saint-Clair's handsome face, which was illuminated by one of the torches, was rooted to the spot

In a flash, Malta saw himself defeated, heart-broken, tortured, perhaps executed. He was courageous, ferocious and vain, but he was determined to hold on to his life. He wanted to fight; he fought. He, who had thought that he was taking his adversaries by surprise, had been taken by surprise himself! It was he who had cried out the savage curse—how could he have imagined that these miserable surface-dwellers would have covered so much ground in a tunnel unknown to them? He had not expected to encounter them until much later, and would then have set a trap for them.

He fought. His rubber truncheon cut through the air, struck Miss Ellen and felled her. He leapt aside to avoid Pilou and lifted his club again. O'Mersey received it full on the skull and fell unconscious.

"The men, Pilou!" Saint-Clair growled, in French. "Light all the torches!" Then, in German, he said: "Hands up, or you're dead men!"

But first, he felled Malta with a bullet to the head. Then, holstering the Browning, he pounced on the motionless young woman. She allowed herself to be pushed to one side, trussed up from her shoulders to her feet, and remained leaning against the rock, stupefied.

At Saint-Clair's command, torches were lit, augmenting the light already provided by the survivors. Pilou brandished his revolver in the black men's faces–two of whom, once they had got a grip on themselves, had begun to fight back. One was half-strangling Saincer, but the sub-mariner sliced his opponent's carotid artery with a desperate slash of his dagger and liberated himself from the terrible hands. The second, a giant, tried to lay Mattol out, but the latter avoided his punch and planted his knife in his opponent's side. As for the other three, having seen Malta killed, they were terrified of the power of the weapon they were facing. Kneeling down with hands upraised, they begged for mercy. The fight was over. It had lasted two minutes. There had been no noise, save for Saint-Clair's constrained growl as he barked his orders, and the muffled fall of the dead bodies,

Having disposed of his adversary, Mattol occupied himself with Miss Ellen and O'Mersey. Malta's club had struck the young Englishwoman on the shoulder; pain and the commotion had caused her to faint, but she recovered consciousness immediately and was completely restored to heath by a mouthful of the rum that Pilou kept in a small flask in the satchel fixed to his belt. As for O'Mersey, he was dead; the truncheon had fractured his skull. His body was set aside, with the face veiled.

On the Nyctalope's orders, the three surviving men were stripped of their jackets and trousers, under which each of them wore a flannel vest and linen underpants. They also gave up their torches and masks, and those of their dead comrades. Then, their arms and legs were securely tied up and they were laid on the ground some distance away from the corpses. They were warned that they must not try to get free, if they wanted to save their lives.

Only Malta's mask was taken, by Saint-Clair, who suspended it from his belt.

"Miss Ellen, and you too, my friends," Saint-Clair said. "Dress yourselves in these jackets and trousers and put these masks on your faces. Would you take charge of the gas-generator, Saincer? It might well be useful. Put your own torches in your pockets and attach theirs to your breasts. Have you got the rope,

Pilou? Good! Get ready to march; we'll continue towards the Hollow Rock–but first, I'd like a little chat with this woman..."

Saint-Clair had not been mistaken on that point; his captive's masculine clothes could not hide a figure and features that were undoubtedly feminine, despite the athletic appearance of her legs and torso. The delicate finesse of her hands and her hair gave her away...

Saint-Clair turned to the captive, freed her rapidly from the bonds he had tied round her when he wanted her to be motionless, and said in German, in a voice that was soft but firm: "Would you care to unmask, Madame?" She obeyed; her forehead, eyes and lips seemed so young to the Nyctalope that be corrected himself, smiling. "That should be Mademoiselle, I think. Your name, please?"

"Grisyl," the young woman replied, with a timidity that astonished her and made her blush.

"Well, Mademoiselle Grisyl," the Nyctalope said, seriously, "your face and eyes have the characteristic features–albeit very feminine–of a race of which I have already seen two specimens. You're a Warteck, are you not?"

Surprised, Grisyl replied: "Yes."

"I won't ask you to serve me, then," Saint-Clair went on, nobly. "I don't suppose you'd answer my questions–but you're an enemy. I must make sure of you. Permit me to set your hands behind you and make it impossible for you to do any harm. The handcuffs, Pilou!"

As quickly as it had been said, it was done. Grisyl remained docile.

"I ought to gag you," Saint-Clair said, "but I don't want to. Listen to this, though: Pilou, don't lose sight of Mademoiselle Grisyl's eyes, and if she looks like crying out, arrest the cry in her throat. You've seen, Mademoiselle, that our Brownings kill without making the slightest noise. I'll say no more. Pilou and Saincer, keep your torches on. The rest of you, switch off."

Everyone obeyed.

"Mademoiselle, permit me to put your mask back on." When Pilou had passed him the handcuffs, Grisyl had let go of her mask; it had been immediately picked up by Saint-Clair. He covered her face with it, then said: "I'll take the lead, a dozen paces in front of Mademoiselle Grisyl, Pilou and Saincer, then Mattol, Girard and Miss Ellen. Very good! Don't forget that we have a chance, at least for the first few minutes, of being mistaken for those we've just vanquished–but the advantage won't last long. All the more reason for me to make the necessary dispositions for the plan that I'm disposed to put into action. We've won the first round, more easily than I dared hope. Let's make sure that we don't lose the second. Forward!"

Followed by Grisyl, whose mind was in turmoil, and his little band of heroes, the Nyctalope resumed his march in the subterranean tunnel that led to the enigmatic Hollow Rock, where Irène de Ciserat and Henri were prisoners.

V. Lucifer's Three Phantoms

On that same day, May 20, in Paris, three events of exceptional importance–equally fantastic but unequally tragic–occurred within less than a quarter of and hour.

The first event involved Laurence Païli. Suspended between life and death since May 16, Laurence had not presented any new symptoms, either of definite mortality or the possibility of resurrection. At 6:02 a.m. on May 20, however, she opened her eyes.

The shutters were closed and the curtains drawn; the room was illuminated by an electric night-light equipped with a screen, whose feeble light made the objects on the nightstand clearly visible, but scarcely penetrated the shadows enveloping the nearest items of furniture and left the depths of the room in complete darkness.

A woman in a white smock and bonnet was sitting beside the bed, facing the bedhead, asleep in a capacious armchair. The light rendered her face as white as her clothing; she might have seemed dead had her respiration not been as perceptible as the sonorous ticking of a clock, whose face gleamed faintly on the dull marble bracket-table.

After opening her eyes, Laurence turned her head slightly to the right, towards the light, then to the left, then to the right again. As she looked at the sleeping woman, she was suddenly conscious of being in an unfamiliar place.

She was lying on her back, her arms by her sides, under a sheet and a light blanket. She wanted to sit up, so she drew up her right arm in order to support herself on the elbow–but she was so weak that, having made the first movement, she was incapable of the second. She remained still, exhausted, with sweat on her forehead and anguish in her heart.

Her eyes closed, perhaps for three minutes, while her heart calmed down. Then Laurence, feeling new strength, opened her eyes again.

Abruptly, she remembered everything: all the extraordinary and terrible things that had happened at Schwarzrock; Saint-Clair's presence in the overhanging tower; the invisible wall; the three servants, Minna, Gertrude and Marie; her own observations; the announcement of Leo's capture and Lucifer's ultimatum; her internal struggle; her plan of action; her decisive summons– "Baron Glô von Warteck. I summon you. Come!"–and her mouth, offered to the lips of the Lord of Schwarzrock; and then...

At that point in the evocation of these extraordinary and terrible things, Laurence was arrested by a vision which emerged before her eyes at the foot of the bed, monopolizing her mind.

"Oh, no!" she said, in a voice as faint as a breath. "No! I'm not asleep any more! I can see! These are real things! I hear myself speak. My fingers are touching the sheet, my chemise, my flesh... This is the material world and my open eyes can distinguish that seated woman in white, asleep in a black armchair, and the brass bars at the foot of the bed, and beyond that... that thing..."

What was it? What was the thing beyond the faintly-gleaming brass bars that drew Laurence's gaze and demanded her attention?

At first, there was nothing but a thin vertical wisp of white vapor, undulating slowly in the half-light, set against the black background of the room's depths. As soon as Laurence's gaze focused upon it, though, it rapidly became more distinct. The white vapor expanded and thickened; its undulations designed a form, and were henceforth no more than a slight vibration. The form was that of a human body enveloped by fabric that was close-fitting and blurred at the same time, white in color, with grey shadows. Although quite opaque, it was suggestive of transparency, and although compact in appearance, it gave the impression of fluidity.

To begin with, the head was merely an indistinct oval of white vapor, but its lines soon became set and fixed; a light coloration added greater density to the vapor; dark touches defined eyes and a mouth. Suddenly, there was a face, living and phantasmal at the same time, in which eyes sparkled, lips were shaped in a sardonic rictus, and red hair was wildly aflame...

"Lucifer!" croaked Laurence.

She tried to get up gain. but her weakness pinned her to the bed, her head raised by the firm pillow. Overwhelmed, but lucid, Laurence Païli heard a voice.

It was definitely the voice of Glô von Warteck, Lord of Schwarzrock, the voice of Lucifer–just as the form floating at the foot of the bed was definitely his phantom, and that fantastic face definitely his. But Laurence did not hear the voice as if it were the phantom's; she heard it as if it were inside her, in her own brain. Even so, the phantom's lips moved as if it were speaking.

"Do you recognize me?" the voice said–and Laurence was irresistibly compelled to reply, as loudly as her weakness would permit.

"Yes," she said, "I recognize you."

"Who am I, then?" asked the voice.

At that moment–at that exact instant–the nurse who was placed in the armchair beside the bed, facing the bedhead, woke up. Whether or not she was roused from sleep by the murmur that Laurence produced in replying "Yes, I recognize you," the fact is that she woke up.

The nurse was Madame Deléglise. She was 42 years of age, sturdy in body and calm in mind. Her character was pragmatic, even a trifle vulgar, as incapable of extravagant imagination as of material baseness. In brief, she was a woman of substance, order and good sense.

Awake, with her eyes open and her ears ready to register the least sound, Madame Deléglise looked at the invalid of whom she was in charge–and was amazed to see that the invalid's eyes were open and alert, even somewhat alarmed. The nurse was about to leap to her feet when a sudden thought made her pause: *What is she looking at?* For Laurence's eyes had the expression of attentive concentration that eyes have when they are strongly attracted to some object.

Madame Deléglise started to turn her head in the direction of Laurence's gaze, but something happened that kept her still. What happened was that Laurence began to speak.

What Laurence said, quite distinctly, was: "*You are the monster that calls himself Lucifer.*"

Having heard these extraordinary words, Madame Deléglise turned her head to see what Laurence was looking at, and to whom these words had been addressed. She froze, feeling the hair stand up on her head and an icy chill run down her spine. For Madame Deléglise immediately heard the phantom's voice, not as if it came from him, but as if it were inside her, in her own brain—although the phantom was speaking to Laurence and, evidently, to her alone!

"For two whole days," it said, "I remained in the same state as you, living and dead at the same time. I am awake now and I know that I shall live. Because I had just enough time, when you struck me, to link your vital substance to mine, you have slept as I have. Now, I awaken and you, too, will live. Do you understand?"

"Yes!" Laurence replied. "I understand, and I hate you!"

Madame Deléglise turned her head abruptly to look at Laurence, whose words she had heard and whose features she saw convulsed with horror—but she turned back immediately to the phantom, which was speaking again.

"I don't want to prevent you from hating me, Laurence. My desire is to possess you of your own free will, despite your hatred, and that is still my intention. Hate me, then, Laurence—but listen to this. Not that you can avoid listening..." There was a pause, then: "I was momentarily defeated despite my power by a woman's love and a man's cunning. It was because I made the mistake of being too impatient, attempting to realize my desire too soon. Listen: do you remember the Machine in the tower? The Teledynamo."

"Yes," said Laurence.

"It does not yet have enough power. With its aid, I can only dominate the relatively inferior will-power of women, children and men whose strength is only apparent or too limited—like the strength of Mathias Narbonne, for example. A Saint-Clair or a Prillant, even a Lourmel or a Mattol—especially if they are distant from me—still escape me. That is why I did not attack them directly. That is why they have been able to fight me. Saint-Clair, especially, whose will-power is of the first order, and who also has other powers of his own to draw from..."

"He will defeat you! He will kill you!"

"No, Laurence, no! Don't cling to that hope! While I was hovering, like you, between life and death, my intelligence was at work, my subconscious active. I only have a few details of mechanics and occult alchemy to resolve. It

230

will be long and difficult, but my Teledynamo will be completely ready no later than June 10. Then, Laurence, I shall only have to wish...! Mattol, Lourmel, Prillant, even Saint-Clair himself, will be like pygmies! They will come on bended knee to untie my shoelaces! And the world–the entire world–will belong to me. I shall avenge my family. All humankind will be, for me and my family, an immense reservoir of slaves. Besides which, I expect that Saint-Clair will fall into the power of my brothers, either today or tomorrow. He'll die immediately. I shall not wait until June 10 to settle his fate..."

"You're mad!"

"I am wise, Laurence. I want you and I shall have you. Listen! There will be stages in the exercise of my victory. So far as you are concerned, there are two alternatives. Either you come to me before midday on June 10, without mental reservations, to kneel at my feet and say: *I am yours!*–and, shivering with hatred, give yourself to me–or, obstinate in your impotent rebellion, you will not come.

"In the first instance, your mother's slavery–for I am in possession of your mother, who is at Schwarzrock–will include neither torture nor violent death; she will live quietly with you and will die a natural death as Destiny wills. In the second instance, however, she will undergo frightful tortures at the same time as I draw you to me, by means of my then-unlimited power. By the effect of my will-power alone, I shall render you incapable of leaving my slightest desire unsatisfied.

"You will, of course, be present at, and fully conscious of, your mother's torture, and she, similarly conscious, will be a spectator of... you understand? Yes, I know you do. You're suffering too much to reply... So think about it. Make your choice. Today is May 20. You have until June 10. Till we meet again, Laurence, in my room at Schwarzrock... or elsewhere!

"In order that you cannot seek to deceive yourself, though, by pretending that what you have just seen and heard is a hallucination or a nightmare, I shall put my mark on you, Laurence, on your left breast, above your heart!"

Then, Madame Deléglise saw the phantom move, float above the bed and lean over towards Laurence, whose bosom it brutally exposed... and the specter bit the left breast. Laurence's body convulsed; she lifted her arms, released a heart-rending cry, and fell back again. At the same time, the phantom faded away.

Madame Deléglise collapsed, groaning, overcome by horror.

Professor Lourmel was staying in the Nyctalope's house. At that moment, he was awake, standing before a lectern in his pajamas with a cup of hot coffee in his hand, writing. He heard the frightful cry and ran to the bedroom, arriving at the same time as Corsat.

While the servant switched on all the electric lamps, the Professor hurried to the bed. He found Madame Deléglise in the armchair, sobbing convulsively, and Laurence on the bed, writhing in a nervous fit. Her breasts were bare, the left one marked by a deep bite, beaded with blood...

The second event involved Mathias Narbonne, who had been stabbed in the hand on May 7 and had then received an ultimatum from Lucifer, which he had rejected. Since the "council of war" held that day, Monsieur Narbonne had been calmly waiting for June 10, the deadline specified in Lucifer's ultimatum. Professor Lourmel and Monsieur Prillant had begged him to utilize the antagonism of milieux explained by Mattol, and to undertake a submarine voyage himself. Narbonne was rich enough to afford the rare luxury of a cruise on a submarine yacht and the Subtransatlantic Company was quite willing to let him hire the *Synancée*, the *Lampas*'s sister ship, with a first-rate crew—but to his friends' suggestions, Narbonne had replied: "Are you two going off in a submarine? You've sent your niece, Lourmel, and you've taken care of your son, Prillant. That's good! But aren't you just as exposed to the diabolical spells of this Lucifer as I am? You're staying, so I'm staying."

Days passed. Narbonne's wound scarred over, and the philanthropist, having ensured the benevolent future of his fortune by means of a will, waited for the fatal date calmly and courageously.

He did not place too much trust in the hope that the Nyctalope would triumph over Lucifer's occult power before that date. At the end of the day, though, if the Nyctalope failed, so what? Narbonne would die at his post, as a benefactor of humanity. His godson and secretary, André d'Arbol, who was younger and more attached to life, was distressed by this obstinacy, which seemed to him to be futile—but he could not change his employer's mind. He took the precaution of making sure that the *Synancée* was still at Le Havre, ready to put out to sea.

The days passed and there was no new manifestation in Narbonne's home. Lourmel and Prillant kept him informed of everything they knew about the Nyctalope's actions against Lucifer.

On May 20, Narbonne got up as usual at 5 a.m., took a bath and eventually went into his study at 6:30 a.m.–where, owing to an unusual lapse on his manservant's part, the windows were still closed and shuttered and the curtains drawn.

Guided by the faint light coming through the interstices of the shutters and curtains, Narbonne was walking towards one of the windows when he was rudely struck on the back of the neck. The blow put him in mind of stiffened fingers. He turned round abruptly... and froze on the spot.

In the scarcely-attenuated obscurity of the room, against the black backcloth of a large doorway, a fantastic and exorbitant white form was floating at least 50 centimeters above the carpet, clearly outlined and agitated by rapid vibrations.

Narbonne became involuntarily chilled by terror.

"Lucifer!" Narbonne exclaimed, in a strangled voice, after the phantom had fully materialized. Lourmel had given him a description of the infernal Lord of Schwarzrock, as provided by the Nyctalope.

And as the phantom's lips moved to respond, a voice resounded in Narbonne's brain: "Yes, Lucifer! I'm substituting my will for yours... It's useless to resist. Walk! Write!"

Conscious of his enslavement, but helpless to resist it, animated by a desire to rebel, but unable to exercise it, horribly unhappy but obedient, Narbonne flicked a switch that illuminated all the electric lamps, walked to his desk, sat down and took up a piece of paper and a pen. His hand, guided by a merciless, irresistible force, began to write, in a calm, orderly, rounded and firm script that was definitely the well-known handwriting of the philanthropist Mathias Narbonne:

This is my testament.

I am going to kill myself, for personal reasons that I do not wish to make known. Before dying from a bullet in the head, I declare that, being in full possession of my reason and my faculties, I annul my previous wills and their codicils deposited at the office of my notary, Monsieur Dubreuil. I leave all my possessions, movable and immovable, without restriction and unconditionally–possessions of which Monsieur Dubreuil possesses the most recent inventory, a duplicate of which is in my safe–to Monsieur Eiger Nott, residing at No. 28, Rue du Mont-Blanc, in Geneva. I write this definitive testament in duplicate, both copies being enclosed in envelopes, one addressed to my notary and the other to Monsieur Eiger Nott.

Made by my hand in Paris, in my study in the Rue d'Orchampt, on May 20, 1921, at 6:45 a.m.

The hand stopped.

"Sign!" said the voice.

And Narbonne signed his habitual and famous signature.

"Now copy it!" ordered the voice.

And Narbonne made a copy of the testament, which he signed as authentically as the original.

Then, obedient to the orders of the phantom–which was still present, although invisible in the glare of the electric lights–he folded the precious pieces of paper, slid them into two envelopes, sealed them with wax, wrote the two addresses, rang for his manservant and waited, apparently quite calmly, although his heat and brain were in tumult.

A few minutes went by, then the door opened and Michel appeared.

"Good day, Monsieur."

"Good day, Michel. Take these two letters and send them immediately by registered post."

"But it's only 7 a.m., Monsieur. The Post Office doesn't open until 8 a.m."

"Go send them from the Central Post Office in the Rue du Louvre. Wait there until the office opens."

"Very well, Monsieur."

"Is André up?"

"Yes, Monsieur."

"Tell him that I want to work alone until 11 a.m. He may take advantage of the liberty I'm giving him by going out for a walk. Don't mention the letters, though."

"Very well, Monsieur."

"Now, go!"

Michel went out.

Having given those orders, of which his soul disapproved but which had been imposed upon him, Mathias Narbonne continued to obey the infernal power. Still calm to all appearances, but entirely possessed by Lucifer's implacable and ferocious will–save for his unconscious, which revolted in vain in the abyss of his interior existence–and suffering an inexpressible torture of which the grave serenity of his face gave no hint, the philanthropist bolted the door connecting his study to the hallway.

Then he returned to the desk, opened a drawer and took out a revolver. He confirmed that it was loaded. Revolver in hand, he went into his bedroom, closing the door to the study with his heel. There was no lamp lit in the bedroom or the adjoining bathroom; the phantom reappeared.

Narbonne bolted all the doors, locking himself in. Who could doubt, after that, that he had committed suicide, of his own free will? Further proof would be provided by the position of his body and the weapon. Baron Glô von Warteck, grandmaster of the occult sciences, had not forgotten that he was operating in a world in which the police and judiciary interested themselves in the lives and deaths of the individuals constituting civilized society, the Lord of Schwarzrock wanted his victim's testament to be unassailable.

To what end? Why use this atrocious means to capture Narbonne's fortune, when the sorcerer could have appropriated many other fortunes simply by the exercise of his will-power? A mystery.[35] The fact is that he had set his designs upon that fortune rather than others, and had decided to kill Narbonne–who had opposed him–before June 10, the deadline imposed by the ultimatum of the May 7. And Narbonne, thus condemned, executed himself.

He lay down on his bed, put the end of the revolver's barrel to his right temple and pulled the trigger. There was an explosion. His arm went slack and fell, but the weapon retained in his clenched fingers. Blood ran out of a hole in his skull. Mathias Narbonne was dead.

The phantom dissipated in the air like a puff of smoke.

A distant clock sounded 7 a.m.

Part Four: Warteck Unmasks

I. The Third Phantom

That morning, Monsieur Prillant had arrived at the Ministry of the Interior before dawn. In the silence of his office, in the semi-obscurity left on all sides by a single screened lamp–whose light was focused on the writing-pad on a desk scattered with handwritten papers–Monsieur Prillant was busy rehearsing the key sentences of an important speech that he had to make in the Chamber that very day. It would explain and win approval for the firm repression of certain Bolshevik conspirators who were threatening Paris, Lyon, Marseille, Toulouse and Bordeaux with fire and bloodshed.

The President of the Council, whose eloquence was universally admired, moved back and forth from the table, consulting sheets of paper and throwing them back, making sober gestures and speaking in a low voice, repeatedly going over the speech–which was not the one that would be heard in the Chamber, but which constituted the main thread of the definitive discourse.

Outside, day was breaking; the Sun rose. The large clock chimed 6 a.m., then 7 a.m. Paris was already beginning to resound with the myriad sounds of its intense life—but neither the sunlight nor the hubbub of Parisian life reached Monsieur Prillant's office. With its windows closed, its double curtains tightly drawn and a single lamp concentrating its light on the writing-pad and a few sheets of paper, the Minister's office remained in almost complete obscurity, and no sound could be heard except for Monsieur Prillant's hushed voice and muffled footsteps on the carpet.

Suddenly, Monsieur Prillant fell silent and stood still, his eyebrows raised and his stare fixed. Something strange was happening away to his right, in the darkest corner of the room.

A thin vertical wisp of white vapor was undulating slowly in the half-light... Then, there was a face, living and phantasmal at the same time...

"Lucifer!" said Monsieur Prillant, recognizing Glô von Warteck from the Nyctalope's description.

Monsieur Prillant–quite calm and absolutely master of himself–drew a chair towards him with his left hand and sat down, leaning on a corner of the table. Still watching the phantom, he murmured: "Eusapia Palladino [36] herself could never show me an incontestable manifestation, but here's one: there can't be any doubt that what I'm looking at is no hoax, for I'm alone in my office and all three doors are locked. It's a manifestation of the perispirit [37] of that nefarious occultist, Glô von Warteck. Very well, let's observe it!"

And he observed it, calmly, lucidly and in full possession of his free will—either because Lucifer had no intention of influencing his will or because his soul was too powerful to allow itself to be absorbed wholly or partially by the soul of the Lord of Schwarzrock. Meanwhile, the phantom glided slightly to the left, thus unmasking almost all the surface of a wall-panel whose woodwork was rendered totally black by the shadows. As soon as the phantom had become immobile again, scarcely agitated by a rapid continuous vibration which did not displace it, a new phenomenon was manifest.

White letters appeared on the black backcloth of the wall. The letters formed words, which formed sentences. Still calm and strong in the face of the terrible emotion that gripped him as the meaning of the inscription became clearer, Monsieur Prillant read:

You know that your son is in my power. Until June 10, he will not suffer, but after that date, he will be slowly tortured to death unless you yield to my demand. Be advised also that after June 10, my hypnotic power will increase to the point at which you will be unable to resist me, and my demands will be imposed on you. You will speak and act, without any possibility of disobedience, exactly as I wish. But then, I shall punish you, first through your son, then in yourself, for having made me wait. You are sufficiently intelligent for me not to need to involve myself in the details, so here is my demand: from today, remain the apparent adversary of the anarchist revolution in public, but further its cause in secret by all means possible. I have spoken. Before my departure, I want to leave you a souvenir of my visit, by means of a feat of levitation whose materiality you will be unable to deny. And remember June 10!

This inscription, which was luminous without being radiant, formed a narrow and tall column on the black background of the wall. It persisted for about a minute after the last word had been written. Then it began to fade and soon disappeared. The phantom evaporated at the same time—but Monsieur Prillant's attention was immediately attracted by a slight clicking sound on his desk. He looked to his side. A heavy silver and ivory seal engraved with his initials, with which he stamped the wax sealing certain letters, and which ordinarily lay in an open box next to a stick of wax and a special lighter near the telephone on the left-hand side of the table, was rising upwards, while the lighter opened and lit up by itself.

The seal climbed into the air and stopped, in such a position that the engraved silver plate was directly above the flame. After a few seconds, the seal rose again and glided through the air towards Monsieur Prillant. Descending abruptly, it struck the back of the minister's left hand, and remained there momentarily, pressing down violently. Monsieur Prillant could not help releasing a small cry in response to the blow and the burn, but immediately contained it and snatched his hand away, pressing it to his chest. The seal came with it, but took flight again almost immediately, glided to the table, descended into its box and lay there, next to the lighter—which was closed, its flame extinct.

Alexandre Prillant's eyes followed the reverse levitation, then looked down at his painful hand: the silver plate had left a monogram composed of the letters A and P, which stood out in purple relief with a red surround, having burned the skin superficially.

Monsieur Prillant moistened the little wound with saliva. Then he looked around. Seeing nothing abnormal, he got up and walked back and forth across his office, his expression grave, his eyes saddened and his brow furrowed—but he collected himself almost immediately and assumed an expression of heroic resolution and serene majesty. A quarter of an hour went by; then he suddenly stopped beside the telephone and snatched up the receiver.

"Hello?" he said, enunciating the syllables in a slow, grave and calm manner. "Yes, it's me. I want Gobelins 26-62."

He waited with the receiver to his ear. Then: "Hello? Gobelins 26-62? Professor Lourmel, if you please, on behalf of Monsieur Prillant... Yes."

After another minute: "Hello? Lourmel? Yes? Good! Something extraordinary and extremely serious just happened in my office. I must speak to you about it as soon as possible... Oh! What? That's abominable!... But of course, my dear friend... In an hour? Very well. I'll be with you in an hour, precisely."

Monsieur Prillant hung up the receiver; then he rang a bell and turned the keys to unlock all three doors. One of them opened wide and an usher appeared.

"Let in some light and air, Firmin," said Monsieur Prillant, gesturing towards the windows. "Then bring me a cup of coffee and a brioche. I'm going out at 8 a.m.; I'll return at about 11 a.m. Tell anyone who wants to see me to wait; I'll see them after noon."

"Very well, Monsieur le Président."

When the windows were open, Monsieur Prillant took a deep breath of pure morning air and filled his eyes with the beautiful light of day. He ate the brioche and drank the coffee that Firmin brought him standing up. Then he smoked a cigarette while pacing meditatively. Then, still on his feet, he re-read the bits of paper on which he had sketched out the essential elements of his speech. Having locked the papers in a drawer, whose key he slipped into his pocket, he rang the bell, asked for his hat and gloves, went out via the private corridor and climbed into his waiting limousine, having said to the footman: "Rue de Nansouty."

Twenty minutes later, Alexandre Prillant went into the Nyctalope's house. Corsat greeted him, took his hat and gloves, and immediately led him to Laurence Païli's bedroom.

"Come in!" said Professor Lourmel, taking him by the hand and drawing him to the middle of the room, into which the air and sunlight entered freely through wide open windows. The nurse was not there. Laurence was still lying on the bed, with the covers pulled up to her neck. She was pale and her eyes were closed, just as Monsieur Prillant had seen her two days earlier.

"She's between life and death again," Lourmel said, in a voice replete with sorrow and repressed anger. "She reverted to that state about a quarter of an hour after her frightful crisis. During the crisis, she saw the phantom of Lucifer. It spoke; she replied. Madame Deléglise, who was on duty, also saw and heard the phantom. She reported everything to me, with exactitude, but she was in such a state of fright that I've entrusted her to the care of Madame Urtu, the other nurse. Listen to this!"

Professor Lourmel repeated the story that Madame Deléglise had told him to Monsieur Prillant. Then he said: "And you?"

"This is what happened, my dear friend," the President of the Council replied, with the sublime calm that he succeeded in maintaining by sheer will-power in the midst of terrible circumstances. He recounted what had happened in his office in the Place Beauvau, and held up his bruised hand.

The Professor muttered muffled but furious curses. "The Nyctalope must be made aware of all this," he said.

"Yes," said Monsieur Prillant. "I'll take care of that." He let his extreme paternal sorrow show on his face as his features suddenly contracted and his eyes became moist. "No one but the Nyctalope can save my little Henri," he said, his voice low and tremulous.

"And Irène! Her too! And both of us, and countless others! All of the civilized world, my dear chap!"

They shook hands and fell silent, profoundly moved–but a distant ringing attracted their attention.

"The telephone," Lourmel murmured. Then: "Let's go–I think poor Laurence can be left alone for a few minutes."

They left the room and went to the Nyctalope's study, where the muted bell was ringing. Professor Lourmel picked up the receiver. "Hello?... Yes... D'Arbol?... What is it?" He gestured with his free hand, and Monsieur Prillant picked up a second receiver. They both heard things hat made them shiver: Mathias Narbonne was dead, a suicide! Dead, perhaps–but a suicide? No, that was impossible!

"Impossible, impossible!" Lourmel repeated into the telephone. "Hold on, d'Arbol. Monsieur Prillant will send you the head of the Sûreté... No, I can't come myself–things have happened here and elsewhere that... No, I'll say no more. It's useless to talk like this. Don't touch anything. Wait for the head of the Sûreté. This afternoon, perhaps, I'll take a look myself... No letter? Nothing? He didn't write to you, or me, or Prillant?... All right–it's not suicide... It's something else... Don't panic, my boy... Soon, I hope... Yes, understood!"

He hung up. Monsieur Prillant did likewise. Then the two men looked at one another.

"You think it was the monster who killed him, don't you?" said the Minister.

"Of course!"

240

"I'll inform the Nyctalope of that too."

"Naturally."

"We can meet again this evening, if you wish, when I leave the Chamber."

"Come to dinner here. Can you do that?"

"Yes."

"This evening, then."

And while Monsieur Prillant went back to his car, Professor Lourmel returned to Laurence's side. Once again. she had become the mysterious living dead woman, who disconcerted all the science and defied all the intelligence of the illustrious scientist.

II. In Lucifer's Round Room

That day, May 20, from 6 a.m. until 7 a.m., Baron Glô von Warteck was in his room in Schwarzrock castle, deep in a deathlike sleep.

The room was very strange. It was perfectly round, with a cupola ceiling. It was not very large–scarcely five meters in diameter and four meters high in the center. It appeared to have no door and was devoid of windows. It was ventilated by means of shafts with invisible openings and silent machinery, warmed by a heater installed in the next room, and illuminated by an unobtrusive ceiling light embedded at the top of the cupola, which emitted an even green radiance. The entire room was painted matt black. Where the circular walls began to curve inwards to form the cupola, a white line about ten centimeters wide began to describe a tight spiral, which wound around the cupola until it was lost in the luminous circumference of the light. There were no pictures or ornaments on the black walls–nothing but dull tenebrous uniformity. It was impossible to determine whether the floor was composed of tiles, flagstones or boards; it was covered in its entirety by a thick black carpet.

This bizarre room contained but one item of furniture: a bed. Set in the middle of the room, its frame was made of solid nickel and the support for its mattress of nickel chain. The mattress itself was made of horsehair and white silk, the pillow of rubber inflated with air; there were no sheets or blankets. The foot of the bed extended into a nickel cupboard with a secret catch, the bedhead into a nickel table. The table bore a square block of ebony inset with numbered ivory buttons: electrical switches whose wires were hidden in the base and feet of the table.

It was here and here alone that the formidable Lucifer slept, whether his sleep was natural or autohypnotic. No other man but he had ever entered the room since the first night he had lain down there.

From whichever part of the castle Glô von Warteck happened to be in, when he wanted to go to the Round Room, he would first go into a large room fitted out as a bathroom, dressing-room and wardrobe. There, alone or aided by one of the young women exclusively reserved to his personal service, he undressed completely and put on a simple druidic robe of white spongy wool. Then he went into a short, narrow corridor; the dressing-room door closed automatically behind him, forming a hermetic seal, while a door opened ahead of him, exactly as broad and tall as he was. Three strides brought him into the Round Room. The door closed behind him, fitting so exactly that its rectangle was indiscernible. A second invisible door, facing the first on the far side of the Round Room, gave access to an identical corridor, from which a spiral staircase hollowed out within the thickness of the wall led to the Machine Room.

Glô von Warteck, 13th of that name, was lying on his back. A night-light, whose electric bulb was in the ceiling-fitting, disseminated a faint green light throughout the room. What a sinister spectacle it was: the funereal chamber with its white spiral; the bizarre bed; the cadaverous man in the white robe, his feet bare, his face emaciated and his red hair twisting like flames–all with a vague green tint.

Somewhere within the thickness of the wall, a clock had chimed seven.

Minutes passed.

Suddenly, the extended body was shaken by a galvanic convulsion. It immediately sat up, its eyes wide open, its thin arms stiff by its sides, its hands flat on the bed.

Facing it, a misty phantom was seated on the nickel cupboard. In order to speak to Laurence Païli, to oblige Monsieur Narbonne to commit suicide, and to write its ultimatum before Monsieur Prillant's eyes, the terrible mage had not merely to materialize his perispirit, thus duplicating himself. No! That would not have been sufficient. He had concentrated all his power, externalized all his vital fluid; he had disincarnated himself. It was his powerful soul, materialized just sufficiently to excite the visual and auditory senses of his victims, that had transported itself with the rapidity of thought from Schwarzrock to Paris. The body that remained behind, on the bed, in the sinister Round Room, really had been no more than a cadaver between 6 a.m. and 7 a.m.

Now, the Baron's soul had returned and his body revived. But human beings are divided. Whether man lives on Earth in the guise of a brutal and ignorant swineherd or a quintessential intellectual, he is, by nature, divided.

Have we not observed, every one of us, that there are two entities in each of us? There is the one that lives and the one that observes life, the one that decides and the other that questions, the first acts and the second controls, and–finally–the one that suffers the consequences of the action and the one that judges the action in terms of blame or approval.

Thus, like every man, Glô von Warteck was divided–but he, unusually among men, had the power to divide himself effectively and to look himself in the face. Generally, the Actor remained within the carnal body and the Judge materialized itself as a white cloud with a vaguely human form. This morning, the carnal body sat upon the bed and the white cloud settled, light and vibrant, on the entablature of the nickel cupboard integrated into the foot of the bed.

"What is your objective, Glô?" asked the spirit being.

"Don't you know, Glô?" replied the carnal body.

And, just as we all debate the least of our actions in two alternating voices in the profoundest depths of our souls, Glô von Warteck, the powerful sorcerer, discussed a whole series of actions face-to-face in the luminous air, in two alternating voices, for a few minutes: the amazing series of actions that Lucifer had accomplished, and those that he had planned, since the moment when the formi-

243

dable Machine–the infernal and divine Teledynamo–in the dungeons of Schwarzrock had functioned for the first time.

The Machine was still rudimentary in the eyes of its brilliant and deadly
inventor, but it would soon be perfected–and so would its operator, in the same
way that the fallen angel is the perfection of evil!

III. Grisyl's Heart

Meanwhile, in the Bermudas, the Nyctalope continued his march along the subterranean tunnel that led to the enigmatic Hollow Rock, where Irène de Ciserat and little Henri Prillant were detained. Behind him came the handcuffed Grisyl, Saincer–who was carrying the gas-projector–Pilou, Mattol, Miss Ellen and Girard.

Where shall we come out at the end of this journey? Saint-Clair asked himself.

They were advancing through the blackest darkness, but they all held on to a rope which extended from Girard's hand to that of the Nyctalope, for whom darkness did not exist. Sometimes sandy, sometimes rocky, the ground presented no awkward obstacles. The tunnel was now almost level and virtually devoid of sharp turns.

They had been walking for half an hour without the slightest incident when Saint-Clair was suddenly struck violently in the back, and heard a painful exclamation from behind him. He turned round and saw that Grisyl had fallen.

"Halt!" he whispered to the others.

He helped the young woman get up and murmured in German: "Have you done yourself any harm, Mademoiselle? I would be extremely sorry–but you will understand that we must march without light. For the moment, though–light up, Pilou!"

Grisyl's mask had slipped down to her chin. Saint-Clair was surprised by the expression in her blue eyes, which was infinite tenderness. He added: "Will you give me your word that when we arrive, you will take no action against us? If so, I'll remove your handcuffs."

"I promise!" she said, simply.

Saint-Clair read sincerity in the strange face of the young woman, which was hard and naïve at the same time. He removed the handcuffs gently and slipped them into his jacket pocket, saying: "Put your mask back, Mademoiselle. It's possible that we'll have to release the gas."

"Oh, those are only soporifics," she replied, with a smile. "They wouldn't do me any great harm. I'd rather remain awake, however, whatever happens, so I'll adjust my mask. Would you answer me one question, though?"

"Willingly."

"You march confidently in the darkness. You turn corners without hesitation and without bumping into the rock. How do you do it?"

"A matter of habit, Mademoiselle," Saint-Clair replied, "and also of smell. I can distinguish the different odors of earth and water, rocks and plants. Then again, I have hands that know how to touch. Light out, Pilou! Here's the rope, Mademoiselle. I'm holding the end. Forward!"

Grisyl had to be content with this explanation, which filled her with astonishment. She admired this man, who was so calm and handsome, so skillful and strong, audacious to the point of folly, chivalrous—since he believed her promise—and endowed with a mysterious ability that permitted him to march without any apparent difficulty through a dark tunnel with which he was completely unfamiliar; this man, whose fine and vigorous features she recalled to mind; this man who had killed Malta, whom she detested.

She admired him and found him more handsome still than the one she had seen sleeping in a bed on the day of the young woman's abduction.

Despite all her scientific knowledge, Grisyl was a neophyte in the realm of the sentiments. Her emotions had the spontaneity, the impulsiveness and the violence that emotions always have in primitive beings. Moreover, she was a woman and she dreamed, as every woman does, of forbidden fruit. For the daughter of the Warteck line, men of the outside world constituted forbidden fruit, while—by an irritating contrast—the male Wartecks never deprived themselves of the satisfaction of their taste for the women of that same world. Slaves abducted from the coasts of the Antilles and South America were passed around within the Hollow Rock, before becoming the prey of enormous octopodes lurking in the cavities of submarine reefs.

These vague reveries on Grisyl's part—which had been provoked for several days past by memories of the dark-haired man sleeping next to the young woman who had been abducted—became more focused and more precise as the young woman's thoughts were entirely preoccupied with the seductive enigma, even more seductive than it was redoubtable, of the man who was marching in front of her through the darkness.

Eventually, an ardent curiosity was born in Grisyl's mind, and she said to herself: *How will this man react to the danger that awaits him, whose nature he surely cannot suspect, and to which he will fall prey? For he will be captured. To warn him about it would deprive me of a spectacle that will allow me to judge the worth of these men once and for all—or, at least, of one of the very best among the men destined to become our slaves. How will he react, this one who is a leader?*

What, then, was the danger to which, according to Grisyl's tranquil anticipations, her conqueror would fall prey?

To be sure, neither the Nyctalope nor his companions were intoxicated by their first success. They knew perfectly well that it had been nothing but a preliminary skirmish and a benign encounter in which victory had been assured thanks to Saint-Clair's nyctalopia. They expected more difficult obstacles and graver perils. The question of exactly what the obstacles and perils might be was one to which neither intuition nor reason could provide an answer. In the Nyctalope's words, they were all taking their chances.

Grisyl, who knew perfectly well that these men could not have any precise knowledge of the Hollow Rock, its extent or its defenses, was amazed that they would take such risks—but they marched on. Then again, their leader, who was so gentle and courteous, but resolute and firm at the same time, was marching steadily and confidently at their head, without a guide or a light in the darkness! For all that she had learned about the enemy, she had never imagined that such a thing was possible.

As they drew nearer to the Hollow Rock, Grisyl shivered with a complex emotion that had far more in it than impatient curiosity about the future.

Finally, the Nyctalope's attentive eyes perceived indications that they were approaching the Wartecks' immense subterranean lair. The walls and ceiling of the tunnel were more and more extensively dressed with something like cement.

A few minutes after making that observation, the Nyctalope stopped, as did everyone behind him. They were in a kind of rectangular room, twice as wide and high as the tunnel, which continued on the other side of it. The two entrances were facing one another, both having been adapted by masonry to form perfect squares of equal size.

The Nyctalope was considering leaving his companions and his captive there, while he crept forward to investigate the tunnel on the far side of the room, when three things happened simultaneously—three very serious things, which even the Nyctalope was far from expecting.

In the hollows of the rocky vault, which the Nyctalope had not examined closely, a dozen electric lamps lit up, filling the room with vivid light. Emerging from a deep crack excavated in solid rock, which Saint-Clair had not noticed as he passed by, an iron grille with enormous bars sealed the doorway through which they had entered, while a large sheet of polished metal slid from another fissure to seal off the entirety of the doorway through which the Nyctalope was about to pass for the purpose of reconnaissance.

"Move to the right, backs to the wall!" Saint-Clair cried, drawing his Browning—but the order could not be obeyed, because the Nyctalope and his companions immediately found themselves in an extraordinary situation.

They all had the sensation of being in the grip of an irresistible force—and were, in fact, caught and sucked up—individually or in groups, just as they happened to be standing, but all at the same time—and abruptly plastered against the polished metal plate. They were stuck together in the most bizarre fashion, breasts against backs, arms and legs everywhere, some parts of their bodies thrashing about while others could not move.

The Nyctalope understood immediately. He was stuck directly to the plate, while Pilou, diagonally placed, was half-stuck to him. "The electromagnet!" he cried. "The plate is magnetized! All the metallic objects we have in our pockets or on our clothing have been powerfully attracted. Disengage your hands, unbuckle your belts, slip your weapons out of your pockets..."

Too late!

A kind of low postern, rendered invisible by the artifice of the masonry, opened noisily in the left-hand wall and half-naked black men poured out, followed and commanded by an albino. The black men were armed with braided leather cords with balls of solid rubber on the ends. They tied the wrists and ankles of the "magnetized" prisoners with such skillful speed that the Nyctalope himself was secured before he could count his new adversaries.

The albino let out a guttural cry.

The plate must have been deactivated instantaneously, but as magnetism persists for some time after the suppression of an electric current, the captives themselves did not fall down. They were seized by the black men, brutally pulled away from the perfidious plate and set on their feet–for the cords binding the ankles left the legs enough play to walk at a normal pace. They were unmasked and disarmed. Their pockets were emptied of everything they contained. Even their wristwatches were taken.

It as only then that Saint-Clair noticed that Grisyl, who had taken off her mask, had not been attracted by the plate–because the young valkyrie was not carrying any metal object on her person. Saint-Clair also noticed that Grisyl was looking at him–and him alone–with a sort of avidity.

For the Nyctalope, though, that was merely a rapid and mechanical observation. His whole mind was immediately monopolized by the gravity of the circumstances. He and all his companions had been taken prisoner–and the manner of their capture demonstrated the incomparable means at the disposal of their enemy. That did not matter–he did not concede defeat. As long as a fighter is alive, that fighter has a chance of victory.

Instinctively, all the others had turned towards him. "We've been taken prisoner," he said to them firmly. "Every one of us must now think of escaping, and, if possible, rescuing the others. In any case, don't answer any questions. Be all eyes and ears, and remain mute! I alone will speak, if I judge it necessary. All of you must be absolutely silent. If we must die, then, we'll die. Our cause is too just for our deaths to remain unavenged. On the other hand, so long as you live, don't forget that our duty is to save Irène and Henri!"

Miss Ellen let out a cry of rage and pain; lifting her feeble bound hands, she attempted to hurl herself upon the albino–who was evidently waiting, impassively, for orders from Grisyl, to whom he had bowed deeply once the captures had been made. Mattol restrained the young Englishwoman.

Meanwhile, Saint-Clair turned to Grisyl. "By the expression in your eyes, Mademoiselle," he said, with a sort of severe dignity, "I divine that you understand the French language, which I have just used to speak to my friends, and which I shall continue to use to tell you that I expect you to show that young woman"–he pointed at Miss Ellen–"the same courtesy and gentleness that I showed you. If you have other sentiments here than barbaric cruelty, you will allow that young Englishwoman to share the prison and the life of the little boy your people have abducted, to whom she is like an elder sister. Will you do that? Answer me!"

Grisyl had listened with a rather puerile and naïve attentiveness. At the captive leader's last words—imperative and suppliant at the same time—she blushed, closed her eyes against the man's gaze, lowered her head slightly and answered in German: "I will do that."

"That's good!" said Saint-Clair—and he turned away from her to place himself between Mattol and Pilou, to whom he spoke in a tone that would, if possible, only be audible to them.

Grisyl only made a single gesture, which caught the attention of the albino. The latter muttered a few words. The black men, of whom there were a dozen, surrounded the six prisoners and marched them off. As the little troop advanced, electric lamps in the cavities of the vault lit up, then went out when they had passed by.

They walked for about ten minutes, then came to a wide staircase with 20 steps, at the top of which Grisyl—who had gone on ahead—opened a narrow iron door. They passed through it one by one into a plastered corridor lit by two ceiling-lights. There was another narrow door, then a large pentagonal room, bare and empty, with five doors. Grisyl disappeared through one of them, after darting a profound glance at Saint-Clair, whose expression surprised the Nyctalope greatly, and which immediately set him thinking hard. He had time to do so; during the march, he had spoken affectionate words of encouragement to his four companions and to Miss Ellen, and had given precise instructions for certain eventualities. He had nothing more to say to them now.

They all devoted themselves to their private thoughts during the long half-hour that went by before any of the doors opened. The black men stood like statues around the thoughtful group of prisoners. The albino, leaning his back against the wall, his gaze inexpressive, was the very image of indifference. A slave of a higher rank, but a slave all the same, accustomed to his slavery, he was the same here as anywhere and he did what he would have done anywhere else.

Finally, one of the five doors opened and Grisyl appeared.

She went straight to Saint-Clair. Smiling with a singular timidity, she said in German: "The young woman will be taken to the child." She hesitated, then continued, making an effort, her eyes suddenly cold and hard: "She will remain with him until June 10."

Saint-Clair shivered. June 10! He recalled the various ultimata given by Lucifer to his victims. June 10 was the date after which, if his demands were not met and he had not yet been defeated, there would be nothing to follow but days of abominable torture and death—but the Nyctalope contained his violent emotion.

"That's good," he said, calmly. "Thank you."

Blushing again, her eyes anxious and timid, Grisyl went on: "Your companions will be well-treated. Our Supreme Lord will decide their fate."

Everyone understood that the "Supreme Lord" was Glô von Warteck; what Saint-Clair knew and James Conquett had revealed were in perfect accord on that matter.

"As for you," Grisyl went on, "the *Grottenmeister*'s waiting for you. I'll take you to him."

"At once, Mademoiselle?"

"Yes."

"And afterwards, I'll rejoin my companions?"

"I don't know. The *Grottenmeister* will decide."

"Very well." He turned to Miss Ellen and said: "Have confidence, miss, and don't let Henri despair. There are 19 full days until June 10. Monsieur Prillant and Professor Lourmel are not the sort of men to give up if I remain captive too long." Then, addressing himself to Pilou, Mattol, Girard and Saincer, he said: "Au revoir, my friends!" Finally, to Grisyl, he said: "I am at your disposal, Mademoiselle."

Pilou, Mattol, Girard and Saincer had only answered their leader and friend with heartfelt expressions. Their gazes followed him as he followed the young valkyrie through one of the five doors, which shut soundlessly behind them.

After that, Saint-Clair could easily have believed himself to be in the town house of some rich family, whose successive members had all been glad to add some embellishment to their old ancestral home. The carved woodwork, Cordovan leather, antique tapestries, beautiful furniture in various styles, paintings and sculptures by old masters contained in the rooms through which Grisyl took the Nyctalope–a vestibule, an armory, a sitting-room, a smoking room, a gallery–all testified to a history of several centuries. But, in every one of these rooms, the chandeliers, lamps and wall-brackets were furnished with electric bulbs; there was a gleaming telephone apparatus on every table; every door opened automatically at the touch of a button inset in its frame, then closed again. The strangest thing about all the rooms was that they had neither windows nor fireplaces.

Finally, having closed a heavy velvet door-curtain behind the captive, Grisyl stopped and stood aside. Saint-Clair saw that he was in a large, brightly-lit oblong room, whose walls were entirely covered, from floor to ceiling, in bookshelves. The books, bound and unbound, ranged in size from folios to tiny miniatures. In the center was an enormous desk-table with four faces, each furnished with numerous drawers. Above the desk was an enormous electric lamp with a green shade. A man was standing behind it, indistinct in the half-shadows.

After a brief pause for observation, Saint-Clair went forward as far as the table. As he came to a halt, four lamps lit up within a chandelier and the man was fully illuminated.

Thanks to what the Nyctalope already knew, and what he was able to deduce, he had expected to find a resemblance between this "*Grottenmeister*" and

Glô von Warteck. He was not surprised by the extent of that resemblance: the shape and complexion of the face, the characteristic deformation of the features, the expression and color of the eyes, the flame-red hair. Without their being absolutely identical, as Glô and the other red-haired man were, the similitude was very remarkable, although there were abundant differences. The *Grottenmeister* was older than Lucifer, not as thin, and slightly taller; instead of letting his hair grow freely, undulating like flames atop his skull, he kept his severely cut and flattened down. Nor did he wear a smoking jacket like Lucifer's, with a turned-down collar of white silk, but rather a sort of red woolen pajama jacket and a grey flannel shirt with a narrow, open turned-down collar.

The commander of the grottoes had an expression in his eyes and mouth as rude and imperious as the one Saint-Clair had observed in Lucifer's eyes and mouth when he had turned round in the sentry-post at Schwarzrock after tying up the red-haired man. He recalled that terrible, already distant, moment, and thought: *Is this one endowed with the same occult powers as the other? We shall see.*

Immediately, he went on the offensive. In an incisive and arrogant voice, he said in German: "You are the father of Glô von Warteck, Lord of Schwarzrock, are you not?"

Without showing the least surprise, the *Grottenmeister*, similarly incisive and arrogant, replied immediately. "Only one man can know that–the one who dared to attack Our Lord Baron in his fortress. So you are Leo Saint-Clair, the one they call the Nyctalope?"

"Yes."

"Good. Without being foreseen, your intervention here was anticipated. I received an order regarding you–for we all recognize the pre-eminence of Glô XIII, our Supreme Lord, and I, Rupert VI, his father, am the first to obey him; just one, single order, imperative and unconditional, to be carried out at the risk of my own death."

"I can guess what it is."

"Yes: to kill you!"

"Your Lord Baron must be afraid of me!"

"A justified fear, which we all have and shall have no longer. In a quarter of an hour, you will be dead."

"Really?"

"Unless..."

"Ah! You are going to make me some infamous proposal, Monsieur."

"Unless you make honorable amends and swear to be the faithful servant and devoted collaborator of Glô von Warteck in all his designs–for you have a strength that..."

"Is that all?"

"Yes."

"I used the right word: infamous!"

"You prefer to die, then?"

"Of course!"

"In a quarter of an hour, you'll be satisfied."

Rupert VI pressed one of the buttons aligned in front of him. The four lamps in the chandelier went out and shadows invaded the large room, now only illuminated by the large lamp with the green shade above the table.

A door-curtain opened to the right. A colossal man appeared.

"One moment!" said the Nyctalope, in a tone of such solemn authority that the *Grottenmeister* held back the words he was about to pronounce. "What will become of my companions?"

"They will be generously treated as prisoners of war," Rupert VI replied, "until midnight on June 10. Then, according to the decision of our Supreme Lord, they will either be set at liberty or destined for experimental torture."

Saint-Clair shivered. His face expressed so much anger and sorrow that anyone but a monster would have been moved–but Rupert VI remained impassive.

"Vile! You are vile!" the Nyctalope exclaimed, with lucid and grievous rage. "But if I die, others are alive who will fight until June 10. I do not want to look at you any longer. I am ashamed to belong to the same species as you. May I be taken away and murdered!" And he walked towards the colossus, whom he assumed to be his executioner.

He was not mistaken. He heard Rupert say, coldly: "Electrocution, in 12 minutes, Sulzar."

The colossus bowed and muttered: "Will the *Grottenmeister* be there?"

"I will be there. But if I am not there, carry out the execution anyway, in 12 minutes exactly."

The executioner put his enormous hand on Saint-Clair's shoulder–and Rupert VI was left alone.

Now, this formidable dialogue and terrible scene had had an audience and a spectator: Grisyl.

When she had introduced the captive, her duty was to withdraw–to leave the room and go immediately to her own bedroom, since the final hour of her daily shift in the listening room had elapsed. However, once the pleats of the heavy velvet curtain had fallen vertically, the young woman had paused on the threshold, preventing the door from closing completely.

She listened.

When Rupert named Leo Saint-Clair, the Nyctalope, she trembled violently and her ears became even more avid to miss none of what the *Grottenmeister* and his captive were saying. When she heard the irremissible condemnation to death, her face contracted, her brow furrowed and her whole body underwent something like a start of revolt.

At Rupert's final "I will be there," she murmured: "I, too, will be there." And she drew away, muffling her footsteps.

Death induced by electrocution is a form of punishment sometimes used in the United States on those condemned to pay the ultimate penalty, but the method is neither generalized, nor imposed definitively, because its victims, during and after their execution, are nearly always subject to reflexive tremors and violent convulsions, at the sight of which the executioners and witnesses wonder whether electrocution might be more painful than hanging or decapitation—and whether, in consequence, it constitutes torture.

Individuals condemned to electrocution are seated in a wooden chair, to the back, arms and feet of which they are attached. Electrodes are firmly applied and solidly fixed to the forehead and one leg. At the hour appointed by the magistrate who directed the execution, an electric current—alternating or direct, but always of great power—is sent through the wires. In theory, the man is rendered unconscious in less than a second, but, in practice, one is entitled to fear that he might live for several minutes. Whether it be rapid or slow, death is ineluctable and certain.

At the Hollow Rock, the electrocution cell was located in the part of the caverns that the Wartecks called the *gefangenenquartier*, or the prisoners' quarter. This sinister region was composed of about 30 grottoes of various dimensions, situated beside or above one another, all connected by tunnels and staircases, disposed in such a manner that one could go directly from any one, without passing through another, to a central cell called the death-cell.

The majority of the cells had no artificial workings and were only furnished, more or less summarily, when they were inhabited. Even then, they were rarely ventilated. The death-cell, however, which was almost perfectly cubic, about eight meters square, was plastered throughout and paneled with polished wood to the height of a man. It was furnished with cupboards, a dozen stools and two high chairs set against the wall directly facing the electric chair.

Massively solid, wide and deep, this armchair was riveted to a platform about five centimeters high, to which one ascended by a stairway with a single step. The electric wires, fitted with insulating sheaths, hung down from the ceiling, the electrodes gathered in a thick glass receptacle on a little table hidden behind the chair. Twenty movable electric lamps suspended from the ceiling or attached to the wall-panels, furnished with shades, little reflectors or screens, permitted the direction and the intensity of the lighting to be varied.

It was to this death-cell that the executioner led Saint-Clair, by way of a series of corridors and staircases. With his hands tied, utterly ignorant of the topography of the Hollow Rock, totally disarmed and gripped by the shoulder by the enormous hand of a brute whose physical strength must have been Herculean, the Nyctalope could not envisage any possibility of continuing the struggle or saving his life.

Twelve minutes, Rupert had said!

When the victim and the executioner entered the death-cell, Saint-Clair estimated that three minutes had elapsed. *Nine minutes to go!* he said to himself. *They carry out their executions without much ceremony here.*

He saw the sinister chair, understood its purpose, and thought: *Although it has nothing in common with occultism, its operation is no less rapid. I'm completely lost this time!*

He saw Laurence Païli, first as he had when he was her lover for a few unforgettable weeks at Cap d'Antibes, then caught between life and death on the bed where he had left her. An inexpressible despair took painful hold of him, so suddenly that he groaned and tears came into his eyes–but he stiffened himself, repressed his tears and walked to the platform.

He tried not to think about Laurence again. He forced himself to evoke Monsieur Prillant and poor little Henri, Professor Lourmel, Raymond de Ciserat and the unfortunate Irène; then his companions, Mattol, Girard, Saincer and Miss Ellen, and his brave servants, Pilou–who would undoubtedly die here–Corsat, Sidonie the cook and her husband Choiffour... Even Wolf. He thought about them all–but they were naught but a parade of shadows on a transparent screen, behind which Laurence was lying, pathetic and so beautiful, living and dead at the same time. Would she come back to life? Would Corsat be obliged by a terrible heroism to plunge a dagger into her heart?

"Ah! Don't think about it any longer!" Saint-Clair said, aloud. "Must I, then, recover a lover, still beloved, and lose her again so soon and die? Ah, at least there'll be no further delay..."

He leapt on to the platform with a single bound and sat down in the chair of death, in front of the stupefied executioner.

One minute had passed.

Without his features expressing and sort of sentiment, save for a bleak indifference, the executioner Sulzar stood at the foot of the platform in front of the electric chair. Abruptly, in a dull and coarse voice, he said: "Herr *Grottenmeister* won't come until the last moment. He hasn't given me any order contrary to custom. You still have seven minutes. The custom is to devote five to satisfying any last wish the condemned man might have, provided that desire can't hinder or delay the execution, and that it's reasonable and easy to grant."

"I understand," Saint-Clair said. "In that case, I'd like to see one of my companions–the one called Pilou. Is that possible?"

"That's possible." Turning to the right-hand wall, where there was a phonograph funnel, he raised his voice to say, very distinctly: "Hello? The condemned man would like to see one of his companions, the one named Pilou."

A metallic voice coming from the phonograph replied: "*Jawohl!*"

Sulzar turned back to his victim and resumed his normal dull voice. "While we wait, I'll strap you to the chair and place the electrodes. I won't put the mask on yet–nothing will get in the way of your talking to Pilou."

Buckled straps fixed to various points on the chair soon held Saint-Clair's forehead, neck, arms, wrists, waist, knees and ankles tightly in place. Pale, with his jaw clenched and his eyes bleak because of the powerful tension of his determination to vanquish the horror of imminent death and overcome the pain of the consequences of his defeat, the Nyctalope watched the door through which he expected Pilou to come, indifferent to his executioner's actions.

Another minute passed, perhaps two; then the door opened. It was Grisyl, dragging a half-naked man along with her.

What happened in the death-cell then had the precision, the speed and the logic of certain nightmares that one occasionally has when one is not yet fully awake, but not entirely asleep.

Releasing the man, who collapsed, Grisyl leapt on to the platform.

"Undo the straps, Sulzar."

The executioner stood there stupidly, his hands suspended in mid-air.

"Undo the straps!" Grisyl repeated, already unbuckling the wrist-straps. She went on to the ankle-straps. "Undo them, Sulzar. You'll be recompensed. Besides, have you not sworn an oath? I command it, Sulzar!"

"I obey, mistress."

In 20 seconds, Saint-Clair was free. Without understanding everything, he guessed. That man collapsed on the floor... The poor fellow...

"Should I undress?" Saint-Clair asked Grisyl.

"Yes." To the executioner, the young woman said: "The mask, the head-clamp, the collar, the gloves—quickly!"

It was, in fact, usual to hide completely the parts of the condemned man's head, neck and limbs protruding from his clothing, so horrid was the sight of the face and hands while the electric current passed through the body.

Perhaps 30 seconds later, Saint-Clair, having divested himself of his own clothing—but keeping his underwear on—put on the blue cotton trousers which, along with something resembling a pair of bathing trunks, comprised the entire costume of the half-stunned man Grisyl had brought with her.

"Quick! Dress him!"

Together, with far more haste than method, the Nyctalope, the executioner and the young woman stuffed the man into Saint-Clair's clothes and shoes. When it was done, Grisyl commanded Sulzar to strap him to the chair and put the mask on.

"But, Mistress," Sulzar stammered, "if the *Grottenmeister* has him unmasked..."

"Perhaps he will. Then you'll say that you don't understand what happened. You'll act stupid. You'll suppose that the substitution took place during an interruption in the lighting that happened in corridor B30 when you were bringing the condemned man back from the library. Understood?"

"Understood, Mistress—but this one will say something!" He pointed at the replacement already positioned in the electric chair.

255

"No–he's mad and can't do anything but groan."

"But they'll come looking for you, Mistress, because you're supposed to be on duty now, in the prison quarter. You'll be held responsible."

"Yes–but by then, I hope, it will all be over."

"So you're risking..." Saint-Clair said.

"Nothing!" Grisyl insisted, forcefully. "Nothing!"

"Is Pilou coming?" Saint-Clair asked.

"No. It was me who answered. Follow me, quickly. Pilou's waiting for you elsewhere."

She hurled herself toward the door. Saint-Clair raced after her. They went from the death-cell into a corridor, turned left almost immediately and climbed a staircase four steps at a time. At the top, Saint-Clair was delighted to see Pilou waiting for him, his hands and feet unbound.

"Don't stop!" Grisyl said. "Quickly! Quickly!"

All three of them ran on. There was another corridor, closed at the end by a grille and a door. Grisyl opened them, and they went through. She closed them again carefully. They were in a large damp cave. They went down a stairway, then through an upward-sloping tunnel. Electric lamps lit up as they passed, going out against almost immediately.

"We're safe," said Grisyl, breathlessly.

They were in front of a little iron door, just large enough for an ordinary man to pass through if he bent down. A Sulzar would have had to get down on all fours and tilt his shoulders.

Grisyl opened it by pressing with both hands, using all her strength, on two stones which seemed no different from any of the others cemented into the cracks in the rock around the doorway. Saint-Clair noticed that the door was fitted very exactly into the deep grooves of a rubber frame. Two meters beyond the doorway, there was a second, exactly similar except that its locking mechanisms resembled those of a ship's hatches.

"Help me," said Grisyl.

In the ceiling, a lamp shone inside a stout receptacle of thick crystal glass embedded in the rock. The walls of the vestibule were extremely damp. Saint-Clair made these observations while he toiled, along with Grisyl and Pilou, to disengage the door's locking mechanisms.

It was rapidly done; they passed through.

Some sort of projector illuminated the right-hand section of a low-ceilinged space, all bare rock without any masonry. A dozen galvanized metal boxes were lined up there, attached to the rock by iron bars. There were six sluice-gates to the left–beneath which, at floor level, there were six valve-openings.

"It must be closed!" Grisyl said.

There were closing mechanisms on this side of the door similar to those on the other; they set about screwing them down. When that was done, Grisyl went to one of the boxes and opened it.

"Look!" she said, with violent emphasis. "Two diving-suits. Put them on."

But Saint-Clair gently placed a hand on Grisyl's shoulder and looked into the strangely ecstatic young woman's eyes. "I understand, Grisyl. This cave will fill with water, and by opening one of these sluice-gates, Pilou and I can get out into the sea."

"Yes," said his liberator, blushing. "Yes. Then you..."

"Wait, Grisyl!" Saint-Clair said, interrupting her with tranquil gravity. "The question of what we'll do once we're in the sea can wait. First, we must consider you. What will become of you when we're gone?"

"What does that matter?" she said, rudely.

"It matters a great deal. Be frank—our escape means death for you, doesn't it?"

She hesitated, but he held her with the magnetism of his gaze and the authority of his hand. She lowered her head and relied; "Yes."

"I don't want that to happen," the Nyctalope said. "You must come with us."

Grisyl shivered and blushed again, quite violently. "Oh, no! No, that's impossible!"

"Why?"

"How can I talk here, when every minute increases the risk that you'll be discovered, pursued, recaptured... and when I'm utterly confused by what is happening to me, which I don't understand?"

Saint-Clair smiled, with infinite gentleness, and said: "Fine! Don't talk. But it's perfectly simple—if you don't come with us, I shall stay..."

"Ah! May destiny make of me what it will!" cried Grisyl.

"You'll come, then?"

"Yes."

"Good—but wait a little longer!"

"Oh!"

"No, no—the danger isn't imminent. If our audacious subterfuge is discovered, Grisyl, it won't be right at this moment. The interrogation of the executioner, the inquiries necessary to link us together, the discovery of our trail, the arrival behind those two doors, the time required to open them... it's not the work of minutes! Nothing is pressing; we can talk. I have duties, Grisyl. I cannot save myself without ensuring their fulfillment—and I must ask you some questions..."

Resigned and submissive, as if exhausted and abandoned, Grisyl let herself fall into a sitting position on one of the boxes, placing her hands by her sides for support. She looked up at the Nyctalope, her eyes moist with emotion. With complete and simple naivete, she said: "I'll answer."

"Can we save Irène and Henri along with ourselves?"

"Impossible–absolutely impossible."

"And my other companions?"

"Just as impossible."

"Will my escape make the situation of Irène and Henri worse?"

"No. Their fate depends on the will of our Supreme Lord. It will not be determined before June 10."

"And my other companions?"

"Their death or survival depends of the fate that Irène and Henri meet on that date."

"Is that quite certain? Will you swear to me on..." Saint-Clair hesitated. He learned forward, very gravely, his eyes searching Grisyl's soul by way of her innocent eyes. He concluded: "...on the sentiments in your heart?"

She stood up abruptly, standing very straight. Her face expressed immense surprise. Almost immediately, though, as if she were admitting once and for all the truth that she finally perceived in herself, she replied in a firm voice "Yes! On the sentiments in my heart!"

"Let's go, then," Saint-Clair said, decisively.

She trembled, suddenly disconcerted. "What will become of me?"

"You will meet your destiny, as you said," Saint-Clair replied. Then, imperiously: "Let's go! The diving-suits!"

During this strange dialogue, Pilou had retreated to a corner of the cave. In response to the Nyctalope's definitive order, he came back, leaned over the box and took out a pair of trunks. Saint-Clair did likewise. Grisyl opened another box. Assisting one another, the three fugitives required no more than ten minutes to put on the diving-suits.

Grisyl's and Pilou's helmets were screwed on first. Saint-Clair was in the process of securing his, while Grisyl was poised over the sluice-gates, reaching out to the lever that would activate their opening mechanisms, thus flooding the cave with seawater, when...

Saint-Clair's fingers suddenly stopped moving, frozen in suspense for a few seconds, and–sure of being heard, for the helmets were equipped with miniature wireless telephones–cried: "Grisyl, Pilou! Hurry! Get out of the diving-suits immediately! Keep the underclothes on, though, in case we're obliged to come back."

In less time than they had needed to get into them, the two men and the young woman got out of their submarine carapaces.

"Grisyl," the Nyctalope said, "I have an idea. We won't leave! Or, rather, we won't leave unless we have no alternative. I need to be sure of what we can and can't do..."

"I understand," Grisyl said, lost in admiration. "If the execution has taken place..."

"Exactly!" Saint-Clair cut in. "If the execution has taken place without your subterfuge being discovered, I'm dead–and dead, Grisyl, I'm all-powerful! In less than an hour, I'll be master of the Hollow Rock! Let's go!"

Lifting his arms and stretching himself, the Nyctalope burst out laughing– the kind of broad and youthful laughter that vibrates with the joy of battle and confidence in victory.

As for Grisyl, she looked at him, admiring him without understanding him, desiring him without being conscious of it, utterly possessed by the kind of ecstasy that sometimes makes a young woman who has previously devoted herself merely to her duties into a literally hallucinated lover, who cannot think of anything but a man and has no other will but his. The instinct of love, which the sight of Raymond de Ciserat had abruptly awakened in her, had been whipped into activity and boldness by the presence and conduct of the Nyctalope. Grisyl was no longer governed by anything but that instinct!

And Leo Saint-Clair had understood that so well that the notion had become the point of departure of his new plan.

"Let's go! Let's go!" he repeated. He felt a thrill of joy imparted to him by the prospect of the tremendous conflict of violence and cunning that he was about to launch, at great speed and sparing no effort, against the mysterious and powerful Lucifer.

IV. A Redoubtable Enigma!

Saint-Clair, Grisyl and Pilou quickly unfastened the door. "Leave it open," the Nyctalope said. "If we're obliged to return, the least delay might be fatal. Run!"

The lamps lit up and went out as they passed rapidly by. Preoccupied as he was with the immediate future, the play of the lamps intrigued the Nyctalope, as it had before. Grisyl was running beside him and he asked: "By what means do the lights...?"

"Yes," the young woman replied, interrupting him as she understood the import of the question before it was entirely formulated. In a voice that was slightly jerky because she was running, she explained: "The displacement of the air caused by the passage of any living creature, human or animal, is detected by sensitive aerodynamic motors integrated into the panels. For as long as the disturbance lasts, the motors serve the function of electrical switches. It's quite simple."

"Indeed it is!" said Saint-Clair. He smiled and added: "But as far as I'm concerned, it's not as valuable as my nyctalopia."

"Certainly! When the *Grottenmeister* named you, I understood how you got through the tunnel from Hamilton–but you're the only Nyctalope. For us, the aerodynamic motors are very convenient."

"Your voice is golden, Grisyl, but stop! We're getting close to places that are inhabited." He stopped, placing a hand on the young woman's shoulder. Behind them, Pilou also stopped.

"My friend," Saint-Clair went on, "go see if my replacement–but as to that, where did you get him from?"

"From among the captives reserved for certain experiments our Supreme Lord carries out when he comes."

"Oh!" said Saint-Clair, raising his eyebrows. "Glô XIII comes to the Hollow Rock?"

"Sometimes."

"In a submarine, no doubt."

"Yes."

"Is it a long time since he last came?"

"Four months."

"Do you think he'll come soon, Grisyl?"

"Perhaps. Unless he prefers that Irène and Henri are sent to him after June 10."

"Of course! I'll make provision for that, Grisyl. But go see if my replacement has been properly executed–which is to say, without raising any question regarding the death of Leo Saint-Clair."

They were at the top of the stairway near the base of which the corridor leading to the death-cell began. Grisyl ran down obediently and disappeared around the corner.

"Boss?" said Pilou.

"What?"

"When she took me from the prison where our comrades still are, that demoiselle asked me whether I understand German, because her French isn't very good."

"And?"

"I said yes, naturally. Then she said this: 'If I should die in this affair, tell your master that I die content if he is safe, in despair if he is recaptured.' I'm telling you anyway, boss, even though she's still very much alive."

"You were right to do that, Pilou–but I knew it. Her eyes told me. She has the kind of eyes that speak, you see, and eyes that speak are, so to speak, not merely polyglots but panglots!" [38]

"You're joking, boss." Pilou said, beaming. "You're pleased, then?"

"Delighted. You see, Pilou, so far we've only been able to wage a guerilla campaign against Lucifer–skirmishes and ambushes. We've assembled a series of anecdotes–but now, it's open warfare, with operations that extend beyond force and cunning... It's going to be beautiful!"

"What a pity Corsat isn't here, boss."

Saint-Clair became serious. "Corsat, my dear Pilou, is manning a post where there might be more danger than there is here." With an emotion very different from the one he had felt a little while before, Saint-Clair saw Laurence on her bed again, between life and death. *Oh, I shall save her*! he roared, within himself. *I shall save her*! And he gathered all the strength of his being for the enormous and enigmatic battle to come.

Grisyl came back, still running. As if everything were normal and going to a plan she had prepared in advance, she simply said: "The man was not unmasked during the electrocution. The *Grottenmeister* had already gone back; he was only there for three minutes and did not say a word. He seemed fretful, as if he were ashamed to have ordered you to be brutally put to death in the same manner as men guilty of the most vulgar crimes."

"Who told you that?" Saint-Clair asked, mildly astonished.

Without the innocent clarity of her large eyes becoming the least bit troubled, Grisyl replied: "My bother Norbert. He assisted in the execution in the role of chief electrician. He saw the burn-blackened face of the dead man–but as he does not know you..." She blushed. "Oh, darling!" she said, giving verbal expression for the first time to the sentiments that had inspired all these actions, "you don't have to thank me. To do something for you gives me such joy–a profound and sweet joy that I have never known before..."

She smiled weakly, timid and audacious at the same time. Leaning slightly forwards, with her arms slightly spread and her hands open, her gaze and everything within her proclaimed her oblation and devotion, the delight of her abnegation and sacrifice.

He took one of her hands, caressed it lightly, and said, very earnestly: "Very well, Grisyl. I accept, totally and definitively, the gift that you're making to me of yourself. Perhaps I shall be obliged to sacrifice you–but I promise that I shall always think of you with gratitude and tenderness, and I shall do my best not to oblige you to sacrifice more than your life..."

He was leaning towards her slightly; she was very pale now, trembling from head to toe. As he pronounced the word "life," he stood up straight and his tone changed. "Let's go!" he said. "Since I'm quite dead now, I must act. Grisyl!"

"Darling?" said the lovesick girl, also standing up straight.

"These are my orders: first, reassure my companions and tell them on my behalf to be ready, mentally, for any eventuality and risk; second, procure for Pilou and myself the weapons that we had when we were captured; third, conduct me to the door of the room in which the *Grottenmeister* can be found. That's all."

"It must be done right away?"

"Yes, right away."

"One plea..."

"Speak."

"Whatever happens, will you spare my brothers Rupert and Norbert, my mother Dorothea and my father Hermann?"

"Yes, Grisyl. But in the case of conflict, how shall I recognize them?"

"Today, and for four days hence, they will each have a black cross on the forehead."

"A black cross?" said Saint-Clair, astonished. "Why?"

"It's one of the rites of our religion, in certain circumstances. It would take too long to explain."

"Fine! The cause isn't important; the effect will have the consequences you desire, Grisyl. Your mother, father and brothers won't come to any harm if I can help it."

"Thank you. You'll wait here?"

"Yes."

"Four minutes, then." And Grisyl ran off, joyfully. Today was evidently the best day of her life.

"Boss!" said Pilou.

"What is it?"

"I don't understand that young woman. After all, she's betraying everything for which she has lived until today. I can't understand that."

Saint-Clair smiled. "That proves, my dear Pilou, that you know mechanics and acrobatics better than you know women. For a woman, to forget is not to commit treason. When a girl falls in love for the first time, she becomes a

262

woman by virtue of that fact alone; then, love alone possesses her, and she is no longer bound to her past in any way whatsoever. The forgetfulness is as complete as the love is impulsive, like a bolt of lightning–but note that Grisyl thought of saving her mother, father and brothers. You would have been much more surprised if she had not mentioned them, but how many young women in the heart of civilization quit the familial apartment between one day and the next to follow a lover? How many of them don't give the slightest consideration to their mother and father? So you see that Grisyl is less incomprehensible than she might be.

"Don't think that I take any pride in being the man she loves. Grisyl was predisposed, doubtless by some atavism, to dream of a life other than that of the Hollow Rock, and of men other than those that dwell here. I arrived with the prestige of a leader. Before her eyes, I killed a man whom she detested–I saw the way she looked at his corpse in the tunnel. I've certainly put flesh on the Prince Charming of her dreams. Then she discovered that I'm the Nyctalope... But then again, you see, we shouldn't seek the causes and reasons of love. I know of no phenomenon that is more disconcerting to reason, experience and logic. We're playing a formidable game; let's accept the trump cards that fall into our hands, without thinking too much about the combinations of cards that destiny contrived in order to deliver those trumps at the right moment..."

He fell silent, meditatively.

Scarcely four minutes had elapsed when Grisyl came back. "Here are your silent pistols and your daggers," she said, presenting Saint-Clair and Pilou with two belts furnished with holsters and sheaths. "Your companions are reassured, as is the Englishwoman who is with the child..."

"And Irène?" said Saint-Clair.

"Irène too, since they put her in the same cell as the child."

"Good."

"But we must make haste, for the guards will do their rounds in the prison quarters in an hour or so, and the officer on duty will discover Pilou's absence."

"Oh, I won't need an hour to succeed or fail," the Nyctalope said, smiling. "In the latter case, Pilou will be dead–and me too, probably."

"And I'll be dead too, my darling," murmured Grisyl. "Rupert VI's victorious will demonstrate his mercilessness. I shall tell you, later, about the intolerable weight that has always borne down upon my soul–I don't know why–here, in the midst of these men of the race to which I seem to belong, but..."

"But we must make haste, Grisyl."

With the serene gravity and relaxed expression of tranquil strength that distinguished the face, voice, gestures and entire attitude of the Nyctalope when he got to the heart of the action, Saint-Clair ordered her to take him to the room where Rupert VI was.

"If you will follow me, darling," Grisyl said, continuing to address the man on whom she had given herself in the manner of a lover.

"Let's go."

At the foot of the staircase, at the place a few paces along the corridor where it turned left towards the death-cell, she turned right. "This gallery," she said, "goes around the prisoners' quarter to the crossroads of the apartments and offices of the general quarters of the Hollow Rock. We won't run into anyone. At this hour, everyone is in bed–except for Rupert VI, who stays up late, and a section of the guard comprising an officer and 20 men."

Saint-Clair and Pilou had lost track of time; they no longer had their chronometers.

"What time is it, then?" the Nyctalope asked.

"Day and night do not exist here," Grisyl replied. "There are neither weeks nor seasons. The year is divided up according to the passage of the Sun through the various signs of the zodiac. We do not say January, February, and so on, as you do on land, but Capricorn, Aquarius, Pisces, etc. At present, it is a few minutes past the 17th hour of the 30th of Taurus..."

"Which corresponds," Saint-Clair said, "to 5 p.m. on May 20." [39]

"Yes. We also count in units of 24 hours, and the usual hours of retirement and sleep are from 16 to 24."

"From 4 p.m. to midnight."

"Yes. The first of Gemini will commence in seven hours." [40]

"Which is May 21."

Grisyl lowered her voice to continue: "The 30 or 31 days of each zodiacal sign are numbered one, two, three and so on, not Monday, Tuesday, Wednesday etc. There are no weekly divisions or holidays... but we're here now!" She stopped outside a door.

"This is the one to which you brought me before, when I was a prisoner," Saint-Clair said, in a low voice.

"Yes–the *Grottenmeister* is in the library. It's the room he likes best and in which he usually spends his time. The doors are open. You have only to turn the handle and enter. But what should I do, darling?"

"Stay here."

"Very well. If you need me, press button No. 5 on the panel on the *Grottenmeister*'s desk. A luminous signal then appears in every part of the Hollow Rock where I can normally be found."

"Even here, in the adjoining room that resembles a smoking-room?"

"Yes, to the right of that perpetually-illuminated lamp. The signal will cause the usual white light to take on a pink tint."

"Very ingenious. Wait here, then, Grisyl. Follow me, Pilou."

And the Nyctalope crossed the threshold of the room whose door had just opened ahead of him, with no more apparent emotion than if he were entering his own study in Paris, at any hour of an ordinary day. He lifted the curtain, which Pilou took from him, and he marched into the middle of the large room.

When the door opened, Rupert VI was slumped in an armchair on the far side of the central table, smoking a cigar that he had just lit, riffling through the pages of a German scientific journal. At the slight noise of the door opening, he turned his head to see who was coming in without the usual preliminary knock. He saw the folds of dark curtain fall back into place and two men outlined in grey against the curtain. One, who remained still, he did not know–but he recognized the other, who came forward, as the Nyctalope!

He could not believe his eyes. He froze. He thought of witchcraft, of a phantom produced by the distant and formidable power of his son, Lord Glô XIII of Schwarzrock. But why? And it was only a thought, like a flash of lightning–for the Nyctalope who was advancing upon him seemed to be flesh and bone, very much alive, and not a more-or-less nebulous entity comprised of a perispirit recalled from the afterlife and materialized...

Swiftly placing the journal and cigar on the table, Rupert VI stood up abruptly.

The Nyctalope stopped and aimed his Browning. His eyes were terrible in their calm fixity. "Don't move, or I'll shoot," he said, his voice cold and contained. "My pistol makes no sound. Move away from the summoning panel, to the right. There! You're close to another armchair–sit down. Sit down! Good. This stool will do for me. We're face to face now. Don't move! Pilou!"

The Provençal came running forward. Without taking his eyes off Rupert VI, Saint-Clair went on: "Unfasten the strings of those two files there on the table. Quickly! Tie his hands and feet, securely. One never knows, with all their mechanisms... Make sure the armchair isn't furnished with an electric wire. Disconnect it. Good! Stay there."

He paused, then resumed in a curt tone: "Now, Monsieur, without wasting time explaining my resurrection, I inform you that your life is no more precious to me than mine was to you. I won't kill you if you don't give me any trouble, but if you do, I'll kill you instantly. I won't ask you any questions and I don't need any information from you, but don't allow yourself to put up any resistance. At the slightest gesture or suggestion of rebellion or perfidy, I'll kill you or have you killed. Is that understood? Good, Pilou?"

"Boss?"

Go tell you-know-who to get you a gas-projector and two masks, right away. Put the machine on your back, put on one of the masks, and bring me the other. Hurry!"

Pilou went out without replying. During his absence, Saint-Clair did nothing, except watch and study his captive. He scarcely even bothered to think; his mind was at rest. The plan of action that he had formulated once and for all could only be modified in response to subsequent events and newly-arisen facts. Calmly, therefore, the Nyctalope waited.

Pilou soon returned, his face masked, the machine on his back, the gas-nozzle in his left hand and a second mask in his right. Saint-Clair took the mask and put it on. Then, his voice muffled by the preserver but quite distinct, he said to Pilou: "Put that man to sleep for me."

The Provençal had only to turn a little tap attached to the nozzle. Gas emerged, as visible as the liquid emerging from an atomizer. It slowly formed a vapor, which condensed around Rupert VI's head, at which the nozzle was aimed from a distance of two meters.

"I was told not to turn it on for longer than a minute," Pilou said.

"So be it!"

Almost immediately after the tap was turned off, the vapor dissipated rapidly. Rupert VI was asleep, his eyes closed and his mouth half-open. His breathing was even but slightly exaggerated, his limp body sprawled on the armchair.

"Very good!" said Saint-Clair. Going to the table, he pressed button No. 5 on the summoning panel.

The door-curtain was pushed aside and Grisyl came running. She darted an indifferent glance at Rupert VI, then immediately looked to the Nyctalope, gazing at him with manifest admiration and love.

"Where can we put him?"

"On his bed–his room's there." Grisyl pointed at a door curtain to her left. "No one will go into that room without being summoned–besides, it's the time when Rupert normally goes to bed."

Saint-Clair had put his Browning back in its holster. He went forward, put his hands under Rupert's armpits and around his back and lifted him up. Grisyl had already opened the door to the bedroom. It was an austere cell: walls paneled but bare; an iron bedstead; a night-stand; an aluminum wardrobe; several overlapping rush mats forming a bedside rug; a globular electric ceiling-light whose cord hung down near the pillow; that was all. A half-open door gave access to a dressing-room furnished with taps, bowls and the usual indispensable objects. The two rooms had no other exit than the one to the library.

"Perfect," said Saint-Clair, inspecting everything rapidly after depositing Rupert on the bed. "Come on, Grisyl!" He turned off the electric light as he went out, with Grisyl on his heels; then he closed the door.

"How long will he sleep?" Saint-Clair asked.

"At least 12 hours."

"And at most?"

"Fourteen, occasionally 15."

"Good. Take me to the prison quarter."

"To your companions?"

"Yes."

"Let's go, darling. We'll make a long detour, to avoid the guard-room."

"As you please."

Grisyl, confident as she was, wore an anxious expression. As for Pilou, whose face was hidden by the mask, he had an insouciance that nothing could ever disturb while he was operating under the Nyctalope's direct orders. The Nyctalope himself, who had uncovered his face, would not have shown Grisyl or Pilou anything but impassive features, eyes that were lively, serious and calm, and lips that were occasionally parted by a smile–the smile of pleasure that one experiences in realizing, step by step, a difficult enterprise which the least unforeseen incident might turn into a shattering catastrophe.

The captives were only slightly surprised to see the Nyctalope arriving in their prison, which was a huge cave with a boarded floor, furnished with hammocks, stools and tables, brightly-lit, well-ventilated and–all things considered–relatively comfortable. Grisyl had done more than reassure them. She had said to them: "The Nyctalope is free and working on your behalf."

The congratulations were brief and Saint-Clair did not offer any explanation. The braided leather ropes were rapidly untied. "Everyone keep his own," Saint-Clair said. "They might come in handy." Then, to Grisyl: "Where are their weapons and masks?"

"In a cell in the arsenal."

"Is it far?"

"No, close by."

"Let's go."

"Ten minutes later, Mattol, Girard and Saincer were masked, armed and content. Pilou was still carrying the gas projector. Mattol, Girard and Saincer asked no questions, From the Nyctalope's face, when he unmasked momentarily, they understood that there was only time for action, not for words, except for commands.

"To the guard-room, Grisyl," Saint-Clair said.

"This way, darling."

She moved off, light of foot and prodigiously happy. Serving this extraordinary man, obeying him blindly, filled her with a voluptuous sensation of absolute surrender. She did not ask herself how far he might go in exploiting her willingness to renounce her family and betray her past by assisting the enemy of the Wartecks, whose name she bore and whose blood circulated in her veins. The Wartecks! Save for her father, her mother and her brothers, she feared them and disliked them; she had never understood the profound reasons for their abnormal existence. Ever since she had learned to read, observe and listen, she had dreamed of living in the sunlight with the men and women of the land, of seeing, touching and smelling flowers, of being dressed in silky fabrics that enveloped the body and hung loosely. In brief, she was a daughter of Eve more than a daughter, sister, cousin and niece of Wartecks.

While he marched to meet his fate–the next inevitable stage in his plan of action–Saint-Clair had a clear intuition of all this, and thought about it.

"Grisyl," he said, abruptly, "is your mother also a Warteck?"

"No," the young women replied, surprised and suddenly very emotional.

"What nationality is she, then?"

"Russian. My father saved her from a shipwreck; he kept her and made her his wife."

"Yes–I understand better now. Thank you, Grisyl."

She smiled and increased her pace, using her haste to demonstrate her zeal to satisfy him.

He reverted to thinking about the guards. "There are 21 men, aren't there?"

"Counting the officer, yes–but we shouldn't talk any more, and we should walk soundlessly."

Pilou, Mattol, Saincer and Girard lightened their step. They rounded a corner in the corridor and crossed a rotunda. A doorless arch gave entry into a room dotted with smoothed and polished columns of rock, between which were camp-beds occupied by full-dressed sleepers. There was a table where four men were playing cards; another, better-dressed man was watching. The whole room was brightly it by lamps fixed to the columns, the ceiling and the carefully-evened walls.

"Hands up, if you value your lives!" Saint-Clair said, in German.

Pilou was already aiming his gas-projector at the petrified card-players, while Girard and Mattol covered them with their Brownings. Saincer inspected the line of beds, weapon in hand, but none of the sleepers woke up. As for the officer, who was covered by Saint-Clair, he had no thought of rebellion. Neither he nor his men had been informed of the details of Malta's expedition and its aftermath. All he knew, from the colleague from whom he had taken over, was that a man had been electrocuted and that four more were imprisoned in cell No. 6; he would have checked on them during his rounds. Four captives? Now he saw five masked aggressors, one of them armed with a gas-projector, and Miss Grisyl, watching and smiling. Genuinely amazed, he stared at Pilou, who was vaporizing the soporific gas beneath his nose. Then he collapsed, falling asleep without having understood what was happening.

Sixteen of the 21 men were left lying on the beds, four slumped on the table and one stretched out on the floor-mats. Some of them had been put to sleep for a minimum of 12 hours and the rest had been bound and gagged before they were in a state to resist.

"There!" said Saint-Clair, unmasking. "That's done. Grisyl?"

"Darling?"

"Do you have some means of communicating with James Conquett–your spy in the Governor's palace in Hamilton?"

"Ah, Schurmer!" said Grisyl, smiling with naïve astonishment. "Have you also captured him?"

"Yes–unmasked and captured. You have telephones, I know, and these telephones are connected with the one used by Governor of the Bermudas himself. That's good–I admire the ingenious audacity of the Wartecks. But when you have to speak to Schurmer, what do you do here? Schurmer did not know and could not tell me."

"We only communicate with him at certain hours of the day and night when he is on duty at the door of the Governor's office and the Governor is not there. We have a special signal, to which Schurmer responds with another signal before any exchange of words. Without the response, we don't speak."

"Yes–I know all that. But where's the apparatus that communicates with him?"

"Schurmer can be contacted from the library or the listening room."

"Let's go to the listening room, then."

"One of my brothers is there..."

"Very well–don't show yourself right away. I'll treat him with respect. Pilou will put him to sleep, and when your brother wakes up, you can tell him some story..."

"He'll be with me, then?"

"Certainly–here or elsewhere, today or some other day. I don't know yet–but your father, your mother and your brothers will be reunited with you. Let's go, Grisyl. The listening room."

"Let' go, darling."

Grisyl led the way; Saint-Clair put his mask back on and followed. Mattol, Girard and Saincer, who were beginning to think that the Nyctalope had surpassed himself, followed him, with as much curiosity as confidence.

In the listening room, Saint-Clair and Pilou had no difficulty taking Norbert by surprise, holding him down and putting him to sleep. He was carefully laid out on the thick carpet that covered the room's floorboards. Then Grisyl came in and reassured herself that her brother was in no danger. After that, she turned up the ventilator to dissipate the remains of the soporific gas, so that they could take off their masks.

"Where's the telephone?" Saint-Clair asked.

"Wait," said Grisyl. She pressed two of the buttons on the table. The telephonographic funnel opened out in the side wall. The young woman pressed a third button.

"There," she said. "The bell is ringing in the Governor's office. If there's anyone there..."

"Captain Wallis has installed a camp bed in there," Mattol said. "And there's the response-signal that Conquett revealed to us, which Wallis is sending."

Indeed, a musical clicking-sound was heard, rapidly ascending and descending the scale.

"Good!" said Grisyl, still addressing Saint-Clair. "You may talk, darling. Speech is picked up from anywhere in the room, provided that the speaker turns towards the funnel and pronounces the words loudly and a little more distinctly than usual."

Pilou, Mattol, Captain Girard and Saincer were passionately interested, as one might imagine. It seemed to them that they were both actors and audience in a powerful drama whose plot and dénouement they did not know. Grisyl was the most avidly curious of all.

"Hello? Hello? Captain Wallis?" said Saint-Clair.

"Hello? Yes, who's speaking?" the voice emerging from the funnel said, in English

The voice was metallic, but Mattol, in particular, recognized it instantly. "Yes!" he said. "Yes, it's really Wallis!"

"Good," said Saint-Clair. Speaking into the funnel, he said: "Leo Saint-Clair. The Nyctalope."

"Hurrah!" said Wallis's voice, surprised and joyful. "How are you?"

"I've won the day," Saint-Clair replied in English.

"Any losses?"

"Yes. O'Mersey's dead."

"Poor fellow! Honor and glory to him! What are your orders?"

"Here they are. Can you write them down as I dictate them."

"Yes, I'm listening."

The Nyctalope dictated his orders slowly. "Firstly, get Raymond de Ciserat's strength back by telling him that Irène's waiting for him here. Tell him to bring the entire crew of the *Lampas*. Understood?"

"Understood and written down."

"Secondly, at the same time, send me 50 soldiers and their officers, with minimum equipment, armed only with Brownings. Understood?"

"Understood and written down."

"A question. Have you any seamen in the *Blue Rose*'s crew who have served on submarines?"

"Yes. Exactly six."

"Thirdly, then, send me those six seamen, armed with Brownings, furnished with proper authorization for a month's secondment and their personal belongings. Understood?"

"Understood."

"That's all. The entrance to the communicating tunnel is open, in the last cellar. The tunnel is about 17 kilometers long. It's necessary that Raymond, his crew and your seamen cross that distance in a maximum of three hours. How much time will you require to summon them, assemble them and get them down to the cellars?"

"Twenty minutes or so."

"Very well—I want everyone here in three and a half hours at the latest. I'll give the officer commanding the English soldiers my explicit and definitive instructions."

"They'll be followed exactly."

"Many thanks, Captain Wallis—and *au revoir*!"

"*Au revoir*, Monsieur Saint-Clair."

Grisyl pressed a button and the funnel closed up.

"There–it's all arranged!" said the Nyctalope, in his normal voice. "I'm very satisfied, Grisyl."

"Darling!"

"Conquett–Schurmer–told me that your electromagnetic submarine is named *Uberalles*?"

"Indeed."

"I imagine that it's ready to put to sea immediately?"

"Yes."

"Where is its crew?"

"At this hour, the officers and crewmen are asleep in the maritime quarter of the Hollow Rock. There are only four sailors standing guard aboard the *Uberalles*, working three hours shifts in pairs."

"Perfect. And the *Lampas*?"

"It's beached in the *Uberalles*' dock."

"Undamaged?"

"Quite intact."

"Better and better. Well, Grisyl, this is what we're going to do while we wait for Monsieur de Ciserat and the Englishmen to arrive... Oh! I've thought of something else. Let me inform you, Grisyl, that a red-haired man whose name I don't know was abducted from Schwarzrock by Pilou and myself, because his perfect resemblance to Glô XIII, your Supreme Lord, interested me tremendously. I brought him to the Bermudas, thinking that he might be useful. He has, indeed, been useful, and I don't want to lose him, even though he's in some kind of bizarre trance, from which he can't be extracted except by hypnotizing him and making him act by suggestion. You'll take charge of him, Grisyl."

Without pausing in response to the astonishment of the young woman's expression, Saint-Clair continued: "So, while we wait for the men from Hamilton to arrive, this is what we'll do. First, you'll take me to Mademoiselle Irène, Henri and Miss Ellen. Then, while Mattol and I remain with them, you'll take Saincer and Girard here, with Pilou, aboard the *Uberalles*, where you'll make it impossible for the four sailors on guard to do any harm. Furthermore, you'll do whatever is necessary–whatever you like, since I have confidence in your ingenuity–to prevent the officers and crew of the *Uberalles* from leaving the cave in the maritime quarter where they're presently asleep. Then, tell Saincer and Girard how they can get into the *Lampas*. Is that possible, Grisyl?"

"Yes, darling."

"Good–you'll give them the information, then, and return to me, with Pilou alone. Is all that understood?"

"Yes, darling."

"And you'll remember it all?"

"Oh, yes!"

271

"Leave your brother asleep there. We'll attend to him and your parents when the moment comes. Let's go to Irène.

"Oh, Saint-Clair!" cried Mattol. "What genius!"

"Hush!" said the smiling Nyctalope. "Crying victory too soon and too loudly might wake some somnolent contrary destiny. We're not yet at the end of the road, and there's still a risk of slipping on a banana-skin!"

Everyone understood now. Mattol, Girard, Saincer, Pilou and Grisyl, all knew the principal dispositions and the consequences of the Nyctalope's scheme. It was, indeed, quite simple. It is true that without Grisyl... But a Nyctalope always finds a Grisyl, as a Napoleon always finds a Barras' Mistress.[41] It is the everyday working of enigmatic destiny: *Audaces Fortuna Juvat*! Yes, fortune favors the bold–at least when she is not capricious, coquettish and perverse, performing some sudden about-face in order to oblige them to fight against her, tame her, possess her and enslave her.

V. Into What Future?

After being put into a deep sleep by the soporific gas, removed from their beds and brought to the Hollow Rock, Irène de Ciserat and Henri Prillant had been deposited on two fine twin beds in a room quite similar to a first-class cabin on a transatlantic liner. This room communicated on one side with a very comfortable bathroom, and on the other with a another double room—beyond which, in sequence, were two other rooms paneled in polished oak, fitted out as a sitting-room and dining-room. The whole comprised a complete apartment, whose sole bizarrerie was that it had neither portholes overlooking the sea nor windows looking out upon the land.

When Irène woke up, she was utterly disorientated for more than a quarter of an hour. Then, by reflection and observation, and the sight of little Henri sleeping in the neighboring bed, she deduced that someone had kidnapped them while they slept. Who? Why? Where was she? The unfortunate woman was beginning to get distressed when someone came in: a man? No, a woman, rather old, disconcerting in her pajama jacket and turned-down shirt, with her hair cut short. The woman spoke very softly, in French, with a bizarre accent that Irène did not recognize. The woman told her the simple truth.

Irène moaned and wept desperately; separated from Raymond forever, she had finally fallen prey to Lucifer. She would rather have died. The woman did not try to console her, but she prevented the unhappy Irène, who was almost mad with sorrow and terror, from injuring herself by the violence of her convulsions.

Fortunately for him, Henri was not a witness to this atrocious scene. More effective on his youthful constitution, the soporific gas kept him profoundly asleep for much longer.

Finally, exhausted, Irène fell into a prostration that led her guardian—who was certainly an expert nurse, perhaps a knowledgeable physician—to deem it appropriate to give her an injection, which soon restored her to consciousness.

For several hours, Irène remained somber and meditative, refusing all nourishment. Then, little Henri suddenly awoke—and Irène, sublime in her abnegation, courage and pity, devoted herself entirely to the care of the child. She told him a plausible and marvelous story of being transported to a subterranean villa to escape the bad magician who had tried to strangle him before.

"And Miss Ellen?"

"Exactly!" Irène replied, heroically restraining her tears and sobs. "She gave chase to the bad magician, whom she was finally able to see in the moonlight—the only light in which magical beings are visible—and she will kill her!"

"Then she'll come back?" Henri asked.

"Yes, of course."

And the hours passed by. In order not to alarm the child, Irène succeeded in controlling her suffering and her terror. She ate and drank, and made him eat and drink. He slept, and she watched over him while he slept. The old woman in the pajama jacket admired her, and gave evidence of that admiration with all sorts of attentive gestures.

Then, a miracle! Miss Ellen arrived.

How? Why? Irène set such question aside for later. Henri was awake and saw the governess he loved so much come in. He threw his arms around her.

"Have you killed the bad magician, Miss?"

Very quickly, pressing her hands against her heart–which was beating as if to break–Irène gave Miss Ellen the gist of the story she had told. The Englishwoman, her eyes full of tears and her voice stammering with contained sobs, assured him that she had killed the bad magician.

Eventually, the child went to sleep on the knees of the martyrized Irène, who was finally able to ask about Raymond.

Miss Ellen recounted the entire adventure: the Nyctalope arriving by aeroplane with the red-haired man who was, unfortunately, only Lucifer's double; the speedy investigation and the discovery of the spy; his interrogation; the expedition to the Hollow Rock. The account was devoid of any significant detail, for she herself knew only the broad outline of events. She had scarcely finished when a powerful young woman in a grey woolen vest and trunks came into the imitation cabin, smiling strangely, and calmly said to the two stupefied women: "The Nyctalope is free. He will be victorious. Be hopeful! He will free you within the hour. I am Grisyl, whom he instructed to reassure you. Don't go to bed. Wake the child. Be ready."

They woke Henri, and told him that they were about to leave.

"To go where?"

They did not know, but surely to somewhere pleasant, now that the bad magician no longer existed.

"To find my father?"

"Yes, of course."

So Irène and Miss Ellen waited for the Nyctalope, with an impatience that tormented them. Irène thought that Raymond, too, would not be long in coming–for if the Nyctalope was victorious, surely he must have sent a message to Professor Jameson. So many expectations, doubts, hopes and uncertainties were diminished by so many hypotheses and destroyed by so many fears.

Finally, the door opened and the Nyctalope came in.

The cry that Irène could not restrain caused Henri to sit up. He recognized "Uncle Saint-Clair." There were exclamations, laughter, tears and embraces. Mattol helped Saint-Clair to calm the two women and the child, who was excited by their example.

Saint-Clair gave them a succinct summary of events. He concluded: "Raymond will resume command of the *Lampas*, in which you will embark, and

274

he will take her into the midst of the Antilles. Saincer will go aboard the submarine to give him the information he needs for the time being, and will then embark on the *Uberalles* with some English seamen and take her to Le Havre, so that the chief engineer of the Subtransatlantic Company can study her and learn how to build new submarines combining the features of the *Uberalles* and the *Lampas*."

"And you?" Irène asked.

"I'm leaving for Paris by aeroplane, with Girard and the red-haired man."

"What red-haired man?" asked little Henri, who was listening avidly.

Saint-Clair smiled at him. "I'll explain that later, my boy. It's very complicated. Listen, but please don't interrupt, all right?"

With "Uncle Saint-Clair," Henri remained a baby of the earliest months when the faculties of logical reasoning, discernment and conscious will are born in the human mind; he was quite docile. "Yes, all right," he said.

"Good!" And the Nyctalope, addressing himself primarily to Irène, went on: "On the day when Mattol's telegram about you reached me, I planned, before returning to Schwarzrock..."

"Schwarzrock?" said Irène.

"That's right–you don't know. It's Lucifer's castle, from which I abducted the red-haired man."

"My God! I'm getting lost."

"Mattol knows everything–he'll give you the details. So, before returning to Schwarzrock, I planned to make a final attempt, with your uncle's help, to obtain some useful revelations from the red-haired man by means of hypnosis. Professor Lourmel and I had already tried three times, in vain. The red-haired man is under Lucifer's influence, which is stronger despite the distance–but the Professor had conducted an experiment at Saint-Anne the previous night. Putting an entranced subject into a radioactive environment multiplies his docility and the power of the hypnotizer a hundredfold. Well, that's the experiment I intend to try in order to resume my direct offensive against Lucifer with a better hand. I only came here to save you and Henri, which will be accomplished once and for all in two hours. Moreover, I've captured the entire Warteck family."

"The Warteck family?" Irène echoed, bewildered.

"Yes–Lucifer's family. They've been swarming inside this Hollow Rock in secret, unknown to the world at large. Mattol will explain... but here's Grisyl!"

Irène was obliged to postpone knowing and understanding everything. The events driving the Nyctalope did not permit him to waste any time with explanations that were interesting but did not need to be offered urgently. Irène also set aside her astonishment; with the Nyctalope, it was necessary to be prepared for anything. For the moment, Irène was content to wait for Raymond; that was sufficient to occupy her mind and her heart.

"Everything has been done as you ordered, darling," Grisyl said.

"That's good. Is there a map of the Hollow Rock?"

"Yes–a map of the whole and maps of the various sections. They're in the library."

"We'll return to the library, then. Mattol and Pilou, you come with me. You too, Grisyl. Irène, my dear, follow us with Henri and Miss Ellen. We mustn't get separated."

They all went to the library, where Irène and Miss Ellen entertained Henri by showing him the illustrations in a magnificent folio edition of Buffon.[42]

Grisyl unfolded the maps on the large table. In response to Saint-Clair's request, the young woman, still smiling and serene, pointed out all the places where the inhabitants of the microcosm that was the Hollow Rock were presently sleeping, first on the individual plans and then on the general one. Asking when necessary for brief items of information and succinct explanations, Saint-Clair outlined details plans for the occupation of the Hollow Rock and the capture of all its inhabitants–put to sleep in advance by means of the soporific gas. The English soldiers would have the enormous advantage of surprise and the entire operation would probably be accomplished without the death of a single man. If not, there would be no misplaced sentiment; if killing became necessary, people would be killed. Since masks would be given to all the Englishmen, however, and they would be equipped with 20 gas-projectors, they would make every effort to avoid bloody conflict.

The moment was now drawing near when Raymond de Ciserat, his seamen and the Englishmen from Hamilton would be approaching the Hollow Rock through the subterranean tunnel. "Let's hope that nothing's holding them up," said Saint-Clair, consulting his wristwatch, which Grisyl had returned to him. "It's getting close to the 24th hour–and that's the hour when the wake-up call is sounded here."

"Yes," said Grisyl.

"Well, almost everything's set. Grisyl, let's go to meet Ciserat. Mattol and Pilou, remain here with Irène, Henri and Miss Ellen."

One can imagine all the animation and pathos of the scenes to which the Hollow Rock served as a theater that night! The meeting of Saint-Clair and Ciserat in the tunnel; the introduction of Grisyl–"my ally," the Nyctalope said, simply–the emotional reunion of Irène and Raymond; the distribution of the English soldiers through the grottoes; the rapid capture, without a shot being fired, of the Warteck family and all their slaves; the installation in the *Lampas* of Irène, Henri, Miss Ellen, Mattol, Raymond de Ciserat and his crew; the occupation by Jacques Saincer and the English mariners of the Wartecks' submarine *Uberalles*–which shared the principal characteristics of all the submarines of the era, save for the motors powered by electricity obtained by a new and admirably simple method–the soporific gassing of Grisyl's father, mother and other brother and their embarkation on the *Uberalles* on stretchers, along with Norbert and Rupert VI, for transportation to Le Havre and then to Paris; the English officers, under orders from Saint-Clair, occupying the caves and evacuating their inhabitants in relays to Hamilton... In brief, all the actions that made the Hollow Rock into an English possession and its inhabitants into prisoners of war, whose eventual fate was determined by a secret agreement between Monsieur Prillant and the British Prime Minister. The only individuals excepted from that agreement were Grisyl and her family and Rupert VI, whose destiny Leo Saint-Clair reserved the privilege of deciding, at least until Lucifer was defeated.

Raymond de Ciserat's first concern was, of course, to defuse the melinite booby-trap he had set before the departure in diving-suits. Fortunately for the inhabitants of the Hollow Rock—and for Irène and Henri while they had been held here—none of the Wartecks who had visited the *Lampas* while she was in the *Uberalles*' dock had thought to touch the tiller; if they had, the detonation of the melinite in the confined space of the basin would have had the force of a volcanic eruption and would have destroyed the Hollow Rock.

It required several hours for all the details of Saint-Clair's plan to be put into operation, but in the end, they were complete.

Everyone said their goodbyes. Irène and Miss Ellen shed tears of gratitude; Raymond's voice was tremulous with emotion; Mattol and little Henri were overflowing with affection. The brief speeches of the English officers and Jacques Saincer's salutes were respectfully admiring. The exclamations of the French and English mariners forming the crews of the two submarines were enthusiastic. All this—which took place while the large cave-harbor was completely dry, although the pumps soon began to refill it, and the great sluice-gates opened so that the *Uberalles* and the *Lampas* could take to the open sea—was for Leo Saint-Clair, who had then to return to Hamilton with Grisyl, Girard and Pilou, to take off soon afterwards in the RC3 for France, and Paris.

Finally, they went their separate ways. The Hollow Rock no longer contained any but the English soldiers and their captives. The *Lampas* headed for the waters of the Antilles, while the *Uberalles* headed directly for Le Havre. The Nyctalope and his companions walked through the tunnel in the direction of Hamilton, where they arrived without having met any difficulty.

The Nyctalope's party went up into the mansion, where they were greeted by Governor Wallis and Professor Jameson. Succinctly, but in a clear and complete manner, the Nyctalope told them everything. Jameson and Wallis congratulated them, as one may imagine. Being in need of rest, Saint-Clair and his companions went to bed and slept for a few hours; then they ate a hearty meal.

While Girard and Pilou busied themselves making various preparations aboard the RC3, in which Grisyl was installed as comfortably as possible—along with the red-haired man, who had been entrusted to her care—Saint-Clair conferred with Wallis and Jameson regarding the final arrangements needed to conclude "the Hollow Rock affair."

Wallis received confirmation by telegraph of his appointment as Governor of the Bermudas in place of the deceased Sir Ernest Bernd. Professor Jameson and his daughter Jessie, who had been hard hit by the death of her fiancé, took ship for New York the following day–where they immediately set out for France, because Jameson wanted to collaborate with Lourmel in the defense against Lucifer, while the Nyctalope launched a new offensive.

The RC3 took off for France at daybreak on May 22, carrying its co-pilot, its engineer and two passengers.

In the Bermudas, the Nyctalope had won the battle against Lucifer. The Wartecks were prisoners; Irène and Henri were on a submerged submarine, sheltered from supernatural molestation–at least, Saint-Clair hoped so, as much as Mattol did. But what was happening now in Paris and at Schwarzrock? How was Laurence Païli faring? How would Lucifer react? As he asked himself that vital question, the Nyctalope hoped that the red-haired man and Rupert VI, hypnotized and interrogated in a radioactive environment, might give him information that would prove useful in his offensive against the sinister and mysterious Lord of Schwarzrock.

As for Grisyl, Saint-Clair made no mistake regarding her sentiments. This young woman, possessed of a scientific mind and a primitive soul, had been suddenly awakened to the life of the passions by the lightning-strike of absolute love. But might that love not be transformed into the most savage hatred, by virtue of jealousy, when Grisyl would find out about Laurence...?

On the immense horizon that delimited the green line of the ocean against the azure of the sky, the Nyctalope could see nothing yet but mystery: the mystery of a future charged with storms, from which lightning might strike, inevitably, implacably and fatally!

Part Six: Love, Magic and Hatred

I. Vision of Spring

It sometimes happens that the hazards of an affair, a visit or a stroll take Parisians who do not live within the trapezoid quadrilateral described by sections of the Rue Denfert-Rochereau, the Boulevard Saint-Jacques, the Rue de la Santé and the Boulevard de Port-Royal into the environs of the Observatory. When these Parisians come to the Boulevard Arago in the upper reaches of the Faubourg Saint-Jacques, they invariably pause, simultaneously seized by astonishment and pleasure, because they are confronted by the most unexpected spectacle of a small wilderness in the heart of Paris: the Observatory gardens.

It is the largest of the few private gardens that still exist in Paris. It is green with hectic grass, shaded by ancient trees, delightfully cluttered with bushes and spinneys, which seem abandoned to their own primitive devices, and which make a flavorsome contrast with the sculpted heads of their carefully-cultivated kin. One can even find brambles and wild grains there, and uncultivated patches of ground where wild flowers gladden the heart, blooming and withering freely.

Moreover, this miniscule paradise and minuscule Paradou [43] seems immense to the city-dwellers, who automatically compare it to the narrow and meager flower-beds in other private gardens that they have noticed in other parts of Paris. It is only separated from the pavement on the right-hand side–the even-numbered side–of the Boulevard Arago by a low wall with a large gate which, while forbidding all access, at least permit everyone to look in.

The garden extends from left to right for a distance of approximately 150 meters, but in extending towards the north it quickly widens out, and one can no longer see its sides, masked by large trees and their undergrowth. The architectural mass of the Observatory, crowned by its domes, looms up at the back, black, grey, white or roseate, according to the season, the hour and the condition of the sky.

It is very rare for the stroller or passer-by, arrested on the pavement outside the gate by surprise and admiration, to see a man in the garden, and even rarer to see a woman. A stroller or passer-by who happened to be there at 11 a.m. on May 23, however, looking towards the Observatory, would have been able to see two women walking slowly through the grass. He would, at least, have been able to catch glimpses of them, for they were moving through the higher part of the garden, continually hidden from view behind bushes, trees or grassy knolls. However brief the vision might have been, though, it would have left a visual impression of elegant shapes and pretty colors and a mental impression of vernal seductiveness, with contrasting tones that made the image stand out and lent clarity to the memory. This was because one of the women–who was young, elegant and beautiful, dressed in light white fabrics, with a red sash around her waist and a large straw hat with muslin gauze and red ribbons attached it its band–was leaning on the arms of a companion in a dark dress and a veil of black lace.

There was something charming, extraordinary, and slightly disturbing about the passage of these two women through the large garden, half-wild and almost always deserted.

At 9 a.m. on that same morning, a military aircraft of the RC series came in to land at Le Bourget aerodrome. The officers, pilots, mechanics and humble soldiers who happened to be on the field had realized even before it touched down that it was the RC3, which had set off on a mission on May 19.

Once alerted, the colonel came running. He gave an order. His own car was brought. The spectators of every rank stood aside. With only two officers, followed by the car–driven by his orderly–the colonel went to the stationary plane.

Pilou got down first, then Saint-Clair, Grisyl and the red-haired man, with Captain Girard bringing up the rear. A few words were exchanged between the colonel and Saint-Clair–congratulations on the part of the former, thanks on the part of the latter for the car. After shaking hands with Captain Girard, Saint-Clair climbed into the car with Pilou, the red-haired man and Grisyl; it got under way immediately. Pilou placed himself next to the chauffeur, saying: "Rue Nansouty, near the Parc Montsouris."

"I know it," the orderly replied–and took the most direct route there, at a swift pace.

On one side of the courtyard of his house, Sinclair had built a lodge whose ground-floor rooms were occupied by Pilou, the concierge Choiffour and his wife, the cook Sidonie, while the first floor was a six-room apartment furnished with comfortable simplicity. The Nyctalope decided to accommodate Grisyl, the red-haired man and Wolf in this apartment, the last-named serving as the guard of the second. While Grisyl stayed there, she would be served, as the captive was, by one of Sidonie's sisters, named Rosine–the wife of a customs-officer at the Porte d'Orléans who sometimes came to help out at the house in the Rue Nansouty. Henceforth, she came every day.

Pilou was acquainted with his boss's decision en route, and charged with implementing them after the arrival. Saint-Clair communicated the decision to Grisyl in a few affectionate words. She was as wonderstruck as a child by everything she saw. She had only left the caves of the Hollow Rock occasionally, always in the interior or the conning-tower of the *Uberalles*, which was sometimes submerged and sometimes sailed on the surface. During the aircraft's flight, Grisyl's eyes had gradually become accustomed to the light of the Sun and now she could look around in broad daylight without squinting overmuch.

She replied to Saint-Clair with a smile, and continued to admire the Earth and the sky.

When the military vehicle arrived, Choiffour–who immediately perceived his master within it–threw up his arms and shouted cheerfully: "Oh, Monsieur, Monsieur! What a great day!" Sidonie, who appeared on the threshold of the house, echoed the sentiment, laughing and crying at the same time.

Saint-Clair felt a surge of emotion in his heart. What could have happened to make his faithful and devoted servants welcome him with such cries of joy and excited expressions?

"Laure!"

Leaving Grisyl and the red-haired man to Pilou and Choiffour, he ran to Sidonie and thrust his coat, hat and large gloves into her hands. Without hearing her exclamation of "But there's no one up there, Monsieur!" he raced up the stairs, taking them four at a time. He did not stop until he reached the room in which, five days previously, he had left Laurence suspended between life and death. The open windows inundated the room with bright sunlight. It was devoid of any human presence; a lace-fringed quilt was proudly displayed on the neatly-made bed.

"Laure!" cried Saint-Clair.

It was Sidonie's voice that replied: "Oh, Monsieur, you went so quickly!"

He turned round. The cook's face was creased with laughter and moist with tears. He took her by the hands. "Tell me quickly, Sidonie. What has happened? Where are Mademoiselle Laurence and Professor Lourmel?"

"I could have told you all that just as well downstairs, if you hadn't set off up the stairs like a madman. It was the day before yesterday..."

"What was?"

"Mademoiselle Laurence woke up, after sleeping quite naturally following an attack of nerves. Quite naturally! Pink cheeks... an angel from Heaven! She ate some food, she got up. She had a good–a very good–night thereafter. And yesterday, with Mademoiselle Luce, who came at the same time as the Professor, Mademoiselle Laurence went out for a walk in the gardens of the Observatory–because, as the Professor told Corsat, the director is a friend of his and the garden, closed off on every side, is like a safe country retreat. She even had dinner with the director–a fine dinner, to which he invited Monsieur Lerond, the director of the Opéra-Comique, and Monsieur Lysor–the composer, you know. It seems that Mademoiselle Laurence sang. Corsat and Wolf, who were in the garden, heard her through the open windows. It was so beautiful they were in tears. When she came back here–Mademoiselle Laurence, that is–she told me that she was very happy, because she had seen you in a dream that night, and that you would come back content... But she didn't know that it would be today– your return, that is–because she went back to the Observatory this morning, with Madame Deléglise, who collected her in the Professor's car, to walk in the gardens, which she thought so beautiful, until noon. Corsat and Wolf, of course..."

But the brave cook could say no more. Overcome by happiness, Saint-Clair seized her in his arms, kissed her on both cheeks and twirled her around. Leaving her stunned, he ran into his study and grabbed the telephone.

"Hello? Hello? Ah, Mademoiselle, I recognize your voice! Good day! Yes! Get me the President of the Council..." There was a fretful pause, then: "Hello? Is that the Presidency? Is Monsieur Prillant there? Monsieur Prillant, on behalf of Monsieur Saint-Clair. Extreme urgency... Yes." There was another pause, and eventually: "Hello? Alex? Yes!... Saved!... Yes!... At the Observatory, until midday... Yes... Here... Two hours? Perfect!... Will you telephone Lourmel and Narbonne?... What? Narbonne is dead?... Suicide?... Surely not!... No! You'll come with Lourmel, then?... Yes! Till then... Oh, me too, the same to you! We'll do it, my old friend, we'll do it!"

He hung up, went into the hall, took a soft felt hat from a peg and went into the courtyard. "Tell Sidonie that we'll have lunch in an hour," he shouted to the concierge, and ran out.

Once in the street, he became conscious of his unusual gait and moderated his pace. At the corner of the Avenue Reille, he saw a taxi with its white flag up. "To the Observatory, driver! Quickly, quickly!"

The director of the Observatory was Monsieur Sudmann, from the ancient and renowned Alsatian family. He was a childhood friend of Professor Lourmel's at whose home Saint-Clair had made his acquaintance. During the journey, Saint-Clair thought: *I'll have to ask to speak to Monsieur Sudmann, for the gatekeeper must have been given strict orders, and as he doesn't know me he won't let me in...*

Saint-Clair leapt out on to the pavement before the taxi had drawn to a halt outside the entrance to the Observatory, and went swiftly to the porter's lodge— but he did not have to ask for Monsieur Sudmann. He recognized Professor Lourmel's manservant, Richard–"Richard the Lionheart," as he was known, because of the courage he had often shown in taking part in some of the Professor's riskier experiments.

This brave fellow was sitting in the lodge chatting to the porter. "Ah, Monsieur Saint-Clair!" he cried, standing up. "They weren't expecting you today. I'll telephone the Professor."

"No need, my dear Richard–it's done, You're here on sentry duty..."

"Yes, Monsieur, on this side of the Observatory, at this entrance. The ladies are in the garden. Corsat and Wolf are there too, hidden in the bushes..."

Saint-Clair knew the rest. No longer having any need to ask for Monsieur Sudmann in order to have the gate opened, he went through. Thirty seconds later, he was in the garden. He selected a winding path at random. Almost immediately, he caught sight of her and stopped.

Dressed entirely in white, with a red sash gathered around her slender waist, Laurence Païli was sitting in a wicker armchair in the shade of an exceedingly tall tree. Leaning on her right elbow, with her curled fingers against her cheek, she was gazing through a gap in the bushes in front of her at a large patch of green grass. Roses were in bloom behind her. Saint-Clair saw her in profile, so beautiful and delicate of complexion, all the lines of her body in harmony: a vision of spring, of love, of youth, of happiness!

He restrained himself from crying out and running forward. Pale and smiling, his heart beating madly, he resumed walking.

At the sound of his footsteps, she turned her head. On seeing him, she immediately got to her feet, releasing a sharp exclamation from her half-open lips. Putting out her arms, she ran towards him. He was already extending his own tremulous arms.

What a hug! What a kiss!

Then they drew back from one another slightly and looked at one another, with their fingers interlaced. Their eyes were so penetrating that it seemed that they were peering into one another's souls.

He was the first to speak, in a profound and caressing voice, which had something captivating and sensuous about it–a voice that was familiar to no one in the world, except Laurence Païli.

"Laure, my beloved, you're exactly as you were at Cap d'Antibes!"

"You too, my love!" she replied, palpitant with emotion. "Oh, Leo..."

Desperately, they seized one another again, united their lips, merged their breath, forgetting where they were and the atrocious dramas they had recently endured. They were transported by the expression in their eyes, without any transition, to the happy days they had spent among the roses on the sore of the blue sea: those incomparable days which they had brought to an end voluntarily, to be sure of conserving an unblemished memory... days that they reconnected quite naturally with the present moment.

"Leo!"

"Laure!"

Lucifer seemed so very far away.

Hand in hand, hips pressed together, leaning on one another and smiling, drunk by the sight of one another and one another's touch, they walked instinctively, without reflection, along a meandering path that led them into the midst of a thick clump of bushes. There was an old bench there; they sat down on it. Laure untied the ribbons of her hat, which fell away. She put her head on her lover's breast. He put his arm around his lover's body. Hand in hand, in silence, with their eyes closed, they listened to the precipitate beating of their hearts...

II. The Red-Haired Man Hypnotized

For another three hours, Laurence and Leo lived as if in a dream of love. It was not dispelled by the arrival of Madame Deléglise, who had been walking alone in the garden for some time, nor by the subsequent conversation they had with her, nor by the journey from the Observatory to the Rue Nansouty in Professor Lourmel's car, which came to pick them up, nor by the joyful utterances of Corsat and Wolf, who had mounted guard discreetly in the garden, and who installed themselves beside the driver, nor even by the lunch served by the exultant Corsat.

In the course of these various scenes and their concomitant conversations, Laurence and Leo were each effectively divided. One part of their being–the most apparent and less interesting–moved, talked, ate, and drank, while the other, less visible but more alive, wildly sang the mysterious hymn of youth, spring, love and happiness...

But the division came to an end, and Laurence and Leo–without interrupting their radiant consciousness of happiness, love, spring and youth–reverted to being La Païli and the Nyctalope. That happened when Monsieur Prillant, Professor Lourmel and André d'Arbol made their appearance in the dining-room just as the two were finishing dessert.

The existence of Lucifer, which had ceased for several hours, so far as the two lovers were concerned, was then abruptly reasserted–and all the problems, threats, dangers, horrors and passions that constituted his abominable, inexplicable and incomprehensible existence besides.

Laurence and Saint-Clair got up as Messieurs Prillant, Lourmel and d'Arbol came in. At that moment, the thoughts of all five of them were so profuse, various and tumultuous that they looked at one another for a full 30 seconds without saying a word. Finally, extending an arm towards the Nyctalope, Monsieur Prillant recovered his voice. "Thank you, Leo!" he said.

The two men embraced, emotionally. Then Professor Lourmel, no less agitated by emotions that he did not attempt to hide, thanked Saint-Clair for the deliverance of Irène.

"You've been working as well as I have," Saint-Clair replied, pointing to Laurence.

"Me!" the Professor exclaimed. "I had nothing to do with that. Haven't you told him, Mademoiselle...?"

"Nothing!" said Laurence. "We have not given one another any explanations at all!"

"Then we must..." Lourmel fell silent, and everyone looked at him, in perplexity.

There were so many things that needed to be said, told and explained! Everything that the Nyctalope had done in the Bermudas, and everything that had happened in Paris. Saint-Clair knew nothing about Lucifer's phantom appearances; the radiotelegram sent to him by Monsieur Prillant had only arrived in the Bermudas after his departure by aeroplane. Where to begin? Who should speak first? Everyone was equally avid to learn, to know–Saint-Clair most of all. He did not know what tragic scene had been enacted in Schwarzrock between Laurence and Lucifer.

But Saint-Clair saw André d'Arbol standing sadly to one side, and he suddenly recalled Monsieur Prillant telling him over the telephone about Monsieur Narbonne's death–his suicide. Henri's father, Irène's uncle and Laurence's lover had what they needed to be happy; only Mathias Narbonne's godson and secretary had cause for pain–so Saint-Clair went to d'Arbol and took his hands. "My dear André," he said, "you must begin. We won't..."

"No, no!" protested d'Arbol.

"Why not?"

"Monsieur Prillant telephoned me regarding your return; I only came here to ask you if you would come to the Rue d'Orchampt tomorrow. The head of the Sûreté will be there, and the lawyer..."

"I'll be there too," said Lourmel.

"What time?" Saint-Clair asked.

"2 p.m.," d'Arbol replied. "With you present, I hope that the tragic enigma can be elucidated–because I don't believe that it was suicide, and I never will believe it."

"No more do I!" said Messieurs Lourmel and Prillant, in unison.

"Nor I," Saint-Clair said, firmly. "Until tomorrow, then, at 2 p.m. at the Rue d'Orchampt, my dear André."

"Thank you."

D'Arbol shook the three men by the hand, bowed deeply to Laurence, and withdrew,

"You, my dear Nyctalope," said Lourmel, immediately, "must listen first. You must, I suppose, be avid to know how, having left your beloved in a death-like state, you have found her again more alive, more beautiful and more youthful than ever."

Saint-Clair remained serious. "That's not all I'm avid to know," he said. "The enigma that Laure presented goes further than that. It was in Schwarzrock that the mystery began."

"That's true," said Lourmel.

"Well," said Monsieur Prillant, "let's elucidate everything, at least so far as will be possible, in one session. We have all afternoon."

Laurence, however, having first gone pale and then pink with embarrassment, said: "No. There are things about Schwarzrock that I can only reveal to Leo in private."

"I anticipated that," Saint-Clair said, supportively. "You can tell me all that, Laure, when we are able to think solely of ourselves. For the moment, our friends have a right not to be kept waiting any longer."

They went into the Nyctalope's study. He was the first to tell his story. Very rapidly, but leaving nothing out, he recounted everything that had happened in the Bermudas. Lourmel and Prillant thanked him again, on behalf of Irène and Henri. By way of a brief epilogue, they discussed the precautions taken to shelter those two victims from Lucifer's spells, and that served as a link to bring them to the most extraordinary case of Laurence Païli.

"Lucifer's spells!" cried Professor Lourmel. "We must ask ourselves whether, following Lucifer's double apparition..."

"What apparition?" asked the astonished Saint-Clair.

"Lucifer has appeared to Mademoiselle Païli and to Monsieur Prillant...y You'll hear about that. The question remains as to whether, after that double phantasmal apparition–which took place, please note, between 6 a.m. and 7 a.m. of May 20–Lucifer is still capable of casting spells..."

"But what about Narbonne's death?" Saint-Clair objected.

"Yes," the Professor said, "I'm attributing that to him–all the more so because it also took place between 6 a.m. and 7 a.m. that morning, and does not modify my hypothesis at all."

"On what do you base your supposition," Monsieur Prillant asked, "that after the double phantasmal apparition, Lucifer will not be capable of casting spells, at least for a certain period of time?"

"Let's recapitulate all that we know ourselves, and all that Saint-Clair has told us," the Professor said, as the others listened attentively. "On the one hand, in the Bermudas, Saint-Clair encountered no occult opposition to his actions after 7 a.m. on May 20. You know that kilometric distance is nothing to Lucifer; thought travels as rapidly from Paris to New York as from Paris to Versailles. As thought is the vehicle of the will, thought and volition often being confused. Since will-power is the agent of Lucifer's actions, and the monster knew perfectly well that Irène and Henri were in the Hollow Rock, he would have been able to read Irène's and Henri's minds if he still possessed his supernatural faculties. He would have known about the Nyctalope's presence in the Bermudas and his victory over Rupert VI, and he would have unleashed all his occult power upon the Nyctalope himself. He would have tortured Irène and Henri in order to thwart Leo. He would have possessed Grisyl, upon whom he certainly has an unlimited influence, and changed her mind. However, during the reversal of fortune in the Bermudas, which were so serious and disastrous for him, Lucifer did nothing. My hypothesis that the Lord of Schwarzrock's occult power was suppressed–at least temporarily–is therefore plausible."

"Quite true," said Saint-Clair, impassively.

"Yes," added Monsieur Prillant.

Laurence said nothing, but she was listening intently.

286

"On the other hand," the Professor went on, "here–and your legitimate desire to know will now be satisfied, my dear Saint-Clair–at 6:02 a.m., Lucifer appeared to Laurence and bit her left breast cruelly..."

"He did what?" cried Saint-Clair, going pale–but he controlled himself immediately and added: "Excuse me, Professor. I'm listening." He took Laurence's hand–she was sitting next to him–and held it in his own, exchanging profound glances with the young woman from time to time.

With a clarity and precise fidelity to detail that proved the extent of his reflection on the case, the Professor gave an account of Lucifer's appearance to the singer, repeating the sorcerer's words and those of his victim–a scene witnessed by Madame Deléglise, who had heard the words spoken. When he had finished, he turned to Laurence to ask: "Is that correct?"

"Exact in every detail," the young woman replied, emotionally.

"Running into the room in response to Madame Deléglise's scream," Lourmel continued, "I found her half-mad with terror and our patient in the grip of a fit. I succeeded in calming her with a sedative injection. I put antiseptic on the supernatural bite. She fell asleep and woke up eight hours later. For me, as a physician, that was the most extraordinary aspect of the whole fantastic story. Rosy-cheeked, smiling, prettier and more lively than ever, delighted by a dream that she related to me–in which she had seen you, Saint-Clair, returning tranquilly from a 'distant island'–Laurence declared to me that she was dying of hunger.

" 'But where am I?' she asked.

"Succinctly, while observing her carefully, I told her that you, Saint-Clair, had taken her out of Schwarzrock and brought her here, to your home, where she had been suspended between life and death.

" 'Oh, yes!' she said, simply. 'It's over, that horror. Nothing remains of it but that bite on my breast. It still makes me feel ill–but soon, there will be neither trace nor memory of it. Leo's coming–and Lucifer must be dead.'

"She got up, wanting to take a bath and get dressed. We ate together, chatting about you, Saint-Clair, about Madame Païli–'my dear mama,' Laurence said to me, 'who is waiting patiently for Leo to come and rescue her!'–of the Opéra-Comique, of Monsieur Lerond and Octave Lysor... Is this still correct, my lovely friend?"

"Exactly so," Laurence replied, smiling.

"I'll conclude. Later that day, I visited her again at your house, Saint-Clair. Laurence went to bed at 10 p.m. and spent an excellent night. From then until now, nothing of interest has happened, save for this: while walking with my sister Luce or with Madame Deléglise in the gardens of the Observatory, at the dinner-table with Sudmann, Lerond, Lysor and myself, Laurence has been exactly as I knew her before May 7, the day of her disappearance; I have not even asked her about the circumstances of her disappearance and her sojourn in the castle of Schwarzrock.

"Lerond and Lysor, on my instructions, have made no allusion to the enigma of May 7. Laurence has behaved as if she has been on a journey, except that she has seemed to everyone to be happier and more serene than usual. That's it! But now, I believe that the time for explanations has come. I shall not ask for them myself–it's to you that they're due, my dear Saint-Clair, for it's you, most of all, who might profit from them from the viewpoint of your battle against Lucifer. We need to know whether he is dead or alive, whether the war is over or whether there's merely a truce. When it's all over, Saint-Clair, you might give me the pleasure of going over everything with me–even confidential matters– in order that I might obtain some scientific insights that will allow me a penetrate a little further into the mysteries of nature..."

The Professor fell silent. There was a long silence. Everyone looked at La Païli, whose hand Saint-Clair still held. The young woman was deep in thought, her eyelids lowered. Eventually, she opened her lovely black, expressive and luminous eyes as wide as he could, and said: "I swear to you that–save for what happened at Schwarzrock, which I shall tell Leo–I know nothing. From the moment when I fell, out there, into the state of living death until the instant I awoke, here, before the apparition of Lucifer, all is darkness, emptiness, silence: a void. Then there was the apparition, the horrid threats, the bite. Immediately afterwards, inexpressible suffering, then sleep, and delightful dreams in which I saw Leo in an aeroplane. Finally, the definitive awakening: the complete restoration of the person I was before May 7, my *joie de vivre*, my tranquility on the subject of my mother, waiting patiently at Schwarzrock for Leo to come and rescue her, and, over and above all that, the impression that the monster is dead or disarmed..."

She trailed off.

"Strange!" said the Nyctalope, profoundly thoughtful.

There was another silence. It was Laurence's turn to take one of Saint-Clair's hands in hers and to caress it gently. Their eyes on the Nyctalope, Lourmel and Prillant waited.

"Well then," Saint-Clair said, suddenly raising his head. "Let's leave the Laurence case, as you call it, for now and continue the examination of the situation. Your turn, my dear Alex. Tell your story!"

Monsieur Prillant told his story; it was soon done. Just as Lourmel had repeated from memory the exact words exchanged between Lucifer and Laurence during that phantasmal apparition, Monsieur Prillant quoted, word for word, the final ultimatum written in white letters on the black background of the woodwork in his office at the Place Beauvau.

When the Minister had finished, the Nyctalope concluded: "June 10! At the Hollow Rock, Rupert VI and Grisyl knew that the Supreme Lord would decide Irène's and Henri's fate on June 10; it's before June 10 that Laure must submit herself to Lucifer; it's no later than the same June 10 that Monsieur Prillant must surrender once and for all. We know, from what Lucifer told Laure, that it is not until June 10 that the machine at Schwarzrock–the machine I've seen, which Lucifer calls the Teledynamo–will be capable of imposing Lucifer's will on everyone in the world, even me, regardless of distance, even at the Antipodes."

He fell silent, shivering. He got up and began to march back and forth across the room, with increasing animation.

"Lucifer is a man! He calls himself Glô von Warteck. He's a Mongol,[44] cruel and proud–and thus imprudent. He believes that he is stronger than anyone else, so he hurls forth his boasts and talks too much! He's only a man, this creature, and is well worthy, in my opinion, of the name of Lucifer! Laure, do you recall the last lines of the letter of ultimatum that was slipped into Irène's hand in Le Havre?" Pausing in his stride, Saint-Clair quoted: "*A woman who will soon be by my side, who hates me–whom you will love, mourn and replace–cursed me one day by throwing in my face a formidable name. That name pleased me. I desire no other, and I sign myself: Lucifer!*" He took two paces, stopped in front of Laurence and said, with a sort of tender violence: "That woman is you, Laure!"

"Yes, it's me," Laurence replied, simply and quite calmly, her wide-open eyes fixed on the Nyctalope's.

"When? How?"

Messieurs Prillant and Lourmel could not repress a movement of excited attentiveness.

"Three days before my departure on May 7," Laurence said, "a man called at my house and sent me a visiting card engraved with the words: Baron Eiger Nott, Chairman of the Board of the Spectacle Consortium, New York. I had never heard of the consortium in question. I assumed that it was one of those formidable trusts that spring up suddenly in the United States and change the face of some commerce, industry or public service completely within 48 hours. The visitor had doubtless come to me to issue some ostentatious invitation. I had not yet made any arrangements for the summer. I had him shown in." She paused, smiled wryly, and continued in a hushed but impassioned voice: "By your decision and my own, Leo, wise or foolish as we may have been–shall we ever know?–you were no longer alive to me and I was no longer alive to you. Entirely dedicated to my art, therefore, I would have accepted an invitation to tour the United States, provided that the venues were worthy of the French masterpieces that comprise my new repertoire."

She paused again, momentarily, but only to modify the tone and volume of her voice. She went on, calmly at first, but with increasing animation, vibrant with indignation, revulsion and retrospective terror.

"I received Monsieur Eiger Nott. He was tall, thin and red-haired: an unknown Mephistopheles.[45] He made my blood run cold immediately–and the antipathy that he inspired in me was such that I resolved to refuse any proposition he made. From that moment on, I had no other aim but to cut the conversation short and send the man on his way. I did not even invite him to sit down. I re-

289

mained standing. We were in the drawing-room, alone; Mama was in town..." Laurence stopped, blushing and hesitant.

"And then?" Saint-Clair said.

"Let me leave out the odious details, Leo. It will be sufficient, Messieurs, for you to know this: Edgar Nott announced straight away that he had invented the name and the position inscribed on his card. He made a few gestures, which plunged me into a sort of trance, during which I nevertheless retained consciousness. He professed the most violent and tyrannical love for me. He gave me proof of his power by moving a few things without touching them: a chair, a trinket, even the armchair into which I had fallen, which was bearing all my weight. From a distance, he caused me to experience the sensation of caresses, kisses and bites on my cheeks, the nape of my neck, my hands and my feet. Eventually, he concluded: 'In three days, I shall call you to me and you will come; if not, I shall make your mother suffer the tortures imagined for the damned.' But my horror and my hatred for that man were so powerful that I was able to overcome the intense hypnotic empery in which he held me. I cried out that horror and hatred; I cursed him, called him demon and Lucifer, at which he went out, laughing mockingly..."

When La Païli paused again, breathless, Saint-Clair said: "What followed?"

"Three days of anguish! On May 7, a telegram was sent to me, which I read and threw in the fire. Immediately, I felt the same sensations, as if invisible hands had seized mine and very drawing me forward–then that infernal grip was transferred to my elbows, my shoulders... and I could not deny the power of Lucifer! The telegram contained terrible threats against my mother." She sighed, and went on, passionately: "What could I do, Leo? You were not there. I thought you were in the depths of Africa. I thought of calling you–but where? How? Then again, if I attempted the least resistance, would not my mother be tortured? I left. The telegram had told me where tm go. A limousine was waiting for me to the right of the entrance to the Avenue du Bois. I got in. Lucifer was in the back of the car–and it was to Schwarzrock that he took me... There, in my luxurious prison, I waited, anguished and rebellious, for violation and death. And then you came!"

Laurence sobbed convulsively; her entire body shook. She hid her face in her trembling hands. The three men looked at her for a few minutes, with love, affection, admiration and pity.

"Laure!" Saint-Clair said, eventually.

She raised her head again. They smiled. She calmed down. Her tears ceased flowing. Sublimely, she said: "You've defeated him, this Lucifer!"

"No, no–not yet!" cried the Nyctalope, who resumed pacing back and forth across the room. "I tell you this," he said. "Lucifer is only a man. And he talks too much! He gives us information. He has said that the power he has, thanks to the Teledynamo, will not become limitless and irresistible until June 10. Today is May 23. There's only 17 days left. That may be too few. And he's working—working with all his strength, all his intelligence, all his will-power. After he appeared to you, Laurence, and to you, Alex, and after having killed Mathias Narbonne by some unknown means, he went back to work on some task—so difficult and so absorbing that his exclusive devotion to it, in the preceding days, prevented him from thinking about the Bermudas. And afterwards—after the exteriorization of his perispirit for the apparitions—he has not had enough vital energy to carry forward any work, but the demonic labor of forging the weapon that he will use to conquer the world!" He stopped in front of Laurence, Lourmel and Prillant, who were seated in a semicircle, and said: "Do you understand? Lucifer is not thinking, and cannot think, about us. He's entirely occupied with his Teledynamo. So we can come and go, think and act freely! And it's very probable that this state of affairs will last until June 8 or 9, perhaps even 10. Do you understand what we have to do during those 14, 15 or 16 days?"

"Act!" cried Professor Lourmel.

"Fight!" said Monsieur Prillant.

"And conquer!" Laurence finished.

"Yes: act, fight, conquer... and not lose a single day, or an hour. In the beginning, I didn't understand the game. I didn't know anything, I wasn't holding any trump cards in my hand..."

"And yet," said Laurence, transfigured by enthusiasm, "you got into Schwarzrock and you rescued me..."

"And you've rescued Irène and Henri."

"And conquered the Hollow Rock."

"And captured all the Wartecks."

"Yes, my friends, yes. All the Wartecks—except for the only one genuinely capable of fighting and winning. But now, I have trumps in my hand. Ah, Glô XIII, Supreme Lord, Baron of Schwarzrock, inventor and constructor of the Teledynamo, Lucifer... The two of us..."

With his arm extended and his index finger pointing in a gesture of threat addressed to the terrible and mysterious sorcerer, who was even now preparing the prodigious instrument of his witchcraft in the dungeon of his formidable castle, Leo Saint-Clair the Nyctalope burst out into insulting, boastful, confident and hopeful laughter. Laurence smiled, as the roses she had gathered that morning opened out in her corsage, filling the immense, sunlit study with their perfume.

III. The Interrogation of the Red-Haired Man [46]

The following day, at 2 p.m., Leo Saint-Clair, Professor Lourmel and Monsieur Prillant, Maître Dubreuil the notary [47] and the head of the Sûreté, Monsieur Sanglier, were received by André d'Arbol in the late Mathias Narbonne's house in the Rue Orchampt. The young man told them everything he knew. Michel, the manservant, did likewise. Maître Dubreuil displayed the seemingly authentic will that he had received by post in the sealed envelope–the will that contained a confession of freely premeditated suicide.

"And the letter to Eiger Nott?" Saint-Clair asked.

"My best agent has gone to Geneva," Monsieur Sanglier replied.

"I suspect," said Maître Dubreuil, "that the letter to Eiger Nott contains a duplicate of the will."

"It certainly does," Monsieur Sanglier affirmed. "We've examined this blotting-pad here; one can distinguish two perfectly similar signatures by Mathias Narbonne, each accompanied by the last two lines of the will. Monsieur Narbonne must therefore have made a copy of the text, which he signed. As it has not been found here, it must have been put into the envelope addressed to Eiger Nott, the heir."

"That's probable," said Monsieur Prillant.

The session proceeded; the examination was thorough. André d'Arbol lay down on his godfather's bed in the position in which he had found the corpse; he explained that he had been obliged to force the door to obtain entry to the room, all the exits being locked from the inside. Professor Lourmel reported that the autopsy had confirmed the cause of death as a gunshot to the right temple. There was a discussion, which arrived at a conclusion formulated by Monsieur Sanglier:

"It is impossible to contest the free and voluntary suicide, and impossible to deny the validity of the will. We have only to await the inquest, and the heir himself, or his legal representative.

"Yes," said Saint-Clair–but when Dubreuil and Sanglier had departed, the Nyctalope drew the others together with a gesture and said: "Now is the time to interrogate the red-haired man. Perhaps he can enlighten us, on this and other matters."

"Everything is ready," said Lourmel. "I've installed a large glass cage in my private laboratory at Auteuil, large enough to hold six people. The workmen have been laboring night and day since you and I decided, Saint-Clair, to use radioactivity in the attempt to render the red-haired man more sensitive to our hypnosis than the hypnotic influence that holds him perpetually in thrall to Lucifer. Everything is ready now–the atmosphere in the cage will be ionized by the action of radioactive substances, and I've established that the respiration of ionized air by a subject renders him more easily hypnotizable." [48]

"Let's go," said Saint-Clair. "You go on ahead to the house in Auteuil; I'll fetch the red-haired man."

Two cars were waiting in the Rue Lepic: a coupé belonging to Saint-Clair and Monsieur Prillant's limousine. The Minister, the Professor and d'Arbol, got into the limousine and set off for Auteuil. The Nyctalope got into the coupé, which headed for Montsouris with Pilou at the wheel.

An hour later, the four friends were reunited at the house in Auteuil. Saint-Clair had brought Laurence Païli and the red-haired man, the latter to speak and the former to listen–and, if necessary, to pose other questions than those formulated by the Nyctalope.

Professor Lourmel's laboratory was a very large room, measuring eight meters by 12, with a ten-meter-high ceiling. There were books and journals–physics, chemistry, history, literature–and instruments in abundance, in rigorous order, in cabinets and cupboards, on tables and shelves. There were two fireplaces, two stoves and an electrical transformer. A photographic and cinematographic studio was installed in one corner.

"Here's the cage!"

There were six huge plates of transparent glass–four for the sides, one for the top and one for the bottom. The five making up the sides and the top were joined together with rubber seals, and the resultant box, open underneath, was suspended from one of the laboratory's exposed beams by a cord that split into four chains attached to rings embedded in the crystalline thickness of he walls. On the floor of the laboratory, directly below the suspended cage–whose bottom edges were two meters above the floor–was the flat plate of glass that would form the bottom of the cage.

"We all need to be on that plate of glass," said Lourmel. Two long-backed chairs had already been placed on the plate. "One for the red-haired man, one for you, diva!" Lourmel added, turning to Laurence.

While the Professor moved the two chairs in such a manner that the young woman was facing the patient at a 45 degree angle, Monsieur Prillant said to Saint-Clair: "It's strange that, through all the fluctuations to which the enigmatic mind of Glô von Warteck has been subject, the red-haired man has always remained in the same state of stupidity."

"It's stranger still," the Nyctalope said, "that Mattol was able to exercise a hypnotic influence over the red-haired man in the Bermudas that was only effective in producing effects other than revelations regarding Schwarzrock. When I needed the red-haired man to say certain words and strike certain attitudes in front of the spy, Mattol instructed him and he obeyed–but afterwards, when Mattol tried to make him talk about Lucifer, it proved impossible."

"What conclusion did you draw?" the Minister asked.

"I concluded that the red-haired man must be under a special hypnotic influence, limited to certain questions. Is it a product of Lucifer's own brain-cells or the working of the Teledynamo? Perhaps we'll find out."

Laurence and the red-haired man were seated. The Professor invited Saint-Clair, Prillant and d'Arbol to take their places with him on the glass plate. It was all taking place, and would continue, without witnesses. The four doors giving access to the laboratory were locked. The large bay windows through which daylight entered overlooked the garden–or, rather, the crowns of the trees therein–so there was no fear of indiscretion on that side. None of the Professor's usual assistants was in the laboratory. The various operations necessary to the experiment were carried out from inside the glass cage, by means of electricity; to that effect, one of the four lateral plates was furnished with a console bearing several switches, which controlled all the mechanisms. The switches were numbered.

"Are we ready?" asked Lourmel, looking around.

The red-haired man was sitting in one of the corners of the glass plate, facing the opposite corner. Laurence was sitting two meters away, while Saint-Clair and Lourmel were directly facing him on the same diagonal. Prillant was to Laurence's left, slightly behind her. The late Monsieur Narbonne's secretary only had to reach out his right hand to touch the bank of switches; he would be the one to press the buttons, in response to Lourmel's instructions.

"Yes, we're ready," said the Professor–and he used his right foot to press a porcelain stud embedded in the plate on which they were all assembled. The suspended class cage immediately began a slow descent. Its lower edges were soon posed in four grooves hollowed out in the floor-plate. A slight hiss was heard, and rubber valves within the grooves sealed both sides of the inferior edges of the cage's side-walls.

The young woman and the five men were hermetically sealed within the transparent prison.

"We're cut off from the exterior air," Lourmel said. "I'll introduce the radioactive gas that will modify our atmosphere in the desired manner. Don't worry about the slight excitation what you'll experience, which will persist until the end of the experiment, and some time thereafter."

No one said a word. They waited, their hearts afflicted by a kind of impassioned anxiety. They looked at the red-haired man, motionless and impassive on his chair, his open eyes expressionless and his thin lips tightly closed. What was going to come out of that mouth? Words of revelation? Or would it remain shut? Would the distant hypnotic empery of Lucifer prove more powerful than the Nyctalope's will-power and Professor Lourmel's science?

"André–No. 1!"

D'Arbol reached out and used his index finger to press button No. 1 on the switchboard. He held it down. A valve opened in the ceiling of the glass cage, from which extended a rubber tube surrounded with an insulating fabric. This tube, supported by a beam, put the cage in communication with a machine similar to an electrical transformer set on a block of concrete at the back of the laboratory.

There was no audible noise, perceptible odor or visible coloration of the air, but he professor had taken a tiny glass tube from his pocket, whose stopper he removed. There was a white substance in the tube. He put the tube in his left hand, which was half-closed. Thus sheltered from the bright daylight, the white material seemed to acquire a sort of phosphorescence, which became more distinct and was rapidly accentuated. Lourmel followed the rapid progression with his eyes.

"Stop!" he said.

D'Arbol withdrew his finger; the button stood up. The valve in the ceiling closed again with a dry click.

The Professor resealed the tube and put it back in his pocket. "Wait five minutes," he said, "for the radioactive principles to penetrate our bodies, and especially that of our subject."

Laurence was the first to feel a prickling sensation in her fingertips. The others saw her look at her hands, and understood–for Saint-Clair, D'Arbol, Prillant and Lourmel almost immediately experienced the same sensation. The nervous excitation climbed up their arms, excited the nape of their neck and seemed to descend along the entire length of the vertebral column, then the thighs, calves and feet, giving them pins and needles.

The Professor consulted the enormous laboratory clock, which marked the months, the days, the hours, the minutes and the seconds. In a slightly feverish voice, he said: "Shall we begin, Saint-Clair?"

"Let's begin," the Nyctalope replied, quivering with excitement.

They were both pale. No longer able to remain seated, Laurence got up abruptly, went behind her chair and set both hands on it back. Her shoulders, half-exposed by the low cut of her dress, were shivering.

Then, concentrating all the power of his will in his commanding eyes, the Professor approached the red-haired man, until he was no more than one step away from his chair. He took his subject's head in both hands, with four fingers at each temple and the thumbs extended along the brow ridges. Authoritatively, pronouncing each syllable distinctly, he said: "I want you to go to sleep! You will go to sleep! Sleep!"

The Professor's eyes sparkled more brightly than the facets of the mirrors of which many hypnotists make use.

"You will sleep! I command it! Sleep!"

And his two thumbs slowly descended upon the red-haired man's eyelids, which had already begun to sag. The thumbs closed the eyelids, upon which they pressed very gently.

The subject slumped in his chair; he was in a state of catalepsy–the first stage of hypnosis.

The Professor persisted in his occlusion of the eyelids, and the red-haired man was soon in the second stage of hypnosis, which is a lethargy characterized by complete muscular relaxation and exaggerated reflexes, in which the muscles contract with the greatest ease under the influence of the feeblest mechanical excitations.

Saint-Clair satisfied himself as to the red-haired man's condition by touching an extensor muscle in the arm lightly with his right hand; the muscle immediately contracted spasmodically. Then, withdrawing his fingers and thumbs, the Professor pressed down gently on the top of the man's skull. The patient's clenched hand resumed its original position. His eyes remained closed; his lips, which Saint-Clair pricked with a pin, gave no sign of the slightest sensation. Drawing back, the Professor let go of the head, which remained motionless and erect, supported by the back of the chair.

The red-haired man was in the third and most complete stage of hypnosis, in which one is entranced and easily impressionable: somnambulism.

"Good!" murmured Lourmel. "That wasn't difficult; now we need to know whether the subject will be docile. Will he talk?" The Professor's emotion was so profound that he could not hide it, despite his strength of character. His voice, his expression and his gestures all revealed it.

Laurence Païli, standing with both hands of the back of her chair, was pale but calm, staring hard and menacingly at the red-haired man. She was undoubtedly recalling the monstrous Lucifer, of whom he was the exact double.

Monsieur Prillant, with his teeth clenched, his back to the glass wall and his hands in his pockets, was observing and listening, controlling his emotions, although he was slightly choked.

D'Arbol, less in control of himself, was also observing and listening, but nervous tremors often took hold of him and his face was already expressing an immense fatigue.

As for Saint-Clair, he had never felt as powerful. It was he who would conduct the interrogation; it was his will-power, above all, that would be exerted upon the hypnotized man. He focused that will-power to one single end, with the sole purpose of succeeding in substituting his own empery for that of the other red-haired man, Lucifer, over this one. He seemed, and really was, as calm and cool as he had been in India when, flanked by Pilou and Corsat, he had faced a tiger ready to pounce, 20 paces from the end of his rifle.

"Will he talk?" Lourmel had said, as he drew back.

"He'll talk!" said Saint-Clair, forcefully. And the Nyctalope took the Professor's place.

There was a minute's pause. If anyone had been paying attention, he would have heard the beating of hearts within breasts and the slight sigh of breath within throats...

Suddenly, the Nyctalope put out his right hand. Placing it gently on the red-haired man's skull, its five fingers entrenched and invisible within the flamboyant tresses, he moved slightly to his left, in such a way that Laurence had a better view of the patient's face, which she was devouring with eyes of black diamond. He spoke in German–a language which all four spectators understood and spoke. "Hear me, you, whom I touch and command! I order you to respond to me, without restraint and without falsehood. I want you to free your soul from all that weighs upon it and overwhelms it. Do you hear me?"

The red-haired man's lips parted slightly; a breath of air escaped, and the expected word was clearly articulated: "*Ja!*"

"But I want you, I order you, to respond to me!" Saint-Clair immediately insisted. "Will you reply to all my questions?"

After the affirmative response, the lips had remained apart. They moved slowly, beginning to close again.

Laurence, Lourmel, Prillant and d'Arbol watched anxiously. Were they about to see the light–that mysterious light of which Lucifer alone, until now, had been the Master? Or would the red-haired man's silence leave them in the darkness in which, until now, they had only been able to act by grace of the Nyctalope's genius, aided by a combination of favorable circumstances–a preliminary battle whose fortunate result would not, alas, last forever?

"Will you reply to all my questions?" Saint-Clair repeated, infusing his voice with a superhuman force.

The silence was terrible.

Then the red-haired man replied, simply: "*Ja!*"

What sighs of relief were heard in the cage of glass, as bosoms heaved! Laurence let out a nervous sob. Two large tears fell from d'Arbol's eyes. Lourmel swore contentedly. Monsieur Prillant, choked as he was, suddenly went very pale, with a smile beneath his moustache and in his eyes.

Saint-Clair shivered, lowered his head and collected himself. This was the formidable dialogue that would soon shine a clear light into the darkness and infernal fulguration of Schwarzrock, where the Nyctalope would soon be risking his life against its Lord and Master, Lucifer.

"Speak, then! How are you related to Glô XIII of Schwarzrock?"

"I'm his younger twin brother," the red-haired man replied, "and his second in all matters–but to the intelligence and power of the Supreme Lord, my part is unquestioning obedience."

"What is your name?"

"Hunter."

"How much do you know about the occult power of Glô XIII? About the machine called the Teledynamo? About the actions past and present and the projects of the man who compares himself so proudly to Lucifer? How much do you know? A little, a lot, or everything?"

Without hesitation, the hypnotized man replied to that cold, monotonous voice, as slow and uninflected as his own: "Everything, no–a lot, yes."

"You can't read Lucifer's thoughts, then?"

"No."

"Can you witness retrospectively actions already accomplished?"

"Yes."

"Good. Rest for a moment." Turning away from the red-haired Hunter, Saint-Clair said to his companions: "There are three series of questions to be asked, three sets of problems to be solved. The first relates to Lucifer's power, his method, his motives, his whims, his idiosyncrasies, his weaknesses and his means, as comprised by the Teledynamo. The replies to those will explain all the mysteries of Schwarzrock. The second concerns Lucifer's intentions and goals, immediate and distant–in short, his life-plan. The third concerns the truth of Monsieur Narbonne's death, Eiger Nott and Mademoiselle Païli's situation."

"Exactly," said Lourmel. "Hunter will tell us everything that he knows by virtue of having seen or heard it, then everything else of which he is ignorant in his waking state but which his perispirit is able to report. In sum, we shall know what we need to know, save only for the secret thoughts of Glô von Warteck."

"We can deduce much of that from the subject's revelations," said Monsieur Prillant.

"I'll continue, then," Saint-Clair concluded. After directing an affectionate glance at Laurence, who smiled at him, he turned back to the red-haired man.

"Hunter! I want to know everything you know yourself about Glô XIII of Schwarzrock, the one you call the Supreme Lord. If I require you to reply, will you reply?"

"Yes."

"Good. Where and how did Lucifer acquire his expertise as a spell-caster?"

"At 16 years of age, Glô left the Hollow Rock to study at the University of Paris. A half-effaced inscription on a stone he found in the garden of the Musée de Cluny, which he deciphered, set him on the road to a great discovery. It took him to the Benedictine Abbey at Cluny, in the *département* of the Saône-et-Loire. There, hiding by day and searching by night, amid many dangers, he finally discovered a bronze casket beneath a gravestone in the monastic cemetery, which contained the scientific testament of Nicholas Flamel, the great misunderstood alchemist of the 15th century.[49]

"This testament initiated Glô into all the mysteries of occultism, save for certain points that were still obscure. Glô resolved to know everything. He spent ten years traveling for the purpose of study. He discovered all the secrets that a transcendental mind was able to discover, working in the synagogue of Amsterdam, the synod of Dordrecht, the library of San Marco in Venice, the Vatican library in Rome and the Hagia Sofia Mosque in Constantinople. He acquainted himself with the Copts of Egypt, the Maronites of Mount Liban and the monks of Mount Carmel; then he went to Sana'a in Arabia, to Ispahan, Kandahar, Delhi, Agra and finally to Benares, where he lived with the Brahmins for five years.[50] When he returned, he acquired the castle of Schwarzrock, installed himself therein, and immediately began work on the construction of the Teledynamo."

"What is this Teledynamo, exactly?" Saint-Clair asked. His companions were listening, as passionately interested as he was.

"It's the machine which, once raised to its highest degree of perfection, will be to the human brain what a giant crane is to the human arm. The muscles of the most powerful athlete can lift between 100 and 200 kilograms, by dint of a powerful effort; the electric crane can lift and move thousands of tons with indefatigable ease. It is the same with the human brain and the Teledynamo; it multiplies the clarity, the intensity, the penetration, the range and the duration of human thought to an incalculable degree. The thoughts of Glô von Warteck, taken in, transfigured and projected by the Teledynamo, will be capable of absorbing, and thus of governing, arbitrarily and without limits, all the thoughts of all humankind. Here is one example–a petty and ridiculous example, but a revealing one.

"Glô and the Teledynamo are in the dungeon of Schwarzrock. Let us suppose that, at the antipodes of the Black Forest–which is to say, not far from one of the Aleutian islands, at the entrance to the Behring Sea [51]–one were to find Leo Saint-Clair, a man about whom I have read anecdotes in magazines, proving his rare power and character. This Nyctalope might, I imagine, be skinning a salmon. He is very hungry and almost naked, having been the sole survivor of a shipwreck, and there are no other living creatures there except for this salmon, caught with enormous difficulty, The Nyctalope must eat this salmon if he is not to become incapable of movement and succumb to the deadly cold. Well, if Glô von Warteck, in Schwarzrock, were to pour into the Teledynamo this thought: 'I want the Nyctalope to throw the salmon into the sea, and I want this French patriot to set about singing, with all his might, the German anthem *Deutschland, Deutschland über Alles*–well, I tell you that Leo Saint-Clair would throw away the salmon and sing the song...'"

Hunter fell silent, and there was a prolonged pause. The example was striking–and its choice proved, either that Hunter had heard Lucifer use this particular example at some time, or that Hunter benefited under hypnosis from a sort of double existence that sharpened his intelligence considerably. Saint-Clair and his companions were violently impressed–but the Nyctalope did not take long to master his emotion.

"Hunter!" he said, forcefully. "Of what is the Teledynamo made, and how is it constructed?"

"I don't know," the hypnotized man replied.

"But you must often have seen the machine!"

"Yes. I know that its base contains electrodynamic devices with accumulators of extrahuman fluids, which are both concentrated in and emitted by grey matter charged with radium, and with a wave-transmitter... But I don't know any more, save that certain Voltaic piles will be replaced by fire-resistant human

299

skulls as soon as Glô has discovered the new combination of grey matter and radium for which he has been searching since a stranger somehow contrived to get into Schwarzrock..."

"And what do you know about that stranger?" Saint-Clair cut in, excitedly.

"He was mad to attack the Supreme Lord!"

"We shall see!" said the Nyctalope, shrugging his shoulders. "Hunter, continue telling what you know about the Teledynamo."

"I don't know any more."

"Explain to me, then, how Lucifer's powers of spell-casting and distant hypnosis are limited to certain persons, and why he is subject to irregularities and weaknesses–why he can cast a spell on a woman and a child but not on that woman's protectors or the child's father."

"It's quite simple. Glô von Warteck–to whom you apply the nickname Lucifer, which he has rightly adopted, since he will be the sole light-bearer among all the living creature on the surface of the globe–is often absorbed by the work of bringing the Teledynamo to its final perfection. The part of his fluidic thought and will that he can exteriorize, and project to a greater or lesser distance, becomes variable and diminished then, often being almost completely annulled. And whenever Glô has to pay attention to several simultaneous hostile reactions, he abandons the least important. It is for that reason that he cannot yet attack certain brains possessed of a forceful reactivity and a powerful will. At close range, he is able to hypnotize the Nyctalope himself, without the aid of the Teledynamo, but he will not be able to do that at a distance until the Teledynamo is entirely perfected–the end of June at the latest."

Hunter fell silent again. Even though the patient was visibly fatigued, Saint-Clair did not give him any more time to rest.

"Setting aside of the Teledynamo and its various potential actions, what do Lucifer's magical powers amount to?"

"He has all of them, save for the transmutation of base metal into gold–for the philosopher's stone is a chimera of human avarice and ambition. Glô can disincarnate himself, send forth his perispirit, or even his soul, to travel phantomatically. Spell-casting and levitation at a distance are mere games to him; he absorbs light to create darkness as he pleases, through opaque and solid matter."

Saint-Clair, Lourmel, Prillant and d'Arbol felt a *frisson*–the same indescribable frisson that the priest of Isis experiences on the threshold of the temple of the ultimate mystery. As for Laurence, shaken by nervous fits that were exasperated by the radioactive atmosphere, she gripped the chair hard with both hands; her face–strained, white and emaciated–would have excited Saint-Clair's pity had he seen it, but the Nyctalope, at that moment, had no thought for anything except the struggle against the mighty Lucifer. And he wanted to know everything!

"More, more!" he cried, violently. Then, immediately afterwards: "Hunter! What is the invisible wall in the overhanging tower?"

300

"The fluidic will of Lucifer, opposed to some will that he wishes to halt, there or elsewhere."

"Hunter! What is it, exactly, that Lucifer wants?"

"To rule the world."

"And his more immediate aims?"

"To possess certain women, to spend certain fortunes, to revolutionize certain nations, France first of all, and to finish the Teledynamo before June 10, the date he has fixed..."

"Why that date rather than another?"

"I don't know."

"Hunter! Did Monsieur Narbonne make his will and kill himself voluntarily?"

"No."

"How did it happen?"

"A phantasmal apparition. An imperative suggestion to write, to die..."

"Who is Eiger Nott?"

"It's the assumed name of Rupert V, the brother of Rupert VI and Glô's uncle." [52]

"Is Eiger Nott really in Geneva, in person."

"Yes, but I don't..." Hunter faltered. He was whiter than a corpse and his stammering voice was becoming feeble.

"You'll kill him, Saint-Clair," Lourmel said.

"No–he can still talk. I sense it; I know it." And, insistently: "Hunter! What is happening to Madame Païli? What danger is she in?"

"She is under his hypnotic influence, living a pleasant existence. She's waiting contentedly for her daughter. She's in no danger–until June 10."

"Hunter! What is the chink in Lucifer's armor?"

"His sensuality."

"Hunter! What is Schwarzrock's weak point?"

"The Zuchts' house."

"Hunter...!" But the Nyctalope cut himself off. The patient's body slumped to the left, slid off the chair, and fell to the glass floor with its knees drawn up. It was shaken by two or three convulsions, then went stiff.

Lourmel bent down, in quest of a heartbeat.

"You've killed him, Saint-Clair!"

"Bah!" the Nyctalope exclaimed. "Lucifer will resuscitate him, if he so wishes." Then, he said to d'Arbol: "Lift it! Lift the cage! Pure air! Pure air!"

He caught the shivering Laurence, who was on the point of fainting, in his arms. On his knees before Hunter's body, Lourmel leaned both hands on the glass plate. Monsieur Prillant was weak at the knees, half-mad. D'Arbol threw himself on the floor to escape from the cage, which was slowly rising. Saint-Clair would have howled in nervous overexcitement had he not controlled himself angrily. Eventually, the cage was raised high enough in the air for them all

301

to step out on to the floorboards of the laboratory. Prillant ran to a window and opened it wide.

Laurence had already raised her eyelids to look at the Nyctalope. "Come on, my dear, my beloved!" he muttered, tears in his eyes. As she smiled at him, he set her on her feet, turned slightly to one side and said, in a terrible voice: "Lourmel, Prillant, D'Arbol! The Teledynamo! Sensuality! The Zuchts' house! Before June 10! Today's May 24. Do you understand? Quickly! We must, go, fight and win! It may be that in Schwarzrock, as in the Aleutians, I shall throw the aliment of my life into the sea and sing the hymn of slavery. Do you understand? You shall see me again as a conqueror–or never!!

Bearing Laurence, who was both ecstatic and terrified, in his arms, he threw himself out of the laboratory, the flame of his genius fanned to the point at which he seemed mad. But as he descended a staircase, went along a corridor and went through the vestibule he calmed down. In the street, when he climbed into his car, still carrying the bewildered Laurence it was in a relatively calm tone that he said to Pilou: "Home!"

IV. Grisyl's Jealousy

Grisyl had been in the house in the Rue Nansouty for more than 24 hours, during which time she had been she discreetly guarded by Wolf and respectfully served by Rosine–but the daughter of the Wartecks had not yet received a visit from her conqueror and master, Leo Saint-Clair.

She had seen him twice, however: the previous day, when he had come back from the Observatory gardens, and today, when he had left for Auteuil. Hearing noises in the courtyard, the young woman had drawn aside the curtain and had seen that on both occasions the Nyctalope was accompanied by a beautiful–a very beautiful–young woman.

For 24 hours, after having slept for a while, Grisyl had done nothing but wait for Saint-Clair. She allowed herself to live and to be served, following the directions and suggestions offered by Rosine, whose simple and slightly ungrammatical language she understood perfectly, but she was indifferent to everything except for what she could see or discover regarding Saint-Clair's life. Alas, she had only seen and discovered one thing: he came in and went out with a young woman, whose beauty seemed to Grisyl to be marvelous.

Grisyl had never read a novel, nor seen a play, nor heard any commentary on the various fine aspects of dramatic and passionate matters. All she knew, having learned it from austere scientific books and journals, was that love was a sentiment that excited the procreative union between two different sexes. She knew that jealousy was nothing but the instinct and pride of ownership, generally more developed in humans than in animals, but rather variable in its expression and effects in human societies, whether they were "savage" or "civilized."

On seeing Saint-Clair accompanied by a woman, Grisyl understood that it was love that had made her Saint-Clair's slave. On establishing that the woman was very beautiful, she began to suffer from jealousy, not because she thought that she had the least right of ownership relative to Saint-Clair, but because she would have liked to be the only woman who belonged to him. It was the jealousy of Eunice, the slave of Petronius,[53] not that of a modern spouse shooting a husband suspected of infidelity.

On that day, May 24, a few hours after having seen the Nyctalope go out in the company of the woman she had noticed on the previous day, Grisyl saw the Nyctalope and the same woman coming back. She drew away from the window, lay down on a large divan, hid her face in the crook of her left arm, and began to weep very quietly...

As he came back into the house, Saint-Clair was still feeling the effects of the terrible scene that had concluded Hunter's interrogation. During the journey from Auteuil to the Rue Nansouty, Leo had clasped Laurence's hands in his, and had delighted in feeling her troubled head resting fondly on his shoulder–but he had not said a word. He was thinking–and his thoughts were making leaps of genius in time and space between the beacons provided by four problematic terms: the Teledynamo; sensuality; the Zuchts' house; June 10.

Since the first pronunciation of these four fateful phrases, a plan of action had begun to form in the Nyctalope's mind: an audacious folly of admirable psychological profundity. This plan had immediately became firmer and more developed; then, during the journey by car, the plan had been divided into distinct phases, each one determining the next, and its principal details had been fixed–so effectively that as soon as he entered his house in Rue Nansouty, Leo Saint-Clair issued his orders.

To Laurence he said: "My dear, telephone your chambermaid and tell her to fill your trunks with what you normally carry when you give a gala performance in London, Madrid, Milan or Rome–as if you were to perform three or four of the most seductive masterpieces in your repertoire. We're leaving tomorrow morning for Colmar. Your chambermaid will accompany you in your car, driven by your chauffeur."

To Corsat and Pilou he said: "We're leaving at 10 a.m. tomorrow morning for Colmar in my roadster, with the usual clothing and equipment, armed for a great adventure. Don't give any more thought to the red-haired man–he's dead. Pilou, go send this telegram."

In the cipher agreed with the Nortmunds, he wrote a message whose translation was: *To Louis Nortmund,* The Willows, *Colmar, Alsace. Will arrive tomorrow or day after with two women, one female servant, three male servants, two cars. Saint-Clair.*

Then, by means of the internal corridor that connected the first floor of the house to the first floor of the lodge, the Nyctalope went to Grisyl's apartment. He met Rosine in the hallway; she was dusting the chairs,

"Where's Mademoiselle Grisyl?"

"In the sitting-room, Monsieur."

When he went into the sitting-room, without making a noise, Saint-Clair was mildly surprised to see that the young woman, instead of reading something from the room's well-stocked bookshelves, was lying on the divan with her face hidden in the crook of her left arm. The surprise was mild, though, for he saw that Grisyl was crying, and noticed that a lace curtain was still lifted up, and he understood. At first, he frowned in annoyance, but within 20 seconds, he put his face straight and a smile played upon his lips. He went straight to the divan, sat on the edge, put a hand on one of the young woman's shoulders, and gently forced her to uncover her face and turn towards him.

Her blue eyes, misted with tears, expressed an infinite sadness. Her swollen lips were pale, constricted by suffering.

Caressing the young woman's bare shoulder with one hand, and raising her head with the other, turning it towards him and looking into her eyes, Saint-Clair immediately began to speak. "Grisyl, you have never lived in the midst of the everyday passions of humankind. But you have read enough, and have sufficient atavisms, to ensure that your first contact with human beings other than the Warteck family would excite and bring those passions into play. You love me, Grisyl, because, despite being your family's enemy, I have been the Lohengrin of your dreams. You love me as some daughter of Prussian barons might have loved one of Napoleon's colonels of hussars entering Berlin in triumph in 1806. You love me because I am the new man and the conqueror–and that is why you saved me and served me in the Hollow Rock. But now you are jealous and are suffering, because you've been watching through that window. You've seen a woman leave the house with me, and return with me... All that's true, isn't it, Grisyl?"

She sighed. "It's true."

He kissed her forehead, languorously. Then, with his eyes weighing upon her and enveloping her, he resumed in a low but forceful voice: "You are not a rebel, Grisyl. You will never rebel. You will continue to love me and serve me..."

"Oh, yes, yes!" she exclaimed.

"I shall never be your lover, Grisyl, but your love will soften my heart, and I shall surround you with my tenderness."

"Your presence..." she stammered, sobbing.

"You will always remain with me, Grisyl–and the one to whom I have given my heart, once and for all, will love you like a thankful and tender sister..."

"Oh! I cannot detest her, since you love her!"

"You are great and noble, Grisyl. So many others would have said the opposite of what you have just said, and so many others would have behaved badly! But if you were one of those, I would have found you out, child! And I would have left you with the Warteck prisoners."

"Oh, darling! Keep me always at your side!" Then, immediately, with melancholy resignation, she added: "Besides, that always will not last long..."

"Why, Grisyl?"

"Because, as soon as I am no longer useful to you, I shall kill myself."

"Grisyl..."

"I shall kill myself! I only ask one thing of you: that you bury me in the soil where you yourself, one day, might rest."

"Grisyl!"

"Oh, please! Promise me!"

She flung her arms around his neck, hugging him recklessly, violently and passionately, pleading and weeping.

He gradually disengaged himself. Meeting the enraptured eyes of the amorous young woman, he said: "I swear, Grisyl. You shall sleep the sleep of death in the same plot of ground in which my body, in its turn, will be laid for the last time. But if I should fall in the battle that I am about to undertake..."

"Shall I take part in that battle?"

"Yes, if you want to."

"I want to, darling."

"It's against Glô XIII of Schwarzrock."

"I want to!"

"Very well. But if I should fail..."

"I shall die after you and beside you."

He took her head in both hands, drew it towards him, and placed his fiery lips on the quivering lips of the young woman–who moaned and whose eyes widened ecstatically. But he got up immediately and let go, letting her body fall back on the divan. Placing his right hand on her burning forehead, he said: "Rest and prepare yourself, Grisyl. This evening, you shall meet Laurence Païli, who is my wife. Tomorrow, we depart for Schwarzrock."

After favoring the amorous girl with a long smile and a profound gaze, he left.

V. La Païli's Love

Saint-Clair found Laurence in the room that she had occupied since her return from Schwarzrock. The young woman was sitting in an armchair with her elbow on the armrest and her forehead in her hand. As her lover came in, she raised her head slightly and gazed at him in a tender and serious manner.

He understood that the time had come for an exchange of confidences. He drew a chair towards him and sat down on it. "I've just talked to Grisyl," he said. "My observations and your intuition were correct; she loves me–and your loving heart has made a accurate assessment of hers: she would sacrifice herself. I told her that you would be her very thankful and tender sister."

"I will be, Leo," Laurence declared. "And I too shall be able to sacrifice myself..."

"You!" said Saint-Clair, shivering. He went pale, fearful of guessing what she might mean.

Laurence leaned towards him and took his hands. In a pathetic and intensely musical voice, which stirred the nerves as much as the soul, she said: "Listen, Leo! First, you must know what happened at Schwarzrock, in the room with overhanging turret, at 2 p.m. on May 16–the moment when you recovered consciousness of your thoughts and your free will in the round room called the room of death..."

She paused, her bosom palpitant with emotion.

"Speak, my beloved Laure, speak!"

She gazed at him passionately. Then, lowering her eyelids to hide her large black eyes, she leaned a little further forward, squeezed Saint-Clair's muscular hands harder with her own beautiful slender hands, and resumed speaking in a bleaker tone.

"I've already told you what I had deduced. I had concluded, correctly, that if I could drown Lucifer's will-power in violent emotion, all his influence would be abruptly nullified. One thing alone could bring about that formidable effect: the total, ardent, prolonged and incessant renewal of the savage appetites that the man had confessed to me, and of which he desired to make me the victim..."

"Laure!"

"Pardon me, Leo! Was it not necessary to save you? Who could do that, if not me? And how could I have done it, if I had not finally resolved to immolate myself... and to die? Yes, certainly! And there was one hope still burning in me. I said to myself: Leo, once he is free, will race here, weapon in hand. Perhaps he will kill the monster before. And it was that hope, too, which gave me the horrible courage to summon Glô von Warteck and say to him: You have desired me; you desire me still; here I am, submissive and consenting; here are my lips, take me!"

307

"Laure!"

"Oh, Leo, let me finish! The monster responded immediately to my desperate summons. I acted abominably, but was it not necessary, to save you? I acted that day as if I were playing the role that consummated my career as an actress. I offered my lips to Lucifer–and to intoxicate him to the necessary pitch, to concentrate his dispersed power of thought immediately and totally and to capture all of that deadly thought myself, I became a courtesan. Fortunate and unfortunate at the same time, because I would save you by losing myself, I played the role of the enchantress who allows herself, little by little to be enchanted in her turn..."

"Laure, my love! Enough! Shut up!"

"No, no–not yet! I understand your black thoughts. You are hesitating, tortured by doubts, between the joy of having found me again and the shame of... Listen! You must know everything, in order to believe..."

Drawing her trembling hands away from her lover's, Laurence slumped back in the armchair and clutched her forehead. With her face half-hidden, she continued breathlessly: "I let him make me his plaything–apparently! Feigning perverse modesty while I was agonized by horror, I pulled away from him and let him draw me back. All the while, internally, I was counting the minutes, taking stock of the passing time. Oh, the slowness, the length of those infernal minutes! His lips and his hands, as intoxicated as his brain, sought me out violently–and every time, I allowed myself to be caught, always holding myself in reserve... But in response to an abrupt audacity that I had not expected, which I could not bear, I was no longer able to hold my theatrical mask in place... Oh, Leo, pardon me! It was then that I was guilty, because I could not suppress my disgust and my terror, because I would seal your fate after having done so much to save you... Yes, I was then no longer either coquettish, seductive or modest. My entire body and soul shuddered with revulsion and hatred, and–pardon me, Leo!–I forgot you and could think of nothing but refusing myself to the monster, of pushing away his lips, of thrusting aside his hands, which had rendered impossible the boundless joy of which he was so certain... I extracted myself from his embrace, escaped him, fled from him to the back of the room..."

"Laure, my beloved!"

"Oh, Leo, my love! Astonished at first, believing it to be a new scene in the passionate game, he burst out laughing, called to me, waited for me, but not for long. My face was no longer wearing the deceptive mask that my will had imposed upon it. My features, my eyes, my mouth, my attitude, everything in me loudly proclaimed my sentiments and their sincerity: my repulsion and my hatred, my contempt and my determination to defend myself, to fight, to refuse. He understood. He ran towards me. He roared and drew himself up to his full height. I dodged past him again. He doubled back and succeeded in grabbing me by the ear. I recoiled violently and my ear-lobe ripped, leaving its pendant in his fingers. He pounced, and fell upon me, thrusting me back on to the divan with all his might. There was a new struggle, ferocious...

"He struck me, mad with desire, and I suddenly lit up with happiness, for I understood that this new phase of our duel would monopolize his thoughts even more than the first. Oh Leo, what strength your love lent to my limbs! For a long time, a long time, I was able to defend myself–but finally, wounded and crushed, I was afraid that I was about to faint. It was the end. I was lost... Once again, Leo, I forgot you! With the sole intention of getting my lips as far away from his satanic mouth as possible, I seized him by the neck with both hands and I squeezed... I squeezed...

"I was half-dead, but my muscles continued to obey my will as my will began to fade. Vaguely, I perceived that my fingers were clasped around something heavy, which slipped out of their grip. Vaguely, I heard shouting–your voice, Leo, your voice! And that was all..."

"Laure, Laure, my joy, my love, my life!"

Saint-Clair got to his feet. He took Laurence in his arms and let himself fall into the armchair, cradling her and caressing her as if she were a little girl, ex-ultant, rapturous, mad with emotion and happiness, frenetic in his tenderness...

"Laure!" he stammered. "My darling, my beloved! Ah, I guessed it, I knew it! Doubt you? No! The black thoughts came but I chased them away–I swear to you that I chased them away!"

Leo Saint-Clair was so rapturous that he did not hear Laurence Païli say, her voice ecstatic and interrupted by sobs: "But if I must, this time, my Leo, to ensure that you are victorious–to ensure that you defeat him and kill him–if I must sacrifice everything... Oh, I shall be more courageous. Yes, I shall sacrifice myself... And then... then... you will let me die... die in your arms..."

No, the Nyctalope was not listening–for if he had heard...

Would he have accepted Laurence's sacrifice, as he had already garnered Grisyl's?

VI. Separation

At 10 a.m. on the following day, May 25, two cars exited from the Rue Nansouty and bowled along the Boulevard Jourdan in the direction of Vincennes, following the inner periphery of the fortifications until they passed through the Porte Daumesnil. The first, a long gray roadster with two flat trunks buckled to its boot, contained Pilou, Wolf, Corsat and Saint-Clair. The second, a powerful limousine, was driven by La Païli's chauffeur, Lucas, who had Adèle, the singer's chambermaid, beside him; Laurence and Grisyl were in the rear compartment.

Once they had passed through the populous agglomerations of the suburbs, the two cars increased their speed, the second always 150 meters or so behind the first. Their average speed was 40 miles an hour–slow by the roadster's standards, but rapid by the limousine's.

At 1 p.m., they stopped by a wood in the open countryside. Corsat and Adèle spread a tablecloth on the grass and unloaded a large hamper. The masters and their servants ate with hearty appetites, and not without a certain pleasure. Even Grisyl, being very affectionate towards Laurence, who was cosseting her, gave voice to vibrant and youthful fits of laughter. Saint-Clair told jokes and related amusing anecdotes. The spring day was very mild, the countryside picturesque, the food exquisite.

They got under way again at 2 p.m. and averaged 50 miles an hour until the next stop. The Sun was about to set. They "stretched their legs" at the top of a hill overlooking a dark fir-wood. The road snaked across an uncultivated green plain ahead of them. The servants prepared dinner and they ate.

With the headlights on, they resumed their route without haste. The damp ground was not producing any dust and Adèle opened the limousine's windows. The night was a marvel of mildness, calm, perfumed and moonlit. Saint-Clair smoked a flavorsome pipe.

At 2:30 a.m. on May 26, the gate of the Nortmunds' villa, *The Willows*, opened to the two cars.

Messieurs Charles and Louis and Madame Blanche Nortmund were waiting up for the Nyctalope. They knew and loved La Païli. Grisyl was introduced to them by her forename alone. Madame Blanche took the two female travelers into a sitting-room between the two rooms reserved for them, where a light warm supper had been set out. Adèle followed and served her mistress. When the cars had been put away and they had attended to their immediate needs, Pilou, Corsat, Wolf and Lucas were invited to supper with the Nortmunds' butler. The Nyctalope immediately shut himself away with the Nortmund father and son in the smoking-room, where *foie gras* sandwiches awaited them, along with fresh water and Lorraine rosé wine, of which the Nortmunds were connoisseurs.

The three men left the smoking-room and went to bed at 4 a.m.; they did not get up until lunch-time.

The Nortmunds' children, Paul, Pierrette and Jacqueline, were present at lunch, when all was smiling cordiality. They talked about a thousand things, but not Lucifer. Adapting rapidly, Grisyl was charming, speaking French with the strange accent of the Bermudan Wartecks, which had more Anglo-American than German influences and contrived extremely amusing sentences. Saint-Clair took the trouble, in the course of the memorable meal, to establish that Grisyl was more Slavic than German; this contributed to the clarification of the young woman's psychosentimental evolution, the depths of her soul owing almost nothing to the German Wartecks.

At 3 p.m., after a few turns around the villa's large and lovely garden, Saint-Clair said, simply: "Pilou, Corsat and Wolf ought to be ready."

With the two Nortmunds to either side, he headed back to the villa at a rapid pace. Blanche, Laurence and Grisyl followed. They all gathered in the small drawing-room. Leo Saint-Clair took Laurence and Grisyl by the hand and said to Madame Nortmund: "My dear Madame, I entrust them to you."

With the same contained emotion, the young woman replied: "And I, Monsieur, entrust my husband to you."

The Nyctalope bowed gravely, kissed the hands that Madame Blanche extended, and said, with masculine assurance: "We shall return together, Madame."

He shook Charles Nortmund's hand, then favored Grisyl with a profound glance and Laurence with an impassioned one. Both of them, very pale, stiffened themselves against their own emotions. They took one another by the hand, hugged one another, sisters in love and dread and accomplices in a project that was theirs alone.

Leo Saint-Clair went out, immediately followed by Louis Nortmund, whose father and wife embraced him. The Nyctalope's roadster was waiting in front of the perron, with Pilou in the driving-seat, Corsat next to him and Wolf on the outside. Buckled in rear were two large, flat wicker traveling-hampers. Four new tires had been fitted. Saint-Clair was wearing the same traveling-clothes as the day before: cap, grey suit and knee-length boots, Nortmund was similarly dressed, except that his waistcoat and trousers were a darker shade of grey.

Silent and serious, with a certain wildness and hardness in their eyes and the set of their jaws, the two men climbed into the roadster. As the door clicked shut behind Saint-Clair, the car drew away, went around the house and along the main drive, through the open gate, and turned left on to the road.

Hands lifted white curtains at two of the villa's upstairs windows; Louis Nortmund's father and spouse were at one of them; the two women who loved

Saint-Clair at the other. All four faces suddenly took on the same expression of ardent emotion; as the car had gone through the gate Leo and Louis had turned round and raised their hands in a final adieu!

VII. Laurence and Grisyl

The car carrying Saint-Clair and Louis Nortmund had scarcely disappeared when Laurence and Grisyl, hand in hand, turned away from their window and went towards Monsieur Nortmund and his daughter-in-law. Without any preamble, in a firm voice, La Païli said: "Would you be surprised, my dear Monsieur–and you, Madame, who have shown yourself to be such a good friend–if Mademoiselle Grisyl and I left you within the hour?"

Monsieur Nortmund and Madame Blanche made the same gesture of astonishment.

Laurence did not allow them to interrupt her. "Our duty," she said, "Grisyl's and my own, that is, is not to stay here while Leo Saint-Clair goes forth to put himself, at any moment–for hours, and perhaps days–in danger of torture and death...

"You, dear friend, are very anxious, even though you know that your husband–soon to be reunited with his gamekeepers, who have already left for the Black Forest–will not be going into the valley of Schwarzrock to confront Lucifer in person. Imagine the anguish, then, that we who love Leo Saint-Clair are suffering, when the Nyctalope has gone off with the sole aim of getting into Schwarzrock and defeating Glô von Warteck! Can we possibly stay here? No!"

"But what, Madame...?" said Charles Nortmund, who was perplexed.

"Ah! I understand!" cried Blanche.

"You understand, then," Laurence went on, heatedly, "that Grisyl and I have also made a plan of action, which we shall put into operation immediately. We too want to get into Schwarzrock! I've already been there, myself–and Grisyl, for her part, knows a great deal. Against Lucifer, we shall not be as strong as the Nyctalope, but we are more devious–yes, devious! In the name of what faith or honor would anyone dare to blame us for employing, against the monster of Schwarzrock, in the circumstances which might arise, the incomparable weapon of feminine perfidy? Grisyl is related to Lucifer! As for me, I shall use his own desire against him, his own passion...and my beauty..."

And how beautiful, indeed, La Païli was as she pronounced these terrible and sublime words! Grisyl looked at her, admiring her ingenuously. Monsieur Nortmund and Madame Blanche were subjugated.

After a brief silence, the singer resumed, more calmly, and with a smile. "This morning, Monsieur Louis–to whom I was able to speak after he got up–went to Colmar to make the necessary preparations, and promised me to keep the secret. He brought papers back from Colmar that will permit Mademoiselle Grisyl, myself and my chauffeur to cross the Baden border without difficulty. Lucas has been alerted; my limousine is ready. We'll leave as soon as we've taken off our indoor dresses and put on traveling clothes. You won't raise any our indoor dresses and put on traveling clothes. You won't raise any objection to our leaving..."

"Of course not!" cried Blanche, with tears in her eyes. "I understand and I approve. If my husband had not been ordered to wait close to Schwarzrock with the car and the gamekeepers–if he had been obliged to go into the castle with Saint-Clair–you may be certain that I would have demanded to go with you, to act with you...,"

"And we would not have consented," Laurence said, cutting her off.

"Why not?" exclaimed Blanche, astonished.

"Because, if your husband were in peril, your paramount duty would be to your children and your father-in-law. How different it is for us! My mother is my entire family and she is in Schwarzrock! Grisyl acknowledges but one master of her heart and her life, and that is the Nyctalope! Nothing could retain us here! Everything summons us out there! Let us embrace you–and, as I know that you pray to God, Madame, pray for us!"

Madame Blanche was weeping. Charles Nortmund did not even think of repressing his violent emotion. Like his daughter-in-law, he embraced Laurence and Grisyl.

Less than an hour later, the celebrated singer's car drew away from *The Willows*, carrying the two women who adored the Nyctalope. Monsieur Nortmund, however, had not wanted Lucas to remain alone, perhaps for several days, in hiding with the car in the vicinity of Schwarzrock's circle of mountains. He had sent along the son of his gardener–a courageous, sturdy and perceptive lad, twenty-six years of age, named Conrad, who knew how to navigate and was familiar with the greater part of Baden.

What was the plan that Laurence and Grisyl had made? How were they going to get into Schwarzrock, and what did they intend to do there? That was the secret of their love.

VIII. The Enormous Stupor

When Laurence and Grisyl left *The Willows*, Leo Saint-Clair and Louis Nortmund were well on their way to Schwarzrock. They crossed the Rhine at Vieux-Brisach, went through Freiburg without stopping and were soon in the Black Forest. The Nyctalope, Pilou and Corsat had followed the same route once before, but on foot. When night fell, they did not switch on their headlights or the internal lights, and the Nyctalope took over the roadster's wheel.

For Louis Nortmund and Wolf, who had never been in such a situation before, it was a bizarre and slightly disturbing thing to travel very rapidly in a car along forest roads in complete darkness. For the Nyctalope, Pilou and Corsat, however, it was child's play; the first could see as clearly as the other two would have with the headlights blazing, while the others knew full well that their boss was an "ace at the wheel."

After running for what seemed like a long time to Louis Nortmund and Wolf, the roadster stopped.

"We've arrived, my dear Nortmund," said Saint-Clair. "We're in the clearing where you were waiting for me in your limousine. Switch on your pocket torch. Good. Do you recognize the abandoned cabin?"

"Yes."

"When do you think your gamekeepers will arrive?"

"They should be here already! Thy left Colmar by train 12 hours before me. From Freiburg to here by motorcycle..."

"Here they are!"

"Ah! Good."

Two electric lamps had just lit up in the woods and two men, immediately picked out by the beam of Nortmund's torch, were advancing towards the car.

"Anything to report?" Louis asked.

"Nothing, Monsieur," one of the two men replied.

"That's good," said Saint-Clair. "Let's not lose any time. I want to knock on the Zuchts' door before dawn."

Pilou, Corsat and Wolf had already got out and were unbuckling the straps holding the two wicker baskets in the boot.

Within a quarter of an hour, Leo Saint-Clair and his three auxiliaries had put on electrically-insulated black leotards over their warm woolen underpants and vests, and strapped silent pistols, daggers, chisels and lassos to their belts, from which insulated gas masks were also suspended. Corsat, as usual on such expeditions, carried his satchel of tools and instruments. The four men wore tiny berets that clung to the skull and espadrilles with rubber soles, firmly secured at the ankles.

"You haven't forgotten any of the articles on the list, my dear Nortmund?" said Saint-Clair.

"None, my dear friend, don't worry. Go–and return victorious! If you haven't returned in 48 hours, or sent me a message..."

"Do what's necessary."

The two allies exchanged a fraternal accolade, while the two gamekeepers doffed their caps respectfully–and Saint-Clair, Pilou, Corsat and Wolf moved off at a rapid pace, the first seeing normally in the darkness and the other three contriving to follow him without hesitation thanks to the clarity of the atmosphere, which allowed a little of the light of the distant stars to reach as far as the path between the opaque walls formed by lines of tall fir-trees.

The woods soon became less dense and the path became clearer as it suddenly broadened out, becoming wide enough for a cart to pass, although it was steep and smooth. Thy were on the slope of the mountain whose circular summit was indented to form one of the passes giving access to the circus of Schwarzrock–the same pass through which Saint-Clair, Corsat and Pilou had come before, and through which they had returned with La Païli, Wolf and the red-haired man on May 16.

Wolf had assured Saint-Clair several times over that he could indicate the exact direction in which the Zuchts' house lay, once they arrived at the bottom of the basin surrounding the castle. While patrolling the towers of the castle, he had often seen a path winding across the green plain, which ended at the old sylvan buildings inhabited–according to one of his comrades–by the Zuchts, "outdoor" servants of the Lord Baron.

It was an emotional moment for the four men–especially the Nyctalope– when they came through the pass and saw the fantastic black mass of Schwarzrock looming up in the depths of the circus.

Saint-Clair was so suddenly and violently affected that he expressed his thoughts aloud. He was standing on the white rock where he had defeated old Zucht on May 16; his three auxiliaries were behind him, and they heard him proclaim: "Lucifer! The first time I got into your lair I only won half a victory! I knew nothing about you then–but now...! Ah, pray God that I can take you alive. Until the last day of the life that God himself may grant you, I shall submit you, as a powerless slave, to the diabolical empery of that same Teledynamo by means of which you planned to enslave all humankind! Sometimes, I shall return your free will to you; sometimes I shall render you conscious–and then you shall see the happiness of Irène with Raymond; the pride of Alexandre Prillant as he guides his son along the road of life, while France is prosperous and the world enjoys harmonious peace; the gratitude of the unfortunate to the memory of Mathias Narbonne; and the radiant face of Laurence Païli, my wife, supported on my arm. Those spectacles will be my vengeance, Lucifer! And you will suffer, as the fallen angel whose formidable name you have taken must suffer–if he exists–in being condemned to look upon the Divine Glory for all eternity..."

A poet in action, Leo Saint-Clair was rarely one in words–but who would not have been inspired to lyricism in such circumstances, confronted by Schwarzrock, the lair of Glô XIII, the master of the Teledynamo?

After a pause, Saint-Clair went on, his voice now bitter and menacing. "June 10! On that day, you hope to be Irène's master, La Païli's lover, the monstrous sultan of all women, the slave-trader of all men, the master of the world! It is nearly midnight on May 27. Thirteen days, Lucifer. Thirteen–the fateful number. It wasn't me who selected that number 13, but the march of events through days and nights. One day, looking forward to the future, you cried: June 10! On that day, Destiny launched me against you, and here we are, facing the final duel. It is 13 days that Destiny has given me to defeat you, Lucifer–or to be defeated by you! I accept the challenge of your occult powers, and I take the field against you, Glô von Warteck of Schwarzrock! Before the last of those fateful 13 days has faded into the past, I shall be victorious–or dead."

And the Nyctalope resumed his march. Who would not have followed him enthusiastically into battle and to sacrifice? Corsat and Pilou were exultant. Even Wolf, who now knew that he was a free man, would have been happy to die if, in dying, he became worthy to hear the Nyctalope thank him.

Lightly, lithely and rapidly, the four adventurers went down towards the castle. The wind was blowing in violent gusts, which swept the atmosphere clean and filled the valley with a thousand moaning sounds. Thanks to the wind, there was not a cloud in the star-studded sky and no mist on the mountains; the Nyctalope's three auxiliaries could see well enough to be sure of their footing, and if they occasionally set pebbles rolling the noise was lost in the sounds of the wind.

The Nyctalope often looked at the castle during the descent to the circus. There was no light burning–not the least chink of light in the sinister architectural mass, which was blacker than the night. Was the Baron asleep, as other men slept?

"He sleeps!" the Nyctalope said, with a snigger. "He may pretend to be Lucifer, but he's only a man if he sleeps, if only for an hour, while I march against him!"

They finally arrived at the bottom of the circular valley, scarcely 150 meters from the rocky base of the castle. The Nyctalope stopped. "Wolf!" he said, in a low voice.

"Boss!"

"We're here. Get your bearings. Don't make a mistake. Where's the Zuchts' house?"

"I've been thinking of nothing else since we started the descent. I'm sure that I'm not mistaken. The Zuchts' house is that way, at the back." He pointed to the north.

"Let's go–and quickly!"

The path was in good condition. It was quite possible that no vehicle had ever passed that way, and it was possible to see that its carefully-laid gravel was not very old. It only required a quarter of an hour for the four men to come within sight of the Zuchts' house. At this hour of the night, the doors and windows were shut; no light showed and no sound was audible through the cracks in the wooden shutters.

"These people must have a dog," Saint-Clair whispered to Pilou. "Imitate the call signal."

Among other talents, the Provençal possessed that of being able to imitate perfectly the yapping sounds made by a bitch to call her mate. The expected result was not long delayed. There was a grunt within the house, then two short barks–a dog's response to his bitch–and, after a pause, a fusillade of furious barking; the dog had scented the unknown men.

Saint-Clair climbed the three steps, knocked on the door, and called out: "Franz! Berthold!"

Heavy footsteps sounded, and a man's voice rebuking the dog and telling it to shut up. Then the voice said, in German: "Who's there?"

The Nyctalope replied in the same language. "Franz Zucht said to me one day: In the absence of any direct order from our father against you–whom I shall recognize in a thousand, if ever I see you again–you may count on the fact that Berthold and Franz Zucht will not forget that you spared our lives. Do you remember? Franz or Berthold, whoever is behind this door, open up!"

There was a brief silence. Then a bar was removed, a bolt was withdrawn and a key was turned and the door opened wide.

With Corsat, Pilou and Wolf close behind him, the Nyctalope went into a large communal room poorly illuminated by an electric bulb set in the ceiling. In the room, there was a man and a dog. The man was neither Franz nor Berthold, nor old Zucht. He was hirsute and somewhat bewildered, dressed in a shirt, trousers and clogs. He looked at the four strapping fellows who had come into his living-room, whose door had been closed by Wolf, the last entrant.

"Where are the Zuchts?" asked the astonished Saint-Clair.

"Who are you?" demanded the man, at the same time.

"Friends of the Zucht family! Where are Franz, Berthold and old Adalbert?"

"Gone."

"Where?"

"I don't know."

"How? Why?"

"I don't know." the man replied.

"Who are you, then?"

"A shepherd from the other side of the mountain. One day, Franz said to me: 'Leave your hut and bring your dog to the house. You can live there with your family. Mother died yesterday; we'll bury her in an hour. After the burial, you can stay in the house. It's Our Lord's orders.' I came, bringing my purse and my dog. They buried poor Adalheid over there, behind the clump of trees next to the house. I stayed here, alone, and the Zuchts went off towards the castle. That was at nightfall. I went to bed. I haven't seen them since."

"What day was this?" asked Saint-Clair, still astonished.

"Tonight is the fourth that I've spent here."

"So the mother was buried and the Zuchts left on May 24," muttered the Nyctalope. He remained pensive for a full minute. During that time, still surprised and quite intimidated, the unkempt man stared at Corsat, Pilou and Wolf, who were impassive.

"Strange!" said Saint-Clair, shaking his head to clear his thoughts, "but let's leave the explanation for later." He fixed the shepherd with his gaze. "What do you know about the castle?"

"The castle?" said the man, fearfully.

"Yes–the castle where the Baron lives."

"Me? Nothing. Nothing at all. I've never been into it. I was born in a hut on the other side of the mountain. When the Baron came to live in the old castle, where there had only ever been a steward, my parents were dead and I was in charge of a flock of sheep. I only ever talked to the Zuchts and the cowherds. There was a lot of work done in the castle–but the workmen who came to do it went in and never came out again. That's all I know, I swear to God." The man raised a trembling hand.

Saint-Clair shrugged his shoulders. "That's all right. Where do you sleep?"

The shepherd pointed to a sort of cupboard under a staircase leading up to the attics, whose door was open. There was a mattress and a blanket inside.

"Go back to bed."

"With my dog?"

"With your dog."

"Are you staying in the house?"

"We're the masters here!" Saint-Clair replied, rudely.

The poor chap had learned, throughout his life, to obey whoever claimed to be a master. His face even expressed a certain instinctive satisfaction at being done with this business, which he did not understand at all. He turned his back, went to his niche and slipped inside, with the dog between his legs, lay down and pulled the door shut. The catch clicked as it fell back.

"Strange!" the Nyctalope said, again–and he looked round, studying the room. The dresser attracted his attention; the item of furniture was disproportionately large.

If I understood the red-haired man correctly, Saint-Clair said to himself, *the Zuchts' house is the easiest means of entry to the castle itself–so this house and the castle must be connected. That can only be by a subterranean tunnel. There don't appear to be any cellars here, so the access to the tunnel must be hidden by an item of furniture or a wooden panel. The enormous dresser? The floor? No–too clean... and a trapdoor is less convenient than a door in a wall. The dresser, then. Let's try that first. If that doesn't yield anything, I'll search more assiduously...*

Corsat, Pilou and Wolf were waiting attentively. The Nyctalope pointed to the dresser. Together, Corsat, Pilou and Wolf were the equal of a Hercules, but their efforts were in vain; the dresser was immovable.

"Oh-oh!" said Saint-Clair. He inspected the place where the dresser touched the wall.

"Hinges!" he exclaimed. "Well camouflaged, to be sure–but I have sharp eyes for that sort of thing. Corsat, the blow-torch–here and here. Pilou, you take the cutter. Get into the dresser at the base and make a hole in the back wall to see if there's solid stone behind it."

A quarter of an hour later, the dresser was eviscerated. Pilou announced that there was indeed a cavity in the wall. After a further quarter of an hour, the dresser was detached from the wall and set aside.

"Bravo!" said Saint-Clair.

There was a narrow porch and a steel door.

"Corsat–the blow-torch!"

During another quarter of an hour's labor, Saint-Clair, Pilou and Wolf waited, pistols in hand, in case the door opened to give passage to some enemy– but no one came, and the darkness of an artificial corridor was revealed.

"Let's go," said the Nyctalope. "Follow me."

Marching at a rapid pace, the four men followed the secret route that Glô von Warteck had followed on May 14, leading little Minna.

The tunnel was capacious, devoid of woodwork or plaster. The rock was bare, oozing damp. If human hands had played any part in making the tunnel, it must have been several hundred years old–but it could only have been a few years ago that galvanized iron brackets supporting electric lights had been fixed to the walls, to the right and to the left, and parallel grooves etched in the rocky floor to channel the trickling water.

The lamps were out, though, and–as in the tunnel between Bermuda and the Hollow Rock–offered no illumination for the passage of men. Saint-Clair handed back one end of his lasso and let it out as far as Wolf, who was bringing up the rear. In this fashion, the Nyctalope drew his little troop through the darkness of the tunnel.

At first, the tunnel was level, then it began to climb perceptibly; then there was a succession of staircases, inclined planes, curved to a greater or lesser degree, and large flat areas whose walls bore black doors, reinforced with iron and enormous locks–locks which Corsat and Pilou rapidly forced open with the blow-torch and the cutter. Then there was masonry, some ancient and some recent, some intact and some repaired, now alternated with bare rock, dry or slick, with no more irregularities or oozing trickles of water. Then there were walls, some made of rock and some contrived, covered with neatly-carved and polished oak panels, evidently maintained with daily care. There were no more brackets, but wrought iron chandeliers with numerous electric lamps–but the lamps were out, and did not light up.

They reached a vast vestibule, where the wall-panels were partly dressed with loose tapestries. The huge central table, sturdy and polished, was surrounded by ceremonial chairs of the sort used by burgraves. There was an immense chandelier, suspended from the vault by a twisted chain, but none of its multitudinous lamps was lit.

The Nyctalope stopped in the darkness of this vestibule, bringing his companions to a halt behind him. His limbs were shaken by a frisson, for he was astonished beyond all expression, and he began to dread being afraid. He fought against the increasing exasperation of his nerves–because for a quarter of an hour, nothing had gone as he had expected: nothing!

The doors had been forced, and no one had been found behind them. The rooms through which they had come had all been empty. There was silence everywhere–the most absolute silence. It was as if there was no one at all behind any of these walls, wooden panels, hangings and doors.

Now, Leo Saint-Clair recognized this vestibule with its cathedral chairs and its enormous chandelier. He had been here before, while running to Laurence after having defeated the skeleton and the *hauptmann* in the Machine Room. Yes–there, behind those curtains, there was a door, a sitting-room, and then the bedroom with the overhanging turret...

We're in one of the hearts of the multiple organism that is the castle of Schwarzrock, he said to himself, *but no one is here. Is there no one to oppose my progress or bar my way? And not the least noise anywhere, nor any sign of life whatsoever! I don't like this. There's too much solitude, too much silence. Things are going too easily, too safely. Where, then, is the threat that I can neither see nor hear, nor perceive in any manner at all?*

As he searched the surrounding darkness, the Nyctalope felt the *frisson*–the cold premonition of fear–for the second time.

"Boss!" breathed a voice nearby, to the right.

Was that Pilou? Or Corsat?

"Boss!" said a second voice, to the left.

"Corsat! Pilou!" said Saint-Clair, finally. "Are you afraid?"

"Light, boss!" stammered Corsat and Pilou.

"All right! Weapons in hand–light up!"

Three beams of light shot forth. Corsat, Pilou and Wolf illuminated one another's white faces and haggard eyes.

Collecting himself, the Nyctalope said, calmly and loudly: "Pull yourselves together! What's frightening you?"

The light, that voice and those words were more than sufficient to stiffen the resolve of Corsat and Pilou, whose example Wolf continued to follow.

The Nyctalope, reanimated himself, felt that he had his three auxiliaries well in hand. "Let's go!" he said. "We won't inconvenience ourselves any further with darkness or silence. Kill anyone who gets in our way. March!"

With some emotion, he went into the neighboring room, then into the next one, which was the large room with the overhanging turret. There, his beloved Laurence had suffered and fought for him! There, he had seen her lying as if dead! From here, he had carried her away! Oh, if only he had lingered for a minute–just enough time to kill the monster and make sure that he was dead, as one kills a rabid dog, without hesitation or pity!

We must not pause, he said to himself. To his companions, he said: "To the guard-room!"

Pistols in hand, with their lighted torches attached to the breasts of their leotards, the three men followed the Nyctalope, who recalled the directions previously given by Kroon, Wolf, Laurence and the red-haired man–which, added together, established much of the topography of the place.

They expected at every moment to see men appear before them, after which there would be a fight–a beneficial fight, of which their nerves were in need. But no! Behind all the doors, which they opened without difficulty, there were variously-shaped rooms–round, square, rectangular or pentagonal–succeeded by corridors and stairways, but not a single human being appeared; Saint-Clair and his companions hard no sound, save for their own footsteps.

The guard-room was empty and silent.

The four men were stupefied.

"Let's see," said Saint-Clair, abruptly. There was a large electric ceiling light, which was off. The Nyctalope could make out the porcelain switch set in the woodwork. He went to it and turned it, but the light did not come on. Six electric bracket-lamps were attached to the walls, each with a switch underneath. In response to a gesture from their leader, Corsat, Pilou and Wolf tried the switches; none of he lights came on.

Amazed, angry and defiant at the same time, the Nyctalope said, loudly: "Isn't there anyone in this infernal castle?"

His voice echoed in the vaults; then there was deathly silence.

"Wolf!"

"Boss?"

"Take us to the kitchens."

In a castle with a garrison and servants, the kitchens are the center of life. Wolf was perfectly familiar with the route from the guard-room to the kitchens. Within three minutes they were in front of the ovens, which were extinct, empty and cold. In the neighboring room, which served as a larder and store-room, there were neither provisions nor leftovers–but there were stacks of sealed boxes.

"There's no one in the castle," said Wolf. That was incontestable now–and it was bewildering.

"Let's go to the Teledynamo," said Saint-Clair, somberly.

Corsat and Pilou were fuming, but they were used to keeping heir feelings to themselves in such circumstances. They kept quiet, attentive to the Nyctalope's words, gestures and expressions.

They returned to the guard-room, from which it was easy for Wolf to lead his companions to the round cell where they had been imprisoned on the sixteenth of May, from whose vault they had got into the Machine Room,

"Strange!" said Saint-Clair, as soon as he went in. "Can you smell that, Corsat, Pilou?"

"Yes, boss."

"It smells like a corpse!"

"Up there!"

"In the Machine Room!"

"Yes."

There was a brief meditative silence. Then Saint-Clair gave his orders. "Best not to lose time finding the normal means of communication and opening the doors. Wolf, your back–Corsat, climb on top of him. Good. You, Pilou, punch out the piece of the ceiling that we cut away the other day."

A blow of the fist knocked through the ceiling.

"The stink's coming from up there, boss," Pilou said. "Someone's put the floorboard back in place, but it isn't fixed. I'll displace it."

"Up, quickly. I'll follow you."

Climbing up Wolf and Corsat, the Nyctalope passed through the oval hole in the ceiling and the square hole in the floorboards, and stood up in the Machine Room.

"Pilou, throw your rope to Corsat and Wolf so they can come up!" Saint-Clair ordered–and he ran to a window, whose double panes he opened wide, thrusting them back into their wooden shutters, for the atmosphere in the closed room, vast as it was, was so heavily charged with the cadaverous stink as to be unbreathable.

Meanwhile, Corsat and Wolf climbed up.

Thanks to their electric torches, the three horrified men saw what the Nyctalope had seen. Three bodies were laid out on the floor, almost side by side. Corsat, Pilou and Wolf recognized them as easily as Saint-Clair.

"Old Zucht!"

"Franz and Berthold!"

The first-named was in a state of advanced decomposition. As for the other two...

"Courage, my lads!" said the Nyctalope. "Take old Zucht's corpse and throw it out of the window. It's poisoning the air. Then, if his sons are still alive..."

"Horror!" cried Wolf. "Their right hands have been cut off!"

"Yes! But Franz and Berthold were able, with their left hands, to make ligatures with their cravats, to stem the blood-flow."

"Watch out, Pilou!" muttered Corsat.

"It's terrible!"

Finally, the three men succeeded in transporting the decomposed corpse and throwing it out.

"Berthold's dead," said Saint-Clair. "Set him aside. Then we'll see... Franz is alive. His ligature is admirably contrived. He hasn't lost too much blood, but with neither care nor nourishment for two or three days... Rum! Ether! The syringe!"

Corsat took two phials and a little box from the depths of his satchel. The syringe contained five cubic centimeters of camphorated oil.

Three minutes after receiving an injection in his left arm, the rum in his throat and the ether in his nostrils, Franz sighed and opened his eyes–but the beams of the three torches converging upon him dazzled him and terrified him. He closed his eyes, howled, and started shivering.

Saint-Clair took his head in both hands. "Franz!" he said, ardently. "Don't be scared, Franz! I'm the man who didn't want to kill your brother, nor you, nor your father, on May 16. I'm Leo Saint-Clair, the Nyctalope. Open your eyes! Ah! More rum, Pilou!"

Another swig of the cordial quickly brought the unfortunate man round. "My father?" he said, in a very feeble voice.

"We shall avenge him!" Saint-Clair declared.

"Dead?"

"Yes."

"My brother?"

"Dead."

"Oh, the swine! That vile Baron! That..."

"Calm yourself, Franz. Calm yourself, and you'll live–for the sake of vengeance. We're the administrators of justice. You'll join us. Was it Glô von Warteck who mutilated you?"

"Yes."

"Why? No–don't reply. We have time. First, we must save you. Wait!"

As he stood up, the Nyctalope passed Franz to Wolf, who held him up.

"Damn! No Teledynamo! As I thought! The machine was here..." He placed his right hand on a rectangular pedestal illuminated by Corsat's and Pilou's torches. On that pedestal, on May 16, he had glimpsed the machine. If only he had broken it then, instead of allowing himself to be petrified for several seconds by the skeleton!

But now, the infernal machine was no longer there. Nor was the skeleton, nor the electric wires. The pedestal and the walls were bare; the floor was covered in blood...

"Let's hope that Franz knows something..."

324

Shivering with an impatience that all his strength of character could hardly contain, Saint-Clair went back to Franz.

"We'll have to get him to a bed."

Propped up by Wolf–who was behind him, supporting him and warming him up, the mountain man was now in an extraordinary state of nervous excitation, which had commenced as soon as he recovered consciousness. "No, no!" he said, "No! He's too terrible! He's all-powerful! If he were to think about me for only a quarter of a second, he'd kill me, even if he were at the North Pole! If he thinks about you, he'll kill you with one slight effort of his will. Perhaps you have some means of defense–but not me! I must speak straight away, then! You must avenge my father, my brother, yes...but above all, you must avenge Minna–dear, innocent little Minna!"

"Franz, Franz! I want you to calm down!" the Nyctalope ordered, firmly, although he was very emotional himself. He knelt down beside the young man, magnetized him with his gaze, hugged him... and the young man became slightly calmer.

"Now speak, Franz. Tell me everything you know, from beginning to end."

The unfortunate man immediately began to speak. He was a piteous and terrible sight, and it was even more piteous and terrible to hear him.

"On the evening of May 23... When was that?"

"Four days ago."

"Oh! Four days, and I'm still alive..."

"Franz! Tell the story!"

"Yes, yes... On that evening, our mother, who had been ill for several days, suddenly had a vision. She saw Minna, my sister Minna..."

"I know!" Saint-Clair put in. "Your sister Minna, whom the Baron had given as a servant to the woman sequestered in the castle."

"A woman? Perhaps... but that wasn't it. No! Listen! Our mother saw Minna, half-naked, beaten with switches and scored by a knout... She heard her howling in pain and calling for help... She saw her weeping and writhing and rolling on a carpet. But instead of naming me, or my brother, or our father or mother in these desperate cries, she was crying; 'Raymond! Raymond!' "

"Oh!" said the Nyctalope, glimpsing the tragic truth in a flash of inspiration.

"And our mother moaned: 'Minna is being tortured. Her torturer looks like an Oriental! And the Lord Baron... Horror! My God, have pity on us! The Lord Baron is ordering him to strike her harder... And he is standing in front of a machine... A machine that is shining... With the heads of seven dead men! Minna, Minna, my daughter!' And our mother wept and sobbed...

"My father, my brother and I were mad with amazement, dread and pain. Then, suddenly, our mother said: 'It's over. The Oriental is carrying Minna away, unconscious. But I've suffered too much... I'm suffering too much... I'm going to die...'

"And our mother did die, a few minutes later. But before she yielded her last sigh, as our father was questioning her, she said, forcefully: 'I swear before God that I wasn't dreaming! I was awake and fully conscious! The vision I had was true! I can still see Minna being tortured and hear her voice calling Raymond! Raymond! Why Raymond?' And our mother died, weeping..."

"Franz! Franz, my friend!" said the Nyctalope urgently. "Tell the rest of the story! Go on! Go on!"

"Yes, I want to tell you everything... but I'm so weak."

"The rum, Corsat!"

After having drunk, Franz continued, relatively calmly.

"All that night, our father, Bertrand and I thought about it, beside our dead mother. Then day broke. We were still hesitant. Finally, it was decided that all three of us would risk the torture and death that awaits all those who displease Our Lord Baron. It was decided that we would go to the castle and demand that the Lord Baron let us see Minna. Father said: 'We'll take our rifles.' I replied: 'If the Baron takes control of our thoughts, what then?' Berthold said: 'Perhaps God will not permit that. Mother has seen, and she's dead. Our cause is just.' That was true...

"So it was that on May 24... Yes, the day after our mother's death, an hour after the burial, control of our thoughts was taken and we were compelled to put order No. 5 in execution..."

"Order No. 5?" stammered Corsat. The striking narrative was making him feel dizzy.

"Damn it, Corsat!" groaned the Nyctalope.

"Oh–sorry, boss!"

"Go on, Franz. You were saying: order No. 5."

"Yes–which is to say: 'Entrust the house to the shepherd and come with your weapons to the castle stables.' That's what we did, after having buried our mother, for our thoughts were not so strictly controlled that we did not have the freedom to finish what we had set out to do..."

Saint-Clair squeezed Franz's hand and interrupted his narrative with a question. "So the capture of your thoughts by the Baron doesn't always have the same intensity?"

"Ah!" cried Franz. "I feel that I can and must tell all now! No, not always the same intensity. Sometimes, we can act freely, provided that our actions do not prevent the strict obedience of the Lord's orders. Other times, our minds are completely imprisoned, and we can't even think of doing anything except that which the Lord inspires in us and imposes upon us in a manner that chills us with terror when we reflect on it afterwards. From a distance, without seeing us, writing to us or speaking to us, he makes his orders resound–yes, resound–in our brains. Do you understand?"

"I understand. But leave that, Franz, and continue your account of events. You had reached the burial of your mother and your departure from the house, bound for the castle stables..."

"Yes, yes! But there, in the midst of a great commotion of horses and men, boxes and bales, comings and goings of women in traveling-cloaks... Everyone was leaving! Leaving! Well, there, we felt–all three of us–that we had regained full possession of our thoughts, totally! Then our desire to see Minna brought back the dread.

"'Boys,' said our father, 'we must find Minna. Why isn't she here, with these women?' And Berthold said: 'I've just heard it said that all the women in the castle have come down.'

" 'Not Minna!' I said.

"No one was paying any attention to us. Our father knew which stairway led from the stables to the guard-room, because he had once been taken up that way by the *hauptmann*. The stairway was very busy, with men going up empty-handed and coming down loaded with boxes and bales.

"We went up. We had our rifles hanging over our shoulders. We were absolutely determined to see Minna. I've always had more cunning in me than my father and brother. In the guard-room, I spotted a *feldwebel*.[54] I said to him: 'We've been summoned by the Lord Baron. Where is His Lordship?' The *feldwebel* stared at us. 'You're the Zuchts?' he said. 'Yes,' said our father. He showed us the way. There was a corridor, then a stairway, a vestibule and a big black door. We heard a loud noise of breaking glass and pottery. The door wasn't completely closed. Resolutely, Berthold pushed it wide open and we went in together.

"It was a big room with furnaces and all sorts of receptacles in glass and porcelain. Dressed like a city tourist on an excursion to the Black Forest, the Lord Baron, with a hatchet in his hand, was going from one to another, methodically smashing every jar and vessel, one after another. He had his back to us. My father trembled. My brother cried out, furiously: 'Minna! Where's Minna!' Oh, how stupid we were! With our rifles in our hands, we had taken a single step forward, as if in some drill exercise. The Baron turned round. He saw us and immediately burst out laughing.

"He laughed like a madman–but it was us who were mad! 'I want to see Minna!' our father said. Then I distinctly heard the Baron murmur: 'Think of everything! How impossible it is to think of everything without the Teledynamo! These men know. How? Ah–their mother is dead! Yes–Minna's perispirit, liberated while she was possessed by Irène's perispirit, went to speak to her sick mother, who was more sensitive than usual...' "

"You heard that!" cried Saint-Clair.

"I heard that! And if I live for centuries, I shall never forget a single one of those words, whose meaning I don't understand..."

"Perhaps I'll explain one day," said Saint-Clair, roughly. "Go on, and don't forget anything."

"Forget? Never! My mind is freer than it has ever been before and I know that the things I'm telling you will make revenge more certain..."

"Oh, yes!" said Saint-Clair, violently.

"So, the Lord Baron murmured what I just said. Then he looked at us and simply gestured us to follow him with his left hand. He still had the hatchet in his right hand. We followed him."

"Freely?"

"Yes. We still had our presence of mind. Room after room... Oh, now it becomes horrible, horrible!"

Tearing his left hand away from the Nyctalope's tremulous fingers, Franz put it in front of his eyes, moaning and sobbing. His right arm, whose hand had been cut off, hung limply at his side.

"Speak, Franz, speak!" said Saint-Clair, softly, but in a pressing tone. "Speak! Time is passing. You're growing weak. We have to take the tourniquet off your wrist, bandage it and care for you, so that you might live to take revenge!"

"Ah, that's true!" howled the unfortunate man.

Feverishly and breathlessly, but clearly and precisely, he continued: "The Lord Baron–curse him!–the Lord Baron took us into a room that was entirely black, with a white bed in the middle. And on that bed was Minna! Minna's lifeless corpse! Her breast was gaping... The black blood congealed...! At the head of the bed, on a table, in the middle of a glass plate, there was a heart pierced by three long needles–Minna's heart! We were dumbstruck with horror, shivering, but our father suddenly brought up his rifle and... Witchcraft, hell and pandemonium! The terrible Lord Baron reached out his arm, opened his hand, and our father, my brother and I were instantly deprived of our will. Oh, we retained our reasoning, our memory, but without the will to act. What torture! To see Minna dead after such abominable torments! To have loaded rifles in our hands and not be able to use them against the monstrous Baron to avenge Minna!

"Suddenly, he seized the plate bearing the heart and stood beside the bed, holding it in his left hand. Then the bed tilted swiftly, for it was mounted on a trapdoor as long and broad as itself, and slipped through it, disappearing. There was the sound of metal bumping into stone walls, then a loud and violent splash. Then silence... A cold draught emerged from the open well. The thought was put into our heads that we should throw our rifles in and we put that thought into immediate action. I knew that this was the castle's legendary *oubliettes*, at the bottom of which a subterranean river runs–but the trapdoor closed again, slowly and soundlessly.

"Then he went out of the room, carrying the heart and still holding the hatchet, and we followed him meekly. We came to this room and our mental compulsion made us put our right hands and firearms on that pedestal. He cut off our hands with three blows of the hatchet and immediately went away, leaving us here. He took our hands and Minna's heart with him. Quickly, I had the idea of making a ligature to stop the blood that was flowing out. I saw that Berthold was doing the same. I wanted to help our father, who had fallen backwards at full length when the hatchet struck him, but I must have fainted... My God! My God!"

Franz slumped into Wolf's arms. He had only been sustained by the fierce determination to tell his terrifying and abominable story. He had lost a great deal of blood. The effects of the injection of camphorated oil wore off rapidly. The young man was soon unconscious.

Saint-Clair, Corsat and Pilou were chilled by horror. For several moments, they stood in front of the unconscious Franz Zucht without moving. Even the Nyctalope had to make an effort to reactivate himself. Wolf, still supporting the unfortunate man, was trembling in every limb.

"Let's go–bring him along!" said Saint-Clair, his voice blank.

"No point, boss," said Wolf, dully.

Saint-Clair leaned closer. "God! Is he dead?"

He unbuttoned Franz's jacket, slid his hand inside his shirt and paused. He put his ear to the young man's lips. There was nothing–no heartbeat, no breath.

"Yes, he's dead!" The Nyctalope drew himself upright, and brandished his fist feverishly. "Ah, Lucifer, Lucifer, when I get my hands on you! What were you doing to Irène when Minna cried 'Raymond! Raymond!' Why martyrize these three men? What did you do with their hands and Minna's heart? Monster! When I get my hands on you, infernal monster..."

Wolf had gently laid the corpse down; he was kneeling beside it, sobbing like a child. Corsat and Pilou, deeply affected, took one another by the hand and wept.

When the echoes of the Nyctalope's furious threats died away in the vault, Pilou cried: "Let's go, then, boss! Let's go!"

"Yes! On your feet, Wolf!"

The four men launched themselves in quick succession through the hole in the floorboards and the hole in the ceiling of the room below, letting themselves drop on to one of the beds in the cell called the "vestibule of death."

They searched the castle until dawn. It was empty; there were traces everywhere of a rapid but not disorderly departure. The castle's personnel had probably not received their orders until a few hours before the general departure, but Baron Glô von Warteck must have been preparing for it for several days. Saint-Clair, Corsat, Pilou and Wolf went into the scientific laboratory where the three Zuchts had seen their Lord breaking mortars, flasks and jars; the systematic destruction had been completed; not a single item remained intact. Why the destruction? An enigma–but a small one by comparison with the great tormenting mysteries whose confrontation made the Nyctalope feel dizzy.

When dawn broke, Leo Saint-Clair and his three companions were on the platform of the northern tower. All around, the bottom of the circus was blurred by slowly-rising light mists. Denser fogs were scattered about the mountain ridges. The pale blue sky, where the last stars were fading out, was opalized in the east by extremely delicate tints of pink and mauve. The air was exquisitely fresh and redolent with sylvan perfumes.

Emerging from that sinister castle and the nightmarish night, the four men were buoyed up by the grace and serenity of nature, even in that wild and primitive setting. They breathed in the fresh air by the lungful, and opened their eyes wide to the light of day. But they could not help thinking about what they had seen and heard, and what they did not know.

"It's frightful!" Saint-Clair said, speaking in a low voice so as not to disturb the majestic silence of the Earth and sky. "Frightful! Why was Schwarzrock abandoned? And where is Lucifer now?"

"May we speak, boss?" Corsat asked, after exchanging glances with Pilou.

"Yes."

"Well," said the Burgundian, "the trail will be easy to follow. Lucifer is carrying his infernal machine and many other things in boxes and bales. He's escorted by a great many men and women, and what we saw in the stables suggests that he's taken some 30 horses. That's no ordinary caravan–it can't go anywhere without attracting attention. It'll be easy to figure out which pass it went through..."

"And once we're on the track," Pilou added, "we'll be moving much faster than the caravan. It left during the night of May 24. It only has between 72 and 80 hours start on us."

"All that's true!" said Saint-Clair. "But I'm not ready yet to seek out the monster's new lair. We've only passed through the large room fitted out as a library, which was the room where Lucifer spent most of his time here. Now that we've refreshed our lungs, our brains and our bodies, let's go back there. If I haven't found anything in an hour, we'll pick up the trail, rejoin Monsieur Nortmund and give chase. Let's go."

They went back into the tower. Ten minutes later, all the library windows had been opened by Corsat and Pilou. Wolf mounted guard outside the door, a silent pistol in his hand–for it was still necessary to be careful, to take nothing on trust.

The Nyctalope stood in the middle of the room and looked around slowly, in order to form a general impression before doing anything else. Of the room's eight unequal faces, three adjacent ones were occupied by windows. Two had doors with large curtains, the spaces above them being filled by paintings in time-worn gilt frames, which represented two scenes from a boar-hunt. One of the three remaining walls–which were much larger than the other five–was between the two doors, the other two being between the doors and the windows. They were shelved from floor to ceiling, accommodating between two and three

330

thousand books, in limp covers or hardbound, in various formats. Its furniture included a wheeled stepladder, which was presently pushed back against one of the sets of bookshelves, leather-upholstered armchairs and oak stools. There were two large and massive square tables, bearing nothing but a bronze writing-set with a pen-rack and pencils–not a single piece of paper. There were also two globes, one celestial and the other terrestrial, each two meters in diameter, mounted on copper pedestals. They were freely mobile, a system of cogwheels and gears allowing them to be turned in every direction without the least effort–as Saint-Clair ascertained by manipulating the celestial globe, which was closer at hand.

Having taken all this in, the Nyctalope began a more leisurely survey. His attention was caught by the wheeled stepladder. It was standing sideways, in the position in which it might have been set by someone who wanted to reach a particular book. His eyes followed the path that the searcher would have taken as he went up step by step, at head height–and picked out an octavo volume bound in red shagreen, which had not been pushed back as far as the other similar volumes on the shelf, so that its spine jutted out slightly.

"Pilou!"

"Boss?"

"Climb up that step-ladder, slowly."

Pilou obeyed.

"Stop!"

Pilou stopped.

"In font of you, there's a book jutting out. Put your finger on it, without pushing it in. That's the one! Good. What is its title?"

Pilou read: "*Investigations of the Earth's Magnetic Poles.*"

"What?" The Nyctalope started. "Repeat that!"

Pilou repeated it.

"Is the author Edmond Cazal?" [55]

"Yes, boss."

"Hold on! Pay attention, both of you! You listened hard to every bit of Franz's story?"

"Oh yes, boss," they replied, in unison.

"Let me see–if I'm not mistaken, Franz definitely used the words 'North Pole' at the very beginning of his tale."

"Yes! Yes!" cried Corsat and Pilou. And the Provençal continued, excitedly: "He said something like: 'Lucifer would kill me, even if he were at the North Pole.' "

"Exactly," Corsat confirmed. "I remember it too."

Saint-Clair's clear and powerful memory was more precise. "Franz said: 'If he were to think about me for only a quarter of a second, he'd kill me, even if he were at the North Pole!' " As Corsat and Pilou opened their mouths, he shouted: "Shut up!"

Turning sideways, Saint-Clair looked at the terrestrial globe. There was a stool beside it, and on that stool, there was a pencil. "If, after consulting the book," he murmured, "he came to study the globe, what then? In the intensity of his concentration, he put the pencil down and forgot about it. The magnetic poles–the two points at which a magnet's attractive force is greatest. The Earth's magnetic poles! The two points at which the electrical fields of the sky, the continents and the oceans are incessantly concentrated, mingling and reinforcing one another in order to radiate immense and powerful currents incessantly into the atmosphere, along incalculable trajectories. Can it be possible? Great God!"

Quivering with the emotion of a Newton glimpsing the law of universal gravity, the Nyctalope walked forwards. He placed himself in front of the globe, to the left of the stool, thus having the pencil within reach of his right hand. He turned his back to the stepladder, as if he had just come from consulting the book–and he looked at the globe.

Directly in front of his eyes was the North Pole!

Part Seven: The Final Flourish Crowns the Work

I. Active Organization

In the valley, Leo Saint-Clair easily picked up the trail left by the caval-cade formed by Baron Glô von Warteck's troop as it drew away from Schwar-zrock. The troop had left the circus by the northernmost pass. Having estab-lished that, they returned to the roadster guarded by Louis Nortmund and his men. The latter left by motor-cycle, while Louis, Saint-Clair, Corsat, Pilou and Wolf were soon on the road descending from the pass into the Black Forest.

They knew all that they needed to know before the day was over. Glô von Warteck, transformed into a citizen of the United States, had passed his troop off as a film company, to which the noble proprietor of Schwarzrock had given permission to "shoot" in and around the castle. At Freiburg-in-Breisgau, after having sold his horses, which would henceforth be of no use, the "director" had embarked the entire company, with all its baggage, on a special express train, hired two days earlier by one of his administrators, who had been sent to Freiburg for that purpose.

The train must have cost a great deal, but everyone knew that American movie directors were undeterred by any expense. The newspapers reported, with astonishment, that the train had been given free passage along the most direct lines all the way to Danzig, via Berlin, and that it had gone at top speed, only stopping to take on coal and water. The papers added, with less astonishment, that a large submarine of a new design, kitted out for "underwater filming and other purposes," belonging to the Cinematographic Consortium in question, was waiting for the company in Danzig harbor.

"It's obvious," the Nyctalope concluded, "that the Wartecks had two sub-marines: the one that I captured in the Bermudas and another, hidden in some hole on the dreary and deserted Pomeranian coast. Lucifer and his Teledynamo are now at sea, heading for the North Pole."

"Lucifer will probably equip himself with sleds and dogs somewhere in Norway," Louis Nortmund added.

"If he doesn't already have them in his submarine," the Nyctalope said, "and if he can't get hold of an aeroplane to ferry him from the northernmost point accessible to the submarine to the Pole."

And that, so far as speech was concerned, was the entire inquest that took place at Freiburg-in-Breisgau. The Nyctalope needed to think. He was worried about what had become of Irène. He was haunted by the image of Minna being tortured, crying 'Raymond! Raymond!'

On their arrival at Freiburg he had immediately sent a telegram to Professor Lourmel asking him to hasten to the Nortmunds' home.

"Return to Colmar," he said.

Night had fallen during the investigation. They ate in the buffet at Freiburg Station and climbed back into the roadster. Saint-Clair and his three auxiliaries were in dire need of sleep. They slept in the car while Louis Nortmund drove, with the headlights full on, from Freiburg to Colmar–and at *The Willows*, Saint-Clair granted himself a few hours' rest.

He still knew nothing about the flight of Laurence and Grisyl.

The two heroines, having arrived at the castle two hours after Saint-Clair and his companions had left, had talked to the shepherd, whom they had met by chance; by this means, they had learned enough to deduce that Schwarzrock was now deserted and that they had no better option but to return to Colmar, to which the Nyctalope would certainly return in order to organize the supreme offensive against Lucifer on a new basis.

Laure and Grisyl therefore returned to *The Willows* before Saint-Clair, who had been held up in Freiburg. Charles and Blanche promised to keep their heroic excursion secret.

On the other hand, Lourmel arrived that afternoon from Strasbourg, where he had landed in an aircraft that had come from Paris. He was carrying a radio-telegram from Raymond, sent from Georgetown in British Guiana,[56] dated the May 27, which was deciphered thus: *Have visited the charming Lesser Antilles. All well. Irène and Henri tranquil and cheerful. Nothing new.*

"But the torture and death of Minna occurred on May 24," Saint-Clair said. He recounted the story to Lourmel, Blanche and Charles Nortmund.

"Frightful! Atrocious!" cried the Alsatians.

"Yes," said Lourmel, "but it may only have been an experiment. This is what I think: while Irène, out there in the Antilles, was sleeping naturally, either at night or during the daytime siesta, Lucifer might have had enough power to draw Irène's perispirit to him and replace it with Minna's perispirit..."

"A disincarnation and partial reincarnation?" said Saint-Clair.

"Yes. In any case, there's no time to lose, It's May 29. We have 11 more days–and it's a long way to the North Pole."

"Lucifer will certainly be at the Pole before June 10," said the Nyctalope. "He must have powerful and rapid means at his disposal. We already know that his submarine, if it's like the *Uberalles*–note that Grisyl did not know of its existence and that the red-haired man made no mention of it–can travel at nearly 200 kilometers per hour. Now, from Danzig to Spitzbergen, by sea, is about 3,300 kilometers. Lucifer might already have reached Spitzbergen. You may assume that he has other means of crossing the polar ice–which is more-or-less compact at this time of year–than dog-sleds and kayaks. From the Spitzbergen land-mass to the Pole as the crow flies is only 1,000 or 1,200 kilometers. That's only six hours in an aeroplane–and why should Lucifer not have the disassembled pieces of an aeroplane, or even two, aboard his submarine?"

After a pause, Lourmel said: "The magnetic conditions at the North Pole are doubtless such as to give the Teledynamo unlimited power, although I don't know how. In order for us to know and understand that, it would be necessary, first of all, for science to deduce certain consequences from the important observations and discoveries made in those regions by explorers, and then to know exactly what the Teledynamo is and how the machine works. Thus far, the Pole has only been reached once, by Peary [57]–and as for the Teledynamo, Hunter told us very little and Grisyl knows nothing about it."

"You might interrogate Kroon," Charles Nortmund suggested.

Kroon–the man whom Saint-Clair and Corsat had surprised and captured in the little red house on the night of May 11–had been imprisoned in the cellars of *The Willows* since that night.

"Kroon's only a lowly subordinate of little intelligence, who made a good jailer and executioner–but we might as well try."

Saint-Clair, Lourmel and the Nortmunds went down into the cellars. In one that was quite comfortably fitted out, illuminated by an electric light–for there was no access of daylight–the man was in the process of eating a meal, guarded by a gamekeeper with a Browning in his fist. Saint-Clair offered him his life, his freedom on June 15 and 100,000 francs if he would reveal everything that he knew about the Lord Baron of Schwarzrock, the Teledynamo, and so on.

Kroon did not hide his disappointment at being unable to win his freedom and the fortune; save for the red house and the odious details of the Lord Baron's brief sojourns there, the prisoner knew nothing. He expressed his regret in such terms, and with such an expression on his face, that his sincerity was obvious. They left him to finish his copious meal and went back up to the Nortmunds' study to continue their examination of the situation and to formulate a precise plan of action.

Their thoughts were preoccupied with the multiple enigmas presented by Lucifer's unexpected departure, as well as by the problems that could only be solved at the Pole. The enigmas were terrible, the problems formidable; on their explanation and solution depended not only the lives and happiness of the people gathered there, and their associates, but millions of others. The victory of Glô von Warteck would indeed be the victory of the true Lucifer, the Spirit of Darkness–the victory of Evil over Good, the death of Liberty, the enslavement of the vast majority of men under the thumb of an invisible tyranny, amid the bloody chaos of the most savage passions granted limitless unbridled satiation.

They examined, considered and discussed the situation until dinner. At table, with Blanche, Laurence and Grisyl, they made every effort to think of other things, but it was impossible; the conversation was slight and the dinner was cut short. When Saint-Clair and Lourmel shut themselves up in the study with the Nortmunds again, Corsat and Pilou were summoned as consultants–for which they had the requisite qualities–and so that the Nyctalope would not have to repeat his explanation of their roles in the final offensive.

At 8 p.m. everyone went to bed–minds need proper rest even more than bodies.

The next day was May 30. "Ten more days!" the Nyctalope said, coldly, on awakening. He had been repeating those fateful words all night in is sleep.

He had ten days to get to Paris, to organize a reasonably well-equipped expedition, to reach the vicinity of the North Pole, to find, attack and defeat Lucifer!

"Madness! You'll never be able to do it!" said the Sancho Panza that lurks within every man to Don Quixote Saint-Clair.

"Why not? Explain!" retorted Don Quixote Saint-Clair.

Ah! Sancho Panza had little difficulty in complacently exposing the difficulties, the obstacles, the danger and the sheer impossibilities resulting from the conjunction of three enemies: the short time, the long distance and the mysterious darkness enshrouding Lucifer's means and actions. But Saint-Clair the Nyctalope replied again, vibrant with the will to win: "My eyes will dissipate the darkness and speed will take care of the brevity of time and the extent of space." And Don Quixote spoke so loudly and so emphatically that Sancho Panza, by virtue of his cowardice, became even more fearful of his master than of the unknown, and raised no further objection.

The roadster and the limousine left that morning for Paris, bearing the men and women they had brought to *The Willows* four days earlier, plus Professor Lourmel. Alerted by telegram, Alexandre Prillant was waiting for the Nyctalope in the house in the Rue Nansouty. He was not alone: General Benoît, Captain Girard and a third military aviator, Lieutenant Romski were also waiting for the Nyctalope. Before Saint-Clair, though, other persons arrived in a large touring car, which had picked them up at the Gare Saint-Lazare from a special train from Le Havre; these were Jacques Saincer, the *Grottenmeister* Rupert VI, Grisyl's father, mother and brothers, and four police inspectors who had been sent to fetch them by Monsieur Prillant.

Everyone was judiciously distributed within Saint-Clair's house and the adjoining lodge. Choiffour, Sidonie and Rosine had received orders the day before; the number of beds had been tripled, extra rooms adapted as bedrooms and the kitchens filled with provisions. The Wartecks and the policemen would probably remain there until–well, it would have been necessary to know a great deal about the future to be able to specify the day in the month of June until which the Wartecks would be forced to remain the guests of Leo Saint-Clair the Nyctalope!

On that same evening of May 30, at 10 p.m., four aeroplanes took off from the military airfield at Le Bourget; they were the four aircraft of the RC series.

II. To The North Pole

The Norwegian Solund Islands, at 61 degrees north latitude, are the west-ernmost point of Scandinavia. To get there, a ship departing from Le Havre needs no more time, traveling at an equal speed, than a ship departing from Danzig; the former, in fact, may travel in a near-straight line, while the latter–whose point of departure seems much closer on the map–must first negotiate the long north-eastern promontory of Pomerania, then go west as far as Bornholm Island, follow the long corridor of the Sund, go north through the Kattegat and then go west again to get around the southern tip of Norway, a crossing not without long and numerous turnings.

The Nyctalope and Lieutenant Saincer calculated correctly, therefore, in estimating that the *Uberalles*, leaving Le Havre five days after the probable de-parture from Danzig of Lucifer's submarine, would arrive in the waters of the Solund Isles five days after that submarine had passed through them.

From the Solund Isles to Spitzbergen, it was only necessary to set a straight course. In estimating that the *Uberalles* would not take longer to follow that course than its sister ship, the Nyctalope and Saincer had only to rely on infor-mation provided by Rupert VI, put to sleep by Lourmel, to the effect that the submarine at Lucifer's disposal was, in terms of power, tonnage and armaments, an exact duplicate of the *Uberalles*.

"By the way," Saincer had said, "With what name should we replace the German word *Uberalles*?"

"None!" replied the Nyctalope, excitedly. "*Above all* is our watchword. Let us, therefore, give that name to the submarine we have captured and which must be one of our means of victory." [58]

The four aeroplanes landed at Le Havre. Crews of mechanics and motor-ized trucks were waiting for them. Two of the aircraft, the RC1 and the RC2, were dismantled piece by piece, transported and loaded on to the *Uberalles* in a matter of hours, part of the hull having been opened up so that a cargo with twice the weight of the two aircraft might be stored in large bunkers.

The eight pilots and mechanics of the RC1 and RC2 embarked with Sain-cer, then Professor Lourmel, with Rupert VI–who might well prove useful–and Laurence and Grisyl, who had easily obtained permission to take part in the ex-pedition. As for the RC 3 and the RC4, they took off again at the same time as the *Uberalles* left Le Havre. The former carried Lieutenant Romski, his co-pilot Sergeant Berge, the mechanic, Corporal Dopp, and Wolf; the latter carried Saint-Clair, Captain Girard, Corsat and Pilou. They flew 1,300 kilometers from Le Havre to Christiana, then 1,500 kilometers from Christiana to Vardo.

Carried by solid wings and propelled by powerful motors, the two aircraft completed the whole of this enormous journey in 20 hours. They touched down at Vardo, at the north-eastern extremity of Norway, at 9 a.m. on June 1–but the eight aviators were exhausted. At Vardo, they entrusted the craft to a few local inhabitants, who looked after them with as much scrupulousness as enthusiasm, and after eating a substantial hot meal, they slept until 7 a.m. the following morning, June 2. Then they took to the air again. They covered another 1,200 kilometers above the glacial Arctic Ocean, replete with icebergs, ice-fields and partly-broken ice-packs. At 1 p.m. they arrived at the English station on Cape Flora, in the south-west of Franz Josef Land, on the 80th parallel. The Nyctalope and his companions were now in the regions of the classic American polar expeditions.

Franz Josef Land, whose extent is not yet fully determined, extends to either side of the 60th degree of eastern longitude, between the 80th and 85th parallels. It was the object of a particular study made in 1895-96 by Fritjof Nansen. The famous explorer and one of his companions from the Fram, Lieutenant Hjalmar Johansen, heroically spent the winter in the extreme conditions of that lost land in the polar sea. In 1894, an English expedition to Franz Josef Land commanded by Jackson had built a wooden hut in the Russian style on the basaltic rocks of Cape Flora, around which they had established dog kennels and storehouses.[59] The principal members of the English expedition, in addition to Captain Jackson, were the second officer, Mr. Armitage, the photographer Mr. Child, Doctor Koetlitz, Mr. Fisher, the botanist Mr. Burgess and Mr. Blomqvist. They were the people who welcomed Nansen and Johansen on June 17, 1896. After that, the personnel of the expedition had to be renewed several times over, but the station was maintained, under its original name of Elmwood. On June 2, 1921, at 1 p.m., the RC3 and the RC4 touched down on a snowfield 200 meters from the hut.

As the first man who came out of the buildings ran towards them, the Nyctalope asked, in English: "Do I have the honor of speaking to Sir Patrick Swires?"

"Yes sir!"

Saint-Clair continued, in French: "Monsieur, would you care to acquaint yourself with the contents of this letter from His Excellency the British Ambassador to the French Republic?"

"With the greatest of pleasure, sir," replied Sir Patrick Swires, bowing.

The temperature was only three or four degrees below zero–a veritable summer's day in those latitudes! The Nyctalope had taken off his gloves, unbuttoned his fur-lined coat and taken a sturdy envelope out of an interior pocket. The commander of Elmwood station took the envelope, slit one side and took out a piece of paper, which he unfolded slowly and read gravely.

Afterwards, extending his right hand enthusiastically and looking at Saint-Clair with an expression of joyful and cordial admiration, the Englishman said: "I am happy, sir, to make the acquaintance of the illustrious Nyctalope. There is no need for orders from my government; your name alone is sufficient to have the entire mission placed at your service. Command, sir, and we shall obey."

"Thank you very much, Monsieur," Saint-Clair replied, with a smile, "but it's not as simple as that. I am here more to consult than command–but we can do that after lunch, if you like."

"I do," said Swires, also smiling.

"It's often windy here, isn't it?" Saint-Clair asked.

"Sometimes–but not today, of course."

"It's unnecessary, then–at least for the moment–to tie down our aircraft?"

"Unnecessary."

"Permit me, then, Monsieur, to introduce my companions."

"And me mine."

The introductions were made with the utmost correctness. The English mission had nine principal members, all of whom were there. When the protocols were complete, they went into the principal hut, where the table-leaves were immediately extended and eight extra places set.

During lunch, the conversation was restricted to voyages of exploration and wintry conditions. Afterwards, though, everyone formed a kind of council, and Leo Saint-Clair was the first to address it.

III. Lucifer and His Mother

At Danzig on May 26, while his company was embarking on the submarine *Kaiser-Gott*–temporarily masquerading as the *Roosevelt*, a submarine belonging to the American Cinematographic Consortium–Baron Glô von Warteck, who was posing as Frederick Alan Schön, producer/director of the aforementioned Consortium, went to No. 183 Schopenhauerstrasse.

No. 183 was a small town house separated from the pavement by a garden and a tall gate reinforced with sheet metal from its base to the tips of its lanceheads.

The Baron took a leather purse from his pocket and extracted a tiny flat key, which he introduced into the lock on the gate. He opened it, went through and closed it carefully behind him. He went straight through the garden, climbed the three steps that led to the door of the house, and opened it with the same key, only putting it half way into the lock. He went in and closed he door.

A bull's eye clock in the hallway marked 10 a.m. Outside, it was a beautiful spring day. Through windows with little panes of colored glass, the Sun projected long rays of yellow, blue, red and green light on to the waxed floor.

Glô von Warteck stood still for a moment, meditatively, his face and body fantastically illuminated by these multicolored rays. He had come in without making a noise. Nothing troubled the silence that surrounded him, save for the monotonous tick-tock of the bull's-eye.

Eventually, the Baron came to a decision. He went rapidly along the hallway and climbed a stairway of waxed wood, whose carpet was held in place by nickel stair-rods. On the first-floor landing, he bumped into a young woman who was making a hurried exit from a room on the left, with a feather duster in her hand.

"Oh! Our Lord!" the young woman cried, surprised, confused and fearful.

"Is my mother ready, Elsa?" the Baron said.

"Yes, Our Lord!"

"Good. Get on with your work."

He went past, took a corridor to the right, and rapped on the first door with his knuckles. Without waiting for a reply, he opened it and went in. There was a minuscule antechamber and another door, curtained on both sides, then a large bedroom with three windows.

A log fire was burning in the grate. A woman was sitting idly in an armchair in front of the fire, clutching the arm-rests and presenting feet shod in sturdy buttoned boots to the warmth of the flames. The chair was placed in such a fashion that its occupant had only to lift her head and turn slightly to one side, on hearing the slight noise of the Baron's entrance, to face her visitor.

"Good morning, mother," said the Baron, with evident respect.

"Good morning, my son," the woman replied, in a harsh voice. "I've been waiting for you. I'm ready. Are we going?"

"Right away?"

"Yes, of course! Right away." She got up abruptly, in a graceless, almost brutal manner.

She was a large, stout woman of about 60. Her white hair was formed into a fringe over her broad forehead and temples and a thick, heavy bun at the nape of her neck. Her face was almost masculine, square and somewhat wrinkled. She had cold grey eyes, an aquiline nose, thin lips, heavy jaws and a prominent chin.

She was dressed in a steel-grey stiff-collared costume with a military cut. With rapid and confident gestures, she took up a plain grey bonnet from a table and fastened it in position, not without a certain cavalier elegance, then donned her gloves and threw a magnificent squirrel-fur stole over her shoulders. In her right hand, she picked up a traveling-bag, which was of medium dimensions but rather heavy, but which the Baron did not offer to carry. "Let's go!" she said.

He bowed as she went past him.

As he had entered the room, the Baron had had his hat in his hand. As he went out behind his mother, he put it back on.

The maid with the feather-duster was on the landing.

"Elsa," said her mistress, "you and Glawitz are forbidden to let anyone into the house."

"Will the Baroness be gone for a long time?" Elsa asked, respectfully.

Diana von Warteck turned to her son and queried: "Much later than June 10?"

"No, mother," Glô replied, with a proud smile. "No. You'll return by aeroplane on June 11, 12 at the latest."

Diana turned back to the maid and said: "You heard my son. But don't forget that, from a distance as from nearby, today, tomorrow and every day, I shall know what is happening here. Do you understand? Woe betide you and Glawitz if you get up to anything!"

Else went pale, her blue eyes suddenly expressing a sharp fear. Immediately lowering her eyelids, however, and bending her knee in a humble curtsey, she stammered: "I'll be sensible, mistress."

"I'm counting on it."

Three minutes later, Diana and Glô von Warteck were in the street.

"A carriage, mother?" the Baron said.

"No. I prefer to walk."

Side by side, they strode rapidly through the town, without exchanging a word, stiffly maintaining impassive expressions.

On the quay alongside which the pretended *Roosevelt* was standing, watched by many idlers, the son went ahead of his mother to guide her through the curious crowd to the submarine's gangway. They immediately became the focal point of every gaze–but not for long, for they went into the vessel immediately.

Then the blast of a whistle sounded.

Mariners in grey uniforms appeared on deck, barefoot and bare-headed, moving about methodically. An officer in a white cap, but similarly barefoot and clad in the same grey uniform, whose long sleeves were marked with three small blue stripes, barked orders at them. In a few minutes, everything was prepared for the submersion. One after the other, like puppets, with the officer bringing up the rear, the mariners disappeared. By that time, the submarine had moved away from the quay to a distance that was about twice as great as its visible length. The whole slender mass came slowly about, turning its stern to the quay– and the fake *Roosevelt* sailed away, while the gawkers dispersed, each one heading for some other idle spectacle or going to work.

When it had doubled the final jetty and left the last signal-beacon far behind, the *Kaiser-Gott* submerged and put on speed rapidly, until it was gliding along beneath the surface at its normal cruising speed of 50 knots.

Glô had led his mother to the apartment that Diana von Warteck had occupied several times before on journeys from Danzig to Stockholm, where she had a summer residence. He went into the apartment with her. Together, they went through a little vestibule, a minuscule dining-room and a miniature sitting-room, not pausing until they reached a bedroom with a single bed, as large as the other three rooms put together.

In addition to the bed, there was a mirror-fronted wardrobe, a divan, a table, wall-hangings and rugs. The luxury of its furnishings was slightly overstated, but it was very comfortable. One of the walls as pierced by three portholes–closed, naturally, since the submarine was traveling underwater–partly masked by lace and velvet curtains. A ceiling-light and three electric lamps, already switched on when Diana and Glô entered the room, filled it with vivid light.

Suddenly, something strange happened. The reciprocal attitudes of the mother and son were completely modified. While she put down her traveling-bag and took off her gloves, stole and bonnet, which she unfastened herself, she looked at her son and smiled affectionately. He no longer had the coldly respectful attitude that he had adopted in the house in the Schopenhauerstrasse and in the street, but the opposite: the free and easy manner of a superior man.

The mother let herself fall heavily into an armchair and said in a soft voice: "Ah, now we have time to chat at our leisure. For several days, I've only had news of you by telephone. How are you?"

He remained standing in front of her, looming over her, and he talked– sometimes standing still, sometimes pacing back and forth, stiff and supple at the same time, anxious, menacing and feline, simultaneously enraged and self-satisfied. "How am I? At the luminous dawn of victory–but still struggling against the darkness! What fumblings! What hesitations! What faults, even! I was nearly killed. Me!"

"By a woman, I'll wager!" Diana von Warteck put in, her affectionate pity leavened with scorn.

He stopped short, furious, ready to react abusively, but she added, very gravely: "Womankind will ruin you, my son."

He shrugged his shoulders, scornful in his turn. "It's your fault," he replied, dryly. "When I came back from India and you learned about my experiments, your ambition and haste to see me triumph were so great that they made you too docile a subject, even though I knew exactly what I had to contend with: the ordinary force of your soul, your personal pride, your rigid will, and the hardness of heart towards me of which you have given me so many proofs since my childhood in the Bermudas. At the end of those experiments, I thought I was much stronger than I am, and instead of waiting until I had finished the construction of the perfected Teledynamo, I wanted to act immediately with the force of my brain alone, solely by the power of my own magnetism, with the cards put into my hands by my occult science!"

He stopped, clenched his fists and looked hard at his mother. She had slumped further into the armchair. Her eyes were open but glazed, like those of a dead woman. Her face was now expressionless. Shrugging his shoulders again, he went on: "Installed at Schwarzrock, I terrorized the 50 brutes and 20 girls that I made into my soldiers and servants. I transformed my brother Hunter into a puppet. I hypnotized servants and made them into unconscious messengers by suggestion. I cast a spell on a son from a distance, to get at the father..."

Diana interrupted him. "Maladroit cruelty!" she said, in a bleak voice. "If you had consulted me, I would have set you straight regarding the father's psychology. You can't intimidate an Alexandre Prillant!"

He did not seem to have heard. He continued: "I cast a spell on Irène..."

Diana interrupted again. "Stupid impatience! When you want to possess a woman, you don't start by rendering yourself odious and inflicting physical suffering..."

Still indifferent, at least in appearance, he was still continuing: "I drew Laurence Païli to me, by the force of my will-power alone..."

Diana cut in again, obstinately. "Puerile contradiction! You force her to come to you and demand that she gives herself to you freely!"

He made no reply. He went on: "I cast a spell on Matthias Narbonne..."

Again she cut in: "Stupid caprice! You could, by simple suggestion, have had all the capitalists in the world sign checks in your favor worth millions, and send them to you."

"I hated Narbonne when he was alive!" he retorted, brutally. "I still hate him now that he's dead!"

"You've killed him?"

"I've killed him."

"Stupidity!"

"Vengeance."

"A Lucifer does not avenge himself–he heads straight to his goal. You've been petty and stupid."

"Mother!"

"Go on, my son."

He ground his teeth with rage. Then, doubtless seized once again by pride in the certainty of his accomplishment, he said: "You may be right, mother. But why did you not make me insensible to material pleasures? Why did you send me out into the world like the sons of other men? Who is responsible for my sensuality, if not you?"

"Haven't I told you, Glô, that it's necessary to be patient and self-restrained? To remain chaste and cold until the day after the definitive victory? What did the Hindu teach you, if not that?"

"I understood it too late. I only understood it when that accursed Nyctalope escaped my power, even at close quarters, just as Prillant, Lourmel, Mattol and others escaped it at a distance. I understood, especially, when Rupert VI, although a captive, managed to operate the electric switch that turned the entire Hollow Rock into a vast multiple echo-chamber in which every sound was instantly reproduced by the microradiotelephone, clearly and distinctly, in the listening room at Schwarzrock.

"Then, mother, I completely abandoned my impassioned and incomplete enterprises after a long conversation with my other self in the Mental Concentration Chamber. I devoted myself entirely to the last necessary experiments in vivisection and spell-casting, transfusing vital fluids into my Teledynamo's accumulators. I reiterated my orders and instructions to Wilfried, who is expecting us at the Pole from hour to hour. Thus–as you desired, mother–I vanquished myself."

"It is on that sole condition that you will vanquish other men, Glô!" the hard and massive woman pronounced, solemnly.

He recovered himself then, diabolically superb: "I shall vanquish! In a few days, my Teledynamo will be established at the magnetic pole of the boreal hemisphere–which is the hemisphere of the old world, where all the world's true powers are: Europe, modern Asia, the United States of America. It's also the hemisphere in which men preserve the sacred traditions of the mysteries of Isis, Eleusis, Moloch, Brahma, Vishnu and Shiva–for Egypt, Arabia and India are all north of the equator. As imaginary meridians radiate across maps of the world, so the all-powerful fluids, irresistible propagators of my will, will radiate from the North Pole to the equator, and I shall capture to my profit the thoughts of all that humankind which swarms upon the Earth, criss-crosses the seas and attempts to scale the Heavens! I shall domesticate their intelligence, direct their will-power according to my whim, destroy or subjugate their organized forces, overturn, drain or dissipate as it might suit me their material and fiduciary fortunes... And humankind entire will eventually obey me, more loyally than a Palatine slave obeyed Caesar!"

He fell silent, standing over Diana von Warteck, domineering and terrible. The monster's mother was no longer slumped in the armchair; her eyes were no longer glazed, like those of a corpse. She was still seated, but was stiff and upright, her mouth arched by the violent contraction of her features. Her grey eyes sparkling, she stared at the man to whom she had given birth, in whom were concentrated, for the purposes of a practical realization that was now certain, all the rancors, hatreds, visions, hopes, wraths and avidities of the tenebrous race of the Wartecks.

"Glô, my son," she croaked, in a voice choked with emotion, "forgive my just and necessary reproaches. I have found you again. This is what I love and admire in you!"

"Oh, mother, so it must be," Lucifer replied, with a mocking laugh. "But afterwards, when I am the omnipotent and omniscient master of living humanity, and when I attempt to extend the tentacles of my science and my power into the realm of the dead, don't come to importune me with your belated lessons if I satisfy, without limit, those passions for blood and flesh which your flesh and your blood have put into me! I know that my appetite for all women has merely been awakened, at present, by Irène and La Païli! My hatred of all men, likewise, is concentrated for the present on one man: Leo Saint-Clair! On the very next day after my victory, June 11, I intend simultaneously to possess Irène and to have Saint-Clair tortured materially, in human terms, with nothing occult about it. That same day, I also intend to possess La Païli and to make Saint-Clair watch me! Ah, how he shall suffer! He has been my rival, and still is. He has failed to defeat me, and fights on. I shall have him, in the end, and he shall suffer! Oh! How he shall suffer!"

He was fuming with rage, joy and ferocious hatred.

His mother made a gesture of indifference and slowly pronounced words that immediately calmed the monster: "On June 11, my son, I shall return to my house in Danzig, where I shall be well placed to enjoy, in a restricted but adequate circle, the universal triumph of the Wartecks." Without pause, she added, in a changed voice that was hard and glacial: "What have you done with La Païli's mother?"

He smiled sardonically. "Unharmed, captive here," was his laconic reply.

"Will you give her to me?"

"I will give her to you."

"That's good–for I too have my petty hatreds. I want the person who was once the beautiful Donella to see me, to recognize me, to beg me in tears and curse me..."

"You may use her as you wish."

"Thank you. And what have you done with Minna Zucht?"

"Experiments–dead."

"And the three Zuchts?"

"Dangerous–dead."

"I regret Berthold. He pleased me."

"You'll find others, mother," he jeered, in a low and ferocious voice.

"I certainly hope so!" she said, simply. And the old woman's eyes had a cryptic and disquieting glimmer. At that moment, the mother and the son–one stout and heavy, the other tall and thin–resembled one another solely by virtue of the frightful and repulsive expressions on their faces.

But at that moment, the man was not worthy of the immense and fulgurant name of Lucifer! And the woman was not worthy of having brought into the world a genius of rebellion! Neither of them, however far they had fallen, had fallen from as high as Lucifer, the Angel of Light who had become a demon of Darkness–but they had both fallen much lower.

IV. At the North Pole

When Commander Peary reached the North Pole in 1908, he only found what he had found in 1906 below the 87th degree of latitude and what Nansen had found in 1895, on the other side of the Pole, at a similar latitude: fields of snow and ice chaotically studded with blocks and crevices, without the slightest trace of land: a scene of terrible and mortal desolation, absolute aridity and continual instability–for the thickness of the immense ice-sheet is often subject to convulsion, deformed by temporary melting and sudden freezing, which incessantly modify its details while preserving a desperate uniformity in the whole.

Neither Nansen nor Perry, although they might have had some slight suspicion, discovered what the infernal genius Glô von Warteck discovered a few years later, and which the science and industry of his formidable family had immediately put to use.

This discovery was that the North Pole is not, as everyone has had to accept until now, for lack of contrary evidence, at a point on the globe occupied by the abyssal waters of the glacial Arctic Ocean. Beneath a layer of snow and ice of relatively mediocre thickness, just above what would have been the maximum level of the Ocean, had some abnormal increase in temperature permitted the immediate environs of the Pole to become liquid, there was land–or, rather a rock: a large rocky plateau linked by submarine mountains to one side of Franz Josef land, which is north of Novaya Zemlya, on the far side of the Arctic circle from Ellesmere Island and Greenland.

In other words, if Peary, when planting the starry flag on the North Pole, had been able to dig down in the ice to a depth of only 11 meters, he would not have found marine ice or water but rock: the very skeleton of the Earth!

Glô von Warteck had discovered this when he had returned from India, where he had spent several years studying the Hermetic sciences. Accompanied by several male members of his family and a few Tibetans, he had crossed Mongolia and Siberia and continued further north, following the approximate course of the 80th meridian east of Paris. On the shore of the glacial Arctic Ocean, he had hypnotized and subjugated to the power of his suggestion an entire tribe of Eskimos. With sleds and dogs, Glô's numerous party had then headed straight for the Pole, passing to the east of Franz Josef Land.

The modern instruments with which the Wartecks were equipped–further perfected by their own researches–eventually informed them that they had reached the northernmost point of the Earth's axis. There, they had only to operate an instrument recently invented by one of the Tibetans, who had completed his education at the University of Paris. This prodigiously sensitive instrument was nothing other than an electrically-powered scientific version of the famous "magician's wand." It could reveal the presence, at distances that could be specified to the nearest millimeter or micrometer, according to the setting of its scale, of any kind of mineral.

The Wartecks and the Tibetans dug down at the exact spot where the magnetic pole of the terraqueous Earth was located. They had electric drilling-equipment, and made rapid progress. In a few minutes, the drill-bit threw up a fragment of basalt torn away from a rocky mass that was covered, at that point, by ten meters and 53 centimeters of compacted ice. Glô von Warteck knew immediately that he would eventually be able to install upon the unbreachable foundation of that secret isle the tower of stone inside which the Teledynamo–whose essential mechanism he had already constructed, in theory–would one day be put into operation to bring humankind under his thrall.

The company of explorers had continued on their way. Leaving the North Pole behind them, they went on to Greenland, which they crossed in its entirety from north to south. The submarine *Kaiser-Gott* was waiting for them at Cape Farewell. Scarcely had they come aboard when the Tibetans were strangled and their bodies thrown into the sea. Thus, the secret of the Pole was the sole possession of the Wartecks–and not all of them, but only those who had taken part in the polar expedition. The Eskimos would never be capable of indiscretion; they had been transformed into slaves.

The following year, Glô and the same four kinsmen–Wilfried, Glass, Durbox and Krieg–left for the North Pole again on the *Kaiser-Gott*, with an assortment of white, Kalmuk and Eskimo slaves. The submarine passed through the Smith Strait between Greenland and Ellesmere Island, which had been explored several times by Peary. They went as far north as they could beneath the ice-cap, and reached the point in the sea beyond which the terrestrial and oceanic ice met and were confused. Then, remaining hidden beneath the ice, having nothing below them but a few fathoms of water and the sea-bed, they opened the upper part of the *Kaiser-Gott* so that human divers and electrical implements could work. The ice was pierced and the men emerged into the open air. They were only nine kilometers from the Pole.

Eight months later, broken up by explosives and melted by electricity drawn from the water and the air, the polar ice was destroyed over an area some 500 square meters. The exposed rock was cut into thousands of cubes, save for a central square 25 meters on each side. The cubes extracted from the inexhaustible quarry were disposed on that central platform so as to form walls and partitions. Construction-beams of iron and wood were brought out of the submarine, along with apparatus of every sort, thick plates of glass, sheets of felt, furniture, cables, electric wires, instruments, casks and barrels of food and drink, bales of ammunition and weapons–in brief, a kind of fort was erected there, 85 meters high, whose upper terrace was surmounted by a crystal cupola with a copper framework.

It was Wilfried von Warteck who was invested by Glô as commander of the North Polar outpost. Glass, Durbox and Krieg were his lieutenants, the white slaves his workmen, the Eskimos and Kalmuks his soldiers and servants. Glô left again, this time for Danzig and Schwarzrock–from which he undertook occasional excursions to France, in the course of which he heard La Païli and saw Irène.

Such was the past, in respect of the North Pole. What would the future hold? For the present, on May 26, the *Kaiser-Gott* was cruising underwater in the direction of Spitzbergen with Glô and his mother, Diana, on board.

Maintaining an average speed of 69 miles an hour, the *Kaiser-Gott* only required some 40 hours to cover the distance which, by sea, separated Danzig from the submarine station that the Wartecks had built beneath the eternal ice, ten kilometers from the North Pole–or from Fort Warteck, as they called the complex of architectural constructions raised at the pole.

Even while keeping to the maximum depth that the submarine could attain, it was necessary to take account of the special dangers of submarine navigation in the Arctic Ocean. There was the risk of collision with the submerged portion of a giant iceberg, or of entering a glacial corridor that had no exit. From year to year, and month to month, the thickness of the ice and its submarine distribution varied enormously; a route along which they would have been able to pass a few weeks earlier or would be able to follow a few weeks later might no longer or not yet exist. In the approaches to the Polar Isle–as the Wartecks called the basalt plateau discovered by Glô–the adherence of the submarine ice to the rocky inclines extended to depths that varied continually. Instead of arriving at the entrance to the canal giving access to the submarine station, it was possible to stray into a cul-de-sac, to become trapped in a pocket of ice that threatened to close up after the submarine had passed, to be struck violently by one of those icebergs that sometimes turn upside-down when the part above water acquires a mass superior to that of the submerged part, or, finally, to bump into an iceberg, free-floating or immobile.

At any rate, once it had passed the landmass of Spitzbergen, where the English and Americans were exploring for oil, the *Kaiser-Gott* diminished its speed considerably. It was not until midnight on May 29 that the vessel's lookout spotted the submarine electric lights shining at either side of the entrance to the canal.

The canal was an extraordinary thing. The Wartecks had, of course, found a means to capture and utilize the electric fluid permanently present in water and air, without any limit other than the power of their extractors, transformers and applicators. They stored this fluid in accumulators, passed it through diffusers or even condensed and projected it, so to speak, according to the specific purpose for which it was deployed–to supply motive force, light or heat–by means of a single machine. Thus, on the slope of the submarine mountain extending five kilometers south from the station, the polar Wartecks had installed veritable conduits of electric heat, and these conduits, constantly and continuously radiating millions of calories, which fanned out to warm the seawater above and around them, created an opening with a 20-meter radius: the canal,

The submarine station was nine kilometers from Fort Warteck as the crow flies, at a depth of a mere 20 meters. Furthermore, between Fort Warteck and the station, the same warming process kept an open trench free of snow and ice, which was furnished with an electric Decauville mounted on high rails fixed to the constituent basalt of the Polar Isle.[60]

The system was arranged in such a way that the submarine, arriving from the south beneath the thickness of the ice-cap, went into the canal, advancing slowly but climbing by degrees along the canal's slope, following the declivity of the ground, to the extent that, about 1,000 meters in advance of the station's magnetic docks, the submarine was no longer moving beneath the ice but in rippling water open to the sky—for the radiation of electric heat elevated the surface temperature above freezing-point.

Once at the station, the submarine surfaced and disembarked its passengers and cargo on to the dock—which was equipped with very comfortable living-quarters—and the closed and heated wagons of the electric Decauville carried the people and their luggage swiftly to Fort Warteck, between two high walls of streaming ice, whose surface melted and froze incessantly, the heat of the conduits radiating to the left, right and upwards to a precise and invariable limit.

Every time it snowed, a bizarre phenomenon was produced: all along the Decauville's trench, the snow stopped dead at a certain height along a certain width, there being transformed into rain—but to the left and the right, on the shelf, it continued to fall as snow, thus making a tunnel of rain with a basalt floor, walls of ice and a roof of snow. But that was only one of numerous strange events caused in the vicinity of the pole by the Wartecks' scientific installations.

Having unloaded those people and goods that were to be disembarked, the submarine usually submerged and went to rest underwater in one of three magnetic berths, connected by watertight tubes to the submarine part of the station—which was itself connected to the terrestrial part by elevators and hoists. This was not, however, the procedure followed by the *Kaiser-Gott* when it arrived in the submarine harbor shortly before 1 a.m. on May 30. It did not surface or unload its passengers and cargo. Instead, by means of a maneuver to which he was doubtless accustomed, the commander of the *Kaiser-Gott*—the Durbox of the polar expedition—took his submarine directly and very smoothly into the central berth.

As soon as the spindle-shaped vessel came to rest, a hermetically sealed tube extended like an accordion from the wall of the submarine station into the water of the basin. Sliding on rails, it quickly engaged its terminal metal rectangle with a magnetic rectangle hollowed out in the flank of the *Kaiser-Gott*. This hatch opened inwards, while the tube's end-piece opened in its turn; communication was thus established between the earthbound and the sea-voyagers.

A man marched rapidly through the tube, which was illuminated by a series of electric lights, coming out of the station and into the submarine. Durbox was waiting for him in the compartment where the triple doors of steel had opened. He extended his hand. In German–for the Wartecks only spoke German between themselves, although centuries of cross-breeding had made them into a Mongolo-Russo-German hybrid so difficult to classify that Doctor Pascal and Emile Zola would have exercised their science of atavistic progress in vain [61]–he said: "Good morning, Glass, we've brought the Supreme Lord. Is the commandant well?"

"Wilfried's well. His cold's over. I was worried about him for two days, but he avoided bronchitis. He's out of bed." Glass was a physician and surgeon, with diplomas from the faculties of Paris and Berlin.

"He's following you?" Durbox asked.

"Yes–Krieg, too."

"Everything's ready, then."

"Everything." After a slight hesitation, Glass lowered his voice to ask: "Is the Supreme Lord in a scientific state?" In ordinary language, that meant: "Is Glô reading our thoughts at present?"

"No," Durbox replied, curtly. "I know that he has to rest his brain. I heard him say so to his mother. He's saving all his power for the day of the Teledynamo."

"That's still June 10?"

"Yes, I believe so."

"And... are there women aboard?"

"No," said Durbox.

"Too bad! Wilfried, Krieg and I were counting on... Eskimo women eventually become repulsive. Such stupid brutes, with oily skin..."

Durbox burst out laughing. Clapping his cousin on the shoulder–for Wilfried, Krieg, Glass and Durbox were the sons of four sisters–he said, cheerfully: "I'm just teasing you, Glass! All the serving girls from Schwarzrock are on board–and I imagine that by June 10, the Supreme Lord will have no further need of experiments in vivisection. You can–we can–have our choice of servants who are slightly better than Eskimos, from every point of view..."

"*Teufel*!" Glass swore. "I should think so!"

Footsteps sounded on the hard aluminum sheets that were set crosswise to form the floor of the long tube, and a shadow was projected through the open doorway to where the two men were standing. They shut up, turned round and clicked their heels as they gave a military salute.

Wilfried, the commander of the Pole, arrived at a rapid stride, followed by the chief electrician, Krieg. Krieg joined Glass, the chief of staff and Durbox, the captain of the *Kaiser-Gott*, in the first compartment, but Wilfried passed through without stopping, offering a stiff salute before disappearing into the vessel's interior through an iron door, which closed automatically behind him.

351

V. At Cape Flora

The *Uberalles*, commanded by Jacques Saincer and carrying Laurence Païli, Grisyl, Professor Lourmel, Rupert VI, the pilots and mechanics from the RC1 and RC2–and the dismantled aircraft themselves, in well-padded sections of the hold–in addition to the crew of 12 Englishmen and Frenchmen necessary to operate the captured submarine, left Le Havre on the morning of May 31 and headed north. In the meantime, the RC3 and RC4, carrying Saint-Clair, Girard and their associates, were heading for Cape Flora in Franz Josef Land. This was some five days after the *Kaiser-Gott* had already arrived at the North Pole.

"I've been from Le Havre to Spitzbergen," Jacques Saincer had said, "in much the same time that the *Kaiser-Gott* will take to go from Danzig to Spitzbergen"–among other things, Rupert VI, in a hypnotic trance, had revealed the name of the Wartecks' second submarine–"and Cape Flora and Spitzbergen are about the same distance from Le Havre. At this time of year, it's often the case that the southern part of Franz Josef Land, including Cape Flora, is free of winter ice. Nothing should delay me. I'll be at the Cape two or three days after leaving Le Havre."

"If nothing delayed Lucifer," the Nyctalope had concluded, "he's been at the Pole for five days; he'll have been there for seven or eight when you rejoin me at Cape Flora. He'll have been able to do a lot of work in that time!" The *Uberalles* had not been slowed down or interrupted by any incident; the submarine had only taken 24 hours longer than Saint-Clair and his companions had taken to go from Le Havre to Cape Flora.

The Nyctalope had put two aircraft and eight aviators aboard the submarine as a prudent precaution. If any accident were to overtake the RC3 or the RC4, or both of them, the RC1 and the RC2 would arrive intact at Cape Flora with the *Uberalles*. They would only have to be reassembled, which could be done in two or three hours, in order to carry through the extremely audacious plan conceived by the Nyctalope in consequence of Rupert VI's revelations. The latter left little margin of ignorance regarding the Polar Isle, Fort Warteck and the submarine station, which constituted Lucifer's polar establishment. The plan could not be executed, however, without the cooperation of the Englishmen at Cape Flora.

Thus, during the afternoon of June 2, Leo Saint-Clair held council at Cape Flora with Sir Patrick Swires, the commander of Elmwood station and his eight principal colleagues. One can easily imagine the Englishmen's amazement when they learned that there was a basalt island at the North Pole, upon which men had built habitations, workshops and storehouses–and also that they had installed a railway in a trench excavated in the ice, kept ice-free by electric radiation, organized a submarine station communicating with the open sea beneath the permanent ice-sheet by means of a canal whose temperature was similarly maintained, electrically, above freezing point.

The Englishmen could hardly believe their ears–and it was another thing entirely when Saint-Clair had given them, with his customary clarity, a summary of recent events and an account of the vicissitudes of his war against Lucifer, in France, the Black Forest and the Bermudas. If the affair had not involved the celebrated Nyctalope himself, and Captain Girard, Corsat and Pilou had not been there as witnesses, and Saint-Clair had not announced as soon as he arrived the probable arrival on the following day of the submarine *Uberalles*, with the illustrious Professor Lourmel, the *Grottenmeister* of the Bermudas, Grisyl and La Païli, the Englishmen would not have believed a word of the unimaginable story, and would have considered its narrator to be one of those dangerous madmen whose liberty of action have to be curtailed as quickly as possible.

In June, the polar night comes to an end and the days are lit for 24 hours, from midnight to midnight, as the Sun makes a tour of the horizon. There is no nocturnal darkness. Had the time not been divided up into regular slices by meals, sleep-periods and so on, the Englishmen of Cape Flora might have spent days asking the Nyctalope for new details of his extraordinary struggle against the fantastic Lucifer. They had dinner–but they ate little, so preoccupied were they with talking and listening. After dinner, the Englishmen posed more questions, which the Nyctalope answered indefatigably–but in the end, Sir Patrick Swires had asked: "And what are you going to do now?"

"That is my final plan of action," Saint-Clair said, getting to his feet. "I shall reveal it to you tomorrow, and request further discussion then, when the *Uberalles* has disembarked Professor Lourmel and Rupert VI."

"Good!" said Sir Patrick. "But that will be June 3..."

"There will only be six or seven days left," observed Elias Carter, the mission's geographer, a trifle ingenuously.

"As the crow flies," Saint-Clair said, "we're..."

"Exactly 1,132 kilometers from the Pole," the geographer supplied.

"And for the *Uberalles*," Saint-Clair went on, "it's 800 miles to the Wartecks' submarine station. It will take me three days, at the most, to succeed– or to die, for I have no wish to witness the enslavement of the human race."

As he spoke thus, solemnly, Leo Saint-Clair was thinking of Laurence Païli as much as the mass of humankind.

"We might as well go to bed, then," said Sir Patrick Swires, abruptly.

"I was about to ask you if we might," Saint-Clair said.

One of the mission's barrack-rooms had been specially prepared during the afternoon to lodge the newcomers. There they found bunks with woolen mattresses, sheets, blankets and heaters.

All morning on the following day, June 3, Saint-Clair and Girard, with Corsat, Pilou, Romski, Berge, Dopp and Wolf, worked to clean, reset, oil and test all the mechanical parts and the overall structure of the RC3 and RC4. Affecting a greater impassivity than they actually felt, all the members of the English mission devoted themselves to their normal occupations and the various tasks planned for that morning, but a lookout climbed up to the summit of the high basalt cliff at the foot of which Elmwood station had been built and kept watch on the ocean, where bergs of every shape and size were floating. The Frenchmen and Englishmen often raised their heads to look up at the top of the cliff.

Suddenly, a British flag was displayed. The *Uberalles* had been sighted. The chronometer showed 11:55 a.m.

Since Cape Flora's ice had broken up, a wharf of wood and iron had been extended from the shore into the sea. That morning, Sir Patrick Swires had ordered the launch of two large launches put at the expedition's disposal, which had a flotilla of 25 small boats, not counting Eskimo kayaks. At 12:35 p.m., Sir Patrick and Saint-Clair leapt aboard one of these launches; propelled by four oarsmen, it sped rapidly towards a long black mass with a metallic superstructure, which was held immobile by two cables. The second launch followed, with a further four oarsmen.

"Laure!"

"Leo!"

Notwithstanding the presence of the solemn Englishman, the two lovers embraced and Saint-Clair kissed Grisyl on both cheeks.

By 2 p.m., the entire companies of the mission and the submarine having worked well in concert, the disembarkation of passengers and cargo was complete. At 3 p.m., after a late lunch, the supreme council of war was finally opened.

Everyone who would have a part to play in the action of the Nyctalope's final battle against Lucifer–some of them doubtless quite unexpected, by others if not by themselves–was gathered in the vast common room of Elmwood House, which had been cleared of everything except the table and chairs: Sir Patrick Swires, who was immediately appointed as the council's chairman; Professor Lourmel; Laurence Païli and Grisyl; Leo Saint-Clair, Corsat and Pilou; Lieutenant Jacques Saincer; Captain Girard, Lieutenant Romski, Sergeant Berge, Corporal Dopp and Wolf; Ensign Donat, second-in-command of the *Uberalles*; Captain Berton and Cadet Dupuis, the pilots of the RC1 and RC2, with their co-pilots Bompard and Sylvain and their mechanics Aymard and Garet; and the eight principal members of the expedition: Elias Carter, the geographer; Anderson, an electrical engineer; Yerkes, a meteorolologist; Ward, a physician; Gaddesden, a naval officer; MacEwen, a botanist; Merton, a physicist and chemist; and Mallory, the chief of staff. There were 28 individuals in all.

At a nod from the Nyctalope, Sir Patrick Swires stood up and opened the session. With extreme gravity, he wished the Nyctalope, Professor Lourmel and their auxiliaries the best of luck in their enterprise, and he terminated his speech–as moving as it was laconic–by placing himself under Saint-Clair's command and putting all the senior members of his expedition, their staff and equipment, at the service of the cause that had brought the Nyctalope and his company to the polar regions.

It was Professor Lourmel who replied, in a manner that was just as grave, laconic and moving. He thanked Sir Patrick Swires and called upon Leo Saint-Clair, the leader, to reveal his plan of action without further ado. He stated, parenthetically, that Rupert VI, who was sitting in a corner of the room, was in a hypnotic trance and could be interrogated, if the need arose, so long as he remained free–as he evidently was for the moment–from any magnetic empery emanating from Lucifer.

"I imagine," the Nyctalope said, "that Baron Glô von Warteck, certain of success on June 10, is devoting all his strength to his preparations and making certain of his victory, and will not be paying any attention to what is happening in the rest of the world."

"That's certainly so, my friend," affirmed Professor Lourmel. "I've been interrogating Rupert VI during the voyage of the *Uberalles*, and I questioned him on that particular matter. He answered me in terms identical to those that you have just used to express the same thought."

"In that case, let's listen first and act afterwards," said Sir Patrick. "Would you care to begin, Monsieur Saint-Clair?"

With an imposing calmness, a clarity that astonished even Professor Lourmel, and a simplicity that made his explanations clear even to Wolf, Leo Saint-Clair revealed his plan.

VI. The Octopus [62]

The Bahama Channel in the westernmost reaches of the Atlantic Ocean is surely one of the most picturesque maritime routes in the world. It is a deep oceanic valley separating the island of Cuba from the Lucayan Islands, or the Bahamas. It is crossed by the tropic of Cancer and the 80th meridian west of Paris. Its green and blue waters are sprinkled with an infinity of little islets and reefs; even though it is easily understandable that it a good 500 kilometers in length, it is sometimes difficult to accept that it is 300 kilometers wide in places; one is so constantly within sight of land that that one has the impression of gliding through the middle of an archipelago.

Having stayed for several hours in the waters of British Guiana, Raymond de Ciserat had the idea of showing his wife and Mattol a little of the Greater Antilles, as he had already showed them the Lesser ones. Afterwards, he set a north-westward course, rounded the island of Trinidad, went diagonally across the Caribbean Sea, went through the Jamaica channel and the Windward Passage between Cuba and Haiti and along the northern cost of Cuba into the Bahama Channel.

At midday on June 3, he came to a stop. The *Lampas* was at sea off the little port of Jibara, at 78 degrees, 15 minutes and 22 seconds west longitude and 22 degrees, 18 minutes and six seconds north latitude. For about four cables to starboard of the submarine, which was afloat with its propellers motionless, at the mercy of the gentle waves, the sea was dotted with reefs; they formed a minuscule archipelago half a kilometer long and 200 meters wide, whose highest altitude was no more than four or five meters above sea-level at high tide.

On the deck, along with Raymond de Ciserat, who was holding his sextant, were his first mate, Luc Bonnery, who was making calculations on a notepad, Mattol, who was staring out to sea, Irène and Miss Ellen, who were leaning on the guard-rail with Henri Prillant between them.

"Oh, look, Miss! Look!" cried the boy with the enthusiastic ardor that made him desire all sorts of things. "Miss! Look at the seagulls over the rocks! I bet they're full of crabs and shrimps! And mussels and limpets too! Madame Irène, will the commander let us get off again?"

On the morning of the previous day, as much to amuse the two women and the child as to see whether Irène and Henri would continue to be free of the torments of abominable memory, "commander" Raymond had authorized a disembarkation that had lasted for two hours on a bank of reefs analogous to the one at which they were now looking. The "expeditionaries" had brought back two basketfuls of crabs, shrimps, mussels, limpets and other mollusks, on which everyone had feasted at the midday meal.

"Madame," said Miss Ellen, "may we ask the commander?"

356

"Of course," Irène relied, smiling at Henri, who had turned his large eyes towards her pleadingly–and she called out: "Raymond!"

Since they had left the Bermudas behind, the naval officer had been enjoying life. For ten days, while idly taking his *Lampas* through the Greater and Lesser Antilles, he had resumed his honeymoon with Irène, to the point at which he had almost completely forgotten the tragic incidents in Venice and the drama of the Bermudas. The young spouses had no doubt that the Nyctalope would defeat Lucifer conclusively, and that final victory was pending. The monster was muzzled and choked, since he no longer cast spells!

Mattol, meanwhile, kept Irène and Henri under observation. He saw them tranquil and happy. He shared Ciserat's and Miss Ellen's confidence in the Nyctalope's inevitable victory–but he feared that Lucifer might manifest himself again before succumbing. Not wishing to trouble the happiness that reigned aboard the *Lampas* unnecessarily, though, he kept his fears and apprehensions to himself. Whenever the young woman and the boy went up on to the emergent vessel's deck, and especially when they went ashore, as they had several times, he went with them, ready to grab the child and draw Irène away at a run and to hurl himself with them into the submarine, which would immediately dive...

"What do you want, darling?" Raymond asked, turning round in response to his wife's call.

She gestured towards the bank of reefs and relayed Henri's request, adding: "I confess that I too would be delighted to catch crabs and shrimps."

"Very well, go!" said Raymond.

"I'll accompany you," Mattol said, simply. "I need to stretch my legs. I'll carry the mussel-basket, if there is one."

"Bravo! Bravo! Thank you, commander!" cried the excited Henri, clapping his hands.

Bonnery shouted an order.

A metallic creaking was audible almost immediately; in the *Lampas*'s bow, a section of deck was raised up and set back and a dinghy rose up slowly, furnished with four oars and a tiller. A sailor appeared on the port side of the dinghy, jumped on to the deck, disengaged the boat from the little mobile dock to which it as attached, and slid it into the water.

"Embark!" said Raymond.

"What about the nets, the knives, the baskets, the beach-sandals?" cried Henri.

"Everything's in the dinghy, Monsieur!" confirmed the sailor, whose name was Martin, and who had the particular responsibility of ferrying and watching over these fishing expeditions and pleasure-trips.

Henri was the first to pass from the deck into the dinghy; Irène and Miss Ellen followed him, then Mattol, and finally the sailor, who cast off the mooring rope before taking up two of the oars. Mattol took the tiller, and the light boat sped towards the reefs. It only required a few minutes for Martin to arrive in a little creek where the water was perfectly calm, permitting a comfortable landing and an easy disembarkation.

When Raymond saw the two women, the child and Mattol leap on to the rocks, he waved to them and called out. They answered immediately, in joyful voices, their white silhouettes gesticulating.

"My dear Luc," Raymond said to his second-in-command. "Stay here, please. If Martin moves the dinghy, make sure you always keep it in view, at the closest possible range."

"Understood!"

After a last glance towards his dear wife, the officer went back into the *Lampas*. He had to write a letter to Professor Lourmel, which he intended to take to Havana, where there was a deep-water harbor. If he did not profit from the hour when Irène was not on board, he would never find the time to write it–which would not please the Professor, who would expect at least eight pages stuffed with details of life on board, Irène's physical and mental health, and a page dealing with Henri and Miss Ellen for the special attention of Monsieur Prillant.

The bank of reefs was everything for which young Henri had hoped: a host of rocks, in the midst of which snaked channels that filled and emptied with the ebb and flow of the tide. Scattered here and there were pools full of multicolored algae, whose sides were replete with picturesque and ludicrous animals. Shellfish of every description–including conches, murexes, scallops, mitres, spindles, cones, abalones of the kind called "Virgin's slippers" and downy limpets–remained firmly in place, while sea-urchins in holes in the rock waved their spines. Crabs fled sideways while transparent shrimps darted hither and yon like rays of light.

What joy! What excitement! What cries of triumph!

Irène and Miss Ellen–and Mattol too–each had a net in hand and a basket that was rapidly filling up. They were amusing themselves as much as little Henri. Everyone had left their shoes in the dinghy, replacing them with the cord sandals that the boy called "beach sandals." Thanks to their culottes, they could go a little way into the water, in order to reach the shells and creatures that were too far way from the edges of the channels and pools.

Engrossed by their fishing, however–which had all the ups and downs of a hunt in full flight–the four explorers gradually drew apart. Miss Ellen always took care never to lose sight of Henri, and often sacrificed her own pleasure to follow his comings and goings, but Mattol–excited by glimpses of an enormous crab lodged in a crack, which occasionally put forth one of its pincers in an attempt to seize a piece of white chiffon dangling just out of range–allowed Irène to get further and further away from him. The young woman had told Henri, childishly, that she would bring back more shrimps than he would have of animals and shellfish of every sort. Using her net skillfully, she went from channel to channel and pool to pool, with the result that she crossed the entire bank of reefs and was out of sight of Ellen, Henri, Mattol and Martin, who were nearby, as well as Luc Bonnery, standing on the deck of the *Lampas*.

Abruptly, Irène became conscious of her isolation. She stood up and looked around at the chaos of the arid reefs, grey beneath the tropical heat of the bright Sun, and the empty immensity of the Ocean. In the distance, beneath flossy clouds, there was a blur that must have been an islet. There was no other sound but the lapping of the silky water in the inlets in the rocks.

"God, it's hot!" Irène sighed.

She suddenly felt exhausted, her limbs weak, her neck aching, her ears ringing. Mechanically, she set down her net and basket on a flat rock. She sat down, her eyes unseeing, her brain devoid of thought, her entire body possessed by a kind of extreme languor. She sat without moving, with her elbows on her knees and her chin in her cupped hands, until she felt a sudden violent frisson and stood up stiffly, shivering.

A voice had resounded within her–a familiar voice, seemingly forgotten but whose tone, accent and least inflection she suddenly remembered. The voice of Lucifer! She recognized it, with horror and alarm.

"Irène! Irène!" the infernal voice called. Almost immediately afterwards, Irène heard it echo again within her–inside her head, it seemed!

"Irène," the voice said, "here I am again. You recognize me, don't you, with no hesitation? That's because I want you too. Listen to me, Irène, because I also want you to answer me, freely, willingly, independently. For me to speak to you, though, I have had to induce the commotion that initially made you feel exhausted... For I'm so far away! Irène, you have all your free will; you have the power to do anything you please, even to refuse to listen to me, to flee, to call Raymond or Mattol, to put yourself to sleep in order to produce the illusion of having confounded my empery–but be afraid for those you love, for their extreme distress..."

There was a silence, and a violent ringing in her ears; then the voice resumed: "Are you listening to me, Irène? Will you listen? Answer me. Distant as I am, I shall hear you."

Clearly, but in a whisper, Irène said: "Yes, I'll listen." Her entire body shuddered again with horror and alarm, and an inexpressible despair crept into her soul.

"Perfect!" said the voice. "Well, Irène, do you remember the letter that one of my men delivered to you in Le Havre, when you got out of the car that had brought you from Paris?"

"Yes, I remember," Irène stammered. Her eyes were dilated, her head tilted back, her hands clenched upon her bosom; if anyone had seen her at that moment they would have thought her mad, or in a painful ecstasy.

"Do you remember exactly what I told you?" the voice continued. "You read that letter so many times before giving it to the Nyctalope–you know it by heart. Tell me what I wrote..."

"No!" The voice had been mocking, sneering; Irène was indignant. "No!" she repeated, proud to demonstrate, now, that she was indeed free. "No, I won't!"

"I like that rebelliousness, Irène," the voice retorted, in a tone that was grave and harsh. "Your voluntary submission will be all the more precious. I shall then recite the letter myself. It's necessary that you understand perfectly the alternatives between which you shall soon have to choose, and that you cannot deny what you know!"

Lucifer burst out laughing–and that diabolical laugh resounded in the unfortunate woman's skull to the point at which she moaned in pain. When the laughter died away, the voice went on.

"Do you remember the date, my dearest? May 7. Today is June 3. Our relationship is 26 days older, and very loving. On May 7, I wrote to you that there were two alternatives between which you would have to choose before June 10.

"Either you would willingly submit to me, or I would kill, at a distance and after 12 hours of terrible tortures, first your Aunt Luce, then your uncle the Professor, then your friend Mattol, and then your husband Raymond. Then I would take control of you, despite anything you might do, and you would live with the remorse and shame of having sacrificed, uselessly, the four people that you love.

"I added that, once you have reached a decision, I would give you the appropriate instructions to render it effective."

The voice fell silent.

Irène wrung her hands. A terrible idea flared up in her mind: to die! *I have only to take a step and let myself fall, mouth agape, without struggling. The sea would soon swallow me up. Everyone would think it was an accident.*

But the voice resumed: "No, no, Irène, you shall not kill yourself. In that respect, alone, I confiscate your liberty. Try!"

She wanted to defy the frightful invisible monster, distant but so abominably present. With a desperate thrust of her entire body, she threw herself...

But she did not fall. It seemed that a wall had sprung up in front of her–a wall as elastic as it was invisible, by which she was first arrested and held upright, then gently but irresistibly pushed back.

The voice went on: "Irène, you will never kill yourself. Other than that, you are free. But to prove to you how merciless I shall be if you do not come to me of your own free will, I shall make you witness an edifying spectacle. Miss Ellen..."

The voice fell silent.

"What?" said Irène, her heartbeat increasing with a new dread.

"Ah, that gets your attention?" said Lucifer. "I counted on it. Miss Ellen is, fundamentally, indifferent to me. I could let her live–all the more so because I'm certain now that I shall snuff out Henri's father, Alexandre Prillant, in a flash, on June 10. Well, Irène, you shall see Miss Ellen die..."

"Oh! Vile monster!" cried Irène, mad with indignation and pain.

"That's right, insult me!" mocked the satanic voice. "How beautiful you are now, my Irène! I only know one woman in all the world as beautiful as you: Laurence Païli. But you'll see her in my home–she'll be your sister and your rival!"

"Monster! Monster!"

"Cry out loud, Irène, as loudly as you can! Your cries have been heard. Miss Ellen is running, leaving Henri to Mattol, who–excellent man!–will had him over to Martin before coming to your aid. He'll arrive too late... Here's Miss Ellen! Her death will be symbolic. Like the animal that will seize her, I intend to extend my tentacles and apply my suckers to all humankind, Irène! But you'll understand that later. For the moment, watch! Look in front of you–I insist!"

Obedient to that voice resounding within her head, which caused the image to surge forth from her memory of a thin, red-haired man in a smoking-jacket, Irène looked in front of her...

Immediately, she let out a piercing scream and leapt backwards. She bumped into a rock, tottered, fell to her knees and, clutching her temples, was petrified by the horror of what she saw.

"Oh, Madame, what's wrong?" the Englishwoman had cried, jumping upon the rock where Irène de Ciserat had been standing just as the latter recoiled in horror.

Mechanically–or, rather, already possessed by the will-power of the distant Glô von Warteck–Miss Ellen looked in the direction in which the thing that had so terrified Irène must be...

And the Englishwoman screamed.

She howled as an exasperated dog howls at the prospect of its own death, in the phantasmagoria of a moonlit night, and in response to that lugubrious howl, Mattol, 100 meters away, shouted: "Irène! Miss Ellen! Hold on! Here I am!"

Already, though, as if fascinated, the Englishwoman was walking into the water beneath the slanting rock. Some four meters away, just beneath the surface of the water, a monstrous creature was moving with hallucinatory slowness. It was a octopus–an enormous octopus, whose tentacles, several meters in length, were moving around it, coiling like snakes. Two huge black eyes stood out against its swollen magenta-striped ochreous body, expressive of voracious cruelty, simultaneously human and animal.

And Miss Ellen was walking towards the octopus!

The unfortunate woman was evidently in a somnambulistic state–a somnambulism from which nothing could awaken her, for neither the coldness of the water or Mattol's appeals, nor those of Martin, who was in the dinghy with Henri and had rounded the reef, rowing with all possible speed, nor the echoes of their cries, could recall the Englishwoman to reason...

When the water came up to her breast, she began to swim, mutely, towards the octopus. Not for long! One of the tentacles shot out of the water, whipped through the air and descended upon Miss Ellen, who was turned over by the force of the blow. Other tentacles immediately seized her and drew her under–already limp, as if dead...

By the time that Mattol and Martin–the former standing beside Irène, the latter in the dinghy clutching little Henri, sobbing and writhing–shook off the invisible bonds that held them immobile by a effort of will and recovered the ability to act, the octopus was sliding sideways, settling its entire gelatinous mass upon Miss Ellen's body. With a gentle movement, it drew away, its tentacles wrapped around her, and sank with her into the transparent water.

A loud blast of a whistle split the air. Mattol and Martin turned their heads.

"The *Lampas*!"

Obedient to the orders he had been given, Bonnery had set the submarine astir as soon as Martin had begin to row. He, too, had heard the screams, understood that something abnormal was happening, and had summoned Raymond. The commander and his second were now on the deck with several mariners and the *Lampas* was coming closer, although it was forced to remain a certain difference from the reefs because of the risk of running into submarine rocks.

"Raymond! Raymond" cried Mattol, getting hold of himself. "An octopus is carrying Miss Ellen away!"

Mad with heroic devotion, Martin launched the dinghy at the rock, threw little Henri–who had almost fainted–into Mattol's arms, and leapt into the sea with a long broad knife in his hand.

A considerable agitation of the water ensued, a few fathoms distant; two tentacles emerged into the air, thrashing brutally. Martin and three other sailors who had come from the submarine, with hatchets in hand and their knives in their teeth, dived repeatedly into the foaming sea for several minutes, but it was all in vain. The octopus and Miss Ellen had disappeared into the inaccessible depths of the abyss.

Raymond de Ciserat was too familiar with the ways of the sea to conserve the slightest hope, except for the recovery of the young woman's corpse. He knew that the class of Cephalopoda–for which the term octopus is merely the common name–included individuals of colossal dimensions and insatiable voracity, whose mouths, which close exactly like a parrot's beak, have edges so sharp that their jaws can cut through a man's limb as easily as a razor cuts through a matchstick. How many maritime writers have recalled that Aristotle measured the length of one squid–a kind of cephalopod–as five cubits, which is more than three meters; that the museums of Trieste and Montpellier hold the skeletons of cephalopods measuring two meters; that our fishermen frequently see specimens whose length surpasses 1.80 meters; and, finally, that according to the calculations of naturalists, one of these animals with a body a mere two meters long would have tentacles longer than ten meters. That really is a formidable monster. For an octopus of that size, Miss Ellen was only small prey.[63]

Even so, Raymond maneuvered the submarine into the depths into which the octopus had disappeared. Suited divers armed with cutlasses came out of the *Lampas* and searched for more than an hour. They did not bring back the octopus, nor the slightest shred of Miss Ellen's white dress.

In a room on the *Lampas*, with little Henri, numb with fright, on her knees and in her arms, Irène wept with her head rigid and her eyes wide open, insensible to Mattol's attentions and Raymond's words and caresses. She thought that she would not escape Lucifer if she did not submit to his demands, and that she would also expose all the people she loved to pain, torture and death.

Eventually, Irène de Ciserat seemed to calm down. She summoned Lili, her chambermaid, and handed Henri Prillant over to her. He had finally fallen into the benevolent sleep of childhood, after which life seemingly reclaims its rights and everything bad is forgotten.

"What a frightful business Raymond! I thought I would go mad with horror and pity. You can leave me alone now. I'm quite calm."

Accustomed to the submarine's routines, Irène knew that her husband was due in the conning-tower in a quarter of an hour. Leaving his wife to Mattol's care, therefore, Raymond de Ciserat went to his post, saddened by Miss Ellen's frightful death, but reassured with regard to Irène, for nothing in the tragic adventure had suggested to him that the spell-caster could possibly be involved in it.

"Perhaps it would be best if you slept for a while, Irène," Mattol said, when Ciserat had gone–but she gestured to him to be quiet and wait.

She listened. When she was certain that her husband had reached the conning-tower, and that it was absolutely impossible for him to hear what she was about to say, the young woman's attitude abruptly changed. She sat up straight in her armchair. Her face took on a wildly forceful expression. In a firm voice, she said to Mattol: "Sit down, Louis. I have to talk to you, because I want to tell you everything, so that later, when I've vanished, you'll be able to save Raymond from madness and despair."

Mattol was stupefied by this speech. He let himself fall on to the edge of the divan, and stammered: "When you've vanished? Whatever can you mean, Irène?"

"Keep a cool head, Louis!"

That was an order. The young doctor was stung by it. He started abruptly, frowned, and stared at a hard-faced Irène he no longer recognized. After a pause, he said: "A cool head? I have one now." Then, in a softer voice, accompanied by an affectionate gaze, he said: "I'm listening, Irène."

Still wild and resolute, the unhappy woman asked: "Did Saint-Clair give you the letter signed Lucifer that was handed to me clandestinely in Le Havre, to bring to the Bermudas?"

"Yes," said Mattol, shivering as a presentiment gripped his heart.

"Have you read it?"

"No, but Saint-Clair recited the text to me."

"And what did you think?" Irène asked, her eyes fixed on Mattol's, as if she were trying to read his mind.

The young scientist did not even think about lying. He simply replied: "I thought that the Nyctalope would set Lucifer straight before June 10."

"Do you still believe that?"

"Yes—all the more so because of the Nyctalope's great success in the Bermudas and the certain guarantee of..."

"Of nothing at all," Irène cut in, trenchantly.

"What!" said the astonished and troubled Mattol, tormented by the presentiment of something terrible.

"Of nothing at all!" Irène repeated. "The Nyctalope's victory in the Bermudas was inconsequential. We're all lost if I don't obey Lucifer. He is the stronger and always will be." She had lost her hard and impassioned stiffness; her voice had become sorrowful and pathetic. Tears glistened between her eyelids.

He took her hands. Authoritative and pleading at the same time, he said: "Now, now Irène, don't say things like that. We have proof that Lucifer is beaten—"

"What proof?"

"What? Your peace, since..."

"Oh, you think so?" Abruptly withdrawing her hands, the unhappy woman, harsh and resolute again, went on: "Lucifer is present here—yes, all around us! Listen to me, Louis—Miss Ellen's death was no accident, as you thought. She didn't fall into the water. She was pushed into it by Lucifer's will-power."

"Irène!"

"Listen, Louis! Lucifer spoke to me, out there on the reefs. He repeated the terms of his odious letter to me—and to give me proof of his power, he hypnotized Miss Ellen, who went voluntarily to throw herself into the tentacles of the octopus before my eyes. You don't believe me? You think that grief has made me mad? Well, Louis, you're mistaken. I'm calm and resolved."

"Resolved to do what?" stammered Mattol, who dared not believe or doubt and was now afraid.

"To obey him."

"Irène!"

"Yes, to obey him! I don't want all the people who love me to be tortured to death and I don't want them to witness my own unavoidable martyrdom in the midst of their infernal torments."

"Irène!"

"No! Lucifer is here, I tell you, all-powerful and..."

She fell silent, and suddenly stood up, facing the white-faced Mattol—who had just got to his feet and was staring at a corner of the cabin: a dark corner, which the electric light could not reach, being masked on that side by a screen. Irène turned her head slightly to look into that same dark corner.

At first, she could see nothing in the relative obscurity but a slender white column of vapor slowly undulating—but as soon as Mattol's gaze was fixed on it, it rapidly became more distinct.

The white vapor expanded and thickened; its undulations acquired a shape. That shape was that of a human body, flat and blurred, white with grey shadows. While being opaque, it was suggestive of transparency; while being compact, it communicated an impression of fluidity. At first, the head was only an indecisive vaporous oval, but its outline soon became more distinct and stable; a light coloration made it seem denser than the vapor, dark touches making eyes and a mouth. Suddenly, there was a face, living and ghostly at the same time, in which eyes sparkled, lips twisted into a sardonic smile, and disorderly red hair seemed ablaze.

"Lucifer!" croaked Mattol, petrified.

"Lucifer!" breathed Irène, who was shivering. Her teeth were chattering.

But their dismay was gone in a flash. As if both of them had been injected with a serum that both animated and tranquilized them, Mattol and Irène suddenly felt lucid, cold and attentive, and each of them knew that the other felt the same. It was then that both of them—each knowing that the other heard it—heard a voice, not as if it came from the phantom, but as if it were inside themselves, in their own brains. The phantom's lips moved, though, for it was evidently that which spoke.

"Mattol believes you now," it said, "since his eyes see and his ears hear. He may listen and judge!" After a pause charged with anguish, it added: "Irène, will you consent to come to me?"

Unable to resist, Mattol turned his head slightly so that he could see both Irène and the phantom. What a spectacle! Like an exhausted body no longer able to sustain itself, the young woman fell to her knees, overwhelmed, her hands joined together in desperate prayer. Her uplifted face expressed distress and infinite sorrow. Her soul was in agony. Given the sublimity of her love for Raymond, her tenderness for her uncle, Professor Lourmel, her affection for her childhood friend, Louis, Irène had decided to sacrifice herself, resignedly making a gift of herself to the implacable monster. But what a martyrdom! To lose everything of which one has dreamed, everything in which one has found happiness, and to go, alone, to the torture and shame of a complete abandonment of oneself to some kind of frightful demon...

"Raymond! Raymond!" she moaned—a last appeal, emitted by her entire being. But he could not hear—and if he had heard, what could he have done? Mattol was there, powerless to attempt a single gesture or pronounce a single word. He looked on, lost in sorrow and fright.

With an inexpressible horror, which chilled him to the core, made his hair stand on end and set his hands and body trembling, Mattol heard Irène say: "Yes, yes! Spare them! I'm yours." Then his eyes were irresistibly drawn to the phenomenon produced in the dark corner: the phantom was slowly fading away.

Soon, when all the vapor had disappeared, Mattol felt something like an electric shock. He passed a hand over his forehead, which was suddenly steaming with cold sweat. He saw Irène lie down on the carpet, inanimate. Very much his own master, he bent down, carefully took hold of the young woman, lifted her up and deposited her on the divan. In the neighboring bathroom, he was able to find smelling salts. He quickly set about bringing Irène back to consciousness.

She opened her eyes, accepted her friend's attentions and tried to get up. They stood up, facing one another, hand in hand. They looked at one another with inexpressible despair.

"Louis," Irène said, eventually, "do you have any more doubt?"

"Alas, no."

"We must say nothing to Raymond."

"I understand why it's necessary to say nothing."

"When I'm gone, Louis, you must keep an eye on him, Uncle Onésime and Aunt Luce."

"Irène!"

"And yourself too."

"I'll die, Irène."

"You'll live, for them, Louis."

"Alas!"

Standing there, looking at one another, they wept–but there was a noise of footsteps and slamming doors, and a voice coming nearer.

"Yes, my dear chap, yes. It's marvelous that you've had the same idea, wonderful! We'll do better than Nansen or Peary. Ah! It's an exploit worthy of the famous Captain Nemo! To the North Pole by submarine. The *Lampas* can do it. Why didn't we think of it sooner?"

Mattol and Irène had just enough time to wipe away their tears, to summon up the heroic strength they needed to stop weeping, and smile. They were still trembling with horror, though, for even as they heard and understood what Raymond was saying, they also heard the incontestable voice of Lucifer resounding in their heads, saying: "Although my phantom perispirit is dissipating, I am present nonetheless. My body and mind are at the North Pole, in a citadel of mysteries and prodigies that I built for myself and my Teledynamo. The Teledynamo is the machine that will make me the all-powerful god of the terrestrial world. From now on, I shall hypnotize the entire crew of the *Lampas*– and your own husband, Irène, will bring you to me at the North Pole!"

Mattol and Irène heard and understood that too–and from that moment on, they were obliged to accept that they had descended into madness: an alienation more extravagant than all the cases of dementia recorded by the world's psychiatrists.

Ciserat and his first mate, Bonnery, came into the cabin.

"Ah, there you are!" cried Raymond, exultantly. To all appearances, he had completely forgotten Miss Ellen's death–and Bonnery had forgotten too, for the young officer was laughing. "I told Luc that you must be here, not in the drawing-room," continued Raymond. His abnormal cheerfulness seemed sinister to Irène and Mattol, who understood its cause only too well. "I've had an idea.

We're going to undertake a polar expedition. Yes, instead of going back and forth through archipelagoes or along continental coasts that have nothing new to show us, we'll attempt to reach the North Pole in the *Lampas*. I've given the orders. Kervalec's at the tiller, and we're heading for the Pole at top speed. What do you think of that?"

Mattol made an effort, and succeeded in saying: "Splendid!"

"Isn't it?" said Bonnery.

The commander's eyes, and those of his first mate, were sparkling with joy. A sort of feverish excitement made them pace back and forth and their laughter had a nervous and insane quality about it.

"My God!" said Irène, who was still lucid. "It's as if they were possessed." She spoke in a whisper so that only Mattol heard her.

"They are, indeed, possessed," he murmured.

"Ah," Raymond went on, "I can see our route as if I had the chart in front of my eyes–but there's no map here, Irène, since it's your room. Follow me! We'll go through the Bahamas and head straight for the Bermudas–ah, the Bermudas! God bless the Nyctalope! We shan't stop there, naturally. Full speed, always full speed, to Cape Newfoundland, which we'll leave behind us in the west. Northwards, northwards! The Davis Strait between Greenland and America, then Baffin Bay–and afterwards, the same route as Peary. The Smith Strait, the Lincoln Sea, the Arctic Ocean, the ice-cap–under the ice-cap, of course! And the North Pole! Luc, have you counted up? How many miles, at the shortest?"

"Five thousand miles–five and a half thousand at the most."

"Ah! The *Lampas* can do 50 miles an hour, so... Bonnery?"

"A hundred and ten hours!"

"A hundred and ten hours!" Raymond cried. "Do you hear, Mattol? Do you understand, Irène? In 110 hours–between four or five days, at the most–we'll be as close as possible to the Pole. Today's..."

"June 3, 17:00."

"On June 7 or 8, then... Ah, the North Pole! We'll have to buy furs, Irène! Bah! We'll find everything we need in Newfoundland! Well, Irène, Louis, what do you say to that?"

"Yes, what do you say to that?"

The two hallucinated and possessed men rubbed their hands in glee.

It required less than an hour for Irène and Mattol to ascertain that all the crew members had similarly fallen victim to Lucifer's hypnotic power, none harboring any thought or performing any action that was not prompted by the distant and mysterious Teledynamo.

In the ensuing days and nights, Irène and Mattol had to hold their tongues. They were alone, aboard the *Lampas*, in being able to think and act freely. But what good was that liberty?

Once and for all, Irène had made the sacrifice of her happiness and her life. Every hour was a station in her abominable calvary, for she was suffering atrociously, and her thoughts, dominated as they were by the red-haired sorcerer, could not be other than painful. She would have liked to be able to annihilate herself in a dreamless sleep akin to death, but she could achieve no more than a superficial somnolence disturbed by nightmares. "Oh, why did the monster not entrance me?" she moaned. "Why is he letting me suffer in this way? Is it not unnecessarily cruel, given that I have consented?"

The depressed and pensive Mattol also asked himself why Lucifer had left him free and conscious. Conscious, yes, he said to himself, but free? To do what? He wanted to experiment with his liberty, to see what its limits might be.

On June 4, while the *Lampas* was heading for the fatal Pole at top speed, its entire hull shuddering, Louis Mattol took it upon himself to talk to Irène, to argue against her decision, to restore her confidence in the Nyctalope and to persuade her, if possible, to cheat Lucifer.

"Wherever Saint-Clair might be," he said, "he's certainly continuing the war against Lucifer."

"What good is that?" Irène replied. "Can he halt this vessel that my own husband is steering towards the monster? No. What, then? Besides, my dear Louis, do you know what has become of Saint-Clair? Since British Guiana, we've had no news of him. How many days have gone by? Do you think that Lucifer would make the mistake of leaving the Nyctalope free to act? Saint-Clair is probably dead."

Mattol was obstinate. "No! Something inside me tells me that he's alive! But let's put Saint-Clair aside–I have an idea."

Irène looked at him pityingly. She no longer belonged to the world in which she had been happy, in which a husband lived whom she adored–but whom she no longer recognized, so extensively had he been changed by the truly diabolical possession whose victim he was. That contributed more than a little to the rendering the poor woman's martyrdom more painful and more desperate.

Condescendingly, she said: "What idea?"

"Would you care to conduct an experiment?" Mattol's voice was hesitant. He was frightened precisely because the experiment, or rather test, would determine the limit of the illusory liberty left to him by the dreadful sorcerer.

"An experiment?" Irène repeated, with a slight shrug of her shoulders. "What would it involve?"

"Putting you into a trace and interrogating you." He got to his feet–and the intellectual's earnest and honest face suddenly reflected such a forceful hope that Irène was impressed.

"My God!" she said, sighing. "Who knows? Put me into a trance? Interrogate me? Perhaps I do, indeed, know things, and can tell you... Oh, Louis, if you could..."

Then they went pale, however, and a great tremor took hold of them. Their eyes, despairing again, filled with tears and they looked at one another, racked by sobs...

They had just heard loud mocking laughter erupt between and around them: the cruel, savage, sardonic and ferociously joyful laughter of Lucifer!

It was indeed Lucifer who was laughing; his laughter, bursting out at the North Pole, was reproduced for Irène and Mattol thousands of leagues away, in the cabin on the *Lampas*. It was indeed the Lord Baron Glô von Warteck, the 13th of that name, alias Lucifer, spell-caster, sorcerer and master of the Hermetic sciences.

On that morning of June 4, he was at the very top of Fort Warteck, in the great copper-framed cupola of thick clear crystal. He was not alone; he was in conversation with the commander of the polar station, his cousin Wilfried.

The crystal cupola was so broad and tall that it formed a globe in which 20 men could have performed exercises under the instructions of an officer on horseback. Its inner edges were embedded between two concentric felt-lined copper rings, inscribed in a thickly-carpeted floor of oak. In the middle of this circular plane was a pedestal three meters square and two meters high. On one of its four faces, a door was visible, which gave access to the cupola. The pedestal's inferior base formed a landing perforated by the head of a staircase communicating with Glô von Warteck's study-library.

The cupola was furnished with two curved divans, several stools—upholstered or wooden—and various cupboards, all set around the periphery, at a height not exceeding that of the circular base of felt-lined copper that supported the immense crystal bell-jar.

Against the side of the pedestal parallel to the one in which the door was set, a flight of felt-lined iron steps climbed up to a cornice, which was a meter and a half wide and furnished with a guard-rail, By means of this cornice, one could make a circular tour of the platform above the pedestal—and it was on this platform that the Teledynamo was set.

Varnished wooden tables topped with thick plates of glass were set against the other faces of the pedestal; Glô and Wilfried were sitting at one of these tables, the former in his smoking jacket with the turned-down collar and white silk shirt and the latter in a grey woolen cycling-costume with grey stockings and grey felt sandals. They were both bare-headed. Both men were leaning over, peering into the clear water in a crystal bowl placed on the table. It was a very large bowl with no supporting feet, which, half-full, held a good three liters of water. A soft continuous snoring sound was audible, coming from above, and that monotonous sonic base was overlaid, at intervals of about a minute, by the crackling of outbursts of electric sparks.

This is what the two men saw as they looked into the transparent water in the bowl: two little people, alive and naturally colored, described with the precision and fine detail of a carefully-focused microscope; two figurines which moved back and forth, sat down, made gestures, and spoke to one another: Irène and Mattol!

Yes, Irène and Mattol, there in the bowl, very tiny, but exactly as they were in their normal proportions, thousands of leagues from the North Pole, in a cabin on the submarine *Lampas*–and around their reproduction, minuscule but faithful in every respect, the décor of the cabin could be seen in the transparency of the water, in perspective, fading away at the edges. In brief, it was an image of Irène and Mattol in their actual present surroundings.

Glô and Wilfried were observing the active life of these two other people in the magnetic bowl. They were also listening to their impassioned words, for two electric wires hung down from the Teledynamo, each one divided at the bottom into two branches, which terminated in microphones embedded in ear-pieces worn by Glô and Wilfried.

The two Wartecks had been there for a quarter of an hour, watching and listening to Irène and Mattol, when Glô burst out laughing–laughter that was loud and mocking, cruel, savage, sardonic and ferociously joyful...

It was at that moment that Irène de Ciserat, aboard the *Lampas*, thousands of leagues from the Pole, had just said to Louis Mattol, "Perhaps I do, indeed, know things, and can tell you... Oh, Louis, if you could..."–and Lucifer's laughter had cut Irène's speech abruptly short.

371

VIII. The Teledynamo

Of all the Wartecks, Wilfried was the only one for whom Glô truly felt and manifested feelings of affection. It was mainly for that reason that the Baron had entrusted to his cousin the command of Fort Warteck, which would one day be the headquarters of his worldwide operations and the receptacle of the Teledynamo.

It is only fair to add that Wilfried had a vast intelligence, that he possessed encyclopedic knowledge, and that his was a character of rare energy. With Glô's mother, Diana, Wilfried shared the confidence of the Supreme Lord, the uncontested head of the Warteck family, and he knew the full extent and ambitions of Lucifer's projects. There was nothing he did not know about Glô's passions, large or small, and Glô had deemed him worthy of knowing every detail of the scientific means at his disposal in placing the entire world at his mercy.

With Irène de Ciserat and the *Lampas* as objectives, Glô had elected to give the Teledynamo a first trial run—and the two men had been able to convince themselves that the experiment was quite conclusive.

After Lucifer had put an end to the loud laughter with which he had greeted Mattol's test of emancipation and Irène's timid hope, he said to Wilfried, who was still leaning over the magic bowl: "That's good enough, I think, my dear chap! You'll observe that Irène and Mattol, struck by my laughter, consider themselves conclusively defeated, since they're turning away from one another and drawing apart. Although they're no longer talking, they're thinking—you can hear the murmur that their thoughts being translated into distinct words make in the Teledynamo's earpieces—and they've given up. Mattol is deciding to follow the desperate adventure to the end, with the clear intention of committing suicide, if he can, when he sees that all is definitely lost, convinced as he is that even Raymond, if I were to return his free will, would not want to survive the disappearance of his wife.

"Poor Mattol does not know, my dear Wilfried, that one second after zero hour on June 11, all humankind will only live or commit suicide according to my wishes. All intentional actions will only be able to reach accomplishment in the measure that I have fixed, both for humankind collectively and for particular individuals. As for Irène, she is definitely resolved to save all the people she loves from torture and from the spectacle of her own degraded existence. Let us, therefore, pass on, leaving the *Lampas* under the ever-active influence of the Teledynamo...

"Get up! I intend not only to authorize you to look at the machine, but also to explain what you didn't understand at first sight." So saying, Glô rose to his feet, imitated by Wilfried.

The two men took out their earpieces, which were small black spheres pierced with tiny holes, just small enough to fit snugly into the auricular canal. These spheres, still dangling from the electrical wires emerging from the Teledynamo, were deposited in the water in the magic bowl. They did not float on the surface, nor did they fall to the bottom; they remained suspended half way, all four of them at exactly the same level.

Glô, who was hirsutely red-headed, with the profile of vulture, went up the ladder that led to the Teledynamo ahead of his cousin, whose flat hair was a dull blond and who had the face of a Kalmuk. When they reached the top of the staircase, whose top step was large and rounded, the two men stopped and leaned back against the guard-rail. The Teledynamo was before them, in such a fashion that all its workings were visible without their having to shift their gaze from one to another.

"You see, my dear Wilfried," Glô said, "that the Teledynamo, as a whole, is somewhat reminiscent of a more complex version of the alternating current generator constructed in accordance with the latest discoveries of the great physicist Nikola Tesla.[64] That's mere appearance, though, as is the similarity that might cause those four coils to make you think of Ruhmkorff.[65] They're certainly transformers, though! That projector up there, at the extremity of the pylon atop the mass of the workings, does not emit luminous rays but magnetic ones, which are comparable, though far superior, to X-rays, in that they can not only pass through a limited number of solid materials but all matter, made up of whatever elements, if I wish. I'm the one who determines the wavelength of the rays; I'm the one who tells them: you shall go this far, and no further–and they obey. I call them *Omega rays*."

"I understand their effects, "Wilfried put in, earnestly. "The Omega rays transmit your irresistible will over long distances. Furthermore, they work in both directions, consequently reporting back to you the distant effects of the manifestation of your will. Such reports recorded by the Teledynamo, and communicated to you by mans of the earpieces and the magic bowl..."

"Very good, Wilfried."

"Yes–but what is the cause, the means of this prodigy? How does your Teledynamo–whose name comes from *tele*, meaning distant, and *dynamis*, meaning force–project your will instead of familiar waves and rays, such as Hertzian waves or Roentgen rays." [66]

"Look at those seven skulls, Wilfried."

Seven skeletal skulls were arranged along the machine's flank, mounted at 25 centimeter intervals on a slender platinum rod, linked to one another by electrical wires, and to the machine by others five times as thick–effectively, small cables. These skulls lent the Teledynamo a macabre and sinister physiognomy. The electrical wires emerged from their dark orbits; the cables went in through the mouths between the polished teeth and came out through the cavity into which the vertebral columns had been slotted when they skulls had been filled

373

with grey matter, furnished with sensory organs and clad in flesh and skin: the living heads of living people!

There was a momentary silence, during which the formidable Glô von Warteck contemplated the skulls with a solemnity equal to Wilfried's. Then the Baron spoke, suddenly and pompously. "There, in truth, is the marvelous discovery which, brought to perfection, will make me master of the world. Listen! In the Wahallarah, the ancient, secret subterranean temple of Delhi–of which the English are ignorant, and which is known to only a dozen Brahmins cut off from the world that thrives on the Earth's surface–I read about a substance that was known some 18 centuries before the Christian Era, which had the property of absorbing human thought and re-emitting it with an amplification subject to infinite increase. I made a thorough study of all the parts of the Wahallarah that referred to this marvelous substance, and arrived at the conclusion that it was none other than *radium*! Yes, our modern radium–the radium that the Curies and Monsieur Bémont have rediscovered, thousands of years after the Tibetan mages experimented with it.[67] Doubtless frightened by the properties of this divine matter, the mages had not revealed its existence, and died without confiding the secret, save to the Hermetic pages of Wahallarah!"

Glô paused. Wilfried was listening with his eyes closed, impassively. After a moment's meditation, the Baron continued: "You must remember, cousin, that three grams of radium were stolen from Edison's laboratory a few years ago–it made a great deal of noise in that sonorous sphere which is the world of men."

"Yes, I remember," Wilfried said, in a low voice.

"And you've guessed that the thief was me. I needed radium right away. Could I extract it? Years of work! Could I buy it? There were only 50 grams in the entire world at that time, a gram here, a gram there, jealously guarded, watched over, eked out in a miserly fashion, infinitely slowly. The greatest aggregation–three grams–was in Edison's possession, so I went to Madison Square. There's no need to tell you how I went about it. I was already a grand master of hypnosis. I obtained my radium. And with the Wahallarah before my eyes, in the unknown temple of Delhi, I worked..."

There was another pause, during which Glô's face became terrible and truly Luciferian. "What long nights! What pains! How many tortures inflicted, how much blood spilled! A thousand human brains, extracted alive from trepanned skulls, were treated according to a formula that I had succeeded in extracting from the arcana of Wahallarah; they produced three grams of a grey substance...

"That was an era, Wilfried, in which a mature man could not stray into the forest around the temple at dusk without being attacked, dragged way, laid on a stone, scalped, trepanned, de-brained...

"Three grams of that grey substance submitted to the emanations of radium for 30 hours made a condenser, an amplifier, and a projector for my thought, by means of a rudimentary apparatus. After that, the Brahmins had no further need to send their slaves into the forest to capture men... I had only to think, and the men came of their own accord.

"That went on for three years. How many did I kill to obtain the grey matter of which their brains were constituted? The English government, which did not understand what was happening, attributed the near-total depopulation of an entire district to a fictitious famine. But I had enough of the grey substance to fill seven skulls..."

He paused again. This time, it was Wilfried who broke the silence. "Why skulls, and not some other, more scientific, receptacle?"

"Symbolism, Wilfried!" Glô murmured, with a smile. "Symbolism, reminiscence, homage... Yes, thanks to the Wahallarah, I had created a human brain of quasi-divine power; that brain I reproduced seven times over. Was it not only just that the receptacles, the tabernacles, of those brains–superhuman, but composed of human brain-tissue–should be human skulls?"

He paused again, then concluded: "The rest, Wilfried, was mere child's play. The combination of magneto-human radioactivity, Hertzobranlian radioactivity and Crookes-Roentgen radioactivity with mechanical means of transmission and reception;[68] the amalgamation of the whole with a captor-condenser-projector–which is there, to the left of the Teledynamo, and which captures, condenses and projects perispiritual fluid–and I had a machine which amplifies the effluvia of my brain infinitely. It manifests with incalculable power all the faculties of spell-casting, hypnotism, thought-reading, suggestion, disincarnation–in sum, those of the Sorcerer Supreme–that I had acquired in my Hermetic studies, from the books of Nicholas Flamel to the wall-decorations of the Wahallarah..."

He fell silent–but almost immediately raised a hand, and said: "But..." Then he fell silent again.

Wilfried had just closed his eyes; after a moment, he opened them again, turned to the Supreme Lord, and queried: "But...?"

"But my Teledynamo isn't perfect," Glô said. "As yet, it can only act at one point at a time, only one! It cannot perform several actions simultaneously. I have seven skulls, Wilfried, but I only have one centralizer-diffuser–there, that crystal-lined platinum box. Do you understand?

"While I'm acting upon the individuals delimited by the hull of the *Lampas*–which I have isolated–I cannot act, for example, upon the Nyctalope, of whom I know nothing since May 21. And I can't act preferentially upon the Nyctalope, because I don't have at hand the appropriate elements to open his mind to me, so to speak. It would be necessary for me to measure, by means of the cephalometer you see there, the fluidic capacity of his will. That capacity, like those of Prillant and Lourmel, is so powerful that it goes off the scale of that cephalometer."

"So?" said Wilfried, almost violently.

"So my artisans are laboring in the workshops of the *Kaiser-Gott*. I'm sure that I'll have six more centralizer-diffusers in six crystal-lined platinum boxes by midnight on June 9. I'll have a 1,000-degree cephalometer–that one's only a 100-degrees. I'll also have six more radioactive crystal bowls, so that we can reproduce and see in their electrified water scenes that I produce simultaneously in seven different places–even if those places are on the other side of the world from me, or from one another, in the remotest depths of the Pacific or at the very center of the Earth! Understand that, Wilfried!

"Even if destiny–for there are still unknowns that destiny has hidden from me–determines that the seven items of apparatus are not all ready by midnight on June 9, I shall nevertheless be certain of defeating the Nyctalope..."

He stopped short, lifted his clenched fists and howled with fury and hatred. "The Nyctalope! My sole enemy! The one who corresponds with the enigmatic predictions of the Kabbalah, which I was only able to decipher last night..."

"Oh!" said Wilfried, excitedly. "You've finally managed to decipher the Kaballah's verbal labyrinth?"

"Yes."

"And what does it say?"

"It says: *Lucifer will only be defeated by a man whose eyes dissipate the darkness. Lucifer will be defeated if the man is not dead at the hour of the day equal to the day of the month, subtracted from the age of the Moon on that day...* It was a lengthy calculation; I'll spare you the details. The result was: the 10th hour of the 10th day of the month, the 16th lunar day, the sixth month of the year. To recapitulate: day, ten; day of the month, ten; the difference between that day and the age of the Moon on that day, six–which, subtracting ten from 16 gives six... Which is, therefore, the sixth month, June–for on June 10, the Moon is in the 16th day of its cycle, which proves the accuracy of my calculation."

"So you must kill the Nyctalope by 10 a.m. on June 10, at the latest," said Wilfried. "If not, you're lost, according to the infallible and irrevocable Kabbalah."

"Yes, Wilfried! But I repeat that, even if jealous destiny should prevent my Teledynamo from being ready by the fateful hour, I'm certain to defeat the Nyctalope."

"How?"

"Simply by leaving the Teledynamo to act on the environment of the *Lampas*."

"I understand, but..."

"Yes, Wilfried?"

"The Nyctalope, wherever he is and whatever he is doing, will fly to the aid of the *Lampas* as soon as he finds out that Irène and Henri are in danger. And you will know that he has done so via someone you can reach who is presently in contact with the Nyctalope–La Païli, for example."

"Yes–or Rupert VI, since I don't know what has become of Hunter, my brother. That puzzles me, too, and it's another reason why I'm impatient for the Teledynamo and the cephalometer to be ready. The field of Hunter's perispirit suddenly vanished on May 24. He was in Paris then, at Professor Lourmel's house. But let's put that aside. You're right–the Nyctalope, once warned, will rush to help Irène and Henri. By then, Irène and Henri will be in the submarine station. An ambush will be set and Leo Saint-Clair will be killed, in some vulgar manner–a dagger-thrust or a bullet from a gun. Killed–even though I promised La Païli that, if she did not yield, she'd be forced to witness her lover's... Yes, yes, she'll see her lover–but as a corpse!"

He fell silent, quivering.

Wilfried said nothing. He stared at the Teledynamo. Little by little, Glô calmed down.

Minutes went by. Eventually, Wilfried said, softly: "Glô, I admire you even more, if that's possible, than I did yesterday–but I'd also like you to hold me in slightly higher esteem with each passing day. You've explained what I didn't understand in regard to your wondrous Teledynamo. Would you do me the honor of accepting something from me which, by sparing you a little work and occasionally saving you a few minutes' time, will be some little use to you and will make you think of me with pleasure?"

"What is it?" Glô asked, astonished.

"When you came in just now, cousin, you did not notice that there was an additional object in the cupola. Look over there!"

"Oh!" cried Glô, visibly pleased. "The beautiful globe! Did you build it, design it and paint it yourself?"

"I did–but wait! What you see is nothing, for you're seeing it motionless, inert and solid. Now, my dear Glô..."

"What?"

"That globe is alive!"

"Alive?"

"Come, Glô."

Preceded, this time, by his cousin and loyal subject, Glô von Warteck went down the steps that led to the Teledynamo. Between the pedestal and a divan, on the opposite side to the one where the table with the magic bowl was set, was a magnificent terrestrial globe mounted in a nickel bracket, whose circumference measured two meters. The mountains were depicted in relief; subtly different shades distinguished the various nations and their colonies, or areas of influence.

"Sit down on the divan, Glô," said Wilfried.

The Supreme Lord obeyed. He was facing the globe, but he raised his head slightly, so that his eyes, looking straight ahead, were fixed upon the equator. If, when confronted by a map of the world, one's eyes are drawn to a particular point, it is always the equator, the center of the field of view.

Wilfried sat down next to Glô, who was now most intrigued, but did not even think of reading his cousin's mind telepathically, as he could easily have done.

"We have Asia before us," Wilfried said, "and a part of Australia. I imagine that you would prefer to see, without having to lift a finger, the region in which the *Lampas* is presently sailing?"

"Yes, certainly," said Glô, smiling.

"Well, be patient for a few minutes. Before I satisfy your desire, let me first tell you an interesting little story."

"I'm listening, my dear fellow!"

"Do you remember Professor Weilich of Berlin?"

"Perfectly–small, jaundiced, peevish."

"Yes. When you left Berlin, I stayed there for another year before joining you in Calcutta. I became very close to Professor Weilich and often went to see him. At his home, I made the acquaintance of Herman Blaff..."

"The botanist who died young?"

"Yes–and this is how he died. His tragic death is connected to the story of this globe.

"After returning from a trip to Paris, during which I had had no news of Professor Weilich or Hermann, I went to visit the young botanist, who had become my close friend.

"A thunderclap sounded as I was going into his workroom. 'You've brought me a storm!' Hermann exclaimed, as he offered me his hand. We both paused for a minute to gaze at the dark sky heaped with enormous clouds–the window was wide open, because of the dull heat of the summer afternoon. The thunder rumbled again as we sat down, Hermann on his rotating chair, me in a low quilted armchair that was next to his workbench.

"It was only then that I noticed an object on the familiar bench that I had never seen before: a terrestrial globe. It was of moderate size, about 50 centimeters tall, counting its oak frame. With a flick of my hand I turned the multicolored ball, whose axis was inclined at 45 degrees. 'That's a pretty globe you have there,' I said. 'Did you buy it?'

" 'No,' Hermann replied. 'I received it today, in my capacity as executor of the will of our old friend Weilich...'

" 'Oh, he's dead!' I said, surprised

" 'Yes and he left me... Hold on! Since you're here, you might be able to solve the puzzle...'

" 'What puzzle?'

" 'Take this and read it–this piece of paper was attached by a bit of thread to the North Pole of the globe.' And Blaff passed me a piece of yellowed paper that had been on the table in front of him. I took it and read these words, written in Gothic script: *Weilich's living globe. Interrogate it; it will answer.*

" 'Well?' he said.

" 'I don't understand,' I replied. Puzzled, I studied the globe. It was new, similar to all terrestrial globes with inclined axes, about 50 centimeters tall, frame included, and about a meter in circumference. The marine currents were marked in a deeper blue than the pale blue of the sea; the trade winds were indicated by hundreds of little red arrows; black lines marked the meridians and lines of latitude; the various countries were distinguished, as usual, by different colors. 'There's nothing extraordinary about it,' I murmured.

"A dull roll of thunder echoed in the sky. 'You'd better close the window,' I said, immediately, with that disquiet which storms elicit from people of nervous temperament.

" 'You don't understand, then?' Hermann said, paying no attention to my request.

" 'No–do you think this means something? Strictly speaking, any mobile globe is a living thing, which turns, speaks to our eyes and mind... *Interrogate it; it will answer*, right?'

" 'What do you mean, right?'

" 'It's obvious!' I cried, a trifle annoyed by Hermann's persistence and his mute refusal to close the window. 'It's not difficult. If I need to know where some city, river or mountain is located, I interrogate the globe, and it answers.'

" 'I thought the same thing,' Hermann replied, mockingly, 'but I knew Weilich well, and he never opened his mouth to say nothing–and yet these Gothic characters that he left me along with the globe aren't saying anything, if the explanation you've given is correct!'

"A lightning-flash zigzagged across the breadth of the window, immediately followed by a violent clap of thunder, and rain began to fall. 'It'll be a lovely storm!' Herman said, getting to his feet.

"I thought that he was going to close the window and rejoiced in anticipation–but he contented himself with darting a glance outside before fixing his eyes on me. Gazing distractedly at the globe, without ceasing to think about the danger of thunderbolts. I said: 'Yesterday's newspapers reported that an extraordinary storm laid waste to an entire village in America. Hopefully, this one isn't starting to go the same way...' I leapt to my feet, my tongue stuck to my palate, my throat suddenly constricted.

" 'What's the matter?' Hermann said.

" 'I...I...' I made a violent effort, and said, abruptly: 'Didn't you see... the globe turn?'

" 'Come on, Wilfried!' Hermann said.

" 'It turned, I tell you–it turned! When I pronounced the word America, it suddenly turned–and now, America is directly in front of me!' We looked at one another and I saw him grow pale.

" 'How pale you are!' he murmured. 'Are you quite certain that you haven't had a hallucination? The storm...would you like me to close the window?'

"I suddenly felt ashamed and calmed down. *Come on!* I said to myself. *We're behaving like children! The globe turned, I'm sure of it–but what's frightening about that? Let's consider the matter, don't you think?* I was no longer thinking about the storm or the open window. I didn't see the lightning flashes zigzagging from minute to minute; I didn't hear the almost uninterrupted rolling of the thunder. 'Look at it, Hermann. You see that America is directly in front of me. Stay where you are, facing it. The globe is directly between us–we are at the antipodes. Now you pronounce the word America–we'll soon see.'

"Hermann stared at the globe, hesitantly. Then, in a blank voice, he suddenly said: 'America!' And the globe turned! Yes, it turned, from right to left. There was a rapid, smooth movement, curtly halted. The Chinese empire and Hindustan were in front of me.

" 'Prussia!' I cried, mechanically. The globe turned through three-quarters of a circle, and I had Prussia before my eyes.

" 'We have to find out how it works!' Hermann howled, with great excitement. 'We have to find out!' Seizing the globe by its base he lifted it up and ran to the window. There, leaning into the brighter outdoor light, he examined the entire surface of the globe, searching feverishly for some opening, some operative mechanism, anything...

"I went towards him, but I was blinded by a lightning-flash. A brutal commotion caused me to stagger–and amid the noise of a frightful clap of thunder, I saw my friend fall, collapsing on the floor.

"I hurled myself forward–but all I could make out was a blackened, rigid, carbonized face–a near-supernatural thing. The lightning bolt that had killed Hermann had burned the rigid colored envelope of the globe, consuming it within a second. The frame alone was intact–and it supported a bizarre assembly of minuscule mechanisms, innumerable and incomprehensible...

"As words and exclamations emerged instinctively from my mouth, my eyes remarked that some of these mechanisms were reminiscent of certain parts of a phonograph, and were marvelously sensitive to the sounds of my voice..."

Wilfried paused for a few seconds, before concluding, with a smile: "I've reconstructed that terrestrial globe on a large scale. Not only does it turn on its ordinary axis, but it is mobile on another axis, perpendicular to the first, which goes through the equator–in sum, it moves in any direction, dipping and coming erect again, in such a manner as to present directly to the eyes of the observer the exact part of the world that he desires to examine. Glô, I offer this globe to you, and beg you to accept it. In order to put it to the test immediately, I have only to press this button to render the globe sensible to the human voice and to the syllables of the geographical terms inscribed on its surface."

So saying, Wilfried got up, marched towards the globe, leaned over it and pressed an ivory button that stood out visibly from the metal base. Then he returned to sit beside the Supreme Lord.

Gravely, he pronounced the word "Labrador!"

The globe immediately dipped, turned, shifted, and suddenly became immobile. The coast of Labrador, in the north-west of Canada, was directly facing Lucifer.

IX. "It Won't Be Easy!"

Coincidences occur. When fortunate, they bring about an eighteenth of Brumaire; when unfortunate, they produce a Waterloo.[69]

On June 4, at the very moment when Glô and Wilfried were under the cupola of Fort Warteck looking at the spectacle offered to them by the magic bowl, a few minutes before they climbed the stairway to the Teledynamo, Saint-Clair, Lourmel and Sir Patrick Swires were with Rupert VI in a specially-prepared cabin on the *Uberalles* at Cape Flora, in a large cage of glass similar to the one in which Hunter had died in the house at Auteuil.

Saint-Clair, Lourmel and Sir Patrick wanted to interrogate Rupert VI while he was hypnotized, in the radioactive atmosphere that put the subject beyond Lucifer's potential control, and which gave the same subject the faculty of seeing at a distance with unlimited range. Before putting his plan for the supreme offensive against Lucifer and Fort Warteck into action, the Nyctalope wanted to know what was happening in his enemy's lair.

That morning, Rupert VI was perfectly docile, and he had lost none of the visual acuity with which he depicted, described and reproduced what he saw and heard.

Sir Patrick was attending such a session for the first time in his life. Not for an instant did he doubt the reality of the visions that Rupert VI registered in his hypnotic state, for the Englishman had heard so many extraordinary things in the preceding 24 hours that he could no longer doubt or be astonished by what was taking place. However, while he listened to the formidable, fantastic and unimaginable speech that emerged from Rupert VI's mouth, reproducing the words simultaneously pronounced at the North Pole by Lucifer as he explained the Teledynamo to his half-brother, Sir Patrick used up the last vestiges of the amazement held in reserve in the depths of his brain. Like a true Briton, though, he let nothing show, remaining impassive.

As for Saint-Clair and Lourmel, they were possessed by conflicting emotions: dread and sorrowful pity for Irène, Henri, Mattol, Raymond and his crew; hope that they might be saved; gravely troubled perplexity as to the means that they might employ–for the plight of the *Lampas* upset part of the Nyctalope's action plan–admiration for Lucifer's genius, mingled with horror provoked by the use he had made of it and terrible apprehension regarding the use he was preparing to make; the joy of learning that the Teledynamo was imperfect, in such a precise fashion–a precision that would assist the Nyctalope in the orientation of his offensive–the desire to know everything that was being done, said and prepared at Fort Warteck; and, at the same time impatience regarding the prolongation of the session while precious minutes sped by...

Eventually, they were party to Wilfried's story regarding the living globe, and the brief demonstration that followed it.

After a pause, Rupert concluded: "Glô and Wilfried are leaving the cupola by means of the staircase in the Teledynamo's pedestal. They're going down. At the foot of the stair, they're turning left into a corridor. A door. A workroom. They're passing through it. Another door. The dining-room. A meal is served. They're sitting down. They're eating..."

"Enough!" said the Nyctalope. "Let's get on. Wake him up, Professor! We must act–but my plan will have to be profoundly modified. We'll have to hold another council, like yesterday's."

"After lunch?" said Sir Patrick.

"No, before. We'll eat afterwards."

"As you wish."

When Rupert VI was woken up, he was so exhausted that he almost fainted, but Lourmel had taken the precaution of putting a small flask of an *ad hoc* elixir in his coat pocket. Rupert VI drank the restorative liquor and recovered immediately. The bell-jar was lifted up and they came out. They left Rupert VI behind, because the radioactive environment, resistant to Lucifer's distant fluids, made it impossible for a subject to project his perispirit, in response to a summons from the Supreme Lord. One of Sir Patrick's launches took the three leaders back to Elmwood.

The council of war was immediately assembled, comprising exactly the same individuals as the day before. Once the session had been opened by the chairman, Sir Patrick Swires, the Nyctalope revealed the substance of Rupert VI's new revelations, without unnecessary details, but comprehensively. He concluded: "The most important thing in all of this, for us, is the Teledynamo–and the fact that Lucifer will be incapable, until midnight on June 9, of carrying out several distant actions simultaneously. For many hours to come, he and his prodigious machine will be entirely preoccupied with the *Lampas*. He will only be able to exercise a very feeble influence on Rupert VI, using his brain alone–his own human brain–without the amplificatory effect of the Teledynamo. And Lucifer cannot make that feeble influence effective because Rupert is in the bell-jar, completely isolated from any magnetism."

"What about me, Leo?" asked Laurence Païli.

"Yes, my darling Laure, Lucifer mentioned you, and the manner in which Rupert VI might, by capturing your thoughts, learn what you knew about me, so that he could use it to send me racing to help the *Lampas*. By that means, Lucifer thought to have me killed in some vulgar manner, as he put it, by the most banal of ambushes. Well, let's leave him to it. If, after having tried in vain to influence Rupert VI, Lucifer passes on to you, Laure, and plants a suggestion in your mind, we'll let him play the enemy and listen to what he inspires you to tell me. As we're now forewarned and won't be fooled, perhaps what you say to me will be useful rather than inimical."

"I hope so!" said Laurence, exchanging glances with Grisyl, who was sitting beside her.

Then the young and hot-headed Lieutenant Romski, seized by a self-sacrificial impulse, took advantage of the fact that Saint-Clair did not resume speaking immediately, and cried: "Messieurs, I understand that our great leader the Nyctalope does not only wish to defeat Lucifer, but to obtain that victory with the least possible risk to our lives–all our lives, whether we are soldiers or colleagues–but what are our lives worth in proportion to the benefit that all humankind will derive from the annihilation of Lucifer? Nothing! Or, rather, they are only worth what they contribute to that victory."

"Bravo!" Sergeant Berge could not help adding, enthusiastically. He had the same temperament and generous character as his immediate superior.

The latter continued: "Now, it seems to me that the Nyctalope is taking too much risk with his own life, and not enough with ours–all of which added together are not as precious as his alone. Do we need to be so careful? No! If our deaths could safeguard the Nyctalope's and ensure victory, we would die happily. This is what I propose, therefore–begging Monsieur de Saint-Clair's pardon for rendering his plan unnecessary." Standing up with his eyes aflame and his face enraptured by heroism, Romski concluded: "The crews of the RC1, RC2 and RC3 will take off in their respective aircraft. They will proceed directly to the Pole at a great height. Once there, they will spiral down above Fort Warteck, getting as close to it as possible, and when they reach the fort, they will release all their bombs. Three times 20 is 60: 60 bombs, of which one alone would flatten the Panthéon in Paris! In three minutes, Fort Warteck will be reduced to a heap of shapeless ruins, and Lucifer, his Teledynamo, Wilfried and all his company to burned and broken corpses! In the meantime, the Nyctalope, Captain Girard, Corsat and Pilou, aboard the RC4, and the *Uberalles*, with Professor Lourmel and its crew, will leave before us in order to launch a simultaneous attack on the Wartecks' submarine station. It will be easy enough for the Nyctalope and Commander Saincer to take possession of the station and the *Kaiser-Gott*. It is highly probable, if not certain, that the detonation of 60 bombs will immediately reduce the RC1, RC2 and RC3 to dust, along with their pilots and mechanics, but so what? You can raise a commemorative memorial to us at the North Pole, on the ruins of Fort Warteck!"

Cheers and applause burst forth; all the personnel of the three aircraft approved of Romski's heroic enthusiasm for self-sacrifice. Laurence and Grisyl had eyes full of tears. Corsat and Pilou envied Romski; Captain Girard shook his hand; the Englishmen admired him; Lourmel cried: "Ah, the brave lads!"

Saint-Clair, who had risen to his feet, went to embrace the Polish officer fraternally, but when the general emotion had calmed down somewhat, the Nyctalope began speaking again, with the necessary authority.

"Before anything else," he said, "let's thank Lieutenant Romski for his generous offer, and also thank these young men who, by their loud applause and cheers, immediately declared their willingness to die gladly in his company. That's wonderful! Personally, I'm touched to the bottom of my heart–and I know that I would have to battle hard against Romski and his noble cohort if all I had to oppose him was an equivalent determination to sacrifice myself... But no, my friends, no. This isn't a matter of dying in order to win, for you or for me; it's a matter of winning in order to live. We run the risk of being killed, that's taken for granted–and I assure you that you will be just as exposed to that risk as I shall be–but a victory of the sort that Lieutenant Romski would obtain, if I accepted his sacrifice, is not the sort of victory we need to win.

"Yesterday and just now, I revealed to you the essentials of my strategy and my tactics. Romski's generous intervention obliges me to specify my objectives, in order that you and he will understand why I will not accept his sacrifice. We must not only defeat Lucifer, capture him–dead or alive–and make it impossible for him to do any harm, and do the same with all his fanatical supporters, but we must also capture the Teledynamo intact, to study it, to make use of it in the cause of scientific progress, while taking every precaution to ensure that no perverse human being will ever again be able to attempt what we have to prevent Lucifer from accomplishing.

"The total destruction of Fort Warteck, which would be the inevitable result of the kind of offensive the Romski proposes, would annihilate not only the Teledynamo but the living globe and many other machines and agencies that it would be extremely useful for us to discover and study. A true victory, on the other hand, would give the conqueror the benefit of all the advantages by which by means of which the enemy nearly triumphed. The real conqueror, in this case, will neither be me, nor you, nor the company of which we are all a part, but the entirety of humankind.

"To these general considerations, I add others. Since it is possible that we might win without risking any of our lives, it would be criminal for me to accept an incomplete victory ensured by the certain death of the youngest among us. We must not forget, either, that Laurence Païli's mother is in Fort Warteck..."

"Oh, Leo!" cried Laurence, so deeply moved that tears were running down her lovely face. "Leo, if my mother could hear us and speak to us, she would say: 'Don't think about me! Kill Lucifer, to save the world!' "

"Yes!" said the Nyctalope. "And I would expect no less of your nobility, Laure–but your mother's presence in Fort Warteck is, for me, merely one reason among others. I won't repeat them, but I say this to Romski: Are you convinced, my friend, that the necessity is not to die in order to win, but to win in order to live?"

"Pardon me, Monsieur!" said Romski, emotionally. "I'm convinced. You will win so that the world may live. But..."

"But what?" Saint-Clair echoed, smiling.

"But it won't be easy!"

"Of course not!" cried the Nyctalope. "If it were going to be easy, you wouldn't have proposed that you and your companions should commit suicide to make it less difficult!" And immediately after that declaration, made with a smile, he said: "Messieurs, the matter is closed. Has anyone else any remark or proposition to make regarding my plan of action?"

No one said a word.

"In that case, Messieurs," Saint-Clair concluded, "here are my orders." And the Nyctalope spoke, no longer as a member of a council but as the commander-in-chief, assuming all the prerogatives and all the responsibilities of power.

X. Laure, Grisyl and Romski

It was 2:20 p.m. on June 4 when the Nyctalope, having finished giving orders and allocating roles in the unfolding tragedy, cheerfully declared: "I'm dying of hunger–let's eat!" Yes, cheerfully–for he possessed the kind of combative temperament for which a fight, on whatever scale and however grave its perils might be, always has an element of ardent vitality, and hence of joy.

"Grisyl!" called Laurence–and as the young woman came towards her, La Païli seized the hand of Lieutenant Romski, who was standing beside her, and whispered: "Follow us without anyone noticing. I need to talk to you." Then, aloud, to Grisyl, she said: "Let's go take a look at the dining-room. We've been too forgetful of the fact that we're women."

The overheard remark generated smiles around her. Saint-Clair made a gesture of approval–from some way off, for he was at the back of the room giving supplementary instructions to Sir Patrick Swires, in the presence of Lourmel and Captain Girard.

Twenty-eight places had been set for the members of the council of war in one of Elmwood station's hangars, on a long table made up of boards on trestles. The English mission included an Irish cook and four Eskimo assistants, whose four wives had been hastily trained as waitresses. Everyone thought that when she left the station's main building, where the council had been held, Laurence Païli was going to the dining-room. No one whose gaze might have followed her, intentionally or otherwise, would have suspected anything else. But once in the "feasting hangar," as Pilou facetiously called it, the young woman drew Grisyl and Romski towards a side door, and immediately said to the Polish officer: "If Saint-Clair, Lourmel and Patrick come in, go over there–no one must see you talking to me."

"All right."

La Païli went on, gravely and rapidly: "Grisyl, you're utterly determined, like me, to help Leo Saint-Clair, even if he doesn't wish it?"

"Utterly," the young woman replied, resolutely.

"And you, Romski–will you put your strength and your life at my disposal?"

The officer blushed like a child, and his blue eyes sparkled as he said: "I'm yours, Madame, with all my heart. And since I feel that we're approaching a critical moment, let me tell you that, since I have known you, I have seen no other solution for me than death. When I offered my life to the Nyctalope just now, it was to you that I was giving it."

"I accept it," Laurence said, simply.

The hot-headed young man and the illustrious seductress looked at one another, the former giving away his soul without asking anything in return, the latter accepting it without promising anything in return.

"Ladislas," La Païli murmured, "if you die in the course of what we are going to do, tell yourself that I, living, shall not experience a single moment of joy that I do not associate with you–and that, should I die, it will be for the same cause as you."

She offered him her hand. He took it, kissed it for a long time, and let it fall back. Coolly and calmly, he became the perfect instrument, which the audacious virtuoso might use without apprehension. "I'm ready," he said.

The dialogue proceeded rapidly.

"You will order Berge and Dopp to cede their places on the RC3 to Grisyl and me."

"Yes."

"You will leave the RC1 and the RC2 to constitute the RC4's reserve and you will fly to the North Pole at top speed."

"Without any explanations?"

"None."

"All right."

"Will it be possible, after we touch down, for us to change places very rapidly, in order to make anyone watching believe that it was me who was piloting the aircraft?"

"Yes, quite easily."

"Good. Grisyl will have ropes ready. She'll tie you up, as if you were our prisoner."

"Understood."

"And you'll have no other role to play but that of a bewildered and resigned captive."

"Is that all?" said Romski, regretfully.

"Until the time when you are about to be killed," Laure added, "or until the moment when, perhaps having need of you, I have you set free or set you free myself."

"I shall hope for the second alternative, but I shall be ever-ready for the first."

"Thank you. That's all, my dear friend."

"Can't you tell me any more?"

"I don't know any more myself."

"But what are your plans?"

"Uncertain, vague and hazardous, as well as mutually contradictory–my plans will only reach the point of choice or decision when Grisyl and I find ourselves confronted by Lucifer, Wilfried or some other enemy."

"Do you intend to kill Lucifer?"

"Perhaps."

"So you'll be carrying a weapon?"

"Yes, a silent Browning."

"And you, Mademoiselle?"

"Me too," said Grisyl.

"I know enough of all these strange things," Romski said, "to think that, on seeing you or learning of your presence, Lucifer will be suspicious, and will probably be reluctant to have you brought to him."

Laurence smiled at the young man's naivete. Prudently, she replied: "We shall see." Immediately thereafter, she added: "Go, Romski!" She opened the door.

The officer slipped out, just as Lourmel and the Nyctalope, preceded by Sir Patrick and Captain Girard, came into the hangar from the other side. Laurence pretended to be talking to a waitress through the half-open door through which the Pole had departed. "Yes, yes," she said, in English. "Do hurry." The Eskimos at the station, to which they had belonged for two years, understood the language of their habitual masters quite well.

Closing the door again, she rejoined Grisyl, who hurriedly set about pretending to put the place-settings in better order.

The other members of the council followed the Nyctalope into the hangar, sat down, and began to eat in relative silence. The food was abundant and tasty. The air of the polar regions sharpens the appetite, to the extent that none of these men and women were inhibited by their personal emotions or the gravity of the situation from taking the nourishment they needed. Everyone knew that they would need their physical strength, without which mental energy and intellectual lucidity cannot long maintain their intensity in action.

After the meal, everyone set about doing what needed to be done to execute the Nyctalope's orders within the allotted time. These were the various things that had to be done between 3 and 8 p.m. on June 4: the gathering together of every piece of white-colored cloth–including furs, sheets and clothing– that was to be found in Elmwood station or the submarine *Uberalles*; the compilation of an inventory of these materials and their distribution, according to individual need, among the 16 men comprising the crews of the four aircraft and the eight Englishmen who were to join these crews by way of reinforcement; and the arming of every individual, in the aeroplanes as well as in the submarine, with two Brownings and ten six-shot ammunition-clips, a hatchet and a knife. Saint-Clair, Corsat and Pilou still had their silent pistols, of course; Captain Girard, Sir Patrick and Elias Carter, who were traveling with them in the RC4, were furnished with spare pistols of a similar type from the Nyctalope's luggage.

When everyone was hard at work and all these various operations were under way, Leo Saint-Clair and Elias Carter, the geographer, went up to the top of the basalt cliff overlooking Elmwood and, for nearly an hour, Saint-Clair looked silently and meditatively northwards, studying the immense polar wastes. Because summer was coming, slightly early this year, there had been considerable breakage of the ice a few days earlier. The contours of Northbrook Island, which constituted part of Cape Flora, stood out clearly. To the north of the island, beyond a chaplet of black reefs, at the opening of the channel leading to the Victoria Sea, was a chaos of stretches of grey water and huge ice-floes with gnarled surfaces, undulating in the waves. Far away in the distance, a large space gave the illusion of open sea, but icebergs calved from glaciers were heaped up on the neighboring land-based ice-sheets; almost everywhere there were long ranges of large aggregations known as hummocks, welded by fallen snow and refrozen to form abrupt slopes, extending as far as the eye could see.

The Sun was low on the horizon, above which it seemed to be rolling like a golden discus along a circular track. It never set at this time of year, its light varying only with the weather; at present, it was projecting over this desolate landscape a sinister Apocalyptic radiance, because it was partly veiled by a sort of mist, which decomposed its light into a spectrum dominated by sallow orange and somber red. Above the glacial expanses, the sky was like a low vault composed of a lugubrious red fog.

"What a spectacle of desolation and horror!" said the Nyctalope, softly.

"It's not always like this," said Carter, long familiarity having rendered him far less sensitive to such terrestrial and solar phantasmagorias than Saint-Clair was. "Sometimes, especially at this time of year, the sky is pure and the Sun clear, and then it's a fairyland of luminous whites and fantastic blues..."

The Nyctalope made no reply. He continued his contemplation. Soon, though, he saw neither ice nor water; the sinister games of the Sun and clouds left him indifferent. He saw with the eyes of his imagination alone: constructions of basalt partly covered by snow and ice; and, at the summit of the tallest of those buildings, a sparkling dome—the crystal dome under which the complex, mysterious and macabre Teledynamo squatted, with its seven skeletal skulls...

"Monsieur," said a voice next to him, "it's time to go back to the station."

Saint-Clair shivered. Slowly, he unfolded his arms, looked at Elias Carter for a few seconds before he recognized him, and said: "That's right—let's go down."

XI. Professor Lourmel's Idea

On the outskirts of the station, Leo Saint-Clair saw Professor Lourmel running towards him.

"Something new, Professor?" the Nyctalope said.

"As regards events, no. In my head, yes." Taking Saint-Clair by the arm, the Professor spoke rapidly, while continuing to walk with him towards the buildings. "My dear friend, cast your mind back to the point you were at when, in the council, you envisaged what we might do with Laurence if your diva, in accordance with Rupert VI's revelations, were to be hypnotized and subject to Lucifer's suggestive influence."

"I remember," said the Nyctalope.

"You said then...?"

"I said, in effect: We'll let him play the enemy, let him plant a suggestion in Laure's mind, and we'll listen to what he inspires you to tell us. As we're now forewarned and won't be fooled, perhaps what you say to me will be useful rather than inimical. That's what I said."

Lourmel cut him off abruptly. "No!"

"What do you mean, no?" said Saint-Clair, astonished.

"You'll see. How do you know that Lucifer, hypnotizing Laurence at a distance, won't be able to read the young woman's thoughts as well? How do you know that he won't learn by that means everything she knows about our plans–your plan, your imminent action?"

"Oh! That's true!" said the Nyctalope, shivering.

"I think so too–so it's necessary to modify it. It's necessary to do something other than what you supposed then."

"How?"

"Very simply. Since Lucifer intends to make use of Laurence or Rupert VI, let's remove Rupert VI and Laurence from his as-yet-limited power. We know all about Lucifer, the Teledynamo and Fort Warteck. We even know that the accursed von Warteck will inform us, via Laurence or Rupert, that Irène, Henri and the *Lampas* are at the submarine station. What good does it do, then, to leave Laurence and Rupert at his disposition? That might be useful to him, but it is not useful to us."

"So?"

"So, enclose Laurence and Rupert in the radioactive bell-jar. Then, when he seeks to plant suggestions in their minds, Lucifer will not find them–just as, previously, there was an interval in which he could no longer find Hunter."

"True again–very true!" Saint-Clair said, approvingly. "But you can't keep them in the atmosphere of the bell-jar indefinitely. Exactly when, and for how long...?"

"That objection's anticipated. Since you agree with me, I'll take Laurence aboard the *Uberalles* immediately. She and Rupert will be in the cabin where the bell-jar is, with me keeping a close watch on them. As soon as one or other of them betrays Lucifer's magnetic influence by their attitude, I'll put them in the bell-jar!"

Despite the seriousness of these conjectures, Saint-Clair could not help smiling, and his smile broadened as a thought struck him. "My dear Professor," he said, "I agree entirely, Yes, that's what we must do. It's all the more necessary to do it because it gives us a good reason for preventing Laure from taking part in my expedition against Fort Warteck. She is absolutely determined to come. How could I oppose it? I had no good reason to make her stay here instead of risking her life with mine–until now, thanks to your idea..."

"It's settled, then."

"It's settled."

"You'll talk to Laurence right away?"

"Right away–but you must come too and talk to her. It will be difficult to convince her."

"Let's go!"

The two men went into Elmwood's main building together. Everyone was working hard on the preparation of the white clothing demanded by the Nyctalope. La Païli and Grisyl were in a group with Romski, Berge, Dopp and Wolf.

"Laure!" called Saint-Clair. The diva raised her head. "Would you come here for a moment? The Professor and I need to talk to you."

The young woman got up, already anxious, for she knew that anything new that came up might derail her plan of action–the enigmatic plan that also involved Grisyl, and into which the singer had so easily drawn Lieutenant Romski, without revealing its entirety. With Saint-Clair and Lourmel, Laurence went into a small room, which normally served as Sir Patrick Swires's study.

"Listen, Laure," Saint-Clair said, gravely, after closing the door to the main hall. Taking his lover's hands in his, he explained the dangers presented by Lucifer's magnetic influence over her, and the Professor's idea, adding further arguments. From time to time, Lourmel lent a supporting comment to the Nyctalope's speech. The more the latter said, the more Laurence suffered, for she could not deny that Saint-Clair and Lourmel were right. She could see no valid argument with which to oppose them, and she could see the implicit consequence of it all: she would not be able to depart on the RC3 with Romski and Grisyl.

Her exasperation was so intense that she interrupted Saint-Clair to say, with the mixture of sincerity and reticence that is not the least of the manifestations of amorous devotion: "But in order to be with you without getting in your way, I wanted to ask you if Grisyl and I might take the places of Berge and Dopp in Romski's aircraft, while they traveled in yours!"

Thus, in Laurence's mind, one detail of her plan was modified; it was not surreptitiously that she and Grisyl would replace Berge and Dopp, but with the Nyctalope's consent—for the young woman thought that her lover could not, in the final analysis, find any powerful reason for refusing to let her take part, with Grisyl, in the expedition. But the reason already existed!

"I would indeed have given you permission, Laure," Saint-Clair said, "but we have to make sure that the Professor does not expose me to the dangers that we would all run if Lucifer were to take control of your mind. We have to yield to the actual necessity—we have to, my darling Laure."

Yes, that would have been the "actual necessity," as the Nyctalope put it, if La Païli's plan had not existed. For her, though, the imperious necessity was to do, with Grisyl and Romski, what she had planned—which would, she thought, ensure a conclusive victory without exposing the Nyctalope to more than a minimum of danger.

She was tempted to reply to Saint-Clair's objections by exposing her own plan, but she kept silent. He would never consent! He would even be capable of putting Romski under arrest to prevent its execution, and organizing a system of surveillance that would make it absolutely impossible for her and Grisyl to act.

La Païli gave in, but reserved the intention of acting on her own behalf, if the opportunity arose. Why should it not arise? she said to herself. Smiling, her eyes moist with emotion, proud of the afterthought that gave her words a meaning that Saint-Clair would not suspect, she murmured: "Whoever has love for a guide and support walks with a calm and sure tread, watched over by the gods..."

"Laure, my darling Laure, my beloved!"

Lourmel had made a discreet exit. The two lovers bid one another adieu, for La Païli was going aboard the *Uberalles*, which would soon depart; she would not see Saint-Clair again until after the victory...

They were entwined, standing face to face, looking at one another, both very pale. He was thinking that he might be killed. She was thinking that she might not succeed.

"Laure," he said, "if I don't come back..."

"I shall die, Leo!"

"No, live! You must live, Laure, if Lucifer is defeated. Swear to me that you will live!"

"If Lucifer is defeated, you want me to live?"

"Yes! Yes!"

"Even if you are dead?"

"Yes, Laure, yes. You owe a duty to your audience, for whom you incarnate such beautiful dreams. You do not have the right to die so young, in the splendor of your beauty, in the daily-renewed marvel of your talent."

"So be it. I shall live, since to live is to obey you. But if Lucifer in victorious..."

"Oh, Laure, my Laure! Not in his hands... You... Not in his hands..."

"He shall not have me, Leo. And if I can avenge you, and defeat him in my turn–yes, defeat him! One Delilah was sufficient against a Samson that thousands of men could not lay low. Judith had but one gesture to make to kill Holofernes, whom armies had not been able to vanquish..."

"Yes, Laure, but..." The Nyctalope's voice trembled as he added: "But Delilah and Judith, before triumphing over their man..."

"I hear you. Shut up! Were my lover dead, beloved, what would my virtue matter? If the sacrifice were necessary to avenge you and strike the monster down, provided that I could purify myself thereafter by dying voluntarily..."

"Shut up!"

Their lips met. Quivering, they mingled their souls. Then, suddenly, he drew away from her. He moved her aside, and after one last glance, he left as if he were fleeing. As he crossed the threshold, though, he pulled himself together and mastered himself again.

Lourmel was waiting for him. "My friend," he said, effortfully, in a low and halting voice, "I leave her and entrust her to you. Do you believe in God?"

"Yes," said Lourmel, unsurprised by the question, so open was his mind, at that moment, to all questions.

"Well, pray to Him that I defeat Lucifer!" And he went outside, to be alone for a few minutes, in order not to see Laurence when she went down to the shore and then, in a launch, to the submarine.

A few minutes went by. In the main hall where everyone was working at their allotted tasks, the Professor waited for Laurence. Grisyl and Romski were watching anxiously, wondering what was happening.

La Païli reappeared, apparently quite calm. She smiled at Lourmel. "My dear Professor, I'll be with you in a moment. You'll permit me to keep Grisyl close by, won't you? Leo has no more need of her–she has no fixed role in the expedition."

"As you wish," said Lourmel.

"Then I'll go fetch her."

And Laurence headed for Grisyl and Romski. She leaned over them, so that they could both hear her, and spoke in a whisper, so that they were the only ones who could hear her. "Nothing essential has changed, but our action will have an unexpected prologue. Don't ask me for explanations; I haven't time. You're coming with me now, Grisyl."

"Fine."

"Romski, be ready with the aircraft, as soon as possible–and be alert. We might have to act under the Nyctalope's very eyes and against his orders."

"I'm entirely yours," whispered the officer.

"Keep an eye on the submarine. As soon as you see us come out, take off. Grisyl will lift up her arms. Leave Berge and Dopp behind."

"Right."

"Can you pass over the submarine, almost grazing the gangway?"

"I see what you're getting at. Yes, I can–but at too great a speed for you to grab hold of the struts supporting the wheels or the floats."

"What, then?" said Laure, tapping her foot. "It has to be done."

"It will be," Romski replied. "I can start off rolling towards the shore, then skim the surface of the water at low speed, stopping close to the submarine–for one second! You can walk along the edge of the lower wing to get to the bucket-seats; then I can move away and take off."

"Very good! I'm counting on you, Romski. I think you'd better bring some furs–the cloaks that we'll have with us won't be sufficient."

"Understood. Has the boss told you the departure time?"

"No, but it will be around 9 or 10 p.m. Everything will be ready at 8, but there will still be dispositions to arrange. Enough talk. Be careful, Romski."

"My life is yours."

"I shall make use of it."

"You may abuse it if you wish."

"That might be necessary. Come on, Grisyl."

The two women walked towards Lourmel. The discussion had lasted less than a minute.

Outside, Leo Saint-Clair had taken refuge behind the corner of the barracks, in a part of the station where he could not be seen by the men working in the open, but from which he had a perfect view of the route that Laurence and Lourmel would take in going to the dinghy that would carry them to the submarine–for the Nyctalope was suffering. He was suffering as a man suffers who, after having lost his adored lover and found her again more amorous and more beautiful than he remembered her, is on the point of losing her again–thus time, perhaps, forever...

Saint-Clair had no illusions about the dangers he would run in his offensive against Fort Warteck. This time, it was the final battle. No feint, no subterfuge, no strategic retreat or evasion could interrupt this combat to prepare for another. This time, it was necessary to win or be defeated; neither result could be postponed. Only five days–six at the most–remained to the Nyctalope to complete his task. After that, it would be finished, with no more hope in the case of defeat, no more apprehension in the case of victory. There were so many mortal risks, known and unknown; it was impossible to calculate the way the dice would fall. What lover would not have suffered amid such conjectures? Saint-Clair was suffering; he wanted to see La Païli–the woman he truly loved–one last time. And he saw her.

Between Lourmel and Grisyl, the young woman walked rapidly over the pebble-strewn and snow-covered ground. She was wrapped in a long white fur coat, with white furry boots, coiffed by a bonnet made of white fox-fur. She was shorter in stature than Grisyl and Lourmel.

Saint-Clair needed all his strength of mind not to call out to her or run after her–oh, to embrace his beloved once more, to see her ardent soul in her beautiful eyes, to savor the disturbing taste of her lips... But no! Destiny had spoken. Saint-Clair did not move.

He only thought specifically about Grisyl when he saw the young woman climb into the dinghy first. Two sailors from the *Uberalles*, who were wandering on the beach a short distance away immediately ran back to it.

Is she going too? he said to himself. *Good idea–I don't need her. She'll be good company for Laure aboard the submarine–but she might come back alone, to ask me for a place in an aircraft. I'll refuse. Better that Laure and Grisyl aren't separated...*

Forcing back the tears that he felt welling up beneath his eyelids, La Païli's lover remained hidden where he was, seeing without being seen, until the moment when the two women and the Professor disappeared into the submarine. Before going down the ladder to the main deck, Laurence turned towards Elmwood station, and waved goodbye.

"Shall I see her again?" Saint-Clair murmured. He strangled a sob, and leaned on the wooden wall for a few seconds–but his weakness was brief. The Nyctalope stood up straight again, his face calm and serious, and it was with the attitude, gait and thoughts of a leader that he walked towards the landing-strip where the aviators were getting the aircraft ready.

XII. La Païli's Plan

Laurence and Grisyl were immediately taken to the cabin that had been modified to accommodate and facilitate the use of the radioactive bell-jar. Rupert VI was still lodged in the bell-jar, drowsing in a comfortable armchair, watched by a man named Chabot.

Chabot was a highly intelligent laboratory assistant of about 30, who had embarked with his employer, Professor Lourmel. In Paris, Chabot had worked on the construction, assembly and experimental testing of the radioactive chamber. During the submarine journey, the Professor had completed his specialist instruction, and was now able to put the utmost confidence in him.

"Good day, Chabot. Anything new?" Lourmel said, as they entered the cabin.

"No sir. Rupert has not come out of his trance. I've given him food and water and even took him for a walk in the crew's quarters while the valves were opened to renew the atmosphere. When he was put back into the bell-jar, he became drowsy. I've taken his temperature and pulse; everything's normal."

"Perfect!"

With the natural interest of an experimenter, combined with the keen curiosity of an indefatigable student of life's marvels, Lourmel was completely taken up with the "Rupert case" for several more minutes. He observed the somnolent subject and interrogated the enthusiastic Chabot further, apparently forgetting Laurence Païli. The young woman took advantage of the opportunity to take Grisyl to one side. She had not said everything in front of the Polish officer because there was no time to spare and because the Professor, who was then attentive to her alone, would have been surprised by a long conversation. She had assumed that Lourmel would not always be so constantly at hand on the *Uberalles* and that she would be able to communicate her entire plan to Grisyl there.

In a corner of the cabin where there were pegs attached to the bell-jar, Laurence and Grisyl took off their coats and hats while the Professor was some distance away. Chabot assisted him to dispose of his own clothes temporarily on a nearby chair.

"Grisyl!" whispered Laurence.

"I'm listening," the young woman replied.

"You're very strong, aren't you?"

"Physically?"

"Yes."

"Quite strong, I suppose."

"If necessary, then, you could overpower Chabot, tie him up and gag him?"

"Yes."

Darting a sideways glance at the two men, Grisyl smiled, expressing scornful pity. Indeed, Chabot, a clever electrician and skillful mechanic, was no athlete. Short and a little too plump, neither wiry nor muscular, he would not put up much resistance to the tall and powerful Grisyl, who has always been extremely assiduous in performing the daily gymnastic exercises prescribed by Warteck law.

"You can use his greatcoat and muffler," Laurence continued. "They're over there, on the other pegs."

"Yes, I see them."

"Good. I'll take care of the Professor."

"Be careful, Laurence!" Grisyl said. "The Professor is tall, well-built and strong."

"Don't worry–I don't intend to get into a fight with him. As women, our best weapon remains trickery."

"What are you going to do?"

"No need to explain–let's stick to the indispensable. Listen, Grisyl."

"Well?"

"Don't leave the cabin, unless it's absolutely necessary. I'll ask the Professor to let you remain with me at all times–outside the bell-jar, of course. We can't do anything until Romski's ready."

"We'd lose everything?"

"Yes."

"So?"

"Romski won't be ready until 8 p.m. We must get out of here between 8 and 8:05 p.m."

Grisyl turned her head and raised her eyes to a wall-clock fixed between two closed portholes on the far side of the cabin. "It's already 6:30 p.m.," she said.

"I know–I saw that as we came in. We must wait until 7:45 p.m. If Chabot isn't here, you'll have to invent some pretext for summoning him. I'll be in the cage with the Professor. When I shout 'Saint-Clair!' you grab him. It will have to be done very quickly–getting out of here, climbing on to the gangplank..."

"What if there's someone else here?"

"There won't be anyone else. I told Lourmel in the dinghy that I didn't want to risk being seen if I fell into a hypnotic trance."

"And once we're out of here?"

"No one will stop us. We shan't give the appearance of running away."

"Understood."

They both knew that what they intended to do, if they succeeded in the preliminaries, carried frightful risks of torture and death, but they were quite prepared to sacrifice their lives. As for the preliminary tortures, they would only last for a while. What is pain, whose end can be foreseen, when one submits to it

398

in order to safeguard the life of the man one loves? Laurence and Grisyl were women, and the adventure into which their love caused them to throw themselves so ardently was, for them, the ultimate game of skill. It would be delightful to play–and besides, why should they not succeed?

Grisyl almost laughed mischievously as she said: "I can hardly wait to see..."

"What I'll do to the Professor?" La Païli finished, pertly.

"Yes."

"Would you like me to tell you now?"

"Oh, yes!"

"Well, when I..." But at that moment Lourmel turned to the two young women and came towards them. Laurence fell silent.

"Excuse me, my dear friends," the Professor said. "I couldn't help giving a little time to the Rupert case, which I find so interesting. It's done, and I'm entirely at your disposal. Let's not stay here. The next cabin is a sort of miniature library, very comfortable. You and Grisyl will be better off there, my dear friend. I'll keep you company, if you'll allow it."

"Willingly, my dear Professor," replied La Païli. "But if I'm suddenly overtaken by... What you're expecting?"

"We have only to take a few steps to bring us back to the bell-jar. Within a minute, you'd be enclosed in a radioactive atmosphere. Pray to God that it will be as easy for me to free Irène and Henri from the monster's potential spells. The *Lampas* has already been heading at top speed for the submarine station at the Pole since yesterday. Oh, there are times–all too frequent–when it seems to me to be impossible that the Nyctalope will succeed, despite all his genius."

Laurence did not reply. She had heard the Professor talking about his niece in agonized terms several times before; Irène was never far from her uncle's thoughts, however preoccupied he was with his scientific work or collaboration with Saint-Clair. But what could she say? Laurence certainly felt sorry for Irène and little Henri Prillant, but the prospects and threats they faced were no worse than those confronting her. It was true that Lucifer was, for the moment, concentrating all his attractive and terrifying power on Irène and Henri, but what were a few days of common imprisonment to individuals who, if the battle they had joined was not won by a specific date, would be condemned thereafter to perpetual solitary confinement or imminent death? Those days were only significant in the context of the war; since Irène and Henri would not have been able to contribute to the struggle, whether Lucifer let them alone or not, it was of scant importance.

Meanwhile, they went into the smaller room. Laurence and Grisyl sat down side by side on a divan. The Professor sat in an armchair.

"I won't offer to find you a book," he said, "and I won't get one myself. We have enough in our heads and hearts to occupy us while we wait..."

Laurence made a sign of assent, and Grisyl smiled.

The two women and the man remained there, silent and immobile, refraining from looking at one another and quickly looking to one side if their eyes happened to meet, waiting for the ever-mysterious and ever-menacing empery of Lucifer.

Half an hour went by. Then, La Païli suddenly sat up straight and raised her head, as if in response to a summons. Her eyelids fluttered, her eyes turned upwards, a groan emerged from her mouth and a corpse-like pallor overtook her face.

"Quickly! Quickly!" cried the Professor, coming to his feet. He shouted: "Chabot!"

On hearing his name called by his employer, the assistant operated the controls activating the mechanism that elevated the glass cage. Grisyl had anticipated the Professor; she took Laurence's stiff body in her strong arms, lifted it up, and ran through the open door, carrying it effortlessly.

Thirty seconds later, the bell-jar fell back gently, enclosing in its transparent shell not merely Rupert VI–who had not emerged from his somnolence or moved from his armchair–but also Laurence, seated in a second armchair, and Lourmel, who stood facing her. Grisyl remained outside the cage, beside Chabot, her eyes fixed on the entranced Laurence, who was rapidly passing from Lucifer's distant influence to that of Professor Lourmel.

He'll question her, Grisyl thought. *It's 7:10 p.m. The hypnotic session shouldn't last longer than half an hour–three quarters of an hour at the most–but Laurence will be very tired afterwards. Will she be able to carry through whatever she planned to do to prevent the Professor from being an obstacle to our departure?* She was very anxious. She heard Lourmel's voice, attenuated by the thickness of the crystal but distinct enough for the words to be clearly perceived by an attentive ear.

"Where are you, Laurence?" the Professor asked.

La Païli replied, in a dull voice that Grisyl heard quite clearly: "I'm in Fort Warteck, in the cupola of the Teledynamo."

"What and who can you see?"

"The Teledynamo, with seven skeletal skulls, a large terrestrial globe, Glô von Warteck and Wilfried."

"What are they doing?"

"They're both leaning over a crystal bowl filled with water. They're wearing earpieces. They're not moving."

"Look! Listen! If they move, describe their movements. If they speak, repeat their words."

"Yes, yes."

There was a pause. Excited and captivated, no longer feeling the anxiety of a few moments before, Grisyl watched and listened, leaning her hands on the transparent wall. Standing next to her, with his hands in his pockets, Chabot was also watching and listening.

400

Suddenly, Laurence's dull voice said: "Glô gestures angrily. He raises his head and turns to Wilfried, who is acting in exactly the same manner. Both their faces express disappointment. Glô says: 'I can't hear anything; I can't see anything.' 'Neither can I,' says Wilfried. They turn back again and lean over the bowl. Glô lifts his head again, takes a step to one side, removes some polished pegs from an ivory console pierced with holes. He comes back to look into the bowl."

The voice paused; thirty seconds ran by.

"Ah... I can see things in the bowl," Laurence resumed, with greater animation. "A submarine gliding beneath the surface, at top speed. Oh! The submarine's interior... There's Irène! And little Henri... I recognize them." Professor Lourmel had shown the singer photographs of the young woman and the child on several occasions. "And that's undoubtedly Monsieur Mattol. They're in a cabin. Little Henri's asleep on a divan. Irène's weeping, slumped in an armchair, her fists under her chin, her eyes staring. Monsieur Mattol seems to be in a hypnotic trance. Oh! Glô is saying: 'You see, Wilfried, the Teledynamo's working. There's the *Lampas*—and it was working when plugged into La Païli. We saw, just for a second, some sort of library, still blurred—but everything vanished before we could distinguish any specific details. Everything vanished; there's been silence in the earpieces, and the water in the bowl's been perfectly transparent, in exactly the same fashion as when Hunter was removed from the Teledynamo's field on May 24. He never returned, despite my calls. It was as if his body and soul had been extinguished...' "

Laurence fell silent momentarily. In a low voice, as if talking to himself, Chabot said: "Right! Once he had been removed from the cage, dead, I shut Hunter in a hermetically-sealed tank filled with radioactive gas."

Grisyl, who was standing next to him, overheard him. She said: "Which proves that Professor Lourmel has found a means of nullifying the power of the Teledynamo. The Teledynamo's waves can't penetrate an atmosphere saturated with radioactive gas, like the one he has composed."

"And Lucifer doesn't know that."

"He doesn't know it yet," Grisyl said, "but he'll investigate and figure it out..."

"If the Nyctalope gives him time, Mademoiselle! Look!"

In her armchair, facing the standing Lourmel, La Païli had started.

"Speak, Laurence!" the Professor ordered.

She obeyed immediately. Her voice was clearly audible. "Glô says: 'Nothing! Nothing! And I can't let the *Lampas* alone for too long. Mattol will be able to react—to damage the ship in such a way that it'll have to surface, incapable of making further progress.' Wilfried frowns. He's says: 'That's true!' Glô snatches the earpieces from his ears and cries: 'Ah, if I could take Irène, I'd bring her aboard! I'd find La Païli again afterwards...' Wilfried also takes out his earpieces. Glô goes up to the machine with the seven skulls. He examines it, walking all around it, followed by Wilfried. He murmurs words that I can't make out. He stops. He looks at Wilfried. He speaks. 'Let's go to the laboratory, Wilfried. I'll branch a conductive wire from the Teledynamo to the laboratory so that, without significantly diminishing the force of the waves holding the *Lampas* and its occupants captive, we'll be able to displace enough fluid to make experiments. We'll combine all the gases that we can produce by decomposition or amalgamation. We'll also test the reactions of the fluid in relation to various electrical stimuli and material substances. I think one of my adversaries–probably Professor Lourmel–has found some means to insulate individuals and their supportive milieux from my investigations. Is that insulating substance a solid? A gas? An element treated in some specific fashion? We need to find out–if we don't, my victory on June 10 will not be entirely complete, since Lourmel will be able to insulate himself and others from the Teledynamo's influence. Let's go!'

"They're going down the stairway that leads to the machine. They're going into the pedestal. They..."

Lourmel's voice, simultaneously gentle and imperious, cut in: "No need to follow them, Laurence. They're going to work. We, too, must do the same. Wake up!" The Professor's face was transfigured; it radiated noble pride and triumphant joy. With respect to an important scientific point, he had undoubtedly put Lucifer and his Teledynamo in check.

When Laurence woke up, Lourmel operated the controls that introduced oxygen into the cage, gradually substituting pure air for the radioactive atmosphere. Then he lifted up the crystal enclosure. As soon as he could slip out under the vertical walls, he came out.

"Look after Laurence, Grisyl. You'll find everything you need–cordial, biscuits–in a cupboard in the next room. If she seems too weak, give her an injection with syringe No. 3, which is filled with a red liquid. Inject all its contents. I'll go confer with the Nyctalope."

"Use the telephone, boss!" said Chabot, with his usual liberty of language. A wireless telephone connection had indeed been installed between the *Uberalles* and Elmwood.

"No," said the Professor. "What I have to say is too important, and it may be necessary to make new decisions. Besides, my presence here isn't indispensable. If, by chance–it's unlikely, because Lucifer is too busy now to launch a counterstrike–but if Mademoiselle Païli is overtaken again, carry her back into the cage, Grisyl, and telephone me immediately."

"Yes, sir."

Having finally dressed himself from top to toe in furs–for he was extremely sensitive to cold, and dreaded the abrupt transition from the warmth of the submarine's interior to the glacial external atmosphere–the Professor ran out of the large cabin. Without responding to the "What's new?" uttered by Commander Saincer–whom he met near the exit–he threw himself out on to the deck, leapt into the dinghy and ordered the two sailors waiting there to row him to shore immediately.

Meanwhile, having opened her eyes and collected herself, Laurence recognized Grisyl. She smiled, and sighed: "My God!"

"Are you tired?" the younger woman asked.

"Yes, exhausted! Did it last a long time?"

"Twenty minutes. It's 7:30 p.m. Can you walk?"

"Yes, if I lean on you. But we must... It's absolutely necessary that in less than..." She caught sight of Chabot, who was waiting in case anyone had need of him, and fell silent.

"I remain at your disposal, Mesdemoiselles," the assistant said, "according to the boss's orders."

"Good," said Laurence, with a smile. Supported by Grisyl, she went into the next room. "Shut the door," she whispered.

"Yes, I think that's best." The younger woman closed the door that connected the little room to the larger cabin where Chabot was waiting.

As soon as she was seated on the divan, Laurence said, in a low voice: "Quickly, Grisyl–revive me!"

"Did you hear the Professor? Everything necessary is here. The injection first–then eat and drink. No need to worry–we have a good 20 minutes."

"But I need to know what I said in the bell-jar."

"Naturally! I heard everything, understood everything. I'll tell you all that while I take care of you. Ah, here's syringe No. 3, red liquid. Do you want the injection in the arm or the thigh?"

"In the arm."

"Very well–here you are."

During the injection and afterwards, while serving Laurence with biscuits and a generous glass of wine, Grisyl repeated, almost word for word, the revelations that the singer had made in her hypnotic state.

"Good!" said the diva as soon as Grisyl had finished. "Didn't I hear that the Professor has gone ashore to confer with the Nyctalope?"

"Yes."

"Then I won't have to play the nasty trick that would have permitted us to part company."

Grisyl smiled. Still in a whisper, she said, curiously: "What would you have done at the time fixed for our departure, if the Professor had still been with us?"

"That's quite simple. At 7:45 p.m., I would have asked him if we could conduct an experiment. If he were in the radioactive atmosphere and I were outside in the ordinary air, could he put me into a trance through the glass wall? I know the Professor well. Any new problem, even if it seems trivial, excites his curiosity. Many a time I've heard him say: 'How can one know how an experiment will turn out if one hasn't tried it?' He would certainly have agreed. Once the bell-jar is sealed and full of radioactive gas, the replacement of that artificial atmosphere with normal air takes time because of the slowness of the relevant mechanisms–plenty of time for you, my dear Grisyl, to make it impossible for Chabot to follow us, and for me to put on my boots, hat and coat. Then we would have gone up on deck. Romski would certainly have picked us up before the Professor got out of the cage and released Chabot. Ah–you're laughing!"

Indeed, Grisyl could not help laughing. Despite the gravity of the circumstances, the notion of the Professor, temporarily imprisoned by glass, watching them tying up Chabot and escaping seemed very funny.

"Yes," she said, "I'm laughing. To make a fool of a man of Professor Lourmel's importance in such a manner–I'm scandalized, but I find it very comical."

"You made a fool of Rupert VI in the Bermudas, to save Leo from electrocution."

"Oh, that was quite different," said Grisyl, blushing. "For one thing, I didn't have to attack the *Grottenmeister* directly. Then again, the Nyctalope would have died in a matter of minutes if... But we're chattering, Laure, and time's passing."

"Dear Grisyl!" Leaning towards the younger woman, who was kneeling in front of her, La Païli kissed her on the forehead and immediately got to her feet.

"How do you feel?" said Grisyl, getting up.

"Very well–no longer tired. My head is straight, my thoughts clear. The injection, the exquisite wine and the dry cakes, have all done me the world of good. My God! I feared that you might never laugh again, Grisyl, and that I would never smile at your youthful gaiety. We're heading towards death, Grisyl, and perhaps something more terrible and abominable than death. Even if we're victorious, we might become victims."

"We'll save the life..."

"Of the Nyctalope? Yes, even if we die."

"Let's go, Laure–time's passing."

"Yes, let's go my friend." Taking the younger woman by the hand, La Païli marched towards the door.

"Nothing has changed regarding Chabot?" asked Grisyl.

"Of course, nothing's changed. He wouldn't stop us going on deck, but he'd follow us."

"All right, Laure; give me time to do it and put my outdoor clothes on."

La Païli opened the door. Grisyl went out first; calmly but rapidly, she went to Chabot, who was sitting on a chair smoking a cigarette, without losing sight of Rupert VI–who was still in the glass cage, in the trance into which Professor Lourmel had put him with the aid of a mild narcotic mixed with his food. Chabot was directly underneath the four pegs from which hung his fringed muffler, his greatcoat, his fur cape and his white fox-fur hat.

While Grisyl went forward, Le Païli went to sit on a stool on the far side of the room, to put her large fur boots on over the light woolen stockings that she was wearing.

As he saw Grisyl coming towards him, Chabot got up, threw the cigarette-butt into an ash-tray set in a corner and was doubtless about to ask her how he might be useful to her when Grisyl seized both his wrists, holding them in one hand, and said: "Not a word, and don't resist, Chabot! This is to help the Nyctalope."

Chabot was petrified. Grisyl quickly secured his wrists to his ankles with a belt, gagged him with a handkerchief and scarf, pushed him into a dark corner and threw on his overcoat, white fur cape and hat. As she did this, she said to him: "Count until a thousand, Chabot. When you've finished, you'll be able to free yourself easily enough by wriggling your hands and feet, for I've made a knot that comes apart when you tug on its ends–but not until you've counted to a thousand. If anyone comes in before you've finished, don't move or breathe a word. Once more, this is for the sake of the Nyctalope."

La Païli was ready. She helped Grisyl to put on her furs rapidly. The two friends left the cabin and went up on to the deck of the submarine. On deck, Commander Jacques Saincer appeared to be complacently watching the activity ashore, around the buildings of the English station. He had his back to them.

"Silence!" said Laurence, squeezing Grisyl's hand.

Grisyl raised her arms above her head and waved; it was the signal agreed with Romski. Immediately, two men standing beside an aircraft–which, as if by chance, was set slightly apart from the others–sprang into action. One of them hastened to get into the pilot's eat. The aircraft, evidently ready to go, rolled over the beach to the water's edge, where its floats took over from its wheels–and the RC3 slid across the calm sea, avoiding the lumps of ice that floated here and there.

"Hold on!" said Commander Saincer, loudly, "what's that chap doing? That's not in the program, it seems to me!"

"Wait, Grisyl!" whispered Laurence.

The aircraft headed straight for the submarine. Still invisible to Saincer, who had his back to them, the two women were on the very edge of the deck, almost at water-level.

"Hey, Romski!" Saincer shouted. "Are you bringing boarders?"

The skillfully-piloted aircraft leaned slightly to starboard for a moment. Its port wing almost touched the submarine's massive double hull as it showed. There was no need for it to come to a complete stop. As it passed by, Laurence and Grisyl grabbed hold of the stays, tension-wires and struts of that port wing, slipped on to it and walked along it lithely. Within 20 seconds, they had reached the two empty bucket-seats behind Romski.[70]

"Take off!" cried La Païli.

The RC3 gained speed, drew away, took off and climbed into the air. It described two great circles and disappeared into a bank of cloud that extended from the north-west to the south-east. Jacques Saincer stood there petrified, while a storm of shouts sprang up from Elmwood.

XIII. The Great Departure

At first, the reaction ashore was a combination of astonishment, incomprehension and amazement.

Romski had been ready for a good quarter of an hour. With Berge and Dopp–assisted by Wolf, to the extent that he could make himself useful–the Polish aviator had got his aircraft into a perfect state of readiness for an immediate departure. When he had nothing else to do but wait for Laurence and Grisyl to appear on the submarine's deck, the officer sent Berge and Dopp to the stores, asking them to look for a small packet of wing-nuts which did not exist.

They'll be looking for long enough, he said to himself, *not to be there when I depart.* As for Wolf, he would be useful during take-off because he obeyed Romski's orders without thought or hesitation.

At that moment, nearly all the Englishmen and Frenchmen present at the station were outdoors, occupied in attending to the aircraft or carrying various objects, comprising an orderly hive of activity. Saint-Clair and Lourmel were slightly apart, standing on the beach a hundred yards away, immersed in an animated conversation.

The first person to notice the RC3 sliding from the beach to the water was Sir Patrick Swires; Saint-Clair and Lourmel were walking along with their backs to the beach. Sir Patrick assumed that a special order had been given for a supplementary maneuver–but when he saw the two human forms throw themselves from the submarine on to its wing, he suspected that something was awry. "Saint-Clair!" he cried, at the top of his voice–but ten seconds more elapsed before Saint-Clair and Lourmel had turned and seen what was happening.

"What's he doing?" asked the Professor.

"Oh!" said Saint-Clair, who had the eyes of a mariner and a lover. "Laure and Grisyl!"

He remained rooted to the spot. He did not understand. Questions rose up in his abruptly-confused mind. *What are Laurence and Grisyl doing? What's that aircraft doing? Isn't it Romski's?* Something like a minute went by before the Nyctalope could make any sense of the incident. As for Lourmel, his eyes went from Sir Patrick to the swiftly-climbing aircraft, and he stammered: "Laure and Grisyl? Did you order them...? Without telling me...? But...but..."

Everyone had heard Sir Patrick's shout. The work stopped short, all heads turning towards the sea and the sky, every face expressing astonishment. When the RC3 disappeared into the cloud, the frenetic Saint-Clair howled: "They're mad! Mad!"

"My friend!" cried Lourmel, seizing the hands of the trembling Nyctalope, whose face was suddenly expressing an atrocious and desperate sorrow. It was then that, as if they were confronted by a catastrophe, all the spectators instinctively set up an immense and violent clamor.

"My friend!" Lourmel begged in a voice so poignant that it had an immediate and salutary effect on the Nyctalope. Tears sprang from Saint-Clair's eyes and ran down his face. Lourmel wiped them away paternally, with touching gentleness.

The Nyctalope ground his teeth and shut his eyes. Something akin to a sob shook him, and he squeezed the Professor's hands hard enough to break bones. After 20 seconds, though, he opened his eyes again and relaxed his powerful grip. "I see it all now," he said, in a profoundly emotional voice. They're going to confront Lucifer. They want to sacrifice themselves to save me, to save us all... Oh, my friend, if we're victorious I shall not survive a victory that might, perhaps, be rendered more difficult by the heroism and sacrifice of those two women..."

"Do you know any of the details?" Lourmel asked, feverishly. "Where are they going–the submarine station or Fort Warteck? What do they hope to achieve? How will they go about it?"

"No, I don't know anything; they're taking their secret with them."

"Sir!" It was the voice of Sir Patrick Swires. He was running towards them, with Berge and Dopp at his sides and Captain Girard and a crowd of men behind him. All of them had an intuition of what was happening, and what it meant.

Drawing slightly apart from Lourmel, the Nyctalope pulled himself together, His calmness was august and terrible. "Berge, Dopp–what do you know?" he said.

"Nothing, boss," the two men replied, in unison.

"Where were you when the RC3 got under way?"

"The lieutenant sent us to the stores..." Berge began.

"To look for something we didn't find," Dopp finished.

"He wanted to get you out of the way," Saint-Clair said. Turning towards Lourmel and Sir Patrick, he added: "Romski's hot-headed, thirsty for heroism and sacrifice. Laurence won't have had any difficulty convincing him. May God protect all three of them, as heroic and voluntary martyrs, if He doesn't find them unworthy!"

He gestured towards the sky, as if to call on the mysterious power that plays inexplicably with the destiny of worlds. Then, returning his gaze to the excited and attentive crowd, he said: "My friends, whatever plan Mademoiselle Païli, Grisyl and Lieutenant Romski are attempting to put into action, nothing is modified in my own plans. The RC3 will not be lining up with the reserves; there will only be one back-up aircraft. Berge and Dopp will take the places of the two Englishmen in the RC1 and Wolf will replace another in the RC2. To work! I want us to be off by 9 p.m. and not a minute later!"

"Long live Saint-Clair!" someone shouted.

"Victory to the Nyctalope!" cried another voice, followed by enthusiastic applause.

Five minutes later, hiding the intense emotion that was gripping his heart, Leo Saint-Clair and Lourmel were aboard the *Uberalles*. Jacques Saincer awaited them on deck. The Nyctalope assured himself that all the desired dispositions had been made, then left Lourmel, whom he embraced for a long time, and Saincer, whose hand he shook, murmuring "Good luck, my friend!" and returned to shore. As soon as he had disembarked, the two sailors rowed back to the submarine.

A quarter of an hour later, having received all the men and objects it had to take aboard via the launch, the *Uberalles* closed its hatches, slid gracefully over the waves, and soon disappeared into the light mist that was extending over the sea.

At 9 p.m., a siren sounded. At that moment, Leo Saint-Clair and Sir Patrick Swires were finishing getting dressed, all in white, in the latter's room.

"Whatever happens to Laurence and Grisyl," Saint-Clair said, "Lucifer won't be able to learn the means we'll use to defeat him, even if the hypnotizes them, since only you, Lourmel and I know what it is."

"We alone," Sir Patrick agreed. "Those of my mechanics who worked on the fabrication of the metal canisters and the adaptation of the diving-suits were personally supervised by me. As you instructed, the work was done in such a way that none of the workmen knew the significance or the purpose of their work."

"Well, for my part," the Nyctalope said, "I'm sure that that the lead seals on the canvas sacks containing the diving-suits and the canisters are quite intact. In the aircraft, each man will have his sack between his legs. When they signal is given, they'll be opened..."

"Ah, it's a fine game, Monsieur."

"Very fine, sir!" said Saint-Clair, gravely. "I'd have a joyful heart if Laurence and Grisyl hadn't had the heroic folly to doubt both Professor Lourmel's scientific genius and my own star."

"Women in love..."

"Yes, I hear you," Saint-Clair said. "But you see, sir, even when she acts mistakenly, a woman who acts out of love is always doing something sublime— even when it's harmful or criminal. That's because love is the most irreducible and independent powers with which nature has equipped the human being."

"The most blind too, Monsieur."

"I agree with you, sir–at least when it's not prodigiously clairvoyant."

They said no more; they were ready. According to the new attributions made by Saint-Clair after Romski's departure with Laurence and Grisyl on the RC3, the crews were made up as follows: Saint-Clair, Girard, Swires, Corsat and Pilou on the RC4; Dupuis, Aymard, Garet, Berge and Wolf on the RC2; Captain Berton, Bompard, Sylvain, Dopp and Elias Carter on the RC1. Furthermore, following a new intuitive estimate of the probable facts, the Nyctalope had modified two details of his plan. No aircraft would now remain in reserve; all three would act together. This meant that Sir Patrick Swires and Elias Carter were the only Englishmen taking part in the airborne expedition; all the others who had previously been designated for that role had embarked on the *Uberalles*. A few minutes after Elmwood's siren had concluded its long and strident fanfare, these aviators took their places in their respective aircraft. One of them held a long staff from which hung, at the same height, the French and British flags.

"May God go with us!" said the Nyctalope, in a resounding voice.

Cries of "Hurrah!" came from all sides.

The motors spluttered into life, indifferent to the very low temperature because the fuel and oil had been prevented from freezing by the addition of a specially-devised alcohol formulated and tested by Lourmel some years before. The propellers began to turn, drawing the aircraft forward.

"Hurrah! Hip, hip hurrah!" These acclamations were still resounding when the aircraft disappeared from view in the direction of the pole.

It was 9:15 p.m. on the evening of June 4.

XIV. Two Women and the Serpent

The distance from Cape Flora, the south-western extremity of Franz Josef Land, to the geographical point called the North Pole is about 1,100 kilometers as the crow flies. Romski's RC3, having left Cape Flora at 8 p.m. on June 4, would cover that distance in a little less than six hours if it maintained an average speed of between 180 and 200 kilometers an hour. If no incident occurred to interrupt its progress it would touch down at Fort Warteck at about 2 a.m. on June 5.

According to Rupert VI's revelations, which were in agreement with information possessed by Grisyl, his adversaries knew that Glô von Warteck usually maintained his regular habit of sleeping from 10 p.m. to 4 a.m. This was not an artificial sleep, but simple and healthy natural slumber–the vulgar sleep of rest and restoration, without which no man can live actively.

Although there are stylites in India, immobile and motionless on their columns, who go for weeks without the sleep to which all earthly living creatures submit, it is because they do nothing–absolutely nothing. It is as if they have temporarily interrupted and suspended all their corporeal functions. It is as if, with their nostrils stuffed with clay and their throats obstructed by their retracted tongues, they are no longer breathing. Given his prodigious cerebral and intense physical activity, though, Glô needed to sleep–and unless exceptional circumstances intervened, he slept regularly every day for about six hours, two before midnight and four afterwards.

The Baron even ate and drank, not in the as-yet-hypothetical and imaginative manner of certain anticipated savants, content to absorb a few pills, tablets and sachets from time to time, but in the omnivorous manner of the majority of human beings. To the extent that he could, Glô ate and drank at regular hours, as if it were a matter of no great importance to him, sitting down at a table on which were deposited, each in the appropriate receptacle consecrated to it by universal custom, foodstuffs prepared by a cook comparable with the best in his profession. In addition, Glô generally preferred the generous wines of the south to those of the north; he was rarely served the produce of the banks of the Rhine, which are much appreciated elsewhere. He did not disdain sparkling wines from the plains of Champagne, provided that they were authentic and of a suitable age, but he was rarely satisfied by meals that were unsupported by vintage Burgundies, and he would demonstrate his disappointment rudely if he could not alternate them, as often as possible, with the traditional nectars of Bordeaux. He enjoyed certain Spanish wines very much, and was familiar with the different tastes of the principal Italian wines.

All of which is to say that Glô von Warteck, no matter how much he desired to be called Lucifer, was nonetheless consciously, willingly and gladly a

411

man, furnished with an educated palate, a solid stomach and a faultless digestive apparatus.

Lucifer loved eating and drinking, but he was not a slave to entirely natural tastes. He knew how to be sober without effort and moderate without regret when he encountered one of those circumstances in which the work of digestion would have done harm, however slightly, to the functioning of his limbs or the intense life of his intellect. An egg or some preserved fish, biscuits, a piece of Dutch cheese, a little jam or a few dried fruits would then make a meal, washed down with a glass of water. Lucifer was, in every sense of the word, a man–but a man who was master of himself.

There was only one flaw in this armor: the sensuality that was both virile and, so to speak, sentimental. Glô von Warteck loved Woman, and since his adolescence had longed to be loved–but he was one of those individuals to whom Destiny gives everything, except what they desire most of all, of which it refuses them even the least particle.

Glô had never, ever been loved–and in its formidable irony, Destiny dictates that men without love cannot do anything at all that does not distance them even further from the love that they crave and pursue with such avidity, passion and fury that only death can put a end to their quest.

Such was Lucifer: a prodigious intelligence, vibrant with genius and wild ambition; a creature gifted with unprecedented power by virtue of that extraordinary machine, the Teledynamo; but a man for whom Woman existed–that Woman whose love is the supreme wealth of conquest.

Glô von Warteck often repeated, in the secret privacy of his thoughts: *I should be superior to all the gods if Laurence Païli and Irene de Ciserat would say to me, with the spontaneous warmth of sincerity: "I love you!"* And it was because he knew in advance, with rage and disappointment, that neither Laurence not Irène would ever, under any circumstances, say to him "I love you!" that he was animated by such a fury of cruel and despotic ambition.

To this infernal genius love was lacking; for this human Lucifer, there was no Eloa.[71] And it was certainly not Laurence Païli who would be that Eloa, eventually affectionate and amorously submissive–not, at any rate, with the spontaneous warmth of sincerity–for if ever repulsion and hatred had embittered and inflamed a woman's heart, that heart was surely La Païli's. She went to Glô von Warteck not to give her heart but to bring death, albeit under the deceptive appearances of love.

Shivering under the warm swathes of fur that enveloped her from top to toe, Laurence held herself immobile in her bucket-seat. The formation of the aircraft's windshield protected its occupants so well that they were hardly affected by the terrible blast of their rapid course. Next to Laurence in the other bucket-seat, Grisyl, similarly muffled, seemed to be asleep–but she was thinking, as La Païli was.

In front of them, Romski was piloting the aircraft. For such a short journey–to this champion of the air, a six-hour flight, even in the polar cold, seemed mere child's play–the Polish officer had no need of any assistant; that is why he had raised no objection when Laurence had asked him not to bring Berge and Dopp. As the RC3 was performing admirably, its engine being powerful, regular, calm and docile, Romski was able to concentrate on maintaining the right heading. On first taking off, he had tried out various different altitudes in order to avoid the great air currents that differences in temperature between ice, water and land generally cause close to the surface of the globe, but once he deemed that he was in a relatively calm atmosphere he had no other thought than to head directly for the pole, so as to arrive at Fort Warteck in he briefest possible time.

Of Saint-Clair's plan, Lieutenant Romski new only what everyone at Elmwood knew; he knew nothing about the principal means of action–which would, in Saint-Clair's reckoning, offer a 99% chance of victory. That secret was known only to Saint-Clair, Lourmel and Sir Patrick Swires. However, Romski assumed that putting that means into effect would oblige the RC1, RC2 and RC4 to take precautions and make maneuvers that would oblige the three aircraft to proceed less rapidly than usual. In the first instance, they would have to fly above the clouds for two thirds of their course, in order not to risk being seen by scouts from Fort Warteck abroad on some reconnaissance mission; afterwards, they would have to fly as low as possible, in order not to be seen by the sentries at the fort; finally, they would have to touch down a few kilometers away from the fort, in order that the Nyctalope could give his companions their final orders. For all these reasons, Romski assumed, there was no chance of Saint-Clair's three aircraft overtaking the RC3 and preventing Laurence and Grisyl from doing as they wished.

Romski was, therefore, perfectly tranquil. To be sure, he did not doubt for a single instant that death awaited him at Fort Warteck–but he had put his destiny once and for all in the soft hands of La Païli. If he died in such a manner as to leave a warm and thankful memory within the singer's mind, he would die happy. *Since La Païli and this Grisyl are risking death for love*, Romski said to himself, *it is entirely natural that I should run the same risk for the same cause.*

Thus reasons passion, with sublime unreason.

The hours passed–9, 10, 11 p.m. The RC3 slid through the cold air in the lugubrious light of the polar regions. None of the three individuals aboard the aircraft had any thought of speaking to the others Everything had been said before they quit Elmwood and the *Uberalles*.

Yes, everything had been said–and there was the roar of the engine...

Midnight! And afterwards, 1, 2, 3 a.m...

The third hour–the sixth of the flight [72]–was marked on the luminous dial of the chronometer in front of Romski, of which Laurence and Grisyl also had a perfect view. Romski brought the RC3 down until he was below the clouds that had been hiding the grey and white ice-clad terrain for some time.

"Fort Warteck!" cried Laurence, in a strangely shrill voice.

Still seemingly distant, a light blazed, like that of a lighthouse with a fixed and continuous lamp. It seemed to be very high in the air, by virtue of an optical illusion that did not deceive Romski, Laurence or Grisyl.

Beneath the blazing light, there were a few smaller luminous sparks set against the rosy clarity of the murky daylight; not everyone was asleep in Fort Warteck.

"It will soon be the time at which Glô, if he's asleep, will awake for a new day," Grisyl said.

Laurence did not hear her, but she had had the same thought at the same instant.

"If nothing alters the usual hour of his awakening," Grisyl went on, "we'll arrive while he's in his deepest sleep." These words, too, expressed Laurence's thoughts. Their arrival at Fort Warteck while Lucifer was asleep was exactly what La Païli had intended. That was also, as La Païli knew, what the Nyctalope had intended for his own company. Like Romski, though, Laurence had calculated that if nothing delayed the RC3, it would arrive at Fort Warteck nearly an hour ahead of Saint-Clair. *I shall have plenty of time to vanquish or be vanquished*, she had told herself.

And now Fort Warteck was there: a black mass, vertically striped with long icicles, like stalactites. It was so close, with its powerful searchlight and its few scintillating lamps, that Romski, seeing a propitious white esplanade in front of him, immediately aimed for it, maneuvering skillfully. The aircraft's wheels brushed snow solidified by the cold and rebounded–but it made contact again in a long skid, slowed down and came to a stop.

Romski turned to the two women–who were already upright–got to his feet and said, calmly: "We've made better time than I expected. I hardly had to look at the speedometer. It's 2:20 a.m..."

"Quickly, Romski!" This came from Grisyl, who removed her gloves momentarily, threw a rope around the officer and tied him up tightly from his shoulders to his ankles, his wrists cruelly scored by the rough cord. Then she threw him into the empty bucket-seat parallel to the pilot's, which was normally reserved for the mechanic.

"What do we do now?" Grisyl asked.

"Get down and walk to Fort Warteck," Laurence replied, resolutely–but before leaving the aircraft she leaned towards Romski. From his smiling mouth to his serious eyes, the aviator's face was visible between his collar and fur cap. "My friend," she said, "I thank you with all my heart."

"I can die now!" sighed the young man.

Grisyl had already jumped on to the ice. Laurence followed suit. Taking one another by the hand, the two women walked towards Fort Warteck. They did had no expectations, and were ready for anything–except for what actually happened.

What happened was this: the two women had only taken 20 steps when a luminous beam of light sprang forth from the white wall surrounding Fort Warteck. This projection enveloped them in bright light, much more vivid than the polar daylight produced by the mist-shrouded Sun. Then they heard a piercing whistling sound, and something fell on to the ice some 20 meters to their right. It was a black object, which burst open like a grenade, without emitting any light.

"A shell!" said Laurence, coming to a halt.

"Soporific gas!" said Grisyl. "Why did I not foresee that? Everything, but not that! What fools we have been!"

Another projectile whistled through the air, immediately falling to their left and bursting open. Two clouds of black smoke gushed out, swelled up and began to spread. A third shell landed in front of them, and a fourth behind–and others fell, one by one, at intervals of about a second, around the two women and around the aeroplane.

Laura and Grisyl did not hesitate any longer. Still holding hands, they ran forwards and slightly to the left, where they saw a gap between two clouds of smoke. But the shells were still falling further ahead, and others to the right and left. The two women found that they were completely surrounded by smoke, which was creeping between their legs and extending above their heads. Already weakening, they understood that no escape into pure air would be possible. With a desperate effort, which they already understood to be futile, they plunged forward with their heads lowered...

It was Laurence who collapsed first, groaning. With enough consciousness left for one voluntary act, Grisyl knelt down beside her friend–but that was only for a few seconds. Losing all awareness of things, the young woman slipped sideways, her eyes closed.

A few minutes went by. Then a gust of wind–a strong air-current, projected as if from a giant bellows–sprang forth from Fort Warteck: a whistling squall which tore through the smoke and dissipated it. A dozen masked men emerged from a door that suddenly opened in the white wall girdling the fort.

Arriving at the two extended bodies, shapeless in their furs, one of these men barked orders in a harsh voice, in a language that neither Laurence nor Grisyl would have understood had they been able to hear it. Then the leader ran to the aeroplane, followed by seven men. After having established–not without a certain surprise, expressed by a dozen shrill exclamations–that only one human being was aboard, trussed up from head to toe, he shouted more orders. The seven men, pulling or pushing, rolled the RC3 over the solid ice.

Twenty minutes later, Laurence, Grisyl and Romski–the former two still fully-clothed, the latter untied but still fur-clad–were laid out upon a long and broad basalt table, in a bare room illuminated by a ceiling light.

The room was fitted out, furnished or decorated–however one might care to put it–in a bizarrely macabre fashion. Skeletons hung from one wall; another was almost completely covered by brightly-colored anatomical illustrations. A third wall was lined with glass-fronted cabinets filled with dissecting instruments, jars, test-tubes, flasks of variously-tinted liquids, bandages and bundles of cotton wool. The floor was concrete, with trenches radiating from the feet of the table to the walls, within which a clear liquid flowed incessantly and soundlessly. Some 20 stools of varying height were distributed haphazardly. The fourth wall was pierced by three doors. There were no windows. Warmed by an invisible heater, the air in the room was comfortably breathable, and strangely perfumed with vervain.

Standing beside the table, in front of the extended bodies, three men remained alone when the porters had gone. These men were Wilfried, the commander of the North Pole, Krieg, the chief electrician, and Glass, the chief of staff and physician-surgeon. They had been asleep when the sentries had alerted them to an unprecedented, extraordinary and utterly unexpected incident: the landing of a biplane about a kilometer south-west of Fort Warteck. The officer of the watch had done nothing but follow standard orders, alerting the three chiefs and bombarding the temeritous invaders with soporific gas-shells. Now, in the dissecting room, the three chiefs were standing before the sleeping captives, whose headgear they had just removed.

"Two women and a man," said Glass. "Strange! We must undress them a little further to get a better look at their faces."

"I don't think it's necessary," Wilfried opined, "to wake them up before the Supreme Lord..."

"Naturally," Krieg said. "Let's not forget the detail that the man was trussed up like a sausage."

They set to work. Within a few minutes, the three bodies were dispossessed of gloves, cloaks and boots.

"Oh!" Wilfried exclaimed. "I've seen that face before at the Hollow Rock! It's Grisyl–the one with the Russian mother."

"And I've seen this one–such perfect beauty!" cried Glass. "On my last trip to Paris, in the foyer of the Opéra, then at a dinner for artistes and in honor of Professor Lourmel, the medical director of the Clinique Molière. It's La Païli! The famous..."

"Silence, Glass!"

"Yes! Silence."

The three men looked at one another. They were not without some knowledge of their Supreme Lord's human passions. And La Païli...

"As for this one," said Krieg, pursing his lips, "it's some aviator."

"What the Devil can have happened?" murmured Wilfried. "The Hollow Rock has been taken by the Nyctalope and occupied by the English. We know that all the Wartecks over there, and all their personnel, are in the power of English and French jailers. We know, too, hat their captivity will only last until June 10 or 11–but why and how Grisyl and La Païli..."

"The aircraft's from the new squadron at Le Bourget," said Krieg. "It might very well have come directly from its hangar, in five or six stages."

"There's no need for further discussion," Wilfried said. "The mere presence of this woman"–he pointed to La Païli–"is sufficient to justify what I need to do."

"Wake up the Supreme Lord?" Glass asked.

"Yes."

"Go on, then. In the meantime, Krieg and I will go through their pockets."

"Certainly–we must make sure that when they wake up, none of them can use a weapon. You never know..."

Wilfried left the room.

Laurence and Grisyl were dressed much as Romski was, in jackets and trousers of a military cut, felt leggings and thick woolen calf-length socks. Grisyl's hair was cut short, but Laurence had been content with braiding her beautiful hair tightly and twisting it into a sort of crown. Krieg and Glass rummaged through all the pockets, internal and external, of their jackets, and then those in their trousers. They patted their arms and legs to make sure that no weapons were concealed under their clothing; they unbuttoned their shirts–uninhibitedly in the case of the man, but rather delicately in those of the two women–and then buttoned them up again. The results of the search were three Brownings of a model unknown to them, six ammunition-clips, three knives and three pairs of steel handcuffs.

"Ha!" said Glass. "I wonder why Grisyl was armed in the same way as this aviator, who was tied up in his bucket-seat while the two women were apparently walking towards Fort Warteck!"

"Let's not discus it, Glass, if you please."

"Quite right, Krieg."

The two men fell silent, studying La Païli's divine features–but Krieg suddenly shivered, and murmured: "I believe, Glass, that we'd do better not to look at her."

Glass blushed and turned away, saying: "You're right, Krieg."

The two men went to sit down on stools, some distance away from the table, placed in such a manner that the furs heaped up beside the aviator completely hid the bodies of Grisyl and La Païli from their view.

A quarter of an hour went by. There was absolute silence in the room, and nothing moved.

Suddenly, one of the three doors at the back opened. Glô von Warteck appeared, his hair uncombed, his face impassive and his eyes gleaming. He was dressed in a sort of white flannel pajama suit, with fur slippers on his feet. Krieg and Glass got to their feet and waited, their attitude respectful but not rigid. After a brief pause, the Baron came forward rapidly. Wilfried followed him, leaving the door to close by itself, but he went to set himself beside Krieg and Glass rather than staying close to the Supreme Lord.

417

Stopping in front of La Païli, Glô remained transfixed for a full minute. His face was expressionless. His eyes, half-hidden by lowered lids, were now invisible to his three relatives and subordinates, who were passionately attentive beneath their appearance of careless submission.

Glô slowly raised his right hand and took hold of La Païli's left hand–but his attention was suddenly caught by a gleam of light close at hand; it was the blade of a dagger half-drawn from its fur sheath. He saw the Brownings, the ammunition clips, the knives and the handcuffs. His bony fingers contracted about Laurence's hand. Raising his head and turning slightly to one side, he fixed his cold eyes upon Wilfried, Krieg and Glass.

If he had wanted to, Glô the Sorcerer could certainly have read the three men's thoughts–but he only indulged in those terrible games, which tired him so, when he judged it necessary. At Schwarzrock, he took pleasure in maintaining his frightful prestige in the eyes of his garrison by frequently showing its men and women that he had no need of words, but here, at Fort Warteck, especially with regard to his three assistants, the Supreme Lord had no need to expend fluid in that fashion. He spoke, therefore, as if he were an ordinary man. In a voice that was slightly gruff, he said: "How were these weapons distributed?"

It was Krieg who replied: "Equally among the three captives; each had a Browning, a dagger and a pair of handcuffs."

"And this one was tied up?" Glô said, pointing at the aviator with his left hand.

"Very tightly," Glass replied. "I untied him. There's the rope, in the corner of the table."

There was a pause, then Glô said: "Wilfried, Krieg, Glass, pick up these weapons and clothes and take them away. Come straight back." He let go of Laurence's hands. His eyes followed the three men as they carried out his order. When the door closed again behind the heels of Glass–the last to go out–Glô shuddered violently. He leapt up and knelt on the edge of the table, leaned over and placed his hands on Laurence's shoulders. He violated her closed lips with a frenzied kiss.

When the three men came back, however, having been absent for less than a minute, Glô was standing up impassively, with one of La Païli's hands between his fingers. Immediately, he said: "Glass, carry Grisyl to my mother's apartment; wait there until my mother wakes up. Tell her what has happened and that you're entrusting Grisyl to her, on my behalf. Then wake Grisyl up."

"Yes, Lord!" said Glass, with a bow.

"Krieg, lock this man in a cell and leave him there, under the surveillance of a guard. When he wakes up of his own accord, have him killed by the Kalmuks. They've been deprived of entertainment for a long time."

"Yes, Lord." Krieg bowed deeply.

"As for you, Wilfried, go make a detailed examination of the aeroplane and its contents, so that you can tell me about it when I question you."

Wilfried made a reverent gesture identical to those of Glass and Krieg. "Yes, Lord!"

Then, outwardly calm but trembling with an inexpressible joy, in the grip of an emotion seemingly capable of turning him inside out, and burning with mad desire, Lucifer took the sleeping body of Laurence Païli in his arms and went out of the sinister room.

A few minutes later, he deposited his living burden on a long and broad blue divan, scattered with silk cushions in every shade of blue. There was a canopy above it, from which hung three light silk curtains, opened almost to their full extent, all in the same delicate shade of blue.

The large room, of which the divan took up the whole of one side, was hung with pale blue silk and furnished very elegantly, with a sort of comfortable voluptuousness. The low bed also had a canopy with blue curtains. There were a few armchairs, some poufs, two tables, a small settee and two wardrobes, all in a new style slightly reminiscent of the aristocratic English style of recent years, but much more graceful in its lines and more harmonious in its contours.

The room was an exact reproduction of the set of a lyrical drama in which La Païli had scored the greatest success of her career at the Opéra-Comique. If, instead of being shielded by masculine clothing of a military sort, the singer laid out on the divan had been wearing the delicate low-cut dress that had formerly hugged the curves of her divine figure while she relaxed, smiling, on an exactly similar divan on the stage of the Opéra-Comique, Glô von Warteck would not have waited for the young woman to wake up, naturally or otherwise! He would have forgotten his formidable role in the terrestrial world, his ambitions, his plans, and everything else. He would have forgotten it all... And the Man would finally have triumphed over the rebel Woman.

What would it have mattered that she was asleep? Why should that give him pause? There was so little difference between this sleeping Laurence and La Païli the performer, awaiting the arrival of her beloved in a near-rapturous state. Yes, if Laurence had been wearing La Païli's dress here... But while La Païli was extended there, Glô von Warteck was abruptly brought back from the dream into which the room's imitative appearance had transported him into reality– because Laurence was presently dressed like a man!

Glô released a kind of roar, threw himself backwards and clenched his fists upon his brow, where pearls of seat were forming, so violent and profound was his reaction. He muttered furiously: "Mad! Mad! Worse than mad! Stupid and ridiculous! What was I going to do? Waste in a matter of seconds that from which I expect ecstasies a hundred times renewed! And while that woman might have knowledge in her head crucial to success and failure, good and evil–which is to say, my life or my death. From her, I shall discover where my enemies are. From her, I shall discover what happened to Hunter and Rupert VI... That's the immediate necessity! Afterwards, will there not be days and nights, weeks and months and years, years to renew my pleasure, provided that I don't extinguish it forever in a few minutes! Come on! First, let's find out why and how La Païli, the Nyctalope's lover, and Grisyl of the Hollow Rock, are here, at the North Pole, with an aviator found tied up in his own aircraft!"

Lucifer, having conquered his lust, collected himself again. He propped Laurence's sleeping body up, supporting it with a pile of cushions. Then he sat on a pouf, facing his victim. Simply extending his hands palm outwards, without making any ritual passes in the air, solely by the force of his will, he caused the young woman to pass from the sleep in which she was plunged into another far less innocent: a third-stage hypnotic trance. In a moderate tone, but forcefully, he said: "Laurence, tell me everything that you have done, heard, seen and said–everything, Laurence!–since I bit you on the breast on May 20. I want you to recall every slight detail, Laurence! Tell me, day by day, everything that has happened between the morning of May 12 and the night of June 4. I'm listening–speak!"

Meekly, Laurence began speaking in a monotonous voice, without inflection or pause, as someone with an excellent memory might recite, without being conscious of it, a patiently-memorized story.

XV. The Nyctalope versus Lucifer

At the moment when La Païli, unconscious and subjugated by Lucifer, began her recitation in the blue room in Fort Warteck, the Nyctalope's three aircraft touched down ten kilometers away.

Leo Saint-Clair had not revealed the whole of his plan in the course of the councils held at Elmwood. He had allowed it to be believed that his offensive would be launched directly against Fort Warteck itself–but he had actually resolved, with Lourmel and Sir Patrick Swires, to strike first at the enemy's submarine station, which was ten kilometers south of the Pole.

Having left Elmwood as if to head straight for Fort Warteck, the RC4, commanded by Saint-Clair and piloted by Captain Girard, soon veered slightly westwards, towards the point of the compass where the submarine station lay. The RC1 and RC2 followed meekly. The three aircraft, at some risk, attained and surpassed their officially-prescribed maximum speed, because the Nyctalope wanted to reduce the lead that Laurence and Grisyl had on him.

"Shall we arrive in time to save them?" he said to himself, anxiously. He did not think about the danger to which he might be exposed by revelations made by Laurence, a marvelous medium in Lucifer's hands. In any case, Laurence did not know the principal dispositions and means of combat that the Nyctalope was employing. She also did not know that Saint-Clair and his companions would be outside the field in which the double sight of the medium and her hypnotic interrogator could operate. Tranquil on that matter, the Nyctalope had only to worry about the lives of Laurence, Grisyl and Romski. Naturally, he was primarily concerned with the perils threatening the diva, which he felt in is heart as a painful contraction.

"Faster, faster! Faster still!" he would have cried to Girard, had he not restrained himself.

Eventually, they arrived. The RC4's chronometer showed 2:35 a.m. when Saint-Clair touched Girard on the shoulder–the signal which meant "land." A red light was shining in the distance: the submarine station's beacon.

The three aircraft had a suitable landing-ground beneath them. They set down without incident. Immediately, having been given orders in advance, Pilou ran to the RC1 and RC2. "Open the sacks," he said, "and put on the diving-suits. Put the metal canisters on your backs. Screw the nozzles into the sockets on the left of the helmets, then open the taps. Buckle your Brownings and knives to your belts. Quickly! Quickly!"

Physical movement and cerebral excitation produce heat–fortunately, for taking off one's furs outdoors, in a temperature of 30 degrees below zero, getting into a leather diving-suit, then putting on fur boots, suspending a metal canister from one's shoulders, screwing the inferior circle of a helmet into the collar of the suit to make a hermetic seal, and manipulating a breathing-tube, straps and buckles, is neither easy nor without danger for any man.

Surprised by the unexpected occurrence—for the Nyctalope's secret plan was known only to Lourmel and Swires—these men felt their excitement increase; obliged to hurry, they moved rapidly. Under their furs, the men were tightly swathed in wool. Within five minutes, all 15 were ready; Saint-Clair, Swires and Pilou, of course, had not needed the whip of surprise to excite them.

The Nyctalope's plan comprised the employment of hermetically-sealed diving-suits, which would be infused with three hours' supply of the radioactive gas contained under pressure in the metal canisters. Because each diving-suit formed a carapace which the external air could not penetrate, the entire bodies of the 15 men would be plunged for three hours into the radioactive atmosphere that even the effluvia of the Teledynamo could not penetrate.

The 15 men assembled in front of the three aircraft, their forms seeming bizarre and apocalyptic in the sinister daylight, with their huge spherical helmets lending a nightmarishly elephantine aspect to their heads. At a distance, though, they would have been hardly visible, for their fur boots, diving-suits, helmets and gauntlets all had the same off-white color as the grey-and-white ensemble of the glacial surface, the foggy horizon and the lowering sky.

The submarine station's sentries were no less vigilant than Fort Warteck's, for the spectral troop had not taken a hundred paces towards their goal when they were detected, located and illuminated. A searchlight-beam sprang forth from a squat tower and enveloped the 15 diving-suits with its rays.

It is hardly necessary to specify that these diving-suits carried none of the apparatus which, beneath the sea, has the effect of making them heavier than water. They had no lead weights on the chest and back, nor did they have lead-soled boots. There were the helmets—but the helmets were relatively light on robust shoulders. As for the metal canisters, they only weighed five kilograms.

As the searchlight-beam shot out, Saint-Clair cried: "Forward, quickly! Straight ahead!" All the helmets were equipped with miniature wireless telephone apparatus,

They broke into a run, Brownings in hand.

A shell fell some way behind the charging troop, burst like a grenade and released its cloud of soporific gas. Others fell, one by one—and the artillerists quickly corrected their range, so that these burst ahead of the troop. What did it matter? The noxious smoke could not get inside their helmets.

With Saint-Clair, Swires, Corsat and Pilou in a line at the head, then Girard leading a tightly-bunched platoon of ten, Lucifer's enemies arrived at the searchlight tower. Beyond the squat buildings, there was a sparkling expanse of water, from which vapor was rising. There was a door at the base of the tower.

Saint-Clair put his left hand into a cartridge-bag secured to his belt. He drew out a gleaming tube with a screw-cap. He turned the cap through a semicircle and set the tube at the bottom of the door. Then he ran towards the squat buildings.

Everyone followed him. They went around the edge of the vast pool. A door opened in the facing wall of one of the buildings and a man appeared. What other reaction could he have to the sight of the white diving-suits save total bewilderment? His thoughts had not finished crossing his mind before he was seized, shoved back inside and handcuffed. The attackers rushed in like a whirlwind.

At that moment, the walls seemed to vibrate. A dull explosion had just sounded and resounded outside, like an earthquake. Men were shouting. desperately calling for help.

"That's the tower blowing up!" said Saint-Clair. He ran on, now followed not by 14 soldiers but only by nine. They were the advance-party. By means of the detailed revelations obtained from Rupert VI under hypnosis, Saint-Clair and Swires knew the basic lay-out of both the submarine station and Fort Warteck; Swires and four other men were sufficient to hold the station; Saint-Clair and his nine men were going on to the fort.

First, Sir Patrick posted Elias Carter as a sentinel at the console controlling telephonic and telegraphic communications with Fort Warteck; he had a Browning in each hand. Thus, Wilfried received no warning of the attack on the station. As for the noise made by blowing up the watch-tower, if it was perceived at the Fort, it was confused with the ever-present cracking sounds emitted by the shifting ice-cap.

Sir Patrick and his four men, benefiting from surprise and the initial victory over the sentries, were adequate to close down the few ill-defended functions of the submarine station. As for the *Kaiser-Gott*, aboard which were 15 crew-members, including Commander Durbox and two officers, it was immobilized in the basin by its magnetic dock and isolated from the terrestrial buildings by the closure of its connecting tubes. The lever regulating the magnetization of the submarine dock was under Elias Carter's control, for the entire control panel was before the geographer's eyes, beside the telephono-telegraphic console. The little room occupied by the energetic and vigilant Elias was the heart of the submarine station, where everything worked by electricity.

By leaving the dock to which the *Kaiser-Gott* was stuck magnetized, they obliged the crew to suffer an indefinite imprisonment, for the escape of any individual through one of the submarine's hatches in a diving-suit would expose the fugitive to deadly gunfire as soon as he emerged from the water. As for the possibility of a collective escape by means of the submersible launch with which the *Kaiser-Gott* was equipped, that was impossible for the simple reason that, being largely composed of metal parts, it would be drawn to and captured by the magnetic docks.

All these considerations, made in advance, had persuaded the Nyctalope to leave only four men with Sir Patrick to secure and hold the station; these four auxiliaries were Carter, Captain Berton, Cadet Dupuis and Wolf. Sir Patrick would much rather have gone to Fort Warteck than stay at the submarine station, but as he was the only seaman on the expedition, that marked him out as the best man to capture the *Kaiser-Gott* and he was destined to his role.

Further means of transport were supplied by automatic electric trams and a double-track line some ten kilometers long, set on foundations of black basalt between two walls of streaming ice, which connected the submarine station to the agglomeration of buildings known as Fort Warteck. Saint-Clair felt no disquiet relative to Swires and his four men as he boarded the carriage that was already mounted on the ascendant rail within its garage.

The Nyctalope set himself at the conductor's post and took hold of the rheostat by means of which the intensity of the current–and hence the speed of the tram–was increased or decreased. Corsat and Pilou stood to either side of him, silent Brownings in hand. Then they were off!

What emotions those men were feeling! What a tempest of suppositions was whirling in their minds! Corsat and Pilou were shivering to the point of grinding their teeth. This time, they were going up against Lucifer himself! At Schwarzrock, during the fist offensive, they had had no idea of what awaited them. At Schwarzrock again, during the second offensive, circumstances had suggested to them from the outset that the enemy had slipped away. Here, though, at Fort Warteck, at the North Pole, it was the end. The beast would be cornered. The net's fall would be definitive, since Lucifer's mother and his remaining relatives would be in it with him. The lair would be swept clean, completely.

But what form would the final battle take?

Corsat and Pilou were so violently overexcited–the radioactive atmosphere in which they were enclosed contributed to that–that they both felt the need, simultaneously, to let their feelings out in speech. The miniature radiotelephones in their helmets permitted that.

"Boss!" said the impulsive Provençal.

"Boss!" said the Burgundian, immediately afterwards.

"What is it, my friends?" replied the Nyctalope, calmly.

The tramway ran almost silently at a speed of 30 kilometers an hour. Six minutes had gone by since the departure; three kilometers had been covered. Only seven kilometers and 14 minutes, remained.

"If anything has delayed the RC3," Pilou said, "we might have a chance of finding Lucifer asleep."

"Why should the RC3 have made poorer time than our own squadron?" objected Corsat. "We'll find Lucifer awake."

"Provided that Mademoiselle Laurence and Grisyl..."

"And Romski..."

Pilou and Corsat had had no more difficulty than Saint-Clair in deducing the goal of the RC3's flight with the two women aboard.

"My friends," the Nyctalope put in, "don't form unnecessary hypotheses. We don't know and can't know what has been happening in Fort Warteck for the last half hour or so, what is happening at this moment, or what will happen in the dozen minutes that still separate us from the moment when we leap out on to the platform..."

"But, boss...!"

"Damn it...!"

"Yes, yes, I know. You both need to talk, because you're overexcited and because we have nothing to do while the tram is running–nothing that would serve to let it out. Well, grit your teeth, stretch your muscles, tense your nerves–and shut up!"

"Yes, boss." This time, the two voices were obedient. Nothing more was heard. Outside the tram, as in the interior, there was silence.

The temperature of the heated air in the trench was the same as that of the air in the tram, whose doors remained open, its thick crystal windows no only slightly misted. On the other hand, the glass visors of the diving-suit helmets remained perfectly clear, because the condensation that the men's breath might have produced was rendered impossible by the radioactive atmosphere–to such an extent that the more studious travelers could observe the walls of the trench. That served them as a distraction for a few minutes, and they exchanged their thoughts on the subject–for they all felt, perhaps unconsciously, a sort of puerile pride in demonstrating that they were not entirely preoccupied by what awaited them at the end of the line. But that game only took up the first five or six minutes of the journey; after that they spoke less, then no longer looked outside at all, then fell silent.

Eventually, the seven men, who had been sitting down, got up–and, without a word of explanation, as if by instinct, separated into two groups. One group, of five men, moved on to the more spacious rear platform; the other, a mere couple, went on to the forward platform to stand behind Corsat and Pilou. Saint-Clair heard them, and turned his head.

"Berge and Dopp," he said. "That's good. Girard will command the others–the second line." He had read the newcomers' names on their breasts, for he and Swires had taken the hasty precaution, at Elmwood, of using a paintbrush and black ink to scrawl the name of each of the 15 men–including his and Swires's–on the front of his white diving-suit, and on the sacks in which they were contained.

"We're almost there!" said Berge.

"Yes!" said Corsat.

The ten-kilometer route was perfectly straight. One kilometer still remained to be covered and nothing could be seen at the end but a white wall as high as the trench. Above it, to the right, was a black, grey and white architectural mass whose base as hidden by the wall of the trench.

"A man!" said Pilou and Corsat, in unison.

"Kill him!" said Saint-Clair, coldly.

They were scarcely 400 meters away. A doorway had opened in the white wall, forming a black rectangle in contrast to the whiteness of the wall and the roseate exterior daylight. The man within it was bare-headed, clad in a military uniform of indeterminate color. He raised his arms and turned round, probably to go back inside and give a signal–but Corsat and Pilou had already taken aim and fired.

The silent Brownings made their usual faint click and the man reeled sideways, falling full-length like a felled tree.

"Some irresponsible subaltern," Saint-Clair said. "He probably didn't deserve to die–but left alive he'd have given us away, and that would have been too awkward. Stop!"

The Nyctalope brought the rheostat's slider to the zero position and used his other hand to turn the brake-wheel. He jumped down immediately, Browning in hand. Corsat and Pilou jumped with him, with Berge and Dopp behind them. The second group was already running forward, Girard at their head.

The exit was a revolving door; they set it turning and passed through. They found themselves in a room that was obviously a guard-room. Two men were sleeping on wooden bunks. In the middle of the room was a chair and a fixed table, on which were a dozen numbered electrical switches. A single ceiling-light gave out a moderate light.

Saint-Clair leaned over the two sleeping men. "Kalmuks," he said. "No need to regret the death of the watchman." He beckoned Dopp, who was nearest to him and came running. "Handcuff these two men! Stay here, Dopp. Orders: kill anyone who comes in."

"Understood, boss!"

Saint-Clair did not hesitate between the four doors that could be seen in the guardroom's interior walls. He remembered Rupert VI's revelations word for word. The doors were numbered; he went towards No. 4. "Forward, my friends," he said, in a calm and incisive voice that was scarcely altered by the microphone.

It was an elevator; the nine suited divers filled it. Their leader pushed the button and the elevator went up.

One floor, two, three, four–halt!

The nine men came out into a long corridor extending to the left and the right, illuminated by ceiling-lights. No one was in it; there was silence.

Saint-Clair knew the only double-paneled door opening on to this corridor–the others had only one section–was that of Glô's personal apartment, his living-quarters. It was immediately under the tower, one floor below the large laboratory-cum-library whose ceiling supported the base of the dome of the crystal cupola, where the Teledynamo was.

How was it possible, given the probable circumstances of that unique night, that there were no sentries or guards there? Within his carapace, the Nyctalope shivered, his emotion increasing. For 30 seconds, his thoughts became vertiginous. Was it possible that Laure, Grisyl and Romski had not yet arrived? That everyone at Fort Warteck, except for the Kalmuks on guard down in the access-bunker, was deep in that peaceful nocturnal sleep in which nothing troubles or threatens the human soul? Could it be that, in a bedroom, in the apartment whose double door was directly facing the elevator, the intangible, formidable, mysterious Lucifer was asleep? Asleep! Asleep, at the very minute when the Nyctalope...

"Is it possible?" murmured Saint-Clair, disconcerted. "Such an easy victory? I know the secret of how to open and close that door and the ones within. Less than a week ago, only three men and one woman knew it–Lucifer, Wilfried, Rupert VI and Diana von Warteck, the monster's mother. Rupert revealed it to me. Lucifer doesn't know that, since he has not talked since then to Rupert, Lourmel, Sir Patrick Swires or me–so I can go in and...so simply? Let's go, then! The die is cast."

He marched towards the double door, and his eight companions followed him.

Wilfried, Krieg and Glass had obeyed Glô's orders with the promptitude and docility habitual to every member of the Warteck family and household. The execution of the orders concerning Grisyl, Romski and the aeroplane only required ten minutes.

In the vestibule of Diana's apartment, Glass installed the sleeping Grisyl on two armchairs, sat down on a third, lit his pipe–which he was hardly ever without–and began smoking in a leisurely fashion, thinking about La Païli, the Opéra and Paris while awaiting the appearance of the maid allocated to the service of the Supreme Lord's mother.

Krieg had the aviator locked up in a subterranean cell by one of the Kalmuk sentries in the guardroom of the access-bunker and went back to his own apartment, where he went back to bed as complacently as anyone in the world and went to sleep.

Meanwhile, Wilfried went to supervise the inventory–which he had already ordered on his on authority–of the aeroplane and its contents.

The "front" of Fort Warteck was, in effect, the side of the complex which faced the railway to the submarine station. The "back" was, in consequence, the side parallel to that face, for the buildings formed a single square. At the four corners of the outer wall, at some distance from the central building surmounted by the tower and the dome, stood four square fortifications forming permanent guard-rooms. It was from one of these small forts that the light had been directed and the rain of soporific gas-shells launched after the appearance of the two human forms which had descended from the unexpected aircraft. It was the garrison of that same fort which had emerged and brought back, along with the three sleepers, the aeroplane itself.

The aircraft was rapidly dismantled–specialists in aviation and mechanics were abundant among the ranks of the slave-workers–and it was introduced, piece by piece, into the large, almost bare room that occupied the ground floor of the building and served as an ammunition store. Inventory was immediately taken of the various objects contained in the aircraft; all Wilfried had to do was recapitulate and confirm this inventory. It took him five minutes.

There was nothing unusual among these objects, because–perhaps fortunately for Saint-Clair and his 14 companions–Romski, Laurence and Grisyl had not brought sacks containing diving-suits; they did not even know of their existence, because the sacks had not been distributed to the other three aircraft until the RC3 had departed.

Once the inventory was signed, Wilfried left the little fort and went back to the central building, where–like Krieg–he simply went back to bed.

Long habit had accustomed these three men not to preoccupy themselves with anything that they were not specifically instructed to do. They had no freedom to act on their own when Glô was present, being entirely submissive to his decisions. This long habit of non-reflection and non-responsibility in the presence of the Supreme Lord had made Wilfried, Krieg and Glass into corporals devoid of initiative, almost indifferent to everything. Obliged to stay awake, Glass stayed awake, consoling himself with his pipe and reminiscences of his trips to Paris. Free to stay awake or sleep, Wilfried and Krieg chose the second alternative, because they were tired after the labors of the previous day and had a human need for sleep.

It was for that reason that, 30 or 40 minutes after the ill-timed arrival of the aircraft, everyone in Fort Warteck who had the right to be asleep at that hour was asleep. The only men on watch were in the four little corner-forts and the access-bunker in the tramway terminus. What happened in the bunker was no concern of the sentries in the forts. That was why Saint-Clair's tram had been able to reach its destination and the invaders were able to dismount without being troubled by anything but the preliminary appearance of a single man, of whom Corsat's and Pilou's silent Brownings had easily taken care. The watchmen in the forts had not paid any attention to the arrival of the tram; it was not uncommon for carriages to pass back and forth during the nocturnal hours.

That was why Saint-Clair and his companions were able to get as far as the door of Lucifer's apartment, having killed only one man and taken only two prisoners. As for the absence of any guards from the long corridors, that was perfectly logical: they were at the North Pole! Fort Warteck was surrounded by defenses. Anyone attempting to get there by walking along the trench would have been electrocuted within 20 yards by contacts embedded and concealed in the basalt floor. The trench was impassable, except by tram–and how likely was it that an enemy might overwhelm the submarine station without Fort Warteck being alerted by a signal almost as rapid as thought?

In taking all these defensive precautions, however, Lucifer had not taken into account the Nyctalope or Professor Lourmel. When the fighting man and the man of science had allied themselves against him, Lucifer had shrugged his shoulders and laughed, for he was at the North Pole and the Teledynamo would be ready on June 10! And finally, when Lucifer had learned at 3 a.m. on June 5 from the submissive mouth of Laurence Païli, that the Nyctalope and Lourmel were at Cape Flora, within 1,200 kilometers of the Pole, he had laughed and thought: *We'll put these crusaders to sleep and gather them up when they come, just as the delightful and naïve Laure, my heart's desire, was gathered up.*

Despite all his science, Lucifer was ignorant of the brilliant application that Saint-Clair had secretly made, by means of humble diving-suits, of the radioactive gas whose antiteledynamic properties Lourmel had discovered, and whose marvelous action La Païli had just described involuntarily. Lucifer had laughed again, then. *Ah! If they all enclose themselves in the glass cage with the radioactive gas and wait for June 10, they will be prisoners and victims of their own discovery!* And that point, the Baron had been utterly convinced of his own power and the definitive weakness of all other men—including such upstarts as Lourmel and Saint-Clair...

Finally, finally, Lucifer had La Païli there, in front of him! And in less than 24 hours, the *Lampas* would come into the harbor of the submarine station, bringing Irène!

It was for all these reasons, in sum, that Leo Saint-Clair, the Nyctalope, had arrived without any significant difficulty at the door of Lucifer's apartment, with nothing between him and the monster but the mechanism of a lock, whose secret he knew.

So the Nyctalope marched up to the door that had two panels, at a calm and rapid pace, followed by his eight companions.

Behind that door and others, beyond several other rooms, was the blue bedroom. In that blue bedroom, La Païli had just completed her recitation, rendering account of everything she had witnessed since her resurrection in the Nyctalope's house in the Rue Nansouty in Paris. When she had finished, Lucifer knew about the offensive that the Nyctalope's three aircraft were trying to mount at that moment, but he was not worried, because there were sentries in the little forts and there was no shortage of gas-filled shells for the pneumatic cannons from which they were launched. Lucifer also knew about the offensive planed by La Païli and Grisyl, with the help of the Polish officer.

He spoke aloud, as if Laurence could hear him consciously, saying: "Romski and Grisyl will be killed, but not you, my perfidious beauty. I shall wake you up and possess you without further delay. When your Saint-Clair arrives, you will display yourself to his eyes, O sublime lover, so that he shall have no doubt of his misfortune!"

He sniggered. He was overwhelmed by such desire and such violent impatience that he forgot his ambition to take possession of La Païli while she was consenting and desperate at the same time. Since he had her here, now, he would wait no longer! Given the state of weakness she would be in when she came out of her hypnotic trance, she would not have the physical strength to defend herself, but she would be conscious enough to take account of the actions of others and her own sensations.

Conclusively resolved, desirous that all should be consummated before the Nyctalope's arrival–when he would be brought in unconscious, by virtue of the soporific gas–Lucifer made haste. First, he undressed the inanimate young woman, rapidly and brutally. When the splendid body was no longer clad in anything but the light silk underwear that La Païli had retained beneath her masculine garments, Lucifer hurriedly made the ritual gestures that would bring the hypnotic trance to an end.

His hands were trembling. His face bore a livid pallor. His eyes were infused with blood.

Extended on the divan, among the cushions, almost in the pose that Titian gave to his Danaë, but with the right leg dangling instead of folded,[73] Laurence Païli woke up.

She released a long sigh, opened her eyes slightly, closed them again, then opened them wide. With infinite lassitude, they expressed all the surprise of which a sleep-clouded mind is capable.

The light emitted by the electric lamps was softened by pale blue shades. Perfume–chypre and violets–floated in the lukewarm air.

"Where am I?" sighed Laurence, trying to sit up. She could only raise herself on to her elbow, but she held her head up and looked around.

"Oh! Is it possible...?"

Her face expressed immense amazement. She recognized the bedroom–it was the one in the lyrical drama that had contributed so much to her fame. A thousand memories flooded her mind. The illusion was so complete that it only awaited the entrance of the Prince Charming to become a perfect replica–so she looked at the door through which he ought to come.

On the back of an armchair, within arm's reach, the singer saw the large silk cloak in which she had wrapped herself at the end of the act. La Païli thought about her dress then, and made the habitual gesture necessary to rectify its folds–but her hand suddenly remained in suspense, for Laurence saw herself, and saw that she was almost naked.

She sat up with a sudden start, her pupils dilated, her head pounding with blows that threatened madness. It was, indeed, only a start; the unfortunate girl was too weak to sustain herself. She fell back on the divan, among the cushions, into her original position, her body sprawling and her thoughts in disorder–but with her eyes still turned to Prince Charming's door.

The door opened–but it was Lucifer who made his entrance!

She saw him. Her clouded mind was cleared, as if by a gust of wind. Her thoughts became focused.

She remembered everything–everything, from the moment of her collapse on the polar ice amid the clouds of soporific smoke emitted by the shells that burst like grenades–and she understood.

She tried to get up, in order to defend herself. She could only reach out as far as the cloak, seize it, draw it towards her and cover herself hurriedly and awkwardly.

He came forward, grave and pale–so pale!

Laurence understood, from the expression in Lucifer's eyes, that she was utterly lost this time. She knew only too well, alas, that she was too weak to put up a fight. She looked around. No Grisyl, no Romski–no one at all. And no weapon...

No weapon? Why, was she not a woman? Was she not a woman in love? Why was she here, if not to save her lover? Ah! She would sacrifice herself; she would save him. And then–benevolent death...

La Païli found the sublime strength to smile. Laurence smiled at Lucifer! Artfully transforming her gesture of horrified defense into a charming gesture of fearful modesty, she stammered: "I have come... as you desired... and I am yours... but wait, wait for..."

She fell silent, frozen by a nameless dread.

Lucifer had cut her speech short with a gesture. "Shut up, Laurence!" he said, brutally. "No need to act the part–you've already spoken, and told me everything, in the hypnotic trance from which you've just emerged. You came with Grisyl to kill me, crudely, with a bullet in the head. No more tricks–it's over. You're mine. Defend yourself if you wish. You can't do much. I'm stronger than you. And you'll be conscious of my strength, in the most intimate depths of your being."

He took a step towards the divan–but stopped short. In front of him and to the left, a door had opened–and framed in that doorway, white in the blue light, was a form both human and monstrous.

"Oh!" Lucifer exclaimed. He was transfixed, his eyes widening and his mind abruptly unbalanced, unable to understand or divine what was happening.

That exclamation, his facial expression and attitude galvanized Laurence. She was able to sit up, turn her head and look. At first, she understood no more than he did–but almost immediately, she let out a sharp cry.

"Leo! My beloved!"

Joy overwhelmed her, although terror and despair had been unable to do so, and she fell back on the cushions in a faint, her body chastely covered by the sumptuous silken cloak.

On the breast of the blanched diving-suit, scrawled in large black letters, was a name that Laurence had read, and which Lucifer now read: NYCTA-LOPE.

Leo Saint-Clair came into the blue room then, and eight similar monsters followed him in. When the door was closed, though, a collective instinct impelled them to line up with their backs to the wall-hangings, to either side of the door.

Saint-Clair came forward alone. Three paces in front of the petrified Lucifer, he stopped. He lifted up his helmet, which he had unscrewed from the collar of his suit in the elevator, in anticipation of this confrontation. With his head free and bare, his eyes fiery and his features set, he took two more forward steps. Then he raised his right hand, placed the index finger on Lucifer's breast–a breast palpating beneath the blue silk pajamas–and pronounced, in an imperious and glacial tone: "I challenge you, Baron Glô von Warteck of Schwarzrock! I challenge you, Glô XIII, master of the Teledynamo! I challenge you, sorcerer, monster, Lucifer!"

As Glô, finally able to react, shuddered and took a step backwards, the Nyctalope advanced by the same margin. "Listen to me!" he said, forcefully. "I could strike you down within a minute with a gunshot. These eight men could fire with me and you'd fall with nine bullets in you, as if before a firing-squad. I could do that–but I have not done it. It's too easy and, in my opinion, it would be cowardly." He fell silent and let his right arm fall back, divinely handsome in his mad bravery and cold determination.

Laurence, recovering consciousness, opened her eyes, propped herself up between two cushions, watched and listened.

Saint-Clair went on: "Me against you! The Nyctalope against Lucifer! My mind against your mind! My will against your will! Me to subjugate you! I'm here. I'm looking you in the face–and I'm waiting. Try me, Lucifer!"

He folded his arms; he was like a statue of Defiance.

Glô von Warteck took another step backwards and he, too, drew his steely frame up to its full height. His eyes gleamed and he raised his arms and extended his hands to make cabalistic designs...

Some 20, 30, 40 seconds went by. Then, everything became vertiginous. Saint-Clair abruptly burst out laughing, joyful, insulting and formidable. While laughing, he quickly made the movements that rid him of the diving-suit. He emerged svelte and vigorous, lithe and agile, dressed in a white woolen pullover and trousers, and slippers.

"Corsat! Pilou! Your daggers!" he cried.

There were two movements behind him, and he suddenly had two blades in his hands: long, broad, sharp and shiny, with black hilts. He threw one of them down at the feet of Glô von Warteck, retaining the other in his right hand. Then, in a sardonic voice, the Nyctalope said: "God's judgment, Lucifer! Since your spell-casting will cannot impose itself on mine, sorcerer, become a man again! Take up that dagger and defend yourself, as best you can. We must revert, for a while, to the Middle Ages, whose spirit you've extinguished with the principles of your accursed science. *En garde*, Warteck!"

Lucifer, still upright, but now with the face of a madman, did not budge. Saint-Clair relaxed and took a step to the left. In a changed voice, cold and scornful, he said: "Baron Glô von Warteck, I warn you that if you refuse to fight me with a dagger, I will have you executed like the common murderer you are. You have killed Mathias Narbonne, the three Zuchts and Minna. Doubtless, they are not the only murders you have committed, but I don't know the other victims and those are sufficient for me. I'll count to ten. Then, I'll shout fire!" He turned his head towards his eight companions and concluded: "Then, all together, you'll fire."

Standing a little further to the left, so as to be outside the line of fire, he began counting: "One... Two... Three... Four..."

Eight hands, each armed with a Browning, were raised as one.

"Five... Six..."

On "seven," Lucifer finally reached down, picked up the dagger and said, harshly: "And if I win?"

"You'll be shot immediately afterwards," Saint-Clair said, "for murdering Mathias Narbonne, the three Zuchts and Minna."

"Why should I fight, then?" sneered Glô.

"Because you'll have an opportunity to kill me—which, I feel sure, would sweeten the bitterness of your own death."

"So it would! But why do you risk your own life when it's so easy to..."

Saint-Clair cut him off. "To enjoy the opportunity of killing you." Then, understanding from the Baron's hateful stare that the duel was accepted, he said to his companions: "Lower your weapons!"

He resumed his place in the center of the room.

"I can see you, Leo," said a soft but firm voice.

"I know that, Laure."

With his left arm raised as a shield and his right arm by his side, his weapon flat against his thigh in the manner of the peasants of Aragon, Leo Saint-Clair advanced on Lucifer.

What a spectacle! What a lesson in philosophy! What a symbol of true humanity! These two geniuses, who had fought with the weapons of science during weeks of prodigious cerebral activity, making heady progress with each passing day, were now brought together by the irony of circumstance and the fatal play of their own characters, to fight man-to-man with daggers, like two peasants from Spain!

Moreover, their passions were running so high, at that supreme moment, that the one forgot his satanic ambitions and the other his universal altruism. They were no longer fighting, now, for the conquest of the world or the liberty of humankind, but simply for the possession of a woman.

Until the last moment, however, Glô von Warteck continued to manifest that cowardice which consists of only exercising force at a distance. He had doubtless taken lessons in knife-throwing from Malta in the Bermudas. The dagger he had in his hand had a well-balanced blade and hilt; Glô had taken account of that when he took it in hand. He did not wait for Saint-Clair to come at him–he raised his right arm abruptly and hurled it forcefully. The blade shot through the air as if it were a ray of steel sprung from his open hand.

"Ah!" The strident cry of horror came from Laurence–but the Nyctalope had been on his guard. If he had not seen it in time, the sharp blade would have planted its entire length in his throat, but he ducked under it skillfully and promptly, and it flew over his head.

"Traitor!" he growled.

Standing erect and leaping forward, he drew back his dagger with a rapid movement and sank the blade into Lucifer's breast, slightly to one side.

The blade remained there. Saint-Clair stood back and folded his arms.

"My God!" gasped Laurence, intoxicated with joy.

Glô von Warteck staggered backwards. His wide-open eyes and screwed-up face expressed hatred and despair. He fell to his knees against a tapestry whose large folds hid the wall between two windows.

He's dying! thought Saint-Clair.

He's dying! thought La Païli and the eight men standing motionless at the back of the room.

There was a five-second interval. Leaning his left hand on the floor, Lucifer lifted the fabric with his right hand, seized a lever, put his entire weight on it, depressed it, and collapsed, croaking: "You'll... all die too!"

"Ah! Laurence, my friends–let's get out of here! Go!" howled the Nyctalope.

Who would not have understood? Presumptuous as he was, sure as he was of his ultimate victory, Lucifer had nevertheless taken precautions against his defeat, doubtless by virtue of some obscure and troubling presentiment, entertained since he had deciphered the prediction hidden in the verbal labyrinth of the Kabbalah. Every room in Fort Warteck was equipped with a mechanism which, once triggered, would provoke explosions, collapse, ruination, destruction and death.

"Go! Get out!"

Saint-Clair lifted up the semi-conscious Laurence. The entire company ran for the elevator, which descended. They went out through the guard-room bunker, on the side opposite the tramway.

"Dopp!" shouted Saint-Clair, as they passed through. Dopp followed, uncomprehendingly–after which the Nyctalope, his mind clear and alert and his gestures sure and lively, wrapped La Païli in one of the fur cloaks used by the Kalmuks, which was hanging from the wall near the exit door.

Outside, in the dreary daylight, a brief glance and a rapid thought sufficed for Saint-Clair to get his bearings. They had come out on the east side; ten kilometers to the south-west the three aircraft were waiting, near the submarine station.

"Go left! Go left!" the Nyctalope howled—and ran.

The large entrance court, like the tramway trench, was hollowed out of the ice and its atmosphere was similarly kept warm by means of electric radiators. The wall surrounding the buildings of Fort Warteck finished to the right and the left at the places where they branched out at right-angles to form the court. Heated galvanized iron stairways gave access to the surface of the ice-cap outside the wall.

"Go left!"

They climbed the left-hand stairway and ran headlong into the compacted snow, heading diagonally south-eastwards, distancing themselves from both the walls and the trench.

Less than three minutes had gone by since Lucifer had fallen dead upon the depressed lever. There was suddenly a mighty roar: explosions; a cataclysmic tornado.

The entire tightly-knit company of fugitives was seized by an invisible cyclonic wind, knocked down, sent skidding. Instinctively, some of the men grabbed hold of one another; those left isolated formed themselves into balls; Saint-Clair hugged Laurence tightly to him and was himself surrounded by the strong arms of Corsat and Pilou; their agglutinated mass slid over the ice and was brought to an abrupt halt by an outcrop of ice standing up like a menhir.

In the distance, flames leapt up from Fort Warteck towards the clouds; black masses soared upwards and fell back to Earth. It was as if a hundred cannons were firing at the same time. Detonations resounded along the entire length of the trench, towards the south, and smoke gushed into the air.

The Nyctalope, who was quite lucid, heard and saw it all. Having been shoved, dragged and rolled by the mighty wind, he was sitting where he had stopped, with his back to the ice menhir. To his right, Corsat and Pilou were taking off one another's helmets. Girard was lodged to his left, motionless. Leo Saint-Clair, the conqueror of Baron Glô von Warteck, alias Lucifer—still hugging Laurence's body, wrapped up in the Kalmuk's cloak—witnessed the total destruction and annihilation of Fort Warteck and, without any possible doubt, all the individuals within it.

"Grisyl! Admirable Grisyl!" Saint-Clair whispered, his heart gripped by gloomy regret. "Madame Païli! Romski!" And immediately thereafter: "What about the station? That must have been destroyed too, along with Sir Patrick Swires!"

"We're alive, boss!" said a hoarse voice beside him.

"We're alive!"

That was Pilou and Corsat.

"And I've killed Lucifer!" added Saint-Clair, with such emotion that large tears sprang from his eyes.

At that moment, Laurence stirred within the fur that enveloped her. She had recovered consciousness a few seconds before, and had heard the Nyctalope's words. She saw the tears running down his ecstatic face.

"Leo, my beloved!"

She raised herself up. He leaned over her. Their foreheads touched, their lips were united...

For them—for an interval that probably lasted a minute, but which comprised years of happiness for lovers who could no longer be separated—the outside world no longer existed...

Epilog

A few hours later, beside the RC1, RC2 and RC4, a short distance from the devastated submarine station, Leo Saint-Clair added up the balance-sheets of the victory and the catastrophe.

On the one hand, the victory: Lucifer dead; his family destroyed or taken prisoner; the liberty of humankind saved; Laurence, Irène and Henri Prillant free to enjoy life and love.

On the other hand, the catastrophe: Grisyl dead, Romski dead, Madame Païli dead, along with Sir Patrick Swires, Elias Carter, Captain Berton, Cadet Dupuis and Wolf; the Teledynamo lost; the scientific discoveries of every sort, for which Fort Warteck and the submarine station now served as tombs, blasted apart to the point where nothing useful remained.

But all that was over. It was necessary to act.

Retaining the RC4, with La Païli, Captain Girard, Corsat and Pilou, Saint-Clair took it upon himself to spend 24 hours exploring the ruins of Fort Warteck, the railway and the submarine station. Some distance away, he found Grisyl's head in the snow, almost intact.

The RC1 and RC2, with Aymard, Garet and Berge, flew out over the sea, where the compact polar ice gave way to the relatively open sea to await for the *Uberalles* and the *Lampas*, which could not be long delayed—because it was probable that Raymond de Ciserat, freed from all enchantment, and Professor Lourmel, warned about the destruction of Fort Warteck by the hypnotized Rupert VI, would not go into the waters beneath the ice-cap. The ignorance of what had happened would leave the former somewhat at a loss, astonished to find himself suddenly in the polar regions; logical deduction would assure the latter that the Nyctalope would undoubtedly send one or two aircraft on a reconnaissance mission, if that were not revealed to him by Rupert VI. That was, in fact, how events unfolded.

Is it necessary to describe the tender scenes that marked the reunion of the *Uberalles*, the *Lampas*, the RC1 and the RC2, soon rejoined by the RC4, with the Nyctalope and La Païli? Is it necessary to describe the sorrow of the Englishmen at Elmwood station when they received news of the deaths of Sir Patrick Swires and Elias Carter, ameliorated by the pleasure of knowing that Lucifer and his family were in no condition to enslave humankind? Is there, finally, any need to register the details of our heroes' return to France, or the exile to a Pacific island of the survivors of the Bermudas, or the fates of the thuggish Kroon, the straw man Eiger Nott and other nonentities?

And would it be appropriate to conclude this epic with a lengthy account of what the world's newspapers had to say about the marriage of the singer Laurence Païli to Leo Saint-Clair, the Nyctalope, at which Monsieur Alexandre Prillant, Onésime Lourmel, Raymond de Ciserat and Captain Girard served as witnesses?

La Païli continued her career as an actress and singer–which did not prevent her from presenting Leo Saint-Clair with three handsome sons during the next five years. Irène de Ciserat traveled a great deal by submarine, with her husband–which presented no obstacle to the birth of a daughter, and then a son, who was baptized with sea-water in the harbor at Rio de Janeiro. Henri Prillant became a brilliant student. In brief, life went on.

And at dawn every year, on June 6, in the garden of their château in Maintenon, Leo Saint-Clair and Laurence Païli kneel down in front of a marble stone surrounded by rosebushes.

There is nothing engraved on that stone but a name: GRISYL. For there is one act more beautiful than the act of love, and that is the act of sacrifice, which is often the consequence, the crowning glory and the purification of love.

THE END

JEAN DE LA HIRE

GORILLARD

Les Grandes Aventures du "NYCTALOPE"

★ Editions d'Hauteville ★

LES ROMANS D'AVENTURE

LES AMOURS DE L'INCONNU

(L'HOMME QUI PEUT VIVRE DANS L'EAU)

par JEAN DE LA HIRE

LE VOLUME 1.25

Not Alone in the Dark:
The Tumultuous Life and Troubled Times of the Nyctalope

Jean de La Hire's Leo Saint-Clair, alias the Nyctalope, is a French character who has not gained the recognition of the more famous Rocambole, Arsène Lupin, Rouletabille and Fantômas–nor, to be honest, did it deserve to, at least on its literary merits alone. Yet, the Nyctalope ought to be remembered as the first, full-fledged superhero in the history of French pulp literature, anticipating such larger than life crime-fighters as Doc Savage by more than 20 years.

Leo Saint-Clair is a fearless French explorer, adventurer and crimefighter, known as the Nyctalope because of his ability to see in total darkness. This, in fact, is the opposite of the real condition of *nyctalopia*–Greek for night blindness–which makes it difficult or nearly impossible to see in the dark. The Nyctalope is said to have eerie eyes, not unlike those of a lynx, with irises shifting colors between brown, yellow and green.

La Hire was notoriously inconsistent in the spellings of his characters' names, even within the same novels. In its first appearance, the Nyctalope is named "Leo Sainte-Claire" and in his second "Jean de Sainclair," but we shall use "Leo Saint-Clair" which is the standard version used by La Hire from the third novel onwards.

French scholar Hubert Juin notes in his foreword to the Marabout edition of *Les Mystères de Lyon* that La Hire was fond of using the name "Sainte-Claire" or "Saint-Clair" in the mainstream novels he wrote before 1908, often as an alias for himself. Whether any of these other "Saint-Clairs" or "Sainte-Claires" can, or should, be connected to the Nyctalope's family tree still remains to be investigated.

In any event, La Hire was not adverse to reusing the same fictional names for different characters in different works. For example, the Nyctalope novel *Titania* (1929) features an evil scientist named Korridès, while La Hire's popular pulp series, *Les grandes aventures d'un boy scout* [*The Great Adventures of a Boy Scout*] (1926), includes a good scientist also named Korridès!

To attempt to piece together a consistent biography of the Nyctalope sometimes requires us to choose between conflicting bits of information given throughout the series, selecting some while discarding or trying to explain away others. Most of these inconsistencies are due to the fact that La Hire chronicled the Nyctalope's adventures between 1911 and 1946. During that time, he was confronted by what is known in comic books today as the issue of the "sliding timescale," i.e.: the clash between the once-topical references and the seemingly agelessness of the hero. Whereas Edgar Rice Burroughs chose to make his Tarzan immortal, La Hire retroactively rewrote his hero's biography.

441

In addition to the spelling of the name "Saint-Clair" in the first two volumes, there are three major inconsistencies in the series: (i) the Nyctalope's birthdate, which appears to have been moved forward as the series went on; (ii) the Nyctalope's father, a French Navy Ensign named "Jean," then, later, an engineer named "Pierre" and (iii) the sudden aging of one of the hero's sons (also named "Pierre") between two of the later books.

We shall deal with these inconsistencies as they arise and try to posit various explanations for them.

Finally, it is worth noting that, throughout the series, La Hire makes it clear that the Nyctalope is a real figure and he, merely his biographer–just as Ponson du Terrail did with Rocambole and Maurice Leblanc with Arsène Lupin. He even specifies in a footnote that the notebook Leo loaned him to retranscribe his adventure was stained with the Nyctalope's own blood.

The saga of the Nyctalope begins with *L'Homme qui peut vivre dans l'eau* [*The Man Who Could Live Underwater*], first serialized in the daily newspaper *Le Matin* in 1909. In it, we meet Jean Sainte-Claire, who is only a supporting character in the story. He is introduced as a young French Navy Ensign, who is serving under Lieutenant Louis de Ciserat aboard the ship *Cyclone*. *L'Homme qui peut vivre dans l'eau* is about two megalomaniacal villains, Oxus, and his brother, the evil monk Fulbert, who are plotting to conquer the world. To achieve their goal, they have grafted shark gills onto an orphaned boy, raised him underwater and misled him as to the nature of the human race; they have turned him into the "Hictaner," a water-breathing man, who is meant to be their secret weapon. Then, posing as "L'Inconnu" (The Unknown), they attempt to blackmail the great powers of the world into submission.

Another protagonist is Charles Severac, a misguided militant anarchist and a formidable engineer, who has designed a super-powerful submarine called the *Torpedo*. As it turns out, Severac is also the Hictaner's biological father. At the end of the story, Severac betrays Oxus and Fulbert, the Hictaner is restored to normality and marries Moisette, Oxus' daughter. Together, they retire to live in peace on a small island near Tahiti. Fulbert manages to escape, while Oxus makes a deal with the authorities.

L'Homme qui peut vivre dans l'eau takes place between February and May of an unspecified year, but several topical references, such as a mention of a King of England as opposed to Queen Victoria, who passed away in 1901, leads us to assume that the story was initially meant to take place contemporaneously, i.e.: in 1908, as was, in fact, the case with most of La Hire's novels.

However, with the next book, *Le Mystère des XV* [*The Mystery of the XV*], first serialized in *Le Matin* in 1911, La Hire decided to reuse the characters and events from *L'Homme* as a springboard for a more ambitious novel.

Oxus now returns as the leader of a secret society of 15 megalomaniacal scientists calling themselves the XV, who plan to conquer Mars, which they have reached by using technologically-advanced rockets. There, they propose to breed a better race of men using smart, young girls kidnapped from Earth. The story takes place on the same Mars as that in H. G. Wells' *War of the Worlds*, which is presented as historical fact. The XV have discovered ways of thwarting the Martians' heat ray and black smoke and are at war with the aliens, who are fighting them back with their famous tripods.

Among the girls taken to Mars by Oxus are Xavière de Ciserat and her younger sister, Yvonne. Xavière is engaged to a bold 33-year-old French explorer named Leo Sainte-Claire, who is nicknamed the Nyctalope, we are told, because of his ability to see in total darkness. Leo also has a younger sister, Christiane, who is adopted. After managing to capture one of the rockets and getting to Mars, Leo confronts the XV and, eventually, proves strong enough to become their new leader. He discovers that Wells' Martians, beings with huge heads and eight tentacles, are drawing their sustenance from other bipedal humanoid Martians, who are an earlier stage of their evolution.

Eventually, the Nyctalope restores peace between the XV and the Martians and frees the bipeds from their enslavement. He marries Xavière under a new Martian rite, devised for the circumstances, while Christiane marries Noël de Pierrefort, a former servant of the XV. Oxus renounces his former ways and rejoices in the peace and harmony of the new-found Martian colony.

Le Mystère des XV takes place from September through November 1910. La Hire now tells us that the events of *L'Homme qui peut vivre dans l'eau* actually took place 25 years prior, meaning in 1885, despite the topical references that had been contained therein. We are told that Fulbert is now dead, that Leo is the son of Jean Sainte-Claire, who died ten years prior (i.e.: in 1900). Christiane, his adopted younger sister, is revealed to be the daughter of the Hictaner and Moisette–and therefore Oxus' granddaughter–adopted by Jean Sainte-Claire after a terrible tornado ravaged Tahiti and killed her parents. Xavière and Yvonne de Ciserat are the daughters of Louis de Ciserat from the first novel, who is now retired.

This abundance of details is a clear indication that La Hire purposefully intended to retroactively move the events of *L'Homme qui peut vivre dans l'eau* from a presumed 1908 back to 1885. Since La Hire states in *Le Mystère des XV* that Leo is 33, this means that he was born in 1877. This would also mean that the Nyctalope would have been 69 by the time of his last recorded adventure in 1946, while still looking much younger and vital. This element, as we shall see, was dealt with in the later books.

After World War I, and an interval of ten years, during which La Hire wrote other novels, the Nyctalope made his return in *Lucifer*, serialized in *Le Matin* in late 1921 and early 1922. In it, the megalomaniacal Baron Glô von Warteck of Schwarzrock, aptly nicknamed Lucifer, the last descendent of a line of evil tyrants, proposes to enslave humanity using his devilish "teledynamo" from his secret lair at the North Pole.

Lucifer takes place contemporaneously, in May and June 1921. Possibly due to some confusion caused by the amount of time that had passed since he had last chronicled his hero's adventures, La Hire called the Nyctalope "Jean de Sainclair." Because Leo looked like he had not aged a day since he met his biographer, La Hire claimed that he was 35, even though in reality, he would have been 44. We also learned that his birthday is on May 7, that his mother died of pneumonia about a year and a half before the story began and that he has just returned from the Sudan. In fact, La Hire enumerates a whole series of unrecorded adventures that have taken place since his last encounter with Leo: the Nyctalope is supposed to have subdued rebel tribes in Southern Morocco, freed the King of Spain who had been kidnapped by terrorists, fought a trio of supervillains in China, etc.

More surprisingly, no mention is made of the Nyctalope's marriage to Xavière de Ciserat or of Xavière herself. Leo appears to be single again and very much in love with the young opera singer Laurence Païli, whom he marries at the end of the novel. La Hire states that she bore him three sons. However, neither she nor any of her children ever made a reappearance in the series.

In *Lucifer*, Leo is assisted by Raymond de Ciserat, a Navy lieutenant, the son of gynaecologist C.-G. de Ciserat. We can only speculate as to the relationship between the earlier Ciserats (Louis and Xavière) on the one hand, and C.-G. de Ciserat and Raymond on the other. They are probably cousins.

The next novel in the series is *Le Roi de la Nuit* [*The King of the Night*], written in December 1922. In it, the Nyctalope flies to Rhea, a heretofore undiscovered planet of the Solar System, in an anti-gravity-powered spaceship. There, he and his crew settle a war between Rhea's winged daysiders and its ape-like nightsiders. At the end of the book, Leo is said to marry Véronique d'Olbans, the daughter of the scientist who designed the spacecraft. The action takes place between June and September 1922.

Le Roi de la Nuit presents us with an unusual problem. The novel was serialized in *Le Matin* in 1943, then collected in book form that same year. No information about a first publication in 1923 could be found. It is obvious that La Hire rewrote it to some extent to conform with later events, because the 1943 edition features no topical 1920s references and includes as supporting cast Leo's Japanese friend Gnô Mitang and his two Corsican bodyguards, Vitto and Soca, none of whom he had yet met in 1922! Also, scholar Pierre Versins noted in his *Encyclopaedia* that the original version made a reference to H. G. Wells' Professor Cavor's cavorite–a second Wellsian crossover–being used to propel the spacecraft, but that reference is missing from the 1943 edition, which labels the antigravity substance "Z-4" and credits its discovery to Véronique's father, Maxime d'Olbans.

We may therefore safely assume that the 1922 account is the real one, and the 1943 version a somewhat made-up version rewritten by La Hire, possibly at Saint-Clair's suggestion, to polish his image during the French Occupation. The fact that the book was published by the Editions du Livre Moderne, the "aryanized" successor of J. Ferenczi & fils whom La Hire had been asked to manage, is telling.

We should therefore feel free to ignore this so-called "marriage" to Véronique d'Olbans–although an affair with her would certainly explain the sudden disappearance of Laurence Païli and her three children. Several times throughout the series, La Hire states that the Nyctalope is what we would call today a "serial womanizer." One might assume that Laurence divorced Leo because of his infidelities and obtained custody of the boys.

The next story in the Nyctalope saga was *L'Amazone du Mont Everest* [*The Amazon of Mount Everest*], serialized in 1925, and obviously inspired by the then-recent exploits of Alexandra David-Néel in Tibet. In it, the Nyctalope, who has just returned from yet another unrecorded adventure in equatorial Africa, embarks on a Tibetan expedition accompanied by French Navy Captain Jean de Ciserat (another cousin?) and his wife, Gaelle. Near Mount Everest, Leo discovers a hidden civilization of Amazons and eventually leaves with their Queen Mizzeia Khali, who has become besotted with him.

L'Amazone takes place in April 1924, and states that Leo is in his early 40ies–he is in fact 47. As always, he appears younger than his biological age. In it, we are told that Leo is already familiar with Tibet, which he has visited before. In fact, La Hire often mentioned Tibet amongst Leo's unrecorded adventures and claims that he is amongst the men "who have lifted the veils of the mysteries of Tibet."

The next novel, *La Captive du Démon* [*The Captive of the Demon*], was serialized in *Le Matin* in 1927. Now, Leo faces an adversary that is even possibly deadlier than Lucifer: Leonid Zattan, Prince of Issyk-Koul, a forbidden city located in the region of Tien-Chan in Central Asia. Zattan is the lord and master of an international empire of criminals, anarchists and evil-doers. He is the Prophet of the Antichrist and stands for pure evil and anarchy. He is opposed by a mysterious mastermind called Mathias Lumen, who lives in a secluded castle located on the island of Ouessant in Brittany. Lumen has unearthed a heretofore undiscovered prophecy of Nostradamus, which predicts that only one man can prevent the coming of the Antichrist and "the heaps of corpses and rivers of blood" that will ensue. That man is, of course, Leo Saint-Clair, the Nyctalope!

In order to fulfill the prophecy and defeat Zattan, Leo must marry the "golden virgin" and father a child with her. The girl turns out to be young Sylvie Mac Dhul, the only daughter of the late millionaire Gregor Mac Dhul, one of Lumen's associates. Zattan, who is equally familiar with the Prophecy, is naturally intent on getting his hands on Sylvie and using her for his own, evil purposes. In the course of the story, Leo teams up with Gnô Mitang, a Japanese who was Gregor Mac Dhul's dedicated assistant. Zattan, on the other hand, is assisted by Diana Ivanovna Krasnoview, the self-styled "Red Princess," a merciless villainess who was once Lumen's lover and now dreams of marrying the

Monarch of Issyk-Koul. The novel ends on a less than conclusive note: Zattan is dethroned and exiled to a tiny island in the South Pacific; Diana succeeds in killing Lumen and escapes. Leo marries Sylvie, as required by the Prophecy. La Hire tells us that the grim fate that threatened the world has now been averted. But has it?...

The events of *La Captive du Démon* take place in March and April of 1926. (Some sloppy editing in the book version occasionally slips in the date of 1919 instead, but that is obviously an error.) When Sylvie first meets Leo, she recognizes him as the man "who defeated the monster known as Lucifer" and "the hero behind the exploration of planet Mars." In that book, Leo uses the alias of Pedro del Campo and poses as a Spanish gypsy. We are also told that he earned the rank of Colonel in the French Army during the Great War, during which he met both Zattan and Lumen and became aware of their interest in the prophecies of Nostradamus; while in Madrid, he heard about Lumen's recent activities, and that information is what propelled him into the story.

Diana Krasnoview returned in *Titania*, which was serialized in *Le Matin* in 1929. In it, she kidnapped Pierre, the newly-born son of Leo and Sylvie. This time, the Red Princess is allied with an evil engineer named Korridès who has invented a death ray and a futuristic, sun-powered helicopter. Together, they try to take over the world, but fail. Diana is ultimately stabbed to death by a young gypsy girl and Korridès commits suicide while in prison. *Titania* takes place soon after *La Captive du Démon*, in May and June 1927.

The next story, *Belzebuth*, serialized in *Le Matin* in 1930, reveals that Korridès and Titania had a son years prior to their encounter with the Nyctalope. He is the savage, yet brilliant, scientist Hughes Mézarek, a.k.a. Belzebuth. Mézarek injects himself, Sylvie and Pierre with a cataleptic serum, programmed to awaken them all 172 years later, i.e.: in the year 2100. The Nyctalope and Gnô Mitang (now a regular sidekick) follow him, using the same method, and discover a future world divided into two blocs: one under Mézarek's control, the other under Leo's. Eventually, the Nyctalope defeats Mézarek, who is stabbed to death by a girl. Interestingly, in the future, the Nyctalope meets a friendly descendent of Oxus. *Belzebuth* starts and ends in June 1928.

Jean de La Hire never tells us how Leo and his family and friends returned from the year 2100 to the present. Instead, he ends the novel by having Leo waking up in bed–as if the entire adventure had been nothing but a dream. But was it? It is possible that the story did take place, but that some as-yet-unknown time traveling entity rescued the Nyctalope and his family from the future, and even tampered with their memories. La Hire, not knowing what to write, filled in the gaps as best he could.

The next novel, *Gorillard*, serialized in *Le Matin* in 1932, takes place in March and April 1931. In it, the Nyctalope fights yet another mysterious supervillain who, despite his plethora of colorful identities, Gorillard, the Mastodon, Ourga, Dan Arlem, etc., is in reality Dominique de Soto, an arch-enemy of the

Saint-Clairs, who has become the master of the Seven Living Buddhas. The self-styled Gorillard uses their secret Oriental science and psychic powers to threaten the West, but is defeated.

Gorillard is the first novel which reveals that, thanks to Sylvie's immense fortune, Leo has founded the C.I.D.–Committee of Information and Defense–an international organization to combat crime, a veritable army of do-gooders at his beck and call. The characters of the two loyal Corsican bodyguards Vitto and Soca are introduced.

The next book written by La Hire was to be the origin story of the Nyctalope–revealed at last! *L'Assassinat du Nyctalope* [*The Assassination of the Nyctalope*] was published in 1933. By then, Leo was a somewhat unlikely hero, a 56 year-old man in an unaging 40 year-old body. Perhaps questions were being asked? One might theorize that, in order to protect himself and his family, Leo asked his biographer, La Hire, to write a story which would make him appear younger than his real age, hence *L'Assassinat du Nyctalope*.

The novel moves Leo's life-story forward in time 15 years by stating that he was 20 in 1912, meaning that he would have been born in 1892, not in 1877 as previously established. More surprisingly, the book states that Leo's father, now called Pierre Saint-Clair (not Jean) is a scientist, who has invented a device called "Radiant Z" capable of recording, storing and manipulating all types of radio transmissions.

A mysterious Asian mastermind named Sadi Khan shoots Pierre, who is left paralyzed, and steals his plans. Leo and his friends pursue the villains to Lausanne, in Switzerland, where Leo is shot in the face by a gang of Russian "anarchists" (Communists) led by Dr. Serge Ivanof. The bullet grazes his right temporal lobe and he is first blinded, before gaining the power to see in the dark, then eventually regaining his full sight. That is when his eyes acquire their mysterious colors.

Young Leo falls in love with his nurse, Aurora Malianoff, who is revealed to be in cahoots with the Communists. (Her real name is Katia Irenovna Garcheff.) Leo is captured and tortured–beaten up, burned–and ultimately stabbed in the heart and killed–on March 21. He is rushed to the clinic of Dr. de Villiers-Pagan who removes the blade and restarts his heart by implanting inside it an artificial device made of metal and rubber and powered by electro-magnets–thus turning him into a proto-cyborg.

One of the unintended consequences of this surgery might have been to extend Leo's natural life-span, hence the necessity to pretend that he was born later than he really was. In that case, it is more likely that the events of *L'Assassinat du Nyctalope* really took place in 1897, despite any topical references. In it, we also learned that Leo was captain of his rugby team at school and studied science at the University. His family already seems to have high-ranking contacts with both the French Diplomatic Corps and the various departments of French Military Intelligence.

447

L'Assassinat du Nyctalope ends tragically: Sadi Khan is never caught and La Hire hints that he might have been part of a greater criminal empire, perhaps that of Leonid Zattan. The Swiss Communist cell also manages to escape, except for Aurora who commits suicide. Leo's father remains paralyzed and dies soon afterwards, unable to complete his wondrous invention.

As for Leo, he has become the Nyctalope and acquired a sense of his mission. Strangely, as he is about to die, having already suffered from a night of torture, he is said to experience a vision of "eternal life" which may be an expression of religious belief or perhaps a precognitive experience of what the future has in store for him.

The next book in the series is arguably the last of the Nyctalope's great battles. *Les Mystères de Lyon* [*The Mysteries of Lyons*], serialized in *Le Matin* in 1933, takes place right after *Gorillard*, from June to August 1931. In it, Leo fights the beautiful Alouh T'Ho, the leader of a pseudo-satanic cult called the Blood Worshippers which is headquartered in Lyon. Despite looking like a 25-year-old girl, Alouh T'Ho may be, in fact, T'seu Hsi, a former Empress of China who ruled from 1861 to 1908. She maintains her youth and vitality by stealing other people's blood and life-force. The Nyctalope is again assisted by Gnô Mitang, Vitto and Soca and the local C.I.D. Alouh T'Ho naturally succumbs to Leo's overwhelming charm, and, at the end of the book, the Nyctalope is satisfied with sending her home and exacting her solemn vow to never return to France.

Sylvie Mac Dhul plays only a minor role in the novel, but Leo's son, Pierre Saint-Clair, suddenly takes center stage. Surprisingly, we are told that he is now 19 and studying at the University of Leipzig in Germany, preparing to be a diplomat and statesman. (His father believes in the Franco-German alliance.) How could Pierre, allegedly born in 1927, be 19 in 1931? There really is only one possibility: If Pierre is 19, then he was born in 1912 and he is not Sylvie's son—but Xavière's! If Leo's first wife died in childbirth in 1912, that would explain both her departure from the series, the continued friendly relations between Leo and the Ciserats (who might otherwise have been upset by a divorce) and the presence in 1931 of a 19 year-old Pierre, who of course would call Sylvie "mother" as was the custom.

What, then, of "baby" Pierre who was kidnapped by Diana Krasnoview and who was the natural son of Leo and Sylvie–as we were told in *Titania*? The Prophecy of Nostradamus unearthed by Lumen in *La Captive du Démon* predicted that, if Leo did not father a child with Sylvie, then horrible events–"rivers of blood and heaps of corpses"–would come to pass in 1929, then three years in the future. At that time, La Hire assured us that Leo was the man sent by Providence, that his victory over Zattan, his marriage to Sylvie, his fathering of a child with her and, finally, his assumption of Mathias Lumen's role would guarantee that the dire events forecasted by Nostradamus would not come to pass.

Yet, what if Leo had ultimately failed in his preordained duty? After *Les Mystères de Lyon*, neither Sylvie nor Pierre (either of them) ever make a reappearance. Leo behaves as if he is single again, although he does not remarry. One is led to wonder if the couple separated, possibly because of the Nyctalope's continued infidelities. Leo's marriage to Sylvie obviously failed. Their baby son might have died. Leo's C.I.D., instead of fulfilling Mathias Lumen's role in warding off evil, all too often became Leo's personal tool. The Prophecy was not fulfilled after all. What if the great evil that Leo failed to prevent took place not in 1929 but in 1939–when Germany annexed Poland and started World War II? The man who had vanquished Lucifer, Zattan and Gorillard never once confronted Hitler–in whom many saw the Antichrist...

After *Les Mystères de Lyon*, the Nyctalope seems almost to turn into a pale caricature of his earlier persona: a somewhat smug and self-satisfied bourgeois, whose adventures are minor skirmishes with the forces of evil, while appearing largely indifferent to the greater evil that is about to be unleashed over Europe.

Le Sphinx du Maroc [*The Moroccan Sphinx*], serialized in *Le Matin* in 1934, takes place that same year. It is a classic colonial espionage adventure in which Leo manages to prevent a rebellion in French Morocco, saves the beautiful Naima and thwarts the evil schemes of Helen Parsons, a.k.a. The Djinn.

The next book, *La Croisière du Nyctalope* [*The Nyctalope's Cruise*], serialized in *Le Matin* in 1936, is interesting because it is an earlier adventure, taking place in June and July of 1913. Curiously, it confirms the Nyctalope's birth year of 1877 because, several times, it states that the Nyctalope was then 35, i.e.: two years older than he was during *Le Mystère des XV*.

In *La Croisière du Nyctalope*, Leo travels to Russia to prevent the beautiful German *femme fatale* Wanda Stielman from stealing the fortune of the pretty Russian princess Irena Zahidof, who owns vast oil deposits near Bakou. We are told that Wanda is a former lover whom Leo thought had been shot by a firing squad *à la* Mata-Hari. In the conclusion of the story, La Hire states that Leo loved Irena, but couldn't marry her because she died on July 28, 1913 from pulmonary congestion. The fact that Leo might have married Irena–if she had lived–is another indication that Xavière had died prior to this adventure.

La Croisière also mentions that Leo's father was a high-ranking diplomat who lived in Russia with his wife and son during and after the Franco-Russian alliance of 1892. While this statement confirms the relocation of the events of *L'Homme qui peut vivre dans l'eau* to 1885, it now gives Leo's father a third career! One would then logically assume that Jean (Pierre) Saint-Clair was reassigned from the French Navy to the Quai d'Orsay and moved to Russia six or seven years after the events of *L'Homme*. He was obviously back in France by 1897 for the events of *L'Assassinat du Nyctalope*. *Le Mystère des XV* then tells us that he died in 1900.

Le Mystère de la Croix du Sang [*The Mystery of the Bloody Cross*], first serialized in *Le Matin* in 1940, takes place in January 1939 in the Perigord region of France–there is, therefore, a five-year gap between it and *Le Sphinx du Maroc*. In it, the Nyctalope saves his friend, Jacques d'Hermont, from the invisible death rays of an evil occultist/scientist, Armand Logreux d'Albury, alias the Master of the Seven Lights, who resides at the nearby Castle of the Bloody Cross, and plots to murder the d'Hermont family, marry young Basilie d'Hermont, Jacques' only daughter, and steal their fortune. In this novel, the Nyctalope is assisted by a tribe of gypsies, for whom he is the "Capo" Pedro del Campo, the same pseudonym he once used in *La Captive du Démon*.

L'Enfant perdu (*The Lost Child*) was only serialized in the magazine *Actu* in 1942 but never collected in book form. It tells of an adventure that the Nyctalope and Gnô Mitang experienced during the June 1940 exodus after France was invaded by the Nazis.

The novella *Rien qu'une Nuit* (*Only One Night*), published in 1944, takes place in January 1941. In it, Leo and Gnô Mitang save the young and beautiful Madeleine d'Evires from the clutches of the evil hypnotist Godfroy de Montluc. It states that the Nyctalope has his own car, adequate supplies of gasoline and all the necessary SPs and *Ausweis* (legal documents issued by the Vichy regime and the German occupation forces) enabling him to move at will between Occupied and Free France, as well as several other occupied countries of Europe. Further, it mentions that Leo is a regular guest at various social functions. Overall, he does not seem bothered in the least by the Nazi occupiers.

In 1954, two years before La Hire's death, his son-in-law began to reprint a number of his works, including some of the Nyctalope's novels in truncated and updated editions. *The Mystery of XV*, for example, was retitled *The Secret of the XII* (!) and the Nyctalope was taken out of the story entirely and replaced by the fictional "Hugues Cendras." This new imprint, however, included two heretofore unpublished adventures.

La Sorcière Nue [*The Naked Sorceress*] was released in 1954. The book takes place in the Languedoc region in mid-1946 and references Maquis battles that occurred there in 1943 and 1944. In it, Alouh T'Ho, despite her solemn promise never to return to France, is back and is again up to her old tricks. She is now calling herself Aya-Li, but it is the same Alouh T'Ho. Her first encounter with Leo in Lyon 15 years before is clearly referenced. Interestingly, there is a mention of a second, unrecorded battle between her and the Nyctalope that would have taken place in Fez in Morocco, although no year is given. This time, Leo's victory is complete and Alouh T'Ho/Aya-Li dies. The Nyctalope is again assisted by Vitto and Soca, but Gnô Mitang is gone. Leo, who seems older and wiser, falls in love with young Dinah Ranson but realizes that their age difference (despite his seeming agelessness) is too great a chasm to be bridged easily.

One cannot help but feel that *La Sorcière Nue* was written prior to or during World War II and the date of 1946 and the topical references inserted by La Hire's son-in-law to make the book seem a little more relevant. Since we will never know the truth, we have chosen to take the dates at face value.

L'Enigme du Squelette [*The Enigma of the Skeleton*] was published in 1955. The book opens when the Nyctalope's friend, Monsieur de Barange, is killed by a mysterious death ray that disintegrates the man's flesh, leaving only a skeleton behind. Leo and Gnô Mitang investigate and eventually expose the murderers, the beautiful Maya de la Cruz and her manipulative father, the Count Albert de la Cruz-Tanguy. The action starts on Tuesday, June 15, which means that the story can only have taken place in 1937 or 1941. Because of the lack of topical references to the Occupation, the earlier date seems more appropriate.

One should not leave out the short-story "*Marguerite,*" written by the undersigned and published in *Tales of the Shadowmen 2* in 2006. It is an anecdote that takes place in early 1942 when Leo, despite his collaboration with the infamous Milice, lets his sense of kindness and honor take over.

This is the story and the strange fate of the oldest French superhero of all. While Leo Saint-Clair the Nyctalope had many heroic qualities, he was also chauvinistic, sexist and racist, like many men of his times, social class and background. He claimed to respect women, but was a serial philanderer. He was all too often patronizing in his relations with non-white or non-western people—although his most trusted friend was Japanese. His undisputed devotion was to an ideal of France and its Colonial Empire that flourished before World War I and was slipping away by the early 1940s. The pursuit of that ideal led him, in the end, to a compromise that many other Frenchmen, including his biographer, embraced and from which he emerged not unscathed.

Superheroes, more than most characters, are symbols; they embody the virtues and vices of a people and of an epoch. Just as Steve Rogers, Captain America, is the incarnation of the Stars and Stripes, Leo Saint-Clair the Nyctalope stood for the ideals of Colonial France between two world wars. He vanished at the same time as France's Empire—deservedly so.

Jean-Marc Lofficier

Timeline

1877 (May 7) – Birth of Leon (Leo) Saint-Clair from Jean-Pierre Saint-Clair and his (otherwise unidentified) wife.

1885 (February-May) – *L'Homme qui peut vivre dans l'eau*. Jean-Pierre Saint-Clair serves as ensign in the French navy under Louis de Ciserat. Oxus and Fulbert use the water-breathing Hictaner to try to take over the world but are defeated by the Hictaner's father, Charles Severac. The Hictaner marries Oxus' daughter, Moisette.

1890? – A tornado kills the Hictaner and Moisette; Jean-Pierre Saint-Clair adopts their only daughter, Christiane. Leo is captain of his rugby team at school.

1892 – Jean-Pierre Saint-Clair is transferred to the diplomatic service and he and his family move to Russia.

1895? – Jean-Pierre Saint-Clair returns to France with his family. Leo takes his baccalauréat and studies science at the university.

1897 – *L'Assassinat du Nyctalope*. Sadi Khan shoots Jean-Pierre Saint-Clair, who becomes paralyzed. Leo gains his powers and an artificial heart after being shot, tortured and murdered by Communists in Lausanne. His first love, Aurora, betrays him, then commits suicide.

1900 – Death of Jean-Pierre Saint-Clair.

1901-10 – Unrecorded adventures in Central Africa and Tibet.

1905? – Leo has an affair with German spy Wanda Stielman.

1909? – Leo frees the King of Spain kidnapped by terrorists.

1910 (September-November) – *Le Mystère des XV*. Leo goes to Mars, takes over Oxus' group of XV and makes peace with the Martians. He marries Xavière de Ciserat. Christiane Saint-Clair also gets married.

1912? – Death of Xavière in childbirth. Birth of Pierre (I). Leo travels to Morocco to subdue rebel tribes.

1913 (June-July) – *La Croisière du Nyctalope*. In Russia, Leo prevents Wanda Stielman from stealing Princess Irena Zahidof's fortune. He would marry Irena but she dies in July.

1913? – Leo then goes on to fight a trio of villainous masterminds in China.

1914 (July)-1918 (November) – World War I. Leo earns the rank of Colonel in the French Army. He first meets Mathias Lumen and Leonid Zattan.

1919 – Leo meets singer Laurence Païli on the French Riviera. Leo's mother dies from pneumonia.

1920 – Leo explores the Sudan.

1921 (May-June) – *Lucifer*. Leo and Raymond de Ciserat defeat Baron Glô von Warteck of Schwarzrock. Leo marries Laurence Païli.

1922 (June-September) – *Le Roi de la Nuit*. Leo travels to unknown planet Rhea and settles a war between daysiders and nightsiders. He has an affair with Véronique d'Olbans.

1923 – Leo explores Central Africa.

1924 (April) – *L'Amazone du Mont Everest*. Leo and Jean de Ciserat discover a hidden civilization of Amazons in Tibet. Leo returns with their Queen Mizzeia Khali.

1925? – Laurence, who had three sons with Leo, divorces him and gets custody of the children. Leo goes to Madrid where he poses as Pedro del Campo.

1926 (March-April) – *La Captive du Démon*. Leo battles Leonid Zattan, Prince of Issyk-Koul. Diana Ivanovna Krasnoview kills Mathias Lumen. Leo meets Gnô Mitang and Sylvie Mac Dhul, whom he marries. If Leo fulfills the terms of the Nostradamus Prophecy, he will prevent the coming of the Antichrist.

1927 (May-June) – *Titania*. Leo and Sylvie have a son, Pierre (II), who is kidnapped by Diana, now allied to evil engineer Korridès. Diana is killed by a gypsy girl; Korridès commits suicide.

1928 (June) – *Belzebuth*. Hughes Mézarek, the son of Korridès and Diana, kidnaps Sylvie and Pierre (II) and takes them through suspended animation to the year 2100. Leo and Gnô Mitang follow and defeat him.

1929? – Death of Pierre (II). Failure of the Prophecy.

1931 (March-April) – *Gorillard*. Leo and Gnô Mitang fight Dominique de Soto, who uses the Seven Living Buddhas' powers to threaten the West. Creation of the C.I.D. financed by Sylvie (to avenge Pierre's death?).

1931 (June-August) – *Les Mystères de Lyon*. Leo and Gnô Mitang fight the Chinese Empress Alouh T'Ho, leader of the Blood Worshippers, headquartered in Lyons. She is eventually driven back to China. Pierre (I) is 19 and studying in Germany.

1932? – Leo divorces Sylvie.

1934 – *Le Sphinx du Maroc*. Leo stops a rebellion in French Morocco and defeats Helen Parsons, a.k.a. The Djinn.

1935? – Leo fights Alouh T'Ho in Fez and drives her out of Morocco.

1937 (June) – *L'Enigme du Squelette*. Leo and Gnô Mitang solve a murder committed with a flesh-dissolving ray.

1939 (January) – *Le Mystère de la Croix du Sang*. Leo defeats Armand Logreux d'Albury.

1939 (September 17) – Hitler invades Poland. Start of World War II.

1940 (June) – *L'Enfant Perdu*. Leo and Gnô Mitang during the Exodus.

1941 (January) – *Rien qu'une Nuit*. Leo and Gnô Mitang save a young girl from the clutches of an evil hypnotist.

1942 (January) – *"Marguerite"* (by Jean-Marc Lofficier). Leo rescues a French Resistant from the Milice.

1946 (May-June) – *La Sorcière Nue*. Last battle between Leo and Alouh T'Ho, who now calls herself Aya-Li; Alouh T'Ho dies.

Bibliography

1. *L'Homme Qui Peut Vivre dans l'Eau* : a. serialized in *Le Matin* (1909) ; b. reprinted as *L'Homme Qui Peut Vivre dans l'Eau* (Felix Juven, 1910) ; c. reprinted as 1. *L'Homme Qui Peut Vivre dans l'Eau*, 2. *Les Amours de l'Inconnu* (Roman d'Aventures (2ème série), Ferenczi et fils, 1926).

2. *Le Mystère des XV* : serialized in *Le Matin* (1911) ; b. reprinted as 1. *Le Mystère des XV*, 2. *Le Triomphe de l'Amour* (Romans d'Aventures (1ère série), Ferenczi et fils, 1922) ; c. reprinted as 1. *Le Secret des XII*, 2. *Les Conquérants de Mars* (Jaeger d'Hauteville, 1954) (*sans* Leo).

3. *Lucifer* : a. serialized in *Le Matin* (1921-22) ; b. reprinted as 1. *Lucifer*; 2. *Le Nyctalope contre Lucifer* (Romans d'Aventures (1ère série), Ferenczi et fils, 1922) ; c. reprinted as 1. *Lucifer*, 2. *Les Drames des Bermudes* (Le Livre National (nouvelle série), J. Tallandier, 1936).

4. *Le Roi de la Nuit* : a. ? (1923) ; b. serialized in *Le Matin* (1943) ; c. reprinted as *Le Roi de la Nuit* (Le Livre Moderne, 1943) ; d. reprinted as *Planète sans feu* (Jaeger d'Hauteville, 1953) (*sans* Leo).

5. *L'Amazone du Mont Everest* : a. (Romans d'Aventures, Ferenczi et fils, 1925) ; b. reprinted as *La Madone des Cimes* (Voyages & Aventures, Ferenczi et fils, 1933) ; c. reprinted as *Le Mystère de l'Everest* (Jaeger d'Hauteville, 1953).

6. *La Captive du Démon* (a.k.a. *L'Antichrist*): a. serialized in *Le Matin* (1927) ; b. reprinted as 1. *La Captive du Démon*; 2. *La Princesse Rouge* (Le Livre National, J. Tallandier, 1929).

7. *Titania* : a. serialized in *Le Matin* (1929) ; b. reprinted as 1. *Titania*; 2. *Ecrase ta Vipère* (Le Livre National, J. Tallandier, 1931).

8. *Belzebuth* : a. serialized in *Le Matin* (1930) ; b. reprinted as 1. *Belzebuth*; 2. *L'Île d'Épouvante* (Le Livre Populaire, Arthème Fayard & Cie., 1930) ; c. reprinted as 1. *Belzebuth*; 2. *L'Île d'Épouvante* (Jaeger d'Hauteville, 1954).

9. *Gorillard*! : a. serialized in *Le Matin* (1932) ; b. reprinted as 1. *Gorillard*; 2. *Le Mystère Jaune* (Le Livre National, J. Tallandier, 1932) ; c. reprinted as 1. *Gorillard*; 2. *Le Mystère Jaune* (Jaeger d'Hauteville, 1954).

10. *L'Assassinat du Nyctalope* : (Le Disque Rouge, La Renaissance du Livre, 1933).

11. *Les Mystères de Lyon* : a. serialized in *Le Matin* (1933) ; b. reprinted as 1. *Les Mystères de Lyon*; 2. *Les Adorateurs du Sang* (Le Livre National, J. Tallandier, 1933-34) ; c. reprinted as 1. & 2. *Les Mystères de Lyon* (Marabout Nos. 1045 & 1046, 1979).

12. *Le Sphinx du Maroc* : a. serialized in *Le Matin* (1934) ; b. reprinted as *Le Sphinx du Maroc* (Les Meilleurs Romans de Drame et d'Amour, J. Tallandier, 1936).

13. *La Croisière du Nyctalope* : a. serialized in *Le Matin* (1936) ; b. reprinted as *La Croisière du Nyctalope* (Arthème Fayard, 1936) ; c. reprinted as *Wanda* (Jaeger d'Hauteville, 1953).

14. *Le Mystère de la Croix du Sang* : a. serialized in *Le Matin* (1940) ; b. reprinted as *La Croix de Sang* (R. Simon, 1941) ; c. reprinted as *La Croix du Sang* (Jaeger d'Hauteville, 1954).

15. *L'Enfant Perdu* : serialized in *Actu* (1942).

16. *Rien qu'une Nuit* : (Collection du Cyclope, 1944).

17. *La Sorcière Nue* : (Jaeger d'Hauteville, 1954).

18. *L'Enigme du Squelette* : (Jaeger d'Hauteville, 1955).

18b. *"Marguerite"* (by Jean-Marc Lofficier): in *Tales of the Shadowmen 2 : Gentlemen of the Night* (Black Coat Press, 2006).

JEAN DE LA HIRE

LE ROI
DE LA
NUIT

24 fr

ÉDITIONS
DU LIVRE MODERNE PARIS

Notes

[1] Eugène Albert d'Aiglun Rochas (1837-1914) was the most famous psychic investigator in France at the turn of the century. He was sacked as the administrator of the Ecole Polytechnique because of his interest in occult matters, subsequently hosting many investigations of spiritualist mediums at his country house in the vicinity of l'Aguelas, near Voiron. Among his guests was the celebrated Eusapia Palladino (see Note 33); as a result of his observations of her apparent ability to project the force of her motor nerves, he wrote *L'exterioriation de motricité* [*The Exteriorization of Motricity*] (1896), advancing "motricity" as a hypothetical mechanism of telekinesis. The fact that La Hire does not use that term, preferring derivatives of *envoûter*, might indicate that his research was a trifle superficial, or merely that he could not expect his readers to be familiar with it.

[2] Charles Gabriel Pravaz (1791-1853) invented a metal syringe in the final year of his life which could be used in association with the hollow needle invented nine years earlier by Francis Rynd. (Previous medial syringes had been used in association with rubber tubes, and were incapable of injecting liquids into subcutaneous veins.) The discovery might have revolutionized medicine had it not been for the fact that early users did not realize the importance of sterilization; surprisingly, Professor Lourmel also seems ignorant of this necessity.

[3] Vercingetorix was the chieftain who attempted to rally the feuding Gaulish clans in united opposition to Julius Caesar's invasion, but accomplished too little too late; he was captured after a long and costly siege and the whole of what is now France was subsequently integrated into the Roman Empire.

[4] When Leo Saint-Clair the Nyctalope was introduced in *Le mystère des XV* (1911), he was already 33 and, therefore, should now be ten years older; but La Hire likely sought to reintroduce the character from scratch in *Lucifer*, including rechristening him "Jean de Sainclair." What made him change his mind and revert to the original "Leo Saint-Clair" version in the next novel is unknown.

[5] La Hire describes Saint-Clair's car–which is an open-topped "touring car", and is carefully contrasted with the numerous limousines and saloon cars featured in the plot–as a *torpedo*, which sounds much better than the Anglo-American "roadster," but I have resisted the temptation to retain the French term.

[6] The *Trouée de Belfort* [Belfort Gap] is a pass at the north extreme of the Jura mountains, separating that range from the Massif des Vosges.

[7] One result of the French defeat in the Franco-Prussian war of 1870-71 was the transfer of the long-disputed province of Alsace-Lorraine to German rule. It was returned to France in 1918 as a result of the Treaty of Versailles, which brought the Great War to a conclusion.

[8] The foremost French military academy.

[9] One might argue that there is no point whatsoever in this sequence of disguises, since Saint-Clair has no reason to think that he is being followed or that Lucifer is on to him; the final disguise he adopts, before introducing himself to the Nortmunds ,proves equally unnecessary; it seems that La Hire is merely establishing that the Nyctalope is a master of disguise like any other vigilante detective.

[10] Strictly speaking, a Kalmuk is a member of a Tartar tribe who stays at home while other members go off hunting or marauding, but La Hire presumably means to imply a greater similarity to the latter party. He appears to think that Kalmuks are bloodthirsty savages–another incarnation of the Yellow Peril–we shall meet some supposedly-literal examples later in the plot.

[11] A burgrave was originally an official appointed to command a burg (a town or a castle), although the title subsequently became hereditary in many of the German duchies.

[12] A mullion is an subsidiary upright within the frame of a window positioned between the lights.

[13] The Nyctalope never does find out, and nor do we. The presence of the windlass in the sentry-box is quite nonsensical, and was obviously improvised *ad hoc* to get Saint-Clair and his companions into the castle–entirely unnecessarily, as it eventually turns out, because a subsequent *ad hoc* improvisation will establish the existence of a much easier entry-route. Such narrative hiccups are inevitably commonplace in *feuilleton* fiction, as is the awkward device of raising the question of explanation and then postponing it indefinitely.

[14] I have left this paragraph untouched, although this statement about the Baron's ancestry is subsequently contradicted in no uncertain terms, to illustrate the fact that La Hire presumably has no idea, at this point, where his narrative might be heading. He may well have been awaiting instructions from the editor of *Le Matin* as to how much further he would need to spin the story out; had reader reaction been indifferent, he might have had to close it down abruptly, contriving a climax within the castle, and substitute a new serial. He was presumably told to keep going, and prepare for a long haul–at which point he had to begin making more elaborate provision for Baron von Warteck's background and ambitions. With regard to the Baron being the "Antichrist," no more is heard of this particular notion, but when La Hire elected to continue the Nyctalope's adventures and had to come up with other villains of even greater nastiness, he employed surnames such as "Zattan" and "Belzebuth" and the concept of the Antichrist was central to *La Captive du Démon* (1927).

[15] A banderilla is a barbed dart, sometimes loaded with explosives, of a type once extensively used in bull-fighting; its use is nowadays considered rather unsporting.

[16] La Hire includes a footnote at this point to translate Wolf's German into French. In English, the staccato speech would go as follows: "Lord! Yes! The sentry, Lord. Yes, the sentry! Rose Laura. Number six. Yes, six!"

[17] The Pleyels were a notable French musical family. The composer Ignace Pleyel (1757-1831) founded a prestigious piano factory in Paris, which was inherited by his son Camille (1788-1855), the husband of the famous pianist Marie (1811-1875).

[18] The story of Judith, as told in Greek and Latin texts allegedly translated from Hebrew–although no Hebrew original has survived–obtained wide circulation in Christendom as an item of Old Testament apocrypha. It was a popular subject in Decadent Art and a frequent reference in 19th-century French accounts of *femmes fatales*. In order to free her native city, Bethulia, from a siege laid by the Assyrian general Holofernes, the seductive Judith pretended to be a traitor and insinuated herself into the general's tent, where she got him drunk (presumably in a euphemistic sense) and then hacked off his head.

[19] There was a popular song of the day about a little frog, whose chorus consisted of the repetition of the nonsense-word *laïtou*.

[20] Sar–which La Hire renders as *sâr*–is a term allegedly derived from the Assyrian, meaning mage-king or "priest-king; La Hire would have been familiar with it by virtue of its adoption as a title by Joséphin Péladan (1859-1918), the head of the most prominent "Rosicrucian Lodge" in *fin-de-siècle* Paris; his successors in that role also adopted it. A popular character published in French pulp magazines in 1909 was the Sâr Dubnotal, a magician who fought a variety of occult menaces.

[21] Omphale was the daughter of the Lydian King Iardanus. After the death of her husband Tmolus, she became ruler in her own right. When Hercules was afflicted with a nasty disease as a penalty for killing his friend Iphitus in a fit of madness, he was informed by the Oracle that he could only be cured by going into service for three years (he had already completed his famous labors, so this was a sort of repeat prescription). Hermes sold him to Omphale so that he might serve out this sentence, and he became so enamored of his mistress that he allegedly allowed her to put on his lion's skin while he dressed in women's clothes and devoted himself to the traditionally female task of spinning wool. The name was well-known in 19th-century France by virtue of providing the eponymous heroine of one of Théophile Gautier's several *nouvelles* featuring beautiful phantom women who offer contemporary men sexual delights that real women cannot provide.

[22] In his haste to send Saint-Clair to Laure's rescue, La Hire has completely forgotten about Lucifer's machine, for which none of his characters has spared a glance–an error of omission that causes him some difficulty in the subsequent development of the plot.

[23] Retrieving the golden apples of the Hesperidés was the eleventh of Hercules' 12 labors. The apples were those that Hera had received as a wedding-gift from Ge (nowadays better known as Gaia), and the garden where they were kept was guarded by the dragon Ladon. Hercules only killed the dragon in some versions of the story; he had no need to do so because he persuaded Atlas to get the apples for him, agreeing to bear the weight of the heavens temporarily in the giant's stead–but then had to trick Atlas into reassuming his traditional burden.

[24] This hasty improvisation raises the question of why the Nyctalope did not observe this opening in the base of the rocky spire during his initial reconnaissance–it might well have served as a more convenient and more plausible means of ingress than the one he actually employed.

[25] As in other instances where La Hire employs this formula in response to some sudden realization, no explanation is ever forthcoming–but La Hire took care never again to lose sight of the possibility that Lucifer might well have such weapons at his disposal.

[26] Although La Hire presumably copied these data straight out of a textbook, it is not true that "any" such reference-work would reveal exactly the same thing. Although my 1903 Encyclopedia agrees that the Bermudas were discovered by Jean Bermudez in 1522, it gives 1611 rather than 1609 as the date of their settlement by Sir George Somers and their chief crops are listed as onions and Easter lilies. The number of islets and rocks is given as 360 and the population (according to the census of 1891) was 15,123.

[27] The spelling of the name Grisyl is later altered to Grysil, but I have retained the former version throughout.

[28] In summarizing the elaborate provisions made by the Wartecks for their survival within the Hollow Rock, La Hire says nothing about their means of procuring a supply of fresh water.

[29] La Hire appears to have anticipated here the phenomenon that later became known as the Bermuda Triangle. The first article of any kind in which the legend of the Triangle began appeared in newspapers by E.V.W. Jones on September 16, 1950, through the Associated Press.

[30] This was a miscalculation in the original text, which we have corrected. The Bermudas are only five hours behind Paris time, according to the time zones agreed by the International Meridian Conference of 1884–a difference that La Hire had misunderstood, claiming that it was a little after 4 a.m., not 11 a.m.

[31] The character's name was initially given as Rupert VII but later became Rupert VI; I have adopted the latter version throughout.

[32] La Hire renders the mate's name as O'Mursée, which is presumably an attempt to reproduce an Irish name by means of French phonetic conventions; I have take the liberty of providing a slightly more plausible spelling. In the original text, Professor Jameson is named "Lytham Jamerson" and his daughter "Jepsie" for which more acceptable substitutes have also been devised.

[33] What was once the huge colony of French Equatorial Africa is nowadays divided into Gabon, Congo, the Central African Republic and Chad. La Hire often refers to past "unrecorded" adventures of the Nyctalope, especially in Africa and Tibet.

[34] Although the British certainly imported African slaves when they colonized the Bermudas in the 17th century, earlier chapters claimed that the Wartecks' original slaves were recruited from the indigenous inhabitants of the islands, who cannot possibly have been black men, and then selectively bred. Similar mistakes are, of course, commonplace in popular literature of a racist stripe— Robinson Crusoe's Friday is often represented illustratively as a black man, although he was actually a Carib "Indian."

[35] Indeed it is, testifying to the fact that La Hire had written his first chapter long before he began to think his plot through. Although La Hire acknowledges the nonsensicality of this part of Lucifer's original plan, and will subsequently make a second attempt to excuse it, he never addresses the even less plausible issue of Lucifer's ham-fisted attempts to promote the cause of anarchism in France. As a would-be tyrant of aristocratic descent and inclinations, Glô von Warteck surely would not have the least sympathy for anarchism, and has absolutely nothing to gain from the demands he makes of Alexandre Prillant. Had Prillant given in to his first demand, or were he to give in to the one he is about to receive, the effects of his capitulation would have become utterly irrelevant on June 10. It is, of course, typical of archvillains in this sort of fiction that they always give advance notice of their plans to their heroic adversaries, thus granting adequate opportunity for their own thwarting, but they rarely do so with so little reason or purpose.

[36] Eusapia Palladino (1854-1918) was the most famous spiritualist mediums of her intensely-fascinated era (and hence of all time). She was an exceptionally histrionic medium, who put on considerable shows of suffering while she manipulated objects in her vicinity, especially when moving furniture. She was recruited 1891 to convince the famous proto-psychologist Cesare Lombroso of the reality of Spiritualism; Lombroso was suitably impressed and she went on to convince a panel of scientists in Milan, including Charles Richet, of her ability to touch them with a living hand while her own were apparently bound. She was subsequently put to the test by many other panels of scientists. The stage magician J. N. Maskelyne, however, pointed out that all the phenomena she produced could be duplicated with a single free hand or foot, and she was repeatedly caught removing her foot from a shoe she had requested a member of her audience to hold. In 1798, Richet arranged a series of séances in Paris for the specific purpose of redeeming her reputation, including some held at the home of the astronomer Camille Flammarion and others at the home of Eugène Rochas (see Note 1). She was invited to the USA in 1909 and was repeatedly caught cheating at séances there, but her champions remained adamant in her defense.

[37] Périspirit–which I have transposed directly into English–was a term coined and popularized by Allan Kardec (1804-1869), a French student of the occult who attempted a comprehensive theoreticization of "Spiritism." The term was introduced in *Le livre des médiums* (1861), the second of the five fundamental works of the alleged science, to describe the ghostly manifestations produced by some mediums, which Kardec rationalized as tenuously material projections of a person's spirit.

[38] I have transposed La Hire's improvised term *panglottes* directly into English, even though its usage–unlike that of polyglotte/polyglot–has never been officially adopted into either language. Its reference, obviously, is to speaking all, rather than merely several, languages.

[39] This calculation is made according to the conventional astrological calendar, whose equivalences were established in Classical times, according to which the Sun is supposed to be in the house of Taurus from April 20 to May 20 (although La Hire must be counting from April 21, since May 20 is reckoned as the 30th day rather than the 31st). Owing to the precession of the equinoxes, the Sun's apparent astronomical position relative to the constellations after which the houses of the zodiac are named has shifted very considerably since then, the Sun's apparent passage through the constellation Taurus nowadays extending from May 14 to June 19. It is perhaps surprising that the scientifically-minded Wartecks were prepared to retain the traditional astrological calendar rather than substituting a modern equivalent.

[40] La Hire has five hours, again demonstrating the unreliability of his arithmetic.

[41] Joséphine de Beauharnais was already the mistress of the influential politician Paul François Jean Nicolas Barras when she met the young general Napoleon Bonaparte and became his lover; Barras helped to facilitate her marriage to Napoleon and gave him the command of the army of Italy. Some have speculated that Joséphine was a spendthrift and Barras may have encouraged the relationship with Napoleon in order to get her off his hands.

[42] Georges-Louis-Leclerc, Comte de Buffon (1707-1788) was the most famous French naturalist of his era. The volume shown to Henri is probably one of the fifteen constituting his *Histoire naturelle* (1749-67), whose later volumes feature a remarkably comprehensive account of quadruped animals.

[43] Paradou–whose name is used here purely for alliterative effect–is a village in Provence eight kilometers north-east of Arles; its name often crops up in word-play likening its name to Paradis (Paradise) but actually derives from the wind-mills used by local weavers.

[44] This statement–which is quite literal and unambiguous, the French version being "*Il est de race mongole*"–is odd. It is partly consistent with the statement La Hire made in Part Three, Chapter III, about Glô von Warteck being the offspring of a "cosmopolitan Hindu" and a Mongol mother, but that allegation appeared to be decisively refuted by the subsequent history of the Warteck family,

in which Glô XIII became the direct descendant of the first Baron Glô von Warteck, who was expelled from Germany as a suspected sorcerer. Glô XIII is definitely the son of Rupert VI, who is certainly not "a cosmopolitan Hindu," and we shall encounter his mother soon enough, who is certainly not from the Orient. The reader will recall that La Hire took the trouble to assure his readers that the first Grisyl was only a "distant cousin" of Rupert and Norbert Warteck, thus establishing that her marriage was not incestuous. Saint-Clair also took the trouble to ascertain that his own Grisyl's mother was a Russian shipwreck victim, in order to establish that she is not a product of inbreeding. We may assume, therefore, that the Wartecks avoided the pharaonic practice of brother/sister marriage by recruiting other such victims into their strange family. Given the Wartecks' own racial prejudices, however, and the inherent unlikelihood of finding Mongolian shipwreck-victims in the Bermudas, it seems highly improbable that they could have, or would have, imported any significant Oriental strain into their family. The fact that Glô XIII is tall, lean and red-haired lends considerable support to this supposition. Why, then, does La Hire make this seemingly-absurd statement? It is one of those little mysteries that defy rational explanation, other than suggesting perhaps some kind of Hunnish origin far back in time? (The Germans were, after all, nicknamed the "Hun" during World War I.) More interestingly, it does serve to suggest that La Hire's imaginary compendium of the attributes of modern villainy includes the nonsensical assumption that diabolical cruelty and pride are essentially Oriental traits.

[45] Mephistopheles is the star part in several operatic versions of the story of Faust; Laurence means "unknown" in the sense that her visitor has not appeared in that role on the stage and is a mysterious, satanic-looking figure.

[46] The previous chapter title ("The Red-Haired Man Hypnotized") implied that the interrogation of the red-haired man was supposed to have taken place in that chapter. The chapters in this section of the book (which is in volume two of the Ferenczi paperback edition) are shorter, on average, than those in earlier sections, so it may be the case that the publisher split them up, and that extra chapter titles were introduced without overmuch thought as to their propriety. On the other hand, it is possible that La Hire's annoying habit of padding by procrastination had enabled him to get to the end of his own projected chapter without actually reaching its intended purpose.

[47] In France, notaries and attorneys are usually addressed as "Maître" instead of "Monsieur;" Maître Dubreuil is the French equivalent of "Dubreuil, esq."

[48] La Hire's mention of "ionized air" seems to be a bluff, intended to convince his readers that he knows what he is talking about. Pierre Curie had, however, discovered in 1900 that alpha particles were helium nuclei–or helium ions–and La Hire might be assuming that such particles can simply be mingled with other atmospheric molecules to produce a mixture that is equally describable as a "radioactive atmosphere" or "ionized air." He does not, at any rate, specify any

other radioactive compound that might be involved; his subsequent comments on the difficulty of obtaining radium imply that he would surely have mentioned it had Professor Lourmel had any access to a supply of that element.

[49] Nicholas Flamel (1330-1418) was a scholar based at the University of Paris. Like many of the proto-scientists of his era, he acquired a reputation as an alchemist and magician that was prodigiously inflated after his death. He was, as La Hire states, *méconnu*–which I have translated as "misunderstood", although it can also mean "unappreciated"–by his contemporaries, although legend has multiplied that misunderstanding tenfold. Modern readers will be most familiar with him by courtesy of J. K. Rowling, he being the philosopher (or sorcerer, in the US version of the title) whose stone is encountered by Harry Potter in the first novel of the best-selling series.

[50] I have transcribed La Hire's reference to the synod of Dordrecht directly into English, although it was actually an event rather than a place; it was the conference held by the Dutch Reformed Church in 1618-19 at which Calvinist doctrine was upheld against the criticisms of the Arminians. I have, however, corrected La Hire's mistaken reference to the Hagia Sofia Mosque (Holy Wisdom Mosque) is Constantinople (Istanbul) as "the Mosque of St Sophia" and have altered his spelling of "Sana" to the more familiar Sana'a; that city is nowadays the capital of Yemen. It is inevitable, in the French fiction of this period, that an itinerary of this sort would conclude in Benares (nowadays Varasani), which had acquired a tremendous reputation in *fin-de-siècle* fiction as a symbolic repository of the Wisdom of the East.

[51] The actual antipodes of the Black Forest are, of course, in the southern hemisphere. If, however, one were to follow the same line of latitude (about nine degrees east) around the globe for a 180 degrees, one would end up not far from the southwesternmost of the Aleutians.

[52] The reader is free to wonder why Glô's grandfather appears to have called both his sons Rupert–although that might make it easier to understand why one of them assumed the name of Eiger Nott.

[53] Eunice, the slave who, unknown to her master, falls in love with Petronius Arbiter at Nero's court is a (wholly fictitious) character in Henryk Sienkiewicz's novel *Quo Vadis* (1896).

[54] *Feldwebel* is a German military rank roughly equivalent to that of sergeant.

[55] Several books credited to "Edmond Cazal," a *nom de plume* commonly used by La Hire, appeared in France between 1919 and 1923, but they do not include a book on the magnetic poles. Presumably, they were all pseudonymous works. Among these are *Joe Rollon, l'autre homme invisible* (1919), a Wellsian pastiche, which is definitely his, and an "anecdotal history" of the Spanish Inquisition. La Hire's final work, published some 20 years after the first cluster of "Edmond Cazal" titles, was still signed "Commandant Cazal."

[56] Guiana was the name of the British colony on the northern coast of South America, now the independent nation of Guyana. The area was originally settled by the Dutch as the colonies of Essequibo, Demerara and Berbice. These three colonies were captured by the British in 1796, officially ceded to the United Kingdom in 1814, and consolidated into a single colony in 1831. The colony's capital was at Georgetown (known as Stabroek prior to 1812). Guyana went on to become independent of the United Kingdom on May 26, 1966.

[57] The conquest of the North Pole is traditionally credited to Anglo-American Navy engineer Robert Edwin Peary, who claimed to have reached the Pole on April 6, 1909, accompanied by African-American Matthew Henson and four Inuit men named Ootah, Seeglo, Egigingwah, and Ooqueah. However, Peary's claim remains controversial.

[58] Because La Hire is writing in French, Saint-Clair translates *Uberalles* as *Pardessus tout* rather than *Above All*, but as the author continues to use *Uberalles* in the text, there is no reason not to use the English translation here.

[59] Major Frederick George Jackson (1860-1938) of the East Surrey Regiment undertook an expedition, usually referred to as the Jackson/Harmsworth Expedition, which established a base on Cape Flora in 1894 called Elmwood, where Jackson and his company played host to Nansen and his companion. The base could not be maintained after 1897, however, because no one could be found to sponsor it. Several of the expedition's members—including Albert Armitage and Doctor Koetlitz from La Hire's list—subsequently joined Captain Robert Falcon Scott's ill-fated expedition to the Antarctic, while Jackson went exploring in Africa (although he took a four year break to fight in the Great War, which he survived). La Hire obviously has a reference copy of one of the two books Jackson wrote about the expedition, and the Nyctalope is evidently modeled on men of that stripe.

[60] Paul Decauville (1846-1922) was the great pioneer of light railways that could be easily erected, dismantled and transported; thousands of miles of Decauville track were built during the Great War, playing a key role in the logistics of the conflict.

[61] Again Le Hire repeats his rather improbable insistence that the Wartecks have imported Mongol blood into their "race." Emile Zola, whose manifesto for literary Naturalism represented it as a quasi-scientific activity, devoted his long series *Les Rougons-Macquarts* to an ostensible analysis of the phenomena of human heredity, largely based on the investigations of Prosper Lucas's *Traité de l'hérédité naturelle* (1847-50), with particular relevance to the preservation of "atavistic" bestial traits in the eponymous dysfunctional family. This analysis reached its climax in *La bête humaine* (1890), in which technological progress is confounded and compromised by physiological fatalities, and the final novel of the sequence, *Le Docteur Pascal* (1893), whose protagonist, Rougon Pascal,

passes judgment on his family in the context of his 30-year study of the phenomena of heredity.

[62] The French title of this chapter is *La Pieuvre*; I have translated it literally, but the reader ought to bear in mind that the word is also applied metaphorically to human beings, in which context it signifies something like "blood-sucker."

[63] This kind of confusion between rumors of giant squids and the actuality of humble and inoffensive octopodes was, of course, not merely routine but virtually compulsory in marine melodramas of the period.

[64] The Austrian physicist Nikola Tesla (1856-1943) went to the USA in 1884, where he became Thomas Alva Edison's great rival as an electrical inventor, eventually selling his key patents to George Westinghouse in order to finance his research. Although his system of alternating current generation eventually displaced Edison's direct current generators, his more grandiose ambitions–especially the broadcasting of electrical power–bore little practical fruit.

[65] The German physicist Heinrich Ruhmkorff (1803-1877) was the inventor of the induction coil.

[66] "Hertzian waves" (radio waves) are named after Heinrich Hertz (1857-194), who first demonstrated the existence of electromagnetic radiation in 188. "Roentgen rays" (X-rays) are named after Wilhelm Roentgen (1845-1923), who discovered them in 1895. Although the electromagnetic spectrum had been almost completely elucidated by 1921, the notion that "thought waves" might belong to another such sector still had considerable currency in pseudoscientific parlance, as a hypothetical mechanism for such supposed phenomena as telepathy and psychokinesis.

[67] Pierre Curie (1859-1906) and his wife Marie, née Sklodowska (1867-1934) published their discovery of radium in 1898; the third signatory of the key paper was the chief financial sponsor of their research, Gustave Bémont.

[68] "Hertzobranlyan radioactivity" combines Hertz's name with that of Edouard Branly (1844-1940), the inventor–in the early 1890s–of the Branly coherer, which eventually formed a key element in radio broadcasting equipment. "Crookes-Roentgen radioactivity" combines Roentgen's name with that of William Crookes (1832-1919), who took up research on radioactivity in 1900 and emulated the Curies in extracting a new element from uranium ores; he was also a key scientific champion of spiritualism, and hence of the kinds of pseudoscience practiced by Glô von Warteck.

[69] The 18th of Brumaire in year VII of the Revolutionary calendar (November 9, 1799), was the day on which Napoleon Bonaparte, having returned from Egypt, overthrew the Directoire; he was appointed First Consul and effective ruler of France the following day. Waterloo was, of course, his final defeat.

[70] The paperback text places Wolf in the plane too at this point, but the subsequent chapter assumes that he was left behind and places him in the crew of the

RC2. The latter alternative makes more sense, so I have eliminated the mistaken reference.

[71] "Eloa" (1824) is an allegorical poem by Alfred de Vigny, in which the eponymous angel feels sorry for Satan and leaves Heaven to console him. Vigny implies that, if Satan had only been able to accept this gift in the spirit in which it was offered, he (and humankind) might have been saved from sin, but instead he seduces her and drags her down to damnation with him.

[72] La Hire's reference to "the third hour" does not signify that it is now 3 a.m., but that it is shortly after 2 a.m., at which point the day's third hour begins.

[73] Titian's *Danaë and the Shower of Gold* (1544) is in the Musea del Prado in Madrid. Danaë is one of the many mortal women seduced by Zeus in different guises, the shower of gold being one of the most plausible disguise in metaphorical terms, though deeply problematic in regard to anatomical practicality. The point of the evocation here, though, is the awkward position attributed by the artist to Danaë's right leg, which would indeed seem far more natural if it were allowed to dangle from the couch, but has to be raised and bent in order to conceal her genitalia. Le Hire is making the point that the particular standards of decency imposed on him by *Le Matin* did not require the leg to be raised, because he had been obliged–presumably against his authorial instincts–to leave his heroine's underwear on.

www.ingramcontent.com/pod-product-compliance
Lightning Source LLC
Chambersburg PA
CBHW030926020726
47498CB00001B/136